NEW ENGLAND

FOUR INSPIRING LOVE STORIES
FROM NORTHEASTERN STATES

LAURALEE BLISS

LYNN A. COLEMAN

JANET GORTSEMA

NANCY N. RUE

BARBOUR
PUBLISHING, INC.
Uhrichsville, Ohio

S

Published by Barbour Publishing, Inc., P.O. Box 719, Uhrichsville, Ohio 44683 http://www.barbourbooks.com

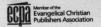 Member of the
Evangelical Christian
Publishers Association

Printed in the United States of America.

NEW ENGLAND

MOUNTAINTOP

Lauralee Bliss

Dedication

To Sarita. God has a great plan for your life!

"And I will give them one heart,
and I will put a new spirit within you;
and I will take the stony heart out of their flesh,
and will give them an heart of flesh:
That they may walk in my statutes and keep mine ordinances,
and do them. . ."
EZEKIEL 11:19–20

Chapter 1

O h no, we're going to drown! Help!!"

Dorothea Shelton's eyes flew open. Outside a terrific noise could be heard pounding the fabric ceiling on the tent above her. A stiff wind rippled the blue material like the wind on the sail of a boat drifting out to sea. Dorothea rolled over to see her younger sister Gail wide-awake, clutching the puffy synthetic cover to her sleeping bag with clenched fists. Her eyes were wide in terror, her mouth poised to unleash another scream.

"Hey, it's going to be okay, Gail," Dorothea assured her sibling. "It's just a rain shower. The tent will keep us safe and dry."

Gail remained dubious of the tent's protection as her dark brown eyes surveyed the weak structure surrounding her. She scanned every nook and cranny of the seams for any water droplets that might have seeped through. "What if this thing leaks, Dorrie?"

"It isn't going to leak," Dorrie assured her. "I seam-sealed it twice before we left home."

Gail's eyes blinked in confusion. "Seam-sealed it? I don't get it. What does that mean?"

Dorrie stifled a chuckle over her sister's ignorance for the great outdoors, which she loved with a passion. "Remember when I set the tent up on the front lawn at home, I rolled that stuff along the tent walls that you thought smelled like airplane glue?"

Gail's eyes rolled in remembrance and were accompanied by a wriggle of her nose. "Ugh, yes I do. The smell was awful."

"Well, that chemical was seam sealant. It's a special concoction that seals the seams of the tent and prevents water from bleeding through." Dorrie yawned once again, dismayed at having to explain to her younger sister the use of seam sealant at two in the morning. Her body ached for a few more hours of shut-eye. "So we're as snug as two bugs in a rug. Roll over and go back to sleep."

Dorrie sighed in relief to hear Gail rustle a bit inside her sleeping bag and plunk her head down on the feather pillow she insisted on bringing. Dorrie listened to the rain beating steadily on the roof of their makeshift home as she stretched her legs inside the cozy confines of her sleeping bag. With the scent of fresh rain seeping into the tent, she felt perfectly content.

Dorrie loved the great outdoors. She did not like the idea of having her civilized sister along on the trip—one who often argued for the comforts of a fancy hotel over a tent and who insisted on putting on her makeup every morning. Yet Dorrie resigned herself to putting up with her sister's idiosyncrasies, for she desired to rekindle a sibling relationship that seemed to have waned since her move to New York City over a year ago.

Since becoming a Christian herself, Dorrie wanted her sister to sample God's awesome creation while showing her the changed life of one devoted to the Savior. When Dorrie suggested a weeklong vacation in the beautiful White Mountains of New Hampshire, where mountain scenery awaited them, along with the famous strip of outlet stores located in North Conway, Gail seemed genuinely intrigued.

"I'll go with you," her sister decided, "if you promise to stay a few nights in a motel instead of tenting every night and give me plenty of opportunities for shopping at the outlet stores."

Dorrie agreed to the ultimatum, but inwardly could not fathom how one might discover the intimate character of God scurrying by women who were in the crowded aisles of a store and who had arms laden with shopping bags. Dorrie groaned at the thought of wasting precious days scouring aisles for clothes and shoes when she might be on a trail, ascending the steep mountainside to the summit, where a magnificent view awaited. From such a vantagepoint, high above the towns and farmlands, God seemed all the more real to Dorrie. She could relish in the magnificent work of the One who made the splendor of the heavens and the earth. If the view from a mountaintop was but a teasing look heavenward, where the Father dwelt, Dorrie knew heaven itself must be spectacular.

Dorrie sighed again. Forget such glimpses of the heavenly realms in the meantime. Shopping was a natural part of Gail's personality, so if Dorrie desired to renew their relationship and display the forbearance of a Christian, she would go along with shopping in the boring outlets. Doubtlessly a part of her would gaze in envy at the splendor of the Presidential mountain range looming before the store window.

The steady drumming of rain slowly died down to an occasional ping, ping on the tent fabric. Dorrie smiled to herself in anticipation of daybreak. There was nothing better than mornings after the rain, when every smell buried deep in the great earth would burst forth. The scent of flowers mixed with the earthy odor of the soil would provide a perfect excuse for hitting one of the many trails in the area. Dorrie wondered if Gail was up to a climb today, but she doubted it after the conversation of the previous evening. Dorrie had scanned the map for hours by the golden glow of the propane lantern, tracing a beautiful route by a raging river that slowly ascended the shoulder of a great mountain and promised a startling view of the Presidential Range once they reached the summit. Gail sat at the picnic table, painstakingly removing her makeup when Dorrie shared her idea of a hike.

"Not a hike already?" Gail had complained, immediately dashing Dorrie's hope for an adventure in the deep woods this early in the game. "I was hoping we might go to Franconia Notch and see that guy way up there on the mountain."

Dorrie stared at her sister, her eyebrows furrowing in puzzlement. "What guy?"

Gail scrubbed her face with a washcloth. "You know, that guy carved out of stone."

"You mean Old Man of the Mountain?"

"Yeah, the Old Man of the Mountain."

Dorrie sighed as she reverted her attention to the plastic-coated White Mountains hiking map, purchased in an outdoor shop before leaving on the trip. "Well, Gail, there'll be plenty of time for that. As long as the weather's this pleasant, we really should hit a trail. The views should be fantastic on the summit. . . ." Dorrie heard the exasperated grumbling, accompanied by the bang of a fist striking the picnic table.

"Then you hike the trail and I'll go see the Old Man," Gail hotly informed her. "Look, Dorrie, I'm not going to spend my entire vacation hiking up and down some mountain, getting myself all filthy, achy, smelly, and for what? Some crazy view or something? Why, there's plenty to see right around here without having to hike a million miles. Like the Old Man."

Dorrie sensed the brewing altercation, something she desired to avoid at all costs on this trip. "Okay, we'll compromise. The first day you get to do what you want, then the next day I do what I want and vice versa."

Gail's eyes lit up. "Great!"

"The only condition to this is that I have reservations for the Lakes of the Clouds hut near Mt. Washington at the end of the week. So you'll have to put up with a few days on the trail. The reservations are already set up and it's costing me a fortune."

Gail tossed the bucket of water in the woods, then proceeded to brush her teeth. "Just so long as I get in my shopping and my stay in the motel, like we agreed."

Right, Dorrie now thought to herself as she lay in her sleeping bag, listening to the sound of Gail's snoring. *The true outdoorswoman—with a purse full of money in one hand and a shopping bag in the other.* Dorrie flopped over on her foam sleeping pad, positioned herself more comfortably, and prayed for sleep to encompass her once more. As her eyelids grew heavy, she murmured, "Lord, help me get along with Gail. Help me be sensitive to her needs and show her the light of Christ on this trip. And please. . .allow me time to witness Your Creation on this trip besides the manmade creation of the shopping center. Amen." A frown tugged down the corners of her lips as Dorrie drifted off into a restless sleep and dreamt of an outlet mall spread out across the summit of her beloved Mt. Washington.

✣

By morning the rain had dissipated, revealing a beautiful dawn and the clear, crisp air refreshed from the storm. Dorrie rose, stretched her extremities, and peeped out of the tent. Birds chirped merrily from treetops that formed a natural canopy of green over their campsite. "What a beautiful morning, Lord," she breathed. Excitement bubbled up for the adventures that lay ahead of her on such a glorious morning.

Next to her sleeping bag, Gail's bag was tossed in a bundle, denoting a young woman in an obvious rush to reach the rest room. Dorrie noticed her sister's makeup paraphernalia gone as well. She snickered, unzipped her sleeping bag, then searched around for her camp shoes. "Gail will be the beauty and I'll look like the beast," Dorrie murmured, forcing her feet into the narrow moccasins that seemed to have shrunk during the night. "She should save her makeup for special occasions, certainly not for the wilds of the Whites."

Dorrie emerged from the tent and once more stretched her hands upward to embrace the skies. Birds darted above her. Yellow and red wildflowers, reflecting the rays of the early morning sun, lent a brilliant color to the campsite. Dorrie hastened over to the rope where she had strung up a bag of food in a waterproof sack to protect the edibles from curious creatures during the night. She enjoyed practicing her outdoor skills whenever she had the opportunity, despite having the convenience of the car parked only a hundred yards away. As she untwisted the rope tied around a tree limb, she recalled Gail's panic at the thought of predators visiting their campsite at night.

"That's why I string up the food, Gail," Dorrie had explained, trying to alleviate her sister's jitters.

"I still don't see why you can't put the bag in the car instead of hanging it in a tree. Are you sure no animal can climb up and get that bag?"

"Not unless it has wings and can fly," Dorrie joked. "I've heard of flying squirrels, but a flying bear or raccoon are new ones to me."

Gail became angry at Dorrie's flippancy. "Don't tease me," she snapped. "I don't happen to like the idea of bears ripping tents and mauling people, Dorrie. It's no laughing matter. . . ."

"Which is why I've strung up the food," Dorrie replied. "This is how hikers in the woods protect their supplies. It's worked for many, many years, so there's no need to worry."

Dorrie shook her head to clear her mind from the thought of last night's conversation. She grabbed hold of the rope and gently eased the foodstuffs to the ground just as a giggle materialized from the woods. Gail skipped along the campground road, all smiles as she swung the handle to the small carrying case containing her makeup. Dorrie noticed Gail's exuberant expression out of the corner of her eye and wondered what spawned the giddiness. *She looks like she's met the love of her life.*

"Oh, Dorrie, you won't believe it!" Gail breathed. "I just met the most gorgeous guy at the rest room."

Dorrie moaned in irritation. *There goes the great plan for a sisterly reunion. She still hasn't let go of her boy craziness from her high school years.* "That's a cozy place to meet. . .the rest room," Dorrie remarked with a hint of sarcasm as she struggled to undo the knot securing the food bag. She thrust a hand inside, retrieving granola bars and orange drink mix.

"I told him we were going to visit the Old Man up there in the mountain. He laughed and said that's where he's going too."

Great, Dorrie thought again, suppressing her irritation as she strode over to the picnic table to retrieve a plastic container with which to mix up a batch of Tang. *Just what this trip needs. . .two lovebirds twirling around the White Mountains.* Dorrie sighed in frustration before silently murmuring a prayer for patience and long-suffering—the two characteristics she sadly lacked at that moment in time. With great difficulty, she asked, "So you plan on meeting him at the Old Man? What time?"

Gail shrugged before disappearing into the tent. "I don't know," came her muffled reply. "He wasn't sure when he'd be going. He says he must stop at the hiker's information booth and check on the condition of a trail he wants to hike."

Dorrie's ears pricked in interest, intrigued by the idea of a fellow outdoorsman interested in hiking. Her hand ceased shaking the container. "He's a hiker, huh?"

Gail emerged from the tent, combing snarls from her curly hair. "Yup. He says he comes to these mountains every summer because he loves to hike in this area." Gail threw the comb into the tent before venturing over to the picnic table, plopping down, and sliding her legs underneath. She picked up the granola breakfast laid out for her. Her mouth opened, ready to sink her teeth into the crisp, spicy bar.

"Hold on, now, we have to pray," Dorrie reminded her sister, taking her place on the bench opposite her.

Gail dutifully bowed her head and closed her eyes while Dorrie offered up prayers of thanks for the beautiful day, for their safety during the rainstorm, and for the adventures that lay ahead. "And thank You, Lord, for this food. In Jesus' name, Amen." Dorrie picked up her tin cup and toasted her sister.

Gail made a face. "I thought we'd be sitting here all day listening to that prayer of yours."

Dorrie opened her mouth, poised to deliver a special monologue she had rehearsed on the importance of knowing Jesus as a personal Savior, then decided it might be ill-timed when she saw the look of disgust emanating from her sister's face. Dorrie recalled the day when she gave her own heart to the Lord and the wonderful feeling of having a close relationship with her Savior.

When she first told Gail of her newfound beliefs awhile back, her sister only

11

wriggled her face and blatantly informed Dorrie not to become religious around her. "I don't need God to run my life. Things are going great right now."

Great to Gail meant having fun with her friends, frequent dates with guys who came calling, or shopping for a new outfit at the nearby mall. Fun for Dorrie meant spending time listening to contemporary Christian music, attending various revival meetings at church, or taking long walks in the outdoors that beautifully displayed God's creative touch.

With Gail's continued interest in the dating scene, Dorrie reflected on her own commitment in that area. Despite the insistence by coworkers that she date, Dorrie committed herself to living a single life for the Lord. She did not want the heartache associated with dating unless she was certain it was the man she intended to marry. Watching the pain and misery that ensued after Gail broke up with her boyfriend of nearly two years, Dorrie tried convincing Gail to change her outlook in the dating arena. "Let God be the matchmaker," Dorrie suggested to her sister. "That way, you won't get hurt."

Gail pointedly told Dorrie she was off her noodle, then rushed out to find another guy to cover up the pain of the broken relationship. Dorrie only offered her sister to the Lord, praying on a daily basis for her salvation. She hoped this trip to the mountains might somehow stimulate her sister's appetite to know God.

"So, what's this guy's name?" Dorrie wondered, now changing the subject as she bit into her granola bar.

Gail cupped a hand to her mouth. "Wouldn't you know it. I didn't even ask him his name. Oh well, I'm sure I can't miss him in a crowd. He's absolutely gorgeous, Dorrie! Blue eyes, blond hair, and a gorgeous set of muscles."

"Humph," Dorrie mumbled. She sat sipping her tin cup filled with Tang while savoring the beauty of the forests, wishing her sister would take a little more interest in the creation surrounding them and not the creation of men.

"He looks like one of those guys who lifeguards at the beach every summer," Gail went on dreamily, closing her eyes as she reminisced. "Tanned, a superb build. . .oh, he's the perfect image of a male model."

"Well, I wouldn't get yourself all excited about Mr. Wonderful. You'll probably never see him again with all the tourists and hikers around."

Gail sat upright and finished her breakfast. "Well, I'm sure gonna try. If not, then I can still dream about him." She cupped her chin in one hand and closed her eyes.

Dorrie snorted softly as she arose from the table, rinsed out her cup, then assembled the necessities she would need inside her daypack: maps, guidebooks, water bottle, first aid kit, and a few extra granola bars. Opening her eyes to observe Dorrie with the pack open on the picnic table, Gail rose and threw in her own possessions for the day: comb, mirror, lipstick, and perfume.

"You shouldn't wear perfume out in the woods, Gail."

"Why not? I happen to like this scent very much."

"It'll attract every stinging insect from here to Maine. You know, there are many varieties of insects drawn to a host by their scent, so. . ."

Gail interrupted the explanation by suddenly ripping the pack from Dorrie's possession, stuffing a hand inside, and withdrawing her favorite bottle of perfume. "There, you satisfied?" she barked. "Honestly, Dorrie, all you can do this morning is find fault with everything." She twirled the bottle of perfume in her fingers, then studied the label before adding with a hint of sarcasm, "Is that what you call being a good Christian?"

Dorrie opened her mouth, ready to issue a stiff retort, then thought better of it. After a quick analysis of the morning's events, she realized she had been quite nitpicky with her sister, who was not accustomed to the rigors of outdoor living. "You're right, I have been rather bossy," she admitted, much to Gail's surprise. "I just don't want you getting all bit up and having a miserable time."

Gail's anger quickly abated. A grateful smile now filled her delicate features. "Thanks for the concern, Dorrie, but I'm willing to take the risk." She deposited the perfume inside the confines of the pack. "I don't plan on smelling like an animal sitting in a manure pile. Disgusting."

Again Dorrie sensed the overwhelming urge as an older sibling to inform Gail she'd regret her actions, but she bit down hard on her lower lip to stifle the words. "Look. . .how 'bout we call this a cease-fire, if it's all right by you?" Dorrie suggested instead. "We're supposed to be renewing a relationship here, not climbing over each other's back. What do you say?"

"That's fine by me," Gail agreed. "Cease-fire."

❧

The two young women jumped into Dorrie's car, preparing to head to the main highway in search of the Old Man of the Mountain. On their way out of Lafayette Campground, where they had spent the night, they passed a small outbuilding on the left with detailed maps of the White Mountains plastered along the outside walls. Studying them intently was a tall, muscular man with a bandanna wrapped around his head and clad in a tank top. When Gail saw him, she squealed with a noise that forced Dorrie to slam on the brake in a hurry. "Would you look at that? There he is! That's him! That's the guy I met at the rest room!"

Dorrie followed her sister's eager finger, examining the profile of the man who stood with a pack resting against his ankles. He studied a map held in one hand, then raised his eyes to compare it with the one fastened to the wall of the building. While Gail sat goggle-eyed over the man, Dorrie admired the pack he owned—an expensive internal frame pack, probably a three-hundred-dollar model by the storage capacity. He appeared ready for a month-long adventure with various accoutrements strung into loops and hooks on the pack itself and a foam sleeping pad rolled up neatly and fastened to the top. Dorrie inhaled a deep breath, wondering what sort of adventure he planned to embark on.

Gail fumbled for the latch to the car and leaped out. "Hey! Hey!" she called out, waving her hand.

Dorrie sat motionless in the front seat as her sister ran up to the man and engaged him in a noisy dialogue. Her fingers tapped the steering wheel, watching her sister's face light up with the rows of even, white teeth smiling at the stranger. "C'mon Gail," she murmured. "We didn't drive all the way up here just to have you fall for some guy you'll never see again in your life." Again Dorrie fought to suppress the impatient urges within her before they exploded into something she would later regret.

Several minutes passed by as Gail chattered on. From the smile parked on the guy's tanned face, he appeared quite amused by her winsome ways. He pointed to the map, then at his pack, explaining his intent. Gail nodded and began sidestepping her way back toward the car.

"Well, okay. . .maybe this afternoon, then," Gail called out to him over her shoulder before parading triumphantly back to the car. She exhaled a loud sigh as she slid into the passenger's seat. "Oooh, what a dreamboat!"

"So what's the dreamboat doing? Sailing the seven seas?"

"Mick's planning a quick hike up the Appalachian Trail across the road over there. He wants to test out his new pack for fit and weight."

"The Appalachian Trail, eh?" Dorrie glanced out the car window, thinking of one of her life's goals—to hike the entire two-thousand-mile distance on the famed foot trail stretching from the state of Georgia all the way to Maine. Of course, her coworkers and her family only laughed at such an idea, yet this did not deter Dorrie. Often she would visit the state park near her parents' home and walk portions of the famed trail, marked by the standard white blazes painted on the trees. She imagined herself tackling the infamous trail on one six-month adventure with a pack on her back and a hiking staff in one hand.

Gail's voice now interrupted her contemplations. "Mick says he's going to see the Old Man this afternoon, Dorrie, so if you want to do something else this morning, that'll be fine with me. In fact, I'll even take a hike with you or something."

"Yeah, sure," Dorrie muttered under her breath, starting the ignition. *Of course, now that the dreamboat hiker is in the picture, she's ready to tackle the trail. Why wasn't she this animated when I wanted to go hiking?* Dorrie glanced at her rearview mirror in time to see the man named Mick shrug on his pack and adjust the wide hip belt encircling his narrow waist. A pang of envy bit her, wishing she might have a pack on her back, ready to attack the famous Appalachian Trail. "He's one lucky dog," she whispered.

"What was that?"

"Nothing," Dorrie answered. Her foot moved to the accelerator. "C'mon, it's too late to start on any decent hike now. Guess we might as well spend money and see the Flume or whatever that water gorge is they advertise around here."

14

Chapter 2

After a bite to eat in the snack bar at the Flume, Dorrie pulled into the parking lot for the natural rock formation called the Old Man of the Mountain. Tourists young and old ambled their way down the paved trails to the various observation points. Gail bounced up and down with more excitement than usual, her eyes carefully scanning every face for the one belonging to Mick. Ignoring her sister's zeal, Dorrie grabbed her camera from the glove compartment of the car and followed the hordes of people making their way to see New Hampshire's most famous natural landmark.

"I wonder if Mick made it back from his hike?" Gail asked, glancing around as they sauntered down the trail.

Irritated at Gail's continual preoccupation with the unknown man, Dorrie retorted, "Well, I wouldn't suffer heart palpitations worrying about it. If you see him, then you'll know he didn't get lost on the trail."

Gail frowned at her sister's snippy remarks. "You're jealous 'cause I saw him first."

Dorrie widened her eyes and laughed outright. "Believe me, I am not jealous. I have more important things to do in my life than track down some weird guy."

"Yeah, but he's a hiker, Dorrie, just like you," Gail pressed. "Didn't you see all his gear? Why, you must be a little interested to learn more about him. Huh?"

Dorrie twirled a forefinger around in midair.

"You're too much," Gail said with a short chortle of her own.

They soon arrived at the circular platform overlooking a pristine lake that reflected the tiny image of a grizzly stone face carved into the mountainside. Dorrie snapped pictures while Gail took up one of the large telescopic viewers for rent, eager to examine the formation close up. She deposited the necessary change, then leaned one eye into the lens. "Hey, Dorrie, you should see this! Why, the rocks really do look like an old man, how about that?" She scrutinized the images for a minute longer. "Hey, it also looks like someone had to wire up all the rocks so they wouldn't fall apart."

Dorrie snapped her last picture, then went over to take a look. "Yup, they sure did," she confirmed as she stared intently through the lens of the viewer, noting every detail of the famous rock formation—from the bearded chin to the crop of stony hair. The face of the man stared forward as if thoughtfully perusing his bird's-eye view far above the rest of creation. "Bet the view is fascinating from up there," Dorrie commented, wishing she might join the Old Man in his gaze of the world around him. "I wonder if people are allowed to climb that mountain for a closer look at the formation?" Dorrie glanced up from the viewer for Gail's reaction, but found her nowhere in the immediate vicinity. Embarrassed by the idea she had been conversing with herself all this time, Dorrie muttered, "Great, now where did she run off to? Honestly, it's like trying to keep an eye on some kid."

A familiar giggle alerted Dorrie to her sister's whereabouts. She noticed Gail striding up the pathway, clinging to the arm of the man called Mick, who ascended the walkway effortlessly with a set of muscular legs and feet clad in sandals. A pair of binoculars swung over one broad shoulder. He wore a red bandanna around his forehead with spikes of straw-colored hair poking out underneath.

"Hey, Dorrie!" Gail called out, grinning from ear to ear. "Here he is! This is Mick."

"Hi," Mick greeted, displaying a bright smile of white teeth that stood out in sharp contrast to his tanned skin.

"Hi," Dorrie answered pleasantly. "So, did you enjoy your hike on the A.T.?"

Mick seemed taken aback by her question. "What? The Appalachian Trail? Uh, yeah, I did. How did you know about the hike on the Trail?" When Dorrie pointed out her sister as the chief informant, Mick nodded his head in comprehension. "Oh, I see. Guess Gail told you my plan."

Dorrie nodded.

"And you are?"

Gail pushed her hand against Mick's strong chest in a gesture of embarrassment. "Oh, I'm sorry, Mick. I totally forgot to introduce you two. This is my sister Dorrie."

"Dorrie," he repeated, sizing her up with a swift eye.

"It's short for Dorothea," Gail went on. "Mother decided to name her after a famous nurse during the Civil War, Dorothea Dix. She was a big history buff back then, which probably had to do with her younger brother—my uncle Bob, who's involved in all that Civil War reenacting. She had a choice between Dorothea or Clara, for Clara Barton. Isn't that cute?"

Dorrie blushed deep red. Inside she fumed, *Thanks a lot for sharing all the family secrets, Miss Quick-with-the-Tongue.*

Mick's grin grew wider as his blue eyes surveyed Dorrie in amusement. "That *is* cute."

Dorrie could see this conversation was going nowhere but downhill and decided to make a fast exit before Gail divulged other stories from their past. "Well, I'm going off to do a little exploring. See you two later."

"Nice meeting you, Dorrie," Mick said congenially, holding out his hand.

Dorrie accepted the hand he offered, surprised by the strength and warmth imparted in the handshake. Wheeling about on one foot, Dorrie continued on down the trail with Gail's silly giggle echoing on the wind that ruffled her hair. "I can't believe she embarrassed me in front of the hotshot hiker," Dorrie complained. "The two of them deserve each other. God, it's just going to be You and me today."

The path led Dorrie by some pretty wildflowers and along a lazy, winding stream that boasted a variety of minnows and other small fish. As Dorrie examined the flora close up, she wished she had brought along a manual identifying the various wildflowers of New England. Bees buzzed to and fro among the assortment of flowery heads, eager to sip up the juicy nectar. All at once, Dorrie remembered Gail's perfume and wondered if she had been attacked by the bugs yet. "What a girl," Dorrie remarked, thinking of Gail's performance up until that point. "Heaven knows why we agreed to do this together. Here I planned for us to renew some type of relationship after a year of noncommunication, only to have this guy plop down right in the middle of it. . . ."

Dorrie sighed and sat in a pretty spot beside the body of water called Profile Lake, which glistened beneath the rocky formation of the Old Man of the Mountain. Here she soaked in the peace and tranquility of an area totally devoid of the busy life she left in New York as a secretary for a business firm. In these pristine surroundings, she could enjoy the beauty and ease the tensions prevailing throughout her body from the mounds of work she was forced to do for her boss.

Dorrie sat for a time, then scooted herself closer toward the bank of the lake, peering at her reflection in the crystal-clear waters. Chocolate brown eyes like all those in her family stared back at her. She shook her short, dark brown, bobbed hair that came just past her earlobes—a cool hairstyle she preferred to wear in the summer. Her mother disliked the cut, saying she looked too much like a man. Gail, on the other hand, possessed the "beautiful, naturally curly hair of a grand lady," Mother remarked to her friends, proudly showing off her youngest daughter. Dorrie would not admit her younger sister was the favorite, but Mother's words definitely substantiated the high ranking Gail held in the family. The activities they shared provided more clues. Mother shopped with Gail, Mother went out to luncheons with Gail, Mother giggled like Gail over some silly thing. . .the list went on and on.

Dorrie picked up a stick and traced a path through the waters, silencing a bitter wave of jealousy that crept up within her. Perhaps Mother did prefer Gail to her, but Dorrie should not feel any lack for she had God, a Father in heaven who loved her. Dorrie pitched the stick into the middle of the lake and rose to her feet, preparing to venture back to the observation platform.

She arrived to find Mick and Gail sitting side by side on a bench, sharing a double-dipped ice cream cone from the concession stand. Gail waved at her. "Hi, Dorrie! Want a bite?"

"No thanks," Dorrie said.

Mick wiped off his mouth on a napkin he held in one hand, then inquired if she would like a cone.

Dorrie smiled and shook her head, conscious of his blue eyes resting on hers for several moments. "No, no thanks."

Gail noticed the silent interaction too, for she thrust the cone once more in his face, successfully disrupting the contact. "Here, Mick, your turn." As he licked the cone, she snuggled up next to his arm and turned her attention toward Dorrie. "Didn't I tell you that Mick looked just like a lifeguard, Dorrie? And guess what? During the summers he watches the young kids at the neighborhood pool where he lives. That's where he gets his fabulous tan."

"That's nice," Dorrie remarked.

Mick shrugged sheepishly, returning the treat to an eager Gail, who bit down on the sugar cone with a satisfying "mm." "Yeah, it earns me a little extra money in the summer."

"What do you do the rest of the time," Dorrie wondered, "besides lifeguard duty and rambles in the woods?"

Mick glanced at her and smirked. "So you could tell I enjoy my hikes."

"Well, it didn't take much to figure out with that fancy pack of yours."

"The pack's a present to myself," he admitted. "Anyway, I teach science at the middle school near where I live."

Gail screwed up her face. "You mean like biology?"

Mick nodded. "That's it exactly."

"Ugh, I'll never forget seventh-grade biology, when we had to dissect those disgusting frogs and worms on those black, greasy dissecting trays." Gail clutched her stomach, feigning nausea. "And the smell of formaldehyde nearly made me sick to my stomach."

"Well, the preservation process is odorless now," Mick told her. "Guess too many people complained about the foul smell."

"I rather enjoyed biology myself," Dorrie interjected, her eyes focusing once more on the stony image of the Old Man perched high above her. "The frog was fascinating. I remember one of my classmates discovering these tiny black eggs inside one of the frogs."

Mick straightened with interest. "The frogs do provide the students with an excellent opportunity to observe the internal organs of a living organism." He went on to explain several incidences in his class where he assisted the more squeamish students with their dissecting procedure and the various discoveries that were made.

Gail noticed Mick's attention drifting toward Dorrie and once more she used the ice cream cone as a diversionary tactic. "Mick, can you finish the rest of this? It's starting to melt."

Mick obliged, taking bites of the cone while continuing to entertain Dorrie with his stories, much to Gail's dismay. Finally, Gail uttered a loud yawn and rose to her feet. "Well, I'm bushed. I think we should call it a day."

Mick threw the napkins into a nearby trash receptacle. "You ready to go?" he asked Dorrie.

She nodded, glancing once more at the scenery before following the pair back down the paved path. Just beyond the platform, a wooden sign erected near a look-out point for the Old Man caught Dorrie's eye. She paused before it, reading the lines twice while allowing the message to sink deep into her soul.

Men hang out their signs indicative of their respective trades.
    Shoemakers hang out a gigantic shoe;
Jewelers a monster watch;
    And a dentist hangs out a gold tooth;
But up in the mountains of New Hampshire
    God Almighty has hung out a sign to show
That there, He makes men.

Attributed to Daniel Webster

Dorrie stood studying the sign so intently, she never heard Mick approach her from behind and peer over her shoulder. His resonant voice in her ear made her jump. "That's one of the most interesting sayings I've ever read," Mick pointed out. "Before I begin my travels in the Whites, I always come here and read it. There's something mysterious about it. . . ."

Dorrie's eyes traveled to the profile of the Old Man's face and head etched in stone on the shoulder of the mountain. "Here in the mountains, God makes men. What do you suppose that means?"

"I've been trying to figure that one out for a long time," Mick admitted, scuffing the toe of his sandal across the pavement. His gaze followed hers across the breadth of the mountain looming before them. "Somehow these mountains change you. They do that physically, of course, because the trails are so demanding. But there must be more to these mountains—maybe a working of the spirit inside of man or something."

"I always love the mountains because they remind me of the power of God's creation," Dorrie remarked.

Mick flashed her a look of curiosity. "God's creation, huh? Guess you're a Christian then."

His observation sent her glancing back in his direction. "Yes, I am."

"I made a commitment like that once," Mick said slowly, "but along the way, God and I split and went our separate ways. I couldn't believe He would allow such terrible things to happen. It had to do with. . ."

"There you are!" Gail's voice shrilled as she came up to them, silencing Mick. "I was wondering where you slipped away. C'mon, it's getting late." She took up Mick's hand, urging him on.

Dorrie followed behind, curious as to what Mick was ready to confess before Gail interrupted. Once in the parking lot, Gail gushed over Mick, telling him what a wonderful afternoon it was. "Oh, I had such a great time, didn't you, Mick? I think it's great we just happened to meet like this, only to find out that we enjoy doing the same things." She went on without drawing a breath. "So, what are your plans in the morning? We're staying at Lafayette Campground again tonight in our tent, site thirty-three, if I'm not mistaken. You take a right when you enter the campgrounds. It's not that far in from the main entrance actually. You should see our campsite, Mick. It's really a nice place, even though I'm afraid some animal might come in the middle of the night and rip open our tent. I've heard about such things, you know, like those terrible grizzly attacks in Alaska and the people who were mauled."

"There are no grizzlies in these mountains, Gail," Mick managed to say before Gail continued to ramble on about her need for protection and how the mountains sometimes frightened her.

Increasingly vexed by her sister's flirtations, Dorrie finally grabbed Gail by the arm and propelled her toward the car. Gail was reluctant to leave, as her feet scuffed the pavement like a child being pulled off a favorite slide at the playground. "Good-bye, Mick!" she said cheerily, waving as he retreated to his own vehicle. Gail sighed as she opened the door to the passenger's seat. "I sure hope I see him again. Isn't he absolutely divine, Dorrie?"

"Well, I wouldn't say he's divine, but yeah, he is a nice guy."

This comment triggered a raised eyebrow from Gail. "Just remember, big sister, I saw him first. He's mine."

"Mick isn't a toy bear you can carry around with you wherever you go," Dorrie commented. "I have a feeling the man's been through a rough time in his life. And quite frankly, I'm kind of curious to know what it is."

Gail blinked thoughtfully. "What makes you say that?"

Dorrie steered the car around, approaching the on-ramp for the Franconia Notch Parkway, which would return them to their tent site at Lafayette Campground. "Oh, just some comments he made or tried to make. Nothing for you to worry about."

Gail crossed her arms, intent on the view out her window. "I will worry about it, Dorrie, if you're taking any interest at all in my man."

Dorrie rolled her eyes. "Gail, I already told you earlier, as far as I'm concerned, you can have the dude all to yourself. I'm not looking for any relationship except for the one I'm attempting to foster with you. . .which we're quite unsuccessful with right now."

Gail remained in her agitated posture and refused to acknowledge her sister. Dorrie knew her words meant little, for she could detect the jealousy and resentment in Gail's facial expressions. How could she convince Gail that she was much more interested in family ties than some strange man?

Gail said little as they prepared their evening meal over the two-burner propane stove, then washed up the tin plates and cups and allowed them to air dry on the picnic table. The evening was picture perfect, with stars glinting between the tree branches that swayed in the breeze. A crescent moon rose in the night sky, bathing the campsite in an incandescent light. Dorrie studied her sister's brooding, wondering what she might say to lighten up the evening. She lit the propane lantern and withdrew her Bible from a stack of belongings. When Gail saw the leather book, she grumbled a few words about hypocrisy and the foolishness of pious living, then grabbed the flashlight and declared she was retiring early.

"Before you go running off, Gail, we need to settle this once and for all," Dorrie said slowly.

Gail shook her head. "I know you. You'll just tell me off and ram Bible verses down my throat."

"No, I won't."

Gail fumbled with the on and off switch to the flashlight, watching the ground illuminate under the yellow beam of light.

"I think it's downright silly getting all uptight over a guy you happen to meet at the rest room," Dorrie went on. "We're here to have fun, Gail, not pick fights. Let's just give it a rest, huh?"

Gail shrugged her shoulders.

"C'mon now, don't let the sun go down on your anger, and already the sun's been down an hour."

Gail flashed Dorrie a look of irritation. "Sounds like a saying from that Bible of yours or something."

"Gail, I only want us to have a good time, okay?"

Gail flashed her a look. "Then if you really want to make me happy, let's go outlet shopping tomorrow. I'm tired of all this camping in the woods."

Dorrie hesitated until the mask of irritation filtered across the face of her sister. "All right, we'll drive on down the Kancamagus Highway tomorrow and see what kinds of outlet stores are in North Conway. I can handle that." She added silently, *So long as we can both put that man named Mick out of the picture and go on with our vacation.*

Gail's face brightened at the suggestion, accompanied by a smile. "Now that sounds like fun."

Dorrie sighed in relief before offering Gail good night, then returned to her Bible study. "Thank You, Lord," she murmured. "I know Your Word says to live peaceably with all men, but Gail is certainly a challenge. I only hope we can continue to avoid these flare-ups of ours while we're on vacation." Dorrie paused, watching several white moths flutter around, attracted by the yellowish glow generated by the mantles of the propane lantern. "Gail needs to be like that," she said with a sigh, returning her attention to the Word lying open before her. "She needs to hover around You, Lord, the Light of the world."

Chapter 3

The next morning, Dorrie stood in front of the propane stove heating water for the breakfast oatmeal, when she heard a cheery whistle and a deep voice offering a pleasant good morning. Startled by these masculine sounds, she snapped up her head at the surprise visitor to their campsite—the tall form of Mick clad in shorts and a T-shirt.

"Well, I did find it," he complimented himself, gazing around their camp. "Nice isolated spot you've got here."

Dorrie stood speechless and dropped her face so her eyes encompassed the pot of water and the bubbles that had just begun to rise to the surface.

"Where's Gail?"

Dorrie turned off the flame, then added the oatmeal mix. "At your favorite stomping ground."

Mick stared at Dorrie quizzically. "What favorite stomping ground?"

"The rest room."

Mick remained puzzled until the comment registered, then a slow smile spread across his face. "Oh, I get it. . .the place where we first met." He spanned the seating area to the picnic table with his muscular legs. "So what's cooking?"

Dorrie whirled the concoction around with a small spoon. "Oatmeal. You're welcome to have some."

"I might snag a bite, thanks. Guys don't cook too well for themselves. I usually survive on power bars when I'm out in the wild."

"Don't you get tired of the same old thing?"

Mick nodded. "Sure. That's why I hit the town restaurant whenever I can. I know every good eating spot in the Whites. Name the town and I'll tell you where to eat."

"North Conway," Dorrie said.

Mick cocked his head, eyeing her in both amusement and curiosity. "Is that a serious question or are you cracking jokes again?"

Dorrie rested her eyes once more on his and noticed they were pale blue to match the morning sky. His honey blond hair appeared unusually brilliant when touched by the rays of the sun. "No, I'm serious. Gail and I plan on driving down the Kancamagus Highway. I promised her we'd visit the outlets in North Conway today."

"Outlet shopping, eh? Too bad. There're some real scenic spots off the highway. Great places to swim too. In fact, there's a favorite place of mine, Franconia Falls, which has a natural rock water slide."

Intrigued by this description, Dorrie ceased stirring the oatmeal and stared at him wide-eyed. "Really? That sounds great!"

"Yeah, it's right next to a walk-in campsite, Franconia Brook, I think it's called. There are nice platforms to pitch your tent. Some of the sites sit close to the river."

Dorrie glanced about the commercial site they had secured for the next several days. "So I take it you have to carry a pack into the campsite?"

Mick nodded. "The trail's real easy, though. Perfectly level. It takes about two hours to hike, I'd say."

Dorrie sighed longingly as she plopped down on the seat next to him. "Wow, that sounds absolutely divine. Unfortunately, my sister is not the roughing-it type. In fact, even this type of camping is a bit too primitive for her tastes. Gail prefers a hotel complete with an indoor pool."

Mick laughed heartily, which sparked a smile on Dorrie's face. "There're only a few women I know of who'd lug all their stuff in packs strapped to their backs just to camp in a pretty spot. I can tell you, the effort's worth it." His hand waved at their campsite. "This is fine for an overnight stay. Once you backpack in the woods, though, it's like stepping out of civilization into the wilds. You carry in everything you need and rely on no modern conveniences. There's nothing but you and nature."

"And God," Dorrie added softly, but loud enough for Mick to hear. He gave her a disconcerting look, then glanced away, pretending to study a crack running along one wooden plank that formed the picnic table.

The silence was broken by the arrival of Gail, who squealed when she saw Mick, then raced toward him and placed herself strategically in his arms. "Oh, Mick, what a nice surprise!"

"You gave me more than adequate directions, Gail," he told her, wrapping an arm around her, his eyes resting on her face.

Dorrie noticed with dismay how the two enjoyed their close proximity. Embarrassed by their actions, Dorrie busied herself with spooning out the hot oatmeal into silver bowls.

"I'm the navigator for all our trips," Gail told Mick proudly, reaching out two fingernails to flick a bit of dirt off his face. "I read the maps and plot our destinations. Dorrie has no sense of direction."

And you have no sense of propriety, flinging yourself into some stranger's arms, Dorrie fumed, but did not verbalize her thought. Instead she kept her gaze averted while setting out the bowls. "Breakfast is on. Enjoy." She then retreated toward the tent to fish out her toiletry bag.

"Aren't you going to eat anything, Dorrie?" Gail asked, a silent hope glimmering in her eyes that read, *It's all right by me if you don't, then I'll have Mick all to myself!*

Dorrie shook her head. "I'm not real hungry this morning. Guess I'll hit the rest room before the crowds arrive. See you later." Dorrie strode away as fast as her legs would carry her, away from the sight of Gail and Mick sharing oatmeal at the picnic table. *Are you really all that concerned about Gail's welfare, Dorrie?* she asked herself. *Or is there a bit of jealousy hidden away inside you, like Gail says?*

Dorrie thrust the questions aside as she banged open the screen door and stepped inside the rest room. The chilly air brought forth goosebumps on her skin. She stood before the sinks, gazing once more at her reflection in the mirror and her boyish hairstyle, as her mother called it. She wondered if Mick might be turned off by her appearance, only to be attracted by the femininity of Gail, with her flouncy set of curls and makeup plastered on her face. Perhaps he did not like the idea of a female jock who loved rigorous outdoor activities.

Dorrie stared again, then unzipped her case and sorted through the junk inside until she found some lipstick. *I'm as bad as Gail,* she scolded herself, *decorating myself just so some man might notice me here in the outdoors.* She traced the color in her lips, observed the effect for a moment, then shook her head and retrieved a tissue to wipe the lipstick away. "I'm just fooling myself," Dorrie mumbled. "I should let Mick take care of Gail and I'll go hike a trail or something."

She withdrew her toothbrush and paste and vigorously scrubbed her teeth. *I can't stomach the idea of the two of them together, snuggling under my nose for the rest of the trip!* Dorrie zipped up the case and sighed. Never before had one of Gail's boyfriends upset her this much. Perhaps deep down inside she did have a longing that a godly man might one day notice her, accept her for who she was, fall in love, and ask her to marry him. While she prided herself on her single-minded devotion to the Lord, the attention shared between Gail and Mick somehow rubbed her in the wrong way. Perhaps this situation was simply a testing of her heart.

Dorrie retraced her steps to the campsite, only to find Mick and Gail snuggling in each other's arms as Gail giggled over something Mick whispered in her ear. Dorrie managed to duck behind a tree before her entrance was detected. Angry tears now smarted her eyes, which she deftly wiped away. *Why God? Why do I have to go through this here, of all places? All I wanted was a quiet family-like vacation in the midst of these beautiful mountains and now I have to put up with this.* Dorrie stood silent, praying to God with all her might for peace to prevail in the midst of these circumstances. She felt her tense muscles relax and a soothing calm replace the irritation. "Thank you, God," she whispered to her ever-present Companion and Friend, finding the strength she needed at the exact time.

Mick seemed embarrassed by Dorrie's arrival at the campsite. He leapt instantly to his feet and out of Gail's reach, swiping back his blond hair with firm strokes of his hand. Gail only glowed and offered a triumphant smile directed toward her older sister. "We saved you some breakfast," she said, showing Dorrie the pot, which now housed a lump of solid mass faintly resembling the oatmeal.

"Yeah, thanks for breakfast, it was good," Mick said, sidestepping away. "Well, I have to get back to my own campsite. Need to get packed up and all."

"You're leaving us?" Dorrie asked, hoping he would leave her and Gail alone so they might continue on with their vacation undisturbed.

Gail reached out and grasped his massive hand in hers. "Mick's offered to be our tour guide around North Conway, Dorrie, before he starts on his backpacking trip. He knows all about the town, so we don't have to worry about getting lost. Isn't that sweet of him?"

Dorrie swallowed a hard lump in her throat, then pivoted on her heel and tossed her toiletry bag into the tent.

The irritation concealed behind the gesture led Mick to comment, "You don't seem too happy about the plan, Dorrie."

"Well, this trip is supposed to be for Gail and myself," Dorrie told him flatly.

"Oh, c'mon, Dorrie," Gail said in a condescending tone of voice, "we've put up with each other for two days now. I think it's a good idea to have Mick come along instead of trying to figure out where to go and what to do once we reach town."

"There's no point in me chaperoning the two of you," Dorrie said icily. "You know the saying—two's company, three's a crowd. If you don't mind, I think I'll check out that trail to the waterfall you mentioned, Mick. Why don't you drop me off at the trailhead on the way to North Conway, then pick me up on the way back?"

Mick stared at Dorrie. A look of concern flashed across his tanned features. "I don't think it's wise for you to hike alone."

"Oh, Dorrie takes care of herself," Gail informed him. "She does this all the time...hiking in the woods for hours. You should see her in the Catskill Mountains in New York when we stay at my aunt's summer home. She hikes everywhere and wears her Walkman, listening to all that religious music of hers. Really, if she wants to do it, let her go."

"I'll be fine," Dorrie assured him, adding silently, *Please, I need to be alone right now...to enjoy my stay in the White Mountains...and not some shopping trip with a pair of lovebirds.*

"Okay, if that's what you want." Mick continued to stare at Dorrie thoughtfully as though he wanted to say more, but did not. Instead, he stuffed his hands in the pockets of his shorts with a look of disappointment overshadowing him. The reaction sent confusion and wonderment soaring through both sisters as they watched him saunter away.

❧

With the concern inherent in an overprotective father, Mick supplied Dorrie with an endless list of dos and don'ts as they sat in the parking lot called Lincoln Woods, where she would begin the hike to Franconia Falls. He gave her his topographical map of the area, pointing out the trail in detail and showing her the natural rockslide into the river. "But you need to be careful," Mick warned. "Those rocks can be dangerous and slippery." He sized up Dorrie's capabilities. "You sure you can do this by yourself?"

Without waiting for Dorrie's response, Gail interjected, "Of course she can. Dorrie's twenty-five years old and quite capable. I tell you she's used to this kind of stuff and really loves it, don't you, Dorrie?"

"I can handle this just fine," Dorrie assured him. "These ole legs of mine have put on about a hundred miles and haven't worn out yet."

"Do you have a first aid kit?" Mick asked.

"Just a small one, you know, with Band-Aids in it, that type of thing."

Mick twisted his face and reached over into his daypack, rummaging for a kit, which he handed to her. "You should have a more complete one than that. Here, take mine. It has everything you need—including an ace wrap, iodine, needles. . ."

Dorrie laughed. "I'm not contemplating major surgery on the trail!" She waved the kit away. "I'll be fine. I've been on dozens of trails, and by the grace of God, I've never injured myself."

Mick poked the kit once more at her, but Dorrie pushed it back into his chest. "Keep it. Who knows, you might need it yourself with all that walking around in the outlet stores. There's bound to be tons of clothing racks. You might trip and fall over one."

Mick flushed red under the sting of her saucy remarks. He surrendered to her pride and tossed the first aid kit back into his pack. "Okay, you win. I guess that's everything. We'll meet you back here around five. That should give you plenty of time for the hike and some recreation."

Dorrie hoisted up her daypack and adjusted the straps around her shoulders. "Well, you two have a good time now."

Gail gave her sister an affectionate hug, whispering, "Thanks for giving us the day to ourselves, Dorrie. You're a terrific sis."

"Sure," Dorrie said, avoiding the look in her sister's eye. "Anytime."

Mick sat quietly in the driver's seat, rapping his fingers on the steering wheel, lost in thought. He glanced up when Dorrie threw a final wave good-bye, then grabbed hold of the steering wheel as Gail jumped into the passenger seat next to him. No one noticed the strange moodiness that suddenly overcame him.

❧

Once Dorrie's feet hit the trail, a sense of well-being soared through her. The day was beautiful, with clear blue skies and a refreshing breeze that caressed her face with soft, sweeping strokes. The daypack bounced up and down on her back as she took long strides with her legs, propelling her forward to Franconia Falls. The level trail appeared like an endless road in the midst of the great forest. As sunlight streamed through the woods, Dorrie noted the various shades of green found in the forest—from avocado, to a sea green, to a rich, deep moss. Birds serenaded the walk from branches overhanging the trail. Occasional passersby would offer a quick hello, with some asking Dorrie how far it was back to the trailhead. In return she inquired of the distance left to the falls. Dorrie relished the comradery she discovered when sharing the trail with fellow hikers. She sensed a unique relationship with those who lived and breathed the great outdoors.

Dorrie observed this with Mick when he offered her his medical kit and graciously provided her his topographical map. As he sat next to her in the car, explaining the route, Dorrie could detect in his voice an excitement for the woods and a distinct yearning to hike the trails he loved. She wondered if he would rather be hiking with her to Franconia Falls than browsing the outlet stores with her giddy sister. "If that were true, well, I wouldn't be doing this journey alone," Dorrie reminded herself, stepping around a rock lying in the middle of the path.

She thought back to her conversation with Mick by the Old Man of the Mountain, wondering what calamity spawned his falling out with God. Hanging around a person like Gail, who did not share a Christian viewpoint, would not restore Mick into a right relationship with God. Dorrie sighed, her steps lengthening along the natural walkway. She should reach out to him, discover the pain of the past, and help bring healing to his heart. Maybe it was possible to turn his life around so it would once again burn with a renewed commitment to the purposes of God.

After several miles of hiking, Dorrie squinted her eyes to see the dark image of a wooden cabin in the distance, signaling the caretaker hut for the Franconia Brook Campsite. She passed several wooden platforms where tents were pitched, surrounded by an assortment of gear. Huge metal boxes near the campsites served as caches for food supplies to keep curious bears from raiding camp supplies. Dorrie stopped to admire one campsite with a baby blue tent. Sleeping bags air-dried over a stout clothesline hung between two trees. A small cooking stove sat next to a fire pit where a huge pile of wood had been gathered, presumably for a roaring fire that evening. The whole scene proved pleasing to Dorrie and one she would love to experience some day.

Reluctantly, she plodded forward until she heard the roar of the water and found the raging river and rocks speckled with people of all ages. Some scampered barefoot on the rocks while others sunbathed or waded in the cool waters. Dorrie hiked along the riverbank until she came to a point where the rocks split wide open to form a perfect chute directly into a deep pool of water below. Excitement bubbled up within her as she watched several young kids glide down the natural rock slide with shrieks of laughter, their arms waving in the air as they splashed into the waters below. Eager to be a part, Dorrie stripped off her clothes, revealing a modest one-piece swimsuit, and came to the riverbank.

"Is the water cold?" she asked one shivering youngster as he grabbed a beach towel off a nearby rock and wrapped it around his wet form.

"Naw, it's fun!" he assured her.

"Where do you go in?"

"Right there." He pointed to a place in the rock just before it formed a steep slide under the rapid flow of the river. "You get in there and slide on down. It's a blast!"

Dorrie smiled at the boy, then joined a line of people waiting their turn at the slide. She splashed some of the chilly water along her arms and across the front of her suit, wincing as the cold shocked her flesh and sent goosebumps rising to the surface. The roar of the water as it dashed over the rocks filled her ears, reminding her of the ocean waves that crashed along the sandy beaches of Long Island.

At the beaches, the crowds were thick like fleas, the sand checkered with various shades of red, yellow, green, and blue from towels strewn across the sand. Umbrellas would poke out of the sand like stunted trees to provide shade, while children and adults alike shouted as they romped in the waters. Dorrie sighed, thankful to be here in the mountains, away from the hordes of people sharing the ocean and the faint outline of the Manhattan skyline visible in the distance. Here there was only the roar of a mountain stream, clear blue skies unmarred by smog, and the refreshing air scented by balsam.

All of a sudden, it was Dorrie's turn at the rock slide. She sat down gingerly in the icy water, shivering a bit, then pushed off. Down, down, down she went, careening into the cold water below. "Woowee!" Dorrie cried in utter delight, shaking the water from her face while pushing back strings of hair dripping water in her eyes. She scrambled up the embankment, eager to try again. After six or so turns plunging into the crystal-clear pool, Dorrie took a break by the riverbank. She toweled off her hair, then nourished herself with a granola bar and some water from her plastic water bottle.

"I wonder how hiker Mick and Miss Gail are enjoying the outlets," Dorrie mused, biting into the bar while watching the children scamper on the rocks. "It certainly can't be as much fun as this." With a bit of nourishment in her stomach, Dorrie found a warm place on the rocks, spread out her towel, and sunbathed for a time, allowing the sun's rays to dry her damp skin and suit. "This is wonderful," she breathed, closing her eyes. "If heaven is even half as nice as this place, it will be marvelous!"

After some time in the sun, Dorrie felt the rock slide beckoning her once more before she had to hike back to rendezvous with the shopping duo by five o'clock. Glancing at her watch in the pocket of her daypack, Dorrie decided she had time left for a few quick trips down the slide before changing back into her hiking attire. The crowds had dissipated by then, leaving Dorrie alone as she ambled up to the starting point. Down she went, her arms flying over her head, and with a splash, hit the pool. She rose quickly to the surface, her eyes scanning the slide above her. "Should I go one more time?" she debated. "Oh, why not? One more time, then I'll head back to meet the lovebirds. Tweet, tweet!" Dorrie giggled.

Slowly she climbed up to the top of the rocky formation once more, conscious of the fatigue that gripped her legs. With effort, Dorrie nestled in the slit between the rocks and pushed off. As she slid down the rocks, a terrible cramp suddenly seized one leg muscle in a painful hold. With a cry, Dorrie lurched uncontrollably into the water, her ankle twisting in several rocks found in the pool below.

Fighting to regain control, Dorrie paddled with her arms while trying to ignore the gnawing sensation of pain rising in her ankle. She managed to reach the shore and struggled onto a rock, where she examined the damage to the injured extremity.

"Great," Dorrie groaned. "I twisted up my leg real good." She managed to scoot herself to the bank where her daypack lay and sat nursing the wounded leg. "Oh, Lord, now what do I do?" Dorrie moaned in despair, glancing around the deserted riverbank. "I can't even walk! How am I ever going to get myself back down the trail like this?"

Chapter 4

The sun began to dip below the trees, with shadows of the approaching night resting across the landscape. After changing out of her damp swimsuit behind a rock, Dorrie limped several yards away from the river's edge to an open area of the woods, where she now leaned up against a stately old tree for support. Her red bandanna, drenched in the cold water from the river, lay swathed around her swollen ankle, but this did little to ease the pain or remedy her predicament.

Dorrie realized the impossibility of hiking without adequate support on her injured ankle. For a time she sat still, her arms crossed before her chest, angry words poised on her lips that she refused to mutter aloud. Instead her mind argued with the question Why? Why did she take that last leap into the water knowing her fatigue from the day's activities? Why did God allow this to happen just when she was having such a glorious time in His creation? She thought of the ace wrap nestled in Mick's first aid kit as her ankle throbbed with pain. Remembering his offer to lend her the kit, Dorrie realized her own stubbornness had prevented her from accepting the one item that might have assisted her in the walk back. "It's all my fault," she spoke aloud, lending a sigh of exasperation.

Dorrie fumbled with the makeshift bandage around her ankle, trying to tie it more firmly. She thought of hobbling over to one of the campsites and asking for assistance, but the mere thought of stumbling into some stranger's camp left her feeling uncomfortable. "Well, Dorrie, old girl, you wanted a camp-out in the woods, and it looks like you might get your wish."

Dorrie sifted through the contents inside her pack, sizing up the food that remained—one granola bar and a box of raisins. A half-filled bottle of potable water sat next to her. Dorrie sighed. "I suppose this'll have to do for dinner. I don't have many options right now." She consumed the sparse meal, then rested against the rough bark of the tree, watching the sun slowly disappear behind a grove of trees. The blue sky melted into colors of orange and red with the coming twilight. Crickets began to serenade her with their nightly choruses. Dorrie shivered with her arms cradled around her legs, wondering how she would keep warm in the cool mountains without a blanket. Inside her pack lay a wadded sweatshirt, which she shrugged on. Her bare legs cramped with the cold, sending ripples of pain shooting down into her injured ankle. "This is not what I had planned, God," Dorrie grumbled in frustration. "How am I supposed to make it through the night like this?"

In a firm determination to try and resume the hike, Dorrie gathered up her belongings and struggled to her feet. A terrible pain gripped her ankle as she fought to take a few meager steps before resigning herself to the reality of her injury. Once more she occupied a space on the ground. "Gail will probably be worried by now," Dorrie decided, readjusting the damp bandanna around her ankle. "Then again, maybe she's thanking God I gave her more time to spend with Mr. Wonderful."

A rustling in the woods disturbed Dorrie's contemplations. She scanned the glade of thick trees that now turned into dark, ominous statues before her. A squirrel dashed from a web of tangled brush, scampered along the ground, then scooted up the nearest tree waving his bushy tail. "Wish I could run like you," Dorrie called out wistfully to the squirrel. Once more a wave of cold air swept over her. "I should build some type of fire," she reasoned out loud, enjoying the companionship of her voice, "but I can't begin to gather up the wood for it so what's the use?"

Dorrie soon drifted off into an uneasy sleep, twitching every so often with cold as she dreamt of Mick dangling an ace wrap in front of her face. She heard voices calling her name in the dream. Dorrie stirred, then bolted upright, wincing at the pain in her ankle. Again she heard the faint voice of someone calling her name.

"Dorrie? Dorrie?"

"Here!" she cried. "Here I am!"

"Keep calling to me," the voice directed.

Dorrie yelled out, "Here, right over here," until branches were batted away and a tall form approached her from the woods. The dark figure was Mick, wearing a daypack and carrying a flashlight. Wrinkles of concern lay etched in deep crevices across his darkened face. Immediately he came to her side, inquiring about her condition in an anxious voice.

"I'm okay, really," Dorrie mumbled, flushing with embarrassment over the idea of her injury requiring Mick to come rescue her like a superhero.

His strong, gentle hands worked across the swollen flesh of her ankle, assessing the extent of her injury. "Might be broken," Mick gravely noted, turning to locate some downed tree limbs. "I'm going to make you a splint for that ankle."

Dorrie shivered again as a brisk breeze blew. Noticing her cold, Mick threw open his pack and pulled out a pair of his sweats for her to put on. "W. . .where's Gail?" Dorrie stammered as she donned the warm fleece over her chilled extremities.

"Well, when you didn't show up at five and at six, I had a feeling something was wrong. I drove Gail across the highway to the campground there and set up my tent. She didn't want me to leave her alone, but I told her she'd be fine in the tent." Mick worked efficiently, tearing up one of his bandannas into strips to tie around the makeshift splint that now cradled her ankle. He then fastened the whole contraption snugly into place with an ace wrap.

"Where did you learn to do all that?" Dorrie noted in admiration as she watched him work.

"Boy Scouts."

"Boy Scouts?" She smiled at the mere thought of the man as a scout in his younger days, wearing a kerchief around his neck and quoting the Boy Scout honor code with raised fingers.

"We had to learn various first aid techniques to earn one of the badges," he explained. With the task completed, Mick sat back on his heels. "How'd you do this to yourself, anyway?"

"I wasn't very smart. I wanted one more slide down the rocks into the water, even though I knew I was tired out. The rock slide's a great place, just like you said it would be."

He nodded his head. "So you injured yourself on the last trip down?"

"Yup, last trip, always the very last one you plan on making, you know." Conscious of eyes perusing her, Dorrie kept her gaze averted, focusing her attention on her ankle and the sticks cradling it, secured by the ace wrap from his first aid kit.

"That's always the way it is," Mick confirmed, rising to his feet. His tall, commanding presence proved comforting in the dark surroundings. His heavy footsteps crushed the leaves scattered across the forest floor as his hands brushed through the downed vegetation, looking for an implement to assist with walking. In a short time he returned with a forked stick. "Okay, let's see if you can walk using this stick as a crutch. If not, I'll run back to the caretaker cabin and ask the guy to radio out for help."

Dorrie blushed at the embarrassment of having to be carried down the trail on a stretcher. With effort and the help of Mick's strong forearm, she hoisted herself to a standing position. She gritted her teeth and said, "It's gonna be slow I'm afraid."

Mick frowned as she hobbled alongside him to the trail, which appeared dark and uninviting with the approach of night. "I don't think this is going to work," he told her. "Let me try to get you back to the caretaker's cabin, where I can get you some help."

"Mick, I'll absolutely die if someone has to carry me out on a stretcher," Dorrie pleaded. "I'll get myself down this trail and back to the parking lot if it's the last thing I do."

Mick grunted in reservation but allowed her to lean heavily on him for support. "This would be fine and dandy if we only had half a mile to go," he grumbled, struggling to maintain his own stability while balancing her at the same time, "but it's over two miles to the parking area. There's absolutely no way you can make it like this."

"Then I will pray, and if you don't mind, maybe you can say a prayer for me too." She began her prayer in earnest, the words jarring from her lips as she fought to keep herself balanced on the uneven path. "Lord, please give me the strength I need to make this walk. Help the swelling go down so I might walk better. Give Mick the strength to assist me. Thank you for watching over us and protecting us in everything we do. In Jesus' name, Amen."

After a time, Mick said, "You're walking a little better now."

"The power of prayer," Dorrie breathed, a grin filling her face. Using the stick for leverage, Dorrie released her hold on Mick and began limping along on her own.

Mick watched her progression in some surprise. After a time, they passed several boulders nestled alongside the trail and decided on a brief rest stop. "Guess the ankle loosened up when you began to exercise it," he noted.

Dorrie laughed. "A true scientific mind at work," she teased him. "You know it's not that. I prayed for help and God answered it."

Mick gulped down the water from his bottle before recorking it with a pound of his fist. "That may be, but more often than not, I've found God to be pretty deaf whenever I pray."

"Depends on what you pray for," Dorrie said matter-of-factly while examining her makeshift wooden splint, oblivious to his growing discontent. "He won't answer something that's not according to His perfect will."

After a few painful minutes, Mick blurted out, "Well, I asked for something that deserved to be answered. I sure never asked Him for all the persecution heaped on us, and finally the. . ." He hesitated, then bent over as if the weight of the secret he carried within proved overbearing. His fingers groped for his feet, looking to tighten the laces that had loosened on his hiking boots.

Dorrie realized Mick sat poised to reveal the reason underlying his strained relationship with God. She waited for what seemed like an eternity before prodding him with a question. "What kind of persecution, Mick?"

"Never mind," he snapped, rising to his feet. He looked down on her, then offered her a hand up. "C'mon. Gail probably thinks we got lost or something."

They continued on in silence as Mick withdrew a flashlight from a side pouch of his daypack and turned it on. The trail glowed before them. An owl hooted in the woods nearby. Evening crickets continued in their singsongs. For a time only the breathing from the exercise was shared between the two until Mick suddenly said, "Sorry I snapped at you back there."

"It's okay." Dorrie then inhaled a deep breath before remarking, "Sounds like you went through a rough time."

"Yeah, I did." Mick flashed the beam of light across the portion of trail Dorrie now hobbled on. "Like I said, it made me even question God's existence. . .why He lets people go through such hard times in life." He paused, then added, "I thought He took care of His children, but it seems like He makes them go through hell on earth first as a prerequisite for heaven or something."

"Even Jesus said we would be persecuted, Mick," Dorrie reminded him. "As they persecuted Him so they will persecute us."

"Yeah, right." His boots pounded the ground in agitation. "I didn't mind the name calling and everything, but when the gang members hurt our family, it became impossible to trust in God anymore. It's like He decided to abandon us."

Tingles shot through Dorrie, sending the hairs on the back of her neck standing straight up. Her curiosity nearly drove her to the breaking point.

"Dad was a good, decent, honorable man," Mick went on, his voice hardening as he continued to reveal bits and pieces of the mystery surrounding his life, "but now he sits in a chair in some nursing home all day long and doesn't even recognize his own family." His breathing became raucous as he flared, "What kind of merciful God would send one of His preachers into a life like that, Dorrie?"

Dorrie gulped. Her hand gripped the stick tightly as she plodded along, dragging her injured extremity behind her. "I. . .I can't answer that, Mick. Was your dad a preacher or something?"

"Yeah, Dad loved to preach. His calling was street evangelism. He had a heart for the gangs of Boston, but the gangs sure rewarded him. They took everything away from him when the leader fired that bullet into his brain." His feet now stomped the ground in anger and hurt. "Dad lay in a coma for over a year and a half. When he came out of it, he didn't know anything or anyone. It's like he reverted back to infancy or something." Suddenly Mick stopped, his fists clenched as he stood straight and immobile, his eyes focused straight ahead. "I hate God for allowing the gang to do that to my father. God put him in that state. Dad gave his life to serve God, then God repays him with a bullet in the brain and a life as a vegetable in a chair." His face now turned to acknowledge Dorrie. "So don't tell me anymore about a loving God or praying to God for help or even believing in a God. As far as I'm concerned, there is no God."

Dorrie felt her heart would break under these statements. Silently she murmured prayers for Mick, but knew nothing could reach a heart hardened in cement from the pain of his past. All she could do was show mercy as she was sure God wanted to show him—the mercy of One who understood even if Mick was opposed to Him. Dorrie cast the stick away and approached him, reaching out with as much compassion as she could muster. "I'm so sorry, Mick," she choked, surprised by the tears welling up in her eyes. "What a terrible thing to have to go through."

Mick accepted Dorrie's embrace, holding her as his muscles heaved under the weight of the burdens he bore. Finally he whispered, "I. . .I've never confided any of this to a stranger before. I don't know why I told you, but it's like I had to tell someone right now. With you being injured and all tonight, it seemed the right place and the right time."

Dorrie disengaged herself from his arms and hobbled back to retrieve her stick. Instead of bitterness for her sprained ankle, her heart found a reason to be thankful. Through the injury, God had opened a door of communication with this troubled man that might not have otherwise existed. "I'm glad you told me, Mick. I'll have to admit, ever since you mentioned a problem in your past back at the Old Man, I was curious to know what happened. I knew you went through some kind of heartache in your life, but of course, I didn't know what."

Mick stared at her thoughtfully. "You seem like someone I can open up to, Dorrie. It's hard to believe you and Gail are sisters. . .you're both so different. Gail is refreshing because she is like a little girl who loves to have fun with life. You, though, you're very serious, you look at things as they are. . . ."

"Some have told me I'm a black and white person," Dorrie confessed. "I see black and white, nothing else."

Mick nodded in agreement. "That's right, you do. You aren't after the fluff or the wide picture. You're a person who looks right at reality without being sidetracked into other things." He sighed, his flashlight acknowledging a painted blaze on a tree nearby. "Guess we ought to get going."

They continued on down the trail, discussing likes and dislikes. Dorrie was amazed to discover they shared many interests, not only for the great outdoors, but also in traveling the United States in search of an exciting adventure or in the area of scientific studies. Mick commented, "Don't mention this to Gail, but I could never settle down with someone who doesn't like to backpack in the outdoors or who doesn't appreciate biology. My hikes and my students are the most important areas of my life right now. They mean everything to me."

After he had spoken these words, Dorrie sensed a strange tingle sweep over her and shoot through her extremity. She realized then how much she loved to backpack and recalled her keen interest in hearing of Mick's escapades teaching biology. In fact, she fulfilled many of his ideas surrounding a perfect companion. Instead of pondering the significance of the statement, Dorrie switched tactics to ease the anxiety mounting within her. "Well, if Gail were to find out how much you love hiking, she'd probably put on her hiking boots and tramp the trails. You know she already thinks you're out of this world."

Mick smirked. "I had a feeling," he agreed, "but I'm not so sure it's meant to be." He then mentioned the incident at the campsite when Dorrie discovered them sharing an embrace. "Sorry you had to put up with all that at the campsite this morning. It was rude and unfair to you." After thinking for a few moments, he added, "Gail can be pretty wild at times. I think she has some idea about us having a relationship, but I don't think that's such a wise idea."

Dorrie could not help but agree, thankful Mick had seen the light where Gail was concerned. "Mick, I think the best thing for all of us is to have you drive us back to our campsite and leave us there to continue on with our vacation and you with yours. In that way no one will feel pressured or unhappy and everyone can have a good time." The moment Dorrie suggested this, she regretted the words. The mere thought of Mick leaving, never to be seen again, saddened her in a strange sort of way.

"I'd rather see how you're feeling before I make my great escape."

"Well, don't ruin your vacation on account of my stupidity, Mick. You should go and enjoy yourself in the White Mountains while you have the time."

There was silence for a few moments before his voice acknowledged, much to Dorrie's astonishment, "I am enjoying myself very much."

❧

Dorrie and Mick arrived at the dark campsite to find Gail asleep on top of his sleeping bag inside the tent. Mick lit his propane lantern, then fished out freeze-dried food for them to eat. Finding herself famished after the long, eventful day, Dorrie gratefully accepted the jerky, apricots, crackers, and other food. Sitting opposite Mick at the picnic table with the food spread out before her, Dorrie contemplated how she would pray for the food and his reaction to the gesture.

In answer to her unspoken dilemma, Mick motioned to her with a stick of jerky. "Go ahead and pray for your food if you want, Dorrie. I'm not going to stop you."

Dorrie shrugged, bent her head, and offered a prayer. Then in an after-thought, she added, "And help Mick know how much You care Lord and how much You love him and his family for the sacrifices they have made. Amen." Dorrie opened her eyes to find Mick staring hard at her, his eyes burning as they reflected the light of the lantern. Even his blond hair seemed to radiate with the flames of anger roaring within him.

"Don't pray for me anymore."

"Somebody has to, Mick . . . ," Dorrie began until his hand came up, silencing her.

"No, nobody has to. I've had many people pray over me. It has already been said time and time again. I know you're just trying to be helpful, but I think it's best if you leave God out of my life."

Dorrie fumbled for the jerky sitting before her. With her vision marred by the tears formed in her eyes, the food wavered like ripples on the water. A large lump in the pit of her stomach silenced the hunger pains. She forced herself to pick up the jerky and chew it while focusing her attention once more on the lantern and the moths attracted to the flame. *Not only does Gail need You, God, but Mick does too. He needs to draw near to You, the light of life, before he falls any deeper into this pit of bitterness.*

Chapter 5

Mick elected to spend the night in his car while Dorrie made herself comfortable on a few blankets spread inside the tent next to the snoring form of her sister. Before retiring for the night, Dorrie ventured shyly to the picnic table where Mick sat absorbed in a trail guide and map. When he turned to acknowledge her, the light from the lantern cast a sheen of white over her.

"I just wanted to thank you for coming out after me tonight."

He smiled. "No problem. Glad you're feeling better. You think you might want to go to a hospital in the morning and get an X-ray of your ankle?"

Dorrie flexed the ankle. "It really is feeling better. I think I just sprained it. Anyway, I was wondering if you had any aspirin, just to avoid any flare-up of pain during the night."

Mick nodded and reached for his daypack lying on the ground, rummaging for his first aid kit. Watching his activity, Dorrie remarked, "Yeah, I was full of pride telling you to keep that kit for yourself when I sure needed the ace wrap stored inside. It's like you had a premonition something would go wrong. . .like you knew I would need it."

"Yeah, what's the old saying, Dorrie? Pride comes before the fall?" Mick chuckled at first, then grew despondent as the words of Scripture sunk deep into him. He thumped his chest as if to ward off the biting insect of conviction nipping his soul, then gave her two tablets and the water bottle. "Have a good night's sleep."

"Thanks, you too."

Dorrie returned to the tent, unaware of Mick's eyes probing her every move, his thoughts reverberating with her simple but powerful confession. Now as he returned his attention to the map before him, he considered her offers of help on the trail to bind the wounds of his past. *Dorrie offered me a bandage too,* he realized, *but how can some stranger repair a heart that has been torn to shreds?* Once more the word "pride" echoed in his thoughts. Mick shook his head. The map before him wavered as visions of his father's attack in a cold, dark alley of Boston now haunted him. He could still hear the sound of the pistol firing behind his father's unsuspecting back and the terrible thud as his dad collapsed onto the hard pavement. Crimson blood dribbled from the head wound. A shiver swept over Mick as he squeezed his eyes shut, trying to blot out the painful memories that tumbled like a car careening off a cliff. Instead, he pictured himself kneeling next to his father's side, trying in vain to arouse him even as one of the gang members threatened him with the same smoking weapon.

"That'll teach him to keep his mouth shut about Jesus," the leader of the gang snarled at Mick.

The wail of a police siren sent the gang members scurrying for cover as Mick hovered over his father's unconscious form, calling his name. An ambulance was summoned, and before Mick realized it, rescue people clad in uniforms whisked his father away to the hospital. Mick could still taste the saltiness of his tears running into his mouth as he stumbled along the street, then drifted down a staircase to the subway station. He wondered how his mother would react to the news that her husband had just been gunned down in an obscure alley of Boston's dark streets.

For years Mom warned Dad to stay away from the gangs for fear he might become a target of their vengeance. The news of laymen and ministers murdered in South America and other parts of the world left her quaking in great fear. Often Mick would hear her murmur prayers well into the wee hours of the morning. . .words that now seemed to have fallen on deaf ears.

When Mick arrived home in Cambridge—a suburb of Boston and home to the prestigious Harvard University—he found his mother on the phone. She cried as a stranger's voice relayed the sad news of her husband's critical state after suffering a gunshot wound to the head.

Throwing the phone into the cradle on the wall, she grabbed her purse, and along with Mick, rushed to the hospital in the center of the great city of Boston. They arrived to find his father in emergency surgery to stop the bleeding in his skull. For hours and hours they waited, huddled together, drawing strength from one another while the delicate procedure was performed.

When the neurosurgeon finally appeared in a doctor's white coat covering the green garb of the operating room, he told the family the news they feared most—Dad suffered an untold amount of damage to the brain. He now lived on life support. They were uncertain he would ever regain consciousness. Mom cried uncontrollably, leaning on Mick for support, until she asked him to contact his older sister, who lived with her family out in California.

Mick telephoned Pamela, who flew in the very next day. In her usual bossy manner, Pam took control of the situation immediately by arranging a conference with the physicians responsible for Dad's care so the family might reason out the situation. On the homefront, Pam fixed the meals, telephoned the neighbors and relatives with the news of the dreadful occurrence, handled the influx of newspaper and television reporters, and maintained order. Mick only found himself paralyzed during the awful time, trapped by the knowledge of this terrible loss and the endless question of why. Why, when Dad gave everything to the druggies and winos and mixed-up kids on the street did God forsake him in his hour of need? Why did God allow such a tragedy to enfold their tiny family unit?

Dad was eventually weaned from the respirator but remained in his coma. Mom visited every day, talking to him, reading from the Bible, sharing the family news, even though his eyes remained closed and he never acknowledged a word she spoke. Mick came less and less frequently to the acute care center where they placed him. Instead he delved into his studies, sent out resumes, and secured a teaching position at one of the area middle schools. During the time he remained at home, he used the money he earned to help pay the bills. Little by little he ceased reading the Bible, praying, or attending church. He did not even acknowledge the church support that went out to the family during the crisis. Several in the church raised funds through bake sales and special collections to help offset the massive medical bills mounting from Dad's care. Others brought over food once a week or came to cheer up his mother, who relished the visits. Yet this outpouring of love from the church family did little to ease the torture afflicting Mick.

Pam offered to move back from California to help manage everything, but Mom refused, encouraging her to continue on with her own life. Mick was secretly glad when Pam left for the West Coast, for she tended to lord it over him as his big sister. Mick held the impression that Pam never considered him an adult but the kid brother who remained interested in playing toy soldiers or hitting a baseball. Even during the height of Dad's illness, she became authoritative, ordering him to do this or that. Mick sighed in relief when he watched her plane take off from Logan International Airport, whispering under his breath so his mother could not hear, "Good-bye, so long, and good riddance."

One day, eighteen months after the initial injury, an exciting thing happened. Mick remembered escorting his mother to his car after a visit with Dad when a nurse came flying out of the entrance to the care unit, waving her arms frantically. "He's waking up, Mrs. Walters! Quick!"

Mick and his mother dashed back inside the facility to see Dad groaning and stirring in his sleep. Mom called out to him in an anxious voice. When his eyes opened, he only stared at her with a blank expression, mumbling some sort of gibberish they did not understand.

"It takes time," the nurse assured them. "Why, he's been asleep for eighteen months. Let's just give him time and see what he does."

However, time only served to show Mick and his mother the true extent of the damage suffered by the bullet that pierced the street preacher's brain. Dad would blubber and bawl, croak out one-word phrases, and sometimes throw temper tantrums by dashing his food to the floor. He was incontinent, requiring adult-size pads to keep him dry. The more Mick witnessed this altered mental state, the more bitter he became. Unable to bear it anymore, Mick moved out of the house, rented his own apartment, and refused to visit his father.

"Mick, really, I have seen changes in your father," his mother would say, begging him to visit his father. "Why, I know he looks at me and answers me when I speak. Please, he needs to see you. He needs you so bad."

"That person isn't my father," Mick told her in a stiff voice, hatred burning within. "That's a stranger, some. . .some baby with an adult face. He doesn't even know who I am! Sorry, Mom, but I can't take it. I won't accept it. As far as I'm concerned, Dad might as well be dead."

Soon afterwards, Mom sold the home that had been the family's for as long as Mick could remember and purchased a small condo near the long-term care facility, where she could be close to Dad. Mick occasionally visited to share dinner with her, but refused to visit his father. Whenever Mom would pray or bring out her Bible, he would scorn her beliefs and inform her that no loving God would have done this to his father, especially when he devoted his whole life to serving Him and the kingdom. Mom cried in response to his accusations, sending waves of guilt washing over Mick. She sent her pastor to Mick's apartment in an effort to reach him, but Mick would only shout, curse, and threaten the man until the pastor was obliged to leave him alone. "His heart is like stone," the pastor informed his mother. "Only God Himself can reach the young man in a way we have yet to see ourselves. Keep him in prayer."

Now as Mick surveyed the tent and the occupants within, he wondered if Dorrie was indeed the answer to the ceaseless prayers offered on his behalf. In a way, Mick prided himself on being the prodigal son—the one who refused to accept his father's condition as the will of God. Mick scowled at the mere thought of Dorrie's Christian beliefs, vowing never to allow her the opportunity to break through the protective barriers encasing his heart in marble.

After awhile, Mick turned off the propane lantern and switched on his flashlight, preparing to venture to the car, where he would spend an uncomfortable night curled up in the passenger's seat. A multitude of stars shone crystal clear in the night sky, indicative of a pleasant day the following morning. Mick wondered what the day would hold as he opened the car door and settled himself inside. Initially, he had planned to begin a backpacking excursion into the vast wilderness, but circumstances forced a one-day delay in his plans. Now as he reclined in the seat with his arms crossed behind his head, he thought of the sisters occupying his tent and how each filled voids in his life he never knew existed.

❧

The next morning, both women emerged from the tent refreshed from the night's sleep, only to find their protector readying his pack for a lengthy hike. Neither spoke a word to him, despite the fact that each sensed a mixture of sorrow and disappointment over his decision to begin his hike. Soon Gail began pleading with Mick not to abandon her just when they were all having a good time.

Irritated by her sister's continual pestering of Mick, Dorrie drew the fretful

Gail to one side and told her that it was time they went on with their vacation and left Mick to enjoy his. "He's spent enough time with us already. We're here to have our own vacations."

Gail glared at her older sister. "Yeah, that's fine for you to say, Dorrie, after spending the whole night out with my boyfriend!"

"He's not your boyfriend."

"Oh, he's not? And just how would you know? Don't think I didn't hear you two chatting and who knows what else, real cozylike at the picnic table last night." Gail whirled away to avoid her sister's startled expression.

"Gail Marie Shelton, all we did was talk!" Dorrie fired back. "That's it, period. Maybe next time instead of eavesdropping, you'll have the nerve to come out of hiding and find out what we're doing."

Gail gave a huff and strode off angrily toward the roar of the river that lay beyond the tent sites. Dorrie exhaled in exasperation, her breath fanning the wisps of dark brown bangs across her forehead.

All at once, Mick came to investigate the commotion. "So am I the cause of the arguing today?" he wondered.

"Gail's jealous. Why. . .I haven't a clue. She thinks we were doing something inappropriate at the picnic table last night to which I promptly set the record straight." Dorrie turned to face him. "Guess between last night's fiasco and the idea you're leaving on a hike today, this gives her enough reason to pout. Honestly, I don't know why we decided to do this trip together. I thought it would be good for the two of us to get out into the woods and renew our friendship, but all we seem to do is get into fights." Dorrie picked up a twig from the ground and pitched it in disgust. "When we get back to the campsite, I might as well pack up the gear and head for home. There's no way I'm gonna endure anymore of this." Then in an afterthought she added, "There's a hundred bucks up in smoke."

"A hundred bucks?" Mick repeated in confusion. "What costs a hundred bucks?"

"For our stay at the Lakes of the Clouds hut on Mt. Washington. I wanted it to be the finale to our vacation. . .a glorious jaunt up to the highest peak of the Presidential mountain range, then a magnificent stay at the most popular hiker's hut. Now, between my ankle and our quarreling, it doesn't look like we're gonna make it."

Mick eyed her in amazement. "That's pretty wild because I have reservations at the same hut midway through my hike. What day is your reservation for?"

"Friday night."

Mick laughed. "Same as mine. Look, Dorrie, today's only Wednesday and you have several days to rest that ankle of yours. Since you really want to do the hike, you can give Gail a little incentive to stick it out by telling her I'll be waiting for her to show up at the hut Friday night."

Dorrie's face brightened. "That's not a bad idea. Just knowing you'll be waiting at the top of the mountain might make the trip easier to swallow for the both of us." Dorrie's gaze drifted toward the river and the faint outline of her sister, skipping rocks by the shore. "Well, I'd better help you break camp and all. I hope you don't mind driving us back to our campsite."

"No problem," he assured her. "I'm going to a trailhead in that general area anyway, so it works out well with my plans."

Together they grabbed hold of the tent poles, dismantled them, then gently eased the shelter to the ground. The poles and fabric were stuffed into a large nylon sack. By the time Gail arrived, the site was spic and span, with remnants of the gear stowed away in Mick's car. While Mick and Dorrie surveyed the site for any remaining camping gear that might have been overlooked, Gail's drawn face observed all of this in growing agitation.

Dorrie waved her arm toward her younger sister. "Let's go, Gail," she called out, sliding into the passenger seat of Mick's car.

Gail stood her ground and shook her head fiercely like a strong-willed child ready to unleash a terrible tantrum.

"What's eating her?" Mick questioned Dorrie, who shrugged her shoulders. Dorrie grasped the underside of her injured extremity, eased her leg out, and stood to her feet. "C'mon now, Gail. We gotta get back to the campsite and make sure no one's ripped off our stuff." Dorrie hobbled up to Gail, who remained in her stubborn stance, her teeth gnawing on her bottom lip. "What's wrong with you?"

Gail sniffed at Dorrie's injured ankle. "I'll bet you just got yourself injured so you'd get my boyfriend all sympathetic," she muttered. "Now he's running off into the woods and leaving me behind, all because of you."

Dorrie's face flushed. "That's not true. Mick's been planning this hike of his all along. If anything, we're the ones who interrupted his plans." She then lowered her voice. "Look, you'll see Mick again in no time, if that's any consolation. He's planning on a stay at the same hiker hut I have reservations for at the end of the week. And he just told me he can't wait to see you again."

Gail's eyes sparkled in anticipation. "Really? What hut is that?"

"You know. . .that hut I've been telling you about since we arrived here in the Whites, the one parked on the shoulder of Mt. Washington called Lakes of the Clouds."

Gail rolled her eyes. "Oh, that one. Yeah, you told me I had to hike three steep miles to get to the thing. No way. I'll never make it."

"C'mon, not even for Mick?" Dorrie asked with a persuasive tilt to her voice. "You wouldn't want to leave him stranded on the summit now, would you?"

Gail's eyes darkened as she crossed her arms tightly before her. "What's the sense, Dorrie, seeing as you've already claimed him for yourself?"

"Look, Gail, we've got to get going. We're holding Mick up. I promise with all my heart I won't even speak to him while we're there, okay? You can have him all to yourself. I won't get in your way. I'll just be like a cloud passing through the sky."

Gail laughed scornfully. "Yeah, right. How do I know you'll keep your word?"

Dorrie sensed the indignation rising within her, but quickly suppressed it with a deep breath. "You have my word. Scouts honor or whatever. Now come on, we're making Mick late for his hike. Go ahead and sit in the front seat if you want."

Gail finally nodded and hopped brightly into the seat next to Mick, while Dorrie gingerly occupied the rear passenger seat, wedging herself beside a box containing camping equipment. The smell of propane assaulted her nostrils, mixed with the musty odor of canvas material. Mick shifted the small car into gear and rolled out of the campground and onto the Kancamagus Highway. Occasionally, his blue eyes would survey Dorrie from the rearview mirror with an expression that illustrated an eagerness to converse with her rather than the chatty Gail, who clung to his arm while her tongue flip-flopped inside her mouth. Soon they were speeding their way through a beautiful area known as Franconia Notch, where steep stone mountainsides split wide open to encompass the thin stretch of highway. The crevices of rock formed unique gorges, while the mountains offered hikers the challenge of climbs that would bring them high into the alpine tundra. Spectacular views from the rock-strewn summits rewarded the climbers.

Mick veered the car off the highway and passed the little wooden hut where the two women first laid eyes on him and his pack, ready to tackle the strenuous trails existing in the region. Finally, he pulled into the campsite where Dorrie's car sat parked. The campsite was none the worse for the wear except for a curious animal that had inspected the remains lurking inside the food bag Dorrie failed to secure yesterday before her ill-fated hike to Franconia Falls. Wrappers and crumbs of granola lay strewn across the picnic table.

Gail's fingers clenched Mick's strong biceps as she squealed, "Oh no. . .a bear! We had a bear at our site! I just knew something like this would happen."

"More likely a raccoon," Mick said, studying the marks made in the soft soil. "These are not the paw prints of a large mammal."

Dorrie hobbled over to the table and promptly began cleaning up the mess.

"You sure you girls can take care of yourselves?" Mick inquired.

"Yes, we girls can take care of ourselves," Dorrie mimicked.

"Mick, are you sure about leaving?" Gail asked, her hold tightening around his arm. "We can still have a great time. I'll hike with you wherever you want to go!"

Instead of acknowledging the young woman who clung to him, Mick leveled his sights on Dorrie, inquiring once more if he should proceed with his hike as planned.

"Of course, of course," Dorrie told him matter-of-factly. "We'll probably leave the campsite and head for a motel in Conway."

"Guess I'll see you both at the hut at the end of the week then, that is, if your ankle is up to the climb."

Dorrie wiggled the extremity and nodded. "I think a few days' rest is just what the doctor ordered."

"You take care of yourself," Gail whispered huskily in his ear, tugging on his neck in an attempt to draw him into a farewell kiss. Mick fought against her gesture of good-bye, much to her chagrin. He waved in the direction of Dorrie, ambled off to his car, and soon sped away with car exhaust filtering over the campsite.

Gail's face fell as her brown eyes burned with tears of rejection. "Well, good riddance to him," she spat. "I hope I never see him again."

Dorrie could not help but chuckle. "That's sure a switch after nearly falling over the guy for two solid days now, Gail."

"Well, it's obvious he isn't interested in me anymore." She flounced her shoulder. "C'mon Dorrie, let's get outta this place and back to civilization."

Dorrie groaned under her breath and continued to pack up the site. To Gail, civilization meant a nice hotel with a heated indoor pool and all the comforts of home. Dorrie sighed, forcing herself to relax. If she wanted any time to hike her beloved Mt. Washington, she must swallow any indignation and plan for a few days' rest to heal her ankle while allowing Gail the comfort of the hotel. Deep inside, Dorrie could not contain the strange eagerness of seeing Mick once again on the highest summit in the Northeast.

Chapter 6

The Zealand Trail provided Mick with an easy two-mile jaunt to his first overnight stay of the trip—the Zealand Falls hut, a hiker's cabin perched on a rise overlooking the raging waters of the Zealand and Whitewall Rivers. His muscular legs easily trekked the fairly level terrain and up a hill. By midafternoon he reached his destination, where he was hailed by the caretakers or "crew" of the hut—two young college-aged men who tended the establishment during the summertime, cooked the evening and morning meals, and provided stimulating conversation to the people who came to visit. It did not take long for Mick to strike up a conversation with the men while assisting with chores around the hut.

Later that afternoon, Mick took a stroll along the edge of the river. He sat down on a large rock perched near the roaring river that eventually dropped over the face of a cliff into a raging waterfall below. He allowed the sights and smells to invade his senses.

Even as he soaked in the rays of the sun and inhaled the earthy vapors inherent in the woods surrounding him, he could not shake his thoughts of Dorrie. He remembered vividly her sympathetic embrace on the dark, lonely trail when he confided in her of his painful past. Now as he pitched rocks into the river, he realized how much Dorrie cared about his internal turmoil over his father's injury. Of course his mother cared, and even those in the church once voiced their concern; but here in the midst of these great woods, a woman who knew nothing about him extended a certain compassion unlike anyone he had ever met.

Dorrie had reached out to him with everything she possessed and he had swatted her away like a pesky fly. Deep inside, sensations of guilt and regret nipped at him. Now Dorrie was left to struggle with an injured ankle and a flighty sister. Mick threw the rocks into the river with greater rapidity. The water splashed upward into miniature fountains of spray that soaked his sandals. Here he basked in the great outdoors while Dorrie sat in a cold hotel room, staring at four antiseptic walls, unable to hike the trails she loved with a passion. "Well, I deserve this time alone on the trail," he rationalized, justifying his own fortune. "Haven't I been through a miserable time myself? Don't I deserve this?"

Yet thoughts of Dorrie continued to tug at his heartstrings as he returned to the hut. He recalled her bravery and her determination to hike back down the trail in the dead of night, despite the trials she faced. He compared her strengths with those in her sister, who seemed fearful of everything. He recalled how many common interests they shared, including their love of hiking. He admired Dorrie's tenacity and independent nature, tempered with the humility to accept his help and to admit her errors. The combination of all these characteristics warmed his heart in a strange way, leaving him consumed with thoughts of her, even during the cheery dinner hour at the hut, when the college-aged crew served up huge platters of spaghetti, Italian bread, and bowls of garden salad to the ravenous hikers who paid for food and accommodations.

Mick tried to ignore the flirting of one young woman at his elbow who continually peppered him with questions about the trail, hoping to spark some interest on his part. At times she would jostle his arm with a quick "Pardon me!" or perform other antics that left Mick feeling warm under his T-shirt. After the meal had concluded, Mick offered to pitch in with the cleanup in an effort to avoid a confrontation with the young woman hiker, who had gathered with the others on the front porch of the hut. He and the crew talked about biology and their college days as they made short work of the supper dishes. Afterwards, the head caretaker gave Mick back half the fee he had paid for the night's stay.

"We usually offer discounts to those who help with the work," he explained.

Mick stuffed the money into his pocket, thinking of an appropriate gift of thanks he might buy Dorrie whenever he reached civilization again. He stepped outside to be greeted by a cool mountain breeze that caressed his face. The other hikers had long since abandoned the porch area of the hut, leaving it vacant and extremely inviting. Mick sat down on the steps leading up to the hut, taking in all the sights and sounds of the evening. An owl hooted in the distance. The trees appeared veiled in white by the rays of the silvery moon rising in the evening sky. The sounds of the rushing river beyond the grove of trees serenaded the night. Nothing could be more peaceful.

Mick was just beginning to relax the tenseness in his muscles when he heard the sound of soft footsteps approaching from the darkness. A petite figure sat down beside him on the step, cupped a chin in her hand, and sighed longingly.

"Great night, huh?"

Mick turned to see the smiling face of the young woman who had occupied the seat next to him at dinner. As the grin pierced his soul, a cloud lifted, revealing her identity before his stunned eyes. He inhaled a sharp breath before exclaiming in disbelief, "Krysta? I. . .I don't believe it!"

Her smile grew broader. "Well, it's about time you recognized me, Mick Walters. Took you long enough. And we just saw each other in the hallway at school a month ago. It's a good thing I'm not easily offended."

Mick felt his guard immediately go up and the color drain from his face. He shifted restlessly on the narrow wooden step. So it was Krysta Anderson who had tried desperately to gain his attention during the meal. Her thin, narrow face with high cheekbones and green eyes sent another round of painful memories spinning around within him. . .memories he thought he had suppressed from two years ago.

During that time, Krysta arrived as a substitute teacher at the middle school where he taught. They conversed at length of their love for the great outdoors. For a time they dated. Soon it became obvious to Mick, after several dates, that Krysta desired more out of their relationship than a few simple dates and conversation. For several weeks, Mick avoided the inevitable, but eventually he became entranced by her feminine ways and her caring attitude, which eased the pain of his father's disability. The attention he received led to an immoral lifestyle. After a time, his guilty conscience burdened him to the point that he finally terminated their relationship, despite her plea that they remain together. Several other times she had tried to rekindle their relationship, but failed.

Krysta folded her arms across her chest and gazed at the crescent moon shining above. "So you've become the silent type, I see," she mused. "You didn't say one word at supper this evening."

Mick pretended to scratch an itch on his leg that wasn't there. "Yeah, well, not much to say. But I wouldn't mind knowing what you're doing here, of all places."

"Don't you remember? You and I always discussed taking a wonderful trip to the Whites one day! I asked your friend Jerry about your plans, and he told me your whole itinerary. Unfortunately, I had to stay here at the hut an extra day waiting for you. Glad you finally showed up. I thought I'd surprise you and maybe even renew a spark in our relationship, huh?"

Mick bristled at the mere suggestion. "I told you almost two years ago our relationship was over."

"Oh, c'mon, don't give me that. We're made for each other. You once told me there would never be anyone else, and I still believe it with all my heart." She flung her luxurious auburn hair over her shoulders—hair Mick once loved to run his fingers through. Now he shuddered at the thought and looked down, pretending to examine the sandals fastened to his feet with Velcro.

"So where are you headed in the morning?"

"I'm sure Jerry told you that as well," he remarked acidly, angered over the betrayal. He wondered how Krysta manipulated his friend into giving out the information.

Krysta laughed. "Actually he did. You have a very caring friend who thinks like I do. . .that we should be together." She curved a small hand under his elbow and gave a slight squeeze. "Look, my friend Cathy and I are supposed to head back to the parking area in the morning, but I'm sure she'll understand when I tell her I've changed plans. How about a hiking buddy?"

Mick shuddered under the touch of her fingers. He disengaged himself from her grasp and stood quickly to his feet. "No, Krysta," he informed her stoutly. "It's over between us." Memories of Dorrie suddenly washed over him. "Anyway, I have someone else waiting for me at the trail's end."

Krysta frowned and narrowed her eyebrows. "A special someone, huh? Well, isn't that cozy. And you were the one who told me you would lead a chaste and virtuous life. What a liar you turned out to be, Mick Walters." Again, she laughed at the very notion while shaking back her flowing hair.

"She happens to be a virtuous woman," Mick remarked, "which is more than I can say for you."

"Or you!" Krysta fired back with a devilish spark in her eye. "Virtuosity is not in your makeup. I am a witness to that."

The comment cut Mick deep to the core. He staggered before whirling from Krysta's view and sauntered inside the hut to the bunkroom.

"How can I get you to change your mind?" she called out after him with a teasing tilt to her voice.

The question chased Mick all the way into the bunkhouse. Krysta's inopportune appearance dredged up all the painful memories he thought were dead and buried. *Why did she have to show up here, of all places, just when I was trying to get my life back in order?* He tried to shake off the haunting illustration of the terrible sin plaguing him by concentrating on Dorrie and her strong Christian values. He knew Dorrie was not interested in the flesh like Krysta or even Gail. Dorrie was a woman interested in his heart and soul. *That must be why I'm attracted to her like no one else,* he decided.

Inside the bunkhouse, illuminated by a propane lantern, Mick declined a game of cards offered by the fellow hikers occupying the dwelling. Instead, he found an unoccupied bunk and settled in underneath the scratchy wool blanket, hoping to rise at dawn and head out before Krysta awakened the following morning. He lay awake for hours, his hands resting beneath his head, unable to sleep. To squelch the memories of Krysta, he concentrated his thoughts on Dorrie, wondering what she might be doing. He envisioned her sitting helplessly by the tree trunk in the dark woods near the river with her ankle wrapped in a damp bandanna, her miserable face brightening upon his arrival. Mick rolled over on his side and shut his eyes. Again he thought about Dorrie's eagerness to hike the trails and her interest when he shared his experiences in biology. Out of all the women he had known the last few years, no one but Dorrie matched his interests as a key might fit a lock. Even Krysta proved pale in comparison, for her interests only fed her flesh and nothing else. Mick frowned as his eyes remained shut. *If only. . . ,* he thought, his hand clenching the pillow under his head, *if only Dorrie wasn't such a fiery Christian with words like thorns of conviction in my soul, there really might be a future for us.*

Mick rose early the next morning in the hopes of starting out on the A to Z

Trail, which would take him to another hiker's hut located in Crawford Notch. In the small, modest kitchen of the hut, the head caretaker stood warming a huge kettle of oatmeal sweetened with sliced apples. Sitting at the long wooden table, studying a trail map, was Krysta. Both glanced up to see Mick as he ventured in and grabbed a spot at the end of the table.

"Well, good morning!" Krysta exclaimed brightly, then moved to a place opposite him.

"Morning," Mick mumbled, hoping to dissuade her interest by his grumpy attitude.

"I was just telling Jeff here how the strap on my pack broke," Krysta went on. "He said he would look at it, but he's pretty busy cooking breakfast. Any chance you could fix it for me?" Her eyelashes fluttered in anticipation. "You always were good with your hands."

Mick ignored the comment and rose quickly out of the seat to pour himself a cup of steaming coffee. Normally he detested coffee, but on a day like today, he felt he needed the strength of the caffeine soaring through his veins. After dousing the liquid with sugar and cream, he returned to his place at the table and Krysta's wide, expectant eyes staring at him. "I'll take a quick look," he decided, slowly stirring the coffee that sent steam rising into his face. He sipped the liquid, made a face, then reached over to the sugar bowl for added sweetener.

Krysta watched his deliberate movements with a small smile. She flipped back her long hair. "I can't imagine how it broke," she went on. "It's always done so well for me in the past."

Mick took another sip. "What kind of pack is it?"

"Oh, one of those internal frame models. It's not very old, either. I'll take it back to the store where I bought it and demand that they refund my money."

Mick placed his broad palms on the wooden table and rose weightily to his feet. "Show me where it is. . .only I don't have much time."

Krysta jumped to her feet and led the way. The pack stood propped up against the side of the hut with one strap hanging loose. Mick bent to observe it, noting the jagged edges as if something or someone had grabbed the strap in its teeth and pulled the nylon apart. "Looks like an animal did this," he observed. "Have you tied your food up at night?"

Krysta knelt down next to him, strands of her auburn hair falling over his shoulder as she observed the cut strap in his hands. She reached out with her fingers, brushing his skin before taking up the torn end of the strap. "I tie it up every night, except of course when I stay at the huts. They have those metal storage bins to hold your food, you know."

Mick fought to keep his attention focused on the pack. "Well, I might be able to sew it back together, but once you reach civilization, I suggest you go directly to an outdoor shop and have a professional restitch it." He rose with Krysta following him like a puppy as he retrieved a sewing kit from his pack and returned to perform the duty. While he sewed the strap to the pack, Krysta gushed over his handling of the job and how well he manipulated the needle and thread.

"Oh, you're fantastic," she crooned, her head dangling over one shoulder as he worked. Her fingertips brushed back wisps of his blond hair as her breath blew in his ear, sending tremors shooting through him.

"Stop it," he told her sharply.

Krysta was undaunted by the response. "Why? I have a very capable and attractive man assisting me. All I want to do is say thank you. Don't be so testy."

Mick kept his eyes focused on his work. As a strong Christian man before his father's injury, he had committed himself to chastity. Now with his heart hardened to the purposes of God after his father's wound, Mick felt his flesh overpowering and his spirit lacking the strength to ward off Krysta's seductiveness. In her presence he felt himself wavering. His fingers worked quickly, hoping to finish the job and hasten away before he lost all his sensibility.

Finally, he tied the last knot and breathed a sigh of relief with the work completed. "There, all set." He glanced around, realizing Krysta had suddenly vanished. Wiping away the sweat that gathered across his brow, Mick rose to his feet, holding Krysta's pack in a powerful grip. He searched around the hut for the young woman as people flocked to the wooden tables, eager for a hearty breakfast before their bodies withstood the rigors of the trail once again. She was nowhere to be found. He finally set the pack down on the porch steps and retreated inside the bunkroom to collect his belongings when Krysta suddenly hopped off a bunk above him like a vulture. Immediately, she flung her arms around his neck.

Mick firmly removed her arms. "What kind of a game are you playing?" he yelled at her laughing face. His feet thumped along the wooden planks of the bunkroom as he gathered up his gear.

"I'm only thanking you for sewing my pack."

"Well, you're not supposed to be in here," he told her flatly, stuffing a shirt and his toothbrush inside a pocket of his pack.

"I most certainly can be," she retorted.

"Look, Krysta, I told you last night. . .I'm not interested in renewing our relationship. It's over. Finished. Done for."

She smiled and shook her head.

Mick thought of praying but decided that was a weak gesture of surrender brought on by a man cornered by his circumstances. He whirled about to avoid her face, only to find her thin arms encircling his waist, hugging him close.

"C'mon Mick," Krysta pleaded. "You're such a great guy. . .strong and good-looking. I know we'll have a great time together, just the two of us, hiking the trails. It'll be like old times again, I just know it."

Mick stood still and silent even as her arms tightened like those of an octopus ready to choke out his life. "No," he again told her, but this time with less resolve.

"Are you sure that's what you want?" her sultry voice whispered.

Mick lurched around suddenly, her face but inches from his. In the dark surroundings of the bunkroom, she appeared demure and appetizing to his weak flesh. He allowed her arms to wrap around his neck, succumbing at last to the temptation of lips that appeared delicious, but in all actuality, were foul and full of poison. A vision of Dorrie flashed through his mind, kneeling in prayer, offering intercession on his behalf. Just as quickly, Mick lurched away from the embrace, the abrupt movement sending Krysta sprawling to the floor. Without another glance, he picked up his pack and fled.

He hiked steadily for hours, his ears acknowledging the soft chuckle in the woods around him and unseen voices that seemed to taunt him through the whisper of the wind in the trees. The hike he endured that day was strenuous, with steep climbs up and down the mountain, yet this did not deter Mick from keeping up a stiff pace. He wanted to place himself as many miles away from Krysta as possible. When he arrived late that afternoon at Crawford Notch, he contemplated staying at the hostel there, but decided against it. Instead, Mick strode out to the bustling highway where cars zoomed by and extended his thumb. He stood patiently waiting for a ride that would take him to Conway and, he hoped, to Dorrie once again.

Chapter 7

I wish you wouldn't go," Dorrie complained as her younger sister modeled her outfit of a short denim miniskirt and rose-colored top, which accentuated her figure, while standing in front of the full-length mirror hanging in the hotel room. With several fingers, Gail fluffed out the curls dancing around her face, then scrutinized her appearance.

"Why not?"

"Because you only met this guy at the pool this afternoon," Dorrie complained. "Who knows what kind of guy he really is." She lay stretched out on the bed, nursing her ankle, which ached after a day of traipsing through the outlet stores with Gail. On the floor lay strewn the shopping bags of items Gail insisted on buying. For her part, Dorrie purchased a better water bottle for use on the hike come Friday and a detailed map outlining the various approaches to Mt. Washington and the Lakes of the Clouds hut. Even now the map lay flat before her on the bed while Gail readied herself for a dinner date with a man she had met during a brief swim session at the hotel pool.

"I still think you should be careful, Gail," Dorrie began once again, only to be met by an irritated look on Gail's face.

"There you go again, trying to run my life just because you're older." Gail flounced her shoulder and reached for her lipstick.

"You know that's not true, so why do you say it?" Dorrie answered in more of an irritated voice than she would have liked. "How many times are you willing to get hurt by all these guys of yours before you decide to give up the games?"

"I don't get hurt, I have fun," Gail retorted in defense, now reaching for her perfume, which she spritzed this way and that. "They pay for the dinner and the movie while I sit back and enjoy it all."

The fog of scent drifting over the room sent Dorrie into a sneezing fit. She reached over for the tissue box and promptly blew her nose. "I hope you'll remember not to stay out late tonight," Dorrie told her, throwing the tissue into a nearby wastebasket. "We'll need our sleep. Tomorrow's the highlight of the trip, remember, the hike up Mt. Washington."

"Maybe for you, but quite frankly, I've found more interesting things to do." Gail tossed the perfume into her cosmetic bag with an air of haughtiness.

Dorrie puffed in anger but clamped her mouth shut just in time to avoid another flare-up of hostility. A knock came on the door, signaling the arrival of Gail's date. When Gail opened it, a man wearing an expensive leather jacket and cowboy boots greeted her. Dorrie only stared hard, sizing up the guy, hoping and praying he would not take advantage of her little sister tonight.

"Wish me a good time now," Gail said with a laugh before hooking her arm around the elbow the man offered. Her giggles echoed down the hall, even after the door slammed shut.

Dorrie returned to her perch on top of the bed, her eyes drifting to the view of the Presidential mountain range through the hotel window. As she gazed at the beautiful sight of majestic mountains framed in red by the sinking sun, tears formed in her eyes. She wondered if it was possible to meet the challenges still lurking before her, namely, a hard climb up the mountainside, dragging her sister in tow while coping with the effects of a sprained ankle. Wiping the tears from her eyes, Dorrie reached over for her Bible lying on the nightstand and thumbed through the pages until she came to a verse in Psalm 121: " 'I will lift up mine eyes unto the hills, from whence cometh my help. My help cometh from the LORD, which made heaven and earth.' " Dorrie knew she must keep her sights focused above, even farther than the mountain peaks looming in the distance, high above into the heavenly realm of God, in whom she could place all her trust. As Dorrie reflected on the Scripture, wisdom slowly sank into her spirit. Down at her feet and the earthly surroundings, with only the painful reminders of her time spent with Gail and the aching of her ankle, life appeared full of disappointment. Yet when she lifted her eyes to behold the beauty of the distant mountain ranges, life became exciting and awesome, filled with the wonders of God and the realization that He held all of creation and herself in the palm of His hand.

A rumbling in the pit of her stomach alerted Dorrie to the fact she had not eaten much all day. She glanced out the window and noticed a fast-food place just a short distance down the street. While she didn't relish the thought of eating greasy food, neither did she like the idea of eating alone in some fancy place. "Maybe they'll even serve a halfway decent salad," she reminded herself as she slowly rose and ventured to the bathroom. She ran a comb through her bobbed hair, then in an afterthought, dug into her toiletry bag for lipstick and applied a faint trace of rose color across her lips. Shrugging at her appearance, Dorrie turned, whirled her purse off the ground, and strode down the dark hall to the elevator.

While waiting for the elevator doors to part, she offered up a prayer on Gail's behalf. As the older sister, Dorrie felt protective of Gail. Many times in the past, Dorrie found herself in a head-to-head confrontation with one of Gail's numerous boyfriends. One such outburst left Gail in tears, swearing she would never forgive Dorrie for her aggressive stand until they discovered later that year the guy had been arrested for grand larceny. "Sister's intuition" Dorrie always called it. Gail never admitted to her error nor did she thank her sister for her timely intervention, but Dorrie knew her response had been appropriate.

The elevator doors burst open before her. Dorrie walked in and pressed M for the main floor. She unzipped her purse to check the money folded inside her wallet as the elevator hummed and the doors parted upon reaching the destination. With her eyes still focused inside the purse, she walked off the elevator, only to plow headlong into a figure coming from the opposite direction.

The contact stunned Dorrie momentarily. Her hand flew to the tender area on her forehead. "Pardon me. . . ," she began until her eyes focused on the familiar face of Mick with the pack on his back. She stared in surprise. "Mick! What are you doing here?"

A sudden flush marred his sleek, tanned face, giving him a fevered appearance. "I. . .uh. . ."

"What happened to your hike? Is everything okay?"

Flustered by the surprise contact, Mick searched in vain for an explanation but found his mind a complete blank.

"Well look," Dorrie went on, oblivious to his embarrassment, "if you've come for Gail, I'm afraid you're too late."

"I'm too late?" Mick repeated in confusion, furrowing his eyebrows.

"Yup. Sorry to bear bad news, but some other guy already claimed her for the evening."

Mick shook his head. "I didn't come looking for Gail. I. . .uh, actually. . .I came looking for you."

Dorrie stepped back in surprise, nearly colliding into other people walking off the elevator behind her. She led Mick to the lobby, where they found seats in two overstuffed chairs. Her eyes narrowed in puzzlement. "You came looking for me? I don't get it. You must've searched every motel around here, and let me tell you, there're a lot of them."

Mick slid his pack to the floor, again finding himself at a total loss for words. Instead, he toyed with one of the many straps looped through the plastic buckles on his pack.

"Did I do something wrong?" Dorrie asked. "I know I messed up your start time for the hike and all, but. . ."

His face rose to meet hers. "No, no, nothing like that. I. . .well, I was worried about your ankle and all. I wanted to find out how you were getting along."

Dorrie sat upright in her chair with lines of disbelief etched across her features. "You mean you came off the trail just to find out how I'm doing?"

"Something like that."

The two sat in silence for several awkward moments. Neither knew how to approach the other with both paralyzed by the anxiety of the moment. Finally

Dorrie said, "Well, that was nice of you, Mick, but as you can see, I'm still on my feet."

"Do you still plan on hiking up Mt. Washington tomorrow?" Mick wondered, breathing a sigh of relief at having found a topic of conversation that was not too discomforting. The meeting with Krysta back at the Zealand Falls hut still left his nerves on edge.

"If all goes well and Gail can make it," Dorrie said. "Unfortunately, Gail fixed herself up for one hot date tonight, so who knows what kind of shape she'll be in for a major hike." Dorrie added with a chuckle, "I'll probably have to force her up the trail like a bulldozer."

"Gail is definitely not the outdoors type," Mick agreed. "Not like you."

Dorrie stretched out her long legs before her and crossed her ankles in a casual posture, unaware that the movement drew Mick's attention like a magnet. "Yup, I've loved the woods ever since I was little. I think it had to do with all those visits to my aunt's place in the Catskill Mountains of New York. I would take little rambles in the woods and such, always on the lookout for some new discovery." Her soft laughter now brought his attention once more to her face. "Yeah, Gail and I are like night and day when it comes to our interests in life. I thought perhaps this little vacation might meld us together, but it's only seemed to separate us even further." Just then, a loud rumbling in her stomach sent Dorrie's hand flying. "Oops, I almost forgot, I was heading out to grab a bite to eat. I'm starved."

"Mind if I join you?" Mick asked. "I haven't eaten hardly anything today."

"Sure. I was gonna grab some fast food down the road." Noting his look of displeasure, Dorrie quickly added, "But if you have a better recommendation, I'm all ears."

Mick rose to his feet. "As a matter of fact, I do. It's a local place, but they serve the best dinner buffet in the Whites. No processed stuff, either. All the food is fresh."

"Hmmm, sounds great!" Dorrie said happily. She pranced her way to the exit of the hotel with Mick lumbering close behind, carrying his pack. "I'm parked right out front," she told him, showing the way to her car. Once there, Dorrie unlocked the trunk and pushed some camping gear aside so he could wedge his internal frame pack among the belongings. With a firm slam of the hatch, she then ambled over to the driver's side.

"I'll drive," Mick offered, pointing to the set of car keys dangling between her thumb and forefinger. "It might be easier if I drive than try to navigate you through Conway at this time of evening."

"Probably better," Dorrie agreed, surrendering the keys to his outstretched hand before slipping into the passenger's seat. "Gail was right about one thing when she said I'm lousy at finding my way around."

Mick flashed her a wide grin that lit his face like beams from the noonday sun. Dorrie swallowed hard and tried not to focus her attention on his handsome features. Instead she occupied herself with the majestic scenery of the mountains framing the bustling community of Conway, New Hampshire. Upon their arrival to the eating establishment, Dorrie squealed like a girl as she pointed out the restaurant's famous decoration, anchored high on the roof. "Why, look up there, a bear!"

"Sure is." Mick shifted in his seat and crossed his arms. "Now I'll tell you a secret. That, my friend, is a huge grizzly, most dangerous of all predators in the western United States. They shot this particular specimen in Alaska." Mick watched Dorrie's reaction with a great deal of amusement. Her dark brown eyes appeared enormous under a pair of thick, arched eyebrows that now arched even further after this explanation.

"Really?" Dorrie started, then frowned and batted him playfully in the upper arm. "Go on, you're teasing me. That's not a real bear." She again eyed the immense structure, squinting a bit to see in the shadows of the coming twilight. "I think it's made of plaster or something."

Mick snapped his fingers and sighed in mock disappointment as he opened his car door and hurried to assist her. "Thought I got you on that one. You're too smart for me."

Dorrie laughed at the joke as she followed him into the restaurant. The interior of the place was not much to rave about, with oblong tables and plastic chairs reminiscent of a high school cafeteria. She was about to say something about the décor until her eyes rested on the bountiful display of food, set to warm in the chafing dishes. Her eyes widened even further when she noticed the chef bring out a real roast turkey and set it before the carving station. "Why look at that! It's real honest to goodness turkey, not that junk made out of congealed broth and fat made to look like turkey breast."

"Hmmm, actually I think it might be made of plaster," Mick countered. "It's the decoration for the buffet, you see."

Dorrie again flashed him a look and flushed under the cheerful countenance that now regarded her. The dancing blue eyes and wide grin gave the impression he liked what he saw. Pushing away the thought, Dorrie remarked, "You always seem so serious, I didn't realize you concealed a humorous streak within you, Mr. Mick. . .what is your last name?"

"Walters," he told her as a waitress showed them to their seats.

"Walters," she repeated, settling herself into the chair and spreading a paper napkin across her lap. "And where did you say you're from? You probably told me once already, but I've forgotten."

"Cambridge. A suburb of Boston."

"Right, right." Dorrie studied the menu, then tossed it aside. "I'll have one of everything," she announced. "The buffet looks so delicious, I'll probably make a pig out of myself."

"A hiker's prerogative," Mick answered after informing the waitress of their orders. "All hikers make pigs of themselves at dinner buffets. That's what gives them the energy to climb these ridiculous mountains around here. I'll never forget the humorous story I once read in a manual describing the Appalachian Trail in the White Mountains. Some joker drew a picture of a guy with suction cups on his feet and hands, trying to climb up the face of a sheer rock cliff. Underneath he wrote the caption 'I love the Whites.' He wasn't too far off track about the suction cups, I'll tell you."

Dorrie laughed once again as they both ventured to the massive food bar, promptly filled their plates, then sauntered back to their seats, where the waitress had already placed glasses brimming with iced tea and a small loaf of freshly baked bread. Before digging into the marvelous feast, Dorrie promptly shut her eyes, thanking the Lord in her heart for the food. She offered an additional prayer of thanks for bringing Mick back, hoping he might be drawn into the presence of God. When she finished her silent prayers, her eyes flicked open to see Mick sitting opposite her, ready to sink his teeth into a hunk of bread slathered with butter. "Okay, you can start," Dorrie told him with a smile.

"Just wanted to make sure God's given His permission before I begin." With great gusto, he began to eat, alternating the bread with huge forkfuls of pasta salad. Dorrie took daintier bites, but managed to clear her plate in record time.

"You're right," Mick sighed in content, resting back in his chair to observe their clean plates. "We are eating like pigs."

"Gail never eats this way," Dorrie confessed after they retrieved a second helping from the buffet. "She likes to impress the guy who's buying by taking tiny bites. Once I actually accompanied her on a date with this one-time boyfriend of hers. I cleaned up my food, then went up for seconds while Gail barely finished half of her first plate before pushing it away and declaring, 'I'm so full! I can't eat another bite.' I felt ridiculous."

Mick picked up his iced tea and gulped down half the contents before placing it on the table before him. "Well, I like to see a woman who eats well. It shows me she's enjoying the date."

Dorrie plunked her fork on her plate, confused by this comment. She had not considered this outing a date, for she was against the whole scheme of dating. After watching Gail go through the pain of broken relationships month after month, she decided long ago to trust God for the man she would one day marry. Despite the idea passed around in wide circles that one must date to find a prospective husband, Dorrie rationalized if she can trust God for her salvation and her everyday needs, why not trust Him to bring her a husband when the time was right? Now she nervously shifted her feet under the table, wondering if she had made a mistake by going with him to the restaurant. The knot that formed in the pit of her stomach suddenly suppressed the appetite.

Mick noticed the change at once. "Did I say something wrong?"

Dorrie brushed her ill feelings aside while forcing herself to pick up the fork and eat. She shook her head. "So tell me all about your teaching job, just don't get too graphic because we are eating."

Mick relaxed and delved into the various aspects of the teaching profession. "The hardest part is the time," he admitted. "Teaching is a very time-consuming profession. When it's not writing lesson plans, it's dealing with some irate parent, or grading tests, or attending faculty meetings. That's why I look forward to my outings every year in the mountains."

"And do you see your parents much?"

Mick placed his fork on the plate with a decisive clink. "I'd rather not talk about it."

Dorrie inhaled a deep breath. "I. . .I think it would be harder to avoid the problems of your family rather than deal with them head-on." The irritated look in his eyes sent her back-pedaling on the subject. "Of course, you have to do what you feel you must."

"Tell me about your job," he said, steering the conversation quickly away from the topic that bothered him most.

A spoon tinkled inside the glass as Dorrie swirled a mixture of artificial sweetener and iced tea around in a whirlpool. "Me? Oh, I'm just a secretary for a big insurance company in New York."

"Where in New York?"

"Downtown Manhattan. Cesspool of the world."

Mick's eyes widened in astonishment. "A single woman like yourself working in the heart of a big city like New York?"

"Well, it's not too bad. I go back and forth with coworkers of mine. I own a townhouse out on Long Island."

"You must make decent money."

Dorrie shrugged. "I make out okay," she admitted, grateful to God for the job that brought her a good income despite the label of a simple secretary. Once she made her move to the big city, it did not take long to realize that executive secretaries for big-name companies could earn almost as much as managers. She attended a business school, spent long hours diligently perfecting her craft, then sought out a position recommended by her school. Dorrie soon landed a job in the insurance company where she now worked. It wasn't long before she found herself in one of the executive positions in the company and able to afford housing out on Long Island instead of the long commute by train from Westchester County, where her family lived.

"So you like working in the Big Apple?"

Dorrie shrugged. "It's okay, I suppose. I like to attend one of those ministry churches near Central Park that reaches out to the gangs and other unfortunates." Dorrie went on to explain the miraculous salvation of a lead gang member by the devout pastor of a church who had a heart for the people of the streets. As she went on to describe the fruit among the depraved of society, she did not notice the strange look that came over Mick's face, nor the way his knees bobbed back and forth beneath the table where they sat.

Each time her voice mentioned the word "gang," it was like a knife stabbing him in the heart. "So this man who outreached to the gangs is still an active pastor?" Mick asked, fighting the pain of bitterness and sorrow surging through him.

Dorrie nodded. "A truly wonderful man of God. . .really awe-inspiring, especially for those of us who work in the city. It's hard seeing all the corruption that abounds, especially on some of the more notorious New York streets that boast the large porno operations and drug dealers. To have the fortitude to go and witness to these people, that really shows the mind and heart of Christ."

Mick swallowed down the rest of his iced tea in a hard gulp. Unable to control the poison festering in his heart, he lashed out, "Then tell me why God chooses to spare some of these godly men of His but yet leaves others to rot in wheelchairs like vegetables for the rest of their lives?"

Caught off guard by the deep rage concealed in his words, Dorrie sat still, her thoughts racing. During her discussion of the church in New York, she had forgotten about Mick's father and his crippling wound at the hand of a gang member's pistol. The look on Mick's face sent her spirit quickly hunting for the right words. "Mick," she said softly, "it's the same wickedness that dealt the deck against God's elect in the Scriptures. You've read the Book of Acts, I'm sure. Remember the apostles of Christ, the faithful men who gave up homes and professions to follow Him, then they were called to preach the Gospel when He ascended to the Father? Do you know how many of those apostles did not end up as martyrs for the sake of the Gospel?"

Mick did not answer but focused his attention on his plate.

"One," Dorrie told him. "Only one lived to be an old man—John, and one who inscribed the visions of Revelation for us on the island of Patmos. God had a purpose for his life. The rest were killed by the sword, crucified, stoned, or killed by some other means. They gave up their lives for the sake of the Gospel. Even Paul says it so clearly, 'for to me, to live is Christ, to die is gain.' For all those who have met death, it is a gain, for they know they live in Christ." Dorrie lowered her voice. "Don't you think to your dad, to live is Christ, even if his body or his brain is dead? He has gained not lost."

Mick felt a fist clench. "Well, I've lost everything," he blurted out. "I lost the man I respected and looked up to all my life. . . ," his words began to choke as they spilled forth, "the one I idolized practically all my life. I used to go with Dad out on the streets when he passed out the tracts to the winos and the prostitutes and the drug dealers. I followed Dad around like he was the greatest thing on earth." Mick bent his head, tears collecting in his eyes. "But now that man doesn't exist anymore. He's gone forever." He swiped up a napkin from the table and blew his nose.

Watching his pain sent watery tears drifting into her own eyes. "Oh, Mick, you were so right to follow in your dad's footsteps and witness his great love for evangelism. But don't you see? It's not him you're supposed to idolize, but Christ in him, the hope of glory. It's only Christ that allowed your dad the strength to do all those wonderful things he did on the streets. It's Christ we must put our faith and trust in."

Her words drove into him like the sharp quills of a porcupine. Mick's bright red face rose to acknowledge her. "The words are real easy to say, Dorrie. You've never been in my shoes."

Dorrie winced under his stiff rebuke, preparing to venture one of her own, but forcing herself to remain quiet. She must allow God to do the work of healing in his tortured heart. In silence, they rose to their feet. Watching the pain in his movements as Mick lumbered over to the cash register to pay the bill, she knew it would take a miraculous intervention of God for this man to let go of his hurt and to reach out to those who desperately needed him.

Chapter 8

Mick and Dorrie endured the journey back to the hotel in a void of silence. After Mick drove the car into the lighted parking area, his hands fell limp in his lap and his head leaned back against the neck rest. Dorrie observed his dejection for a few lingering moments before fumbling for the handle to the door.

At the abrupt movement, Mick glanced over at her.

"I want to turn in early tonight," Dorrie said softly. "Tomorrow's a big day."

His blue eyes regarded her and the stout witness she was, even in the dark interiors of the car. If it was not for her firm faith that convicted him with every blink of her long eyelashes, he would not hesitate to allow a feeling of love to come forth. Yet his own stubbornness prevented him from embracing her or the words she spoke. He only watched in pained silence as she opened the car door and rose to her feet. The knowledge of her departure suddenly yanked a cord within his heart, unleashing emotions within him. Despite her convicting words of the night, Mick did not want her to walk away until they resolved their differences. "Dorrie, wait a minute, will you?"

Dorrie bent down and glanced through the window of the car. "I can see our conversation really isn't going very far tonight. Why don't we leave it alone?"

Her gentle face and sad eyes wrenched his heart. "I don't like how things are right now," he confessed. "I can see I've upset you. I'm sorry that I just don't bear witness with all the things you've been telling me. You're probably right in saying them, Dorrie, but honestly. . .sometimes I feel I'm too far gone."

This dubious pronouncement sent Dorrie flying back into the passenger seat of the car. Her eyes blazed in a righteous fury. "No, you're not too far gone, Mick Walters, and I won't have you confessing such things. Sure you've been through major heartache in your life. It takes time to get all these things sorted out. God's not in a hurry, but I know He wants you to come back to Him. He understands your hurt more than anyone else." She leaned close to him, staring with a steadfastness directly into his eyes. "You've got to believe this, Mick. You've got to let go of your hurt and reach out to Him." Dorrie sat so intent on these words, she did not even see his hand reach out to cup her cheek and the warmth of a kiss that came calling on her lips. Sensing what had just occurred between them, Dorrie jerked away from his touch. She sat stunned by this tender display.

"I'm sorry," Mick faltered, surprised by his impulsive action during their serious discussion, "but you looked so beautiful just then. Your spirit, your character, and then the look in your eyes. . .I couldn't help it."

Dorrie crossed her arms before her, shaking her head fiercely. She stared out the window at the glow of the streetlights illuminating the hotel parking lot. "I was trying to be serious."

"I know you were. And I can see you care a great deal. . .more than anyone I have ever known." His eyes drifted away as he sat back once again in the driver's seat. "That's why I left the trail, Dorrie. I know you care about me. When you held me on the trail to Franconia Falls, I sensed the compassion and love in you." He sighed. "I haven't been able to shake off the encounter since."

Dorrie sensed a flush filling her cheeks. "But the reason I did that was to show you how much God cares about you and your situation."

"I know you care too, Dorrie." He picked up her hand in his. "You're more than just a friend to me. Way more."

Dorrie did not know what to say or think. She desperately wanted to see Mick restored, yet she did not intend to foster any type of relationship with him other than that of a caring friend. Now he appeared willing to cross a line that scared her to death. *I can't possibly have the kind of relationship he wants,* she reasoned silently. *He's from a different world than mine, with a heart imprisoned by the past. After this weekend it will all be over! How can we allow this to go on, only to watch it fall apart once our time here in these mountains is finished?* "Look, Mick," Dorrie finally said, "you know as well as I we aren't meant to be together. You and I, well, we're from different areas, different planets practically. Once our vacations are over, you'll go your way, and I'll go mine. It doesn't make sense to begin a relationship that's bound for the dead zone before it even begins."

The remark stung Mick. He looked over at her with hurt in his eyes. "So you don't think we have a chance, huh?"

Dorrie stared at him, choking back a chuckle within her throat. "Are you kidding? For two people as different as we are. . ." Her words were suddenly interrupted by a scream of tires as a car sped into the parking lot. Gravel flew in every direction. Mick and Dorrie watched wide-eyed as a car door lurched open and some bedraggled figure tumbled out, falling flat onto the road. The door then shut firmly and the car sped away, leaving the unknown person a hopeless mess in the middle of the parking area.

Mick and Dorrie did not hesitate but simultaneously opened their respective car doors and hurried over to the figure sprawled in the road. A disheveled denim skirt and rose-colored top met Dorrie's anguished gaze. "Gail!" she cried, kneeling next to her sister's side.

Breath laced with the overpowering stench of alcohol reached Dorrie's nostrils. The front of Gail's skirt was smeared with sticky vomit. Gail batted one eye open, then loudly bawled, "Dawrie. . .oh Dawrie. . .he stole my money. . .he. . ."

"Shh, it's going to be all right," Dorrie told her sister soothingly, tenderly brushing back wisps of curly hair with one hand. She helped Gail to her feet with Mick supporting the other side. Together they managed to assist the wobbly Gail across the parking lot to the hotel entrance, balancing her as her feet stumbled over pebbles and debris.

"Dawrie. . . ," Gail moaned. "Help me!"

Dorrie and Mick struggled her onto an awaiting elevator, then down the corridor to the hotel room. Once inside, Dorrie assisted her sister to the bathroom, where she began to clean her up while Mick waited patiently outside, ready to be of assistance if needed.

"Dawrie. . .I can't believe this happened," Gail continued to sob.

Her tears dampened Dorrie's shirt as she scrubbed her sister's face clean with a washcloth, then assisted her out of the foul-smelling clothing. "Shh, it's going to be okay," Dorrie told her reassuringly.

"Is she all right?" came Mick's concerned voice from behind the closed door.

"I think so," Dorrie answered, "but she's pretty drunk."

"You think she needs to go to the hospital?" Mick wondered.

Dorrie bit her lip, trying to suppress the anguish at the thought of the man raping her poor sister while under the influence of alcohol. "Uh. . .I'll see if she'll talk to me and tell me what happened." As Dorrie worked, Gail sat listless on the toilet, her head slumped over, her hair hanging in curly ringlets around her face. "Gail," Dorrie began softly, kneeling next to her sister, "I have to know something. . .just in case we need to get you to the hospital. Did that guy. . .did he harm you?"

Gail sniffed and shook her head, blowing her nose into a tissue. "No. He. . .he tried." She burst into tears. "He said I couldn't have my purse back unless I did what he said. I told him no. Then I got sick all over his car. . .and he got mad. That's when he left me. . .right there in the road!"

Dorrie closed her eyes, crying tears of relief. Her arms held her sister close, fostering a silent bond between them. "Shh, it's gonna be okay, Gail. I'm so glad you're safe and sound. Don't you worry about anything."

"But I ruined your trip, Dorrie," Gail finally said. Her eyes, encircled with lines of runny black mascara, stared at Dorrie like a raccoon. "I. . .I should've listened to you. I never listen to anything you say because you're older. Now look what's happened! I ruined everything."

The compassionate side of Dorrie overshadowed any anger she might have otherwise felt toward the foolish girl. "Hey now, we went on this trip to be together. I'm just glad you're okay. You're the only sister I've got, and I'd rather have you more than any ole trip." Dorrie slipped a flowered nightshirt over Gail's tear-stained face and wrestled her arms into the sleeves.

A muffled voice floated out from behind a tissue as Gail croaked, "Dorrie, I want to go home. Please, let's go home, okay? I've had enough. This just isn't going to work out. I know what you wanted to do and everything, but I'm just not cut out for this kind of vacation. I'm sorry."

Dorrie sat back, staring into her sister's bloodshot eyes and runny nose. "You really want this?" she repeated softly, her heart falling into a pit of disappointment. This surprise announcement sealed shut the door for a hike up Mt. Washington and the stay at the Lakes of the Clouds hut.

Gail nodded.

Dorrie tried to mask her disappointment. "Well, we'll talk more about it in the morning. Right now, let's get you to bed."

Dorrie fumbled for the door where Mick stood waiting, eager to assist Gail to bed, where she promptly fell into deep sleep. Sighing, Dorrie stared at Gail for a time, watching the rise and fall of her chest, unaware she was trembling until Mick's calm hand found hers. His grip tightened, imparting a strength that relaxed her jitters.

"Is she okay?" Mick whispered.

Dorrie nodded. "The guy didn't rape her, thank God. I. . .I prayed for her after she left, Mick. I. . .I'm so glad I prayed for her." Dorrie closed her eyes, allowing the tears to fall. She didn't resist Mick's strong arms cradling her, soothing away the tears of relief coupled with sadness. "I knew something like this might happen. Somehow I knew. Gail becomes a terrible mess if she has anything to drink, and I didn't trust that dude the moment I laid eyes on him. Gail says he took her money."

"Sounds like we should notify the police."

Dorrie winced with this suggestion. "I don't know if they'll believe her, Mick, with her so drunk. I'd rather wait 'til she wakes up sober in the morning and can tell us the whole story."

Mick thought on this for a few minutes, then said softly, "Guess Mt. Washington is off tomorrow?"

Dorrie observed her sister's sleeping form and with a sniff replied, "It looks that way. Gail says she wants to go home." She emitted a long, loud sigh, then walked over to the window, gazing out at the golden glow of the night with the lights of Conway illuminating the streets. In the distance she could see the red and white lights of the observation building on the peak of Mt. Washington—the summit where her hopes lay for a glorious ending to her vacation. Now it appeared unattainable. *Why, God?* Dorrie wrestled inside her heart, biting her lip to suppress a wave of bitterness coursing through her. Despite her best efforts, nothing appeared to go right on this vacation. She had to contend with an endless stream of injuries and trials. The peaceful vacation turned out to be no vacation whatsoever, but only a painful lesson of the heart.

A deep sigh next to her alerted Dorrie to the fact that Mick still remained by her side as she gazed at the crystal-clear view outside the hotel window. "Guess you'd better find a place to stay, Mick."

"Already taken care of," he told her. "I got myself a room earlier today when I first arrived."

Dorrie wiped away a stray tear from one cheek. When she turned about, she realized their close proximity and his azure eyes staring down in sympathy. "At least you can go on to Mt. Washington tomorrow. There's no sense in you forfeiting your stay at the hut. As it is, you've given up a lot of your vacation already."

"I haven't minded in the least," Mick told her, yet Dorrie was too distracted by the events of the day to notice the sincerity in his voice.

"You go on and go," she insisted. "Enjoy it for me, anyway. Maybe one day you can write and tell me what it was like."

Mick stared at her thoughtfully for a few moments, his mind buzzing with possibilities. "Look, there may be a way we can both enjoy Mt. Washington while caring for Gail's needs at the same time."

Dorrie shook her head. "That's impossible, Mick. My reservations are already set for tomorrow night. Gail's in no condition to hike. Besides, she's already told me she wants to go home. I'll be driving us back to New York first thing in the morning."

"What if I told you I would foot the money to fly Gail back to New York?"

Dorrie flashed him a look of disbelief. "Are you crazy? Whatever for?"

"I have an idea," he said simply before striding for the door. "I'm going to make a few calls early tomorrow and see what I can come up with." His hand sat poised on the knob as he turned to regard her for a few lingering moments. "I'm going to find out if at least a small part of this vacation can be rescued, Dorrie. Night, now."

Dorrie stood paralyzed, hugging her arms close to her even as the door shut with a firm resolve. "Dear Lord," her voice wavered, "who is this man You've suddenly thrust into my life? He rejects You for the hurt in his life, yet he wants to be with me. What will come of all this in the end?"

❧

"Are you sure this isn't a problem?" Gail asked, nursing a pounding headache with a few sips of orange juice. The threesome sat cozily in a booth, enjoying a bit of breakfast before the long drive to the Manchester airport, where Gail would begin her trip home to New York.

"It's all set," Mick assured both Gail and Dorrie. "I've already made the reservations and everything. You'll have to switch planes in Boston, Gail, but it shouldn't be too much trouble. Dorrie has already contacted your mother, so she'll be waiting for you at La Guardia around four."

Gail stared at Mick incredulously. "I can't believe you're actually paying for all this." Her eyes focused with great curiosity at both Dorrie and Mick. "Guess you want to spend time with my sister real bad to deal out this kind of cash."

This comment brought a flush to both their cheeks. Mick cleared a frog in his throat and shifted in his seat, glancing in Dorrie's direction. Dorrie pretended to study her plate of scrambled eggs and home fries. This conversation was becoming almost too difficult to handle. When she first learned that Mick had secured a plane ticket for Gail, then arranged to switch their Friday night stay in the hiker hut on Mt. Washington to Saturday, she couldn't believe it.

"How did you manage that?" Dorrie gasped in astonishment when Mick shared his secret with her earlier that morning over the telephone from his hotel room.

"Well, the weather outlook for Saturday is pretty poor, so there were several cancellations at the hut. I found you a place inside the overflow bunkroom of the hut, and I'll be staying in the dungeon."

"The dungeon?" Dorrie repeated. "It sounds ominous."

"The hut has several bunks in the basement that they rent out to hikers for a reduced fee," Mick explained. "They call the area the dungeon. I've got a spot reserved."

"But if the weather's going to be bad on Mt. Washington, maybe. . . ," Dorrie began, recalling her reading about the severity of summer storms that struck the highest summit in the Northeast. High wind gusts and severe lightning posed the greatest danger to those traversing the exposed ridgeline.

"The weather looks fine until late afternoon," Mick assured her. "They're forecasting some thunder on the mountain, but we should arrive at the hut well ahead of the storm. Sunday is shaping up to be a decent day with some nice views from the summit. What do you think?"

Dorrie wrestled the idea around in her heart, wondering if she dare accompany him on a trip such as this. Did she trust him enough to allow them this length of time alone together on the trail? What if they found themselves thrust into a situation neither could handle? Yet, he had put forth a tremendous amount of effort and money to secure them places at the Lakes of the Clouds hut—the portion of her vacation that Dorrie had eagerly anticipated the moment she arrived at the White Mountains. Her heart wrestled back and forth within her as she contemplated all this. "I guess the next question I ought to be asking is, why go through all this trouble just for me?"

"Because with all the problems you've faced on this trip of yours, you deserve a chance at Mt. Washington." Dorrie's silence on the telephone triggered a sigh of puzzlement from Mick on the other end. "Maybe I was wrong. I should've asked your opinion first before arranging all of this, huh?"

Dorrie managed a polite "No, it's a thoughtful gesture, Mick, thanks," despite the doubt assailing her. When she hung up the phone, she only prayed the right decision had been made.

✺

Mick and Dorrie stood side by side, waving to Gail as she walked through the doors leading to the sleek commuter that would transport her to Boston and the first leg of her journey home. "Hard to believe she'll soon be in my neck of the woods," Mick commented, watching the hatch slam shut and the small aircraft maneuver about, ready to taxi down the runway.

"That's right, you said you lived in Boston." Dorrie chuckled a bit, attempting to conceal the nervousness welling up inside her. Now she was alone with this man, dependent on him for all the arrangements he had made with their hike and accommodations on Mt. Washington. The very thought left Dorrie with an uneasy feeling. She lapsed into a thoughtful silence for most of the trip back to the mountains. Sensing her distance, Mick chose to leave her alone, pondering instead his own questions. Was she angry at him for taking the initiative of flying Gail home? Did she find him too forward in his eagerness to climb the highest mountain in the Presidential Range with her? He considered the possible answers to these and other questions until he could no longer stand the stillness inside the car. "So what's wrong? You having doubts or something?" Mick held his breath, his muscles tensing as he awaited the explanation behind her aloofness.

Dorrie shrugged. "Guilt, maybe. Here I planned a vacation to be with Gail, who I haven't seen much of lately, then I end up putting her on a plane and leaving with you."

"I wouldn't feel guilty at all if I were you. She doesn't like the outdoors anyway, and after going through what she did last night, it was the best thing for her."

"Maybe. I hope so."

"Look at it this way, now you can enjoy a hike in peace. I know she was kind of a nuisance to you, especially when you wanted to go on a real hiking trip here in the Whites. There's nothing to hold us back from Mt. Washington now."

Dorrie swallowed down a gulp of air as she wrestled with the magnitude of this statement. "Mick, I know you're trying to be helpful and I appreciate it. Believe me, I do want to climb Mt. Washington, but I don't know if I should go with you. We've spent a little time together, but quite frankly, I hardly know you."

He raised an eyebrow. "Well, do you think it's wise for you to hike Mt. Washington alone with that bad ankle of yours?"

Dorrie flexed the damaged extremity, which had begun to mend after several days of rest. She wondered how the ankle would hold up under the tremendous strain of a steep hike up the rock-strewn trail. "No, it's unwise to hike alone. I found that out the hard way, especially when faced with the prospect of an overnight stay in the middle of the woods with no shelter. But I don't think it's wise for us to be alone the entire weekend, either."

"I see." He focused his concentration on the large semi in front of him on the freeway before directing his eyes toward the side mirror in preparation to pass the massive vehicle. "Guess I should've let you drive your sister back to New York, then."

"Look, I do want to hike Mt. Washington. You've been very generous. I'm just not sure about us being together like this."

His fingers gripped the steering wheel of Dorrie's car, which he insisted on driving. "Okay, then let's have it all out in the open, Dorrie. If I were a good Christian man, committed to your God and everything, then would you go with me?"

She paused before saying, "Maybe. He would understand the Bible's instruction on chastity and I think I could trust him."

Mick's face colored at hearing these words, remembering the encounter with Krysta at the Zealand Falls hut and the kiss spawned by his weak flesh to her seductive ways. He knew his life did not reflect the characteristics Dorrie desired to see in a Christian man. Yet the very idea of Dorrie finding someone else to hike the trails, share joyous laughter, or snuggle close to beside a roaring campfire proved too heart-wrenching. Despite this, he reluctantly answered, "I guess I can see your point. I suppose you have no reason in the world to trust me, seeing as God and I are not on good terms right now. I just thought we could have some fun enjoying what we both love to do." His voice melted away into a silence that echoed his disappointment.

The stillness continued until Mick drove the car up through Franconia Notch. When Dorrie flashed him a look of alarm at the change of route, he calmed her fears by informing her of his plan to retrieve his car. "I figured you'd probably feel better driving yourself around," he stated flatly, his eyes staring straight ahead. "Then you can decide what you want to do with the rest of your stay here without me bothering you anymore."

"Mick. . . ," Dorrie began, then paused as he turned her car into a parking area where his own vehicle rested near the trailhead that led to Zealand Falls. Wordlessly, Mick walked to the rear of the car and hauled out his gear from the trunk before depositing the set of keys into Dorrie's hand.

"Guess this is good-bye, then," Mick said, standing by his car with his hands jammed into the pockets of his khaki shorts.

Dorrie sensed the turmoil within her. A part of her wanted Mick to stay while the other believed it was right for them to go their separate ways. Inhaling a deep breath, Dorrie thanked him for everything. Again she reiterated the wisdom of going their separate ways.

"Sure," he retorted with a hint of bitterness, whirling about on one foot.

"Mick. . . ," Dorrie began again, then shook her head and retreated to her car. She sat still in the driver's seat for many minutes, even after the sound of Mick's car faded in the distance. The whisper of the wind in the trees now filled her ears. She felt isolated in this vast wilderness surrounding her. Shrugging her shoulders, Dorrie brushed off the pangs of loneliness with determination. "Well, God, it's just You and me once again."

Chapter 9

The area known as Pinkham Notch, nestled at the foot of Mt. Washington, proved a hiker's domain. Here beneath the awesome peak of the highest mountain in the Northeast, hikers from all walks of life gathered together to plan their treks up to the summit. A lodge, cafeteria, store, and hiker information center provided the would-be enthusiasts with everything they would need for the steep climb that awaited them.

Dorrie steered her car into the parking area late that Friday afternoon. She found it difficult locating a place to park. With the start of another summer weekend, the crowds in Pinkham Notch were thick like fleas. Finally, she managed to find a place at the very end of the large gravel lot, then sat back and sighed. After Mick left in his car, Dorrie decided to go through with her plans to ascend the peak on Saturday, hoping her ankle would hold out until she reached the Lakes of the Clouds hut. She decided to hike the general approach to the hut via the Tuckerman Ravine Trail, which offered her a good climb while being populated by other friendly hikers in case of any mishap along the way. As she rose from the car, her eyes scanned the variety of people milling about, some lugging huge packs on their backs, others talking in groups, dressed in hiking attire and stiff mountain boots. For an instant, she caught sight of a guy with blond hair and wearing a red bandanna crossing the parking lot enroute to the main lodge. Her heart leapt wildly within her. Upon closer inspection, she discovered the man wasn't Mick. "Now you're being silly, Dorrie," she chastised herself, locking the doors to the car and heading over to the lodge, where she might obtain information on the hike in the morning and available accommodations in the lodge. "Stop thinking about Mick. He's gone. You neatly severed the relationship. Go on."

As Dorrie passed couples walking arm in arm around the various pathways connecting the rustic buildings, a pang of regret nipped her. *Mick wanted to be with me and I drove him away.* Again she scolded herself for wasting time on her emotions rather than on the nature of the circumstances surrounding the troubled man. "The man hates God, Dorrie. You can't possibly have a relationship with someone who is not serving God right now."

Dorrie walked into the crowded lobby of the information area. Her senses were assaulted by the sights and sounds of people milling about and the announcements blaring over the sound system, alerting people to members of their parties awaiting them at the front entrance. Dorrie ventured up to the desk and inquired if any accommodations were available.

"We have room left in one of the bunkhouses," said a guy wearing broad, wire-rimmed glasses. "Sleeps four."

"Guess I'll have to take that," Dorrie decided, plunking down her money for one night's stay and breakfast.

The guy took her cash while scrutinizing her thoughtfully for a moment. "You plan on hiking up the mountain tomorrow?"

Dorrie looked up, startled by his question. "Yes. I have reservations at the Lakes hut."

"Hope you plan on leaving early," the guy warned. "There's a cold front coming through tomorrow afternoon. Could get stormy on top of the ridgeline."

"I plan to be up before the rooster crows," Dorrie answered, then quickly left before he asked anything further.

A well-stocked campstore met her curious gaze. Dorrie walked over to sift through the various equipment and other hiker's paraphernalia, wondering if she might need anything for the trip. Bags of freeze-dried food, matches, flashlights, insect repellent, and other necessities met her eyes. Shelves brimmed with spanking new hiking boots and racks held outdoor clothing. Dorrie gasped at the prices on some of the outdoor clothing, especially the parkas made of a waterproof material that was guaranteed to keep one dry in inclement weather. Dorrie had debated the idea of purchasing such a coat back in New York but settled on a cheaper version of a rain slicker. She hoped it would suffice if the weather turned as nasty as everyone predicted.

Next she investigated the reading material for sale. A variety of hiking guides and manuals were aligned neatly along a rack for her perusal. Picking up one that detailed hikes in her native state of New York, Dorrie inspected the contents with a curious eye, flipping through the glossy pages that described some fascinating walks in the Catskill and Adirondack mountain regions of New York. As she read one section detailing a hike up Slide Mountain, the tallest peak in the Catskills, Dorrie closed her eyes for a moment, reminiscing about her hike during late March a few years back and her surprise at encountering snow that came up to her thighs. Struggling to make it through the cold, snowy drifts, she pondered the idea of giving up on the hike altogether. Somehow she found the strength to continue on, eventually arriving on the rocky summit where a stunning view awaited her. Certainly the scenery itself was worth it. Dorrie nodded and opened her eyes, focusing on the page inside the manual. There was no doubt in her mind that the sheer effort of climbing Mt. Washington the next day would yield her similar rewards.

She placed the book on the stand, then walked over to study the huge relief map of Mt. Washington. The network of trails appeared like a great spider web, all of which intersected at the primary goal—the sharp pinnacle of Washington's rocky summit. Studying the terrain made of plaster and painted colors to depict the vegetation, Dorrie examined the trail she would take and the position of the Lakes of the Clouds hut, situated on the shoulder of the great mountain. Other visitors also gathered around to point out the geographical features portrayed in the relief.

"But what if the weather gets as bad as they're calling for?" Dorrie overheard a young woman complain to an enthusiastic guy who was obviously trying to sell her on the idea of a weekend excursion.

"We'll be fine. There're plenty of places to stay if the weather gets rough. And I'll be with you, protecting you. I know this region like the back of my hand, Honey. Don't worry."

The woman snuggled under the arm offered by the man. Dorrie twisted her face at the display of affection and turned away. When she did, she found herself staring face to face with a familiar set of blue eyes and blond hair.

"Fancy meeting you here."

Stunned by the encounter, Dorrie stood speechless.

Mick now commented with a grin, "Need some protection on the trail too? I will offer you my services and at a reduced rate."

Dorrie turned away from his eager face. "I. . .I haven't even decided yet if I'm going."

Mick stared at her in amusement. "Oh really? I heard you tell the guy at the information desk you'd be up before the rooster crows. Sounds to me like you're planning on a trip."

Dorrie's face colored. Indignation rose up within her at the very thought of Mick eavesdropping on her plans. She whirled around. "What, were you spying on me or something?"

His features softened. "I'm just concerned that you're gonna mess yourself up if you try to tackle that trail alone and with all this bad weather coming."

"I appreciate your concern, but I can take care of myself," she answered, walking away. "I have hiked many trails in my lifetime. . .alone, without the need of a guide."

Mick refused to be intimidated by her independent demeanor. "Yeah, and I've witnessed firsthand how you take care of yourself. You think you're ready to conquer the world, then you end up almost breaking your leg at Franconia Falls. You haven't learned the dangers of soloing yet, have you?"

Dorrie bristled, ready to lash back with a comment until she saw the curious faces staring at their disagreement. Instead, she marched out of the lodge, conscious of the footsteps plowing the ground behind her. Whirling about, Dorrie fired back, "Mick, leave me alone."

"The truth hurts, doesn't it?"

Seething from the question, Dorrie's mind now buzzed with an assortment of harsh rebukes until she lashed out, "All right, let's talk about truth while we're on the subject. Instead of following me and invading my privacy, why don't you go home to Boston where you're needed? The real truth is that you're so busy being the wayward son who feels sorry for himself, you have no time left to devote to the real needs of your family. They're the ones who need your undivided attention much more than I ever will."

Once Dorrie spoke of the hurt buried within him, Mick jumped back as if he had been struck. Evening shadows muted the rage building across his face before he whirled about in a start. His feet pounded the ground with every step he took.

"Dorrie, ole girl, now you've done it," she said sadly, plunking down on a stone step with a great heaviness. "You know Mother's always yelling at you for having the biggest mouth this side of the Mississippi." She knew the sting of her biting words must have felt like a dagger to a man struggling with the pain of his family. "He was just trying to be nice, and look what I did." Despite the truth concealed within her statement, the words would never bring forth the healing and renewal he needed in his life.

Dorrie lay wide awake in her bunk that night, disturbed by the giggles of several girls in the neighboring bunks who refused to settle down. Pushing the tiny switch to illuminate the timepiece on her digital watch, she noted the late hour. *Great,* she thought with a groan, flopping over on her other side. *I'll never get to sleep. Between thoughts of Mick and the racket of those two girls, I'll be lucky to catch a few hours.*

Dorrie tried not to dwell on the reasons for her insomnia but screwed her eyes shut and dwelt on the hikes she had taken over the past few years. She recalled the beauty of the woods, the babble of a rushing brook flowing over the rocks, and the sweet smell of the earth after a rainfall. Often on her rambles she would play praise music through a set of headphones on her Walkman, thinking how perfectly the music fit the scenery around her. Once on the summit of a great peak, she sang loud praises to the Lord, unaware of the other hikers who stared at her strangely. Some even refused to approach the summit but turned and scampered away like frightened mice. Dorrie shrugged, smiled smugly to herself, and picked up her daypack. "Light can't mix with dark," she observed. "Either that or they think I've lost my marbles from dehydration."

As she continued to dwell on these pleasant memories, Dorrie felt herself sinking into the sweetness of sleep until visions of Mick and his concerned face suddenly sent her eyes springing open. She heard his voice reverberating over and over, "I'm just concerned. . .I don't want to see you messing yourself up." Dorrie sighed and turned over once more. The springs to the bunk creaked beneath her shifting weight. "I wonder if I've made a mistake," she whispered and began to pray for the situation. Dorrie sensed a peace drift over her after the prayer and a relaxing of her tense muscles as sleep finally won over her troubled mind.

※

Unbeknownst to her, Mick likewise spent the night hours in sleeplessness, contemplating Dorrie's words. While he cared greatly for her, he knew it was pointless to even pursue a relationship with a root of bitterness concerning his father's accident inhabiting his heart. Dorrie's biting words were true. If he could not even care for his own flesh and blood family during the most traumatic times, how could he possibly care for anyone else? He knew a relationship and a subsequent marriage were based upon a union with God and a deep, abiding love that would see the couple through the difficulties inherent in everyday life. Conviction stirred heavily within him. As much as he wanted to be with Dorrie, he knew he must first deal with the obstacles in his path—foremost, his relationship with God, and secondly, his indifference toward his family. The rest of the night he spent in tearful, conscientious prayer before the Lord of heaven and earth, repenting of his sins and allowing the love of Christ to cleanse his tortured soul.

※

The next morning, Dorrie rose early to repack the items she would need for the hike into her large daypack. In it she placed the usual necessities such as a change of clothing, toiletry articles, water bottles, and a flashlight. She would not need to lug a cumbersome sleeping bag or a great deal of food. The hut would provide her with blankets and meals.

Other hikers were also busy assembling packs for the climb that day up Mt. Washington. Many gathered around a scale to weigh in the packs they would carry on their backs for the lengthy journey. By the appearance of the large quantities of gear toted by some hikers, Dorrie decided a few were planning a lengthy walk in the mountains or perhaps even a hike down the famed Appalachian Trail, located in this rough section of the White Mountains.

Dorrie headed into the cafeteria for breakfast and joined a line of hungry hikers eager to delve into the usual fare of eggs and sausage, fresh fruit, juice, and coffee. Balancing the items on a tray, Dorrie slowly entered the seating area, only to hear a voice call out her name. She noticed Mick Walters rise from his seat and wave her over.

Dorrie gulped, almost losing her grip on her tray. *After last night, I thought he would never speak to me again.* Yet there he was, tanned, handsome, with an ever-ready smile poised on his face. Dorrie thought of her prayer last night to God and wondered if this acceptance on Mick's part was His answer.

"Here, let me get that," Mick offered, taking the tray from her hands and placing the food down on the table with the efficiency of a waiter in a classy restaurant.

Dorrie tried to hide her discomfort. "Thanks," she mumbled, taking a seat opposite him. From the quantity of food spread out before him, Mick appeared ready to internalize enough nourishment to last a week.

"I decided to make a pig out of myself," he noted rather sheepishly as she stared at the food.

Dorrie could not help but smile, remembering the comment from their first dinner together at the buffet restaurant. She sat down, offered a quick, silent blessing for the food, then picked up a fork to eat.

"Aren't you going to pray?" Mick inquired.

Dorrie glanced up at him in surprise. "I did."

"Oh, I didn't hear you."

"It was the quiet kind," she told him, sprinkling salt and pepper on her eggs before placing a large forkful in her mouth.

For several minutes, they ate in silence while their eyes wandered about the establishment, watching others enjoy their meals or engage in exciting conversation about the events that loomed ahead of them that day. Finally, Mick rested his fork on his plate, leaned his elbows on the table, and folded his hands. His blue eyes shone like a clear mountain lake in the bright sunshine as he gently said, "Dorrie, I owe you an apology for last night."

Dorrie almost choked on her eggs. She reached for her orange juice and took a large swallow before sputtering out, "An apology? For what?"

"Well, for spying on you when you were at the information desk, then for rubbing it in about your accident at Franconia Falls." His eyes dropped to his half-eaten food sitting before him. "I'll be perfectly honest. I like being with you, and the thought of you hiking up this mountain alone. . .well. . ." He paused and flushed under the awkwardness of his explanation. "Look, I also wanted to say I think you were right yesterday, telling me I should care more about my family than my hurt. I can see now that I've been pretty selfish these last few years." His eyes rose to meet hers. "You've really helped me see the light."

Dorrie finally set down the glass of orange juice she had been holding. "I'm sorry I spoke out so harshly last night, Mick. I guess I'm just trying to find out God's will in all this. . .if we're meant to be friends or what. I guess I need time to sort it all out."

"Well, I also wanted you to know. . .I made peace with God last night." He rubbed his eyes from fatigue. "I didn't get much sleep, but it was worth it. I had a lot of junk I needed to clear up with Him, especially how I've slipped away from the beliefs I once held onto so strongly."

Dorrie could not help but reach out and grasp his hand in a tender move that startled him. "You bet it was worth it! Mick. . .I'm so glad to hear this!"

He smiled at her enthusiasm. "Well, it took a young, caring, godly woman by the name of Dorrie to jar my brain and get my thoughts off yours truly. I know

I have a long way to go to make up for lost time."

"God is patient, Mick," Dorrie assured him, then dropped his hand when she realized how tightly she had been holding on. "He will help you if you trust Him."

Mick returned to his plate of food, consuming several more bites before saying, "Well, I still don't like the idea of you hiking alone, Dorrie, but since you're so adamant about it, I'll take another route or something. I can always drive over to the trailhead for the Ammonoosuc Ravine Trail, which provides another access to the hut. Maybe I'll see you at the top, eh?"

Dorrie thought silently on this. Now that Mick had rededicated his life to the Lord, perhaps this was a sign from God that they should ascend the mighty mountain together as a team. "Well, honestly, Mick, you've helped me see a little of the light too," Dorrie finally admitted. "I was struggling with some pride—wanting to accomplish this hike on my own without any assistance. The accident at Franconia Falls was real embarrassing for me—Miss Hikerette, who has tackled the tall peaks of the Catskills without any problems. But I think it's wisdom to hike in pairs in such rugged terrain, don't you?"

Mick's broad grin and bright eyes sent a crimson tide flooding her cheeks. "I think it's great wisdom, Dorrie."

Chapter 10

The sky looming above the majestic peak of Mt. Washington lay strewn with high cirrus clouds intermixed with patches of clear blue. The trail before Mick and Dorrie appeared all the more inviting, with the glorious sky framing the tall balsam pines, contrasting the green pine needles against a backdrop of blue and white. As was typical for a Saturday during the summer months, the Tuckerman Ravine Trail was jammed with hikers eager to conquer the steep slopes that comprised Mt. Washington. Pausing for a moment to gulp down liquid from their water bottles, Mick and Dorrie savored the invigorating mountain air while silently contemplating the journey that lie ahead. Dorrie was relieved to find her ankle holding up well under the strain of the pounding from the steep ascent that tested every part of her body. Mick offered to carry the heavier items, which eased her burden. The internal frame pack on his back appeared overbearing to Dorrie, but Mick managed it without complaint and with the energy of one used to strenuous activity. Neither conversed much during the hike, with their labored breathing providing needy muscles with adequate oxygen intake during the prolonged exercise. Occasionally they passed fellow hikers taking it slow during the steep climb, while others in better physical shape strode up the mountainside with little or no effort.

The trail leading them to Mt. Washington was a rock-strewn pathway, wide enough for an all-terrain vehicle in some parts. As Mick and Dorrie climbed, the trail gradually narrowed and the rocks became larger. At times, great boulders rested near the border of the trail, some with flat surfaces that provided a pleasant resting place. Other boulders beckoned Mick with a quick rock climbing adventure. Dorrie watched with some apprehension as Mick rested his pack next to her, then took off using hand- and footholds to climb the rock. When he reached the top, he waved at her from his lofty perch.

Dorrie shielded her eyes from the rays of sun poking through the clouds. "Who do you think you are, the king of the mountain?" she joked.

Mick laughed. He cupped his hand to his forehead and exclaimed, "What a view! You can see the lodge at Pinkham Notch from here, Dorrie. The cars in the parking lot look like matchboxes. Wanna come up and take a look? I'll help you."

Dorrie shook her head. "No thanks. I'm thankful my ankle is holding up as well as it is. I sure don't want to take any chances with it now, especially rock climbing."

Mick eased himself back onto solid ground again, where he took the water bottle from Dorrie's outstretched hand. As he drank thirstily, Dorrie could not help but notice the sweat outlining his thick biceps and his crimson face with perspiration trickling down each temple. Observing her out of the corner of his eye, Mick arched an eyebrow and flashed her a grin. Dorrie hastily looked away. A hot flush filled her cheeks as she focused her attention on a tree extending its leafy branches like an umbrella. Hoping to diffuse the embarrassing moment, she commented, "So you looked like you actually knew what you were doing on that rock. Have you rock climbed before?"

"I spent some time with a wilderness adventures group when I was a young kid. They train you in all sorts of sporting activities, including canoeing, search and rescue, swimming, and rock climbing. I went on to earn a lifesaving certificate in swimming so I could work as a lifeguard at the town pool where I live."

Dorrie remembered Gail's claim that Mick possessed the body of a lifeguard. Somehow the very thought left her uncomfortable. She chastised herself for dwelling so much on flesh rather than on character and promptly thought of Scriptures to ease the tingling sensation now sweeping over her. "Well, I guess that's enough playing for now. We'd better get going if we want to reach the hut before the weather turns bad."

"Right you are," Mick agreed, shrugging on his pack with a grunt and adjusting the hip belt around his waist.

The trail became steeper as they marched onward. Dorrie felt her legs tighten into knots, alerting her to the painful realization that she was not in terrific shape. Mick slowed his pace and paused every so often to allow her time to catch up. Struggling with each step, Dorrie resented the way Mick stood watching her progression. Gasping for air at the next turn, Dorrie leaned against a tree in frustration and waved her arm. "G. . .go on, Mick. Don't wait for me."

Mick ignored her request and stumbled back down the trail to her side. "No, we agreed to do this together, Dorrie. We can rest as often as you need to."

"Well, as you can see, I'm not Miss Muscle," Dorrie complained, pushing away the water bottle he offered from a side pouch.

"Dorrie, you need the water. Drink it."

"Why aren't you drinking any?"

"I don't need any right now. Besides, we're running a little low. When we reach the Hermit Lake shelter, I'll fill up the water bottles at the spring."

Dorrie sensed her pride firing up within her. "Well, if you're not going to drink, then I won't either."

Mick sighed in exasperation. "Dorrie, this is not a contest to see who is stronger or who can go without water the longest. It's a simple fact of life that men are stronger than women. You don't prove a thing by being stubborn."

"Really now."

"Yes, really. I'm a biology teacher, you know. Men possess a greater muscle mass and a greater volume of blood than women. Why do you think male runners achieve faster race times than women? Why can men lift heavier weights? It's because we're built differently."

"Well, this woman can definitely keep up with you anytime, anywhere," Dorrie informed him, enjoying the prospect of a challenge as she reached down for her pack and flung it onto her back. She began a stiff pace up the trail with Mick following close behind.

"This is ridiculous, Dorrie," he huffed, the bandanna around his head becoming drenched with sweat. "I thought we were hiking this trail to enjoy ourselves."

"I am enjoying myself," she returned, inhaling several quick breaths. "I'm enjoying the prospect of beating you to the lean-to."

Mick increased his pace, hiking stride for stride with her, observing her as her respirations quickened and sweat poured off her face. "You've got to stop this, Dorrie," he protested. "You'll collapse from heat exhaustion if you keep this up."

As they neared the shelter, Dorrie eyed Mick and suddenly thought up a little dramatic episode that might exploit his concern while gaining her an upper hand in the challenge she had created. She suddenly moaned and placed a hand across her sweaty forehead. "Oh. . .my head! I feel so faint!" She then sank to the ground.

Mick rushed to her side. "Dorrie, are you okay? Dorrie? What's wrong? Is it your ankle? What?"

Dorrie opened one eye, soaking in the concerned expression on his face with pleasure. She added a few more moans. "I. . .I can't go on any further, Mick, I just can't. It's hopeless. You're gonna have to carry me all the way back down to Pinkham Notch."

Mick knelt by her side, eyeing this sudden malady in confusion, until Dorrie leapt to her feet and began racing along a level section of the trail toward the lean-to.

"Why, of all the. . .!" Mick shouted, grabbing up his pack and dashing after her. When he arrived at the Hermit Lake Shelter, Dorrie stood with one shoulder leaning against the sidewall, her arms crossed, laughing at him.

"What took you so long?" she mocked good-naturedly. "Weren't you the one who claimed men are stronger and faster than us measly women? I'd say the success of this little experiment proves your theory in error, Mr. Science."

Mick frowned and tossed his pack onto the ground before striding up to her. As she stood there with sparkling eyes, crimson cheeks, and cherry red lips grinning at him, he thought she was the most perfect vision of beauty there in the midst of the rugged terrain in the White Mountains. Instead of rebuking her devious antics, he only placed his hands against the stout wooden walls of the structure, pinning her against the lean-to. "So. . .you think you're pretty clever, eh?"

Dorrie's laughter quickly melted away under his tender expression. Before she could react, he was kissing her, enjoying the taste of her salty lips against his own.

"S. . .stop it, Mick," Dorrie sputtered, ducking underneath his arms to escape the encounter. "Please don't do that."

He turned, reached out for her hand, and drew her toward him. Strong arms encircled her in a hearty embrace. "Why?"

Dorrie shrugged out of his arms. "Look, I didn't agree to go on this trip just so you can take advantage of every situation that pops along." Dorrie averted her eyes at his confused look. "This is what I was afraid of," she whispered. "This is the very thing I wanted to avoid."

"I'm sorry, Dorrie," Mick apologized. "I didn't think a harmless little kiss would bother you."

"Well, it does. I promised myself I wouldn't date a man unless I married him. All I needed to see was my sister go through some major heartache before God opened my eyes. Then I did a little reading of my own in the Bible. You remember the story of Isaac and Rebekah, how Abraham sent out his servant with a specific order to find the right bride for his son? The servant asked God to help him find the perfect woman. The Bible says the servant prayed specifically to God that if a woman comes to the well and draws water for himself and his camels, he would know this is the wife God selected for Isaac. Sure enough, Rebekah came and offered water, just as the servant prayed. Isaac and Rebekah never dated, but God divinely brought them together through the servant's prayer."

"Looks like you've spent a lot of time thinking about this."

"Well, when you work in the kind of company I do, surrounded by men eager for relationships, you have to foster principles to live by, then make up your mind to abide by them no matter what."

Mick considered her rationale. "I suppose a majority of us don't have the kind of faith you do," he mused, "but I can see what you're saying. I guess I should be thanking you for warning me about this ahead of time. I didn't realize you felt so strongly about the no-dating rule." Disappointment filtered across his face, for he had hoped Dorrie might want to date him. As one who just recently rededicated his own life to the Lord, he felt his faith weak like a newborn and lacking the strength to accept the ultimatum she laid out before him.

An emotional distance was evident when they took up their packs to renew the journey. Preoccupied by his mixed feelings, Mick stayed several paces behind Dorrie as they walked along the narrow trail. He could not deny the strong attraction he held for her, but knew he must temper whatever feelings he possessed. Dorrie held all the cards when it came to having any type of a relationship, and he had to abide by her wishes. He only prayed that God had indeed selected them for a much greater call.

After hiking through a bed of alpine plants on a relatively level portion of the trail, they soon encountered steep talus slopes in a bowl-like configuration that comprised the headwall of Tuckerman Ravine near the summit of Mt. Washington. As they gazed at the spectacle before them, Mick pointed out the steep terrain to Dorrie, telling her of the many people who hiked up the trail with skis on their backs, eager for a little downhill practice in the rugged area during the winter. Dorrie's eyes widened in astonishment, trying to imagine the skis carried on someone's back, and then the steep march up the hill to a point where one might glide down the snow-covered slope. "There are no ski lifts here, either," she observed. "That's a lot of effort for one quick trip down the mountainside."

"Yeah, but many do it anyway. I for one could never get myself interested in downhill skiing. I'm not much for winter activities. Pam enjoyed downhill skiing, but it was a struggle for me just to put on the skis."

Dorrie now turned to regard him. Her eyebrows furrowed in puzzlement. "Pam? Who's Pam?"

Mick noted the cautious tone to her voice and could not help but make the most of the moment. He smiled roguishly. "You mean I never mentioned Pam to you?"

A sinking feeling suddenly overcame Dorrie at the thought of other women in Mick's life. "No, you never did." Dorrie glanced away, hoping he would not detect her disappointment. "Is she a friend of yours or something?"

"Sometimes my friend, other times my worst enemy."

Dorrie glanced back, unable to comprehend his meaning.

"Pam's my older sister," he finally explained with a slight grin.

Dorrie frowned when she realized she had been misled. "Well, you might have told me that right from the start, Mick Walters, instead of leading me on." She brushed by him and strode up the trail that climbed steeply to the right of the Tuckerman Bowl.

"Would it have made a difference?" Mick could not help but ask, puffing as he hiked behind her.

"As far as having open, honest communication. . .yes," she answered, breathless from the exercise.

"Well, call it payback time for your little stunt at the Hermit Lake Shelter."

Dorrie could not help but smile as she wiped away the collection of sweat accumulating on her face. Together they watched a bank of fog rise up over the mountainside and spill down into the bowl like great fluffs of cotton candy. "We won't have much of a view from the ridgeline," she noted in disappointment. "All this effort for nothing."

"You're right. The weather's getting worse. We'd better try to keep up a good pace if we're going to beat the storm. The weather's projected to be quite nasty."

Dorrie wasted no time but trudged on, conscious of the growing fatigue in her legs and the twinges of pain in her ankle. The next portion of the trail proved the steepest by far. When Dorrie glanced up, the rocky trail dared her to come master its dizzying heights. Deep gullies from washouts and the numerous rocks made the going all the more treacherous. "I. . .I'd never make. . .make it up. . .this thing if. . .if I were carrying a loaded pack," she stammered.

Mick was equally breathless in his response. "B. . .be glad we have. . .a place to stay too. . .once the rain hits."

At the summit of the bowl they continued on, maneuvering through large boulders on a crossover trail. At one point they decided on a lengthy rest by one of the boulders. Mick hauled off his pack and promptly collapsed onto the ground. Dorrie opened her daypack and fished out food for them to eat. They munched beef jerky and hard cheese while Mick surveyed his map. "We're here." He pointed as Dorrie hovered over his elbow. "I'd say we have about a half mile left to reach the hiker hut, maybe less, and it should be downhill most of the way." He folded the map and turned to acknowledge her, conscious of her warm presence. He felt the tremendous urge at that moment to take her in his arms, hold her close, and kiss her wet lips moistened from a thirsty encounter with a water bottle. Instead, he reached for her hand, which he grasped tightly in his own. Thankfully, she did not draw back. In a soft voice, he said, "You've done a great job on this trip, Dorrie. Ever consider a long-term profession in the area of mountain climbing?"

Dorrie laughed with a sound like bells tinkling in his ear. Her warm breath fanned his face. "Actually I have considered a long-term hike on the Appalachian Trail."

His eyes widened. "Really?"

Dorrie nodded. "When I was a kid, I was fascinated by the thought of spending six months hiking and camping in all those shelters while walking two thousand miles just for the fun of it. I used to buy books on the subject and even went to the headquarters for the trail in the town of Harper's Ferry, West Virginia, to check out the possibility."

Mick laughed. "That's funny because I've considered it too. Unfortunately, I would have to take a semester's leave from teaching. I don't think the school board would think too highly of someone asking for leave time just to traipse around in the woods for six months." His thumb gently stroked her skin, which felt like velvet to the touch.

Dorrie relaxed against a firm boulder positioned behind them and closed her eyes. "Maybe one day," she murmured. "It's a goal I have in life, to walk the Appalachian Trail from Springer Mountain, Georgia, all the way to Mt. Katahdin in Maine."

Mick again suppressed the deep desire to kiss her as she sat relaxed and at perfect peace in the rocky surroundings above the treeline. He could think of nothing better than spending six months on the Appalachian Trail with this woman beside him. *Not six months,* he told himself. *A lifetime. Even a lifetime with Dorrie would not be enough. God, I know I'm in love with her! Please, somehow, help Dorrie find a love for me.*

Chapter 11

The ridgeline sat completely covered in a thick blanket of fog. Both Mick and Dorrie contemplated the beautiful views they were missing from the rocky slopes as they walked the last leg of the journey to the Lakes of the Clouds hut—a name that proved quite apropos that day. Through the cloudy mist, the exhausted hikers could see an outline of wood and stone comprising the largest of the huts in the White Mountains, nestled beside twin alpine lakes. A few other hikers milled about the establishment when Mick and Dorrie arrived.

"Glad you made it before the storm," the caretaker greeted them after confirming their reservations. He then brought them cups of hot coffee that sent steam swirling into their faces. Dorrie and Mick took seats on the rustic benches inside the hut and helped themselves to the trail mix set out in bowls. "We're receiving news of rather rough weather headed this way," the caretaker said. "The observation tower on the summit says visibility is decreasing and the winds are beginning to pick up."

Dorrie chewed and swallowed a handful of trail mix. "I've heard it said that the peak sometimes receives wind gusts well over one hundred miles per hour."

The caretaker nodded. "Not only that, but Mt. Washington holds the record for the strongest wind gust—231 miles per hour back in 1934."

With great eagerness, the young man delved into his favorite topic—meteorology. Mick and Dorrie endured stories of the changing Gulf Stream and sinking troughs until their minds could no longer ingest anymore. They politely excused themselves and wandered about the hut, noting the many bunkrooms and the small library of books. Dorrie then followed Mick outside and through a door that led to the basement, nicknamed the dungeon, where hikers could spread out their own sleeping gear on bunks for a modest six-dollar fee. Already, the small area was crowded with hiking gear. Mick found one remaining bottom bunk against a far wall, where he took up residence.

"Real cozy down here," Dorrie noted sarcastically. "Looks like the rats would love it."

Mick observed the dark, dank room. "What do you expect for six bucks? This isn't the Hilton."

"That's for sure. Hope you can get some sleep. I don't think I could sleep in a place like this, packed in like sardines. Better you than me."

"I'm glad you have a space in the bunkroom, Dorrie. You should be pretty comfortable."

"If I don't end up with a bunch of chattering girls as roommates like I did at Pinkham Notch." As Mick unrolled his sleeping bag, Dorrie inquired if he and his older sister got along.

"Well, Pam always thought of me as the proverbial kid brother. Of course, I wanted her to play the usual male-oriented activities with me, you know, football in the fall, baseball in the spring, that sort of thing. Pam is four years older than me, so she was always busy with her own activities or playing with her friends."

"But you had friends growing up, didn't you?"

Mick spread out his sleeping bag along the bottom bunk, rested back on his heels, and nodded. "I had a few friends. But I was the son of a street preacher, so that didn't make me popular in high school. You kind of pick up the label of a religious freak for having a father who roams the streets trying to reach out to the scum of the earth. I didn't mind it, though. I thought Dad was the greatest." Mick lowered his head, suddenly lost in thought. "It will be hard seeing him again, sitting there in a wheelchair, unable to do anything. I. . .I don't know if I'm ready to handle it."

"Just pray and trust God, Mick. That's all you can do."

Mick glanced up at Dorrie and stared into her dark eyes. "I wish you could come with me for moral support, but I guess that's impossible."

Dorrie nodded. She knew there were only a few days left to her vacation, with her boss expecting her back in the office bright and early Tuesday morning, ready to tackle the word processor. "Yes it is. You know I have to be back in the office or the boss will. . ."

"Oh, I understand, Dorrie. This is something I have to do on my own." He found her hand and gripped it soundly. "But thanks for all you've done." He brought the hand to his lips, kissed it gently, then returned the hand to her side. "I hope that wasn't out of line."

"No, it was really sweet, Mick," Dorrie managed to say, thankful the dim surroundings masked the flush creeping up her neck and spilling into her cheeks.

❧

Unbeknownst to Mick and Dorrie, as they shared these quiet thoughts in the corner of the basement, a shadowy figure watched their interaction through the door at the top of the stairs. The figure wheeled about and vanished once Dorrie announced her need to use the facilities. Mick finished separating her belongings from his inside the confines of his pack. He did not hear the sound of the intruder venturing back down the stairs and into the room until long fingers clasped his shoulders and a giggle drifted into his ears. Mick lurched away in a start, falling backward onto the hard floor as he stared up into the face of Krysta Anderson.

She laughed at his startled expression. "Hi, Mick!"

Mick's eyes immediately darted to the basement stairs. "Krysta, get out of here," he whispered furiously, watching for Dorrie.

"Why? I paid for my night's stay here, same as you. I can go wherever I want." She glanced about the room. "Dungeon's crowded tonight. I was glad to see you finally made it. The caretaker was kind enough to let me know you'd be here tonight instead of Friday."

"Look, I'm giving you ten seconds to scram before. . ."

She whirled her head around, her eyes blazing. "Before what? Before your new girlfriend finds out who I am?"

"Who you were."

"No, who I am. Look, you can't just snap your fingers and pretend we never happened."

Mick gulped hard, again looking toward the stairs, praying Dorrie would not appear and find them together. He returned his attention to Krysta, who stared back in expectation with her hair cascading over one shoulder in a sea of reddish brown. "Now look, I won't have you following me like this. I meant what I said back at Zealand hut. Our relationship is over. You may think you need to live in the past, but I won't. I've gotten things right with God. I'm starting with a clean slate."

Krysta burst out laughing. "You've gotten things right with God," she repeated, mocking his words. "Since when has religion ever meant anything to you, Mick Walters? You were supposedly this pious man when we met at school and now you think you're somehow different?" She leaned over, her hair brushing his face. "Well, I know differently. You forget I happen to know everything about you, much more than that new girlfriend of yours does. I know what makes you tick inside. And I also happen to know everything you've been through. You're no different at all, Mr. Walters. The quicker someone tells your little girlfriend about us, the better it will be for everyone."

Mick's face reddened with anger. "You just keep quiet. . .I mean it."

Krysta's eyes widened. "Why? Is it because she won't be able to swallow the truth about us? Well, I believe in truth. I think she has a right to know where we stand and that nothing has changed between you and me." Before he could respond, she strode out of the basement with a haughty air to her step.

Mick sat still on the floor, staring hollowly into space, wondering what to do. Dorrie would inevitably find out that the son of a street preacher once lived an immoral life, then what would she think of him? *She'll have nothing more to do with me,* he thought miserably. *Dorrie is a godly woman, a keeper of the word, one who will not even date so she might keep herself unstained. And look at me. Look at what stains me. What am I? I'll be nothing to her but filth.*

A little while later, Dorrie found him still sitting on the floor of the basement, clothed in a dark garment of depression. "What's the matter, Mick? You look like you've seen the devil or something."

"You're close. . . ," he mumbled, unable to meet her concerned expression.

"What's that supposed to mean? Are you sick? Did something happen?"

Mick considered confessing his sin right then but found himself unable to speak the words. Instead, he coughed and reached for the water bottle to quench his dry throat, which felt like sandpaper when he swallowed. He recorked the empty bottle and thrust it back into a side pocket of the pack. "I'm all right," he mumbled.

"You're okay my foot. I don't believe you for a minute." Dorrie paused and listened to the swirling wind as it whistled around the eaves of the hut. Rain pelted the walls of the structure with a sound not unlike the shots of a rifle. "Hear the storm? It's a doozy."

"Yeah, a doozy," he repeated, his mind in a daze.

Dorrie frowned, then jumped to her feet. "Well, when you feel like being your old self again, let me know. I'll unpack my stuff, then check out the small library of trail guides and nature booklets they have. Come on up when you're recovered."

Mick motioned to her belongings. "Here're your things, Dorrie. I didn't know what you would need."

Dorrie stooped to pick up her belongings before giving Mick one more curious glance. "I hope whatever's bothering you, you'll tell me." She strode off, leaving Mick wallowing in a pit of depression.

Upstairs in the bunkroom, Dorrie busied herself with arranging her sleeping area when a woman with long flowing hair ventured inside. She observed Dorrie's movements silently for a few minutes, then stepped forward and said hello.

Dorrie glanced up. "Oh, hi."

"That's a nice daypack you've got there," the woman complimented. "I like the twin pockets in front. Good places to store water bottles."

"That's what I thought too," Dorrie agreed, glad to have found a woman eager to converse about hiking. For several minutes they talked over equipment and the various trails they had hiked in their past.

"Oh, by the way, I'm Krysta, from Boston," she said.

"I'm Dorrie. . . ," Dorrie began, then paused. "Did you just say Boston?"

"That's right. Actually I live in a suburb of Boston called Cambridge. Ever hear of it?"

Dorrie furrowed her eyebrows. "Isn't that a coincidence. The guy I'm hiking with is from Cambridge too."

The woman's face became serious. "That's what I want to talk to you about."

Dorrie stared at her. "What do you mean?"

"Dorrie, this guy you're hiking with. . .Mick Walters. . .well, I know him quite well. In fact, he and I were supposed to get married. I had plans all ready for our big day and everything."

Dorrie stood frozen in place, stunned by the announcement. "You can't be serious. You must have this Mick mixed up with someone else."

"I'm afraid not. This is Mick Walters, a science teacher who works at the same school I do. His father lives in a long-term care facility after being shot in the head. I know all about his life, you see."

Dorrie's face fell. A chill coursed through her.

Krysta sniffed, "He's the same one who ditched me too." She continued on with her tale. "Yeah, we met in the middle school where we both work. I was a substitute teacher and he taught science. We hit it off pretty well, you know? We spent a great time together. He and I decided to get engaged, then poof, he ordered me to leave. I was so hurt by it. I really loved him, you know? I couldn't understand why he would break it off until. . . ," she paused, "I found out he was fooling around with other women behind my back. I couldn't believe he would do such a thing!"

Dorrie stared at the young woman aghast.

Krysta went on. "I asked him if I could please come back. I didn't care about the other women in his life, I only wanted him. I knew in his heart he still loved me. I think he just needed time, you know? I was willing to give him all the time in the world. I wanted to forgive him and get married like we'd planned."

Dorrie's mind was a whirl of confusion. Her hands began to tremble. *This can't be true!* "So you. . .you two were supposed to get married?"

"Of course. I knew we had the chemistry. Everything was so right." She sniffed once more. "I'm hoping somehow I can turn things around. He knows we need to renew our relationship and go on with our lives." Krysta shook her head, glancing up with satisfaction at the painful expression now filtering across Dorrie's face. Before Dorrie could detect her deception, Krysta immediately lapsed into a sorrowful mood. "I'm so terribly sorry, Dorrie. I can see that Mick never told you any of this, but that's not surprising. He's not one for confessions or keeping a commitment. I hope I haven't ruined your hike or anything."

Dorrie stood to her feet as though she had been stung by a hornet. Her eyes fogged over with angry tears until everything around her became a blur. "No, I'm glad you did tell me before it was too late." Quickly she began stuffing her personal belongings into the daypack.

Krysta stood by, watching her. "What are you doing?"

"I. . .I can't stay here. I can't go on like this, not after what you've told me."

"If you think that's wise. . . ," Krysta began.

"Yes, I do. I'm leaving right now. He'll never see me again."

"I'm sorry, but I felt you should know what's going on." Krysta gave her one last look, then wheeled about on one foot and left the bunkroom.

Dorrie shook her head. Her entire body trembled under the weight of this revelation. Angry tears smarted her eyes and ran down her cheeks. *Of all the. . .*, Dorrie thought, shoving her belongings into the daypack as fast as she could, then donning her rain slicker. *I can't believe it. He never told me he was engaged to be married, never told me he ran out on the commitment to be with other women, and now he cozies up to me?* Dorrie thrust her arms through the straps on the pack. *Who does he think I am? Well, I'm getting outta here fast. I hope I never lay eyes on that man again as long as I live!*

The fierce weather outside matched the torrent of emotion sweeping over Dorrie as she stumbled around blindly. She decided not to venture back down the steep trail through the Tuckerman Ravine, but chose instead the Ammonoosuc Ravine Trail, which would lead her swiftly off the mountain and out of Mick's life forever. Raindrops splattered into her face. Water streamed down the neck of her jacket. How she wished she had purchased a waterproof parka as a stiff wind blew, thoroughly soaking her clothes. Lightning bolts struck the ground all around her feet. "Dorrie, how can you do this?" she moaned to herself. "Because I can't see Mick anymore, not after all this." Mud oozed into the tops of her boots. The trail soon became a river of water gushing down from above as Dorrie slipped and slid along, at times only taking small steps to avoid falling. "I'm a fool," she cried into the rage and fury of the storm all around her. "I'm a fool for allowing him into my life and believing he had changed when all he'll ever be is a selfish, deceptive man."

Dorrie paused, drawing in a deep breath, watching twigs and leaves whirl in a frenzy, mixing with the steady rain. As she stepped off, she felt her ankle twist beneath her. A tremendous gust of wind sent her tumbling uncontrollably down the embankment along with the mud and the water. Branches from the scrub brush tore gaping holes in her slicker. The strap on her daypack broke. Dorrie screamed, trying desperately to grab onto something to break her descent. Her hands reached out wildly, searching for anything, until her head plowed into a large rock and a deep, dark void silenced the storm of wind, rain, and turmoil all around her.

※

Mick soon came to the conclusion that it was better to tell Dorrie about his past mistake rather than have her risk a major confrontation with Krysta. He ventured upstairs and into the main living area of the hut, searching around for her. Instead, he found Krysta sitting at a large wooden table, absorbed in a book.

She glanced up at his arrival and smiled. "Hi, Mick. You should see what I've been reading here, all about the species of wildlife found in the White Mountains."

Mick ignored her. He went inside the bunkroom, anticipating Dorrie to be arranging her bunk, but found her absent. He then made a thorough search of every nook and cranny of the hut but could not find her anywhere. *That's strange. I wonder where she could be?*

Krysta cornered Mick inside one of the bunkrooms, her eyes narrowed to sinister slits like that of a cat who had just found a mouse. "What's the matter, Mick?" she asked, fluttering her lashes demurely.

"Nothing."

"You lose something?"

"Well if I did, I wouldn't tell you about it." He tried to sidestep her only to find her barring his path.

"C'mon Mick, don't play so hard to get," Krysta teased. "That's just kid stuff, after all."

Mick sensed the irritation rising up within him. "If you don't mind, I'm looking for my friend."

"Friend, huh? What kind of friend is she? One-night-stand friend, weekend friend?"

"That's none of your business."

Krysta shrugged and took a dainty step to one side. "You shouldn't be so nasty to me." She wheeled about on one foot. "I may have a hint or two as to where this friend of yours might be hiding." She sauntered away, only to hear the footsteps of Mick following her.

"Where Krysta?"

Krysta stopped and turned, a knowing glimmer in her eye. "We had quite a pleasant conversation, your friend and I. She understands our situation. You and I belong together. It's better this way, believe me. . . ."

"Just what is that supposed to mean. . . ," he began until the reality of Krysta's words sunk into him like a fist planted hard into his stomach. He closed his eyes. Dorrie knew about their sinful past.

Krysta shrugged as if his pain was of no consequence. "I would feel sorry for you, Mick, but after all, you ought to be honest about these things. Dorrie needed to leave so we could be together."

His blue eyes widened in alarm. "She left?"

Krysta nodded. "She knows you've already made a commitment. . .to me. So now maybe we can. . ."

"No!" he shouted as he dashed for the door and opened it wide before him. Raindrops stung his face. The wind ruffled his hair. "Dorrie!" he yelled into the blinding swirl of rain. A thick bank of fog marred his vision. *Dorrie couldn't have left in this weather. . .and with her bad ankle to boot.* Mick turned about and grabbed Krysta by the shoulders, startling her. "Tell me right now. Did Dorrie leave the hut?"

"Yes, she left. I already told you."

"When? Tell me when."

"I don't know. . . .a half hour maybe. Look, Mick, she doesn't want anything to do with you. It's the two of us now. Forget about her."

Mick closed his eyes in disbelief. *I can't believe this happened! She's crazy to leave in weather like this. . . .* Suddenly, he realized his fault in the situation. *I drove her away by all the secrecy, right out into this destructive storm.* He opened his eyes to acknowledge the severe elements. *There's no time to lose. I must find her quickly before she gets any farther in this storm.* Mick raced through the driving wind to the rear of the hut and clattered down the stairs to the basement room, ignoring the sounds of Krysta following him. He tore open his pack to put on a rain jacket, jammed his gear quickly inside, and thrust the pack onto his shoulders.

"You can't go out there in this, Mick!" Krysta told him, watching his frantic actions. "Are you crazy? Why, it's terrible! You can't even see your hand in front of your face!"

Mick did not respond. All he could think about was Dorrie and her safety. He had to find her, no matter what. Pushing past Krysta, he fled into the depths of the storm that howled mournfully in his ears. *God, how could I have done this to Dorrie? Why wasn't I honest with her? God, please, help me find her!*

Chapter 12

Mick retraced the path to the junction with the Tuckerman Ravine Trail but found no trace of Dorrie anywhere. The lone hiker he met on the trail only shook his head when Mick asked him if he had seen a woman hiking down toward Pinkham Notch.

"Hope she's not caught in this," the hiker told him. "As it is, I'm barely gonna make it to the hut myself. The footing is treacherous, I'll tell you."

Mick continued to stumble down the trail and call her name. After a time, he stopped to ponder his next move. Reaching absentmindedly for his water bottle to relieve a nagging thirst, he found the bottle empty, having forgotten to fill it at the hut in his haste to leave. He muttered to himself and unfolded the wrinkled topographical map, wiping away the rain droplets collecting in the crevices to scrutinize the network of trails in the area. It made sense she would venture this way, but the hiker he questioned denied seeing her on the trail. Mick itched a scratch on his damp head of stringy blond hair. *Did she decide to continue on to the observation area on the summit of Mt. Washington, hoping to find shelter? Or did she hike out by some other route?* Either way, Mick knew she could not have traveled very far in this weather.

He climbed back up the trail and hiked toward the Lakes of the Clouds hut once more. Instinctively, his feet turned onto the Ammonoosuc Ravine Trail. Just a short distance from the hut, he noticed a couple making their way up the trail using forked sticks to help stabilize the treacherous footing on rocks now coated with mud. One of the hikers held a bulky object in one hand. As Mick neared, he discovered the man held a daypack that looked strangely familiar. When he asked the two if they had seen a young woman walking alone down the trail, they looked at each other and shook their heads.

"But we found this," the guy said, holding up a daypack with the torn strap. "It was lying in a puddle."

Mick took the pack with shaky fingers and unzipped it. His face paled when he recognized Dorrie's belongings. "It's hers all right. Something's happened. Where did you find this?"

"About a half mile down the trail. But I tell you, you can't go too far in this weather. It's slippery and. . ."

Mick did not wait to hear the rest of the man's warning. He took off down the mud-filled slope, hoping, praying, begging in his heart that Dorrie was all right.

Knowing she already suffered from an injured ankle, a bad fall might explain the condition of the daypack found by the hikers. His feet sloshed along the trail. Mud stained his clothing as the water became a swift current around his feet, nearly sweeping him down the steep embankment. Over and over he called Dorrie's name, praying for her faint voice to respond as she once did when he searched for her in the woods near Franconia Falls.

Only the sound of the howling wind and driving rain met his ears. Mick held his hands up before his face to shield him from the mighty tempest, battling both the rage of the storm and the panic in his heart. *I have to find her. . .I must find her. . .*, he repeated over and over in his mind, using the energy within the words to spur him onward.

A colorful object bobbing in a puddle of water down the trail caught his eye. Sloshing through the water, he retrieved a bright red bandanna similar to what Dorrie kept tied to the ring of her daypack. Now he scanned the terrain of rocks and scrub brush all around him. "Dorrie!" he yelled. "Dorrie! Please, answer me!" He stood still, waiting and listening for any sound that might help him locate her whereabouts. He then glanced down at his feet, watching the water part before him to form two distinct paths in the shape of a Y. He noticed off to his right how the water flowed around a bush that appeared to have been trampled by some sort of heavy object. Mick's heart began to race. He followed the trail of destruction until he stumbled upon a figure lying against a rock, covered in mud. "Oh God!" Mick cried, trudging through the brambles until he came to where Dorrie lay unconscious. The wound on her head told him she had smashed it against the rough surface of the rock after a tumble of several hundred feet over the thorny brambles. Blood covered her face. Her clothes were saturated with mud and water. Lifting up her delicate wrist in his massive hand, Mick felt frantically for a pulse and was relieved to find one. He cradled her limp form in his arms, hugging her close. Salty tears mixed with the raindrops that fell on her face. "Dorrie, I'm so sorry, I'm so sorry," he told her over and over. "Please forgive me. Forgive me for not being honest with you." He kissed her bloody cheek. "I love you so much. Don't give up on me now. Please God, let her live."

Her clammy skin and blue lips told him she was dangerously hypothermic. Struggling to reach his pack, he fumbled for a dry sweatshirt tucked inside. He carefully removed the wet slicker from her, placed the sweatshirt gently over her bloodied head, then negotiated her limp arms through the sleeves. Mick winced as a faint trickle of blood ran down one side of her temple from the gash on her head. Removing his own parka, he slipped this over the sweatshirt for added warmth. He realized he must get her out of the elements and into a warm, dry place as quickly as possible. Glancing at his pack, then at Dorrie's unconscious form, he realized he could not manage both on the treacherous journey back to the hut. He abandoned the pack by the rock and hefted Dorrie's unconscious form, draping her across his upper back in a fireman's hold.

With great determination, Mick began the mountainous climb. The weight of Dorrie's form on his upper torso nearly toppled him to the ground. Sweat poured off his brow and he staggered under the load, yet nothing would deter him from seeing his beloved brought to safety. Groaning with the weight he bore, his spirit called on God for strength while he repented of every sin he could think of, including the affair with Krysta and the neglect of his family. *Please, help me, God,* he pleaded in his heart as he collapsed on the ground. Once more he took the unconscious Dorrie in his arms and found her skin cold. "She. . .she's worsening." He shuddered, rubbing her arms, trying to warm her up. "Gotta. . .gotta get her to a warm, safe place. . .or I'll lose her." Mick fought to keep his fears from consuming him. Summoning a hidden strength left within him, Mick again hoisted her up across his shoulders and slowly, with great effort, covered the rest of the journey in the pouring rain, reaching the hut before he collapsed in complete exhaustion.

⅔⅗

Murmuring voices and the smell of hot chicken soup drifting into her nostrils set Dorrie stirring on the cot made up for her in the corner of the dining room. A thick pile of wool blankets covered her. One of the caretakers who was EMT certified opened an eyelid and flashed a piercing light directly into her pupil, temporarily blinding her.

"Hey, what's going on?" Dorrie called out, batting at the light until a terrible pain gripped her. "Ouch, my head!"

The EMT sat back on his heels and sighed in relief. "She's finally awake," he told the anxious residents of the hut who kept a vigil with him.

Dorrie's confused eyes scanned the array of unfamiliar faces hovering over her. Her hand felt the gauze bandage wrapped around her head. "Ouch!" she complained again. "What happened?"

"You took a nasty fall," the EMT told her. "You're suffering from some mild head trauma and hypothermia. Rest easy now. Don't try to move. As soon as the weather clears, we'll transport you off this mountain and to a hospital."

Dorrie tried to sit up until a wave of dizziness overcame her. Reluctantly she rested her head back on the pillow. "I remember falling," she murmured dreamily. "I couldn't stop myself. The next thing I remember is being here."

"Well, your boyfriend went out after you," the EMT told her. "He should receive a medal for carrying you half a mile up the ravine in this weather. I still don't know how he did it."

Boyfriend? Medal? Dorrie pinched her eyes shut from the pain shooting like electrical currents through her head. *He must mean Mick. Mick went out after me and had to rescue me again.* Dorrie kept her eyes shut as she ruminated on this information. *It would've been his fault if I died out there,* she thought until she pondered the terrible finality of her statement. *Hold on, you almost did die out there. . . . Are you kidding? Mick saved your life. But why?* Exhausted by these rambling thoughts, Dorrie found herself sinking once more into sleep, dreaming of Mick carrying her in his arms through the splendor of heaven's gate.

The EMT tried keeping her in a conscious state, but Dorrie slipped into a sound slumber. He sighed and wiped the sweat from his face, mumbling to the other hikers, "The sooner we get her to the hospital, the better I'll like it."

"H. . .h. . .how is she?" came a trembling voice. The EMT glanced up to find Mick shivering in a wool blanket, his bloodshot eyes staring down in concern.

"Well, she woke up for a minute or two, then went right back off to sleep again. I'll feel better when we can get a rescue team up here and get her checked out at a hospital. She might have suffered trauma inside her brain from the blunt blow."

Mick swallowed hard as he knelt next to her cot. "Did she say anything?"

"Yeah, talked about the fall. At least she's responsive and lucid, which are good signs." Again, the EMT checked her pupillary reaction with his flashlight. "Her pupils are equal and reactive. Wish I could get her to stay awake."

"I'll try and wake her." Mick gently shook Dorrie's arm. "Hey, Dorrie, c'mon now and wake up. It's time to go on our hike, remember? Wake up or you're gonna miss it."

Dorrie's eyelids fluttered as she stirred once again. A firm "too tired, leave me alone" came from her lips.

The EMT looked at Mick and grinned. "Stubborn, isn't she?"

"You're not kidding." He nudged her once more, but she had drifted off to sleep.

"We'll try again later," the EMT decided. "Meanwhile, you'd better get some hot soup in you. You don't look too good, either."

Mick obliged, rising slowly to his feet and shuffling over to a bench, where the caretaker gave him a bowl of soup and crackers to go along with it. For a time, Mick allowed the steam to caress his face before he picked up the spoon and began to eat. After a few minutes, Krysta came and sat next to him, her face drawn and her green eyes wide with concern.

"Mick. . . ," she began.

"Leave us alone, Krysta," he told her flatly. "Haven't you done enough damage for one day?"

"That's what I wanted to talk with you about. I'm really sorry about Dorrie's accident and all. I. . .I never wanted any of this to happen. Please believe me."

"Right. Well, it did happen."

"I know and I'm very sorry." She rose quickly from the bench. "If there's something I can do, anything at all, let me know, okay?"

Mick rested the spoon in the bowl and closed his eyes, overwhelmed by exhaustion and worry. *Dorrie, please be okay. Please, God, please heal her. I. . .I couldn't bear to have another loved one hurt in the mind again.* Waves of anguish coursed over him, remembering his father and the extensive brain damage from the gunshot wound. *Please, God, I will do anything, anything at all. . .only somehow restore Dorrie to me once again.*

❧

Mick and the EMT stayed by Dorrie's side all through the night. Dorrie awoke twice, asking where she was and complaining of a terrible headache, which she described as hammers pounding her head. During each of these occurrences, Mick gently reassured her anxiety while the EMT performed pupillary reaction tests on her eyes.

The next morning, with the storm gone from the mountains, Dorrie was air-lifted out via a chopper to the nearest hospital. Mick, on the brink of total exhaustion, accompanied her. He remained at the hospital while Dorrie went through a battery of tests including a CAT scan, X-rays, and lab work to determine the extent of her injuries. Mick made himself comfortable on one of the waiting room couches, catching periods of sleep whenever he could. Finally, he was allowed in to see her once the physician briefed him on her injuries.

"She's one lucky young woman," he confirmed. "We detected no injury to the brain, but she did receive quite a concussion, so we'll keep her here overnight for observation."

Mick sighed in relief. "So she's gonna be okay?"

The physician nodded as his hands slid into the pockets of his white lab coat. "On X-ray we did find a fracture in her right hand. We reduced the fracture and applied a cast. Other than that and the laceration on her scalp, which we sutured, she's in good condition."

Mick nodded, thanking God for this encouraging report. Now he inhaled a deep breath as he walked into Dorrie's room. She sat quietly in the hospital bed with her head elevated, staring out the window when he entered.

"Hi," Mick managed to say, drawing up a chair by her bedside. Dorrie did not acknowledge him but continued in her fixed gaze. Her lack of response unnerved him. "Dorrie, are you okay? Are you in pain?"

Now she turned her head and said stiffly, "Well, you can see I'm not okay." She lifted her arm encased in fiberglass. "What is this thing on my arm?"

"I just saw the doctor. He said you have a broken bone in your hand."

"They had to cast my entire arm for a measly broken bone in my hand?" Dorrie blew out an exasperated sigh. "Great. I'm in big trouble now. How am I supposed to do my work? My boss'll have a fit! He'll probably use this as an excuse to fire me."

"Don't you have any sick leave available?" Mick wondered, trying to keep his voice as gentle as possible.

"A few days, maybe. I'm sure I'll have this thing on more than one week." She closed her eyes in tearful frustration. "I wish I had never taken a vacation in these mountains."

Mick sat still for a few moments, unable to think of the words to say. It was evident to him that Dorrie remained upset over the events on the mountain, events triggered by his own dishonesty. While he cared greatly for the woman lying in the bed before him, he feared she would never care for him.

"So how did I end up here in the hospital?" Dorrie inquired, the question disrupting the depressing thoughts now circulating around Mick's mind.

Mick straightened. "You were taken out by helicopter, Dorrie. The EMT at the hut didn't think it was wise to try to carry you down by stretcher. The trails were a mess after the storm."

"I don't even remember that! You mean I missed my first flight in a helicopter?" Dorrie shifted about in the bed. "Well, it was foolish to go out in that kind of weather. I should have known better, but at that moment, my brain seemed to have turned to mush." She felt the bandage on her head. "Guess I needed a good bump on the head to bring me back into reality. Ouch."

"This was my fault, Dorrie," Mick was quick to tell her. "I. . .I should have been open and honest about Krysta at the onset. I'll admit it, I was a coward. I knew you would look down at me for what I did in the past and. . ."

"So it's true. You were supposed to get married?" Dorrie suddenly interrupted, focusing her dark eyes on him.

Mick seemed startled by the question. "What? No. Krysta and I. . .we were never engaged or anything like that. We talked about an engagement once, but the relationship was wrong. I had abandoned the code I once lived by. At that point, I was pretty miserable with my life. We broke up and haven't been together since."

"Huh. Well, this Krysta whatever told me quite a different version of the whole tale. She said you were quite the womanizer, always dashing off with some lady on your arm, that sort of thing."

Mick gaped in shock. "That's not true, Dorrie. None of that is true. I never had any other girlfriends after we broke up."

"I suppose it doesn't matter now, with our vacations over, Mick." Dorrie closed her eyes. "What a disaster! If God had told me before I started out on this trip with Gail that things would turn out this way, I would've never gone. I'd have remained content to huddle on some crowded beach out on Long Island with everyone else. Gail might have liked it better too."

"I think it was a good vacation, Dorrie," Mick countered.

Dorrie turned her head and raised her eyebrows. "A good vacation? Are you crazy? Tell me something good that happened on this vacation."

"I met you. . .the most wonderful person there is."

Dorrie opened her mouth wide, prepared to counter the statement, but seeing the look of sincerity in his eyes, decided against it.

Mick continued. "I met the one person who could open my eyes to my own selfishness and pride. How can I not help but say it was a good vacation? I am not the same man who first came to these mountains."

At that moment, Dorrie remembered the plaque they both viewed in front of the stony image of the Old Man. "And I know I'm not the same, either. I guess both of us have learned something, haven't we?" She then inhaled a deep breath and added, "Guess we can truthfully say, Mick, that in the mountains of New Hampshire, God makes men."

Mick acknowledged her with wide eyes, remembering the inscription on the plaque. "That's right!" he exclaimed. "I'd forgotten about that little saying we found in front of the Old Man of the Mountain. It said something about signs, like a shoemaker puts out a shoe, a dentist a tooth."

"But in the mountains of New Hampshire, God has hung out a sign to show that there He makes men." Dorrie shook her head in wonderment. "How true, Mick. We've both been through that firsthand, haven't we?"

Mick nodded in agreement. "I'll say. When I came here, I was just a selfish kid with eyes on the number-one person in my life, me. Now I have eyes for three. . .God, my family, and. . . ," he hesitated, then picked up her casted extremity in his hand, "a woman named Dorothea."

Dorrie screwed up her face and howled. "Please don't even say that name, Mick! Ugh, I can't believe you remembered it."

Mick laughed softly before becoming serious. "It's the name of a strong woman, Dorrie, a nurse who served wounded men in the Civil War. I think the name fits you well."

For some reason, the comment spurred Dorrie to rest a weary head on his shoulder. This tender display stirred up a hope within Mick that perhaps all was not lost, despite his many mistakes. His fingers gently stroked her cheek. "I love you, Dorrie," he whispered.

"Mick. . . ," she began, jerking her head upright to rest once more on the pillow. "I still don't know what to do about us, Mick. I. . .I need time."

"I understand. Take all the time you need, Dorrie. After all that has happened to us, I'll wait as long as I have to."

Chapter 13

After Dorrie was released from the hospital, Mick suggested that they ride a bus back to Pinkham Notch and pick up her car. He would then drive her to her family's home in Westchester County, New York, where she might recover from her harrowing experience. Dorrie protested at first, but Mick would hear none of it. He cited her casted extremity and the dizzy spells she suffered since the concussion as reasons enough for a chauffeur.

During the trip home, Dorrie was shocked by her appearance in a mirror at a rest stop on the interstate. When she removed the bandage encircling her head, she found a section of her brown hair had been neatly shaved away, revealing the ugly suture line on her scalp.

Mick became alarmed when Dorrie emerged from the rest room with tears streaming down her face. "What's the matter, Dorrie? Are you in pain?"

"No, I'm a freak!" Dorrie wailed, pointing at her unusual hairstyle. "I look like a punk rock star. Why didn't you tell me? How can I go home like this?" Mick tried to reassure her that she looked beautiful to him, but his words did little to relieve her anxiety. What would her family think? More than likely her mother would either faint when she arrived at the door or have her arrested as a drug addict from the inner city attempting to impersonate her daughter.

Mick burst out laughing when Dorrie confided in him of these reactions. "Keep looking up."

"Yeah, so long as I'm not looking in a mirror," Dorrie grumbled. She played with a piece of loose cotton poking out the front of her cast as the car sped down the freeway toward New York. She then decided to switch subjects rather than dwell on herself. "Are you anxious about seeing my family?"

Mick shrugged. "From what you've been telling me, it should be an interesting encounter. But I'll take it all in stride, as I'm sure you will."

Dorrie sighed as she stared out the window at the Massachusetts countryside. She was unsure of the reception they would receive upon their arrival home. "Gail will probably scream when she sees me," Dorrie commented.

"Out of jealousy?" Mick wondered, giving her a sideways glance.

"Maybe. . .when she sees you. Actually, I was thinking more on the line of my appearance. Gail's pretty persnickety about appearances, so she'll probably tell me how to improve my looks. 'Don't wear your hair that way, Dorrie, wear it like this!' " Dorrie said, mimicking her sister's high-pitched voice to perfection.

" 'No, this is a better shade of lipstick for you. And please put on some perfume, will you? You smell like an ox.' "

Mick laughed heartily. "I've got to hand it to you, Dorrie, you sure make the trip go quick. You're better than any entertainer on television. Ever think of becoming a stand-up comedian?"

Dorrie shook her head. Her face beamed with pleasure over the compliment. "That's a job I never considered, Mick."

As Dorrie predicted, Gail screamed when they arrived at the modest ranch home in Westchester County. She stared wide-eyed at Dorrie—from the casted arm to the hair shaved from Dorrie's head, baring the red suture line that ran across her glistening white scalp. "You look like you were mugged, Dorrie! What on earth happened?"

"I had an accident," Dorrie told her in exasperation.

"I should say you did! Your face looks perfectly dreadful. Mother will have a fit! C'mon, I know just how to fix you up before Mother comes home from work and sees you." Gail ushered her older sister into her bedroom, where a dresser sat littered with name-brand cosmetics and perfumes. Dorrie managed to slip Mick an "I told you so" look, which he acknowledged with a grin.

The Shelton family was particularly quiet that evening over dinner. Mother made a few comments, including a quick chastisement for Dorrie's male-oriented feats in the mountains. Dorrie's father proved more sympathetic—giving her hugs of reassurance and asking about her injuries. Later he drew Mick aside and spoke to him for a few minutes while offering thanks for his care of Dorrie during the traumatic time. When Mick announced he would take a night bus ride back to Boston, Dorrie's father offered to drive him to the bus station. The family then retired to the family room to watch television, allowing Mick and Dorrie a bit of privacy before the scheduled departure. They moseyed on outside and watched fireflies dart by, flashing their bright beacons of light. They slapped at the hungry mosquitoes that came calling on their exposed extremities.

"So how are you getting your car back?" Dorrie wondered.

"I'll take another bus up to the Whites in a few weekends and drive it home. It's still at Pinkham Notch in a pretty safe place. I can catch rides with friends in the meantime. I'm not concerned."

They stood in awkward silence, each heart contemplating the whirl of events that had transformed them over the past week.

"Well, Dorrie, guess this is good-bye," Mick finally said.

"Guess so."

Mick sighed and ran a hand through his hair. "I have some difficult things to do when I get back to Boston." He added a bit wistfully, "Wish you were coming with me."

Dorrie chuckled. "I think your parents could do without seeing a punk rocker, Mick."

He shook his head, then on impulse, gathered her in his arms and cuddled her close to him. "What am I going to do with you?" he teased, then whispered, "Come see me in Boston sometime."

Dorrie disengaged herself from his grasp and shook her head. "I don't think so, Mick. Our meeting was just for a season, you know? God used us in the mountains, but I believe He has other plans for our lives right now."

Mick stared at Dorrie with sorrow evident in his eyes. "I'm not so sure I agree with you about that. . . ," he began.

"Well, I'm sure," Dorrie informed him, patting his arm with her good hand. Her father beeped the car horn. "Go on now. Dad's waiting."

"Guess. . . ," he mumbled, "guess you wouldn't consider kissing me good-bye?"

Dorrie considered his request for a moment, then stood on her toes and planted a swift kiss on his rough cheek before hurrying into the house.

Mick scuffed his feet along the ground to the awaiting car, forcing a smile toward Dorrie's father. *Some things just take time,* he reasoned to himself. *Then why do I have this terrible feeling inside that I'll never see her again? Dorrie will only be but a passing memory for me, a memory of another life lost to me.*

❧

The days and nights proved long for Dorrie following her adventures in the White Mountains. Summer became fall as she continued her job in New York City. The leaves on the trees turned their brilliant shades of red and orange before fluttering gracefully to the ground in the cool autumn breeze. Dorrie occasionally took walks by herself along the sandy beach of Long Island, vacant of the beachcombers and sunbathers with the arrival of cooler weather. An ace wrap swathed her arm after the cast was removed. Her hair had begun to grow back, but Dorrie decided to shorten it in hopes of masking the effect of the damage caused by the fall. Her mother was horrified at the effect, claiming she could not tell from the back whether Dorrie was a man or a woman. The boss at the insurance company where she worked proved reasonable about the whole accident, allowing her less time on the word processor and more involvement with other activities such as filing until she was fully recovered. A new guy in the office named Andy asked her out on a date, but Dorrie refused.

On Sundays, the church near Central Park provided a wonderful inspiration for Dorrie. Watching a few gang members amble in during the middle of the service, Dorrie could not help but think of Mick and his father and all they did to reach the lost in the streets of Boston. At times she would lay awake for hours inside her townhouse on Long Island, thinking about him. Despite her friends and her job in exciting Manhattan, where nothing boring ever happened, Dorrie found herself consumed by thoughts of him.

One day a letter postmarked Boston, Massachusetts, arrived in the mail. Dorrie withdrew it from the box and scrutinized the handwriting. "It's from Mick," she breathed, tearing open the envelope to peruse the contents, even as her heart began to beat furiously within her.

Dear Dorrie,

Hi! So how goes it in New York City these days? Can you guess who this is? I know you're probably wondering where I got your address. Surprise, surprise! I found an envelope with your address on it inside your car and I kept it. Hope you aren't mad.

I just had to write you and tell you what's been happening.

I hope you're feeling better. I imagine by now you probably have the cast off your arm. Hope your boss didn't rake you over the coals when you returned to your job. I've gone back to teaching science at the middle school. The kids are crazy after their summer vacation. It's hard trying to settle them down so they'll learn something. Sometimes I wonder if I should hire an assistant to help me. If you ever want to change jobs, let me know!

Dorrie shook her head and lifted her eyes for a moment, imagining herself standing next to Mick as he taught the students from large charts displayed at the front of the classroom. The very thought of his rich voice and bright blue eyes addressing the students sent a flush crossing her cheeks. With her hand shaking, she returned to the note.

I wanted you to know that I've been back twice to see my dad. I wish I could say we had a nice visit, but it was very hard. He sits in a chair all day long staring and only yelps when I try to tell him something. He can't feed himself or use the bathroom. Mom insists he's much better, but I find that hard to believe. At least she is very happy to have her "wayward son" back again. I've gone back to church and received quite a warm welcome. I hope you don't mind, but I shared with the church what happened to us in the mountains. They believe as I do that God's hand was on us, and I think it still is.

Dorrie's hand shook violently. She inhaled a deep breath to steady the tremor.

I know you probably don't want to remember those times in the Whites, but I'll never forget them as long as I live. This may seem strange, but the most tender time I shared with you was by the rock, in the pouring rain, when I held you in my arms and told you how much I loved you. I know you were not conscious at that moment, but still it remains as vivid to me now as it did then.

Dorrie's hand fell to her side as the last few sentences of the letter rang in her heart like a bell. The words spoke of a man desperately in love, yet she did not know what to do about it. She contemplated answering the letter but somehow could not bring herself to put the words onto paper. Once more she decided to trust her future in the capable hands of God, who never disappointed her. *Lord, if it is Your will that Mick and I be brought together, if it will fulfill some great purpose in both our lives, please make it clear to the both of us. If it is not Your plan, then please take this man away from my innermost thoughts and especially from my heart. And please, do the same with him. Amen.*

❧

Time passed and soon the long Columbus Day weekend loomed before her. Weary of her job in Manhattan and sensing the need for a new direction in her life, Dorrie decided on a quick getaway and managed to secure a four-day weekend. Thursday night, Dorrie pondered where she might go. Normally she would consider a drive home to Westchester County to see her family, but her traveling bones decided to do something totally unique. Flipping through the pages of her road atlas, her eyes focused on Massachusetts and the city of Boston. "Boston. I could go to Boston. . .maybe see some of the historical sights or something." She drew in a deep breath, wondering if she dare surprise Mick with an impromptu visit. Would such a thing be out of line? She recalled the eagerness in his eyes when he invited her to come visit him. Perhaps it would even work out that she could meet his famous street-preaching father in the long-term care facility.

Having in her possession Mick's address from the envelope that concealed his letter to her, Dorrie plotted out her journey, then called her family with her plans. Only her father wished her luck with the trip. "I had a feeling about that young man when he was here, Dorrie girl," her father told her, using an affectionate name for his eldest daughter. "There are very few caring people left in the world. Don't let a good man like that slip away from you now."

Dorrie buried these words of advice deep within her as she selected her outfits for the trip. Perusing her reflection in the mirror, Dorrie wondered what Mick would think of her short hairstyle. As she settled behind the wheel of her trustworthy Mercury early Friday morning, she prayed that Mick had not planned a separate getaway of his own.

The trip went well until she reached the suburbs of Boston. No one told her what a headache Boston was to navigate. She promptly became lost in the complex streets of Cambridge, which all seemed one way with no street signs showing her where to go. Finally, Dorrie pulled into Mick's apartment complex after stopping for directions at a gas station. The complex was fairly new, complete with a pool and tennis courts. She drove around, finally locating his building at the end of a cul-de-sac. Dorrie found a space opposite the private entrance to his apartment. She could not steady her jitters as she sat behind the wheel, working up the courage to march up to his door and ring the bell. "What am I doing here anyway?" she questioned aloud. "This is really a crazy thing to do. I hope he doesn't think I want to settle down with him or something. Somehow I have to convince him I'm only here for a friendly visit. . .a quick stopover while I'm touring the sights. I don't want to give him any false impressions." Dorrie finally chastised herself for her cowardliness. In determination, she climbed out of her car, strode up to the door, and rang the doorbell. She waited for thirty seconds, then rang it again.

"Great, he's not home," Dorrie fretted as she walked back to the car. "I should've called and warned him I was coming. He probably decided on a getaway this weekend after all." Through her eyes filled with tears of disappointment, Dorrie noticed her camera sitting beside her in the passenger's seat. She decided if she couldn't see the man in person, she would snap a picture of where he lived to add a bit of nostalgia to her photo album. She grabbed the camera, rose out of the car, and focused for a shot. Just then, a compact car zoomed into the empty parking spot directly in front of her, blocking her view of the building. Dorrie was about ready to ask the driver to move when Mick jumped out of the driver's seat, clasping a two-liter bottle of soda in one hand and a newspaper in the other. He stared at Dorrie and the camera quizzically for a moment or two, until a curtain suddenly lifted from his eyes. All at once, he dropped the soda and the paper on the ground. Dorrie snapped a picture at that instant, laughing at his startled reaction until she heard the sound of the plastic bottle rolling away. She realized then that her sudden appearance had rattled his nerves.

"Oh, Mick, I'm sorry," Dorrie apologized, chasing after the soda bottle as it rolled underneath a parked car. When she emerged with the bottle in hand, Mick was there to take her in his arms.

"Dorrie. . .I can't believe it. You came. You really came." He murmured this fact over and over while holding her close to him, his hands rubbing circles around her back and shoulders.

Dorrie was taken aback by this tender display of affection. She disengaged herself from his arms and meekly handed him the soda bottle she had recovered. "Here's your soda, but I'm afraid your newspaper is gone with the wind."

"Who cares? I have you! Dorrie, you don't know how much I prayed that one day you would come here to see me. I can't believe it."

"Well, it's me. Like my posh hairdo?" Dorrie twirled around. "I grew tired of the punk style I wore a few months ago. This takes all of three seconds to wash and run a comb through. Mother can't tell if I'm a man or woman, or so she says."

"You look fantastic," he breathed, reaching out his arms only to find Dorrie withdrawing from his embrace. Instead of questioning her standoffish behavior, Mick gestured her to his apartment. "Well, come on in," he told her, "just don't laugh at the mess you see inside. I'm grading papers this weekend."

Dorrie cautiously went inside, standing close to the door as she observed the usual clutter of a typical bachelor pad. Ugly striped curtains adorned a bay window where a withered plant stood. A huge mound of papers lay in disarray on the small dining table. Boxes stood stacked in one corner. The living room was littered with junk food wrappers, soiled cups, hiking magazines, and a weeks' worth of the *Boston Globe*.

"Sorry about the mess," he apologized, bundling up the papers to be recycled and throwing the rest of the trash into a wastebasket. "As you can see, I. . .uh, wasn't expecting company."

"Don't worry about it. I know I came unannounced. I was in the mood to see some of the historic sights and decided as long as I'm here, why not come by and do a little catching up?" Dorrie contemplated sitting on one of the two sofas in the living room, but instead maintained her cautious vigil by the door.

Mick noticed her discomfort. "Look, I haven't got a thing in the fridge, so why don't we go out and grab a bite to eat. You like Chinese?"

"Sure," Dorrie said with a smile, relaxing for the first time since her arrival.

"And don't worry. . .we'll just call this a friendly meeting, not a date."

"I appreciate that." Dorrie turned, preparing to head out the door, when she noticed his muddy pack resting against the wall. A note dangling from the zipper caught her eye. "Sorry about what happened," she read aloud. "I hope this makes amends. I'm leaving for the West Coast, got a full-time teaching job. Take care. Krysta." Dorrie looked over at Mick questioningly.

"Yeah, I found it on my doorstep shortly after I got back. Krysta was really upset about what happened on the mountain, Dorrie. I guess she found my pack by the rocks and brought it with her when she came home."

"She found your pack?" Dorrie repeated. "I didn't know you had lost it."

"Actually I had to leave it at the spot where you were hurt," Mick explained. "I couldn't handle both you and the pack on the trip to the hut."

Dorrie could not believe her ears. "You mean you left an expensive, three-hundred-dollar pack lying there in mud? What if somebody ripped it off, Mick?"

"Dorrie, I consider you much more precious than any three-hundred-dollar pack," he told her, staring her straight in the eye. "To me, you're worth it. I'd do it all over again if I had to and leave a thousand three-hundred-dollar packs."

Dorrie stood stunned by this display of genuine concern on her behalf. Again her father's words echoed in her thoughts. *There are very few caring people left in this world. Don't let a good man like that slip away from you now.* "Wow, that's really. . .well, quite touching."

105

"C'mon," he gestured. "There's a restaurant about five blocks away. I think you'll like it."

Dorrie followed him out the door yet remained bewildered by all that she had seen and heard. Perhaps God was indeed trying to lead her in this matter of the heart, but once again, she found her questions and doubts blocking the way. How would she know His will for sure? There must be a way to discover if her path in life was indeed leading her straight to Mick Walters.

Chapter 14

Dorrie savored every drop of the delicious green tea served in tiny cups at the Chinese restaurant, then set to work on her eggroll while Mick filled her in on his classes for the new term. "They're a rowdy bunch," he confessed, dipping his roll into a dish of hot mustard. "Every new group seems to test me as the teacher, trying to decide if I'm a pushover."

"Are you?" Dorrie wondered, wiping off her lips with a napkin.

Mick winked his eye. "Now that depends on who's in my company."

Dorrie had not meant to make a leading statement and now found herself blushing. She averted her gaze and tried concentrating on eating her eggroll, but with much less enjoyment.

"Do you think I'm a pushover?" he asked.

Dorrie laughed. "Definitely not. Once your mind is made up, not much can change it. A pushover goes wherever the wind blows. Mick is one who follows his heart." Again, Dorrie found herself flustered when his blue eyes softened under the glow of the light glimmering over their booth.

Mick laid down his eggroll and reached for her hand, which she instinctively placed on her lap. "Dorrie, I've tried so many times to tell you what's going on in my heart. . . ," he began.

"I know. Unfortunately, it takes two to tango. Mine is only full of questions. You can't make a decision when all you have is questions."

"If you have a question, I'll do my best to answer it," he told her. "I know I made a big mistake by not telling you everything about my life. As far as I know, there are no more skeletons left in the closet."

"I've forgiven you for the past. My question really has to do with God's will for my life. I want to be sure it's His will and not some wild emotional whim, don't you?"

"I know His will," Mick said defensively, "and it is no emotional whim. I've tried many times to tell you, Dorrie, but you won't stop long enough to listen."

Dorrie's mouth went dry. She reached for her glass of ice water, gulping down the cool liquid before replacing it on the table. *This is not going well at all,* she thought to herself.

He sensed the restlessness stirring at the table. "Look, forget about it for the time being. I wanted to tell you I'm planning to visit my dad tomorrow. You interested in going with me? You can meet my mother afterwards; she's hosting a picnic at a nearby park for the church."

The sudden change of topic threw Dorrie into a confusing spin. "Well, yeah, sure, I guess so. I mean, yes. I really do want to meet your father and the picnic sounds very nice."

"I've already told Mom about you and what happened during the vacation. She thinks you're the living end since you rescued her wayward son from his mountain of sin."

"Well, did you tell her you actually performed the hands-on rescue on Mt. Washington?" Dorrie wondered.

"Yeah, but that's beside the point. To my mom, who's been praying for me solidly since Dad's accident, it's the best news she's had in a long time." He then inhaled a deep breath. "Dorrie, I want you to know I've been thinking a lot about us. I think we have a lot in common. We're right for each other, I know it. I would really like to give Mom more good news tomorrow if I could. . . ."

Sensing what he was about to say, Dorrie shook her head and rose quickly to her feet. "I didn't come all the way here to Boston to get backed into a corner, Mick Walters. The answer's no."

Mick also came to his feet, even as Dorrie fumbled to retrieve her coat thrown over the back of her chair. "Please wait, Dorrie. I won't mention it anymore. It's just. . .I love you so much. I don't want you to slip away from me."

"Please, Mick, no more. What time should I be ready to see your father?"

"I'll leave around noon," he mumbled, sitting down hard in his seat, nearly upsetting his water glass.

"Okay, I'll come by your place around noon." Dorrie observed his dejection as he stared into his plate of uneaten food. With mechanical movements, he pulled out a few bills from his wallet, rose, and walked over to pay the cashier. Dorrie stood waiting as he paid the check, then followed him to his car without comment. When Mick pulled into the parking lot of the apartment where Dorrie's car sat, he turned and eyed her.

"Dorrie, I have just one question to ask you. The truth. Why did you come all the way here to see me?"

Dorrie's eyes widened. She felt herself shrinking under his penetrating glare. In a shaky voice, she said, "Why. . .a f. . .friendly visit, pure and simple."

"A friendly visit, pure and simple, huh?" Mick sighed. "Okay, I'll take your word for it."

Never before did Dorrie endure such emotional turmoil over a man. She spent the remainder of the evening in her motel room thinking about the conversation. She knew Mick was poised to ask for her hand in marriage, yet the very thought sent shivers racing down her spine. "I can't marry him, God," she told her unseen Friend and constant Companion. "I have a life in New York, he has a life here in Boston. In fact, he's only now beginning to get his life back together. How can I make him see that a lifetime commitment just isn't right for two people as different as we are?" Dorrie flipped over on her side, tossing a pillow over her head. "Why can't we just be friends. . .two friends that like to hike and eat out and share good times? Why do we have to become entangled in this love connection, which only causes heartache and grief?" These questions reflected the doubt burdening her heart. They were questions she could not make Mick understand, for he was too wrapped up in his own emotion to even consider them.

※

The motel phone rang the next morning just as Dorrie emerged from the shower with a towel wrapped like a turban around her head. She nearly knocked over her suitcase in her haste to pick up the phone and offered a breathless hello.

"You sound like you just ran the hundred-meter dash," Mick joked through the receiver.

"Just about."

"Look, I make some pretty wild blueberry pancakes. You interested in a brunch over at my place? Then we can leave from here to visit my dad."

Dorrie hesitated until the growling of her stomach overshadowed any resistance to the idea. "Sure, that sounds great."

A sigh of relief drifted over the phone. "Look, I also want to apologize for putting you on the spot last night in the restaurant. It's fine with me if we just stay friends. The Lord knows we can use friends nowadays."

Now it was Dorrie's turn to sigh, thanking God in her heart for his decision. "Great, Mick. See you in about half an hour."

"All right then. See you." The phone clicked in her ear to be replaced by the buzz of dial tone. As Dorrie returned the receiver to the cradle, she smiled to herself, then skipped over to the sink to apply her makeup and blow-dry her damp hair. "Thank goodness," she breathed.

※

The smell of pancakes wafted in the air when Mick, clad in a chef's apron with a spatula in one hand, greeted her at the door. Dorrie could not help but giggle at his attire. As she strode into the kitchen to observe the batch of crisp pancakes he had prepared, she nodded her head in satisfaction. "They look wonderful, Mick. I thought you once said guys couldn't cook."

"Well, pancakes is about the only thing I can cook," he confessed, using his spatula to flip over the next batch. Above him the microwave whined, followed by a buzzer. "Would you mind getting that? It's maple syrup."

Dorrie was more than impressed when she removed a small pitcher of real maple syrup and placed it on the table. Mick had taken great pains to set the table with matching dishes and silverware. She gazed around the apartment, now transformed into decent living quarters, and complimented his hard work. "This is really something, Mick," she observed, sitting down happily at the table. He placed a huge platter of pancakes before her. Sausage links sat in another dish. "Yum, yum, looks scrumptious."

Mick sat down opposite her, bent his head, and offered a simple blessing for the meal—the first words of prayer Dorrie ever heard him utter. A warmth flowed through her heart when she thought of the great transformation that had occurred within him. When she first met Mick in the White Mountains, he was an embittered man who could not stand the idea of prayer or someone offering prayer on his behalf. Now he spoke the words with a confidence and ease as if praying was the most natural thing in the world.

He rose and served her pancakes and sausage, then offered her the warm pitcher of syrup. For a moment, Dorrie could only stare at the food on her plate, thinking of the love and care that went into the preparation of a simple meal. The very thought sent tears welling up in her eyes.

Mick watched her reactions thoughtfully. "Are you okay, Dorrie?"

She jerked herself upright and wiped the tears away with the corner of a paper napkin. "Oh sure, Mick, sure."

He gestured with his fork. "I hope you like sausages. I think I remember you eating them back in the cafeteria at Pinkham Notch."

"Yeah," she responded absentmindedly.

Mick did not know what to make of her strange reaction. He ate silently, yet cast curious glances every so often. Dorrie also consumed the breakfast without offering conversation, immersed in deep thought. Finally, she broke the silence by asking Mick about his father's condition.

"He looked pretty bad to me the last time I was over there. The visit didn't last too long. I told him about myself and how I had gotten right with the Lord. Sometimes it seems he is listening to me, but I can't tell. He says a strange word like 'yow' or something like that. Then he howls and shifts around in his chair." Mick shrugged helplessly. "I don't know what to do. I told him I loved him and everything, then I left."

"And you say he can't do anything for himself?"

Mick drank some orange juice before continuing. "The nurses leave him dressed in a hospital gown because he can't use the. . .well, you know, the bathroom and all. He has problems sitting up, so they have him in some type of reclining chair, a lounge chair I think my mom called it." He blinked before adding softly, "I wish you could know him the way I used to know him, Dorrie."

Dorrie offered a compassionate smile. "Well, if he is anything like his son, I'm sure he must be a great person."

Mick's face softened upon hearing this uplifting comment, then he returned to his stack of pancakes. After swallowing several mouthfuls, he said, "You always seem to know the right words at the right time."

Dorrie smiled as she carried her dirty dishes over to the sink. Rolling up the sleeves to her shirt, she proceeded to wash them while Mick carried the rest of the plates over and deposited them into the soapy water. For a time Mick stood and watched her work. He wanted to make some witty comment, such as how perfectly she fit in with the surroundings, but decided against it. Knowing Dorrie the way he did, she would undoubtedly think the comment presumptuous and overbearing. He sighed and retrieved a dishtowel to wipe up the dishes that now sparkled in the drainer. How he agonized over the woman standing before him. Dorrie stood so close to him but she seemed so far away at the same time—as if it would take a long, arduous journey up a steep mountain just to reach her heart. He enjoyed her warm presence and found himself fighting off the nagging urge to hold her. He had made a commitment on the phone to remain friends. Now it was his responsibility to keep his word despite the longing in his heart.

Just before departing, Dorrie again noticed the stack of boxes piled high in the corner of his apartment. She inquired if he was moving into another place.

"No," Mick responded, striding over to one of the open boxes and withdrawing a pamphlet. "I ordered these when I came back from the mountains." He handed one to her.

Dorrie took the booklet from his outstretched hand and perused the contents. "Why, this is a tract."

"These are the same tracts my dad used to give out on the streets before he was shot," Mick explained.

Dorrie's eyes widened as she stared first at the tract, then at Mick. "Are you thinking of going back to the streets?"

He nodded. "I'm considering it. Right now I'm in the midst of taking an evangelism class at my mom's church. One can get pretty rusty in the things of God after backsliding for two or more years."

"Wow, this is wonderful, Mick! What a great mission field. I can't tell you how much I admire the work that goes on among the gangs in the streets of New York. They are a group right here in America in desperate need of missionaries willing to reach them."

"Yeah, well, I decided if my dad can't do the work anymore, someone oughtta be willing to take up where he left off." Mick took the tract from her and placed it with the others inside the box.

"Have you told your dad what you're doing?" Dorrie asked.

"Told my dad?" Mick snorted as if the suggestion seemed ludicrous. "He doesn't understand anything I tell him, Dorrie. I don't even think he knows who I am. Mom always tells me he knows. She can see it in his eyes or hear it when he yells. I think it's just wishful thinking on her part, to be honest."

Dorrie retrieved another tract. "Well, let's tell him about your call and see how he responds, Mick. It can't do any harm, can it?"

111

"I suppose not."

He held open the door for her as she ventured out, clutching the booklet tight in her hand. Warm, bright sunshine greeted them. Colored leaves swirled around before finding resting places in the grass or on the blacktop of the parking area.

"This is going to be a glorious day, Mick," Dorrie declared, settling down in the passenger seat of his car. "I can just feel it."

So long as you're with me, he thought. *We could have a glorious life too.* He kept the comment tucked away inside where it belonged.

The long-term care facility where Mick's father lived was filled with the scent of antiseptic, freshly starched sheets, and other odors Dorrie could not identify. She followed Mick to the elevator, conscious of her own anxiety. Mick likewise appeared nervous about the visit. His neck muscles were taut and his finger shaking as he pressed the button labeled three. Neither of them spoke a word as the elevator beeped and they stepped off to be greeted by a terrible noise echoing down the corridor.

Mick sighed. "That's Dad you hear," he whispered to Dorrie.

Dorrie's eyes flashed wide. "You mean that howling is coming from your dad?"

Mick nodded and gripped her hand as they walked down the carpeted hall together. Approaching the solarium where patients sat in wheelchairs watching television or catching a brief nap, Mick gestured her over to the far corner where a withered man lay howling in a lounge chair. Dorrie glanced up at Mick's face and saw the tears swimming in his eyes.

"It's okay, Mick," she whispered, squeezing his hand in reassurance.

"I. . .I don't know if I can take this, Dorrie," he whispered. "That. . .that stranger isn't my dad."

Just then they were interrupted by one of the nursing assistants on duty. She recognized Mick at once and said hello.

"This is Dorrie," Mick said. "Dorrie, Debbie here takes care of Dad quite a bit."

"Hi, Debbie," Dorrie said brightly.

"Sorry, but your father is not in the greatest of moods today," Debbie sadly informed them. "He fought with me most of the day. I'm afraid we had to place him in a vest restraint for his safety."

"Vest restraint?" Dorrie wondered.

The pain in Mick's face was very evident as he choked out, "Yeah, sometimes when Dad is really off, he gets restless. The nurses are afraid he might fall and hurt himself. Sometimes they have to use the restraint."

Dorrie was shocked. "You mean they tie him in his chair? Oh Mick, that's awful!"

"It's only for his protection, Miss," Debbie informed her. "Maybe if he calms down during your visit, we can take it off."

Dorrie swallowed hard. This was indeed worse than she had imagined. The man she saw in the chair wore a simple patient's gown with an afghan draped over his lap. Spittle ran out of his mouth and down his neck. His gray eyes were glazed over as he stared into space. Dorrie tried to picture the man walking the streets of Boston, handing out tracts and telling others about the Lord. Her heart could not help but cry out for God's mercy to overshadow this pitiful man.

With great trepidation, Mick approached the bedraggled figure, knelt down next to the chair, and in a soft voice, greeted his father. Dorrie watched the interaction between father and son. She noticed the man move his eyes ever so slightly, followed by the loud word "eyow!"

Unprepared for the noise, Mick jumped to his feet. Trembling, he tried to regain his composure. "D. . .Dad, I want you to meet a friend of mine. This is Dorrie."

Dorrie stepped up and smiled down at the man. "Hello, Mr. Walters."

The man offered no response as he stared listlessly past her.

Dorrie drew in a breath, glancing at Mick for support. After an awkward moment, she decided to communicate with the man as if he could understand everything. Mick looked on as Dorrie explained who she was, where she worked, how she met Mick, and how she loved the Lord. At this, Mr. Walters swiveled his head slightly and emitted another ferocious "eyow!"

Dorrie's heart began to race with growing excitement. *I think Mick's mother is right! I think he does understand what I'm saying!* She then remembered the tract in her possession and withdrew it.

Upon seeing the familiar booklet in her outstretched hand, Mr. Walters strained against the restraint that held him in the chair and emitted another frightful "eyow." Everyone in the solarium glanced over in their direction. Some of the residents shouted at him to be quiet.

"What are you doing, Dorrie?" Mick scolded her. "You're getting him all upset."

"No, look again, Mick, and this time listen carefully to him." Once more, Dorrie showed him the tract and explained how Mick was thinking of going back out to the streets.

"Dorrie," Mick whispered furiously, "why did you tell him all that? He doesn't understand, I tell you."

"Look, Mick!" Dorrie exclaimed excitedly.

His father twisted and turned into contorted positions and yelled several additional "eyows" before he suddenly began to howl like an animal.

The nursing assistant rushed over to find out the reason for the commotion. "I'm afraid this visit is really upsetting him," Debbie observed in dissatisfaction. "Maybe you shouldn't talk to him. Just sit quietly and hold his hand."

"No!" Dorrie fired back. "Debbie, this man knows what we're saying to him.

Every time I mention something from his past, he says the word 'eyow.'" She turned to the man who now lay in the chair. "Isn't that true, Mr. Walters?"

Again, he roared an "eyow!"

"You see, you see?" Dorrie exclaimed in excitement, clutching Mick's arm. "That means, yes. Right, Mr. Walters?"

"Eyow!"

Mick and Debbie stared incredulously, first at the man, then at Dorrie. Now, Dorrie knelt beside the man and pointed to the restraint. "I bet you dislike this thing, don't you, Mr. Walters?"

This sent the man into a fit along with more "eyows."

Mick needed no further convincing. "Take it off right now, Debbie," he ordered.

"I'm not sure if that's wise. . . ," the nursing assistant began.

"Take it off. If there's any chance at all my father understands what we're saying, then he must understand what is happening to him. Take it off now."

Debbie obliged to the echoes of "eyows" screeched by Mick's father.

"Let's roll him to his room where we can talk in private," Dorrie suggested.

Mick agreed, and together they steered the massive chair through the doors and down a hallway to his private room, overlooking the skyline of downtown Boston. Once in his room, Dorrie began to investigate the closet, searching for something to dress the man in besides the flimsy hospital gown. Finding no clothes in the closet, she asked Mick if his mother might consider bringing in some shirts and pants.

"Dorrie," he whispered, leading her by the arm over to one side of the room, "you can't dress him. He, well, he'll soil his clothes."

The comment sent his father into another wave of howls. Dorrie smiled when she heard the reaction. "You see, Mick? See how well your father can hear? And I tell you, he doesn't want to be dressed in an ugly old hospital gown. He wants to feel like a man again, don't you, Mr. Walters?"

"Eyow!" came the reply.

Dorrie went to the dresser and shuffled through bottles of aftershave and old toothbrushes until she found a comb. "Mick, how does your father wear his hair?"

"Parted on the side I think, uh, don't you, Dad?"

The man swiveled his head around and responded with the customary "eyow" for yes.

Dorrie combed out his hair, parted it to one side, then found a mirror so he might view his appearance. "How's that, Mr. Walters?"

"Eyow." He relaxed in his chair.

"You see, Mick? What did I tell you?" Dorrie then studied the man resting before her for several moments. Suddenly, as if the sun had risen, bringing light into the midst of darkness, she began to understand the poor man's plight. "I. . .I think I know what's going on inside you, Mr. Walters," she said softly. She knelt next to the chair, holding a bony hand in hers as she spoke directly to him. "You know everything that's going on. I don't think you've lost your thoughts or memories or ability to understand. What you lost is, well, like a road. . .a road linking thought with action. I've even heard about it. . .those people who have been in comas for years, then wake up and come to an understanding of what's happening around them. After extensive rehabilitation, they are able to talk about how their bodies were like shells, even prisons." Her grip strengthened around his withered hand. "Maybe you've even wondered, 'When, oh God, will someone realize I'm trapped in this body? I can think, I can feel, I can understand, but I can't tell anyone.' " Dorrie sniffed, overwhelmed by the words she spoke. " 'I want to tell people I'm alive, but this body is a prison with no way out.' "

At that moment, Dorrie saw a great tear fall from the man's eye and plop onto her arm. Mick saw it too, and immediately came to his father's side, breaking down into tears. "I'm so sorry, Dad. I didn't understand. Mom. . .she believed. . .she believed you. I. . .I only wanted you back the way you used to be. I was mad at God and. . .and mad at you. Please. . .forgive me for abandoning you, for not caring, for not being there when you needed me most."

Again, another tear slipped out of the man's eyes. "Eyow, eyow, eyow," he cried, along with the weeping pair next to him. No one knew the thoughts circulating in the head of the street preacher at that moment of triumph. *Oh God, at last, at last,* his mind cried. *Thank You for restoring me to my son. Thank You for my family, for through this angel of mercy which You gave understanding to, I can now be understood by my son. Thank You, merciful God.*

Chapter 15

Mick did not want to leave his father's side but reluctantly bid him good-bye, accompanied by a kiss on the forehead. He then told his father about the picnic Mom had planned at a nearby park. "Wish he could come with us," Mick said to Dorrie as they found their way out of the brick building and into the sunshine that glowed even more brilliantly after the visit.

"There's no reason why he can't learn to sit in a wheelchair so you can take him out places. It looks like that nurse, Debbie, is a blessing. She seemed quite open to hearing new ideas on how to care for your father. She's willing to dress him in decent clothes using those adult pads and everything. This is a new day in his life."

"It's a new day in all our lives. I can't wait to tell Mom. She'll be so excited to hear this. Mom has spent nearly every waking hour of her life with Dad. I know she'll be glad to hear that I now understand what's going on and that Dad does too."

"It will be a wonderful surprise for her," Dorrie agreed.

The park on the other side of town was crowded with members of Mick's congregation, who had gathered together for a Columbus Day picnic. Grills were fired up, ready for one final barbecue before winter settled in over the New England city. Checkered tablecloths, lying across the picnic tables, fluttered in the autumn breeze. When Mick and Dorrie arrived, Mrs. Walters came over to greet them. She was a tall woman with chestnut brown hair, bobbed in a style similar to what Dorrie wore before her accident on Mt. Washington. Dorrie sensed an immediate bonding with the woman as Mrs. Walters bestowed a warm hug, thanking Dorrie for all she had done.

"You won't believe our visit at the nursing home, Mom," Mick said, eagerly filling her in on the restoration between himself and his father that afternoon. As he spoke, a small crowd from the church gathered around to hear the story, then exchanged hugs with an exuberant Mrs. Walters.

Tears of joy ran down her cheeks. "Oh, Mick, how I've prayed that one day you would understand your father and how much he loves you. I'm so glad!"

"I would have never understood, Mom," Mick said slowly, turning toward Dorrie, "if it had not been for this terrific lady here."

"How can I ever thank you, Dorrie? You've been such a blessing to me and my family."

116

Dorrie only smiled, embarrassed by all the attention she was receiving from the people around her. "I'm just glad for you," she managed to say.

Mick wrapped his arm around her and gave her an affectionate squeeze. "She's been a godsend to me, Mom," he agreed.

"She's definitely an answer to prayer," Mrs. Walters added with a twinkle in her eye. "Well, Dorrie, you must be hungry. Come, there are hamburgers ready."

Dorrie eagerly helped herself to the food, then became immersed in conversation as people inquired about her escapades in the mountains. After it was all over, Dorrie collapsed inside Mick's car, spent from all the flurry of activity and the emotion of the day. "Wow, I'm bushed!"

"Me too."

"What a great day. You have two wonderful families, Mick—your real family and your church family."

"I have wonderful friends too, Dorrie," he added with a sideways glance toward her.

Dorrie looked over at him and considered his words. Somehow, after the events of the day, the word "friend" did not seem to fit Mick Walters anymore. What was he, then, if he was not a friend? He was not a brother, of course. Was he someone else. . .a special someone that now began to tug on her heart?

The two of them spent Sunday once more surrounded by Mick's two families and also visited Mick's dad at the nursing home for a lengthy time, sharing Scriptures and the message from the pulpit that morning. The nurses remarked how calm Mr. Walters had become since their previous visit and marveled at his transformation. Debbie had him dressed in some of his regular clothes with his hair parted to one side. Both Mick and Dorrie sensed that dignity and hope had been restored to the man who once gave everything in his life to others less fortunate.

"He looked real good," Mick commented over a steak dinner in a fancy restaurant that night—his going-away present to Dorrie before she was obliged to leave early for New York the next morning. "This has been quite a weekend."

"Yes," she agreed, stirring a packet of artificial sweetener into her iced tea.

Mick stared at her thoughtfully, then inquired if she was looking forward to returning to New York.

Dorrie shrugged, growing suddenly despondent with the thought of returning home.

"Well, I have something for you," Mick told her with a mysterious look in his eye.

A strange fear welled up inside her until he handed her a clear plastic egg. She stared at it in confusion. "What is this?"

"Got it out of one of those quarter machines the other day," he told her as she opened the egg to reveal a plastic ring. He added quickly, "Thought it would make a good friendship ring."

Dorrie snickered, shaking her head at him. "How silly."

"Well, I wanted to give you a souvenir rock from Mt. Washington, but I figured that wouldn't go over too well." He returned his attention to the healthy-size portion of steak on a stone platter in front of him.

Dorrie eyed the ring as she twisted it around her finger. A strange sensation swept over her. When she glanced up to see Mick busily chewing his meal, his blue eyes twinkling, she knew what the sensation was that now fell on her like a gentle rain. It was love, pure and simple. Dorrie knew without a doubt she was in love with the man sitting before her.

After dinner, Mick dropped her off at the motel. "I'll come by early to see you off," he promised before returning to his car.

"Okay." Dorrie closed the door to her motel room, then withdrew the ring from her purse. Did this ring speak of a friendship or a longing for a deeper commitment? Dorrie relaxed on the bed, thinking of the exciting things that had happened over the course of her stay in Boston. She remembered how the eyes of Mr. Walters shone when Mick discussed his plan to return to the streets of Boston and share the gospel with those in need. Truly Mick had become a changed man—one who now looked heavenward to the eternal things of the Lord rather than the carnal things of this world. How different he had become since that night on the trail after her ankle injury. How different she had become during these last few days. Dorrie felt her reservations slowly melt away as her questions were replaced by an assurance that this was indeed God's will at work in their lives.

The following morning Mick arrived as promised, with bagels, cream cheese, and juice for a quick breakfast. Dorrie could barely spread the cheese on a bagel. Her heart overflowed with a love that seemed to affect her in everything she did, from packing her suitcase to brushing her teeth to eating the food he had lovingly brought. Now, she set the bagel down and closed her eyes.

Mick noticed her lack of appetite right away. His gentle eyes narrowed in concern. "Did I get the wrong kind of bagels? Maybe I should've asked you what flavor you like."

Suddenly, Dorrie burst into tears. Mick sat stunned, holding a bagel in one hand. Quickly he placed it on a napkin and sat beside her. "Dorrie, what's the matter?"

Unable to bear it anymore, she turned and threw her arms around him. "I love you, Mick!"

"Dorrie. . . ," he began, slowly allowing his arms to enfold her in an embrace.

"I'm sorry it took me so long to see." She laughed a little. "Guess the bump on my head up there in the mountains did something to my vision. I could not even see the terrific guy sitting right underneath my nose."

Mick could only smile and thank God in his heart for this revelation.

Dorrie turned, zipped open her purse, and handed him the plastic ring. "Would you like to exchange this for a real one, instead?" he asked her softly.

Dorrie nodded. "Yes!" Mick bent over her and their lips met in a passionate kiss as a signature of their commitment to one another. When they parted, Dorrie clung to his arm as if she never wanted to let go. She praised God that indeed He had purified their hearts and their very beings in the great and awesome majesty of His mountains. Soon, He would bring them together as one in the high and holy calling of the marriage covenant.

LAURALEE BLISS
A former nurse, Lauralee is a prolific writer of inspirational fiction as well as a home educator. She resides with her family near Charlottesville, Virginia, in the foothills of the Blue Ridge Mountains—a place of inspiration for many of her contemporary and historical novels. Lauralee Bliss writes inspirational fiction to provide readers with entertaining stories, intertwined with Christian principles to assist them in the day-to-day walk with the Lord. Aside from writing, she enjoys gardening, cross-stitching, reading, roaming yard sales, and traveling. Her other published works include a novel for **Heartsong Presents**—*Behind the Mask*, a novella *Island Sunrise* in the collection *Rescue*, and a novella *Ark of Love* in the collection *Tails of Love*, all by Barbour Publishing. Lauralee welcomes you to visit her website: http://lauraleebliss.homestead.com/lrbweb.html

SEA ESCAPE

Lynn A. Coleman

Dedication

First, I want to thank the Lord for the inspiration.
Secondly, to Paul, my hero, my husband of over twenty-five years,
for his loving support and encouragement.
Without him my writing never would have come into being.
And last, but not least, I want to thank a very dear friend
who helped me fine-tune my writing, Tracie Peterson.
To each I say thanks, and I love you all.

Chapter 1

Alex's senses tingled from the swirling salty breeze. Perched on the upper deck of the ferry, she leaned forward into the wind, taking in a deep breath. Her nostrils flared at the exotic, briny air. Across the vast expanse of the sea, she saw the land rise before her in the distance. Gentle slopes with tawny beaches hugged sandy cliffs crowned with captains' houses. Mated together, they presented a glorious picture of God's handiwork. Never had she seen anything like it. Chilled, she rubbed her bare arms, feeling the sea spray drying on her skin. This was such a different sight from the vast farmlands draped across Kansas.

Martha's Vineyard, a small island off the coast of Massachusetts. Alex smiled. She remembered researching the island in the encyclopedia when she was eight. "You're finally here," she said into the wind, squinting at the sun.

She watched a sea gull gliding alongside the boat. *How can it maintain that speed for so long without a flap of its wings?* she wondered. The gull seemed to be watching her as much as she was watching it. Some small children ran up to the rail, holding out crackers. Alex opened her mouth to correct them, but as soon as she did, the gull swooped down and took the treat. The children bounced up and down shouting, "Look at that, look at that, it took it!"

The girl in the trio, maybe around nine, Alex guessed, cried out, "Jonathan, let me have a turn!"

"Wait, Sarah!" the older boy asserted himself. "I want to do it again."

Alex snickered to herself as Sarah stood her ground. She swung her hands to her hips and said, "Mom said we *all* could feed the birds."

The older boy seemed to be judging whether or not his sister would tell on him. Reluctantly, he pulled out another cracker and handed it to her. "Here."

The girl's eyes twinkled. She reached out past the rail, standing on her tiptoes. Without hesitation the gull flew to the hand holding out the cracker.

She dropped it.

"See, I knew you couldn't do it," the older boy teased. "Watch me!"

The younger boy meanwhile had figured his own strategy; he grabbed a deck chair and pulled it up to the rail. He asked his brother for a cracker, stood up tall, and thrust his arm out over his head.

Instinctively taking a step forward, Alex wanted to grab the boy from the rail. He was teetering dangerously over the edge. Or so she thought. Out of the corner of her eye she observed a man, whose hair matched the boys', watching them with paternal intensity. He beamed when the youngest had achieved his quest.

"Daddy, did you see that?"

"Sure did, Timmy. Good job, but it's time to get down, okay? Your mother is waiting for us."

"Okay."

The little girl pouted, "I got scared and dropped mine."

Alex watched the interchange between father and children. A smile curled her lips, but a dull ache of longing buried deep within struggled to the surface. Would she ever have children of her own? *Oh Lord, how long do I have to wait? How soon will I come to terms with the fact that I'm not to have a husband or children of my own? Isn't that why I'm still single, Lord?*

"Daddy, can I try again?"

"Sure, one more time. Jonathan, give your sister another cracker."

"That's no fair, I get another cracker too," the younger boy protested.

The girl stood on tiptoe, right hand on the rail, the other arm stretched out. A gull swooped in from her right for its treat. The young girl's eyes bulged with expectancy.

Plop! "Eww, Daddy, the bird pooped on me!"

Alex laughed out loud. Bridling her laughter, she turned so as not to embarrass the child.

The boat's horn blasted mere inches from her. She jumped at the spine-jarring assault and covered her ears. Realizing they were entering Vineyard Haven Harbor, she decided to make her way down below to the car. Scanning the sky for any more miscreant birds, she headed for the nearest bulkhead.

Two decks down, she rejoined her car. Every vehicle was packed in bumper to bumper, impossibly tight. She remembered her fear when the stewards kept signaling her to come forward. When she got out she'd gasped, seeing only a four-inch clearance.

Alex opened the door, maneuvering her body sideways, and slid into the driver's seat. Weary after the long drive from Kansas, she moaned and fastened her seat belt. Her only stops along the way had been in Indiana to visit a cousin and again in New York to visit an elderly aunt.

A year's sabbatical. She sighed. "Lord, You know how much I need this year off just to get my head on straight." *And what better way to relax than to search out my family roots?*

Her thoughts drifted back to her patients. She had left her practice in the care of another pediatric physician. They had worked side by side the whole summer, allowing her patients to meet the new doctor. Many of the children said how they would miss her. Giving hugs and kisses, several whispered, "I love you, Dr. Alex."

Alex brushed a tear from her eye. She was losing perspective. Her own desires to have a family, compounded with working with children day in and day out, only magnified the ticking of her biological clock. Seven years in her own practice, seven wonderful but lonely years.

Even the Bible spoke of taking the seventh year off. No, she knew it was the right decision. Fear and uncertainty about her future loomed in front of her, and yet excitement and a sense of urgency to explore the land and history of her own family roots already seemed to provide the solace for which she searched.

The car rocked as the steel ferry bounced off the pilings. Alex gripped her steering wheel, wondering if the captain had misjudged. She looked at the others around her. No one seemed a bit concerned by the ricocheting off of the pilings, nor with the creaking they made.

Easing her grasp, she settled back in her bucket seat. The noisy cranking of metal cables and the clanging rush of steel chains broke her reverie as the heavy ramp leveled off to meet the ferry's deck. She released her pent-up breath, unaware she had been holding it.

Drivers turned their engines on; she did the same. One by one, passengers drove off the boat. Amazed by the speed of their exit, she kept a sharp vigil, awaiting her turn.

Brad and Phyllis Trainer's directions lay on the other seat. Her friends owned the beachfront property that would be her home for the next year. Noting that the first turn was almost immediate, she scanned over the paper one more time. *When you get to Five Corners, you take a right.*

"Five Corners, what kind of a place is that?"

"Yo!" A man tapped her hood. Alex jerked. "Come on, Lady, get a move on." She popped her car into gear and it bucked forward. Her cheeks flushed. She followed the line of traffic down a roped-off path through the parking lot. The street immediately before her continued on, but the sign said, "Do Not Enter." She turned left with the rest of the traffic. Stopping at the intersection, she counted, then snickered at herself. Sure enough, five corners.

Alex relaxed in her seat, turned on the directional, and slowly worked her way forward. There was no traffic light. *How could there be for a five-way?* she reasoned. Besides, the thought of traffic lights certainly would take away from the charm of the area. She drove on, picking up the directions again.

"What?"

Stay on this road following signs for Chilmark; but when you reach the first bend where there are two signs, both having directions for Chilmark, take the right. This will allow you to stay on State Road. She checked the directions again.

"Phyllis," she complained to her absent friend, "I should have had Brad write the directions. I can't understand these."

Alex continued to drive, certain she was completely lost, when she rounded a bend and saw the signs for the town of Chilmark confirming her progress. *This island's not as small as the encyclopedia made it seem!* Thirty minutes had gone by since she left the ferry.

Phyllis's directions said there would be a huge red buoy marking their street. She slowed. Her tires bit into the dirt road and grumbled along, but her Ford Bronco made relatively smooth work of it, she noted with gratitude. Charmed by the grassy mound growing in the center between the well-worn tire treads, she drove deeper into the woods.

An unfamiliar place, the growing darkness, and the week-long travel from Kansas left her exhausted. She needed a good night's rest, but not until she took a long, hot shower.

Finally, pulling up to a saltbox structure, she turned off the engine. Her body vibrated. She got out, stretched her back, hoisted her overnight bag onto her shoulder, and headed up the deck stairs. Brad and Phyllis had talked so often about the pleasure of sitting under the stars on their deck and hearing the surf. Alex now found herself straining to listen for distant breakers. Was the ocean really out there in the darkness?

The gentle rhythm of the waves whispered through the brush, filling her with anticipation for what the morning light would unmask. The smell of salt in the breeze soothed her travel-weary bones. Yes, she was here. She was finally here, to track down the seafaring Captain Luce, the grandfather of Alex's distant grandmother, Elizabeth Luce O'Connor, who'd left the island in 1858 to join the man of her dreams. They had gone west to Kansas to find their fortune with an offer of free land.

In the moonlight, Alex counted the silver-gray shingles, two down from the door knob and over three. Pulling the shingle, the silver key plopped into her hand. As she entered the house, Alex tossed the key on the table. Moving into the still darkened hallway, she groped for the wall switch. With the flick of the switch, she quickly found the electrical panel and the breakers for the hot water heater and stove.

In the living room, her hand glided over a tea wagon, the wood well worn from the years. On the top of the wagon lay a white crocheted doily with a complete fine china tea set. The work on the floral pattern, so delicate and intricate, of pink and white apple blossoms with green leaves, was set off with gold leaf on the handle. The cup was extremely thin, almost translucent.

Gently she grasped it, turning it over in her hand. Her eyes widened as she read, *Havilland Limoges, made in England/France.* From what Alex knew of classic antiquities, she estimated this was made around the 1850s, about the same time her ancestor Elizabeth Luce O'Connor had left the island.

After a brief tour of the Trainer home, she unpacked her overnight bag. She pulled out a long flannel nightgown and went into the bathroom, praying the water was heated. It was and she showered, but she quickly exhausted all the hot water.

Grumbling, she made her way to the kitchen, fixed a cup of tea, and opened the sliding glass door facing the surf. The cool ocean breeze penetrated her robe. She grabbed a woolen blanket folded over a chair in the living room. Snuggling deep into a chaise lounge, her fingers curled around the warmth of the mug, and she sipped her tea.

The stars peppered the sky with shimmering brilliance, and the ocean lured her into tranquillity. She rested her head back, closed her eyes, and drifted between awareness and sleep. Words from her grandfather's journal came quickly to mind. *The sea sings the sweetest lullaby.*

"Aye, Grandpa Luce, I see what you mean." Alex grinned and tried to picture the old sea captain in all his glory. There were no photographs of him, no paintings she had ever seen. And yet she pictured him clearly, skin well-leathered from the sun and sea, a barrel-chested man wearing a deep blue wool coat with large black buttons going down the front, wind-blown brown hair, and a reddish-brown beard.

The morning broke bright and crisp. Alex slithered back under the bed covers. Wrapping the warm blanket and sheet up to her chin, she nuzzled the pillow and tried to stay asleep. The trip from Kansas had taken a week, after all; she deserved a day of rest.

But the nagging sunlight drew her from her cocoon. Once dressed, she made herself a cup of tea and strolled out to the deck. The ocean lay before her in all its glory, the blues and sea-greens meshing with the play of light reflecting off the waves. Alex followed the path from the deck to the shore and discovered the land fell away abruptly. She was on a cliff. A steep, narrow stairway led down to the beach. The wood, well weathered from salt, was gray with sparkles of silver.

The sun was so bright, the air deliciously warm, that Alex decided to test the September water. "Man, that's cold!" She jumped back to avoid the roll of the next wave. She touched the water with her hand, bringing her fingers up to her lips. A slow smile formed. It was salty, just like the air.

She walked the shore for awhile, noticing various shells, stones, seaweed, and sponges. *I'll have to purchase a book that will tell me what all this stuff is,* she thought.

Aimlessly, she headed down the shore, not caring about the time. For once, she had no schedules or appointments to keep. She was free, free to do as she wanted. No longer a med-school student pushing herself or an intern doing her time. No longer Dr. Alex always on call, always needed by others but never needed intimately. Never needed as a person.

This is going to be an incredible year. Just what the doctor ordered to put my life back on track. . .to accept God's leading about being a single woman. . .to not be jealous or resentful toward my patients who have children—wanted or unwanted ones. Here, Lord, I'll learn to relax.

She headed toward home and came upon the boathouse the Trainers had mentioned. Their caretaker was building a boat, she had been told, and now she saw its wooden ribs arched toward the sky like the skeleton of a beached whale. Alex calculated it to be twenty-four feet long and maybe eight feet across at its widest point. The bottom hull was already boarded, plus a couple of rows up the sides. *What a lot of work!* She pondered the skeleton boat, curious about the man who would want to make such a thing. Surely it would be a whole lot easier just to buy one. She shrugged her shoulders and continued back to the house.

※

Over the next couple of days, Alex found the local grocery store, post office, and gas station, the basic necessities of life. A map she had purchased now lay sprawled out across the dining room table. Soft rays from the late afternoon sun slanted through the window onto the map as she plotted her course to Edgartown, where the Vineyard Museum and the old historical society were located. Tomorrow she would go down-island and begin tracking her roots.

After supper, Alex decided on a long bubble bath, something she rarely treated herself to. She poured the scented oils and the thick lather piled high up over the edges of the tub. Slowly, she stepped in. "Hmm," she moaned, "heaven on earth." She slid down under the bubbles, their tiny popping noise bringing a smile to her face. The bubbles, so rich and thick, heaped inches high above her shoulders. She fastened her hair up on her head and lay back, closed her eyes, and relaxed.

The water quickly went cool, however. Alex stomped out of the tub, dried herself off, and calmed her frustrated nerves. What was it with the hot water in this house?

In her room lay an assortment of frivolous purchases she had made that day—a mud mask to rid oneself of worry lines, cleaners, clarifiers, and an assortment of things she wasn't even sure how to apply. She read the instructions and applied the mask heavily on her face. Wrapped in her robe, she lay on the bed, applied cucumber slices to her eyes, and relaxed.

※

Jared worked his jeep over the rough mounds of his driveway, mumbling to himself about his need to repair them. Having been off the Vineyard for the past week, visiting family and purchasing supplies for the catboat he was constructing, he was glad to be back home. Next to him on the seat sat his notebook containing the figures for the craft, which he'd rechecked at the Cotuit historical society. While he loved crafting something with his hands, he liked getting it right the first time.

As he passed through the last thicket of trees, a light to his right caught his attention. "What on earth?" He scanned the dark hillside. Sure enough, someone had a light on in the Trainers' home. He took the right fork just before his cottage and ground his way up the cliff toward the Trainers' house. The house seemed still and undisturbed except for the lights on in the kitchen and master bath.

Concerned the house had been looted in his absence, he crept silently up the deck stairs. Cupping his eyes with his hands, he peered through the sliding glass doors. . .everything looked to be in order. He walked around the side to the kitchen door. Locked. Instinctively he went to the shingle where the key was kept.

"What's going on here?" he mumbled to himself.

The key was missing. Whoever had broken in found the key, he figured. His fingers slid down the door jam, checking, just to be sure, for signs of a forced entry. Flustered and confused, he reached into his pocket and pulled out his own set of keys. Fumbling in the moonlight, he at last produced the one he sought.

The smell of a spaghetti sauce greeted his nostrils. Muscles tense, he scanned the shadows in the living room, grabbed a poker from the fireplace, and stealthily worked his way through the house, determined to find the intruders and boot them out. Someone was setting up house; his suspicions were confirmed by a large T-shirt and a pair of jeans draped on the stuffed settee in the living room. The master bedroom door was slightly ajar. He moved past it, down the hall, checking each of the other bedrooms. Nothing had been disrupted. Walking back to the living room, he noticed the main bathroom door was shut. Beneath it, the glow of a warm light radiated softly.

Jared grinned. *Caught ya*, he thought.

Drawing his body up to the door and raising the poker, he listened. Not a single sound. Tired of the game, he turned the knob and flung the door wide open.

Nothing!

Confused, he scratched his head. Someone was in the house or had been recently. The fresh scent of roses coming from the bathroom and the small mounds of bubbles in the tub made it obvious.

He stood back in the hall, and again he noticed the bedroom door. Cautiously, he crept forward. The door flew open with a thud, a woman shrieked.

Was it a woman? *What on earth is on her face?*

"Who are you and what are you doing in here?" he demanded of the green-faced apparition.

Again the woman screamed, but this time she threw a pillow at him as she jumped up from the bed. Flustered, he yanked the door shut.

Chapter 2

Jared paced the living room, glancing down the hall every few moments. He couldn't believe someone had taken up residence in a vacant house. A woman, no less!

What am I going to do? She must be a homeless person or something. But I can't have her living here in the Trainers' house. He tried to roll the tension out of his shoulders.

The sight of her face plastered in green with cucumber slices placed on her eyes resurfaced in his imagination. He suppressed a chuckle.

❧

Still in shock from the hostile invasion, Alex numbly worked her way to the master bath and washed off the facial. The image of the man with the raised fist and a stick. . .no, it had been something metal. . .*what was it? Who on earth was he?* she wondered.

Alex dried off her face with a thick towel. Too angry to be frightened, she stuffed the towel back on the rack and stormed out of the bathroom.

"What *is* your problem?" She hadn't gotten a good look at him before, but now her anger disappeared, and fear crawled up her spine. The man was huge, his shoulders broad and his pectorals like molded steel. Girding herself against intimidation, she stood rigid, eyeing a hasty retreat if necessary.

"Me! Who do you think you are? This isn't your home, Lady. I suggest you pack up your bags and move outta here before I call the cops."

"This *is* my home, at least for the next year. So, who do you think *you* are barging into it?"

"For your information, I'm the caretaker of this place. I know who belongs here, and you don't. Now pack your bags and get out," he stormed, pointing toward the door.

Aware now of who he was, her fear subsided. "For *your* information, Mr. Caretaker," she quipped, "my name is Alexandria Tucker, and I have the permission of Brad and Phyllis Trainer to be in their home for the next year." She planted defiant hands firmly on her hips, watching the bluster fade from his face.

Stunned, the guy is actually stunned, she realized with satisfaction. His facial muscles relaxed from anger and changed into. . .what? Worry? "That's right," she pushed on, "the owners, Brad and Phyllis Trainer. Call them. But get out. I resent the fact that you not only walked right into my home, but marched through it like you owned the place. And what on earth were you thinking, flinging the door open like that? Don't you have a shred of decency in you? Are you some kind of Neanderthal? Do you just do whatever you feel like, not giving any thought or respect to others?"

Her adrenaline was pumping now. She had the upper hand and she knew it. Pleased with her newfound ability to go toe-to-toe with such an Atlas, she fought back a grin. But the thundering pulse in her ears signaled she needed to calm down and gain control.

Heat radiated high in Jared's cheeks. Apparently, this woman knew the owners. On the other hand, a discreet search of the town records could have produced the name of the people who owned the property. He narrowed his gaze on her. Maybe she was simply some very crafty thief. "Look, Lady, I don't know who you are or what you're doing here, but I know one thing and one thing for certain: If, and I do mean if, the Trainers were allowing you to stay in their home, they would have called me. Which they didn't do. Which means you are a trespasser. Which means you don't belong here. Now, for the last time, pack your bags and get out."

"What do you mean they didn't call you? I was there when Phyllis placed the call. She left the message on your machine."

Jared took a step backward. He had been away for a week. Maybe there was a message. Maybe this woman was telling the truth. "I need some identification. Do you have a driver's license?"

Alexandria marched into the master bedroom and came out almost immediately. "Here." She jammed her license in his face.

Jared took it from her and held it a foot from his eyes. *Alexandria Tucker, MD.* Renewed heat flushed his cheeks. Brad was a hospital administrator in Kansas. Alexandria's license was from Kansas. Jared's heart sank. "Fine, I'll call them. I guess you can stay until I hear from them."

"Well that's awfully magnanimous of you."

Jared headed for the kitchen door. His shoulders slumped. *Why didn't I check my messages first? Why didn't I knock before entering the house? Why am I always a bull in a china shop?* Frustrated with himself, he held his tongue and left her steaming in the living room.

He worked his way around the back of the house to the driveway. *I should have checked this before storming into the house.* A black Bronco sat in the dark shadows of the trees. Jared squatted behind the car and strained to read the words *Land of Oz* in blue lettering against a panel of white. He let out a deep sigh, frustrated with himself, and shuffled his way through the new-fallen leaves to his truck.

Once home, he grabbed his phone and dialed the Trainers'.

Phyllis answered immediately. "Hi, Jared, how's the Vineyard?"

"Fine. I was wondering about. . ." Not wanting to play the part of a fool, he decided to ask about the audacious doctor. "I was wondering about Dr. Tucker."

"She should be there by now." Concern rose in Phyllis's voice. "She is there, isn't she?"

"Yes, I was wondering if she was planning on staying through the winter?" He knew the answer to his question before he asked. He shifted uncomfortably on his feet.

"Definitely. Is there a problem with the house?"

"Nope, the hot water heater element should be in soon, and the other items we spoke about I'll take care of shortly." His eyes scanned the caulk and wood preservative he had purchased before going off the island, piled near the door. Caulking the storm windows would take half a day, applying preservative to the deck, the other half. He wondered how he was going to keep Dr. Tucker off the surface until it was dry.

"Fine, do what you need to do. And if Alex needs anything taken care of, you've got my go ahead."

"I understand."

As if sensing his hesitation, she asked, "Jared, is there a problem with Alex and you?"

He paused. "Well, if you must know, I didn't get the message she was coming. I was off the island for a week. Anyway, I saw a light on in the place, and I just sort of marched in to check if you'd been robbed."

"I see. So basically you barged in on Alex?" Hearing a slight chuckle in Phyllis's voice, Jared's face flushed again.

"Uh-huh," he admitted. "I'm really sorry about that. I didn't mean to cause a problem." Jared raked a hand through his hair.

"I'm sure she'll get over it. She's a good friend, Jared. Her family actually hails from the Vineyard. I think you'll like her." Phyllis wasn't holding back her laughter now as she said good-bye.

Jared hung up the phone. *Man, I'm such an idiot! But I didn't get the message*, he justified himself.

❦

Alex answered the phone on the first ring. Expecting it to be Jared with an apology, she was surprised to hear Phyllis on the other end. "So, you had a surprise visitor tonight."

"What kind of a man is that?" Alex sat down on the bed.

"An embarrassed one, I'd say. So tell me what happened. It *is* his job to care for our property, you know. I'm sure he thought it was being robbed or someone had set up housekeeping."

"I suppose. But, Phyllis," Alex lamented, "I was lying on the bed with my face plastered with green goo and cucumbers!" She set some pillows up against the headboard and made herself more comfortable.

"Green goo! A facial mask?" Phyllis stifled a giggle.

"It's not funny." Alex fought back a grin.

Phyllis's laughter filled Alex's ear. "He's gorgeous, isn't he?"

"Stop it, Phyllis." Alex remembered the hulk of a man who had stood before her in the living room. "I can't believe how big he is," she admitted. "Is he on steroids or something?"

"Nope, it's all him. He works hard. I've seldom seen him when he wasn't working. Well, that's not quite true. There was a time, once. . ." Phyllis's words drifted off.

"What do you mean, 'There was a time once?' "

"Nothing. Look, he's a great guy, Alex. Give the man some slack."

"Fine, but he's not going to be allowed to just walk in the place whenever he feels like."

"Alex," Phyllis said, still giggling, "the place is yours. You set up the ground rules. He will need to get in there from time to time to take care of some things for us, but you'll work that out with him."

"Just as long as he understands that where I come from, people are civilized. We knock on a door before we enter."

When they had said their good-byes, Alex replaced the phone on the night-stand. She thought back on the conversation. Phyllis's comments on how handsome Jared was brought his image to her mind. He was handsome. His blond hair with dark highlights and his dark blue eyes. . .the massive chest, thick arms, and hands. . . Most of the men she knew were slightly built. Seldom had she run across someone who obviously worked out. Pediatrics wasn't the place for well-honed bodies, and few fathers brought in their sick children. Most of the doctors she worked with could hardly be called well developed. Several were trim, but in a lean sort of way.

Alex grinned as she realized Jared's build was much the same as Arnold Schwartzenegger's in the movies where he played an ordinary guy. He was quite a contrast to herself and her tall, thin frame. Next to him she would appear small and fragile, whereas at the hospital she held her own with the men. Jared certainly had a way of making his presence known.

Picturing him again as he had stood in the doorway of the bedroom and his accusatory tone only bolstered her resolve to keep her distance from this guy. Phyllis might find him an excellent caretaker, but he wouldn't be taking care of her, she resolved. Despite how handsome he was, she wouldn't cross that barrier. Nope, Jared was definitely a man to stay away from.

Besides, this was the year she had set aside for growing closer to God and finding His plan for her life. As much as she loved her career, she still ached to have her own family. But time was running out. Her biological clock was ticking, and there were no apparent men standing in line wanting to sweep her off her feet. No, God help her, she needed to get used to the idea she would be single the rest of her life. Maybe someday there might be a man in her life, but certainly no children. "Oh, Father, help me be content with Your plan for my life. Help me trust in You, not in a man, for my happiness. Help heal the ache in my heart for children, family, and my own home. Help me, Lord; I don't know that I can do this alone."

With the fleeting prayer still on her lips, Alex settled under the covers and allowed sleep to help ease the aching in her heart.

৵৻

The next morning Jared paced back and forth in his small kitchen. He had to apologize to Dr. Tucker, but how? Arguing with himself, he considered the straightforward approach. The idea of giving her wildflowers as a token of his sincerity was quickly discounted. *No, then she might think I'm interested in her. It's bad enough the woman thinks I'm some sort of Peeping Tom.* He envisioned her coming at him with fire in her eyes. She was beautiful—after she removed the gunk. "Oh, Lord, please take that image away from my memory."

Alexandria Tucker was more than a feisty woman, he admitted to himself. Many women had tried over the years to get his attention, but no one had, not since Hannah. "No, I'm just getting my life back on track with You, Lord. I don't need a woman to complicate things. Not now Lord, not now."

He jammed his eyes shut, forcing Dr. Tucker's image out of his thoughts. Raking his hands through his hair, there was nothing left to do but simply go up to the house and apologize. He had made a mistake. That's what it was, a simple mistake. *How was I supposed to know she was coming?* Which made him wonder when the Trainers had decided to let Dr. Tucker stay in their home—and why.

With large ground-gaining strides, he worked his way up over the rise. The distance between his place and the Trainers' was minimal, good for the lungs. A brisk pace set, he trudged up through the beach grass. The view from this area was breathtaking, but Jared refused to take the time to admire God's handiwork. He had a job to do and it was time to get it over with, no matter how uncomfortable it was.

Taking the back steps two at a time up to the kitchen, he reached for the door and knocked. Seeing her fully clothed and in the kitchen, he marched straight in.

Chapter 3

D r. Tucker. . ."

Alex cut him off. "Don't you have any social graces at all?"

"I came to apologize." A sarcastic retort would have been easier.

"Fine, but who do you think you are? You just walked right into my house, again."

"I knocked."

"While you were already opening the door. You might have waited for a response. Did you grow up in a barn?"

"Whoa, Doc, hold it. Number one, I noticed you were in the kitchen. Number two, what's your problem?"

Alex was about to protest, but he wasn't going to let her have the last word today.

"There's no need for sarcasm. Henceforth, I will gladly await your precious response before entering your home. However, I do have to work on this place."

"No sarcasm, huh? You can do your precious work anytime I'm not around. I don't take kindly to people just barging in on me. You've done it twice now. I'll not stand for it another time."

"Fine, it won't happen again." He took a step back, reaching for the door.

"Fine."

Jared stormed out of the house. *Boy, that went smooth, Madeiras. Maybe you should try again. Yeah right, and get my head chopped off by the wicked witch of Kansas. No, thank you very much!* He bristled all the way to the boathouse.

He needed to work. He needed to expend some energy. Verbal boxing matches with the pretty doctor was not his idea of a good time. No, this was time to work hard, work off his frustration, and most important, work off his anger.

He hadn't been this mad at anyone since releasing his anger toward God about the death of Hannah, the one woman he had loved. The one God took away days before their wedding. He was young then, only twenty-two, but no one since had ever come close to her. She was his soul mate, God's choice for him—and yet before they became husband and wife, God took her away.

His fist slammed the stern of the boat. *No, God, I don't want to remember that. I don't want to remember the pain. It's over; let it die!* Emotional shutdown had been his answer. He refused to allow it to hurt any longer. Hannah was dead. There was no future for them. He ground his teeth and went to work firing up the steam baths; he needed to soak the wood before he could begin.

⟡

Alex threw the frying pan into the sink. *Just who does that man think he is!* She huffed out loud, willing herself to calm down. *Why does he rile me so?*

Thoroughly exasperated with her own behavior, her confidence in herself as the calm, level-headed sort was shaken. *For Pete's sake, I've dealt with aggravating people every day at the hospital...egotistical colleagues, or worse yet, money-grabbing colleagues, who don't care one hoot about their patients. So why can't I handle some country bumpkin?* Her reputation in the medical field stood for control and discipline, someone not easily irritated. This reaction to Jared was not normal. Not for her, anyway. She needed to take a more professional approach.

"Later, I'll think about this later," she muttered at the ceiling. "Today, I'm going to begin my search for Grandpa Luce."

Heading into the dining room, she pulled out her map of the Vineyard and reviewed her course to the historical society, deciding to pick up South Road at Bettlebung Corners to the Edgartown–West Tisbury Road. They were the island's back roads, but they still seemed the most direct route. Being the tourist area it was, streets were well marked. A bunch of purple grapes in the upper center of the state road signs made them easy to recognize.

Alex grabbed her keys, map, and purse and headed into her family's past. "Oh Lord God, make this a better day than it's started out so far," she prayed as she bounced out the dirt path now familiar as the Trainers' driveway.

As she drove past the Chilmark Library and Community Center, she turned onto roads she hadn't yet traveled. She passed a small pond on her left, decoratively laced with swans and ducks. Her tires squealed as she rounded a big bend in the road that curved to the left at almost a complete right angle. Stone walls lined both sides of South Road. On her right, past the open fields, were ponds, then sand dunes and beach grass looking out over the ocean. The view was breathtaking.

A horn blared, bringing her attention back to the road. "Alex, old girl, you'd better keep your eyes on the road. The surf will be there another day." She calculated the next time she could come back around here and take in the view. "Relax, you've got a year. You've only been here a handful of days."

Easing back into her bucket seat, she continued her trip. Noting the sign for the fairgrounds in West Tisbury, she decided to make that another place she would have to stop. Her eye caught a strange sight: An artist had turned his yard into an outdoor exhibit. Alex smiled. Life on the Vineyard was not going to be boring. There were plenty of new things to explore and find.

Alex pulled onto the grass outside the Vineyard Museum and tucked her map between the seats. Grabbing her purse and other items, she marched through the white-gated fence. In front of her was a truncated lighthouse. After reading the information on the plaque, stating that it was in fact the actual top to the old Gay Head lighthouse, she went inside and looked at the prisms. *Amazing,* she thought. Simple lantern lights, fueled with whale's oil, refracted through the prisms to warn the ships of old. She pictured her Captain Luce depending on them to warn him of the rocks and shoals. Alex marveled at the realization that light is still measured in terms of candle power, one lumen equaling one candle.

As she made her way to the back of the property, she came upon an open structure with various sleighs, boats, and wagons. Three lone gravestones stood near the building. Wondering who was buried at the historical society, she meandered over to read the markers. "Chicken tombstones?" she chuckled. "Someone buried chickens? Oh no! It was a Luce, a Nancy Luce. I wonder if we're related? She called them her 'beloved chickens.' Unbelievable!" She snickered and made her way to the main building. The library and gift shop were located inside.

The historical librarian, Beatrice Arno, was quite helpful, pulling out logs and journals that Captain Thomas Luce had written. Alex had a transposed copy that one of her great aunts had passed on to family members years ago, which eventually got passed down to her. That was probably the key item that spurred her on to further her knowledge about the sea and Captain Luce. Now she could see the originals.

She spent hours poring over the information. A map of Holmes Hole, 1858, now known as Vineyard Haven, a village of Tisbury, was shown to her. She found her grandfather's home on Main Street, north of Church Street and on the harbor side of the road.

"Excuse me, can you tell me how I can locate this house?" She pointed to the spot on the old map.

The older woman with snow-white hair placed her glasses high on the bridge of her nose and leaned over the map. "Oh, I'm sorry, Miss, but that house was burned down in the Great Fire of 1883. There's another home on that spot, I believe. Let me check who it belongs to."

"No, that's okay." It wouldn't be the house her adventurous ancestor had been raised in. She had left the Vineyard in 1858 with her new husband bound for Kansas. Alex's excitement about possibly seeing her ancestor's home sank into quiet disappointment.

"I'll be glad to help you with some more research on Captain Luce and that time period if you wish."

"Definitely, I'll be back. Tell me, did everyone go to sea back then?"

The woman nodded. "There's an oral history by Stan Lair, and he talks about every male in Vineyard Haven going to sea at one time or another."

"Makes sense." Alex thumbed the old leather diary lying beside her. "Back then the sea was the primary income of the island."

The woman nodded again. "There were some farmers, of course, some factory work, but mostly the ocean was their provider."

"Whaling?"

"Primarily yes, but the whaling industry was ending about that time. Oil had been discovered and westward expansion was being encouraged."

"I know. I'm from Kansas. My ancestor left the island with her new husband for the promise of land and wealth."

Beatrice gave her a knowing smile and told her a little about some of the historical sites she could find in Edgartown; the old Whaling church, the Sculpin Museum, the row of captains' houses. Alex decided a walking tour of Edgartown in the bright afternoon would be in order. Leaving her car parked outside the museum, she headed to Main Street and up a little on her left to the old Whaling church. There was no way to mistake it. The huge white columns out front stood a couple stories high.

⁂

A sheen of sweat covered Jared's body, not only from his labor, but also from running the steam baths. Soaking the wood softened it for curving against the ribs of the hull. Steaming sped up the process. The last boat he made had been modern, using molded fiberglass. Actually, it had been a replica of an ancient vessel rumored to have crossed the Atlantic. But this new boat was going to be something quite different, a catboat, used on the cape for fishing. The low draft was built exclusively for use on the shoals of the cape and islands. The men could drag scallop dredges, rake for quahogs, or go into deep water to fish for cod. They even pulled up lobster pots with them. In other words, it was a great multipurpose boat for the area.

Finding the wood from area trees had been his hardest assignment. The cape and the islands no longer had the amount of trees needed to support a wood mill. Getting wood grown the closest to the area the boat would be used in was best for protection from the various sea worms and other wood-eating critters.

Jared ran his rough, callused hand over the area he had been sanding. Originally, his plan had been to build the boat in the same way they had been made in the mid-1800s. However, the many hours of hand sanding versus power sanding was an allowance he decided to fudge on. The ridge between the seams felt smooth. Content with its appearance, he placed the sander down beside him on one of the supports holding the frame of the boat in place.

He unrolled the blueprint of the catboat across his workbench and checked and rechecked his work, since details—all the details—were important. The copy of his plans had come from the Cotuit historical society. The Cape Cod town had been one of the largest builders of catboats during the mid to late 1800s.

Jared had decided on a twenty-four-foot vessel. Large enough for a cabin so he could make an occasional sail out to Nantucket or Block Island. He placed a small piece of oak on the upper right-hand corner of the pages, while his left arm held down the opposite side.

He smiled; she was coming along well. Jared lifted his left arm and the plans curled over the block of oak. "Name. . .what shall I name you?" he pondered, scanning the boat from bow to stern. The name *Alexandria* leaped up in his head. He snickered. "I don't think so. Alex isn't a controllable woman. You will be controlled by me—the captain!"

Jared pulled a mug of coffee toward him. "The poor man that marries that woman." He wondered if Phyllis and Brad knew how bossy and hard that woman could be. *Doesn't matter anyway, she's their friend and she's going to be here for the better part of a year, old boy, so get used to it.* Raising the mug the rest of the way, he took a sip. It was cold and bitter; one sip was enough. He placed the mug back on the workbench.

The sound of an approaching car drove him out of the boathouse and around to the back of the building. "Jared, old boy, when did ya get back?" called a man's voice.

"Last night." Jared smiled. John Poole was an old, dear friend. A friend to his parents, a man that stood by him when Hannah and his parents died. John had been on the water since before he could walk and had more salt water running in his veins than Jared did. He'd worked on his family's fishing boat since he was old enough to spit. A small gold earring looped through his right earlobe. John had it long before it was a fashion statement. In fact, the gold earring was a seaman's badge of honor.

"What brings you out here?" Jared asked.

"Wondering what's going on with your fancy new neighbor."

"What do you mean?" Jared questioned with a smile. Apparently nothing escaped the island gossip lines.

"Pretty thing. A doctor, I've heard tell, from Kansas."

"That's about all I know. She's a friend of the Trainers and they gave her the run of the place."

"Heard her say she was researching her family roots—claims to be a descendant of Captain Thomas Luce."

"You know more than I, John."

"You mean a pretty thing like that walks by you and you haven't noticed her?"

"I noticed, but I'm not interested."

"Well, I'll be squid for dinner. If I was forty years younger, I'd ask her out myself."

"She's all yours, John. Let me warn ya, she's got a temper."

"Oh does she now?" John's white bushy eyebrows rose high on his forehead.

Jared shifted his weight uncomfortably. "You want to help me with the catboat?"

"Of course. Don't think I left Martha's good cooking just to check into your love life, do ya?"

Jared wanted to protest that he didn't have a love life, but he knew John would get the best of him and let it drop. "Come on, I'll show you what I found." Jared placed his arm around John's shoulder.

The man had become the grandfather he'd never known. John understood him like no other. Smiling, he led him to the bench and showed him the antique brass compass, winches, and other assorted treasures.

❧

Inside the church, Alex noticed the old wooden floors, the floorboards wide and thick. The pulpit was off to the side on a small raised platform. The pews were huge; she couldn't recall ever seeing any with that wide of a seating area or any as long. In her mind she pictured a preacher standing up front preaching about the dangers of the sea and how a man ought to be right with God before he left the harbor.

The ninety-two-foot clock tower was said to be visible far out to sea, according to a brochure she acquired. All in all it was an impressive building, showing the money the whaling industry had brought to this area. The church was built in 1843, fifteen years before her grandma Elizabeth left the island. Alex wondered if she had ever attended this church. It was possible, but having learned that her relatives primarily lived in another town, she thought it was doubtful.

Alex left the church and headed down Main Street toward the harbor, musing how communities reflected their people by size of houses and the intricacies built into the houses or structures. She marveled that she was walking on brick sidewalks, very old and very worn red bricks.

At the base of Main Street was a parking lot, and the Edgartown Yacht Club sat on a wooden pier. Turning left onto Dock Street, she worked her way to the Chappy Ferry, a small three-vehicle flat barge that crossed back and forth across the harbor. "Chappy," she quickly learned, was the local nickname for the small island of Chappaquidick on the other side of the Edgartown harbor.

The swirl of the tide rushing past made the water appear dangerous. The only other time she had seen water moving that fast was at a river that often sported white-water rafting. Reading the name *On Time* on the ferry, she sat on a bench watching it and getting a feel for the harbor. This was one of the main whaling harbors of the past. Chappaquiddick, on the other side, helped to enclose the harbor. Behind her sat the Old Sculpin Gallery with a whaling boat on the grassy lawn.

She tried to visualize how the scene must have looked back in the 1800s. The gallery, she read, made whaling boats right there. In fact, two of them were now in the Smithsonian. The fine hairs on Alex's neck stood on end as she realized just how much history was in this area.

After spending some time in the gallery, she made her way up Daggett Street, up the hill to North Water Street, where the row of captains' houses still stood. She stared at the widows' walks, picturing wives looking out to sea, waiting for their husbands' return. She looked for doorways that would lead onto the widows' walks and failed to see one. Noting the area, she decided to find a captain's house she could tour. She thought back to her Captain Thomas Luce and wondered if his wife had a widow's walk too, if she had fretted for the return of her husband. Alex shook her head, recalling that an average whaling trip lasted three to four years in the 1800s.

At one point on North Water Street there was a break with no house on the opposite side of the street, closest to the harbor. The view was breathtaking. . .the green of the sea grass, with small patches of beach sand, the water, a white lighthouse glistening in the sun. The top of the light was painted black.

She looked at her watch, then returned to Main Street, following North Water Street. A small group of tourists stood outside a store window. Alex's curiosity was piqued. She stopped and watched. The place was called Murdock's Fudge, and the confectioner was making the largest batch of fudge she'd ever seen. In front of him was a long, narrow table with a marble top. The fudge was folded over and over again upon itself.

The temptation was too great. Alex stepped into the shop. In the glass case were many varieties of fudge. She picked chocolate with walnuts, then noticed a pink fudge with red berries inside. The sign read cranberry fudge. The woman behind the counter gave her a small sample. Alex decided to add some cranberry fudge to her purchase. *Well, it wouldn't be right to pass up items unique to the area*, she justified.

Fudge in hand, she continued back to her car. The shops, the street, the area had too much to offer for one single afternoon. Finding the museum and her car were simple feats, but driving through the one-way streets to the Edgartown–West Tisbury Road challenged her internal compass. She soon made it, however, and headed back up the island to her home away from home.

At the house, she thumbed through the pages of an island history and folklore book she had recently purchased and looked up Edgartown. The area excited her. No wonder it was so popular with tourists. The setting was beautiful, the shops quaint, the people friendly, and everything was so packed with history. The Vineyard actually had some of the oldest towns in the United States.

Thomas Mayhew founded the town of Edgartown in 1642. In hopes of gaining favor with the king, he had named it after the three-year-old son of King Charles I. However, unbeknownst to Mayhew, the boy had died the month before.

Closing the book, Alex made herself some dinner.

✾

Jared's stomach knotted when he heard Alexandria pull into the Trainers' drive. Torn, he debated with himself. Should he attempt another apology?

"Why bother?" he muttered.

On the other hand, if she had found favor with the locals, maybe he'd just caught her on a bad day. He shook his head. *No, she can just stay right there. I'm keeping to myself.* Ambling back to the blueprints, he scanned over them once again. His concentration, however, was almost nil.

A late afternoon delivery brought the needed part to fix the hot water heater, and again he found himself in debate. He really should repair the heater for her.

Maybe a cold shower or two will help to calm that woman down, he thought. *And then she'd have to come to me about the repairs.* That thought stirred up a sense of false pride. He snickered at himself and set the part down to make his dinner. It could wait until morning. *Besides, she told me not to come except when she was not around,* he justified as he nuked another frozen dinner in his microwave. A luke-warm shower would be fine for her. It wasn't like she would catch a cold from it.

Irritated that someone was living so close to him, he shuffled his way through his cottage. He got along with the Trainers, but they had their own lives, their own set of friends. Jared rarely ever saw them. This woman, however, was a bother. Not only did she have a low opinion of him, not that it bothered him, but she also was disturbing his thoughts.

The entire day. . . Where she was—what she was doing. No! He had to stop this! He didn't like it. Not one bit.

"How can one woman be so. . .fascinating?"

Bewildered, he forced himself to stop thinking about her. "Lord, please help me here. My mind is exhausting me."

Chapter 4

The day's sweat, dirt, and salt on her body made Alex yearn for a long, hot shower. She hoped the hot water heater would provide the needed warmth. The few baths and showers so far had been lukewarm. Standing in the bathroom, she reached into the stream of water and set the temperature. It seemed warmer, she thought as she stepped into the shower. She relaxed under the pulsing stream. Lathering up her hair, she leaned back to rinse.

The water started getting colder. Irritation flared its ugly head. She snapped off the cold water faucet. Tepid was the best she could call the water temperature.

Gritting her teeth, Alex rinsed her hair. Quickly, she scrubbed her body from the top of her head to the bottom of her feet. Showers this short belonged to her college days, when she'd always been in a hurry to get to class, having overslept due to a late night of studies.

She turned off the now cold water, teeth chattering, and dried herself off. "I need to call a plumber. I can't live like this," she muttered on her way to the bedroom.

Once dressed, she placed a call back home to Brad and Phyllis. Brad informed her that Jared was well aware of the problem and had to order the part needed for the repairs. The idea of approaching that man for anything was not very appealing, however. Granted, he was a sweet diversion to her eyes, but the gall of the man was something she just couldn't tolerate. Besides, it was late. There was no need to contact him this evening. No, she'd wait until morning.

She browsed through the various books Brad and Phyllis had in their library. One, in particular, caught her attention. *Lost at Sea*, by J. Madeiras. The back cover revealed that the author had been attempting to cross the Atlantic when his ship, caught in a bad storm, capsized and left him stranded in the elements for eight days.

A good book would be a perfect distraction. The image of the handsome but annoying caretaker weighed too heavily on her mind. Alex seized the book and brought it eagerly into the living room. She lounged across the couch, tossing a lap blanket over her legs.

Opening to the dedication, she read, *To those I've lost. They will never be replaced, nor will my love for them be diminished.* Alex's heart tightened. She wondered who had died and if they had perished on this tragic journey out to sea. She turned the page and began to read.

The man was educated—she realized that right off by the words he chose. *And he has a sense of humor.* She smiled, nuzzling deeper into the soft folds of the couch. This was going to be a good read.

※

Jared woke with the sun, far from rested. Dr. Alexandria Tucker had plagued him all night. He really had gotten off on the wrong foot with the woman and needed to apologize. If not that, he needed at least to calm the storm brewing between them. She didn't need to come begging for his help. He was being childish about the hot water heater. Chastising himself for his behavior, he decided to make peace with his neighbor.

He grabbed the heating element and hiked up the hill to the Trainers' home. The smell of bacon filled the air, and his stomach grumbled. He knocked on the door and waited.

There she was, pretty as a three-masted schooner with her sails full and the waves rolling down her sides. Her mouth was tight, almost tense, he assessed. She wasn't looking forward to seeing him, and he knew why. "Dr. Tucker, I came by to fix the hot water heater. May I come in?"

Alex opened the door to him.

"Thank you. It won't take me too long."

"Did Brad call you?"

"No, is there a problem?"

"No, I called him last night about the hot water heater. He told me that you were aware of the problem and I should speak with you."

So, she was avoiding him as much as he was avoiding her. "I'm afraid I need to drain the heater before I can replace the heating element."

"No problem, do what you need to do. I like my hot water."

Jared smiled, then quickly removed the smile. He was gloating. Obviously, she had had a miserable shower or bath, lukewarm at best. "I'm sorry. I could have come by last night, but I. . ."

"It's okay. I think we both needed a night to cool off."

He hesitated, then sucked in a deep breath. "Dr. Tucker, I'm sorry about walking in on you. I really was just concerned about the Trainers' belongings. They have many valuable antiques."

Her face softened. "I know. I overreacted. I'm sorry. Shall we begin again?"

"I'd like that."

"Me too. Did you have breakfast?" she asked.

He shook his head. "But I wanted to fix your hot water heater immediately." He eased his breath out slowly.

"I've got plenty of food. Would you care to join me?"

He shrugged. "Thanks, don't mind if I do. Let me start draining the tank and I'll be back."

Alex went to the kitchen and added some bacon to the frying pan.

Maybe we can be neighbors after all, Jared thought as he went outside to get the hose. Ten minutes later he was wiping his hands on a cloth, joining her in the kitchen.

"Smells great."

"Thanks, it's just bacon and eggs."

"There's nothing 'just' about bacon. It has to be one of my favorite meats."

Alex laughed, the first laugh he had heard from her. The lilt of her laughter flooded his senses. This was a mistake, he realized; it was better if she were his enemy.

He sat down wearily at the table, while he closed down his heart and his emotions. No one would ever be allowed to enter it again. He had lost too many people in his life. He couldn't deal with the pain of anymore loss. Resolute in his conviction, he fired off a quick prayer, murmuring his thanks to God for the meal, then he forked the eggs into his mouth.

Her head was bowed in prayer, he saw. *For pity's sake, she's a believer too! Lord, what kind of test are You putting me through?*

❧

Alex wolfed down her breakfast in fierce determination to leave the house as soon as possible. Jared's presence in the house awakened desires in her that long had been under control. As a doctor, she understood chemistry. This, however, didn't make sense. Never in all her days had she been attracted simply by the way a man looked.

Well, maybe when she was a teen in high school and a certain rock and roll star had caught her interest. How her mother ever tolerated her placing all those pictures on her bedroom wall she would never understand. When she had grown past that phase, her father had had to repaint the wall. All the tape marks, missing paint, and various holes from tacks and small nails had made it appear like a scatter bomb had gone off. But that was her only time for such foolishness, and after all, that was puberty; it was only natural.

This, however, was different, strange, and completely unnerving. No, Jared needed to work, and she needed to clear her head. She jumped up and placed her plate in the sink. She realized she had been a bad hostess, not offering a single word of conversation during breakfast. "Sorry to eat and run, Jared," she blurted. "I need to get some errands done."

His gaze pierced right through her. He knew she was uncomfortable, she sensed, but thankfully, he couldn't read the thoughts she had been having, thoughts about how his arms might feel wrapped around her. No, it was certainly better he didn't know that! She was too vulnerable. Hadn't she just left home to find herself, to make peace with God's plan for her to remain single the rest of her life? After all, time was running out, there was no way she would be having children, a husband, a happy life ever after. No, she was being called to be single.

True, she hadn't heard a definite word from God on the matter, but she would be silly not to realize His purpose when He had not seen fit to provide the man she had been praying for since she was thirteen. That was twenty-two years ago. Here she was thirty-five and acting thirteen. Goodness, she didn't need this now.

"Thanks for fixing the hot water heater," she murmured.

"Welcome, have a good day." His mutter was equally terse.

Escaping back into her bedroom, she grabbed her purse, keys, and a sweater. "Time to explore the island," she called to him as she stood by the door, tossing the keys around her finger into the palm of her hand.

She heard him in a back room, and she wasn't certain he had heard her. No, she wasn't going to go find him and tell him good-bye. She thrust herself out the door. Fresh air, the smell of the salt, calmed her nervous reactions. She paused and took a deep breath. She was being silly.

Silly or not, she did want to take in the sights. A trip to Gay Head and the clay cliffs was on her agenda for the day.

Jared repaired the hot water heater in record time. Alex's obvious uneasiness with him gave him a resolve that the next time he was to see her, he would go out of his way to be nice. There was no sense having the lady afraid of him.

Back at the boathouse, he fired up the steam baths again for the day. An hour later, he removed the steaming planks that would make up the sides of his boat. Setting each one in place, he hammered it to the ribs. They curved nicely against the frame.

The day was unseasonably warm, and the steam from the baths added to the heat. Removing his shirt, he continued to work. It was a long process, something that wouldn't be a problem if he'd simply gone out and bought a boat like most people.

His compulsion to build things with his hands had been with him ever since he could remember. His father was a similar man, and rumor had it, so was his grandfather. Having built his own boat before he had left the family, his grandfather had sailed for parts unknown after an argument with his wife.

Jared's father, Michael, was left with the impression that the man simply ran out on his family. Michael Madeiras quit school and went to work to support his mother, brothers, and sisters. He was the oldest, so it was his responsibility. He started working as a fisherman, but the pay wasn't very good. He went to work for a contractor, then finally went out on his own. By then the rest of the siblings were grown. He fell in love and married Jared's mother. They were a good match; she mirrored his stubborn streak with her own brand of tenacity. They worked through their differences and stayed united in their efforts to raise their children.

His father was a good man, a man Jared was proud of. In fact, the only thing his parents had ever done that really bothered him was when they had gotten themselves killed in a freak accident when a deer had leapt in front of their car.

Jared's throat tightened. They were gone. Hannah was gone. He accepted those facts. He just didn't know why God hadn't prevented it, why He had chosen to take away the people from his life he cared about most. It didn't make sense. Not when others he had grown up with still had their parents, when the same people were allowed to marry their sweethearts. It just didn't seem fair.

But spending those eight days at sea, Jared had learned a little bit about God's fairness. At the same time, he had found that he was a fighter and didn't want to die. He accepted that freak things, such as storms, unexpected deer, and aneurysms, happened in this life. He had made his peace with God. But he wasn't ready. . .no, he would never be ready to open his heart to another. The pain of the loss was too much to bear. He couldn't—he wouldn't—go through that again.

The image of Dr. Alexandria Tucker and the lilt of her laughter flooded over the darkness of his thoughts. She was beautiful, and what a captivating smile! But she was afraid of him. It didn't make sense. If he were some kind of deviant, wouldn't he have harmed her that first night? Why didn't she see the logic in that argument?

He left the boathouse and walked down to the shore. The gentle roll of the waves lapped the edges of his work boots. He squatted down, sitting on his haunches, then picked up small stones and shells, tossing them into the water. He was a good man, an honorable man. No one ever before had been afraid of him. He made her nervous, though; how was he going to handle that? "Lord, I don't want to frighten the poor woman, but I can't exactly allow her too close. Her beauty, her mannerisms disturb me as if I were a teenager all over again. What can I do to change things?"

A wash of calming peace rushed through him. In his mind he felt as if God were saying to simply wait and give her time to get to know him for who he really was.

"I reckon I can wait, Lord."

❧

Alex scanned the clay cliffs in front of her. They were so different from the pictures she had seen of them many years ago. A large red cliff that should have been in the foreground was missing. She looked to the shoreline below and saw the sea was full of red clay. Of course, she pondered, erosion must have taken its toll on the red cliff. The remaining cliffs were beautiful hues of whites and yellows, some with a hint of green. She scanned the short distance from the edge of the cliffs to the bottom of the Gay Head lighthouse and wondered how many years it had left to stand in its present position before erosion would relentlessly lay its claim. This lighthouse was so different from the one in Edgartown. It was painted brown for one thing, and the rail up on top was black.

She stopped in the little shops the local Indians maintained to rid tourists of their money. In spite of herself, she bought some trinkets for her friends and family, and with her arms full of bundles, she headed toward the car. The view before her, running down the south side of the island, took her breath away. . .the large rocks lining the shore and protruding from the water, the bright white sand that made up the beach. Green bushes lined the way back to the paved road.

She turned her attention toward the north side of the island. The air was so clear she could see across the bay to Chilmark, probably right to the area where the Trainers' home was.

She had been wrong to clam up this morning with Jared, she realized as time and distance gave her a better sense of perspective. She had made Jared uncomfortable, as well as herself. She needed to rectify that situation upon her return.

She placed the items in the back of her Bronco and got in, not certain how she was going to ease the situation between her and Jared. As she made her way home, she discovered a few small buildings that made up the town of Gay Head.

After the car was unloaded, she headed toward the boathouse, assuming she would find Jared there. Along the path to the boathouse, on bushes of varying height, she saw some purple berries. Curious, she picked a few and continued down the path. She reached the boathouse and came upon him.

And there he was—all six-foot-one, two hundred and thirty-five pounds of him. His chest was huge, the muscles on his back and arms playing an alluring, hypnotic dance. Stunned, she stood still and watched. His movements were swift and agile. Med school had never prepared her for a man that looked like this.

He turned and smiled. "Can I help you?"

Alex fumbled for words. "I, I. . ."

"Yes?" His grin was disarming. She sensed he knew what his body was doing to her, and he was eating it up.

"I wanted to apologize for breakfast. I–I wasn't very talkative, I guess."

"No need to apologize. I know you don't think highly of me. I'm sorry."

"It's not that." What was it that made her feel so nervous around him?

Jared grabbed a rag and wiped off his hands.

"I'm just a little uncomfortable around you." If he only knew how uncomfortable, she would be at the mercy of this man. She couldn't let that happen. "Thanks for fixing the hot water heater."

"Not a problem."

Alex felt the berries in her hand. *That is a safe subject,* she thought. "Can you tell me what these are?"

Jared stepped closer and held her hand in the inside palm of his huge masculine grip. Her body almost gave her away as she felt her fingers start to tremble, but she caught herself and kept them still. With his other hand, he picked up one of the berries. "These are called beach plums."

"Are they edible?"

"Yes, although you generally make them into jellies, jams, and sauces. The seed is large and the fruit is tart. There is very little of the fruit between the seed and its skin."

"How can I make this jelly? How many of these things would I need to pick?"

"I believe Phyllis picked up a book called *Plum Crazy* a few years back that's filled with recipes."

Alex belatedly realized she had left her hand in his and she jerked it free. She decided to look for the book and attempt to make this local delicacy. "Well, thanks," she said awkwardly.

"Welcome."

Alex rushed away from the boathouse and found the cookbook. She needed ten cups of the berries and two cups of water to make juice for the jelly recipe. Grabbing a container, she went back to the bush. The beach plums were plentiful, and within an hour she was done.

She had worn a pair of shorts and a short sleeve blouse while picking. She looked at the scratches from the briars. "I should cleanse the wounds well in order to prevent infection," she murmured to herself.

❧

Jared turned off the baths for the evening. The day had been a productive one; he was pleased with how many planks were in place. He thought back on the beach plums Alexandria had picked, and scanning the bush she had probably picked from, he spotted some poison ivy. There were still some leaves, but because it was early fall, most of the leaves were off the plants.

He ran down to his house and picked up a bar of Fels Naptha brown soap. *She's going to need to wash with this immediately*, he thought. He ran back up the hill and rapidly pounded on the door.

He saw her approach and smiled when she opened it. "Hey, Doc, did you pick those beach plums yet?"

"Yes, I've got them in the sink. I just rinsed them."

He looked at the scratches on her legs. "I don't suppose you folks have poison ivy out in Kansas, do you?"

Chapter 5

She narrowed her gaze, knitting her eyebrows together. "What is it you're trying to tell me, Jared?"

"I believe while you were picking the beach plums you probably rubbed up against some poison ivy." He handed her a yellowish-brown bar of soap. "I stopped at the bush where I think you were picking. Please take this soap and scrub with it. It helps!"

Alex had already begun to itch, but she had chalked it up to the scratches. She looked down at her legs. If the poison ivy had gone into her bloodstream, she was definitely in for an extreme case of it.

"Alexandria, you're a doctor—can you call in a prescription? I think some cortisone would be in order."

"I suppose I should. I'd better wash."

"Can I get you anything? Go to the drugstore for you?"

"Thanks, maybe I should call in the prescription first." Alex went to the phone and pulled out the local directory. She felt foolish; she should have noticed the poisonous plant.

Jared left after she placed the call, and she went into the bathroom, stripping off her clothes and placing them in the washer first. Once in the shower, she scrubbed, thankful the water was finally hot—until she realized the hot water would open her pores, allowing more of the poison to sink into her skin. Groaning, she turned the faucet knobs, knowing she would have to endure a cold shower. She lathered herself twice, then gave herself a final rinse. Teeth chattering, she gave in and turned up the heat.

She set the washing machine and headed into the kitchen, her legs tingling. Unsure if the itch was caused by the poison ivy or the mere thought of it, she attempted to ignore the impulse to scratch. She decided on shorts. Feeling the rub of the fabric against her legs would only increase the desire to scratch.

Jared returned after she was all showered and changed. In his arms were a pizza box and a couple of bags. "I hope you don't mind, but I took the liberty of ordering some pizza for us. I also picked up some calamine lotion to help with the itching. And a few more ointments, all claiming to help."

She gave him a grateful smile. "Thanks, that's really sweet of you."

"How bad are the cuts?" he asked, straddling a chair beside the table.

"Not very deep, but they sting. I honestly didn't see any poison ivy. I wish you had warned me."

"If I thought you were going to pick immediately, I would have. But I honestly didn't think about it until I was closing down the steam baths."

"Tell me, why do you have to steam the wood?"

Jared went into a description of crafting a wooden-hulled boat—the process of steam-bending the wood, how it enabled the oak to be more pliable, and the research he had done concerning this particular craft's history on the cape.

Alex listened eagerly. "I'm here doing research on my family roots. I've always known about my ancestor being a sea captain and his living on Martha's Vineyard. Since I was small, I wanted to come and experience the ocean and the place where my relatives had grown up. Particularly the one who moved to Kansas. . .she had very fond memories of the place."

"So you're a Luce, then?"

"Well, one of his descendants anyway."

"Have you been to the historical society yet?"

"Yesterday I spent the entire day in Edgartown."

"What did you find?"

Alex went over all her discoveries, glad to share them with someone. Finally, she mentioned the row of captains' houses with their widows' walks.

Jared broke out in laughter. "Tell me, Doc, do you honestly believe those women had nothing better to do with their time, knowing their husbands were out for years at a stretch?"

"No, I figured they only used them when they knew it was about time for their return."

"Sorry to burst your romantic bubble, but widows' walks were not built for searching for husbands."

"They weren't?"

"No. In fact, they had a far more practical use. They were used to extinguish chimney fires in the winter. If you noticed, the roofs in the area tend to have steep peaks."

"Yes, I noticed that. Why?"

"Because of snow. The steeper a peak, the less likely the snow and ice would build up on your roof. Anyway, if you got a fire in your chimney, it was virtually impossible to make it up the roof in the winter. So the more well-to-do families put in these walkways between the chimneys. At the base of each chimney was a bucket of sand to be poured down the flue to extinguish the fire."

"Really?"

He seemed pleased with her interest. "Really. I see we have something in common. We both love history and, in particular, island history and some of the folklore that surrounds it."

"How did the story of widows' walks ever get started in the first place?"

"I don't know. Probably some writer one time looked at the old sea captains' houses and just assumed. Even though it's not true, it does give quite a romantic side to sailors and their loves, don't you think?"

"I suppose, but wouldn't it make more sense to simply tell everyone the truth?"

"Probably." Jared chuckled. "But fiction is sometimes more interesting."

She smiled. *Strange*, she thought, *how this man can be so charming*. Absent-mindedly she scratched her legs.

"Stop that," he bellowed.

Startled, Alex jumped.

"Sorry, I didn't mean to scare you. But you can't scratch. Those abrasions are bad enough. If any of them were made by a poison ivy twig, you are going to have a very bad case."

"I know. I forgot."

Jared scraped the chair backward, got up, and grabbed the bottle of calamine lotion. "Come on, let me rub this on you."

"Yes, Doctor," she teased.

"Well, one of us ought to be."

Alex pointed her leg toward him. He squatted in front of her. He poured the lotion onto a couple of cotton balls and dabbed it on her open wounds. His touch was gentle but very methodical. Once he finished one area, he moved on to the next. Over and over he repeated the process. Aware she was feeling too much pleasure from his attention, she thanked him and pulled her legs back under her chair.

"You're welcome. Good night, Alexandria. Here's my number if you need anything."

"Thank you, Jared. I'm sure I'll be fine."

"I'm sure you will be too, but just in case."

❧

He slipped out the door slowly. Being so close to her, feeling her skin, sensing her vulnerability was too much. He wasn't going to allow himself to get that close to the woman again. *Sure, we can be friends, but that's it.*

But whatever he told himself didn't work. He was concerned about her poison ivy reaction, and something almost primal developed in him, a powerful urge to watch over and care for her. It felt natural, instinctive, almost spiritual. *Maybe that's it, God giving me a tender heart to aid the sick.* That must be it. Jared relaxed. He was simply living his Christian life and putting it into action by coming to her rescue and tending to her needs. There was nothing more, just good, common, brotherly love that Christ gives His people for one another.

At peace with this revelation, he settled in for the night. He had his devotions, said his closing prayers for the day, and fell fast asleep. This was the first night since Dr. Alexandria Tucker imposed herself on his life that he actually was going to get a restful sleep.

The next few days went smoothly between Alex and Jared. He continued to check on her. The first couple of days she was quite sick, but there wasn't much he could do for her. It was a simple case of waiting out the poison in her system. After the first night's application of calamine lotion, neither one of them had wanted a repeat performance. She was feeling better now, and the poison ivy was drying up. She felt well enough to continue her research at the historical society.

Each evening she read a couple of chapters of *Lost at Sea*. The story captivated her, not so much because of the terror of the ordeal but because of the author's openness about his fears, anger, and past grievances with God. And yet, the man never seemed to gain release from the anguish of losing his loved ones. He at last accepted his loss as God's timing, but he still wouldn't allow his heart to be vulnerable again.

Having taken her evening shower, Alex cinched her bathrobe and wrapped her wet hair in a towel-turban high upon her head.

"Alexandria?" Jared yelled as the door slammed against the inner wall.

Anger, fused by embarrassment, fueled her sharp response. "What on earth are you doing plowing in here again?"

"Sorry, it's important."

"No, Jared, it's not so important that you couldn't have knocked."

His cheeks flushed and his neck turned crimson. "There's a nor'easter coming, possibly turning into a hurricane."

"What?"

"Sorry, I didn't mean to barge in, but I need your help. We need to protect the houses."

Flustered, pushing down her surge of anger, she said in level tones, "I'll get dressed. What can I do?"

"I need you to help hold some plywood in place. We need to board the windows and especially the sliding glass door."

"I'll be right out." Alex hurried into the bedroom, pulling her robe off as she walked. *What was a northeaster?* she wondered. The fact that it could turn into a hurricane was enough of a warning. She remembered news footage of Hurricane Andrew in Florida a few years back and various other hurricanes in years since. She knew the potential dangers. "Oh, Lord, protect us. We are on the shore, the first houses to get hit."

Dressed in mere moments, she hurried outside. *There is a steady breeze, but nothing major,* she thought. She ran around the house looking for Jared.

"Jared?" she called. Nothing, no response. She ran down to the boathouse. He wasn't there. She looked down the hill toward Jared's home, which was closer to the shore and lower on the bluff. Seeing him working around the house closing the wooden shutters over the windows, relief washed over her. Something about his presence was reassuring. For the first time in her life, she actually saw working wooden shutters. All of her experience had been with decorative ones.

When she joined him at his cottage, he explained how to secure the shutters. She took over that job and he gathered various outdoor items and placed them either under the house or inside it. The items under the house he secured with tarps and rope, tying them to circular concrete columns that obviously supported the building. Once his place was done, they headed up to the Trainers' home; she carried a couple of hammers and a bag of nails while he carried a few sheets of plywood. The wind was gathering its strength, and the plywood he carried became like wooden sails.

"Can I help?"

"No, I've got them, thanks."

Mr. Macho probably figures he can handle them easier without my help, she reasoned, forgoing an argument with him about how strong she was.

At the house, the first thing Jared boarded up, after placing the deck furniture in the living room, was the sliding glass door that faced the ocean. Under the deck, he pulled out precut pieces of plywood with numbers on them. "Alex, that's window number one."

She nodded.

"We start there and work around the house. Each board is cut for each window."

"I understand. Do you want me to nail or to carry the wood?"

"I'll carry and help you set the first couple nails. Then while I'm gathering more boards and securing the outdoor items under the deck, you can finish securing each board."

"Fine. Show me the way, Captain."

He grinned. Alex smiled and quickly averted her gaze. Instead, she went straight to work. Sprinkles of rain started to fall on her cheeks. She looked to the sky in the direction of the northeast. Sure enough, on the horizon, were intense black clouds.

"Alex, I can finish. I need you to prepare for loss of power. The water is from a well and is pumped by an electric generator, so if we lose power, we lose water. Fill every tub and sink. Go to my place and do the same. Also, at the Trainers' take every pitcher and tall container that can hold water and get us a few gallons for drinking."

"Okay. What else?"

"Locate any candles and flashlights, and turn the refrigerator up to high. Get it really cold. Place some water in large plastic bags with those fancy zipper-type seals into the freezer and make some blocks of ice."

"Sure." Alex knew about preparing for loss of power, having lived through enough windstorms and tornadoes in Kansas. She assumed the same kind of preparations needed there would work here as well.

"After that, run to the store and pick up some nonperishables. If we lose power, we could be without it for several days. When I'm done up here, I'm going to the boathouse to secure things down there."

"All right." Alex fought back her desire to challenge his ordering attitude. *He's simply focused*, she told herself. Typical male. She nodded and headed into the house.

❧

Jared placed the last board up on the Trainers' home. Down at the boathouse, he secured the loose planks, tying them together and placing them alongside the walls. The boathouse only had three walls, the fourth was open to the sea.

Jared gathered his tools, loaded his wooden toolbox, and brought the rest to his house. He secured the steam baths that lay along two walls. Having made them himself, he hated the thought they might be lost.

After storing the toolbox inside the cottage, he returned to the boathouse. Rolling up his blueprints, he placed them back inside a cardboard tube. He gathered together additional items to take out of harm's way. Various shades of ominous gray filled the sky, streaked with occasional lightning. He thanked the Lord there was no evidence of circular movement, thus little threat of a hurricane, yet he knew that northeasters could have winds as strong as hurricanes.

Hearing the latest news update in the shop reminded him he needed a battery-operated radio. "I can't forget that." He placed it on his mental to-do list. The ribbed hull of his boat lay like an empty skeleton before him. He winced, knowing it would be hit, hoping it would be spared the pounding of the waves. He sighed. "Oh well, Lord, it's in Your hands. I can always rebuild."

In his cottage, he deposited the items he had gathered from the boathouse. Anything that could become a missile propelled by the wind was now neatly tucked away or tied down. Grabbing his radio, he checked the batteries. They were weak. He searched through his junk drawer for some fresh batteries, grateful to find a few. He also retrieved a camping lantern, which he set aside to be taken up to the Trainers' home. Turning his refrigerator on high, he placed some water jugs in the freezer.

He paused suddenly, realizing he hadn't asked Alex's permission to stay with her through the storm. He rolled his shoulders and stretched his neck, hoping she wouldn't take offense, counting on her being happy with his company through the rough hours of the storm.

The increased wind howled through the shutters. Rain began its gentle drumming on the roof. Scurrying through his cabinets, he grabbed some canned goods and the steak that was thawing on the counter for dinner. He drove his truck to the backside of his house, furthest from the assaulting winds, trusting that the house would help protect it from flying debris.

❧

At the grocery store, some folks were panicking, others taking a more carefree

155

approach, as if it were just another day. Alex picked up sodas, dehydrated and canned juices, fresh vegetables and fruit that would last without refrigeration, canned meats, soups, and canned vegetables. The shelves were sparse, at best, as she went through the aisles. She calculated for three days' supply, since Jared said if they lost power it could possibly take that long for the electricity to be restored. With her shopping cart full, she stood in line. Every register was open. Five people stood in front of her waiting their turn with the cashier.

One woman talked serenely about how she'd been through many storms like this and worse. Her words calmed a nervous mother with children.

Alex glanced over her shoulder and saw a mother with a small child standing behind her in line. Her cart was nearly empty, her eyes glistened with tears. Other carts behind her were nearly empty as well. "Excuse me," Alex said, "is that all you could find?"

The woman nodded her head.

"How many children do you have?"

"Four."

"Do you have more nonperishable food at home?"

"No, tonight is grocery night. I couldn't get to the store until my husband came home with his paycheck."

Alex scrutinized the array of food in her own cart. There was far more than two people could eat or needed to eat over three days. "Here, take some of mine." The young mother looked on in wonder. "Please, take what you would like from my cart."

"I can't. It's yours." The woman's eyes looked away from her as she bit her lower lip.

"I merely reached the shelves before you were able to. Please, I really don't need all of this food. I want you to have it."

"Are you sure?" She searched Alex's eyes for affirmation.

"Yes." Alex played with the little girl standing in the cart. She had a headful of blond curls and one of the deepest sets of brown eyes Alex had ever seen.

The young mother tentatively reached into Alex's cart. Alex's heart was full, and she knew she had done the right thing. There was no way she could have lived with herself knowing a family of six would possibly go hungry for the next few days.

Gradually, the mother's actions became more relaxed. She took most of Alex's purchases. "Are you sure this is all right?"

"Yes, it's only myself and one other. And there's enough food back at the house."

"Thank you. I simply don't know what else to say."

"Thank the Lord, and do something nice for someone else when it comes your time to give and serve."

She nodded. Alex was next. She placed the remaining items on the conveyer belt. She noticed her act of kindness was caught by others in line. People started sharing their acquisitions with other customers around them. *Storms have a way of making you hoard things, or they pull people together*, Alex hypothesized.

The cashier ran her order through the scanner and winked at her when she paid.

"Thanks again," the young mother said as Alex gathered her bags into her arms.

"You're welcome. I'll pray for you and your family to weather the storm safely."

The young mother nodded and concentrated on getting her groceries ready for the cashier.

Confident in having done the right thing, Alex walked with her shoulders straight and her heart full of Christian love.

Chapter 6

His home secure, Jared worked his way once again up the hill to the Trainers' house. Stopping on the bluff, he stood scanning the horizon. The clouds were gray and deepening to charcoal. The dance of lightning highlighted the clouds and showed their tumultuous drift toward shore.

Memories of a similar storm flickered with bits and pieces of the past. Images of that fateful storm momentarily paralyzed him. He was back on the *Kontiki Too*. Working the rigging, lowering the mainsail, trying to keep the boat pressed into the wind. Waves crashed over the bow; she was taking in some water. He had been fighting the storm for hours, but he continued struggling with the rudder despite the weariness of his body. Fatigued, he held the tiller with what strength he could muster. He had prayed the storm would soon be over, even though the horizon was obliterated by the black, ominous sky.

A forceful gust of wind jarred him back to reality. He squeezed his eyes shut and let out a deep breath. *Today's storm takes precedence; keep yourself in the present, old boy.* With determined strides, he marched toward the Trainers' home.

His hands full with the items from his cottage, he tapped the door with his leather workboot. The chill of the wind seeped through his rain-drenched shirt. "Hi. I've brought a few things."

As Alex held the door open for him, he turned sideways and stepped through. "I've got a lantern here, another flashlight, and a few canned goods." He placed the bags on the table. "Also, I was thawing a steak earlier today so I thought we could share it for dinner."

"Planning on camping out?"

Is she upset? He turned and caught the twinkle in her eye. "If you don't mind, I thought I'd spend the worst of the storm here with you rather than on the beach."

"Sounds great. Jared, I didn't get much from the grocery store."

"I hoped you would get there before it was wiped out."

"Well, not exactly. The shelves were pretty sparse, but there was this woman. . ." Alex retold the incident.

"I would have done the same. I'm sure with what you and I have together, we'll be fine."

"I'm glad you understand."

"The good Lord wouldn't want it any other way." He smiled.

"Can I ask you another question?"

Her eyes were not quite looking straight at him, and Jared assumed she was nervous, maybe embarrassed to be asking whatever question she possibly had in mind. "Sure."

"Are you a believer? I mean, you know, a born-again Christian?"

"Yes, although I haven't always lived in a manner that was pleasing to the Lord. You are also, aren't you?"

"Yes."

He had known she must be. Aware that they now had two things in common, he believed God was using this woman to strengthen him as a Christian. "I thought so."

"How?"

"Little things said and the way you prayed over breakfast the day I fixed the hot water heater."

"Oh."

"Well, how about that steak?"

"Sounds great to me. One thing I'm not worried about—with propane tanks for the stove, we'll be able to cook."

"You're a wise woman. Let me clean up and I'll give you a hand with dinner."

"Sure, how do you like your steak?"

"Rare, what about you?"

She chuckled. "The same."

❧

The wind whistled as it rushed through the plywood sheets across the slider. Rain pelted the house from all sides. Alex found herself a little disoriented. With all the windows boarded, an eerie feeling seized her, like being shut up within a darkened elevator. "Jared, how long do these northeasters last?"

"The better part of a day, generally, but sometimes they've lasted a couple." Getting up from the table, he turned on the Trainers' stereo. "Let's check on the status of the storm."

Alex listened to the crackle of the static as Jared tried to get a clear fix on the area radio station. Once located, they listened, learning the storm would continue for hours. Most of the island still had power as the more intense part of the storm was just about to hit shore. She thought about the book she had been reading, about its description of the storm, about being on a small boat in the middle of a raging sea. Thankful she was on dry land, she allowed her uneasy feelings to dissipate. "How many of these northeasters have you been through?"

"I suppose we have at least one a year. Although, this is early in the season for it."

The power cut out. Jared turned on the flashlight. Alex grabbed the matches and lit the lantern and a few candles.

Tree limbs snapped around them. Lightning cracked right outside the house. Alex jumped. It sounded so close. Mere milliseconds later she heard the ripping of wood. *Thump!* The house groaned. Something large had just landed on the roof over the back bedroom.

Before checking out the damage, Jared lifted the phone. "It's dead also. Someplace down the road the phone and power lines must have been knocked out where they merge."

The intensity of the storm escalated. Between the darkness and the loss of power, they were totally at the disposal of the elements. *Relax!* Alex chastised herself.

Jared went back to check on the damage. She sat alone. The howling of the wind, the waves crashing on the beach, the rain, everything seemed crystal clear. She could picture it even though she sat completely blocked from seeing anything outside.

"The ceiling looks fine. I don't know how bad the roof is. We'll have to check periodically for leaking," Jared said, as he walked into the glow of the candlelit room.

Alex blinked at Jared's shadowy hulk. He would be an intimidating man if she didn't know him. "I don't mind telling you this is a little frightening."

"I know, but I've been through worse."

"When, what happened?"

Jared sat down beside her on the couch. "Imagine yourself being out there," he pointed toward the ocean, "on a fairly small vessel in the middle of the sea and a storm of even stronger winds comes up."

"Oh my, what happened?"

She watched him close his eyes. Slowly he opened them. "It was awhile ago. I had built a ship to cross the Atlantic. Actually, the goal was to sail around the world eventually, but. . ." He paused for a moment, then continued. "I was seven days out when it started to rain. I grabbed my foul-weather gear and trimmed the sails. A little rain never killed a sailor. The entire first day was light rain with some occasional downpours. The wind picked up as the sun went down. I battened down the boat, rigged up an autopilot of sorts, and went to sleep, hoping the storm would be over by morning."

Alex thought back on the story she had been reading. It was the same technique used by the man who was lost at sea. "What happened?"

"When I got up the next morning, the skies were far more threatening. I had sailed smack dab into the heart of the storm. Of course, I didn't know it at the time. I took in the jib, lowered the mainsail some more, and headed straight into the wind. The seas were rolling twelve to fifteen feet at this point. It's an awesome sight seeing a wall of ocean water right over your shoulder."

"I think it would be a terrifying sight."

"That, too, but it's amazing how water moves."

"I suppose. What happened next?"

"That went on for hours, with the waves increasing in size. I was getting nowhere. Not that I was really trying to do anything more than stay afloat, of course."

"How small was this boat?"

"The main hull was about sixteen feet."

"What? Are you crazy? You were trying to cross the Atlantic in a sixteen-foot boat?"

Jared grinned. "I was trying to prove a historical point."

Alex laughed. "What was that, that a man is just as ignorant as his forefathers?"

"Now, hang on, Alex. I did a lot of research and I modernized the hull, making it fiberglass and more seaworthy. Plus, it was a tri-hulled vessel."

Her mind was back on the book. That boat was also small, also had three hulls, and had also been caught in a storm. It couldn't be, could it? "Jared, what's your last name?"

"Madeiras, why?"

"I've been reading a book about a man who was lost at sea for eight days, written by a J. Madeiras. I take it, that is you?" *And you've stolen my heart,* she refused to tell him. How could she possibly tell him that she had fallen in love with the man in the book?

"How on earth did you find a copy of that book?"

"Brad and Phyllis have a copy in their library. It's yours, right? You're the same man?"

"Yes."

Compassion seized her heart. She remembered the longing she felt for this man, how he still needed to get over some of his hurts. She wondered if they still remained. "You said in the dedication, it was to your loved ones lost. Who were they?"

"My folks, and. . ."

And who? she wanted to ask.

"Hannah, my fiancée."

Alex reached out and gently touched his forearm. Her fingers tingled from the contact. She pushed the sensation out of her mind. "I'm so sorry, Jared. What happened?"

"If you don't mind, I prefer not to talk about Hannah."

"All right." This was crazy. Every ounce of her being wanted to know what was behind those darkened eyes. Had Hannah run off with someone else? No, it couldn't be that. He said "lost." Hannah must have died. Did he feel responsible in some way? She longed to ask more questions, but the man she was getting to know demanded to no longer be approached on the subject. Not now, not yet. *I've pretty near a whole year to get it out of him, if need be. After all, it's not like I'm willing to tell him about Peter.* Calming herself down, she refused to allow herself to feel slighted by his unwillingness to talk about Hannah.

"Do you understand?" He searched her eyes.

His deep probing made her uncomfortable. "Let's just say I have some things I'm not quite ready to discuss with you either."

"Fair enough."

"So, tell me, why the Polynesians? What sparked your interest in them and their vessels?"

Jared went on to explain how he had read a story about the *Kontiki* in high school, how he researched it, and finally built his replica, with some modern-day advances, of course. "Basically it came down to the type of storm and how strong it was. No one in that size of a boat, or even in some larger vessels, would have made it safely through. It took the rescuers eight days to locate me because I was so far off course."

"I simply can't imagine it. I mean, I read your book and I could picture it, but there's no way I can truly understand the anguish of bobbing up and down on the ocean for eight days with no control."

"It's a humbling experience." His voice sounded contrite.

❧

The storm was abating. Jared looked at his watch. He and Alex had played competitive games of rummy, Scrabble, Monopoly, and now chess. As he tapped the black rook, he moved in for the kill. "Check."

He loved how Alex bit her lower lip when she was thinking. She moved her queen into a vulnerable spot.

He took his castle and captured her queen. "Check again."

He watched in astonishment as she moved her knight. "Checkmate," she smirked.

His face fell, even though he tried not to show his amazement at her sneaky victory. He examined the board, looking for a possible move that would get him out of the trap she had laid. Nope, she had him pure and simple. "How did you do that?"

Alex chuckled. "Years of practice."

"With whom?"

"First my father, then when I was on my college chess team."

"You competed?"

"Yes. I suppose you think I should have warned you first."

"It would have been nice knowing in advance I was headed for a slaughter." She was a complicated woman; he was beginning to discover that.

"Men."

"What's that supposed to mean?" *Maybe not that complicated, if she lumps all men into one category.*

"Nothing, I suppose, but it seems every man I play just hates to lose to a woman."

"That's a sexist statement if ever I heard one."

"Maybe, but it's held true for me. I watched the guys in competition for years. They had no problem being sacked by a guy, but as soon as a woman, or myself in particular, beat them, then they were outraged. Sorriest bunch of losers you ever did see."

"I was not bellyaching about losing to you."

"No, to your defense you took defeat like a man. However, I did see your face fall in shock."

"I was shocked by the move, not that you are a woman."

She seemed to ponder this for a moment. "I take it back. You're one rather unique man."

Jared twisted a smile. "Thanks, I think."

"Trust me, it's a compliment. What time is it?"

"A little past midnight. Getting tired?"

"Yes."

"I'm going to go outside and inspect the damage. If you want, I'll go to my cabin right afterward, then you can rest."

"Do you think the worst is past?"

"Yes. Do you need me to stay?"

"No, I'll be fine. Thanks for offering, though. Please stop back in and let me know what you find before you go back to your place."

"No problem." He hesitated, realizing he had been hoping they would talk more. He had wanted to share about Hannah as the evening wore on. There was something about Alex that compelled him to open himself up. *But it would be foolish to say something after making such a fuss about not saying anything,* he reasoned.

He got up and took the large flashlight with him. "I'll be back in a few."

As he stepped out the door, he held the screen door tight. The force of the wind was still something to contend with. He worked his way around the back of the house, stepping over downed limbs. The beam of light showed the debris scattered across the path to the back of the house. A large pine tree lay across the back corner of the roof.

There was damage. He decided the ceiling would probably need repairing after the water seeped its way in. The damage to the house was just as Jared expected.

The wind howled through the trees; the rain stung his cheeks. He fought his way around the corner of the house, walking into the wind. The oak and maple leaves made the ground slick. He turned and examined this angle of the house. Dimly, the flashlight showed the fallen tree, a gaping hole of broken wood and missing shingles. Obviously, as the storm continued to blow, it continued to damage the weakened roof. Jared tried to step up on a log and get a better angle, but the wind was too strong. His footing slipped and he fell to the ground.

The storm was picking up again. Getting himself up off the ground, he turned toward the shore. It was still too dark, so there was nothing to see. No stars, no moon, only dark clouds surrounded him. Rather than go back the way he came, he decided to cross the front of the house and see how the deck was faring.

As he turned the corner, he received the full impact of the wind. Pressing each step deeper into the ground, he worked his way to the stairs. The deck was covered with debris, broken limbs, pieces of trash.

Crack! Jared turned just in time to see a limb propelling itself toward him. He tried to duck. He went down. Darkness enveloped him. His mind flashed back to another dark time, his lungs burning under the water, constricting from lack of air.

❧

Alex paced. *Jared should be back by now. Where is he? Why hasn't he come back?* She looked at her watch and realized he'd been gone for half an hour. *Something's not right.* Alex ran to her closet, grabbed a raincoat, and took the other flashlight.

The screen door wrenched out of her hands as the wind caught it. Grunting, she wrestled it closed. The wind pushed her quickly off the back of the deck and around to the rear of the house. Swinging the flashlight from side to side, she probed the darkness. No Jared.

"Jared!" she yelled. "Jared!" But no response. She forged her way to the back corner of the house where the tree had come down. As she rounded the corner, she called again.

"Jared!"

Concern merged with apprehension as she bent low and leaned headlong into the wind. Bits of sand stung her face. Reaching the front corner of the house, she wondered if maybe he had simply headed back to his place. But she was positive he'd said he would return.

Uncertain what to do, she stood frozen with trepidation. Maybe he'd walked around to the front of the house while she walked around the rear. She maneuvered herself against the wind.

As the beam of light fell on the steps, she saw him collapsed with a limb near his head. "Jared!" She ran to him. Her heart slammed in her chest with fear. "Oh, Lord, let him be all right."

Chapter 7

Her fingers worked through his thick locks, feeling for a wound. She knew he was bleeding; she didn't need to turn the flashlight on to see it. Over the years she had felt enough blood. Tenderly, she worked her fingers around the wound, testing to see how bad it was. "Jared, can you hear me?"

Knowing he was unconscious, she needed to talk to see if she could help bring him to. "Dr. Tucker" came alive. She kept talking, telling him each and every thing she was doing, checking his pulse, his breathing. He was stable. She lifted his arm across her back and placed her right shoulder under his left armpit. "Come on, Jared, help me here. Ugh, you're built like an ox."

Alex was stronger than most women her size and proper training in emergency rescue gave her the expertise to lift an adult body. But Jared was solid muscle. She was going to need all her strength and concentration to walk him back.

"Come on, Jared, wake up. I need some help here."

She raised his body up slightly.

"Lord, help me. Wake this man up."

"Jared, we're going back to the house now. Step forward with your right leg."

Jared mumbled, and his leg moved forward. He wasn't fully conscious, but it was enough.

"Great, now the left. Super, Jared. Come on, a few more steps. Perfect, you're doing perfect. Stay with me, Jared." She was thankful they were only twenty feet from the door. "Don't fall back to sleep. Come on, fight it. That's it, great."

Alex unlatched the screen door and the wind caught it. She was grateful they had been walking with the wind, not against it. She opened the interior door and helped Jared through. "Let's go to the couch, Jared. That's it, a few more steps. You're doing wonderful."

She eased him down on the couch. He was waking, though still groggy. The wound needed to be cleansed and a thorough exam of his injuries needed to be assessed. In her bedroom, Alex retrieved her black bag: It was always accessible whether on vacation or a simple errand to the mall. Of course, she left it in her car most of the time, but it was amazing how often she had used it.

She worked quickly and efficiently. Two years of ER training had been a wonderful teacher, not to mention the numerous cuts and spills her regular patients had taken over the years.

"Ow, that stings!"

"Glad to have you back among the living. What happened?"

"Other than a huge hunk of tree plowing into my head, not much."

"Have you ever heard of ducking?"

"I did. It would have landed on my chest if I hadn't."

"Well, at least this way it hit a nonvital organ," she teased.

"Anyone ever tell you, you have a lousy bedside manner, Doc?"

"Nope, you're the first one. Now hush for a moment while I stitch up the last couple of sutures."

"Yes, Ma'am."

"It's not too bad, Jared. Although we should probably have it X-rayed to be sure."

"Is that really necessary? Can it wait until morning? Personally I'm not up for a drive."

"Yes, it can wait, unless you start showing some other signs—then there's no argument, okay?"

"Fine. Doc, do you mind if I spend what is left of the night on your couch? I don't quite have the stomach to walk to the cottage."

"Are you nauseated?"

"No, not really."

"I'll want to spend the night watching you anyway. You can stay here. How about the guest bed, though, instead of the couch?"

"I wouldn't want to put you out."

Alex laughed. "You've got me performing medical aid with no electric lights, nothing of modern medicine, and you don't want to put me out."

"Well, that's all in the line of the Hippocratic oath, isn't it?"

"Jared, you can be such a stubborn. . ."

"So can you, Doc, so can you. How did you get me in here?"

"I'm stronger than I look."

"Yeah, right. You're one pretty skinny little thing."

"Thank you, I think." She was thankful the lights were dim so he wouldn't see her blush. She realized he had sized her up, even as she had noticed him. "You stay down while I make up the bed with fresh linens." Not waiting for a response, she hurried off to one of the other bedrooms, stopping by the linen closet along the way.

❧

Jared's head throbbed with pain. He reached behind and felt the swollen bald spot.

"Try not to touch it."

"Alex?"

"I'm here, Jared."

"Have you been up all night?" He raised his head to look at her.

"I slept some. How are you feeling?"

"Like I got hit by a Mack truck."

"Good."

"Easy for you to say."

She smiled. Jared's heart leaped.

"How's your vision?" Her eyes probed his.

Jared scanned the room. "Fine. Everything is crystal clear."

"Great." Alex held a flashlight in her hand. "Can I look at the wound?"

Rolling to his side, he gave her a better view of his injury. "How's it look?"

"In this light, pretty good. I don't see much infection. I cleansed it a couple of times hoping to get all the bits of bark and debris out."

"Thanks. It's kind of nice having a doctor so close."

Alex chuckled. "You won't think so when you get my bill."

"Hmm, then I withdraw the comment and reserve the right to alter it after I see the bill." Her eyes sparkled with mirth. He took her hand. "Thanks, Alex. I really appreciate your help." He stroked the back of her hand with his thumb. Her silken skin was soft and smooth, so unlike his own hard, callused hands.

"You're welcome, but I'm sure you would have done the same for me."

"I would have helped you, but I'm not a doctor. I'm not sure what I would have done with a head wound." He tried to sit up. Dizzy, he grabbed the sides of the bed.

"Hang on there, big fella, you can't move that quickly. You'll black out."

"Now you tell me."

"I didn't know you were going to try and get up."

"You're right. Okay, Doc, what do I need to know?"

"Tell me if you're nauseous, if your vision blurs, or anything that is different than normal."

"I can do that. Can I walk?"

"Yes, but slowly. It was a fairly deep wound and you lost a bit of blood. You'll live, though."

"Thanks, I think." Jared rubbed the back of his neck. "I don't hear the storm. Has it stopped?"

"Finally."

"Can I go outside and inspect?"

"Only if I can tag along." Alex stood with her hands on her hips.

Man, she's a beautiful woman. "Okay."

"Need a hand?"

She held her hand out to him. He didn't think he really needed it, but the memory of how her hand felt in his encouraged him to grasp it anyway. "Thanks."

"You're welcome. Now take it slow. You'll be feeling better in a few more hours, unless there's something more going on up there."

"Like what?"

"Oh, a cracked skull for instance." She winked.

ॐ

The walk around the house exhausted Jared. Alex wondered if she had allowed him to do too much too soon. "Jared, I want to take you to the hospital and have your skull X-rayed."

"Is it really necessary? I feel fine, just tired."

"I thought we went through this last night. It's just a precaution, but one I would really like to have done."

"All right, I'll be a good patient. But we'll need to take a chain saw with us. There might be downed limbs in the road and I'll need to clear a path for us to get out."

"You can't do that kind of work yet."

"Then we sit here."

"Let me try getting out the driveway first, then I'll come back and get you. If we can pass, fine. If I can't move the limbs, then we are sitting right here." There was no way she was going to allow him to exert himself and get that wound bleeding again. Not yet; it was too soon. He needed a day of rest.

"I don't need to sit down. I'm fine."

"Jared, are you going to be a difficult patient or are you going to listen to me?"

"You're a pediatrician, right?"

"Yes."

"Well, kids may need a rest, but a man doesn't."

Alex laughed so hard she bent over, grabbing her sides. "Men, my dear Jared, are the biggest kids of all. You'll take my advice or I'll strap you down in that chair."

"You and what army?"

"I don't need an army. Remember, I got you into the house by myself, didn't I?"

He looked at her, knitting his eyebrows. His gaze scrutinized her arms and legs, trying to assess her strength.

"I'm stronger than I look."

"Apparently."

"Will you behave and stay put while I check on the road?"

"Yes, Doctor."

"Thanks. I don't want to come back and see you've fallen and undone my fancy embroidery."

Jared laughed a deep, barrel-chested laugh. Alex loved the sound, so warm and comforting. *Watch yourself, Alex, you're going to fall for this man if you're not careful.* "I'll be back as soon as possible."

"Be cautious, okay?" Jared grabbed her hand.

His touch was electric. She squeezed his hand, trying to counter the emotional charge he was giving her. "I will." Pulling away, she mentally switched gears;

she needed to get him to the hospital.

She blinked her eyes against the bright sun. The sky was a rich blue, laced with fleeting, pure white clouds. At the sight of her Bronco, a sick feeling washed over her. Something had smashed her rear window. She examined the car more closely. A chunk of brick, about the size of her palm, lay on the backseat. The bits of glass seemed to be contained to the rear of the car. But as a precaution, she ran her hands across the driver's seat. The thought of sitting on a piece of glass was painful enough, but the prospect of having it extracted even more embarrassing. The seat was clear. She made a mental note to check the other one before Jared sat in it.

The long drive out to the main road was littered with small branches and tons of leaves. Slowly, she worked her way through the debris. Occasionally, some larger limbs blocked her path. Each time she encountered one, she would get out and move it over to the side.

A large tree with a trunk nearly a foot in diameter lay completely across the dirt road. Spotting a house through the trees, she turned off the Bronco and headed through the woods. She found a middle-aged man working in his yard. "Excuse me. I'm Dr. Tucker. I'm staying in the Trainers' home this winter. I need some help. There's a fallen tree in the road and I need to get Jared Madeiras to the hospital."

"Is Jared okay? How bad is he?"

"He's fine, I think. He was hit in the head by a tree limb last night. I've treated the wound, but I would like to have X-rays done."

"Let me grab my chain saw and my boys. We'll have the tree moved in a few minutes. Where is it?"

Alex turned and pointed to her Bronco. "Just in front of my car."

"Okay, the rest of the road is clear. We'll take care of that. You go back and get Jared. Hopefully, by the time you get back, we'll have enough of it clear for you to pass."

"Thanks, I really appreciate this."

"No problem. Anything for Jared."

Alex smiled. She wondered if that meant if someone else were injured he wouldn't be so quick to help, but she tossed the thought aside. From her experience so far, these islanders didn't have a problem lending a hand.

Back at the house she found Jared asleep in the chair. His face, even with its day-old stubble, stirred in her a longing to reach out and caress him. Resisting the urge, she simply placed her hand on his shoulders. "Jared, the road is clear."

He snapped his eyes open. The corners of his lids crinkled in the hint of a smile. Her palm suddenly warmed, and she pulled it off of his strong muscular frame as if it would catch on fire.

"Okay. There weren't any branches in the road?"

"A few. The smaller ones I moved. Some of the neighbors are removing a tree."

"Which neighbors?"

"I'm not sure. I didn't get their names."

"Doesn't matter, I'll find out later."

"Let's get that head of yours examined." *And maybe my own. Goodness, I'm falling for this man, and fast.*

※

Jared nodded in and out during the trip to the hospital. He was fine, he knew he was, just tired and weak. He figured it was due to the amount of blood he lost. Somehow, he wasn't quite sure how, Alex had him change his shirt, or maybe she had done it. That reminded him of her hands on his shoulders moments before they left the house, waking him with the searing awareness of her touch. He needed to guard himself. She was too captivating. He was falling for this woman.

The hospital was in chaos, so many people, so many needs. He watched as Alex gave a hand helping with the emergency patients. He marveled at her care and compassion, and her professionalism, all embodied in a delicate female frame. Rolling his eyes away from Alex, he realized he needed to get his mind off of her. Moment by moment, movement by movement, she was drawing him into her web. *I won't do it. I'll not allow another in. Too much heartache. I can't go through that again, Lord. Help me keep her at bay.*

Two hours went by before his X-rays. He wondered if it would show what was wrong with his thinking, letting a woman get under his skin. How could he open his heart to a woman, to anyone? The mere thought made him nervous. She was his neighbor. That made for further complications. They would be seeing each other on a daily basis. Panic infused his body. His torso stiffened. *How on earth am I going to keep from falling in love with her?* Every time he caught a glimpse of her, he was drawn into her snare. With a hopeless sigh, he tossed down the magazine he had been trying to read. *Oh, Lord, give me strength. I'm not sure I can endure this test. The woman sets my mind a-buzzing. I need help here, Lord.*

After the X-rays, which showed no internal bleeding and no fractures, he was ready to go home. But Alex wasn't. She was needed here. He loved how she worked. So careful and tender with her hands. She really did have a wonderful bedside manner, especially with the children, helping them, calming them down. She was a natural. "Alex, can I drive home? I'll come back and get you. There's nothing I can do here."

"Actually there is, Jared, if you want to lend a hand."

"What can I do? I'm no doctor."

"Let me show you." Alex led him to the entrance. "See all these people? They need to be registered and signed in. As you can see, the folks here are working their fastest, but the hospital is packed."

Jared nodded, not quite sure what she was getting at. She knocked on the window of one of the registrars. "Excuse me, I've got a volunteer here who is will-ing to lend a hand with light stuff. He has a head wound, so no lifting, okay?"

The woman was surprised, but she accepted the doctor's offer.

"She'll tell you what to do," Alex told Jared. "I'll be in the ER."

"Okay. Alex, you're. . ." He cut himself off; what was he going to tell her? She's a great doctor? Or her heart was so tender and loving to people?

Jared worked for several hours until weariness overtook him. He stretched and rubbed the back of his neck, figuring if he was tired, Alex must be also. The number of new patients coming in had dropped considerably in the past hour. "Melissa, I'm going to find Dr. Tucker and take her home. The woman has been up all night taking care of me, and now she's worked almost another six hours straight in the ER."

"Sounds good, Jared. Thanks for your help."

"You're welcome, no problem."

Jared searched the ER and found Alex leaning against a wall with her eyes closed. "Alex?"

"Jared. How are you feeling?" She stood erect and appeared to be ready to go back to work.

"Fine, but you're exhausted. I'm taking you home."

"I really should stay and help."

Her shoulders slumped. She was tired and he knew it. "No, you've been help-ing enough. Now you're exhausted, so you are going home. That's an order, Doc."

"Aye-aye, Captain," she said with a mock salute.

Alex said her good-byes and the staff thanked her for her help. The hospi-tal administrator gushed over her so with his appreciation that Jared eyed him suspiciously. Was he hitting on her? Alex offered her phone number, informing him how long she would be in the area and suggesting that if they found them-selves short sometime to give her a call.

"I'm driving," Jared insisted as they walked through the parking lot.

Alex tossed him the keys. "Sounds like the Jared I know. You must be feel-ing better."

"Must be." There was no way he was going to tell her how protective he felt of her. He knew she must be dead on her feet.

As he drove up the island, she fell asleep almost immediately. He watched the tension ebb from her body. She was an altogether desirable woman. The rest of the trip he glued his eyes to the road. Refusing to look at her was the only safe way to keep his thoughts in check.

"Wake up, Alex, we're home."

Chapter 8

The annoying sound of an engine made Alex cringe under the covers. Sunlight poured through the window. "Sunlight?" She strained through closed lids at the window. The plywood had been removed. *When did Jared take them off?* she wondered. Moaning, her feet hit the floor. The irritating noise outside continued to grate on her nerves. "Why can't the man simply wait until someone is up and awake?" she mumbled, heading into the bathroom.

A shower, a nice hot shower. Her mumbling turned to a whine. The tub was still full of water. There was no power, there would be no shower. She boiled some water and proceeded with a sponge bath. "Dear Lord, thank You that I was born in the twentieth century. Would You mind terribly hurrying along those repairmen?"

After dressing, she noticed every window was unboarded. Certain it was Jared making that irritating noise, she went outside to track down the source of her discontent.

Turning off the chain saw, he called out to her. "Hi! Sleep well?"

"Until a few minutes ago. What on earth are you doing making all that racket?"

"I'm cleaning up after the storm. Sorry I woke you, but it is noon."

"Noon? Don't tell me I slept the morning away."

"Yup. Alex, I need to take care of this tree in order to repair the Trainers' roof."

"Of course. Did you have breakfast?"

"Yes. But some lunch would hit the spot."

"Give me fifteen minutes. I'll fix something, okay? By the way, how's the head?"

"Fine. I'll be in shortly." Jared yanked the pull rope and the chain saw engine sputtered back to life, settling into a low droning sound when he placed it on a log. Somehow it wasn't as annoying now that she knew what he was doing.

Alex marveled she had slept so long and remembered the sleepless night before. She had worked on adrenaline at the hospital until Jared had insisted, thankfully, on taking her home.

Lunch was simple fare—some thick, chunky soup, bread and butter, instant orange juice—calculated for Jared's hearty appetite, she hoped.

He knocked and came through the door. Maybe the man would never learn to just wait. On the other hand, it didn't bother her like before. She knew him, trusted him, and certainly wasn't afraid of him. He washed up in the bathroom and joined her at the table.

Linking their hands in prayer, Jared thanked God for His protection and their many blessings.

"How's your boat?" Alex asked, stirring her soup to cool it.

"Considering the storm, not too bad. There are some boards that will need to be replaced. Some sanding too. The wind really pelted the stern—it's pitted in places."

"Can I help?"

"Sure, I never turn down an extra set of hands."

"What about the roof?"

"The damage up there is pretty superficial, but if you wouldn't mind being a gopher, it would speed up the process."

"A gopher?"

Jared grinned. "Yeah, go for this, go for that."

"I'm probably the only gopher with an MD."

"I like educated gophers," he smirked.

"You're bad." Her heart warmed.

"Seriously, though, you could save me time, especially if I don't have to go up and down the ladder so often."

"I don't mind lending a hand. Besides, growing up on the farm teaches you a lot about humility."

"How's that?" Jared sopped up the last of his soup with his bread.

"Well, nothing like taking care of manure to put you in your own place." *Maybe I shouldn't have mentioned manure at the dinner table,* she worried. At home it was easy to have this kind of table discussion, but would Jared take offense to it?

"Suppose so. So you grew up on a farm?"

Alex released her breath, unaware she had been holding it in. "I thought I told you."

"Nope, learning something new about you every day." Jared got up from the table and carried his bowl and cup to the sink.

Alex followed, discussing growing up on a farm, what it was like to get up with the chickens and feed the animals before you fed yourself.

Jared's work on the roof went quickly with her passing along the items he needed. She found she liked being his gopher. There was something special about helping him.

※

He ripped off the last of the broken shingles. Until they had power, he couldn't cut out the damaged section in the plywood. Well, he could, but he didn't want to take all day doing it. *Tomorrow the power should be back on,* he reasoned.

"Alex, hand me that tarp."

"Sure."

She hadn't complained once. The woman was not ashamed of hard work,

173

not at the hospital and not here working beside him. She never let up, but worked diligently.

"That should hold until we have power. You still up for helping with the boat?"

"Sure."

"Great," Jared said, stepping off the ladder.

The woman was nothing less than amazing. More than her beauty was playing havoc with his senses now; her inner beauty, who she was as a person, was so different from his first impressions. Not that he blamed her any longer for being upset that a man, a stranger, had barged in on her. *That was enough to unnerve anyone,* he supposed.

His stomach knotted as the image of his weather-beaten ship stood before him. True, he had seen it last night after they returned from the hospital, but in the light of day. . . He sighed.

Alexandria placed her hand on his forearm. "You can rebuild, Jared, and I'll help you."

"I know, but it's hard when you've given so much of your time and effort and have to regroup and try again."

"I understand. I had a case once where the child was extremely sick. She would start to gain ground, then would fall back and we would try other meds, other treatments, repeating the process. I tested that poor child for everything. I even sent my notes to some of the best specialists. In the end it was simply a case of waiting it out and much, much prayer. God, after all, is still the great physician."

"Let's hope we don't have another storm this season. I'd hate to have to repeat the process again."

The music of her laughter, the warmth of her hand, eased the loss of his hard work.

"Where do we begin?" she asked timidly.

Taking in a deep breath and letting it out slowly, he walked toward the battered hull. "First we need to clean out the boathouse and get rid of all this sand and debris."

They worked for hours sweeping, shoveling, removing everything under the sun that didn't belong. They worked up a sweat.

"Are you thirsty?" she asked.

"Parched!"

"How about if I run up to the house and bring us something to drink?"

"Sounds like a plan. If we still have a two-liter of soda, bring a bottle down."

"Sure."

As Alex left, Jared ran to his cottage to gather his tools. It was time to rip off the broken boards. Since the power was still out, he left the power tools in the house. He returned to the boathouse and pulled out his crowbar, a cat's paw, and a hammer. Taking the crowbar, he worked to pull a plank off the ribs he had adhered it to. Several planks had been split due to flying debris.

"Here ya go, Jared. I even chipped some ice for the drinks."

"Great, thanks."

They sat outside the boathouse sipping their cold drinks.

"What's that?" Alex pointed toward the ocean.

Jared followed her finger to a boxed crate on the shore.

"That, my dear, may be tonight's supper. Let's go see."

"What is it?"

"It's a lobster pot." Sure enough, there was one good-sized lobster in it. "Do you like lobster?"

"Yes, but I wouldn't have a clue how to cook it."

"I'll cook the lobster. You can handle the rest of the dinner."

"Sounds fine with me. Tell me how this works."

He knelt down beside the lobster trap. "See the netting on this end?"

Alex nodded.

"Well, lobsters can swim. They swim through this opening that you see gets narrower deeper inside the pot. The bait is tied down here, in the center of the pot. . .see that spike?"

She nodded again, her eyes wide with interest. *The woman has an incredible appetite for knowledge*, he thought.

"Now you see this second net. Well, as the lobster feeds on the bait, it will work its body around and make its way backward into the opening of the second net. Then it falls into the area where you see the lobster is now."

"Why don't they just swim out?"

"Sometimes they do, but most of the time their big claws are hard to maneuver. Lobsters walk and feed on the ocean floor. Like crabs, they are scavengers."

"So how do these traps stay on the bottom—I mean wood floats, right?"

"Yes. Take a look at the center of the trap where the bait is tied down. That's a concrete ballast. It's enough weight to keep a pot on the bottom, most of the time. Once in awhile a storm like the one we had moves them."

"So those buoys in the water are all lobster pots?" Alex pointed to the various small buoys bobbing up and down on the surface of the water.

"Right. Each lobsterman is assigned colors and he paints his buoys accordingly."

"It seems like it would be very easy to steal someone's lobsters. I don't see any kind of police on the water."

"The coast guard are the 'police'; however, most men look out for each other. Sort of a code of honor. Say, Joe is fishing his pots and sees a stranger fishing others. He'll report it. Most have radios on their boats. For the few that don't, they'll memorize the numbers and get as good a description of the poacher as possible."

"But I hardly see anyone out here."

"True, most guys only come once, maybe twice a week to check their pots. It takes awhile to lure the lobsters into the pot."

"This is so interesting. You said you're building your catboat to do some fishing with it. Are you planning on doing some lobstering?"

"Yes. You can't stick with one kind of fishing unless you are a deep-sea fisherman. Which I don't intend to do."

"I see."

"I need to get back to work, Alex. You don't have to; you've already helped a lot."

"No, I'll help. What do we do with the lobster?"

"Leave him in the pot. If the owner comes by today, it's his. If not, we'll have it for dinner."

"But isn't it stealing?"

"Maybe, except that is Stan's pot. He's a friend, and I'll be telling him about the pot being washed onshore and the lobster we took from it. If he wants to be reimbursed, I'll pay him for it. Although I doubt it. We grew up together."

"It seems to me most islanders know each other."

"The locals tend to. But there are quite a few folks down-island I don't know. I mean, I might know their families somewhere along the line, but not them personally."

"Well, it is a small place."

"Yup. Shall we?"

Alex marveled at the lobster pot. How ingenious. She wondered who developed the trap. She turned to the ribbed hull of the catboat Jared was building, noticing the pitting the sand had done to the stern; the planks had been cracked from the storm. She longed to help but was no carpenter. Cleaning was the easy part, but to do much more she didn't think was possible for her. "What can I do now, Jared?"

"Let's get the baths up and running."

"How are they fueled?"

"Propane. Let me check the lines before I fire them up. I haven't smelled any gas, have you?"

"No."

She watch Jared lie down on the ground, reaching under the long wooden pots he called baths. She had already learned from him that the steaming actually sped up the process of soaking the wood so it could be shaped. He worked his way to the end and repeated the process on the other bath. He followed the lines to the back wall and headed back to the opening. "Where are you going?" she asked him.

"The tanks are on the back of the building. I need to check the connections, plus turn on the tanks. I turned them off for the storm."

"Oh." Embarrassed, she chastised herself. *Why did I have an uneasiness about him leaving my side? Why did I try to get back here so quickly with the drinks? Why do I like just being in this man's presence? This is not good. This is how mistakes are made.*

Jared came back into the boathouse. His body, his strength, and his mind were all the things Alex had hoped for in a man. But wasn't she here to learn to adjust to never having a man in her life? To accept God's will for the single life? She forced her eyes toward the floor, closed them, and prayed, *Oh Lord, give me strength.*

"Are you okay, Alex?"

She swallowed. "Yes."

"You sure?"

"I'm fine, Jared. Tell me what to do."

"Well, while I'm soaking up some boards, we could be sanding some of the rough spots caused by the sand."

"Okay, where's the sandpaper?"

Jared walked to his workbench and opened a drawer, pulling out some sheets. "Here, you can start with this." He ripped the paper in two and folded each half into thirds, giving her a small rectangle of paper to work with. After Jared pointed out where and how she should sand, she went straight to work.

Jared fired up the baths and placed a couple of planks in each tank. He grabbed the other piece of sandpaper and started sanding also.

They worked with no words spoken between them. Alex fought to concentrate on the sanding, but all she could do was think about Jared, about the strength in his fingers, about the gentleness he managed to get out of such powerful hands.

"Ouch."

"What's the matter?"

"My eye, I think I got sawdust in it."

"Let me see."

He wiped his hands on his jeans and cupped her face. She wanted to melt into his arms.

"Close your eyes gently, not tight."

Alex obeyed.

Jared's warm breath flowed over her eyelids as he blew gently. *What on earth is he doing? Driving me crazy, that's what. No, he's just removing the dust. Nothing more. Calm down, Alex, you are on sensory overload here.*

"Which eye?"

"My right."

He eased the lid open. She kept the other eye closed. She couldn't bear seeing him up close like this. They were too close; she was too captivated. He was too near; she was too attracted.

"Alex, has anyone ever told you what beautiful eyes you have?"

Oh no. She couldn't afford to hear this, not now, not when she was so vulnerable, when she was about to lose all her self-control. "No."

"They're as blue as the Caribbean, glistening in the sun."

Alex opened her eyes now. Jared's fingers caressed her face, his thumbs working their way to her lips. Gaining her voice, she spoke. "Your eyes are darker than mine, more like the Atlantic behind us."

As his eyes searched hers, her body tingled. He was going to kiss her—or was she going to kiss him? It didn't matter; they both moved toward each other. All the passion and pent-up desires from days of longing were caught in the sweetness of his embrace. His lips were soft and tender, sweet as honeycomb.

Chapter 9

Com Electric says just about everyone's power has been restored on the cape and islands after the nor'easter. . . ."

The blast of the radio startled Alex as it unexpectedly surged to life. Jared pulled away and Alex jumped back. It wasn't just the radio that frightened her. His kiss burned on her lips. Never had she responded to a man before in that way. Heat rose in her cheeks as she searched for something to focus on, anything but Jared. Why had she kissed him? Why had he kissed her? It was a mistake, a definite mistake. She would never let that happen again.

Jared left her side in haste, as if lightning were about to strike. He turned off the radio; the silence between them was deafening. How could she have let physical desires control her so? Alex's stomach knotted.

"Alex."

She turned.

"I–I. . ."

"I'm sorry too, Jared. It won't happen again. I think I better check the house and see what was left on when the power went out."

"Sure. But we need to talk."

"Later." She couldn't deal with her own feelings now, how could she possibly deal with his? What were his feelings? Why had he kissed her? Could he possibly be attracted to her? Dazed, she walked up the hill.

The house was well lit, the stereo tuned to the same news station as outside. Relief washed over her as she heard the newscaster report that no deaths were caused by the storm. She hadn't realized how much concern she felt over the elderly gentleman she had worked on at the hospital the day before. Granted, she only stabilized him, the surgeons were the heroes, but she was glad to know he had made it through the night. The old man's neighbors had brought him in and informed his family. She was falling in love with this place and its people, she realized. She liked being in a small community.

She liked it here, yes, but it was tempting too. Maybe she had never had to deal with temptation before because she was always busy, busy with work, busy with school, busy with chores. When had she even had a chance to fall for someone? Maybe this sabbatical wasn't such a good idea after all. Maybe this sabbatical was the very thing that was wrong with trying to understand God's obvious plan for her life. After all, she was running away from her life, her real life, just by being here.

Besides, as long as she was here, Jared would be too real, too present. Every day she would see him. Every day she would be confronted with temptation. This was not good. Maybe she should pack it up and move back to Kansas. She had already found out so much about her distant relatives and their lives on the Vineyard in the 1800s. It wasn't like she had to stay.

Confused and exhausted, she sat down in a chair and attempted to pray. "Oh, Father God, what just happened? Why am I so attracted to this man? How can I survive this test?" She reached for her Bible and searched the Scriptures, praying, asking for God to show her answers to her many questions. She read about lust, she read about marriage, she read about death, and about an incredible battle in the Old Testament. Praying and reading, she searched for answers, but nothing came. She was still as lost and confused as when she sat down to pray.

"A hot shower, I can finally have a hot shower!" Alex got up and hurried to the bathroom, turned on the tap, and stripped off her clothes so fast, as if it had been a year since her last shower. Stepping into the steaming stream, she tilted her head back. The warm water poured over her chestnut brown hair, and she sighed with content over the delicious pleasure. She cleansed her hair of the grease and oils of several days, working a rich lather of shampoo soothingly with her fingers. Massaging her scalp, she rinsed the suds from her hair as Jared's kiss flooded back to mind.

"Oh dear." Alex turned the hot water off and stood under the stream of now cold water.

❧

Jared pounded his fist to the hull. "Why did I kiss her?" *She obviously wanted to be kissed. Maybe that was it, she was tempting me.* No, he knew better than that. Alex had been plaguing his mind since she arrived. The woman was the only one to break through the past, to get beyond the memory of Hannah. He shouldn't have kissed her; he knew better. *I'm never getting married. I promised myself I'd never do that.*

Why did I promise that? "Because you don't want to feel the pain of another loss," he argued with himself.

We don't know each other, so why that kiss? She's made it clear she's not interested—or has she? The way she stares at me when she thinks I'm not looking, a man would have to be blind not to notice. But why does it feel so good to have her look at me that way?

Jared walked to his cottage. He needed to talk to her. He had wanted to talk immediately, not that he knew what to say, but she left. What was he going to say, though? *Gee, Alex, sorry about the kiss, you're just too enchanting! Oh, I got it, "too beguiling." No, that wouldn't work.* Jared raked his fingers through his hair. The sawdust, dirt, and grime from the past few days had taken their toll. Time for a shower.

His shower was both relaxing and unnerving at the same time. He couldn't shake his need to talk to her.

He slammed his hand to his forehead: the lobster! He rushed down the shore, pulled the pot out of the water, and retrieved the shellfish. "You, Sir," he said, holding it up in the air, "are my peace offering."

With lobster in hand, he gained ground in seconds. His large, bold strides worked their way up the hill and onto her deck. His knock was timid at first; the second, bolder.

He studied his shoes. *What am I going to say?*

"Jared."

He held the lobster up. "The three of us had a date."

Her cheeks flamed.

"Alex, we need to talk, please let me in."

She stepped aside. He walked past her, ever so careful that their bodies not touch.

"First, let's make dinner. We can talk while we eat."

"Okay."

Jared wasn't comfortable with the cat and mouse game they played with each other during the dinner preparations, but he wasn't ready to broach the subject of their kiss anymore than Alex was.

"The lobster smells great." Alex leaned over the red, fully steamed lobster.

"Can't forget the butter." A step and a half later, Jared was at the stove grabbing the small pan in which he had melted butter. He poured it into a small, clear custard dish and placed it on the table.

Alex had made some potatoes au gratin and cooked up several frozen vegetables, since they had partially thawed during the power shortage.

When they had sat down at the table, Jared didn't attempt to take Alex's hand for the prayer. Instead they clasped their own hands and bowed their heads. "Father, thank You for Your bounty and we ask that You bless this food to our bodies. In Jesus' name, Amen." *And, Lord, bless our conversation also*, he added silently.

He broke up the lobster, dividing it equally. She passed him some potatoes. He took a smaller portion than usual. Was he going to be able to eat? His throat felt constricted.

"Alex, I'm sorry I was so forward today," he breathed. *That wasn't so bad now, was it? Nope, heart surgery would have been easier.*

Her eyes assaulted him. "We were both guilty."

"Maybe so, but I'm the man, I'm responsible."

"It's the twenty-first century, Jared, equal pay for equal work. In other words, we are equally responsible for our own actions."

"Alex, don't take this wrong, but I don't want to get involved."

"Neither do I."

"What?" *Why wouldn't she want to get involved with me?* Never had he imagined that someone wouldn't want to. All the women before he had to fight off with a stick. Well, maybe not a stick, but still, this was different. It wasn't vanity. At least he didn't think it was. He was a fairly attractive man, or so he had been led to believe.

"Jared." She placed her fork on her plate and clasped her hands. "I came here to sort out my life. I believe God has called me to be a single woman. I don't see marriage in my future."

"Why?" Granted, he wasn't going to be her husband, but the woman had a lot to offer a man. It would be a shame for her to live her life single. At least he had a good reason why he would remain single.

"It's like I said, I believe God is leading me that way."

"How do you know?"

"Look at me, Jared. I'm thirty-five years old. My biological clock is ticking. . . ." She cut herself off.

There was more, he knew it, but it wasn't really his business to pry, was it? "Alex, you can't go second-guessing God."

"I'm not. I'm accepting or trying to accept His will for me."

He felt her reasoning was askew, but how could he tell her? "I don't see that, but it's your life. I really don't know you all that well, so I'll leave it alone. As for me, well there are reasons why I can't get involved."

"What are they?"

Jared swallowed hard. "I was engaged once."

"What happened?"

"She died. She died three days before the wedding."

"Oh, Jared, I'm so sorry." Alex's heart lurched. She had known there were things in his past, but she had never guessed that. "Tell me, what happened?"

"Hannah had an aneurysm in her brain."

Alex closed her eyes. She knew what that was, she knew the pain, the process. "I'm sorry," she whispered.

"I blamed God for taking Hannah away from me. Then not too many years later, I lost both my parents in a freak accident."

She took his hand; she had to comfort him in some way.

"When I was lost at sea, I made peace with God about my losses, but I could never open myself up to another again. I know I could never survive another loss."

And he thinks my reasons for believing God wanting me single are wrong. "Jared, you won't necessarily lose the next person you love."

"Maybe. I can't take the risk. So you see, no matter how attracted I may be to you or you may be to me, we can never be anything more than friends."

He's attracted to me. Alex squelched a smile. "Tell me, are you better than Job?"

"What?"

"You know, Job, in the Bible."

"I know who you're talking about. I just don't see the connection."

"Well, the way I see it, your life, in a way, was like Job's. You had Hannah, your parents, life was going well. Then your world crashes in. You lose Hannah, you lose your parents, you're lost at sea, the sun and the salt eating away at your flesh. All sounds very familiar to me."

Jared simply raised his right eyebrow. He was definitely not liking where she was going with this.

"Don't you see, after the time of testing, God provided Job with a new family. He can do the same for you. If you allow Him."

He didn't speak for several moments, or was it minutes? Time seemed to be dragging by.

"Jared?"

"Sorry, I was thinking. Maybe, but I'm not ready."

"How long ago did Hannah die?" It had to be some time ago, she knew; even the shipwreck was over five years back.

"Fourteen years ago."

"Well, maybe it's time."

"Maybe, but I'm not ready."

"Fair enough."

"Alex, I like you, I like you a lot. You fascinate me in more ways than I can put into words but I, we, well, we can't get involved."

"I agree." She smiled. "I wasn't saying you and I should get involved, you know. Only that you shouldn't be closed to the possibility with *anyone*."

He shrugged, absorbing her words. "But, I don't want to lose our friendship. I'm getting used to having someone around. I love your hunger for learning new things."

He loves something about me, at least. What does it matter? You're not going to allow yourself to fall for this man either. Relax, Alex, keep this in perspective. "I want us to be friends too."

"So, how do we do this?"

"We keep our hands to ourselves?" *And definitely our lips.* The kiss came flooding back to her memory; she fought it down.

"Agreed."

"We're adults, Jared. This shouldn't be a problem." Who was she trying to kid? Every ounce of her being wanted to get to know the man beside her. It was wrong to want that, she knew. Being single forever, she couldn't help but hope she was adult enough to keep her impulses under control with God's help.

His smile nervously crept up his cheek. *Maybe he's not sure he can handle his emotional responses, like me.* He nodded his head but didn't say a word.

Alex rose to clear the dinner dishes. "The lobster was great, Jared, thanks."

"Welcome. That reminds me, I should call Stan."

"You're welcome to use my phone if it's working, of course."

Jared walked over to the kitchen phone. "It's activated."

Alex nodded and continued cleaning up the dishes. Jared helped while he held the phone to his ear by his shoulder. She tried not to listen, but his easy conversation with his friend was obvious. There was so much about him that intrigued her.

She filled the sink with hot soapy water and began to wash. Jared stepped up to the sink beside her and dried. He placed each dish, glass, silverware, and pot into its rightful spot. *How often had he been in this house?* she wondered. He was so at home here.

"Brad and Phyllis!" she nearly shouted.

"What?" Jared said as he hung up the phone.

"Brad and Phyllis must be going nuts. I'm sure they heard about the storm."

"I better call them." Jared tapped out the Trainers' number.

"Brad, it's Jared. Fine. Some, a little to the roof, but I'll have that repaired in no time." Jared's hand touched his wound. Alex's stomach tightened, her knees locked. She had forgotten about his injuries. Maybe tonight wasn't such a good night to discuss their kiss.

"Alex is fine. The boat? Nothing that can't be redone. . . . Thanks, hopefully by spring."

Jared sat down at the table. "No, I hadn't heard that."

Alex made her way to her room; it was too easy to eavesdrop. After all, she needed a break from Jared. He couldn't seem to move or say anything that didn't awaken senses. *Lord, this is going to be the hardest test You've ever put me through. Please give me the strength and grace to endure.*

"Alex!" Jared hollered. His hand was cupped over the mouthpiece when she came back in the room. "Brad wants to speak with you. I'm going home. I'll see you tomorrow, okay?"

She nodded, then took the phone. "Hi, Brad, how's everyone?"

❧

Jared was out the door and catching his breath as the chill of the evening air hit him in the chest. He had to work out. Days had passed since his last workout, and his body craved the exercise. He didn't exercise by going to a gym; he simply did push-ups and pull-ups, one-handed of course.

At his cottage he worked his muscles until they ached. It felt good, the blood pumping through his veins, his muscles bulging in all the right places. Although never having competed, he had been tempted a time or two. But his father's caution about vanity and temptation of worldly pursuits had always kept him away.

His thoughts wandered to the house up the hill, to a certain woman with Caribbean-blue eyes and chestnut hair. *Does she like how I look? Stop it, Jared, this is dangerous territory*, he told himself. He remembered her fingers tentatively exploring his shoulders. "Oh, Lord, Alex said we are adults and can handle this. I'm not so sure. I don't think the temptation to drink ocean water while I was stranded was a greater temptation than to touch that woman's sweet and wonderful lips. Why, Lord? Why did You put her in my path?"

God didn't seem to be answering.

The sheen of sweat over his body spoke of the need for a second shower. Later, dressed in his pajama bottoms, he took out his Bible and read his daily reading. After those passages, he moved over to the Book of Job and began to read. *Could it be God is testing me as He tested Job? No, I'm not worthy, not nearly as righteous as Job.* He closed his eyes in prayer, his Bible open across his lap. His mind whirled with questions and confusion, with Scripture and prayer. His stomach knotted as Alex's comparison of him with Job sprang to life again.

"Am I ready to trust God again?"

Chapter 10

For the next month, Alex and Jared maintained minimal contact with each other. They waved or spoke briefly about the weather and other trivial things. It was November now, early winter was settling in, and the holidays were around the corner. Alex would soon be flying home for a month. She had promised her parents she would return and spend the holidays with them.

In spite of the fact that she and Jared weren't really talking, she didn't want to leave him alone for the holidays. How could she approach this? Maybe she should stay? No, she couldn't; she promised her folks. She wrapped a warm wool sweater around her and headed to the boathouse.

"Hi." She marveled at all the work Jared had accomplished on the boat. The hull was finished. He was inside the boat and working below.

"Hi."

"I was wondering what you were doing for the holidays?"

"Same as always. I go off the island and spend it with my sister and her family."

"Oh, okay." *See, he doesn't need you*, she chastised herself.

"What about yourself?"

"I'm flying back to Kansas."

"I thought you were staying for a year."

"I am, but I promised my folks I'd return for the holidays."

"So you're coming back?"

She nodded. Maybe he was still interested in her friendship. "Jared, can we go out to dinner somewhere? Not a date, just as friends. I've missed your company."

"I've missed yours too. And, yeah, dinner sounds fine. I know a few nice restaurants."

"I'm sure you do." She laughed and wagged her head. Man, did she miss his humor. "So what's a good time for you?"

"How's six sound?"

"Sounds great." She waved a hand at the boat. "She's looking good, Jared. When do you hope to launch her?" She rubbed her hand across the stern.

"Not until spring. I'm hoping to get the hull painted before the temps get below freezing, then during the winter I'll work on the galley."

"Too bad this wall was missing—you could have a heater in here."

"I may put up a tarp, depends on the winter. Some are mild, some are bitter cold. How's your research going?"

"Well, I've read just about everything in the historical society on the Luces and the early 1800s. I'm thinking when I return I'll concentrate on the island after Elizabeth Luce O'Connor left."

"So the island itself is interesting you now?"

"Yup, it's a fascinating place. In Kansas our history only goes back to the 1850s. There are a few records of the Indians and early explorers, but not nearly enough to quench my appetite for history. Here it goes back three hundred and fifty years and more."

"Well, when you're on your next search of island history, remind me to tell you about the time the entire island population became pirates."

"Pirates?"

"Yup, I came across it when I was researching various ships. It's a really funny story."

"You've got my curiosity piqued. How about telling me over dinner?"

"Sounds like a plan. I'll pick you up at six, okay?"

❧

Jared arrived promptly at six. He knocked on the door and waited, timid about his approach to her. *We need to take this slow and easy*, he thought. "Ready?"

"Most of the way. I'm trying to decide if I need my long wool coat or my down jacket."

"It's a little chilly but still a nice night. Where we are going to eat is down-island and away from the shore, much warmer."

"Where are we going?"

"Vineyard Haven, a place called Louis's. Good food." *And no romantic atmosphere*, he said to himself. *The place will be safe.*

Alex settled on her coat and hung the jacket back up. "Ready."

"Great." Jared held the door open for her, then thought twice about it. He saw Alex raise her eyebrows. "My momma raised me to be a gentleman. Sorry."

"I'll have to thank your momma when I get to heaven. Being a gentleman is a lost art today, I'm afraid."

"It's hard. So many women would just as soon take your head off than find out you hold the door for older men and children too."

"I know. I have a couple of friends like that. Funny, deep down, I think many of them like men opening the door for them. They think of themselves as special in a man's eye just by virtue of being a woman."

"Well, my dear, you are the weaker sex and we are to treat you with respect. What's that old saying? God didn't take woman out of Adam's foot so that she was beneath him, nor out of his head so that she was above him, but out of his rib so that she was equal but close to his heart."

"I like that. So tell me about Louis's."

"It's in what used to be a residential home. The food's great. He's open year-round, which makes him popular, and the prices are reasonable."

Alex nodded her head. She was beautiful, but he stayed in control. It was nice having her riding beside him, talking with him. It had been too long. They both had not made much effort to talk since the day they shared that kiss. The memory of it still seared his lips. But he was in control now; he was certain of it.

"When do I get to hear about the pirate story?"

"Hmm, let's savor it over dinner."

"Oh, Jared, you can be such a tease when you want to. I'm dying to hear about this, and you know it."

"Maybe." Yes he did know it, and he was teasing her, but he felt the story would be great dinner conversation and would keep them on calm waters.

"How long has your family been on the Vineyard?" Her voice was steady but not angry.

"You know, I've never done a genealogy on my family. I know my mom was a Norton, and there are Nortons quite a ways back. I'm not sure about the Madeiras line, though."

"I've long since moved in my research from direct descendants to some aunts, uncles, and cousins. It's really fascinating. By the way, Nancy Luce, the one with the chickens, was a distant cousin."

"I'm sure that's a relief. You wouldn't want craziness running through your blood now, would you?" He winked.

"You know, she wasn't crazy, just eccentric."

"Eccentric, my dear, was the term once used to describe family members with Alzheimer's and other forms of dementia."

"True, but she seemed to have the rest of her faculties in place. Just those silly chickens were unusual."

"She must have been lonely. Who else have you found out about?"

"Well, there was a Jonathan Luce who loved to dress in very rich clothing. When he traveled to Boston, they referred to him as Count Luce because of his finery."

"So vanity runs in your family lines."

"He probably got it from Captain Thomas's wife. She spoke of her husband as 'merely the son of a woodcutter' and always spoke of him as 'the Captain.'"

"You know, the women referred to their spouses in a very formal way when they were in public and even in their own homes in front of the children. Familiarity with one's spouse, calling him by his first name, for example, was for the bedroom only." *Bedroom, oops! What was I thinking? I shouldn't have referred to that.* Jared concentrated on the road ahead of him. The moon was out, the sky was clear; hardly anyone was out tonight.

"I know, so strange, so different from our culture today. My parents showed their affection to each other in front of the kids, lots of kisses and hugs."

"Same with mine. Speaking of folks, when will you be seeing yours?" There, back to a safe subject.

"I leave a couple of days before Thanksgiving."

"Need a ride to the airport? I'll be glad to take you—that way you won't have to leave your car parked there for a month."

"I may take you up on that, thanks."

Jared pulled the car into a parking space behind the restaurant. "Here we are."

Jared led the way, careful not to wrap his arm around her as he was inclined to do. So many little things he needed to guard himself against. He could make this work, he assured himself, and opened the door to the restaurant for her.

❧

Alex was amazed; the amount of tables and chairs in the place was mind boggling. The restaurant was about half full. Smells wafting past her nostrils made her stomach gurgle and her mouth water. Jared was right, the food would be good. She noted, with relief, that it was not a romantic place. There were too many tables in one common room. She was thankful that he was trying just as hard as she was to remain friends. Nothing more, nothing less. She did so enjoy his friendship. He was such a knowledgeable man. Not at all the sort of person she had thought he was when they met the first day. How could she have ever called him a Neanderthal? She followed Jared behind a pleasant hostess to a table.

"It smells great."

"I think you'll enjoy the food."

Alex opened the menu and scanned it. She settled on the fettucini, Jared on a large steak. Once their orders were placed, she met his eyes. Did she dare ask him again about the pirates?

"Okay, okay, I see it in your eyes, you want to know about the pirates."

"Well, how about it?" *How can he read my eyes so well?* Alex stifled the growing realization of the connection between them. It was obvious, no matter how cool they played the game.

"Well, back in 1918, during World War One, there was a British ship bound for New York. It was to meet up with a caravan of other ships bringing supplies to the troops in France. This ship, the *Port Hunter*, left from Boston. As she sailed passed the Vineyard, a tugboat rammed her. I'm assuming it was foul weather, but I don't rightly know how and why a tugboat could ram the vessel. I just know it wasn't intentional."

Their drinks came. Alex took a sip of her cola. "And?"

"Well, the captain knew of the shoals off the Vineyard and ran the ship over them. This would allow for the recovery of the cargo, if not the recovery of the vessel itself."

"Sounds smart."

"It should have been. I got the account from old Stan Lair, who was a teen at the time. He had gone into town one day and saw all these British sailors. So he's looking in the harbor for their boat, but there wasn't any. He starts asking around and finds out about the ship sinking. According to Stan, it didn't take long for things to start floating up on shore."

"What kinds of things?"

"Crates full of clothing for the army, candles, mess kits, anything and everything a soldier would need."

"So what's this got to do with pirating?"

"Well, in Stan's words, somehow one of the cargo holds must have popped open and the cargo started to float. That 'somehow' must have been one of the locals. Where the boat lay on the shoals, the water was nearly waist deep if you were walking on the deck. Wouldn't take much for someone to walk in the water and pop the hold."

"No, I imagine it wouldn't. But still, pirates?"

"Hang on, Dear, there's plenty of piracy that went on. Only thing is, no one quite saw it like that. Seems the locals were taking their boats and fishing in the hold, pulling out crates, anything that would float. In some of these crates were leather vests. They'd sell them in the harbor for a buck apiece, the black leather jackets went for two dollars."

"Isn't that salvaging rights?"

"Not exactly. The company, or the government, finally sent some men to investigate. But by the time they did, all the clothing and floatable crates were long off the vessel. There were boats coming in from New Bedford to purchase the ill-gotten goods."

The waiter came with their plates and placed their meals in front of them. Alex took a mouthful of the fettucini and groaned in pleasure.

"Good, huh?"

"Wonderful. Please continue."

"Well, old Stan said he and a couple of boys later that day had heard some of the crates were floating up on shore, so they went down to check it out. There was this one old guy pulling in crates, writing his initials on them, but then a group of others hiding in the bushes took the crates from him."

"Good grief!"

"Exactly. It gets worse. Not only were they pulling things in off the shore, they were pulling them off of the boat as well. Fishing took on a whole new venue. You've heard of the illustrious 'box fish,' haven't you?"

"They tried to call it that?"

"No, that's my take on the whole thing. Back then there were about four thousand island residents. Stan said that nearly everyone got in on the act, whether it was the hauling of loot off the boat or the selling of it. He said eventually the leather coats got up to five bucks apiece."

"You're kidding."

"Nope, that's a fact. The price was so high, if you had purchased a jacket and had it drying on your line, you'd lose it. He even said that not only would your jacket be stolen, but the rest of your laundry too."

"What people will do for money. What happened when the officials came?"

"Best as I can piece it all together, the islanders all became ignorant. No one was going to tell on their neighbor or family member."

"So no one got caught?"

"Not that I saw in the records."

"That's amazing."

"They managed to recover a few small things, but nothing of significance. Stan also said that several houses were built off the profits from that boat. He called the whole island a bunch of pirates. I think he included himself right along with 'em, too."

Alex laughed. The thought of stealing someone's laundry was a hoot. "So is this Stan a relative of yours?"

"Mine? My dear, are you asking if I'm a descendant of a pirate?"

Alex pictured Jared, dressed in old sea captain clothes, the Hollywood representation of one, of course. She could imagine the bright bold colors, his shirt open, exposing his bronze chest, a sash for a belt, and him standing on the deck calling out orders. He was the captain of course in her fantasy; she smirked at her overactive imagination.

"What? What on earth is going on in that pretty little head of yours?"

"Oh nothing, just picturing pirates with swords and a captain giving orders."

"Ah-hah."

She didn't say more. She figured he'd read her mind if she let on anything else. "So were there any Luces involved with this pirating adventure?"

"I'm certain, but I couldn't tell you who."

"I'll have to look that up. Thankfully, my line left the island before this, so I'm not the descendant of any pirate."

"I see. So I'm the rogue of society because my ancestors went crazy over some ill-gotten gain?"

"Could be. Tell me, is that why salt flows through your veins?"

"That, and probably the fact that I've grown up on the water. I can't get enough of it. I was on the mainland for a few years while I attended college. It was too far inland. The only water I found was fresh. It was pretty, don't get me wrong, but it lacked a little character not having salt in it."

"I see, so salt is the essence of life."

"My dear doctor, you more than anyone must know."

"Know what?"

"How many parts saline solution we are."

He'd done it again, amazed her with his knowledge. He was right. The human body was primarily made up of saline solution. "Touché, Jared, touché."

Chapter 11

The holidays went by quickly. When the time came to leave, she hated to leave her parents, but she was anxious to get back to the Vineyard to see Jared again. She had to admit it to herself, she was in love with the man. There was no denying it—but there was no point in proclaiming it either. He was not interested in a relationship and never would be. She had to admit to her mother, who read her like a book, that she had a fondness for Jared. Even though she never said the word "love," she was certain her mother knew.

If she hadn't talked about him so often maybe her parents wouldn't have suspected anything. She explained to her mother the situation with Jared and his desires never to love again, to which her mother simply stated, "If God has destined for you two to fall in love, there will be no stopping it, no matter how hard either of you try. Stop being so foolish. At thirty-five one doesn't play games." Unfortunately, she'd had to agree with her mother, but when she thought of Jared and the possibility of him opening his heart to her, it all seemed pointless.

Maybe she should stay in Kansas. Her practice was going well. She spent some time with her patients and realized they loved Dr. Bob, and he loved them also. She missed her work, but not as much as she missed Jared.

Alex's stomach tightened as she gripped the shoulder strap of her carry-on bag and hustled through the airport. When had she fallen so hard for Jared that he was more important to her than her patients? *Oh, Lord, help me out here. I don't know what to do!*

She boarded the plane back to the Vineyard. The farms, covered with snow, with their little specks of houses and cattle, passed silently beneath her. What was she going to say to Jared when she returned? *I missed you and oh, by the way, I'm in love with you.* No, she couldn't do that. Alex chewed on a nail until the polish was off. She hadn't chewed her nails since high school. *Maybe in New York I should just turn around and go back.*

"No, it's time to grow up, face my fears, face his too."

"What, Dear?" a frumpy little old lady sitting beside her asked.

"Sorry. I was thinking to myself. I didn't realize I had spoken out loud."

The woman nodded her head and didn't pry, but she tapped Alex's hand with her own well-wrinkled, soft skin. "God will get you through, Dear. He always has for me. Sometimes, I wasn't so pleased with the length of time He took, but in the end He seemed to know what He was doing."

Alex smiled. "I suppose He does, doesn't He?"

"Yes."

"Where are you heading?" she inquired of the elderly woman. Probably going to visit her grandchildren, Alex assumed.

"Me, well I'm meeting up with an old friend. He and I used to date back in high school. His wife passed away several years back, and well, my Vincent, he died nearly ten years ago."

Alex saw the twinkle in the woman's eye. "Are you going to refire a lost love?"

"Oh goodness, I don't know, Dear. We dated, just casually. He had dreams and I had another set of dreams. My Vincent was my soulmate. We had five beautiful children together, and we now have sixteen grandchildren and a couple of great-grandchildren. Jason is an old friend. I don't see us being romantically involved. . .but you never know. Right?" She gave Alex a knowing look.

Alex blushed.

"Come on now, Dear, I may not be the pretty little thing I was when I was a teen, but when you're older, friendship is of primary importance. Sex, well it's great in a marriage, one of God's gifts. But the best part in a marriage is friendship. To have your spouse be your best friend, that's the key to a happy marriage."

"I suppose you're right. I've never married."

"Why not, Dear? You're pretty. I'm sure there were men who were interested in you."

"Oh, there were, I just didn't notice them the way a woman wants to notice her husband. At least, no one until now."

"So you've found him?"

"Yes, but he doesn't want to get involved with anyone, ever."

The elderly woman took Alex's hand into hers. "Dear, few men want to get involved; it just happens. You can't make it and he can't stop it. Love is a very strong gift from God. If this is the man, God will work it out."

"Thanks, I suppose He will. I'd given up on finding someone, figured I was to be single all my life."

"Tell me, have you read the Bible?"

"All the time." Alex grinned.

"So you're aware of what the apostle Paul says about being single as a gift from God. Tell me, has the Lord specifically called you to be single? I'm not talking feelings, I'm talking about an absolute, beyond the shadow of a doubt calling from God."

Who was this woman? How could she ask such direct questions? The heat on Alex's face started to sting. "No, I just assumed it because of my age."

"Then it's simply a case of waiting on the Lord. I realize, Dear, you are feeling your age, but our age means nothing to the Lord."

"I suppose."

"Trust me. Why do you suppose God had me sit beside you today?"

Why *had* that happened? She could have sat next to anyone and yet here was a woman who was older and wiser, who understood her fears. Having lived longer, this woman was forward and yet truthful. Obviously, this encounter was God-ordained. "Because I needed reassurance?"

"I call it encouragement. I suppose it's the gift of exhortation, but it's not like I was correcting you for going down the wrong path. Although, self-doubt is a problem. 'Trust in the LORD with all your heart,' Dear. You know the verse."

" 'And lean not on your own understanding.' "

"Yes, and 'he will make your paths straight.' I've taken many detours in my life, I'm afraid. But God has always been faithful to pull me back, showing me the right path."

"Thanks."

"Thank the Lord. So, tell me about this handsome hunk of a man that's driving you crazy."

Alex laughed.

※

Jared paced the small building known as the Martha's Vineyard Airport terminal. Her plane was supposed to be on time. It had left New York on time. The knot in the middle of his gut intensified. "Lord, please keep her safe." Twenty minutes had crawled by since her plane was scheduled to land. Tempted to inquire again, but embarrassed about being a pest, he resisted pursuing the matter. He had asked twice already. Two planes had landed since he had arrived, enough to get his hopes raised and dashed.

Jared had been miserable during Alex's absence. Never had he missed someone so much. It was funny how accustomed he was to just having her around. Her laughter, her smile, the cute little dimple on her left cheek. . . Everything about her was so vivid in his mind. He knew he was caring too much for this woman, he knew he was sinking, and yet, he still wanted to hold on. It wasn't like he wanted to get married or anything. No, he just wanted a friendship. Someone who was his confidante.

A commuter plane's wheels screeched as it landed on the tarmac in front of him. As it taxied around, he walked over to the counter. The woman behind it nodded. Hustling out the doors, he reached the gate. The plane's door slowly opened. He strained to see if Alex was on board. His heart pounded. At last, nothing stood between him and his desire to see her once again.

A smile broadened across his face. There she was, just as he had remembered her. Her long chestnut-brown hair, tropical blue eyes, and the way her smile lit up her face. He waved. She returned the gesture.

He hopped the wooden split-rail fence that made up the gate and traversed the distance between them. "Hi, let me get those bags for you."

"Thanks."

"How was your flight?" Jared slung her suitcase strap over his shoulder.

"Fine, except there was a bit of turbulence between here and New York."

"You must be exhausted—that's a long day of travel."

"I'll sleep well tonight. How are you?"

"Fine. Boy, you're a sight for sore eyes." He searched her delicate face. *Had she missed him too?* he wondered.

She rubbed the back of her neck. "Thanks, it's good to see you too."

"How many bags are we waiting for?"

"Just a couple. Did you bring my car or your truck?"

"I took yours."

"Great. I'm going to need to do some shopping before we go back."

"It's all taken care of."

"Jared?"

"It's my welcome home gift for you. Relax, enjoy. Besides, I figured I can get a meal or two out of you for it."

"You did, did you?" Her smile deepened. "Well, if you bought enough, I'm sure you can. You do have quite an appetite."

"But there isn't an ounce of fat on me, Doc. You have to admit, I don't overeat."

"Maybe. Maybe you simply exercise harder when you've pigged out."

"I'll never tell," he teased. Man, he'd missed her and the playful bantering between them. He ambled up to the luggage cart that had just been unloaded from the plane. Her bags were full, but the volume of weight was not a problem. The size of the bags and balancing them in his arms—that took a little more finesse. "Did you bring home some of Kansas?"

"Just a little. I've a little something for you in one of the bags."

"A present, you brought me a present?"

"Yes, you mean to tell me you didn't buy me one?"

Jared laughed. "You know, I did, but it's at the house. You'll have to wait."

"In that case you'll have to wait too."

Jared loaded the bags in the back end of the Bronco. "Would you like to drive or would you like me to?"

"You can drive, I'm beat."

Inside the car, her delicate perfume tantalized his senses. He still hadn't put a name to the scent. He had been tempted to check out her perfumes while she was away, but he'd thought better of it. His thoughts shifted to the gift he'd purchased. He hoped she would like her present. It was a bold one, but he hoped she wouldn't mind. He figured at the very worst he could keep it if she wasn't pleased.

"So, how's the boat coming?"

"I can't do too much on her now. The weather has been uncooperative."

"Did you put up that temporary wall?"

"Yes, but it's still been too windy. There's been a lot of arctic air from the north." Jared turned right and headed for home. "So tell me, how are your folks, the farm?"

"My parents are great. They want to come to the Vineyard. I don't know if they'll get a chance this summer or not, but they'll be planning a visit."

"Great, you can show them the sights."

"Naturally. I know just about everything on this island now."

"Oh, really? Tell me, Doctor, where are the nude beaches?"

"What?"

"Not that you or I would be going, but it's good to know where they are so you don't accidentally come across them."

"They allow that sort of thing here?"

"It's a privately owned beach, but somehow along the way it became a nude beach. Unfortunately, many tourists seek it out."

"Well, please tell me where and how to avoid it."

"I'll show you."

"Jared, I don't want to go there."

"No, we pass it on the way home."

"We do? I drive this road all the time. I never, I mean how. . . ?"

"Hang on, there isn't a sign saying 'this way to the nude beach.' Word gets around and people flock."

"That's sad."

"Yup."

When they passed the road to the beach, Jared pointed it out.

"That's so huge."

"Isn't it? When I was just a kid it was a footpath. About twenty years ago it got so popular, they widened the road. Too many people were getting stuck trying to get around each other. Eventually, it became what you see now, with two lanes and room on each side to park. The owners now charge people for access."

"Wow, it's hard to believe sin can make so much money, but it does, time and time again. You read about it, see it, even the Bible talks about it."

"Sin is profitable, but death is certain because of it." Jared looked over at her. "Alex, don't you see sin in your practice of medicine?"

"Yes, I hate it. But it's a part of caring for others. You see the evidence of sin everywhere. Children beaten to death, or near death, burned, whipped, raped. . . it's very, very sad. I'm thankful that most of my patients' families are not like that. It's hard to witness that kind of abuse of children."

"It's very hard, I know. Unfortunately, I dealt with it with Hannah and her family. She had an uncle that needed help. The family got it for him, and as far as I know, he's doing fine now."

"We live in tough times."

Jared turned on to the Trainers' driveway. "On another note, your present, well, it may attack you."

"What?" *What on earth did he get me?* she wondered.

"Attack is probably too strong a word. Let's just say it might be excited to see you. Of course, it could be terrified to see you also."

"Jared, what did you do?"

"I took a chance. It's a demanding gift. Something that will take lots of your time and gives little in return, and yet, it gives so much."

Other than an animal of some sort, she wasn't sure what he was talking about. *But he wouldn't buy me an animal, would he? He knows I work long hours. My work, my life isn't good for an animal. He couldn't have, could he?* "Don't tell me you bought me an animal?"

"Not quite."

"How do you 'not quite' buy an animal? You either did or you didn't."

They sat in the parked car, her eyes searching his. He was up to something. Something mischievous, if she could tell correctly. "Jared. . ."

"Come on, I'll show you."

He opened the door to her house to find a bouncing golden pup leaping out. *A dog, the man bought me a dog. How could he? But he's so cute.* Alex knelt down on the porch. "Does he have a name?"

"Captain."

"Captain?"

"Yup, you came here in search of a captain—it seemed only fitting."

He was so right. She came in search of Captain Thomas Luce on her first trip, and now she came in search of another captain—Jared. She ducked her head so he wouldn't read her thoughts. "Come here, Captain."

The puppy pounced over to her and licked her face, his tail wagging back and forth. His fur was soft like silk. "What kind of dog is it?"

"It's a he, and he's a golden retriever, about three months old."

"He's adorable. But, Jared, I don't have a life that's fair to an animal."

"You do here. If you can't take him back to Kansas, I understand, and I'll raise him. While you're here, you can enjoy him, can't you?"

With every part of her being she wanted to enjoy this puppy. She loved animals, she loved dogs. Did he know that retrievers were said to be the best dogs for children? "It doesn't seem fair to the dog, to have him get attached to me and then leave him." *But maybe she wouldn't have to leave him. Maybe she and Jared would get together and then there would be two people to care for the dog. . . .*

"It's not like Captain won't know me. I'll be around. He'll adjust if you have to leave him."

Adjust, just like Jared had adjusted to living single the rest of his life.

"Thanks, Jared, I love dogs, I really do but. . ."

"Please, don't say no just yet. Let him grow on you. He'll be great for companionship. He'll love to walk the beach with you."

So Jared was aware that she walked the beach nearly every morning. "Okay, how can I turn down those wonderful round puppy eyes?"

"They're great eyes, aren't they? Such a deep brown. Reminds me of your hair."

"Actually, I was referring to your puppy eyes, but Captain has great puppy eyes too." That should set him off balance just a touch. Alex smiled as Jared's eyes widened. She'd scored another point, hitting him in a way he hadn't expected. *Why do I like doing that to him so much, keeping him off balance?*

She rose from her knees and proceeded into the house. "Come on, Boy, and bring your friend."

"Are you talking to the dog or me?"

"The Captain," she winked.

※

The dog might have been a mistake; never had he seen Alex so bold in her affection. *And just who was she talking to just then, me or the dog?* Muttering, he said under his breath, "Captain, I think we're heading into stormy waters. Brace yourself, Boy!"

Chapter 12

Captain was growing in leaps and bounds, and Jared, true to his word, spent as much time with the animal as possible. They seemed as close as Alex and Captain were.

Every morning, Captain would join her for her walks down the beach. Occasionally, he would catch a sand crab. He loved to bark and paw at the poor things. Of course, they held their own against their loud attacker, and more than once Alex had to clean wounds on Captain's nose.

He was a great companion. She could confide in him when her heart ached to tell Jared the truth of her love for him. But that wasn't to be. He was still as confident in his resolve not to get involved as he had been before she left for Kansas.

Spring was in the air, and the crocuses popped their white and purple heads out of the ground. The days were brighter and definitely warmer, the wind ceased blowing from the north as often, coming more from the west or occasionally from the south. The buds on the oak trees were peeking out.

Captain would spend his days with Jared when Alex went down-island to work on her research. But she was going less and less. Instead, she spent more of her time at the house, working with Jared on the boat. She was so proud of him and his talent with his hands. The boat was beautiful. It still had some work before it was finished, but it was nearly ready to be launched.

The colder days, Jared spent with her and Captain, showing her some island sights and helping her with research.

"Mrs. Arno, how long have you been working here at the historical society?" Alex inquired one day. It wasn't like she could ask her curious questions about Jared straight out; that would simply imply too much.

"Goodness, Alex, it's been fifteen years since I retired from teaching. Call me Beatrice, Dear."

"Okay, tell me. . ." Alex searched for the right words. "Do you know a Jared Madeiras?"

"Ah, yes. I had Jared in my class; he was a bright boy. . .loved reading and history, but like most kids, he had a hard time doing all his homework."

"Oh really?"

"Funny how that happens. I mean, when he was a youngster, he did only what he had to do. Now, however, the man is very thorough in his research. Much like you are, Dear. So, tell me, where'd you meet Jared?"

Alex felt her face flame. "He's the caretaker of the place where I'm living."

"Oh, so you're staying in the Trainers' home."

"Yes."

"He's a good man, Alex. He's had some tragedy in his life, but he's honest, trustworthy, and a hard worker. Not to mention he's a pretty handsome specimen of the male species too." Beatrice winked and headed back to her research.

Well, that was obvious, Alex, she chastised herself, then attempted to concentrate on the papers before her. Today, Alex had spring fever worse than she had ever known it before, even worse than in college. She didn't want to work, she didn't want to read, she simply wanted to take the day off and relax, enjoy the sunshine, and be totally free of commitments. She hurried home to Captain's greeting.

"Come here, Boy, want to go visit Jared?" The dog wagged his tail so hard his backend wiggled with it. She loved this dog so much.

"Let's go get 'im." Alex opened the screen door and the dog was off, running down the porch and heading toward the boathouse. He was in a full run as she rounded the corner. She heard a whistle and turned.

It was Jared. She looked back at Captain, who tumbled trying to stop himself. Back on his feet and clawing his way back, he sniffed the air. His head turned in the direction where Jared stood, and he barked.

"Come on, Boy," Jared called out.

Captain was in a full run again in a matter of seconds. Alex laughed. The poor dog had so much energy. He was getting bigger, but he still had some growing left in him. He would be a good-sized dog.

Captain pranced up and down around Jared. "Where's Mommy, Boy?"

Captain stood alert and his snout pointed in Alex's direction. "Get her, Captain," Jared pointed toward Alex.

The dog came barreling back to her. She patted him. "Good boy, you found him." She was so tempted to call Jared "Daddy," but that would make her fantasy of them getting together too real, too hard to deal with on a day-to-day basis.

"Hey, Alex, how are you this morning?"

"Lousy."

Jared put down his wood cutter, his voice alarmed. "What's the matter?"

"Nothing, really, just a bad case of spring fever."

"Ahh, I know the cure."

"What?"

"Pack an overnight bag and a picnic lunch."

"You're crazy."

"Probably. Come on, Alex, it will be fun. Don't you trust me?"

"I trust you. Do I need warm clothes, coats, gloves—anything else?"

"All that, plus pack some food for Captain."

"Okay."

"I'll be back in an hour or so. Be ready."

"Where are we going, Jared?"

"It's a surprise, trust me."

"Okay. Do you want to take Captain with you?"

"Sure. Come on, Captain, we've got work to do."

The dog left her side and followed Jared. Alex scratched her head. What on earth could he possibly have in mind that involved an overnight bag?

Jared drove his old truck toward Menemsha, eventually pulling into John Poole's scallop-shelled drive. The shells were so old and weathered they had become small chunks of sun-bleached shells now. "Hey, Jared, what brings you out this morning?"

"Need a favor, John."

"Anything. What's up?"

"I want to take Alex to New Bedford. Can I borrow your boat?"

"Sure, let me get the keys. Both tanks are full. I think the water is probably too shallow at your dock, though."

"I agree. I'll leave the truck in the parking lot."

"When ya coming back?"

"Probably tomorrow night. It's still too cold to take her over in my boat, but your cabin cruiser with the wheelhouse enclosed will be like a luxury liner."

"You know, Dr. Tucker has been doing all that research on whaling. I bet she'd love the museums over in New Bedford."

"That was my thinking. Nantucket is another possibility, but it might be better when the weather's warmer."

Captain jumped out of the truck and sidled up beside Jared.

"Hey there, Captain." John reached out to the dog. The golden retriever licked his hand. "Friendly pup, aren't you?" He looked at his friend. "Jared, what are you going to do with the dog?"

"Take him."

John looked down at the dog, pulled his ball cap off, and patted the pup's head. "I don't know, Son, seems to me the dog wouldn't be allowed in the museums and stuff."

"I hadn't thought about that."

"Say, I'll watch him for you. I'm sure the wife won't mind."

"You sure? I wouldn't want to put you out."

"I'm sure. Come on, Captain, let's meet the missus." John opened the door for the retriever and he stepped right in. "Martha, we've got company."

"Jared, it's so good to see you." Martha hugged him with a friendly embrace.

"Good to see you too, Martha. Although, I'm not the guest John's referring to."

"Oh!" Martha looked at her husband, then at the dog. "John, no, you promised no more animals."

John's belly rolled up and down with laughter. "He's only visiting, Honey. He's Jared's."

"Actually, he's Alex's, but we kind of share him."

Martha raised an eyebrow but held her words. Jared thought about correcting her obvious misconception, but he decided that would just take too much time.

"Jared's borrowing the boat to go to New Bedford. I offered to watch Captain for a couple of days, if it's all right with you, of course."

Jared caught John's wink to his wife. A coral blush painted Martha's cheeks and Jared thought how wonderful it was when people stayed in love with each other over the years.

"Oh, John, really, like I could ever say no to you. Come here, Captain." The puppy stomped over to her and wagged his tail. "I take it he's house-trained?"

"Yes, Ma'am."

"Then he can stay." She turned to the dog and bent down. "Would you like to visit for a few days, Captain?" she cooed.

Jared went down to one knee. "Captain, you be a good boy. Do as John and Martha tell you, okay?"

Captain licked Jared's face and nuzzled into his chest. "I love you, too, Boy. I'll see you in a couple of days."

"Thanks, John." He extended his hand. "Thanks for everything."

"No problem. Here's the keys. Have fun."

"I think we will."

Jared kissed Martha on her cheek and returned to his truck. *Dog food! They're going to need dog food. We can drop it off on our way to the boat.* He rushed back home, packed an overnight bag, plopped it into the rear of his truck, and drove up the hill to Alex's. He hadn't even reached the door when she opened it to him.

She looked around. "Where's Captain?"

"At some friends'. Where we're going we might have trouble taking a dog."

"Jared, where *are* we going, and *who* has my dog?"

"John and Martha Poole. You met John once when he was helping me on the boat."

John seemed like a nice enough man, and if Jared trusted him with Captain, he must be. But still, didn't she have a right to say what did or did not happen with her dog? She squelched the desire to argue with Jared about this. Another time, another place would be better. "I'm ready, I think!" she said, hoping her nervousness didn't show in her smile.

"Relax, trust me."

"I'm trying, Jared, I really am. I'm just not very good with surprises."

"We've got to take Captain some food, so you'll get to say good-bye to him and meet the Pooles in their home."

Somehow this made her feel better. Seeing that Captain was in good hands would help her relax. She grabbed her bag, and Jared carried the dog's food. "Come on, Alex, this is my world-famous cure for spring fever. You're going to have a ball."

"If nothing else, I won't die of boredom."

Jared roared with laughter. It warmed her down to her toes. The idea of spending the day and the next with him was comforting and exciting, both at the same time.

After a brief stop at the Pooles', all of Alex's fears for Captain were laid aside. They were like the perfect grandparents—retired, kindhearted, and spoiling their grandchildren. Already Martha had given Captain some steak. "Can you believe she was feeding him steak?"

"Yup, they're good folks, Alex. They've been like a set of grandparents to me."

"Are your grandparents still alive?"

"No. Well, I'm not sure. My grandmother died awhile back, before my folks did. My grandfather, well, he was another story. Seems like family responsibilities got to be too much and he just up and sailed off one day. I really don't know much about it. Dad never liked to talk about it. I guess it was hard on my father. He became the head of the household, quit school, went to work, and provided for the family. I never really knew my mom's folks. I saw them when I was a child a few times, but they died young."

"Goodness, Jared, I don't think I've known anyone with as much death in his family at such a young age."

"I've accepted it. Now, you ready for your surprise?"

Alex looked around. They were at Menemsha harbor, parked toward the beach but facing the wharf. "Yes. What are we doing here?"

"John owns that boat over there."

Alex followed where Jared was pointing to a cabin cruiser with a wheelhouse on top, all blocked in, shining bright in the sunlight. "What are you saying?"

"We're going out to sea, Alex."

"What? It's March, and it's freezing out there on the water!"

"Not really. The boat is heated. It's very modern and quite comfortable. As you can see, the wheelhouse is enclosed, so it's warm up there as well."

"Where are we going?"

"Well, that's the second part of the surprise."

"Jared, I don't swim well."

"Relax, we aren't going to sink. Besides, with hypothermia you wouldn't need to swim long anyway."

"Oh, you're horrible." *Great, if we sink, we die from the elements. This is a fun trip*, she thought sarcastically.

"Alex, trust me?"

If she heard him say "trust me" one more time. . .

"Come on, you country farmgirl, you."

I should never have agreed to something I didn't know about first. I'll never, ever do that again. She grabbed her overnight bag and prayed, *Oh God, please let Jared be as good of a captain as he thinks he is.*

"Nervous?"

"No." Okay, she lied. But no way was she going to tell him otherwise.

"Right. Come on, let me show you around."

Jared helped her aboard. The swaying sensation of the boat beneath her feet felt odd, but the boat settled back in place quickly enough. Jared unlocked the cabin first, and she stepped inside. "Oh my, this is incredible." Before her lay plush carpet, a couch that wrapped around a table with some chairs, a kitchen, and another doorway down a couple of stairs.

"It's nice, isn't it?"

"This is a floating house?"

"Basically, yes. Awhile back John and Martha retired and lived on board for several years, going to Florida in the winter and back here in the summer. Now they pretty much stay here year-round, but they still go out for long trips every now and again." He pointed. "The bedroom is past those doors, and I'll be staying there tonight. You, on the other hand, will be safe and sound on land."

"What?" she questioned. He started to open his mouth, but she interrupted before he could speak. "Don't you dare say 'trust me' again or so help me, I'll. . ."

He raised his hands in defense. "I promise, I won't say it again. But I've got a plan, okay?"

She wagged her head. "Okay."

Alex watched Jared get ready to leave the dock, removing protective covers, starting the engine, checking everything thoroughly. With each action, her confidence in him and his abilities to captain this boat increased. Finally, he removed the lines and stepped on board. He climbed back up to the wheelhouse and shifted the engine into gear.

The water gurgled off the stern as they pulled away from the dock. Alex joined Jared in the wheelhouse. "This is an amazing view."

"Menemsha's always been one of the prettiest harbors. She's small, but with the pond to our left, the inlet over there toward Lobsterville. . .I don't know, it's just been a special place for me."

"Did you learn to pilot boats in this harbor?"

"Yup. When I was a kid I used to walk down here all the time. I'd spend hours fishing off the docks, catching squid, mackerel, and some junk fish. Once in a while I'd catch a flounder. As a kid, the fish you caught always seemed to taste better."

Alex smiled. His life, his growing up was so different than hers. "So where are we heading?"

"Have you ever read nautical maps?"

"No."

"Come here, let me show you." Jared pulled out a map that concentrated on the water, its various depths and other markings. It was so unlike a road map, where the land was a simple color with no markings except for place names. He showed her the path they were taking, how to navigate by the compass.

Once they were out in open waters, Jared put the boat on autopilot, then turned to her and said, "So what did you bring for lunch?"

Alex stared at the man. "Don't you need to watch where we're going?"

"I did. The horizon is clear, autopilot is on, I have a few minutes before I'll need to check again."

"I'm sorry I'm so nervous. I don't know why—you obviously know what you're doing."

"Come here."

Alex took a step toward him.

He grabbed her shoulders and turned her around. He worked his hands at the nape of her neck and gave her a gentle massage. "I know you read about my accident at sea, but that really was the only time I've had anything major happen."

"Jared, it's not that."

"I know, you weren't brought up on this stuff like I was. To me this is the same as stitching up a laceration would be for you."

She turned back and faced him. They hadn't been this close since the time they had kissed. Everything within her wanted to kiss him again. She searched his eyes. They seemed to be saying the same thing, but she held back.

"Jared, where are we headed?"

Chapter 13

Was she asking about them as a couple—or about their destination? In either case, he wasn't ready to answer. "After lunch, Alex. I'll tell you then."

"You and your incredible appetite." She winked at him.

"Feed me or I die, it's that simple."

"I doubt that, but I'll get our lunch. Would you like some coffee?"

"That would be great. Thanks."

Jared watched Alex take the stairs. Her hands didn't clutch the rails quite so tightly this time. "You know, I could prepare lunch if you want to stay up here and watch," he called after her.

"I think I'm more comfortable in the kitchen."

"Okay, I'll let you get away with it for now, but later you're steering this vessel." He patted the wheel.

She paled. "I don't think so." The look of terror in her eyes made him more determined to help her break this fear.

Jared scanned the horizon again. Nothing was out there, though way off in the distance he could see some fishing trollers. But they wouldn't be moving across his path. He sat back and prayed, "Father, please help Alex relax and enjoy this gorgeous day."

She returned shortly with a cup of hot coffee. "Jared, they have everything in there. I just boiled the water. I wasn't sure if I could use the microwave or not."

"You can, but it's not as efficient. Usually that's used in port when you're hooked up to power at a slip."

"Gotcha. I'll be right back."

"Thanks."

When she returned with their food, he stepped away from the wheel and helped her. "Don't you need to hold the wheel?"

"Nope. It's on autopilot," he reminded her. "Watch." Jared saw Alex's eyes widen as the wheel moved back and forth. "Works the same on planes."

"I don't even want to think about that," she mumbled as she stepped onto the upper level of the wheelhouse.

He chuckled; he couldn't help it. "You're a wonder, Doc. You work on the insides of a human being and yet you fear the ocean."

"I know it doesn't make sense, but believe it or not, I'm liking it out here."

"Come on, sit down here." Jared led her to the captain's chair. He stood behind her and worked her tense muscles around her neck and shoulders.

"You have marvelous hands, Jared."

Her voice, soft and alluring as her scent on the ocean breeze, caressed his heart. He'd come to know her so well. *Maybe we should take this relationship further?* he thought. "Alex. . ."

She turned to him. He knew his gaze was intense. The reaction in her eyes was equal to what he felt in his heart. He explored every freckle, every eyelash, the soft creamy texture of her skin. "Oh, Alex, may I kiss you?"

Tentatively, she reached out to him. She hadn't spoken a word, she didn't need to. He leaned down and drank in her lips, so moist, so tender and sweet, just as he remembered them.

She moaned—or was it him—he wasn't sure. He drew her closer. There was no denying his attraction to her any longer. They both knew it. They'd been foolish trying to hide it. She placed her hands on his chest. At first they explored him, but now she was pushing him back. He didn't want to stop kissing her, but she was right. He stepped back and released her. Cool air chilled his heated skin. Sitting down in the other deck chair, he waited for her to speak.

❧

Alex closed her eyes and tried to focus. Mind, body, soul, and spirit longed to be back in Jared's embrace. But the fire between them was far too intense. Her self-control was being taxed. He was waiting for her response, but what could. . . should she say? The reaction to their first kiss had been a disaster she didn't want to repeat. "Jared, I like you very much." *Actually I love you, but you're not ready to hear that.* "And I believe you like me. Are you ready to bring our relationship to the next level?"

"Alexandria, you don't know how ready I am. I've wanted to start dating you, get closer to you, but you said you weren't interested."

"Jared, you said the same to me. I've kept you at bay because I thought that's what you wanted." *You mean to tell me, I—we could have been enjoying these wonderful kisses for months now?* she wanted to ask, but she wasn't bold enough, not yet.

"Well, aren't we a sorry case?"

He was right. Weren't they too old for these silly games? But then again, were they ready a couple of months ago, days ago, in fact? Who could tell? But now. . ."I guess that means we're moving on to the next step in this relationship." She broke her gaze from his. She wasn't sure she was ready to hear his answer.

"Are you as terrified about that as I am?"

"Yes and no. If we are meant to be a couple, Jared, God will guide us through this."

"I haven't felt these emotions since Hannah."

"Tell me about her, Jared." Alex handed him a sandwich and one for herself. "Please, tell me. She's a part of you, of your past, who you've grown into. I want to know her."

"She was just a kid. I suppose I was too, for that matter. We met in college. It was love at first sight. I didn't do anything without thinking about her first. It was great; we had so much fun together. We decided to get married after I graduated from college. It seemed like the best plan at the time, but I would never recommend to anyone a two-year engagement. It's not healthy."

"Two years?"

"Two years, and a young man. You're a doctor, you know the combination. It was an incredible test of my convictions, but God was gracious and saw me through it. Two weeks before the wedding, I went home to the Vineyard while she returned to her home to prepare for the wedding." Tears welled up in his eyes. "I wasn't there when it happened. The call from her father, crying on the phone, was my darkest moment. I literally fell to my knees, held my sides, and screamed."

Alex stood beside him and held him in her arms.

"The pain was so intense. I felt guilty for not being there, angry that God would take her away from me like that. It just wasn't fair."

Gently she kneaded his shoulders.

"My parents were a big help. We went to the funeral, of course. The image of her lying in that coffin, so peaceful, so beautiful—I wanted to crawl in and be buried with her. As far as I was concerned, my life was over before it even started."

She kissed the top of his head. What else could she do? "I've never known that kind of loss. My heart aches for you, Jared, it truly does."

"I'm afraid to love, Alex. I'm afraid if I give my heart to others, I'll lose them. Do you understand?"

"I think so. But, Jared, you won't lose me."

"You don't know that, Alex, anymore than I do. I want to go further in our relationship—goodness, I have no choice. I see you in the morning, during the day, and at night. You're always around me."

"What are you saying, Jared? You only care about me because I'm always around?"

"No, goodness no! I meant in my mind's eye. I can't get you out of it. You're always there. You're so beautiful, Alexandria. You've awakened me in ways I thought were long dead."

"You're a pretty handsome guy yourself." She wanted to tell him she loved him. Loved him for who he was and not what he looked like, but she was afraid the words would scare him off. She held back her heart and caressed his cheek.

"It's not just your beauty, Alex, it's your mind also—who you are, everything about you. You drive me crazy."

Alex chuckled. "Ditto."

Jared laughed. "We're quite a pair, you and I."

"As long as we're a pair, I think I can live with that."

"Alex, if I had my way, I'd haul you to a justice of the peace and be married by the end of the day. But I'm not ready for that. I know I've got a lot of baggage with regard to Hannah and my parents. Can we take it slow and see how our relationship develops? Continue as friends, but allow ourselves some kisses, maybe a tender caress once in awhile?"

"Sounds like a plan," she said through a grin, giving his favorite response. "Mind if we share another kiss now?"

He took her in his arms, possessive yet tender. This time the kiss was more gentle, the driving passion under control. Just maybe she could handle the physical attraction to this man.

❧

When at last they parted from the kiss, she asked, "So where are you taking me?"

"Patience is not one of your virtues." He slid her hair behind her shoulders.

"I never said it was."

"New Bedford."

"New Bedford? Why?"

"Well, my dear, there's a great whaling museum there and I thought you'd like to see it."

"Love to! So you said earlier you would be sleeping on the boat—where is it that I'm going to be staying?"

"I thought we could get you a room at a hotel on the water. Hopefully, one with a dock so that I can be close by."

"Sounds like fun. How long will we be staying?"

"Just one night. I figure we can head back late afternoon and get in just before dark."

"Great. So, are you going to teach me how to steer this thing?"

Happiness didn't come close to what Jared was feeling in his heart right now. The woman he was falling madly in love with was standing beside him, trying to conquer her fears; she wanted to learn how to steer. He helped her into the captain's chair. "Okay, see the compass there?"

Alex nodded.

"That's our heading. Now when you steer, it's just like a car, except with really loose steering. You'll see." Jared turned off the autopilot and stood back.

"Did you do what I think you just did?"

"Uh-huh."

Alex hurriedly grasped the wheel. "Oh dear, what do I do?"

"Just remember the heading, Alex. Keep the compass heading in the same direction."

She worked so hard to keep it on course. He wanted to laugh, but she was trying. He couldn't help but take her as seriously as she took the job herself. Man, did he love this woman! "Excellent, Honey, you're doing excellent." He stood behind her again and her shoulders relaxed.

"How long does this trip take?"

"A couple of hours."

He noticed she was shivering. "Are you cold?"

"A little." She rubbed her arms to warm them.

"Did you bring your heavy jacket?"

"Yes."

"I'll get it for you. Is it in your overnight bag?"

"Yup, thanks."

Something was so right in having her so close to him, in opening up his heart again. He wondered if he could keep it open, or if the years of shutting down and keeping out others would win in the end.

Down inside the cabin, the air was warm. He opened her case and pulled out her jacket. It smelled like Alex. How he'd grown to love that scent. He peered out the porthole; they were close to the harbor now. Catching himself foolishly sniffing her jacket, he snapped the overnight bag closed and carried the jacket up to her. Their talk remained light the rest of the trip.

※

Walking the cobblestone streets by the whaling museum drew Alex back to a time far more rustic. Still, it was hard to picture this harbor in days of old with all the modern factories and working wharves on it. She enjoyed the museum well enough, but the best part was just spending the day with Jared. They had moved to a new level in their relationship, and she knew that the words the elderly woman spoke on the plane were coming to pass. "In God's time, everything will work out."

Jared talked of Hannah and his relationship with her. He filled in all sorts of details about what they did on their dates, where they liked to eat. They had been college kids back then, and they'd acted and lived the part. For her part, Alex hadn't told him yet about Peter and how he had broken her heart, but she figured she could save that for another day. Today, they were beginning their own relationship; she didn't need to mar it with her ugly past.

※

The first month after their trip to New Bedford flew by in a blur of romantic evening meals, long walks along the shore holding hands, and occasionally yielding to their kisses. They played endless games of rummy and chess. Though he still lost to her consistently, his knowledge of chess ever increased.

Around the middle of May, Jared finally launched his boat. The name for the boat remained a constant inner battle for him. *Hannah* had always been a possibility, but somehow it didn't seem right with his relationship with Alex budding. *And what was it budding into?* he wondered. If he didn't watch himself, they would be an old married couple without the actual license. Every evening they spent together until bedtime, every day they assumed the other would just naturally be there.

This could be a dangerous thing, Jared worried, often taking the concern to prayer. "I accept my physical attraction to the woman, Lord, and I like her company, but I'm not ready to marry. I'm scared to death of it. I know, I know I'm supposed to trust You, but how can I? Everyone I ever loved has been taken from me. Pretty soon Alex will be packing her bags to go back to Kansas. I can't live in Kansas, Lord. And she's a doctor, she has patients back there. They are depending on her to return to them in a few months. It's not right. We can't, I can't ask her to leave her life and join me in mine."

What was he going to do? He had already lost his heart; her leaving would completely rip it apart. And yet he couldn't take her career, her patients, her business away.

Alex's parents were due to come in a couple of weeks, during the early part of June. Jared worked feverishly to finish the boat before they arrived. The sails had come the week before. Some of the rigging still needed to be placed on the deck. The mast had been set a couple weeks back, thanks to the help of a few friends.

Jared let out an ear-piercing whistle. Captain charged toward him. "Hey, Boy, where's Mommy?"

The dog barked as if he understood the question.

"Is she coming down here?"

The dog barked twice. Jared looked up the cliff. There she stood, her tall slender frame that fit so perfectly beside him silhouetted against a sea of blue sky. *But it will never work, she's got to go back.*

"Tell Alex I'm busy, Boy, go on. Shoo!"

Slowly the dog ambled off the dock, his nails clicking on the boards as he made his way to shore. Jared knew he was in a foul mood and he had no business taking it out on the dog. "Come here, Captain. I'm sorry."

The dog ran back and jumped on the deck of the boat. "Woof!"

Jared marveled at how the dog loved being on the boat, as if *he* were the captain. "Sorry, Fella, but on this boat, I'm the captain." Wagging his tail, the dog soaked up Jared's attention, raising his hind quarters for a deeper petting.

❧

"So what was that all about?" Alex stood with her hands on her hips. Something was bothering Jared. She had never seen him push Captain away before.

"I've just been having a bad day."

"What's wrong?" He was tense, his back as rigid as the mast.

"Alex, I don't want to talk about this now."

"So, it has something to do with us?" She searched his eyes for answers. He hid them from her scrutiny.

"Woman, are you a mind reader or something?"

"Or something. Jared, I read you like a book. From on the cliff I could tell something was eating away at you. That's why I sent Captain down. Figured seeing him would cheer you up."

"He did, sort of."

"You're doing it again, Jared."

"What?"

"Closing down."

No matter how much it hurt, she was going to see him through this. Maybe he would never be able to totally open his heart to her, but for as long as she had left on the Vineyard, she was going to fight for him to break free at last.

"Me! Goodness, Alex, you've got something tucked away so deep inside of you, you won't let me in either."

"Me? When did this become about me?"

"Look, Honey, I don't want to argue. Please, just drop it."

"Jared, we can't keep doing this. Every time there's something we aren't comfortable with, we stop talking. That's no basis for a relationship."

"What relationship? You're going home in a couple of months. Where does that leave us? What's the point, Alex? You've got your life, I've got mine. Maybe we're just too old."

Old? He thought she was old? *Doesn't he know I'd leave my practice and start one here? But I can't, not if he won't let me into his heart.*

"Who was he, Alex? Who hurt you so bad you won't tell me about it?"

Every muscle in her body tensed. She had wanted to tell him about Peter, she had intended to, actually. But the right time never seemed to present itself. Or maybe she just didn't have the right words.

"You say I'm closing down, I've closed off my heart," he persisted. "Well, Honey, there's a piece of your heart you've never let me into. Not even a glimpse."

"Jared, I wanted. . ."

"Wanted what? For me to lay all of my life before your feet, tell you all of my wounds so you could use them to cut me off from probing into your own?" Jared stood in front of her and held her shoulders tight. "I know I'm right, Alex, whether you admit it or not. You are the one with the heart that has closed down. Trust me, I know what it looks like."

Tears burned at the back of her eyes, but she refused to cry. She wasn't going to show any weakness, not now. She'd won the battle with Peter, she had gotten on with her life. Such as it was.

"Fine, don't tell me then."

Within seconds he was on the shore walking away from her. Her heart was

SEA ESCAPE

breaking. Why hadn't she told him about Peter? Why had she waited so long?

But she had waited too long. His heart was closing again; she'd seen it over the past few days. Verbal jabs about anything and nothing routinely passed his lips. He hadn't kissed her in nearly a week. He was pulling away.

Maybe it was time to return to Kansas. The tears fell freely now; her cheeks stung with the salt. "Come on, Captain, I think I'm going to pack."

The climb up the stairway in front of the cliff took forever; every step felt as though she were lifting a load of lead. She needed her entire concentration to focus on moving one foot in front of the other, to climb up the stairs, away from the sea, away from her captain. Some escape this trip to the seashore had been. She had made a wreck out of her life and the life of another. "God, I was right the first time—I was meant to be single. Why on earth did I ever believe there was hope for Jared and me?"

Chapter 14

I need to leave for a few days," he told himself. She was everywhere. He couldn't breathe without catching a whiff of her scent. Her presence so flooded his soul it was mind-boggling. He knew what he had said to her was right. Perhaps he didn't say it right or bring it up at the best time, but someone had hurt her. *She doesn't trust. She gives of herself constantly, but doesn't trust someone to come in and hold her heart.*

He loved her. He knew it with every salty, briny section of his being. But she was right too: A relationship has no foundation if one or both can't trust their hearts to the other.

"Well, this is fun, Lord. I open myself up and get slapped in the face! You brought a woman into my life who has so much damage done to her that she can't open up and talk about it." Jared rattled around in the kitchen, picking up a cup and placing it down a few inches away, not really preparing to cook, not even doing the dishes, just expending mindless, useless energy.

He sat in his cottage all evening until around three in the morning, when he finally went to bed. He fought with himself to go and talk with her again, argue if he had to. Something needed to break in this relationship, or it was over.

❧

A persistent rapping at his door drove him out of his bed grumbling. The early morning sunlight made him blink. Alex stood before him with reddened eyes.

"Captain will be much happier here with you." His back went rigid at the sound of her cold and controlled words. The dog walked through the opened door. Alex pivoted sharply and left.

"Alex!" *What is going on here? Wake up, Jared, the woman is leaving, and she's leaving the dog with you.*

Her shoulders stiffened, but she continued to walk away.

"Alex, we need to talk."

She didn't respond. She was shaking now, grasping her sides, but still walking away from him. Away from "them" and any possible hope for a future.

"You're running away!"

Again no response; her pace quickened.

"For pity's sake, Woman, don't do this!" Jared ran out the door and grabbed her in his arms. She stiffened like a board. He caressed her cheek. "Alex, please, can't we talk? Where are you going?"

"Home."

Jared's body tensed.

"I was wrong, Jared. I never should have gotten involved with you."

"Why? Because I'm forcing you to look at something in your heart that hasn't been resolved, in the same way you made me face myself? I don't think that's fair, Alex."

"In my case, things are different. It is resolved. It's over. Everything that happened between Peter and me is over."

At least I got his name out of her. That's something. "Honey, I don't think it's over."

"I haven't seen the man in seven years. Believe me, it's over, Jared." Her anger gave her strength. She pushed away from his embrace.

He tightened his hold, perhaps a little too tight. Her eyes lit with fear. His stomach heaved—she had been attacked. This Peter character had attacked her. He knew it with every ounce of his being. His heart softened. All his cruel words felt like ballast, sinking him further away from her. "Alex, I'm taking you into my place where we can sit down and talk this out."

She shook her head no.

"Honey, I don't know what that creep did to you, but I know one thing for certain, and deep down in your heart you know it too. I will never force myself on you."

Tears welled in her eyes as they darted back and forth. She was reading him, trying to figure out how he knew. "You know, don't you?"

"I suspect the man forced you in some way, am I right?"

The tears flowed down her cheeks now and she sniffled out a "yes."

His hold around her became more protective, firm but gentle. Then he scooped her up in his arms and brought her back into his cottage. Placing her on the couch, he squatted in front of her. "Can you tell me about it, Alex?"

"Oh, Jared, I was such a fool."

He placed her chestnut hair behind her shoulders, wiping her tears with his thumbs. "Shh, none of that. If he took advantage, he was the fool, not you."

"I should have seen it coming."

"Why? Honey, a creep like that is very manipulative in attracting people. You had no idea that in his heart he was ugly and not much of a man."

To this day she still blamed herself for what happened. Jared was right, though: Peter was a master of illusion. "Why couldn't I see?"

"Tell me about it, everything, and maybe I can help you sort it out."

"I wanted to tell you since the trip to New Bedford. I figured I would someday, but you were right, I kept putting it off."

"I should have been more patient. I'm sorry."

Alex proceeded to tell Jared about her relationship with Peter, how he used her from the start, at first wanting her to cover for him and his lack of studies. Then, the final night of their relationship, he tried to force his way on her. She blamed herself too, because she had been tempted, wanting to explore some of her own sexual desires.

He held a finger to her lips. "No, Love. The man was wrong. When you said no, he continued to press. That's when it was his fault and not yours."

"But don't you see, I wanted to for—a little while."

"Honey, we all want to at one time or another. It's how we control those desires that makes us successful against temptation or defeated by it. Alex, you've dealt with rape with your patients—what do you tell them?"

She felt a lightbulb go on in her head; she had never applied her knowledge to her own experience. "They are the victim, they may have made a mistake, but the perpetrator is the one who was responsible."

"See, you know it here." He tapped her temple. "Now apply it here." He pointed to her heart.

"How?" Of course she knew the answers for her patients, but she had been unable to get past this for the seven years and more it had been haunting her.

"Forgive yourself for one thing. Your only mistake was being a poor judge of character, which in these cases is always difficult."

"I know, but. . ."

"What's the problem, Alex? Why haven't you released this stuff? You know all the psychological information regarding abuse and such. So, why do you think you haven't moved on from Peter? Did you date after the attack?"

"No. Like you, I retreated into my own world."

"So, what are we going to do about it?"

"We?"

"Yes, you have your baggage, and I have mine."

"I suppose we have to trust God, trust Him to forgive, trust Him with our hearts."

"Right. So how do you propose we do that?"

"I don't have a clue. We're a sad lot, you and I."

"Maybe. Or maybe we're just more honest than a lot of folks. We didn't bury our feelings and go into meaningless relationships afterwards, trying to find what we lost. Instead, we separated ourselves until we were ready to deal with this."

"Are you ready to put Hannah aside and allow someone else in?" *Oh, Jared, I love you with all my heart, but I'm still afraid to tell you that,* she thought, probing his face for his answer before he gave it. She searched those deep, dark blue eyes she'd grown to cherish.

"I want to, Alex. I thought, no, I believe, I have been doing it. The mere fact that I would allow myself to get involved with you at all is evidence of that."

"I've let you in too. But that doesn't seem to change the fact that we've both been holding onto pieces of our past."

Jared got up and sat beside her on the couch. "Alex, we took a big step today.

You've shared something with me that you've shared with no one else. Let's not push ourselves too hard, too fast."

"I'm going back to Kansas, Jared."

"I know. Will you be staying here for the summer—or are you leaving now?"

"What would you like?"

"Personally, I want you to stay here the rest of the summer. That will give us more time to heal and possibly get closer."

He's not ready to simply throw the relationship away. He did fight to have this conversation today. Maybe I should stay and see if there is more between us. Maybe I need to heal before I can completely trust another. Remember, you are the one who wanted to run. He wasn't running, he was waiting. Besides, even if I wanted to go home today, I'm in no condition to drive halfway across the country.

"I'll stay for now, but I won't promise the rest of the summer."

"Fair enough." He stood from the couch. "Now, let me get to work. I want to have the boat ready for your folks." Jared took her in his arms and hugged her. She longed to hear him proclaim his love for her, but nothing came. He was a man who held tight reins on his heart. *Can I survive this, Lord?*

❧

In the days following, they shared many more heart-to-heart discussions, learning to trust each other, themselves, and the Lord.

Finally, the boat was ready, everything was done. Jared planned for her maiden voyage, but one thing still remained. The name. He couldn't believe he was, after all this time, not content with any name that he had come up with. He thought of naming it the *Alexandria,* but it seemed too noble a name for a work boat. And somehow *Alex* just didn't fit either. Many evenings he and Alex went over all sorts of names, from A to Z, up and down the alphabet, searching through literature, the Bible, old movies, anything and everything. Nothing stuck. And yet Alex, and everything about her, seemed so interlocked with the boat. He even thought of calling it *Dorothy* because she came from Kansas. And, like Dorothy in *The Wizard of Oz,* Alex had tried escaping from her life there.

His hand glided along the tiller, the varnish smooth as glass beneath his touch. He had sanded and sanded again, applying many layers, then buffed to a high gloss. Scanning the boat from bow to stern, he smiled with approval. She was a good vessel, rugged and sleek. The waves tapping against the hull made a rhythmic, slapping sound.

Alex came down the cliff, her every movement captivating his heart. How was he ever going to deal with her departure in a month? During their visit, he fell in love with her parents, and while he wanted to take them on a sail, he decided the maiden voyage would be the two of them alone. There was so much he still wanted to talk about, and yet, there were always interruptions. The hospital had taken to calling Alex whenever someone was going on vacation. More days than not she was working, frequently long, hard hours.

Captain would stay with him during these times, but as soon as he heard her Bronco pull up, he was prancing at the door to go see her. Often Jared was jealous of the dog's close contact with Alex and his ability to have no inhibitions about running up and kissing her. "Lord, she's beautiful," Jared muttered as he waved to her.

Alex smiled and returned with a hearty gesture. She was wearing jeans, a cotton shirt, and a sweater tied around her neck. "Fine looking vessel, Captain." Her eyes sparkled with excitement, lit up with the June sun glistening off the ocean.

"Why thank you, Ma'am. Would you like to come aboard?"

"May I?" She fanned her hand over her chest.

Jared roared. Her imitation of a southern belle dressed in jeans was so contrary. He took her hand as she stepped on board. "You look wonderful, Alex," he said.

"Aye, you ain't so bad yourself, Captain," she winked.

"Southern belle to pirate, without batting an eye. You're multitalented, my lady." Alex laughed. "Honey, I deal with children—I need to be diversified."

"I reckon so." Jared pulled her to himself and kissed her tenderly. "I've missed you. You've been working a lot."

"I know. Remind me later I have something to bounce off you. But let's get going. I can't wait to have my first sail."

"Your first and her maiden voyage—only fitting."

"You still haven't named her yet?"

"Nope, but I'm working on it."

Alex wagged her head. "When you do come up with the name, it's going to be a good one. Nobody takes this many months to name a boat."

"How do you know?" Jared teased.

"Hmm, I'll have to ask around and verify my hypothesis."

"Okay, let's shove off then. Time's a-wasting, and the sun will be setting in a few hours."

❧

Alex sat in the stern and watched as Jared released the lines and pushed the boat into deeper water. He pulled the mainsail up to the top of the mast and secured the line on the cleat. She had learned so much about the boat, working on it with Jared. Lines, sheets, cleats, and winches were a part of her everyday vocabulary now. She spied her Christmas gift to him, an antique sextant, in the hold. It added a sense of authenticity to Jared's careful reconstruction of the historic vessel. He stood beside her, pushing the tiller over to the left to catch the wind.

The whipping of the sail evened out as the wind filled it and pushed the boat forward. It was so quiet on the water, nothing at all like the rides on motorboats.

"Alex, we're going to tack soon. When we do, you shift from one side to the other. I'll say 'ready about,' and if you're ready you say, 'ready.' Then I'll say, 'hard to lee,' and you shift positions, okay?"

"Sure, but why?"

Jared smiled. "Because, my dear, everyone on board will prepare for the shift."

"But why those terms?"

"Well 'ready about' means, is everyone aboard, or 'about' this ship, ready. And 'hard to lee' means we are moving to the lee side of the boat, the side that is sheltered from the wind."

"Gotcha."

"Ready about?" Jared watched the bow.

"Ready!" Alex stifled a giggle.

"Hard to lee." Jared pushed the tiller away from him and the boat spun to the right. The sail flapped loudly until it filled with wind again. Alex managed to scramble from one side to the other. Her heart raced. This was fun! She marveled at how easily Jared pointed the bow and the sail filled.

He pulled the tiller toward himself and the sail started to flap. "You didn't say 'ready about'!" she protested.

"Nope, this is called 'falling off.' It allows you to slow down the sailboat."

"Awesome. How did you learn all this stuff?"

"Honey, I've been sailing since I was in diapers. My mom was afraid I was going to grow gills."

"Oh, Jared, stop it. You're such a tease."

"Want to try?"

"I can't sail, Jared."

"Sure you can. I'll teach you." Jared patted the bench beside him.

Alex slid closer to him. "What do I do?"

"Here, hold the tiller."

She grabbed the tiller and Jared let go.

"Okay, push away from you."

She did, and the boat veered in the opposite direction. She panicked. "Jared, grab it, I'm going the wrong way!"

He placed his arm around her shoulder. "No, Dear, with a tiller you do the opposite of where you want to go."

"Oh."

"Pull it toward you now." She did. "See?"

"Yes. . .this is so strange."

"I know, but you'll get used to it. Now look at the forward corner of the sail."

She stared at the white sheet. It was flapping a little, not full like when Jared was sailing. "Why isn't it tight?"

"Because you're 'falling off.' Point the bow into the wind."

She pulled the tiller too hard and too close. The boat jerked and turned to the side. "Jared, help!"

"Relax, you simply pulled too hard. Ease off, that's it. Great, Honey, you're doing great."

"I'm terrified."

He worked his strong hand over her shoulder muscles. "Trust me, you're doing just fine. You'll be a sailor in no time."

Alex watched the sail, scanning the horizon, staying alert.

"I like your folks," Jared said. "They're great people."

"Thanks, I'm kind of fond of them myself."

"What do they think of the island?"

"They love it. They think they're in paradise."

"Well, they are, aren't they?" He nibbled her ear.

"Jared, behave."

"Sorry, you're just so irresistible."

Alex was more relaxed now and reclined in her seat. "It's a gorgeous day."

"Perfect." He was staring at her, examining her up close, making her feel so loved and adored. If only she could tell him she loved him.

The hospital had offered her a position today. They wanted to hire a pediatric physician as a part of the medical team for the Vineyard. The offer was tempting. She'd take it in a flash if she knew she and Jared had a future together. When they were together and not thinking about jobs, careers, futures, it seemed so right. He seemed to be an extension of her. But when he brought up her career, the atmosphere between them always became tense. He had made it clear on more than one occasion he'd seen enough of the world. The Vineyard was his home and he wasn't leaving it.

She searched his eyes—so deep and brightened by the sun.

"So, do you like the quiet of the sea?" he asked.

"It's great. Very tranquil."

"I love it. It calms me down. It's my escape from pressures. It's like the waves take my troubles away."

Alex could feel that too. She wanted to ask him about their relationship. Did he want to go further? Or was he content with her moving back home in a little over a month?

"You're doing great, Honey. I want to go up front and check some lines. Just keep pointing into the wind like you've been doing, okay?"

"I don't know if I'm ready to go solo."

"You've been doing it for thirty minutes all by yourself. You can handle it, I'm sure of it."

She nodded. She was too nervous to speak. Every cell in her body stood at attention. Every hair was raised like an antenna, alerting her to potential trouble. *Trouble, how do I know if there's trouble? I don't know what I'm doing.* Gnawing her lower lip, she tried to stay focused.

As her confidence was building, a speedboat crossed their bow very close, raising the bow of the boat out of the water. As it dropped back down, the boom bucked. She watched Jared, in the bow, grab for a line. He missed. "Oh Lord, no!" she screamed. "Jared!"

Chapter 15

O h dear God in heaven, let him be all right." She saw him splashing to the surface of the water. "Thank You, Lord."

He was waving at her, yelling something.

"What do I do now?" Her hand trembled on the tiller; Jared was getting farther and farther away.

Fall off, Alex, fall off, but how do I do that? She was trying to remember Jared's instructions. Her mind raced, her fears raged. She pulled the tiller toward her, and the boat turned too far to her right. She pushed the stick away from her and the boat started to go sideways.

Panic-stricken, she stood up. Jared was swimming toward her. She leaned over the side, her knee pushing the tiller away from her some more. The boat was turning around. "Thank You, Lord."

"Jared!"

❧

"Oh, dear Jesus, no!" Jared swam as fast as he could. Alex was standing in the boat; danger hung in the wind. She was tacking; the boom was about to hit her in the head. "Get down, Alex!" he yelled.

He was certain she couldn't hear him. His chest aching, he propelled his body harder than he had ever done before. The thudding sound of her skull being nailed by the boom sickened him. *Don't think of that now*, he berated himself. *I've got to get to her, and fast.*

He kicked harder, reached farther, straining with each stroke. The boat lay idle in the water, gently rolling in the waves. He caught a glimpse of her floating face down in the ocean. "Oh God, no. Don't take her away too! Please, God, let me save her. Help us. I love her. Please!"

Tears poured from his eyes. He reached her and lifted her head out of the water. He held her in his arms, kicking hard to keep them both above the surface of the waves.

"Alex! Please, Alex, breathe!"

He turned her around and placed his arm across her chest. He fought his emotions and forced himself to concentrate, trying to remember the lifesaving course he had taken as a kid. Covering the distance to the boat seemed to take forever, yet that was an illusion, he knew, and he continued to press on. When he reached the boat, he pushed her body up so it draped over the stern, then pulled himself on board. He noticed a small pool of water under her head. "Please, Lord, let that be from her lungs."

He grabbed her lifeless body and laid it tenderly on the deck. His body trembled with so many emotions. *She can't die, God, please don't take her away now! She's far too important to me*, he pleaded.

CPR, clear the passageways. Come on, Jared, you can do it. He pinched her nose and blew fresh air into her lungs. "Come on, Alex, breathe, Woman. I love you. Don't you die on me now! Breathe!" he yelled.

He worked on her for what seemed to be an eternity, though in reality it took only a couple of seconds. She coughed.

"That's it, Baby, breathe, come on."

He rolled her to her side and rubbed her back.

She was breathing now.

"Thank You, Lord."

"Jar. . ." She coughed again.

"Shh, Honey, it's all right, you're safe now. Everything is going to be all right." He kissed her forehead and cried.

They sat there, exhausted, the boat adrift in the middle of the ocean, its lines clapping against the mast. Minutes passed with no words.

"What happened?" she asked.

"You tacked and the boom hit you in the head, knocking you overboard." She felt the back of her head for the lump.

"Yes, my dear, you will be going to the hospital to have that looked at."

"But you were in the water too." She looked up to him and he explored her eyes. The pupils were dilated, but slowly responding to the sunlight.

"Shh, Alex. God was good. I was able to get to you. Relax."

Jared's body quivered, the shock of nearly losing her overwhelmed him.

"Hold me, Jared." Her voice, raspy and hoarse, steeled his senses.

He gathered her into his arms. *I can't let you go, Alex. You mean too much to me.* He brushed her soggy hair away from her face. Her breathing was evening out.

❦

Alex savored the strength of his arms, the warmth of his chest. The thumping of his heart, still working hard, told her he was frightened. She had been frightened too, but no matter what, she had to tell him how she felt. "Jared."

"Hmm?"

"I need to tell you something." Her voice grated past her lips. Her mouth could barely shape the words.

He held her tighter and rocked her back and forth.

"When you went overboard. . ." The tickle in her throat made her cough again.

He lifted her chin and his lips descended to hers. The kiss was tender; she felt so loved. "I love you, Jared." There. At last she had said the words.

"I love you too. Alex, I can't live without you!"

Alex wept. How was it possible to love someone so much?

"I'll even move to Kansas, if that's what it takes for us to be together," he offered as a whisper in her ear, his breath warm and soothing.

"No, my love. Remember I had something to tell you?" She searched his eyes. He nodded.

"I've been offered a position at the hospital and it will allow me to start my own practice here."

"When?"

"Today."

"You mean you'd live here with me?"

She nodded her head and wrapped her arms around him. "Only on one condition."

"What's that?" He eyed her curiously, pushing her back a little to see her face.

"Well," she let the word linger for a moment. "It isn't proper for a lady to ask." She traced his jaw with her fingertip.

"Oh! Well, I don't know. . .that's asking a lot, you know."

She playfully punched his shoulder. "You!"

"First, let me ask you, how do you feel about kids?"

"I love them, of course. Why else would I be in pediatrics?"

"Hmm, so you wouldn't mind having a few of your own?"

"Few! How many are we talking?"

"Well, I never told you this, but twins run in my family."

"Twins, huh?"

"Yup." He toyed with the corners of her mouth, his feather-light touch sending an electrical charge over her skin.

"What if we just take them as they come and negotiate along the way?"

"Hmm, sounds like a plan."

"So, are you going to ask me?"

"It's a possibility."

"What?" They were playing a game; she loved him, and she loved him for it.

"Now, Alexandria, a woman of your social graces knows there is a proper time and place for everything."

"Don't give me that. Marry me or I go back to Kansas."

"Is that a proposal?" he asked.

"Nope, that's a threat."

"Well, then, Dr. Alexandria Rose Tucker, would you do me the great honor of becoming my wife?"

"Yes."

He smiled and captured her lips once again. Alex was certain she would never get enough of this man's kisses if they lived to be a hundred and two.

"I've got a name for the boat, Honey. If you approve."

"What's that?"

"*Sea Escape.* You came here to escape on the sea; I find the sea an escape from my stress. And here, right now, we've escaped from the bonds of our past. What do you think?"

"I like it. But you're going to have to teach me to sail. I don't want our children sailing circles around their mother."

"Hey, your folks are here. Why don't we get married right away?"

"And where are we going to spend our honeymoon?"

"Right here on the sea, my dear."

Alex laughed. "Of course, what was I possibly thinking? Sounds like a plan."

Epilogue

Six years later

Alex bent over in pain. She knew this feeling, remembering two other times when she had experienced it before. "Michael Thomas! Mommy needs you."

A small golden-haired boy ran into her bedroom. "I'm here, Mommy. What's the matter?"

"It's time, the baby is coming. Could you go get Daddy?"

"Okay. Mommy, can I come to the hospital this time?"

"No, Honey, I need you to help Papa John and Nana Martha watch your sister."

"But, Mom, I want to go," he pouted.

A sudden sharp pain attacked her, not even five minutes after the first one. She grasped the bed frame and supported herself. "Honey, if you don't run and get Daddy, Mommy isn't going to make it to the hospital."

His eyes widened with fear. "Mommy, are you okay?"

"Yes, Honey, but I need you to go now, please."

"I'll get Daddy, Mom." Alex had never been so proud of her son. At five, he was growing into quite a little man. She reached for the phone and placed a call.

"Hi, Martha. It's time."

"Goodness, Alex, John just pulled in the drive. You've got great timing."

Alex chuckled. "I'm not sure. The contractions are coming about five minutes apart. I hope we make it to the hospital."

"We're on our way."

Alex heard the phone slam down before the line went dead. John and Martha Poole had become dear friends and adopted grandparents to their children.

❧

"Daddy! Daddy!" Jared saw Michael running toward the dock.

"Hey, Son, what's up?"

"Mommy. . ." He gasped for air. "Mommy. . .baby!"

"Mommy's going to have the baby?"

Little Michael vigorously nodded his head.

Jared dropped his power sander, turned off the generator, and scooped Michael up. "Let's go, Son."

"Daddy, why does Mommy hurt?"

Jared was not ready for this question. His mind worked hard for a good honest answer that wasn't too revealing. Thinking was difficult when he needed to get to Alex. But his son needed answers. "Michael, when mommies have babies, it hurts them a little, but it's only for awhile, then there's no more pain."

"Mommy will be okay?"

"Yes, Son, Mommy will be just fine."

"Did Mommy hurt when I was born?"

"Yes."

"And Megan too?"

"Yes, Son." Jared was on the porch opening the door. There Alex stood with the bag for the hospital all packed. "How far apart?"

"Four minutes."

Concern gripped him. Alex's labor for Megan had only been three hours. "Honey, are we going to make it to the hospital?"

"I hope so, but I don't know."

His knees locked. God would get them through this. "Do you want to stay here to have the baby or risk getting to the hospital on time?"

"If John and Martha get here right away, I think we have time."

As if on cue, Martha ran through the door. "How far apart now?"

"Four minutes," Alex repeated.

"Papa John!" Michael ran into John's arms.

"You two get going, we'll take care of the kids." Martha ushered them toward the door.

"Thanks," Jared said as he grabbed the bag.

"Mommy!" Megan ran to Alex and grabbed her at the knees.

Jared picked his daughter up and held her tight. "Pumpkin, can you do Daddy a favor?"

Megan nodded.

"Nana Martha needs help making a special treat for Mommy and the new baby. Can you help her?"

"Okay, Daddy." Jared's heart tightened. In his daughter's eyes he saw so much love. He hugged her close and passed her over to Martha.

"Thanks, Honey. Mommy and I will be back real soon. 'Bye."

※

Alex winced at each and every bump they went over as Jared made their way out the dirt road. "Jared!"

"Are you okay?"

"Yes. No. Honey, can't you avoid the bumps?"

He took her hand. "I'm trying, Dear. Relax. Have you started your breathing?"

"When did I have time?" Alex felt her temper rising. She knew her anger had to do with the labor and tried to fight her emotions.

"We'll breathe through the contractions together, Dear."

"Sorry."

"Honey, I understand."

She wanted to snap at him. He didn't have a clue what she was going through, but she fought off the urge.

They made it to the hospital in record time. She didn't want to ask Jared how fast he was driving.

"Dr. Madeiras, good to see you. Is it that time?" the receptionist asked.

"Yes, stat!" Alex called out.

The receptionist placed a call and the door flung open to a man pushing a wheelchair. She and Jared were ushered to maternity.

❧

The pain was gone the instant the doctor proclaimed, "It's a boy."

Jared kissed her. "He's beautiful, Alexandria. Have I told you lately that I love you?"

"Not in the past few minutes," Alex beamed. "I love you too."

Alex held her newborn son up to her breast, and he began to suckle. Jared wrapped his protective arms around them both. "Thank You, Lord, for another blessing and another to love. Bless him one day with a woman as wonderful as his mother."

A tear formed in Alex's eye. Seven years ago she had left Kansas, convinced God was calling her to a single life. And yet His plans were a mystery, at the time, to her. The frumpy old lady's voice on the plane played back in her mind, "They that wait on the Lord, Dear. . ."

LYNN A. COLEMAN
Raised on Martha's Vineyard, Lynn now calls Miami, Florida, home. She is a multi-published award-winning author, and the founder and president of the American Christian Romance Writers, an international writing organization. She is a minister's wife who writes to the Lord's glory. She has three grown children and seven grandchildren. She also hosts an online workshop for writers of inspirational fiction. Lynn invites you to visit her website: www.lynncoleman.com.

MOCKINGBIRD'S SONG

Janet Gortsema

Dedication

For Martha,
and for all us other Marthas,
whatever our names.

Chapter 1

On February 23, Ewald Phipps proposed to Martha Hollins. This surprised Martha greatly because February 23 was a Friday and Ewald always proposed on Saturday—every Saturday. Perhaps he'd thought a Friday proposal would surprise her into acceptance, but Friday or not, Martha's answer was just the same as always: "No."

What, he wanted to know, was she waiting for? He was doing well as an accountant, they had known each other all their lives, and they were expected, by all who knew them, to marry. He had waited long enough—through high school and college, through her beginning years of teaching biology here in Empton, Indiana, and through his beginning years at the office. Now he was twenty-nine and she, twenty-seven, and he was ready to set up his own household.

And Martha? She didn't know why she didn't say yes. She just couldn't. Ewald was a nice man, a good man. He was organized, intelligent, kind. She had known him all her life. Wasn't that enough?

Home again that night, in the small upstairs bedroom she had always had, she asked herself that question. She looked her mirrored self straight in the eye and asked—out loud, of course (she did occasionally speak out loud to herself)—if that wasn't enough. Her mirrored self had no answer. Martha studied the reflection intently, trying to find the flaw that made her behave so perversely.

The girl she saw was nice enough looking, tall and straight and trim, with green eyes that could reduce a class of high school biology students to quiet. She peered at her soft peach skin, accepting the few light freckles and feeling pleasure at its smoothness. It was, she thought, her one good feature. Of course, her hair was a problem. It wasn't red and it wasn't brown, but something in between, and it went where it wanted to go in a mass of untamable curls, kept short in self-defense. She looked reasonably good, she guessed, reasonably normal.

She was steady and dependable, a daughter who remembered her mother's medicine, a sister who was always available for babysitting, a teacher who worried overtime about her students, a church member who attended every Sunday. She loved books and quiet, always had, just as she had always tried to keep peace, to be reasonable, to do what she was expected to do.

Now she was expected to marry Ewald.

"You're a lucky girl to have Ewald," said her mother.

"Ewald will make a fine husband," said her father.

"How many other chances do you think you will have?" said her sister.

So, she guessed she should just go ahead and marry him and be done with it. But. . . .

Did she love him? She supposed she must, but it wasn't like the love she had always dreamed of. She didn't count the days, much less the hours or minutes, until they met again. His touch did not make her tingle. Worse, neither did his kiss—singular, one each date. Did he tingle at her touch? Good question. If he did, he had never mentioned it.

Was she to go from childhood to marriage without even a brief period of excitement and/or romance? Evidently. She sighed twice—once for what was and once for what was not to be.

That was Friday. On Monday, she noticed the flyer announcing a one-time special summer program for biology teachers, a work/study program, sponsored by the National Park Service, at the National Seashore installation on Cape Cod. A few "carefully selected teachers" would work on-site for this one summer, "with a view toward sharing their experiences with their colleagues and students on their return to the classroom." *Imagine,* she thought, *a whole summer on Cape Cod. How lovely for some fortunate teachers.* Not her, of course, since she always spent her summers helping her sister with the children and her parents with the house and the garden. She was very busy. She couldn't possibly find time to go. Besides, she would never be selected.

On Tuesday, in a wild gesture, she mailed her application. Then, having done that much, she erased it from her mind. It was fun applying, pretending she could go, but she was too practical to hope for more.

In early May, to her total astonishment, she received official notice of her acceptance. She was going, really going. Alone. She hadn't thought of that before. She had never gone anywhere alone, not even to college. She had commuted to college from home.

"What will Ewald say?" asked her mother.

"Are you sure you know what you're doing?" asked her father.

"How can you do this to me when you know how much I depend on you?" cried her sister.

"I guess I won't go," Martha said, until Ewald told her she must go, so she would have her taste of the world and be ready (he hoped) to settle down. He expected her to go.

So, in early June she went. She loaded her possessions into her blue Chevy sedan, kissed them all good-bye, and drove off for Massachusetts.

It was quiet in the car, even with the radio for company. She wished she had someone along to talk to, to eat with, to read the map. Her mother had insisted she stay overnight with a cousin in Pennsylvania, and she was glad she did. Other than that, she was alone. She drove and thought and thought and drove.

What was she doing alone out here where no one knew her? Having an adventure, that's what. Serious, cautious, old Martha was having an adventure. Old? Twenty-seven is not so old. It just sounds old if your name is Martha. She had always disliked the name. When she had been small, she had asked her mother, "How could you name me 'Martha'?"

"You know," her mother had answered. "You're named after my favorite sister and after Lazarus's sister."

"Martha? The sister who was too busy to have time to sit and listen to Jesus? The one who was doing all the work while her sister sat and enjoyed the company?" Martha had groaned.

"I wanted you to have a Bible name," her mother had said.

But Mother, she thought now, *a Martha would not have green eyes and soft peach skin like mine, would not be a slender five foot, eight inches tall, would not have the embarrassing habit of talking to herself. A Martha would look like. . .like Martha Washington.* Martha's russet curls bounced in indignation as she resisted, again, the idea that anybody could see her as a Martha. She wished she were someone else, someone different, someone fun and carefree, maybe a little fluffy. Not very fluffy, but a little, instead of reliable and practical and dull.

"I don't want you to be somebody else. I like you the way you are," her mother would have said.

"I don't," said Martha to the car. "I'm nobody going nowhere. I need to be out there with the rest of the world, doing things, having fun. Living."

"You are living," her mother would have said.

"Mother," she said to the car, "I'm twenty-seven years old and still doing the same things I've been doing all my life. My friends have all moved on with their lives and I'm standing still. I need to change. I need to learn a new way to be. I can be anybody I want to be for one whole summer. The National Park Service will never know the difference."

"You'll know," said the mother in her imagination.

"I hope so," Martha said to the car.

That's it, she thought. This one time she wanted to forget what she had been and who she was and reach for what she wanted. And what was it she wanted? She wasn't sure. But she knew it wasn't what she had and what she was. Martha didn't dream of fur coats and trips to Paris. Her wishes were more modest and more difficult to achieve. She wanted to be young and in love and. . .different. She wanted to have a good time, just for one summer, before her life snapped shut.

What she needed, she decided, was a disguise so she could be someone else for awhile—not forever, of course, just for awhile. But then she decided it wouldn't work. Too complicated, too melodramatic. Maybe she could just pretend she was someone else. Or maybe she could just call herself another name, a name that fit the person she thought she'd like to be. If she had a different name, maybe she'd feel different—or maybe other people would see her as different. It had possibilities.

All day she played with other names, and by nightfall she had found one to wear for the summer: Muffie. It sounded light (fluffy?), frivolous, fun, new. It sounded just right. By the end of the two long days on the road to Cape Cod, she had made up her mind to change, just for the summer. She would be a Muffie.

What a Muffie would do, she would do. What would a Muffie do? For one thing, a Muffie would like the new popular music. She could start there. She practiced with the radio, experimentally trying to tune her ears to what was (to her) abrasive music on the car radio. She was not successful. *I'll get used to it*, she thought. *I've spent my life in quiet too long.*

She'd get used to the efficiency apartment in Wellfleet too. The apartment found and reserved for her by the summer program administrators was scarcely more than a room added by remodeling the upstairs of an old gray shingle house. At first glance it was depressing—hot, stuffy, drab—but she made up her mind she would learn to like it. It would be fun, kind of like camping. Closets were not really necessary, not really. Neither was a full-sized refrigerator. And the tiny stove (stovelet?) would be plenty big. A wall or two would have been helpful, though, to separate the kitchen from the rest of the big room that was living room and bedroom all in one. Ah well, there were three windows and a private entrance at the top of those outside stairs. If the stairs shook like a rope ladder, that was all part of the fun. Best of all, it was undeniably different.

The apartment came complete with a roommate—a tiny, perfect, blond with delicate bones and beautiful blue eyes and enough clothing to outfit Martha's entire fifth period class. Bree, her name was, short for Brianna, and she was in her third summer of lifeguard duty at the Seashore beach.

Perfect, thought the new Muffie. *Bree is just perfect. She's everything I want to be and if I watch her, I can learn to be just like her, except for the smooth curtain of silky blond hair and those tiny bones, of course. I can't copy those. But I can dress as she dresses, think as she thinks, and do as she does.*

"Bree's a great name," said Muffie.

"Muffie's good too," said Bree. "What's it short for?"

"Summer," said Muffie, and laughed. "It's my name for this summer. I want to have a good time here."

"We can do that," said Bree. "Good times are my specialty. We just have to get you acquainted with the gang and you'll be on your way. I have just the man for you to meet." With that, Bree began what turned out to be an entire summer of conversation, chatting of men and clothes, and men and parties, and men and the beach, and men.

For lack of closets, she and Bree were forced to find other places for their things. Muffie put up a clothesline above the end of her bed and stacked grocery boxes on their sides, open ends out, under the window. Most of her few things were stowed neatly away in these places.

She did the same for Bree, but that clothesline was full and so were Bree's grocery boxes, and the overflow still covered the tattered sofa, both chairs, part of the little table, and various sections of the floor. Bree seemed to have an inexhaustible supply of clothing and zero interest in taking care of it.

Bree took care of paying the rent to "Old Briggs," since she seemed to know him from another year. It took the whole whirlwind weekend to get settled, begin to get used to each other, buy groceries, make plans, and locate Jack, Bree's romantic interest from last summer. By Monday, Bree was on duty and Muffie was ready for orientation. In a few days, she was at work in the Salt Pond Visitors' Center, and by Saturday, she was ready for her first group presentation on the great storms here along the coast.

Standing just inside the shelter at Marconi Station, waiting for her first "class," she felt the flutter of nervous excitement she always felt on the first day of school. "Ready," she said to no one, and quickly looked around. *I'll have to watch that talking to myself or they'll think I'm crazy*, she thought, fixing her Smokey-the-Bear hat firmly on her head against the brisk sea wind and taking her position in front of the scale model of Marconi's transmitting tower.

She stood quietly, watching the group gather. The family of five on the lookout platform moved toward her, directed there by the Protection Ranger now disappearing over the dune on his rounds. Two older ladies strolled slowly up the walkway in almost matching culottes, straw hats, and walking shoes. The two ladies smiled as they entered the shade of the shelter and settled themselves on the bench attached to the low wall. The family tumbled in and found perches on the top of the low wall in the "window" between wall and roof.

Muffie checked her watch and pulled the map of shipwrecks from her backpack. She'd wait a few more minutes for the young couple down the walk, then begin. As they arrived, she directed them to another perch on the wall.

Muffie cleared her throat and began, "Good afternoon and welcome to Cape Cod National Seashore. I'm Ranger Muffie Hollins, and I'm an interpretive ranger. I'm going to tell you about shipwrecks here on the coast of Cape Cod, but before I do, let's get to know a little bit about each other. I'm from Indiana. Is anyone else here from Indiana? No? Tell us where you're from. How about you?"

Muffie indicated the ladies on the bench, who smiled and responded. *Each one*, Muffie reminded herself, *remember to ask each one*. Drawing on her teaching experience, she worked to establish a friendly atmosphere before going on.

Her small group was warming to each other and to her. When each person had spoken, she spread out her map and held it up so they could see it.

She took a deep breath and began, "Here is a map of the known shipwrecks in this area. You can see that there are many of them all along the coast from the tip of Cape Race, on the north, to the southernmost point of the cape, the elbow. A famous writer, Henry David Thoreau, once described Cape Cod in this way. . . ."

They were paying attention, sitting quietly, expectantly, in front of her, waiting to learn. *It works just like school,* she thought with satisfaction, and went on.

Intent on getting it right, she heard the footsteps but was unwilling to interrupt the flow of her narrative. She merely nodded acknowledgment in the direction of the three latecomers. At a pause, she looked up with a welcoming smile. It was Bree and Jack and—who was this tall, tan, dazzling mass of muscles?

Muffie faltered. The three stepped quietly into the shelter and took places against the wall. The handsome stranger nodded slightly, encouragingly. She found herself gaping foolishly, or at least that's the way she felt, and struggled to break eye contact, to look away from his soft brown eyes.

Where was she? She tried to collect her thoughts. Oh yes. . .up to the part about the waves, her favorite part. She took a deep breath.

"We're going to make some waves," she said to the little group. She stepped to the edge of the shelter and scooped up a double handful of sand. "Now, I'm going to give each of you some sand, so I want you to help me by holding your hands cupped together like this."

She scooped sand from the dune outside the shelter and allowed a small stream of sand to flow through her hands into the waiting hands of the smallest boy, then of the second boy, and so on. Jack and Bree obediently accepted sand. The mass of muscles held out his enormous tanned hands too, and Muffie poured sand into them. She glanced up as she stopped the flow of sand, hands poised above his.

He was grinning.

She looked away quickly. He was laughing at her! She felt a rush of embarrassment warm her face. Her hands trembled, losing some of their sand in a sudden lurch.

She glared at him.

He laughed, showing perfect white teeth.

What nerve he had!

She set her jaw. *He is not going to make me lose control on my very first lecture,* she thought. *First I'll do this and do it right. Then I'll deal with him.* She faced the smallest boy. "Now," she said, "hold your hands like this and rub them together. Harder."

She got through it, somehow, demonstrating the abrasive action of wave-driven sand on the bottoms of the ships. She covered the importance of the Nauset Lighthouse and the Lifesavers with their breeches buoy and their motto, "You have to go out but you don't have to come back." She showed the photos of the tanker *Emmaday*, stranded on the beach one winter, and the photos of damage done by a nor'easter.

She covered it all and, with a relieved sigh, asked if there were any questions. There were a few, including "How do you get to be a Lifesaver?" and "If I find a sunken treasure, can I keep it?" She knew the answers and felt the group was satisfied with her presentation.

"Good-bye and thank you," they said and left at various speeds down the path, leaving her with Bree, Jack, and the grinning mass of muscles.

Now for him, she thought grimly, and turned with hands on hips.

"You were great," Muscles said before she could speak. "Really great!"

"This is Charlie Cooper," said Bree, beaming like she was offering a gift. "He rooms at Jack's house. He's in P.E.—Physical Education. Charlie, this is Muffie. Shake hands nicely and don't crush her hand before you even get to know her."

"Does that mean he'll crush it later?" asked Muffie, hands behind her back.

He laughed, obediently holding out his hand in greeting. "I never crunch up feisty little redheads. Too dangerous."

Muffie smiled, in spite of herself, at the thought of anyone thinking of her as either feisty or dangerous and held out her hand to be enveloped in his massive paw and kept there. She looked up in protest. He smiled down at her with a slow, confident smile that made her uneasy. He gave her hand a little squeeze, then slightly relaxed his hold, allowing her to pull free.

"Most people call me Coach," he said. "You can, if you want to."

Muffie didn't answer. With difficulty she drew her eyes away from that mocking smile and shifted her one hundred twenty-four pounds away from him to stand slightly behind Bree.

"We came to hear your first lecture," said Jack. "It was Bree's idea. She thought it would be fun. Hope we didn't make you nervous."

"Of course not," Muffie murmured.

"You did fine," Bree said, "but of course you would, being a teacher and all. Want to go to P'town with us to celebrate your success? You've never been there and it will be fun."

"Go where?"

"P'town. . .Provincetown. We thought we'd look around a little, catch a bite to eat, show you the town. What do you say?" Clearly, Bree had already decided; the question was a formality.

"My car. . . ," began Muffie.

Bree said, "You can't run around P'town dressed like Smokey the Bear. You can make a fast change at the apartment and leave your car there. Jack's driving. Come on." Bree grabbed Jack's arm and started down the path toward the parking lot, her enthusiastic hopping little step making her long, silky blond hair bounce and shimmer in the sunlight. Muffie hesitated. This Charlie and his big white teeth intimidated her. She was not at all sure she was safe with him. *On the other hand,* she thought, *if I wanted to be safe, I should have stayed in Indiana. I said I wanted a new life and here it is staring me right in the face. I got what I wanted and now I'm afraid to take it. What's the matter with me?*

Charlie was dangling her heavy backpack lightly from three fingers. "Ready?" he asked.

"Ready," she answered and hoped she was.

She gritted her teeth when he draped one heavy arm possessively over her shoulders and swept her at half-lope after the others. In the parking lot, she watched the three climb into Jack's roofless, sideless white four-wheel-drive and roar away in a sandstorm of their own making.

Her ordinary blue Chevy looked sedate and tired compared to Jack's white dust thrower. Rebelliously, she jerked the Chevy into reverse and jammed her foot down on the accelerator. The engine shuddered and stopped.

Flooded, she thought. *Serves me right. Poor old car just isn't made for the fast lane. It's good enough to go back and forth to school until it wears out, but it's not much in a place like this. If I'm not careful, I'll be like that—just good enough to go back and forth to school until I wear out.*

"Not me," she said to the car. "Not if I can help it."

The Chevy's progress to the apartment was maddeningly slow. They were waiting for her out front when she got there. She rushed upstairs and reached for her new lavender shirtwaist dress, the one she had made especially for this summer. On second thought, she opted instead for clothes as much like Bree's as she could manage. She exchanged her gray uniform shirt and gray-green pants for a soft spring-green blouse and white soft pants. She took a quick pass at her face with the washcloth and tried to brush smooth her tangled copper curls. It would have to do.

She dashed down the stairs only a little out of breath and climbed into the backseat of Jack's car as Charlie held the door open. (*Do I call this a car,* she wondered?) She expected Charlie to shut the door and let himself in on the other side, but he slid in after her, so she moved to the far corner to make space between them. He moved over too, filling all the space she had made and then some. There was a lot of Charlie.

He was overpowering, breathtaking. She tried not to look at him, but sat quietly, listening to his voice as he joked easily across the front seat barrier.

"Want to stop at the dunes and let Red here try the big-time sandpile?" he was saying.

"Muffie," she said firmly. "My name is Muffie."

"I told you she was feisty," he said to the front seat. To her he said, "Okay, I'll call you Muffie. You call me Coach. Deal?"

"Coach?"

"Not good?" he asked.

"I'd feel like one of your students," she said.

"Okay then, call me Charlie. Deal?"

"Okay. . .Charlie."

He grinned and went back to his conversation with the front seat, allowing her an undisturbed opportunity for a better look at him. In profile, he was too handsome to be real, a magnificently carved animal with great strong white teeth flashing against a rich tan. The sun had apparently bleached his hair from a light brown, which was still visible where the wind blew the top layer of pale yellow hair every which way to expose the original color underneath. The hairs on his massive arms were bleached too, as though he had absorbed the sun, become part of it.

Though tousled by the wind, he had that flawless, carelessly perfect polish of the wealthy. No T-shirt for him. He wore one of those short-sleeved, safari-type shirts she had so far seen only in magazines, and plaid cotton trousers that virtually shouted for notice. Nobody she had ever known had dared wear such trousers. To do so was to invite laughter. She knew, instinctively, that Charlie would enjoy the laughter, would join in and make it his own.

How wonderful, she thought, *to be so confident, so free to do as he chooses.*

He turned at that moment and saw her smiling and smiled back, a genuine smile of open friendliness. She saw that beneath sun-bleached brows his eyes were a warm brown and that they still danced with mischief. This time she found their laughter appealing and laughed back.

"That's better," he said and stretched his enormous arm across the back of her seat. "You and I will have a good time together. We'll make a great team. Stick with Ol' Charlie and you won't be disappointed."

But will he be disappointed in me? she wondered silently. This was no Ewald Phipps, satisfied with holding her hand on the way home from church. This Charlie was strong, dynamic, demanding. She knew she could handle Ewald, but Charlie was another animal altogether.

Her heart lurched. Fear? *Excitement,* she told herself firmly. This is what she had come here for. All she had to do now was follow Bree's lead and she'd be all right.

In the front seat, Jack rested one hand on Bree's shoulder, idly brushing her cheek while he drove. Now and then he turned to look at her, and she gazed into his eyes and crinkled her adorable little nose at him.

I wonder if that would work for me, thought Muffie, giving an experimental crinkle to her classic nose. *No use. Bouncy cheerleader types like Bree can get by with that cute stuff, but I'd feel silly instead of adorable. I'd better stick with normal.*

Normal can't be so bad, she reflected, thinking of the men in Indiana who had said she was attractive. *According to them, green eyes and reddish-brown curls were a pretty combination. But then, they were tame men looking for a tame life with a tame girl. All I know how to be is tame. I'm not exciting enough for this dangerous man with his air of knowing confidence. My one advantage is that he doesn't know how really dull I am. He probably thinks that if Bree and I are friends, we must be very much alike.*

Wrong. But I can watch her and learn. I can fake it. I can act sophisticated like one of those women selling perfume on television, and if I don't make a fool of myself, I just might convince him that I'm a little dangerous myself.

Relax, she told herself, and tried to relax. *Now smile when he looks at you, but only slightly. Let him think you're deciding whether or not he's interesting enough for you. Good. Now look away. Don't look back. Relax.*

This is foolish.

Of course it's foolish. That's what vacations are—chances to look foolish without having your friends watch.

Muffie giggled nervously to herself, then heard her own soft giggle and looked back quickly to see if he had heard.

He was watching. She smiled, carefully, slightly. His interest showed in his eyes and he leaned toward her, abandoning his conversation with the driver.

Her heart lurched again. *Watch it,* she cautioned herself. *Don't overdo it. This man is a handful.*

Charlie pointed ahead on the right where huge bare dunes rose close to the highway. As they came nearer, Muffie could see that while part of these dunes was closed off by snow fence, a large section was accessible to the public.

"Here's your sandpile, Fluffy," Charlie said.

"Muffie," she corrected.

"Right."

Jack explained, "This is one of the few places where the dunes are actually supposed to be climbed on. Dunes look permanent, but they are actually very fragile. Any traffic at all on the dunes, even an occasional barefooted walker, breaks down the thin protective layer of vegetation that holds the sand in place. When that happens, the dunes disintegrate. They move or blow away with the winds or collapse into the sea.

"This little section of dunes is open to satisfy everybody's natural desire to climb on a dune and see for himself what it's like. I suppose the conservationists hope that people will stay off the other dunes if they sacrifice this one.

"You can tell I teach earth science," Jack laughed, slowing the car to a stop in the parking area at the foot of the dune.

Before the car was fully stopped, Charlie had jumped out. He ran around to Muffie's side of the car.

"Pick up your feet," he ordered, grasping Muffie's waist with two huge hands as she rose to get out of the car. With no visible effort at all, except for the muscles shifting under the tan skin of his massive arms, he lifted her out of the car and set her on the sand.

"About one hundred twenty pounds, I'd guess," he said, his hands still on her waist.

She grasped his wrists to pull his hands away. It was like grasping stone. He smiled down at her.

"Am I close?" he asked, not moving.

"Close," she answered, thinking, too close. Then he released her and began to climb, leaving her to struggle in his wake through the deep sand.

It was difficult going. Her feet sank so far in with each step that she had to take giant climbing steps to get anywhere at all. At ten feet up, she pulled off her sandals rather than ruin them. At twenty feet, she leaned forward to scramble up on all fours, shoe straps clutched in one hand. At forty feet, she was hot, out of breath. She looked up to see Charlie grinning down at her from another twenty feet above her head.

"Need help?" he asked.

"No," she said, standing still, ankle deep in sand.

His grin widened. He slid down almost to her and reached out one hand to help her. She took it and felt herself lifted until her feet skimmed lightly over the heavy sand, climbing easily to the windy crest.

"Thanks," she said as she straightened to look around. "I guess I'm a little out of shape."

"Don't worry; I'll have you toughened up in no time. They don't call me Coach for nothing."

She shut her eyes against the thought of toughening up, especially if it involved more climbs. *How did Bree manage to climb this?* She looked behind her to discover that Bree and Jack were still in the car, vehicle, whatever. "They didn't climb," she said inanely.

Charlie shrugged. "They've seen it before. When you've seen one dune, you've seen 'em all. Race you down?"

"I just got here," she objected, "and I'm probably never coming back." On the other side of the dune lay more sand, then the Atlantic Ocean, stretching forever into the horizon and past it. "Ohhhh," she breathed, captured by the majesty of the sea.

"Nice view," offered Charlie. "Ready to go?"

Muffie sighed and reluctantly turned away to begin the slip-slide descent. Reaching up to her this time, Charlie held out a steadying hand, which she grasped without hesitation. Going down was easier than going up, but it still took effort.

"Thanks," she said again at the bottom. "I can manage from here."

He seemed not to hear. He did not let go of her hand until they reached the car. She was afraid he was going to lift her in, but he only opened the door to allow her to clamber in, then he slid in after her. It seemed reasonable for him to assume his usual two-thirds of the seat.

"P'town?" asked Jack.

"Right," answered Charlie and Bree in what must have sounded like a unanimous vote to Jack, who promptly revved up the engine and roared out of the sand and onto the highway.

With the jerk into action, Muffie's head snapped backward, then snapped forward at the first gear change. She struggled to regain her poise. *No one noticed. That's a blessing,* she thought. Or was it?

Blessing. She hadn't heard that word around here, and she wasn't likely to hear it unless she was the one who said it. Losing that word from her vocabulary would take a little work. She had grown up with it, had been taught to say a blessing before each meal, had been told to "Count your blessings," had heard over and over the expression, "It's a blessing that. . ." According to her mother, there were blessings everywhere.

"Amen to that," her father would have said.

Well, maybe they were right about their lives being full of blessings, but to Muffie the same life was just stifling. As she had grown to feel more and more closed in by it, she had lost interest in the details of that life. She no longer cared about the height of the corn by the Fourth of July nor about the date of the first hard frost. She wanted out, if only for one free summer. If "out" meant a summer without blessings, that was fine with her.

Wasn't it?

When she had second thoughts like this she wondered if she really did know what she was doing. She must stop this.

"No second thoughts," she said.

"What did you say?" said Charlie.

"No. . ." Muffie unfuzzied her thoughts and returned to reality to find Charlie leaning toward her attentively.

"No what?" he prodded.

"Um. . .no. . .um. . .no cloud in the sky today," she invented.

He looked up. "Nope. Perfect day for the beach."

Bree swung her head around. "You and your beach. Is that all you think of?"

"Nope," said Charlie, studying Muffie's face intently until she looked away in confusion.

"Don't turn away," he said. "I like that funny face of yours. I was just counting your freckles." He reached out to touch her gently on the cheek.

She sat very still, not looking at him, not looking anyplace.

"You don't like that, do you," he said, and it was not a question.

"I don't know you well enough to like it," she answered.

His finger traced the side of her cheek. "You will," he said. "I promise." He tapped her lightly on the nose and chuckled. Then he slowly sat back in his own two-thirds of the seat.

Muffie released a long slow breath as quietly as she could. *He scares me,* she thought. *Why? Because he does things and says things I'm not used to? So does Bree, but she doesn't scare me. Because he's so big? Maybe that's it. That must be it. It's this feeling that he could crush me with one hand if he wanted to. That and the fact that I don't know whether he might just want to.*

Don't be silly, she scolded herself. *If Bree thought he was dangerous, she wouldn't have brought him along for me.*

Relax. Smile. . .slightly, mysteriously.

Chapter 2

The mysterious smile was stiff on Muffie's lips by the time they reached the center of Provincetown. The powerful white car chortled to slow motion on tight old streets lined with houses from at least a hundred years ago. They slowed for approach and came to a standstill at the choked intersection of the old whaling village's primary shopping street, appropriately named Commercial Street, and the wider street to the municipal pier.

People thronged the intersection, the sidewalks, and the middle of the shopping street itself as far right or left as Muffie could see.

"What's happening?" she asked, looking for fire trucks or parade barriers.

"Saturday night in P'town," said Jack. "This is where it all happens."

"Where what happens?"

"Anything. Everything. It's a good-time town—part Disney, part New England, part pure craziness. I'll drive down Commercial and you can see for yourself." Jack eased the car carefully through a right turn onto the shopping street and she looked.

Ice cream stands and souvenir shops competed with T-shirt displays and craft shops. Pedestrians and bicyclists twined and intertwined their paths, now and then very casually moving aside to make barely enough space for a car or two to creep through. A blasé teenage boy coasted by on skates, grazing the curb on one swerve, nudging a car on another, all without change of expression. Although the car crept through the crowd only slightly faster than someone walking, she couldn't look fast enough to see it all.

"Is it always like this?" she asked.

"Only in summer," answered Jack. "The Cape is a different place in winter. Then we locals take over again, and the town belongs to the fishing fleet and the artists and the other full-time residents. I think I prefer the winter, really."

"But there's nothing to do here in the winter," objected Bree. "I don't know how you get along."

"Just like everyone else in the world does, I guess," said Jack. "We store up enough fun in the summer to last us through the cold."

"Not me," said Bree. "I like action and people and good times. Don't you, Muffie?"

"Definitely." Muffie sounded determined, even to her own ears, thinking that she too, had to store up enough good times for the cold, maybe even enough for the rest of her life.

"I like the way you girls think," agreed Charlie. "Let's grab up the good times."

At the end of the most crowded section, Jack turned right again to get to a faster street two blocks over. After a few blocks, he drove into a parking lot. "The only way to see the town is to walk," he announced. "Everybody out."

Crossing the street, they descended a few stairs and cut through a side walkway almost too small to be a street, although it boasted a street sign. On both sides were two- and three-story houses that looked quite old. Many were remodeled into vacation apartments, studios, and rooming houses, with modern skylights and decks stuck here and there in old walls and roofs. At the end of the short "street," they found themselves in the midst of the strolling crowd on Commercial Street.

For the most part, the strollers moved along with easy, relaxed grace. With no sense of urgency, no hint of intent to arrive at a particular place at a particular time, people seemed to walk and look for the mere pleasure of seeing and being seen.

Along the sides, on curbs, benches, railings, and porches, people rested and watched the passersby. Some sat in open windows above the narrow street. Dogs trotted back and forth in loose proximity to owners. A monkey peered down at Muffie from his perch atop a passing shoulder. Babies slept in backpacks while their parents enjoyed the evening. Old people and young moved side by side, forward and across and back. The human tide moved and milled in the amiable ease of a crowd in relaxed pursuit of pleasure.

"Belgian waffles," read Charlie. "Sounds good to me."

"All food sounds good to you, Charlie," laughed Bree, crinkling her nose at him.

"True, true," Charlie said, passing the Belgian waffles by. "This is Muffie's first taste of P'town, so we ought to eat whatever she wants. What'll it be, Muffie?"

She answered immediately, "Anything. Anything at all, just so it's real food and something I've never tasted before."

Bree skipped a couple of steps in excitement. She said, "If you mean that, I've got the very place for you—the little place on the corner next to the sandal maker. You know the place I mean, Jack?"

"The raw bar?" he asked.

"Right," said Bree. "The very thing."

"I don't know about that," Jack said.

Bree said, "Sure. She'll love it. Won't she, Charlie?"

Aware of a glint of mischief in Bree's blue eyes, Muffie asked, "A bar?"

"No," said Bree, "a place that serves raw fresh food."

"Fine," said Muffie. "I like salad."

Charlie laughed loudly. "Did you two hear that? She says she likes salad. Let's get her some salad."

"What's funny?" said Muffie.

Charlie only laughed again.

The raw bar was far down the street, and they were in no hurry. Along the way they wandered in and out of whatever shops caught their attention. In one arcade, Muffie stood entranced by shelf after shelf of seashells from all over the world, labeled and priced. Bree lingered over silver earrings. Charlie paced up and down the aisles, restless, while Jack found acquaintances among those behind the counters and stopped to pass the time of day.

The fragrant aroma of fresh bread drew them to the Portuguese bakery, but Bree pulled them past it, promising to return if they were still hungry later. She intercepted Charlie's move to the empty table at the sidewalk café too.

Near the town hall/police headquarters, they heard music and wandered around to the other side of the building to stand with others for part of a folk music concert. At a break in the music, Bree pulled them back to the main street, herding them past the open door of the salt water taffy shop.

"Kites!" shouted Charlie, and he disappeared. The others followed up the steps to a big old house bedecked with windsocks and oriental kites catching the evening breeze from poles in the front yard.

Inside were more kites: plastic ones, and paper, and floating silk. They hung from the ceiling and covered the walls and took up space on the uneven wooden floor, leaving a meandering path among the displayed wares. They found Charlie in the back room, gazing up at five silk triangles attached one above the other.

"Aren't those triangles something?" he demanded.

"They're lovely," agreed Muffie, "but aren't they a little tricky to fly?"

"Of course. That's the fun—much better than a single delta. A delta's so stable it'll fly all day tied to a chair. Boring."

"How about a small dragon?" suggested the salesgirl, who had come up behind them. "That's a rainbow dragon right above your head. They're responsive and frisky without being difficult to manage."

"Sounds like the perfect woman," said Charlie.

He's brash and crude, Muffie thought. Her face showed her objection to Charlie's comment. "Charlie. . ."

He laughed. To the clerk he said, "She's feisty." Then he laughed again at Muffie's glare and pointed to the ceiling.

Muffie looked up to see a long, tapering kite suspended loop after loop across the ceiling. "It's beautiful," she said, "like a silken ribbon. But it's so long. I don't think. . ."

"Of course you can," said Charlie. "We'll take it."

"It's too expensive," she objected.

"We have mylar dragons," said the clerk. "They're much less expensive than nylon and fine for beginners. . . ."

"Fine," said Charlie. "The fifty-foot one, and string and a swivel."

"Twenty-five foot," said Muffie.

"Twenty-five foot mylar and string and a swivel," said the clerk, who knew what the customers should have even if they didn't know.

"Thank you," said Muffie, as Charlie paid.

He said, "Here. It's yours. You carry it. Now let's eat."

The raw bar was just across the main intersection, identified by a home-made sign that was easy to miss. The little wooden shack was not more than an open stand with no seats out front and no door to go inside. There was only a rough counter with holders for paper napkins. Oil drum trash containers flanked the ends of the counter. To Muffie it looked rough and shabby, but customers crowded so thickly around it that she couldn't see past them to the inside.

With help from Jack and Charlie, they worked their way up to the counter where Muffie could see what people were eating. "What are those things in clam shells lying on the crushed ice?" she asked.

"Clams," said Charlie, "raw clams and oysters. That's why they call this a raw bar."

"Where do they cook them?" Muffie asked, looking for and not finding a stove.

"They don't. You eat them raw."

Muffie's stomach lurched. "Raw?"

"Raw and alive. That way you're sure they're fresh. What's the matter?"

Muffie couldn't take her eyes off the clams. "But Charlie, you don't even kill them?"

"You do if you bite into them. Otherwise, I guess your digestive juices kill them. They're supposed to be eaten this way. Come on, Duffy; I'll show you."

"Muffie," she said, backing up a step. "That's okay. A hamburger would be fine."

Bree taunted, "I thought you wanted to try something new."

Muffie felt queasy. "I do, really. It's just that. . .they look so. . .slippery."

"Try one, just one," said Charlie. "I'll order a dozen and you can have one of mine."

The dozen on the counter in their little paper container looked bigger and bigger. Muffie watched Charlie, then Bree and Jack as each picked up a clam, shell and all. She peered in to see if the little mollusks were breathing. She couldn't tell.

Charlie squeezed lemon on his clam and held the shell to his mouth. He tipped it up, swallowed, and put the empty shell on the counter.

"See?" said Charlie, "nothing to it. Here." He held out a shell to Muffie.

Muffie's stomach heaved uncomfortably. Bree laughed and upended her shell. She was still laughing as she chewed. Muffie felt a little green.

Jack said, "You don't have to eat one it you don't want to. I don't eat cabbage. Can't stand the stuff."

"Maybe another time," said Muffie.

"Maybe never," said Bree, daring, challenging.

"Nothing to it," said Charlie.

Muffie gulped. Now or never, she thought. If I don't try. . .

She took the wet, slippery clam from Charlie and pulled it out of its shell, tugging it loose, certain it was hanging on for dear life. In her fingers it was not as slippery as she had expected. *Quick,* she thought, *before I change my mind.* She popped it into her mouth and clapped her hand over her mouth to keep it there.

It sat on her tongue. She blinked, half expecting to feel it move. She tried to swallow, but it wouldn't go down. She could feel her throat start to close.

"Chew," said Bree, so Muffie chewed.

I killed it, she thought and chewed some more. She was grateful to discover that the clam was muscular and not slippery, and it helped to know that the thing was now dead. A few more desperate chews, then a giant swallow and it was gone. She resisted an almost overwhelming urge to bring it back.

Cheers from Charlie and Jack made her feat official. She smiled shakily, tasting the strange flavor still in her mouth and hoping the clam would stay where it was.

At her elbow Bree said, "Another one, Muffie? Only one left."

"Mine," said Charlie, and swallowed it whole. "Now, let's see about some real food instead of just appetizers. What next, Muffie? Fried crab?"

She hoped not.

"I could go for one of Mario's wedges," volunteered Jack. "How's that?"

"What is it?" asked Muffie, trying not to sound cautious.

"Basic stuff—a fat sandwich. Some places they're called heroes, or submarines, or hoagies. It's okay. Honest."

Jack sounded believable, so Muffie voted for a wedge. A few minutes later, she was sitting on a step with a normal-looking ham and cheese wedge in her hand.

"Beer for everybody," announced Charlie, putting four cans down on the top step.

"No thanks," Muffie said lightly.

"No beer? You don't like clams and now you don't like beer." Charlie shook his head. "What kind of life do you live out there in Indiana?"

"Life there is just like it is here, only different," said Muffie, trying to answer without actually explaining.

"That clears it up," said Jack, and they all laughed. "Now get the lady something she can drink, Charlie. She's earned it. Lemonade?"

Muffie nodded and Charlie obligingly went for lemonade.

"Charlie doesn't understand anybody who can turn down a beer," said Bree.

Jack studied Muffie thoughtfully and said, "I have a feeling there are quite a few things about you he's not going to understand."

Privately agreeing with him, Muffie's only response was a rueful half smile. Adapting to this new lifestyle was more difficult than she had expected. She never knew when one of her cautious old ways would trip her up and betray her. *When in doubt*, she thought, *be quiet*.

Bree said, "If you ask me—"

"Hey, there's the professor! Professor! Over here, Professor," Jack shouted, jumping up and waving his arm.

Bree groaned aloud, "Oh, no!"

An arm waved back above the heads, then a face emerged from the crowd. As the professor came closer and stopped next to the step she sat on, Muffie caught her breath.

He was lean and tall, very tall, so that even though she sat on the top step and he stood on the ground on the other side of the railing, she still had to look almost straight up to see his face.

As Jack introduced them, the professor looked down at her and she saw that his eyes were blue and deep as the sea itself. His mouth smiled politely, but the serious eyes studied her intently.

"Muffie?" The professor was verifying her name.

She nodded vaguely and offered her hand for him to shake.

He looked at the proffered hand, which still held her nibbled-on ham and cheese wedge. "No, thank you," he said politely as he took a closer look at this slender young woman. His glance rested on soft full lips and smooth skin and returned to the startling green eyes. He added, "If you don't mind, I'll join you for a few minutes."

He sauntered easily around the railing and settled his lanky frame on the step below Muffie's feet, resting his back against the railing.

"Are you here for a vacation?" he asked Muffie.

"No. . .yes. . .sort of," she answered.

He waited for further explanation, but Muffie thought of none.

"She's a seasonal interpretive," explained Bree.

"Interpretive," he repeated, sounding as if he thought it unlikely. She wondered if it was because she hadn't made sense. "Do you teach in the winter?"

"Um—" she responded.

"Yes, she does," said Bree.

"I see," said the professor, sounding as if he didn't see at all.

Charlie returned with lemonade for Muffie, greeted the professor, and sat down to inhale his wedge. Muffie listened as the conversation moved quickly from light chat to serious talk as Jack compared notes with the newcomer on recent sightings of some kind. As the professor became more and more animated in the discussion, his lean face came alive and the blue depths of his eyes sparkled with interest. He talked with his hands, using them to emphasize his words. They gestured with sinuous grace, and she found herself fascinated by their movements.

Everything about him was intense, she decided: his eyes, his black unruly hair, black except for a trace of white at the temples, his straight dark eyebrows, his wide, serious mouth. Everything but his clothes, which were clean but careless, almost shabby. His jeans were worn to threadbare spots at the knees, and his faded sweatshirt sported holes in the elbows to match the holes in his jeans. He dressed as if what he wore was too unimportant to occupy thought or time.

Her eyes returned to his and found them watching her with the same intensity she had felt in his talk. He seemed to be waiting for an answer to some question she had been too preoccupied to hear.

She looked at Bree, who was regarding her with some amusement. Bree spoke for her again, "Not yet. She hasn't had time. She and Charlie are. . ."

"You're with Charlie," the stranger said, blue eyes steady on Muffie's green ones. Muffie nodded. The professor looked Muffie over, assessing, frowning slightly, and she felt sure there was some obscure disappointment in the look, some disapproval behind his scrutiny. "Hmmm," he said, and turned back to his conversation with Jack.

Feeling as if she had been dismissed, Muffie refused to be shut out and began to follow the conversation. As she listened, she learned that the sightings they found so engrossing were sightings of whales. Putting one piece with another, she came to the conclusion that "the professor" really was a professor and that he was involved in some kind of study of whales.

Whatever it was, it totally absorbed him and she found it gradually began to interest her too. She scarcely noticed Charlie's departure and return with another wedge. She forgot her earlier dazed reticence and, urged by her natural curiosity, began to ask questions. Her knowledge of whales was book knowledge, a smattering of information about their biological functions but little about their world. Although her questions were no doubt elementary, the professor answered her with as much respect as he would demonstrate in answering difficult questions from his colleagues. She was unaware that he phrased his answers carefully so that she would feel comfortable in asking more. She knew only that he and his whales were fascinating.

Shuffling and pacing next to her, Charlie was impatient to be done with the conversation. Bree was too. Finally, brought to awareness by their blatant signaling, Jack stood, saying with regret, "We have to go."

The professor nodded in understanding and took his leave. He took three long steps away from them and turned back. He spoke to Muffie alone. "If you'd like to see the whales sometime, come out on the boat."

"I'd like that," she said.

Almost as an afterthought, he spoke to the others, "Come anytime. Just let me know." He nodded a general good-bye and strode off, the only person on the street moving with purposeful speed.

Bree said irritably, "Next time we see one of Jack's professors on the street, try to pretend we don't know him. We wasted more than an hour with his boring whales."

"I didn't think they were boring," said Muffie.

"We know," said Bree. "If you had asked one more question, I was going to step on your fingers. Let's go. It's almost seven-thirty and we've covered only half of this place."

"Wind's up," said Charlie, lifting his face to the sharp breeze. "I say we fly the new kite awhile before we do anymore shopping."

Charlie led them to the municipal pier, then off into the sand of the beach behind the shop buildings of Commercial Street. There he fixed the swivel onto the arched face of the dragon and firmly attached the cord to the swivel. He tossed the kite into the air, allowing it a little string for a start, and tugged and coaxed it until it hung like a rainbow in the sky over the beach.

The long, many-colored tail unfurled as the face pulled it skyward. It rippled and stretched, moving like a live thing against the clouds. When Charlie was satisfied that the kite was properly in place, he beckoned Muffie to him. Placing the twine roll in her hand, he stood behind her, reaching around her to demonstrate the method for flying kites.

He was too close. She felt trapped, smothered, confused. He seemed not to notice, but went about the business of placing her hands correctly and explaining when to tug and when not to tug. Gradually, she resigned herself to his closeness and began to pay attention to his instructions.

"Now you've got it," he encouraged, and he let go, stepping back. Relieved and confused all at once, she let out the loop of string she had held in her right hand. Immediately, the kite dived. "Pull," he ordered. She did and was amazed to see the kite rise steadily upward again.

"Do that again," he instructed. "Let out some string."

Again the dragon plunged toward earth.

"Tug," he said, and again the dragon rose and steadied.

"I've got it; I've got it!" she cried. Experimentally loosening and tugging, she played the kite into dips and dives and loops and climbs until her arms ached.

For almost an hour she played like a child next to this giant, and he had patiently led her into it. She looked up at him, astonished. This was a side of him she hadn't expected. She had thought he would demand attention for himself all the time, but he'd obviously enjoyed her pleasure in the kite. He was kind—a little crude, but kind. And fun. There was more to this man than just muscle.

She watched him carefully fold the kite as she held the rainbow ribbon taut in the stiff breeze. Bree and Jack appeared from up the beach where they had wandered while the dragon had been in the air.

The four drifted toward the shops of Commercial Street again and wandered up and back, covering every shop that was still open, which was most of the shops. Instead of dispersing, the crowd thickened and became a huge party. Some sang and laughed as they strolled, and Muffie absorbed the mood of it, humming little snatches of tunes to herself now and then.

They sampled and tasted South Seas frappe, which was the most delicious kind of milkshake Muffie had ever tasted—fruit-flavored and luscious; fried whole crabs, which squished in her mouth like enormous spiders; cranberry sherbet to erase the taste of the crab; salt water taffy; and Portuguese deep-fried dough. She tasted it all.

Charlie stopped them for another beer at an outdoor café. Uncomfortable with the drinking, Muffie stuck to lemonade. *Grow up,* she told herself. *You're out in the big world with people who know how to have fun. Mother's not watching and there's no one to tell you not to drink beer if you want to.*

She was less uncomfortable when Jack also ordered lemonade. *I'll get used to it,* she thought, and sipped her lemonade.

"Who's the professor?" she asked during a lull in the conversation.

"My marine bio prof from grad school, Professor Stowe," said Jack. "The best teacher I ever had. He's here for post-doctorate research on cetaceans. Stays here in P'town near the research ship."

"Did he mean what he said about going out with him on the boat to see the whales?" Muffie asked.

Bree said, "Of course. He's always trying to get people to go see his whales. It's almost a mission with him. You ought to go once. You might like it."

"Let's all go," Muffie suggested.

Bree said, "We've all been."

"If you've seen one whale, you've seen them all," said Charlie, making Muffie wince.

Somebody suggested leaving and they drifted toward the car, taking a half hour to get there. The night was chilly with the breeze from the sea, and the car was even chillier as it sped through the night.

There was little banter in the car. Absorbed in each other, Jack and Bree left Charlie and Muffie to their own conversation in the backseat.

As Charlie crowded nearer, taking three-quarters of the seat and moving toward four-fifths, Muffie sought nervously for ways to divert his attention. She spoke of the kite and of Provincetown and of the traffic and of the weather. The weather was a poor choice because Charlie pointed out that she was shivering and that she might get warm if she got closer.

Instead, she searched her brain for something to distract him. "Get a man started on his favorite subject and he'll talk for hours," her father always said. But what was his favorite subject? She tried music. No. Politics. No. Travel. No. Football. Yes! One or two prodding questions got him started and that was all it took. As he warmed to the topic, he forgot that she might be cold. He talked on and on about his old days on the university team, his wins and losses, his hopes for a pro career, his injuries. He was still talking enthusiastically when they pulled up in front of the gray-shingle house in Wellfleet.

"I'm home," she pointed out to him and laughed at his surprise. When he apologized for boring her, she laughed again and said truthfully that she wasn't bored at all. She added, "I can't get out."

"That's the idea," Charlie said.

"Not my idea," she answered, pulling her feet up under her on the seat so she could climb up and over the side of the open car. As she stood, Charlie growled in resignation and ordered her to wait for him. He climbed up and over his own side and came around to lift her out on her side.

"Put me down, Charlie," she ordered, clutching at his hair to steady herself. Instead, he sat her on his shoulder, and with Muffie frightened and wobbling at the height, climbed the stairs to the apartment door, where he demanded the key.

"No key, Charlie. You can't come in. Landlord's orders. Put me down, Charlie. Please." She hoped he would.

He lifted her off his shoulder and held her against the door, her face almost level with his, and leaned toward her for what she knew was about to be a very determined kiss.

"No, Charlie," she said, beginning to panic.

His face came closer. She could not escape the smell of beer.

"NO!" she said loudly, bringing her arm up to push against his throat.

Unexpectedly, he laughed aloud. "Okay, Stuffy, you win, this time," he said and lowered her slowly until her toes touched the floor before he let her go.

"Muffie," she said.

With another laugh, he patted her on the head like a small child and trotted off to the car, where he vaulted into the backseat and settled down to wait for the other couple to finish saying good night.

She was trembling as she took her key from her pocket and had to steady her hand against the door to ease the key into the lock. At last, she got the door open and slipped quickly inside.

That was close, she thought, but she had escaped. This time. What about next time? Maybe there wouldn't be a next time. But he was so beautiful, like something from a book.

"Make up your mind, Stuffy," she said in the dark room. "First you want to run on the fast track, then you don't. If you want to have fun like Bree and see for yourself what real life is like, you'd better get used to more than raw clams."

I can't, she thought.

You can, she told herself, switching on the light in the living-sitting-eating-junk-work room.

What a mess! She surveyed the heaps and piles of clothing, boxes, and other paraphernalia with the same dismay she always felt when she came into the room. Muffie sighed and plucked a yellow sandal from the sofa back, wondering idly where the other sandal was.

From the small front window she could see the white car still parked in front with Charlie stretched out in the backseat and Bree and Jack together in the front seat. Bree might be a mess with her clothes, but she certainly knew how to live. No quiet life for her. No insecurities. No long, empty summer days. Or evenings. Bree knew how to get along.

Bree wouldn't have minded a little kiss from Charlie.

"There must be something wrong with me," said Muffie to the window.

Bree was getting out of the car. Another kiss or two at the door, and she'd be here in the room all happy and bouncy and wide awake, asking questions about Charlie and how Muffie liked him.

"Not tonight," said Muffie. She pitched the yellow sandal into Bree's corner and scrambled to change into pajamas and get into bed before Bree could catch her for a long, late night of interrogation. She dived into the narrow bed and pulled up the covers. Remembering that she had dropped her clothes in disorder, she jumped up to snatch the discarded clothing and stuff it hurriedly into the laundry bag and hop back into bed.

She listened. There was no sound at the door. She stretched and turned toward the wall. When at last Bree came in, Muffie seemed to be sound asleep.

Chapter 3

A particularly loud bird woke Muffie. Six-thirty, her watch said. She lay listening to the bird's song rise and fall in complicated patterns and trills, all unfamiliar to her.

She concentrated, trying to find the beginning of the song and frame it in her mind to keep, but she found it constantly varied and wondered if he made up his song as he went along. She figured he must be a wonderfully beautiful little bird to sing like that—perhaps one of those little yellow-and-black ones she'd glimpsed a few days ago. After all those biology courses, she knew a lot about cells and amoebas and very little about the birds, fishes, and mammals around her. Some biologist! There was so much more to know.

She quietly rose, selected the top pair of jeans and the top shirt in each pile, and dressed soundlessly. Finished with the quick grooming, she scribbled a note for Bree, snatched an apple with one hand and her sneakers with the other, and slipped like a shadow from the room and down the stairs in the chilly morning.

She stopped to put on her sneakers and take the measure of the morning air, then headed at a steady pace down the road toward the harbor. In the cool morning, Charlie seemed never to have happened.

West Main Street, Wellfleet, was almost as quiet as her room. The dozen or so shops were closed and the lively activity of the typical business day was almost entirely absent. Only one car passed her, going the opposite way, then a battered pickup truck with a golden retriever in back sniffing the air rattled toward the harbor.

She was passing the Lighthouse Restaurant, which apparently had nothing to do with lighthouses, when the Town Hall clock struck six. Six? She looked at her watch, then remembered that she had read about the clock, that it was the only land-clock in the world to strike ship's time.

Her watch said seven, so six bells must mean seven o'clock in ship's time. Six bells. She liked that. Even the clock here was different from the one at home.

She passed the corner general store and turned down Commercial Street (another one?), where art galleries in old houses hadn't yet opened for the Sunday tourists. Farther on, Lobster Hutt's (with two t's, which she wondered about) mannequin fisherman pulled his net to the boat fastened to the roof of

255

the popular restaurant. At last, over a little rise, she glimpsed the sea—Wellfleet Harbor on Cape Cod Bay, to be exact.

Small houses on the left and a restaurant on her right failed to catch her interest. She looked to the sea and picked up her pace in her hurry to reach it.

The parking lot at the municipal pier was dotted with the cars of those as eager to be at the sea as she, and a few people already moved about the docks or on moored boats. Out on the pier itself, she recognized the pickup truck that had passed her, the dog still in the back.

From the edge of the pier, she looked down at the boats below. They weren't the sleek fiberglass sailboats she had expected. They were grubby and worn, with great hooks and pulleys and rusted tangles of metal. Working boats, belonging to the local shellfishermen, she supposed. Surprised that they were working on Sunday, she decided it must be harder to make a living at fishing than she had thought.

She watched men ready their boats, listening to their companionable banter back and forth from boat to boat. Two men or maybe three to a boat, they started noisy engines, dropped their lines, and chugged away toward the bay. There seemed to be no pattern in their going and not all boats left.

Perhaps they had to catch the tide. Muffie knew about tides but, again, only from books. Was the tide up now and going out, or was it still coming in? She couldn't tell. She tried to determine the direction of the waves, but to her they seemed to go up and down, not in any other particular direction. She wished she knew.

With most of the fishing fleet gone, she settled down on the outside edge of the pier, leaning against a piling, and lifted her eyes to the smaller boats bobbing about on tether in the harbor. These were more what she had expected to see—pleasure craft, mostly sailboats with bare masts. In the outer harbor one large sailboat rode toward the bay and several small ones with colorful sails played with the wind.

How lovely, she thought, *to move across the surface of the water without the grinding noise of an engine, to feel the sail catch the wind.* In her mind she sailed with them, trying to know the feeling secondhand. She imagined it must feel almost like being a human kite.

Maybe someday she'd go out there on a small boat with a rainbow sail. Someday she'd know someone who'd say, "Let's go for a sail," and she'd say, "Sure," very casually, as if she did such things every day.

Maybe Bree knows somebody with a boat.

She took a bite of her apple.

She blinked.

"The professor," she said. He had a boat, or at least he used one, and he had invited her to go out on it. Actually, he'd invited all of them, but she couldn't help feeling that the invitation had been especially for her—maybe it had been the way he had seemed to speak directly to her, as if the others hadn't been there. No, it had been something in his eyes.

Those deep blue eyes looked back at her from her memory, and she felt again the shock of their gaze. She had looked up to find him next to her and the next few minutes had become a blur of deep blue eyes and dark unruly hair and lean, expressive hands. Even later, when she had been more accustomed to his presence on the step below her and had recovered from the initial daze, she'd felt unusually drawn to him.

Nonsense, she thought. *It must be my imagination.* Or the raw clam. That would have made anybody feel strange. Or maybe it was the ambiance of the place and the time.

Either way, clam or influence of the evening, he had invited her to go out on his boat to see the whales. Last night she'd enjoyed hearing about them and now she found the idea of learning more about them intriguing. If the whales turned out to be boring, she would at least have had a chance to get out in a boat. The more she thought about it, the better it sounded. She just might go.

She looked at her apple with its one bite gone and finished it. She'd go.

She rose, crossed the pier to drop her apple core in the trash container (along with a candy wrapper she found lying on the pavement), and started back to the apartment, stirred by one of those streaks of energy that she got when she made up her mind to do something. As she marched along, she sang under her breath and made plans.

The town clock struck two bells as she crossed the yard to her stairs. Nine o'clock, her watch said. *Ship's time,* she thought, and smiled.

A church bell pealed not far away. It was Sunday and time for church, just as it had been every Sunday morning of her life as far back as she could remember. Except for rare days of illness or accident, she had been in church at least once, usually twice, almost every Sunday. Her family had always gone together, four of them when her sister still lived at home, then three.

Two of them this morning, she realized, her mother and father side by side, no doubt thinking of her, praying for her.

For the first time since she'd left, she was homesick. She missed them. She wondered who was seeing that her mother took her medicine and who was feeding Whiskers.

Not that she would go back right now—not when things were going so well here. But she would miss going to church. She'd missed it last Sunday, even in the confusion of getting settled here. So why not go to church here? But of course she didn't know anyone here in these churches, wouldn't even know which to go to. She'd probably feel lost in a church full of strangers who'd see her as one of the summer people, one of the outsiders.

What was she thinking of? Something serious and sensible! No. She had put that behind her and had come here to try a new lifestyle. Church belonged to her Empton life, not her Cape Cod life. Besides, she had agreed to work today. There might not be an evening service to go to when she got done.

She would phone home later and see how they all were, say hello. Then her mother was sure to ask where Muffie—Martha—had gone to church and Muffie would have to say she hadn't gone and. . .

She wouldn't call. She'd write.

The persistent church bell was still pealing as she went up the apartment stairs. Bree was up and dressed, ready to go. She was "on" today too. Maybe someday Muffie would get to the beach, but it wouldn't be possible today because she would be working at the information desk. Besides, she didn't like beaches in the hot sun. She didn't tan; she burned and freckled. She liked beaches in the early morning and the evening.

Bree was still sleepy but beginning to chat in her fast, funny patter, picking up momentum as she came more and more awake. Rather quiet herself and from a quiet family, Muffie found this habit amusing and annoying by turns, alternately wishing she, too, had the gift of small talk and that she could have a little quiet now and then. She had solved this dilemma by disappearing to solitude occasionally. The rest of the time, she enjoyed the chatter.

Bree was now on the subject of Charlie, and Muffie only half listened as she hurried to change into her uniform.

"Let's go to work," Muffie said, flicking a comb through her curls.

Bree said, "You haven't answered me."

"You can ask me in the car," said Muffie, holding the door open.

"So?" asked Bree, as the Chevy pulled away from the curb. "What do you think of Charlie?"

"Big," said Muffie.

"Oh yes," agreed Bree. "Definitely big. And gorgeous. Don't you think he's gorgeous?"

"I suppose so," said Muffie.

"You suppose so!" Bree was shocked. "You ought to see him in his bathing suit. That man is impressive! He can rescue me anytime."

"He certainly has the muscle for it," said Muffie, thinking of the way he had lifted her from the car.

"He likes you, Muffie. I can tell. You just might have a good chance to snag him for the whole summer, if you work it right."

Muffie laughed. "What makes you think I want to snag him?"

"You're a fool if you don't. Half the girls on the beach are in love with him. He can go out with anybody he wants. Always could, I guess. All he has to do is walk by and smile, and they'll follow him all the way to Boston."

Muffie considered. "It takes more than muscle to make a man," she said.

"It's a good start," said Bree. "Major man in college, four years on the football team, fraternity man—like out of the movies. There's nothing wrong with his looks. Or his money—he's got plenty of it. And he's fun. He's always doing something or going someplace. Never a dull moment with Charlie around."

"That's true," said Muffie, thinking that some of those moments were too exciting.

"Yeah," said Bree, wistfully.

Muffie shot an appraising glance at her and said, "You sound like you are a little fond of him yourself."

Bree laughed awkwardly. "Yeah. Well, we went 'round together a couple of summers ago, but after that he kind of moved on. Charlie has a new girl every summer. Then I met Jack and well. . .Jack's a nice guy. We get along pretty well together. He likes me; he wants to get serious, get married, but that's not for me. I want a good time for a few more years before I get stuck with dust and diapers. That's about the only thing we really argue about."

They rode in rare silence for awhile before Bree began to talk again, this time about their trip to P'town the night before. She laughed over the raw clams, declaring Muffie to be a good sport. She offered tidbits about the social life there and toyed with the idea of returning to buy a pair of silver earrings she'd seen in one of the arcade shops. Eventually, she mentioned the professor.

"Aha," she said, looking sharply at Muffie. "Your interest perked up when I mentioned the professor, didn't it?"

"I'm just listening. That's all," said Muffie.

"You listened like crazy to his conversation last night too," Bree said, looking wise. "You hung on his words like whales were the thrill of the world."

"I did not."

"You did so."

"Well, the whales sounded interesting. I've never seen one except in pictures and I don't know much about them. It was entirely new to me and I'd like to find out more. Maybe I'll go out on that boat and take a look."

"At the whales or at the professor?"

"At the whales, of course," said Muffie.

"Uh-huh," answered Bree. "Sure. But let me warn you about the professor. First of all, he's dull. He chases whales all day and studies all night. Lots of girls have been fascinated by him and his big blue eyes, but the only thing he cares about is those whales. If you had a spout and fins he might be interested in you, but as it is, you're just one of the crowd. And he's old. He must be at least thirty-five, maybe even older."

"I'll remember that," said Muffie, thinking thirty-five wasn't so hopelessly old.

"Do that. And stick to Charlie. You'll have a lot more fun. By the way, Charlie said for you to be ready at eight tonight. He's taking you out to eat."

"This is the first I've heard of it." Muffie was indignant. "You tell Charlie I said that if he wants to take me out, he can ask me."

"You can tell him yourself when we pick you up."

"We'll see," said Muffie to herself.

"What?"

"Nothing."

Muffie was at the desk for most of the day, answering questions and offering copies of *Summer Sandings,* the Cape Cod National Seashore newspaper, which listed activities. She felt comfortable behind the counter and felt good about the day.

She had forgotten to bring lunch. She thought about dashing out at noon for a quick sandwich, but she was still a stranger to the area and didn't care to hunt about for an uncrowded place. Bree would spend her lunch break (without food) at the beach, working on her tan, so Muffie could go there just to get away from the desk for awhile, but that didn't appeal to her. Charlie would be on the beach and she had a mental picture of him strolling up and down with bikini-clad girls following him as a tail follows a comet. She decided to avoid that scene. Instead, she walked along the path that led to the salt marsh.

The sharp yellow-green of the grasses and the constant chatter of birds filled her with a summer kind of pleasure. She inhaled the air, pungent with an awful smell, possibly rotten. Then, as she got accustomed to it, the smell intrigued her. It was unique, entirely its own smell. She sniffed and listened and watched, trying to memorize smell, sounds, and sights. Before she got enough of this strange atmosphere, her time was gone and she had to hurry back to the Visitors' Center.

The afternoon was so busy that it was closing time before she knew it. At 5:45 she helped close up and by six she was out the door. Bree would be going home with Jack, so Muffie was on her own for a couple of hours until she had to be ready to go out with Charlie.

Had to be ready? What was she thinking? He hadn't even asked her out. He had sent word with Bree, telling—not asking, telling—her to be ready to go out for dinner at eight. He'd ordered her like he'd order a hamburger. It was a wonder he hadn't told her what to wear. Who did he think he was?

He knew who he was—the hero on the beach. *Maybe,* she reflected, *if you're important enough, you don't have to follow the rules other people play by. Maybe. But what arrogance!*

Although, to be fair, he wasn't arrogant when he was with her—just different. And demanding. Definitely demanding. Like a spoiled child.

"It's not really his fault," she said to the hot car as she turned the key in the starter.

Maybe I'll go, she thought. *Bree seems to think Charlie is worth it. I shouldn't be so stuffy that I pass up the fun side of life just because I wasn't properly invited to it. On the other hand, it can't be good for Charlie to have everybody do what he wants. Someone should treat him like an ordinary mortal.*

She thought it over as she drove north toward Wellfleet. Then, on impulse, she turned right, down an unfamiliar road flanked by scrubby little pines set in sandy soil. She followed it up and down hills and around bends until it ended at a crossroad. She turned left, for no particular reason, and found herself on a road paralleling the dunes next to the sea.

For a long time she drove aimlessly, stopping once near a small lake, where she pulled off the road next to a mass of wild pink roses and sat watching families enjoying the water. Another time she parked in a beach lot. Leaving the car to stand on a bluff high above the beach, she looked out over the Atlantic, peering toward the horizon as if she could see England out there if she looked hard enough.

From up high, the sea looked more vast than it did from the edge of the foamy wavelets. Children down below played along the edge, chasing the gentle little waves. It was hard to imagine those waves destroying a large ship in a matter of days or less, but she knew they could. A shipwrecked man might last only a few minutes.

Standing there, she felt insignificant, puny, and powerless. *"What is man, that thou art mindful of him?"* The familiar words of the eighth Psalm came to her unbidden but with new meaning, as though she hadn't really understood them until now.

Across that ocean were places she had only read about, ways of life stranger and more exciting than hers. *The world is a magnificent place,* she thought, *and I've seen so small a share of it. How can I go back to my little world?* Ahead of her stretched day after day of blackboards and attendance, one day indistinguishable from the other, years of evenings with Ewald. Once this one summer of adventure was over, she must go back to that life.

"I can't," she said to the ocean, but only the roar of the waves and the cries of the gulls answered.

You can and you will, she told herself. *It's a good, secure life. And you love to teach. Be grateful for what you have.*

She sighed.

Her watch said seven-thirty. Charlie'd be at the apartment in half an hour. She'd better get going.

Instead, she sat down on the sand at the top of the bank overlooking the sea. *I should hurry,* she thought, motionless. *You're throwing it all away,* she argued with herself, but she stretched out her long slender legs toward the sea and scrunched more comfortably into the sand.

A small boy and a man, perhaps his father, got out of a car nearby. The boy pranced and hopped about, reaching to touch the kite his father carried. She watched them ready the yellow-and-blue delta and throw it into the winds atop the dune. It steadied and held its place above her, growing small as they let out more string.

She checked her watch. *If I go now, I can just make it,* she thought. She looked up at the kite again where it hung painted on the sky, as steady as Charlie had said deltas would be. It wasn't moving. Neither was she.

At eight she thought, *He's about there. If I go now, my lateness will show him that I object to the way he set this up, but I can still go out with him. Maybe it's not too late.* She stood, brushed the sand off her uniform, and hurried to the car.

At her apartment there was no sign of Charlie, no note on the door.

What did you expect? she asked herself. *Did you think he would sit down on your doorstep and wait for you? Him? The golden boy from the beach? You wanted to show him you're as important as he is and now you're stuck here alone. Serves you right.*

The apartment was empty and hot and messy. It smelled of not-quite-clean cabinets, stale crackers, and inferior plumbing. She could hear the *drip, drip* of the shower. She sat in the middle of the mess on one of the laden chairs, crushing a week's worth of Bree's clothing. She stared at her shoes. Now what?

There was no "now what." There was only Sunday evening alone in a hot room in a strange town. She wished Bree were there. Bree always had ideas of things to do. Muffie could imagine what Bree would have to say about this.

Well, no point in staying in these hot rooms, she decided. She might as well get cleaned up and go out for a bite to eat on her own. She might even find something to do. There was a program on whales tonight at the Visitors' Center, but that was about to begin at 8:30, just as she had been telling people all day.

She'd find something. A shower and fresh clothes would make her feel better, then she'd see what she could do.

What she did was walk. The little Lighthouse Restaurant was open, so she ate there and strolled around picturesque Wellfleet. At three hundred years old, the town was still young and alive. Although some houses leaned a bit and some shops were uneven or in need of repair, its quaint old buildings were still in use. Residents continued the fishing trade as Wellfleeters, whale fleeters, had throughout most of its history. Wellfleet oysters were still famous.

New mixed compatibly with the old. Artists had carved out a place in the community and had brought a fame of their own kind to the little town. Paintings and pottery, along with homey crafts like candle making and quilting, drew crowds of discerning and casual browsers to the village, making it a center for the arts and crafts.

At ten o'clock on this Sunday night, people still wandered about, and she felt quite comfortable alone. It wasn't exciting, but it was pleasant, much better than an evening in the room.

By the time she returned, she felt better. Annoyance with her own foolishness had given way to regret and embarrassment. She'd handled the whole thing badly. She knew that now. It would have been better if she'd been there and told him how she felt instead of trying to make her point by her absence. Next time she saw him, she would explain.

In front of her house was Jack's car and sticking out of it were four heads, two close together in the front seat and two even closer in the backseat. On careful inspection she recognized Jack and Bree in front. The two backseat heads moved, and the light from the street lamp caught them. One head, the one with the long dark hair, she had not seen before. The other was Charlie's.

She hoped they wouldn't notice her, but they did. Jack saw her first, acknowledging her presence with a discreet waggle of his fingers, a private greeting that said he realized she'd rather not be seen. Then Bree called her name and added, "What happened to you?"

"Hello," Muffie ventured, as casually as she could. "Hello, Charlie."

"Hi." He didn't seem surprised to see her nor particularly interested. At least, he wasn't interested enough to let go of the brunette, who was now looking resentfully at Muffie. Muffie must have been an unwelcome interruption.

She saw no point in prolonging this awkwardness. She kept on walking, starting across the yard.

"Muffie," called Charlie. She stopped and turned to listen. "Sorry I couldn't keep our date tonight. I had other commitments." His voice didn't sound sorry. The dark-haired girl giggled.

Muffie said nothing. She couldn't think of anything to say. She climbed the stairs and entered the dark apartment without looking back, although from the top of the stairs she thought she heard the car door slam.

"That man!" she muttered to herself. "That egotistical, arrogant ape. Who does he think he is!"

Leaving the apartment light off, she went to stare out the window at the car. It was driving off. The door opened and Bree burst in.

"What's the matter with you!" Bree demanded loudly. "Do you know what you've done?"

Muffie didn't answer, so Bree went on to tell her, in full detail. The gist of it, made short, was that Muffie had ruined her chance with Charlie.

"Not only that," Bree finished, a long time later, "but now he's mad at me for fixing him up with you. I do you a favor and you cause me trouble. Some friend!"

"I'm sorry," said Muffie, "but—"

"But nothing. Any girl in her right mind would jump at the chance to go out with Charlie. He asks you to dinner and you don't show up because you don't like the way he asks you. Stupid. That's what it is. Stupid."

"But—"

"Do you know how long it took him to get another date? Do you? Five minutes, that's how long." Bree went on and on about the other girl.

Now and then, when she could get the word in, Muffie said, "But—" That's as much as she could say before Bree started in again. At last her patience gave way.

"All right! That's enough." Muffie cut through the barrage of Bree's words. "You've been telling me how stupid I am for long enough. Now you listen. I'm sorry if this caused you trouble, but I really don't think it matters that much to Charlie or to Jack. By tomorrow it won't matter to anyone but me.

"Maybe I should have been here, ready to go out like you said, and maybe not. I'm not used to being told secondhand about my dates. I don't like it." Muffie paused before adding, quietly, "I'm also not used to anyone like Charlie."

Bree's anger had passed as she listened. At this last she said, with the ring of personal experience in her voice, "Nobody is, Honey. Only Charlie is used to Charlie." Then Bree laughed. "On the other hand, I'll bet Charlie isn't used to anyone like you, either. You should've seen how mad he was. You must be the first woman he ever met that he couldn't control with a snap of his fingers. He may never recover. It was almost worth this mess just to see it." She laughed again.

"You can laugh," said Muffie. "You've got all kinds of friends around here. I haven't."

Bree said, "You just wait till it gets around that you stood Charlie Cooper up. Everybody will want to meet you, if only to find out if you're really crazy."

Muffie groaned. "Don't tell anybody. Please? It would only embarrass Charlie."

A juicy bit of news like this was prime stuff on the gossip circuit and Bree hated to waste it, but at last she agreed to keep it quiet and to ask Jack to do the same. "Only you have to tell me what Charlie says to you next time."

"There won't be a next time," said Muffie, and she went grimly to bed.

She was wrong. Next time was the next day. Muffie was standing behind the information counter when Charlie came in. She saw him immediately. He blocked so much light in the doorway that there was no way to miss him. Just as quickly, she knew he had seen her. She thought of taking refuge in the office, but since he was part of the staff, just as she was, he would have followed her there. She had no choice but to stay where she was and face his wrath.

"I thought I'd find you here," he growled.

Not if I'd known you were coming, she thought, but what she said was, "About last night—"

"Yeah," he said. "That's what I wanted to see you about. Jack says maybe you didn't understand."

"Maybe I didn't," Muffie said.

"Didn't you get my message?"

"I got it."

"Then where were you?" he demanded. ~

"Someplace else. Anyway, you said you had another commitment."

Charlie ignored this reference to his parting shot from the evening before. He said, sounding genuinely puzzled, "I thought you wanted to go out with me."

She said, "I thought if you wanted to go out with me, you'd have asked me, not sent me an order by way of messenger. I'm not used to being treated like that."

"I'm not used to begging for dates," he snapped.

"I know. You whistle and the girls come running."

"But you don't."

"I don't. If you want a date with me, you'll have to ask me."

"Don't hold your breath, Babe."

"And don't call me babe."

Charlie looked at her in disbelief and anger. He towered over her, big enough to snap her in half and looking as if he'd like to.

She stood her ground, grateful for the counter between them. She gave him as steady and calm a look as she could manage. She wondered if he could see that she was shaking right down to her knees.

He sized her up, seeing one hundred twenty-four pounds of offended dignity, matching him look for look, nerve for nerve. He shook his head and slammed his meaty hand down on the counter with a crash.

She jumped, but her look never wavered.

He shook his head again, turned on his heel, and stamped out.

She exhaled slowly, feeling flattened.

"Wow," said Mary Lou, coming out of the office. "What was that all about?"

"He doesn't like my attitude," said Muffie.

"Wow," said Mary Lou again.

Definitely wow, thought Muffie, turning to a somewhat astonished middle-aged man who had been standing there watching. She smiled, although it took effort, and said, "May I help you?"

Good old steady Martha, she thought to herself. *A Muffie would have enough sense to cry.*

Chapter 4

Charlie sent no more messages and appeared no more at the Visitors' Center. No one else showed interest in spending time with her, either. It was like she had the plague. Or maybe like she was the plague. In the social vacuum that followed Charlie's appearance at the Visitors' Center, Muffie had plenty of time to reconsider her actions. She replayed them like a tape in her mind until she had nearly worn this mental tape out. She decided she had been wrong on Sunday night, but that on Monday, in the Visitors' Center, she had been as reasonable and calm as she could manage. No matter who was right or wrong, Charlie was gone and so was the fun he had promised.

Bree rode around in the car with Jack. The others on the staff, seasonal and permanent, paired off very quickly. By the end of her second week, the temporary social structure of summer had been established and the crowd, without Muffie, were packing their free time with parties, picnics, and other social events.

She wasn't entirely left out. General all-staff invitations naturally included her. However, there were no invitations for her specifically. No one asked her out and no one showed special interest. Even the other girls lunched without her unless she pushed her way into their group, and she didn't often do that. Most of the seasonals were younger than she, many in college, so it was possible her age had something to do with it. She also suspected that her friction with Charlie had intimidated virtually every other male who might have asked.

At first, Bree offered to find someone else for her, but Muffie steadily refused rather than feel like an ugly duckling who had to accept whatever she could get. Even if she was an ugly duckling, she didn't want to feel like one.

And Charlie? He was doing fine with the little brunette. Gossip said Anita had won him for the summer. Gossip also acknowledged that it was only for the summer. Charlie was not interested in serious involvement. For that matter, Charlie didn't seem interested in anything serious.

That was the trouble, Muffie decided. She should not have insisted on behaving like a serious Martha instead of a fluffy Muffie. This was her chance at fun, her vacation to remember. Ha! What it looked like now was just a job away from home.

Home looked better and better. At least there she had some value, even if it was only for being reliable and useful. She had a family who loved her, and friends, and church. And there was always Ewald Phipps.

266

"Yuk," she said to the piles of Brec's clothing—yuk to the clothing and yuk to Ewald Phipps.

Do something, she thought. What would a Muffie do? A Muffie would find people and join them. On vacation a Muffie would do whatever vacationers do. A Muffie would have a good time no matter what. Would a Muffie attend the evening program called "Portrait of a Coast"? Probably not, but that was the only thing Muffie could find to do on Monday evening, and it was a start.

By eight-thirty the seats in the small indoor auditorium were more than half taken, probably most of them by campers who were glad to be anywhere indoors, out of the drizzle that had started midafternoon. She had never been in a wet tent, but it sounded depressing. She looked around for familiar faces and recognized two who had asked her about the program earlier that day. They seemed not to recognize her out of uniform.

The ranger who introduced the film was a graduate student she knew only slightly. From the film itself she expected very little, so she was pleasantly surprised. She watched as tides and currents and storms changed the coastline, and she found herself caught up in the influence of humankind on this change. She liked the film and liked learning and went home more satisfied with her evening than she had been with the last several evenings.

So, the next night she went to the next program. This one, as she told people all day, was on "Whale Strandings." She didn't know this speaker, who was not a ranger but a naturalist with the nearby Massachusetts Audubon Society Sanctuary. His approach was different, more secure, more mature. Experience made the difference, she supposed—that and his huge fund of information.

She watched the slides with interest, appalled by the number of whales lying on the grassy beach. In slide after slide they lay there, dying in spite of the efforts of would-be rescuers to return them to the sea. Although some were saved, most died. A close-up of slicker-clad workers showed concerned faces, intense purpose. One man, a tall, thin one—

Stop, she wanted to say. *I think that's*— But the slides went on before she could be sure that the tall man in the shabby windbreaker was the professor.

Wait, there he is again.

"It's the professor." Fortunately, her words were soft and the background music covered them. She thought, *I'm sure that's him. I recognize those lean gesturing hands. Maybe he'll be in some more slides.*

She missed the rest of the lecture. She was too busy watching for the professor. There were no more pictures of him, none that she recognized anyway, and none of those had shown what she wanted to see. The slides were too far away, too impersonal. Maybe. . .

By the next morning, she had decided to go on the whale lab boat. If tourists went on whale sightings, she would go too. Thursday was her day off so, following Bree's instructions, she telephoned from work for a reservation for Thursday morning on the *Minke II* out of Provincetown.

The professor had said to let him know, anytime, but Muffie didn't do that. She figured he had probably forgotten all about her by now, and she felt uncomfortable pushing herself on him. She would buy a ticket like the other tourists and if she happened to run into him, fine.

Thursday was clear and hot, a perfect beach day. Dressing for the temperature, Muffie donned cool slacks and a light sleeveless shirt.

"You'll freeze," said Bree, pointing out that the temperature out in the bay was likely to be several degrees below what it was on the sidewalk in the middle of Wellfleet. The blouse wasn't right, according to Bree, and neither were the shoes. The pants would do, but wouldn't the blue ones be better? Especially with the soft blue blouse with the little anchor on the pocket?

"What difference does it make?" argued Muffie. "The whales don't care what I look like."

"You never know who you'll run into," said Bree, nodding wisely.

Whom, thought Muffie, but she didn't say it because Muffies don't worry about grammar.

Bree fussed and selected and Muffie did what she was told until Bree stepped back satisfied. "Here, take my blue slicker," said Bree, snatching it from the bottom of the pile on the sofa and pressing it under Muffie's arm. "You'll look like a New England fisherman."

Muffie protested that the slicker was hot and that it was not raining and that she didn't want it and that she had a tan raincoat of her own and that it was too much trouble to carry and that it probably wouldn't fit. Besides, don't fishermen wear yellow slickers? Nevertheless, when Muffie left, she carried the blue slicker over her arm.

Driving in Provincetown was only a little easier on Thursday mornings than it was on Saturday nights. All the parking places on the streets were full, but the big lot on Macmillan Pier was still open. She parked there and locked the car, reaching in for Bree's blue slicker at the last minute because she knew Bree would ask later.

Macmillan Pier was large enough to support several shops and a restaurant. It reached out from the center of town into the bay and ended abruptly in a large building. The *Minke II* ticket booth was about halfway down the pier, on her right, just as Bree had said, and the *Minke II* itself was tied alongside. About a dozen people had already formed the beginnings of a line for boarding, and others came immediately after she got in line.

On board the boat, which was about ten times bigger than she had pictured, several young people moved and straightened things and otherwise prepared for the trip. Their ages and attitudes reminded her of the seasonal rangers. They were youngish, relaxed, and good-humored and went about their tasks with easy competence.

None of these people were the professor. Perhaps this was not his boat after all. Or perhaps this was his day off. She felt unaccountably disappointed, although she would have hastened to assure Bree that she hadn't come to see him particularly and really had no reason to expect him to be there. If she had wanted to see him, she would have let him know she was coming, wouldn't she? At the same time, she was both disappointed and surprised that she was disappointed.

On the back deck were worktables and unfamiliar charts. Ahead of that, the center of the boat was enclosed, with benches on the inside and a counter that offered minimal snacks.

It was stuffy in there, so she stepped outside on the wide open deck that ran along the entire length of the boat on each side. She found a place on one of the benches attached to the outside wall of the enclosed section and sat. Then, restless and curious, she rose again to explore the front of the boat, where crew members were handling ropes and making ready to sail. They cast the lines off and pushed away. The boat shifted direction. The light breeze stiffened to a gust, then became a steady wind in her face. Some announcement came over the loudspeakers, but she could barely hear it. Other passengers were moving to the back of the boat. She followed.

On the rear deck, a young man was introducing himself as a naturalist with a special interest in whales and was offering to provide information that might make their trip more profitable. She listened as he touched on the major kinds of whales and told them that if they were lucky, they would see whales close up, probably humpback whales, or the less commonly seen Minke. If they were really fortunate, they might even be able to recognize particular whales by the markings on their flukes, their huge tail flippers, since these marks are known to be as individual in whales as fingerprints are in humans. Some of the crew knew these great whales by name and would identify them over the loudspeaker if they could.

The rough, light brown, woodlike material in his hand was baleen, the substitute for teeth in certain types of whales. He demonstrated the way the whale took in huge mouthfuls of water and let it run out again through the baleen, straining out (or in, in this case) small organisms in the water. These it ate, feeding on small animals, although it could easily have swallowed large fish whole.

Or a man, she thought, remembering Jonah. She thought of him as she held the piece of baleen for closer inspection. To a whale, little Jonah would have been only one bite. Less.

The small chart she received with pictures of the different kinds of whales, so that she could identify them, was a puzzle. These whales didn't look the way they were supposed to look. Most of them had low, concave foreheads instead of the great smooth domed heads she usually saw on tieclip whales and story-book covers.

"When you've seen one whale, you've seen 'em all," Charlie had said. Evidently Charlie was wrong. She must have read about these different whales somewhere, but somehow the specifics had escaped her.

Would she be able to identify a particular whale? She doubted it, unless the whale came completely out of the water so she could get a look at its whole shape, and that was not the least likely. She folded the chart and stuffed it into the slicker pocket, and now that the boat was underway, went to find a place on the long side benches, near the middle in the sun, where she could watch the water and peer out toward the horizon in search of whale spouts. The wind was stronger and colder, and the air smelled different in some way she couldn't explain. It smelled like the sea, she supposed, with some special qualities belonging only to the sea.

As the *Minke II* rounded the point of Cape Cod and moved out into the deeper waters of the bay, the water grew much rougher. The waves slapped the sides of the boat and threw sea spray into the air, wetting those people unfortunate enough to be standing in the wrong place at the wrong time. Most people went inside.

Muffie put on the slicker, grateful for its dry warmth and the independence it gave her. As spray spattered the slicker, she pulled up the hood and snuggled into it.

"Mind if I join you?"

The voice was familiar and so were the sea blue eyes. For a moment, she saw nothing else but those eyes. Then, slowly, she gathered awareness and the pleasure of seeing him. She moved over to make a little more room, although there was plenty, and he sat.

"I came to see your whales," she said, looking out at the horizon.

They—really, he—spoke of whales for the next half hour or more as they cruised to Stahlwagon Banks, where whales frequently gathered. Basic stuff to him was new and exciting to her. His enthusiasm was contagious, and she found she was even more fascinated with whales than she had been when she'd first listened to him talk with Jack.

Gradually, the conversation changed slightly to an explanation of his studies of the cetacean population, and she was struck again by his intensity. Some of what he said was obscure to her, some of his vocabulary too technical. She didn't ask what the words meant; she just listened, savoring his joy in his work.

A shout from the pilot's cabin above them interrupted his stream of talk. "Over there!" shouted a man nearby. "A whale has been sighted on the left, about ten o'clock position," said the voice on the loudspeaker.

The professor pointed and Muffie looked, but she saw nothing. Squinting against the sun, she stared at the horizon, not blinking for fear of missing the whale. In the distance, she saw only the sea and the sky and the birds that circled and dived from one element to the other.

"Closer," said the professor, pulling her to stand at the railing and pointing to the water about forty feet from the boat.

As she stared, a gray curved shape broke the surface of the water and spouted. She gasped. Again it surfaced, closer. No, it was a second one. Two, both at the surface, closer, closer, then right next to the boat. By leaning over the railing, she could see that one was much larger than the other.

"A baby," she said, grasping the professor's forearm.

"That's probably Melissa and her calf," he said, looking oddly at her hand on his arm. His other hand hovered over her hand as if to light on it and cover it, but unconscious of this, she pulled her hand away to reach toward the whale.

He cleared his throat. "She brings her baby to us to amuse it, I think, the way we take our children to watch the monkeys in the zoo. Mothers with calves often approach our boat. Watch now; she may sound. You might get a glimpse of her flukes and we can verify her identity."

More of the huge gray back appeared, then disappeared. Her enormous flukes rose to stand at right angles to the surface of the water and vanish into it with little splash.

"M," said Muffie, reading a letter made by the blaze of white on the underside of the fluke.

"Exactly. 'M' for Melissa," he said. "Excuse me." He left her standing in the sea spray, watching for another whale.

Altogether she saw six more whales up close and sighted another dozen farther off—more than that, counting spout sightings. Those watching on the other side of the boat saw some of the same and some different whales. There was no bad place to stand except inside.

The loudspeaker announced too soon that they must return to shore. She stood at her place by the railing, straining her eyes to see for a long time after the *Minke II* turned in a large half circle and headed for port, but she saw no more whales. Unwilling to go in, she resumed her seat on the bench and scanned the waves, just in case she saw a spout.

"Magnificent," she said to the sea.

"Yes," said the professor, "they are magnificent."

"Oh," she said, startled. "I didn't know you were there. I was just—"

"Talking to yourself?" He smiled. "I do it all the time. That way I know somebody's listening, even if it's only me listening to myself."

She looked sharply at him to see if he was laughing at her. He wasn't. Not at all.

"You were telling me about your weekly helicopter flight over the water to maintain a whale census," she said, hoping he would pick up where he had left off.

He did. He was still enthusiastically explaining whale migrations to her when the *Minke II* bumped the dock gently and tied up. He stopped then, although it was clear that he could have gone on for quite awhile.

She stood uncertainly and held out her hand. "Thank you," she said and smiled up at him.

He took her hand. "I'm afraid I've bored you," he said, still holding her hand.

"Not at all," she said. "I enjoyed it. It was the loveliest day I've had since I've been on Cape Cod."

"It's only half a day," he pointed out, "and you haven't had lunch. How about sharing mine—that is, if you don't think Charlie will object."

"He won't," she said as she pulled her hand free. "Charlie and I aren't—I'd love to share your lunch."

He looked at her curiously, but she said no more. He followed her up the gangplank and walked along slowly with her to the beach where she and Charlie had flown the kite.

"Wait here," he said. "I'll get lunch."

She found a place on the sand away from the walkers and swimmers and settled down where she could watch people come and go on the pier. The sun was hot on the blue slicker, so she took it off and spread it out for a picnic table.

Good thing I have it, she thought as she smoothed the flattering blue shirt and pants Bree had insisted she wear. Bree must have known it would be cold out there. Bree must also have guessed she might see the professor. Bree seemed to know these things.

Soft, sandy footsteps behind were a warning before the shadow fell across the slicker. "Ah, Professor. Back already?" she said, looking up. But it wasn't the professor. "Charlie!"

"Bree said you'd be here," Charlie said.

She had no words. He folded himself down to sit across from her and waited.

Finally she said, "Yes?"

"Yes," he answered. "Well, Jack says—I mean maybe I—um, about that last time we met—"

"Yes," she said, then out of pity for his struggle to say the right thing, she added, "Let's forget it."

"Right," he said, looking uncertain but much relieved. "Listen, I'm on lunch break, and I have hardly any time. I came to ask what you're doing Saturday night. I mean, would you like to go to the party with me Saturday? It's not really a staff party—just some of the gang."

"What happened to Anita?"

"Never mind Anita. Would you or wouldn't you?"

"I would like to go out with you Saturday, Charlie. Thank you for asking," she said, very formally.

"Don't overdo it," he said. "We'll pick you up at eight. Okay?"

"Eight would be fine," she said.

"Right. Hello, Professor," Charlie said, looking over Muffie's head and rising to his feet.

The two men exchanged chilly greetings before Charlie strode off in the direction of the parking lot. She expected the professor to comment on Charlie's unexpected appearance, but he didn't. He only looked at her questioningly. She shrugged, and he seemed to accept that as her answer.

She helped him unpack the lunch—ham and cheese sandwiches and lemonade for two—the same food she had been eating the night they first met. *Observant of him,* she thought, and wondered what else he had noticed.

She unwrapped her sandwich and raised it to her lips before she realized that he was waiting. To her astonishment, he bowed his head and said grace over their little lunch.

"You're surprised," he said, when he finished.

She said, "I didn't expect it. I thought I left that behind me in Indiana."

He said, "I don't usually pray in public like this either. I like to keep my prayers for places and ears that are open to them. With you it felt right."

She blushed and nervously began to talk about home and her family and the Christian atmosphere in which she had been raised. He was a good listener, making her feel that what she said really mattered. The lunch was long gone when at last she came to a stop.

"I've talked and talked," she said. "I've told you all about me and you've told me all about whales and I really should be going. Thanks for the lunch, and thanks for listening, Professor."

"Adam," he said.

"Adam," she repeated.

He walked her to the lot where her car sat baking in the sun.

"If you really want to know more about whales, you might like to visit the little historical museum in town here sometime," he suggested. "It's not exactly a whaling museum, but since this is an old whaling town, there's quite a bit about whaling in the museum."

"I would," she said.

"Now?"

She tossed the slicker into the backseat and relocked the car. "Now," she said.

They walked down Commercial Street to the little white frame building set on a slight rise above street level. "Why, it's an old church," she said.

"That's not so strange," he answered. "It's only natural that whaling communities need their churches. They are very much aware of God, these whalers and their families, and all 'They that go down to the sea in ships, that do business in great waters; These see the works of the LORD, and his wonders in the deep.'"

"Psalms?" she ventured.

"Psalm 107," he confirmed. "God feels very close out there on the sea." He fell silent and she left him to his thoughts as they wandered upstairs and down, through the exhibits of the little museum.

The silence between them was comfortable, companionable, with no feeling that the silence must be filled in with words in order to keep the link between them. Muffie was very aware of that link. It intruded on her thoughts, dominated them, until the main thing she saw in the museum was Adam.

At the door they both hesitated.

"The Pilgrim Monument might still be open," he said slowly.

"I really—"

"You've seen it," he said.

"No, but—"

"You're right. There's not enough time to do it properly. The exhibit on whaling is very fine. The scrimshaw is—I'm sorry. I get so involved in whales and whaling that I forget that other people aren't."

"Now that I've seen a whale up close, I think I can understand," she said.

He studied her for a long moment before giving a slight nod that might or might not indicate approval. "I believe you do understand," he finally said.

She began again, "I really must go. It's been a fascinating day—a wonderful day—but I think I've taken too much of your time away from your work. I don't want you to be sorry I came."

"I'm not," he said.

They walked slowly back toward the parking lot. As they passed the raw bar, she told him about her first clam on the half shell, laughing at herself when she told how cautious she had been and how she hadn't wanted to try it.

"Why did you, if you didn't want to?" he asked.

"I had to," she said. "I can't spend all my life being afraid of trying new things. Not if I'm going to live the life I want to live. Not if I'm going to fit in with Bree and, well. . ."

"Charlie," he finished.

"Yes, and Charlie," she said, wondering why she felt defensive about saying it.

"What if you never fit with them?"

"I will."

"What if you don't?"

"I will. I do."

He said nothing more. *I do fit,* she thought. *I have no doubts. Not really. Not after today when Charlie actually tried to apologize and ask me out in spite of his anger. Charlie must like me and he must think I fit. Still. . .*

"I've offended you," Adam said, breaking into her thoughts.

She said, "No. I just think you're wrong."

He said, "Maybe I am. I hope not."

They walked the rest of the way in awkward silence.

"Thanks," she said again as she rolled down her car window from inside the hot car. She started the engine.

He put a hand on the burning hot window sill and quickly jerked his hand away. He leaned down to say, "Would you like to see the Pilgrim Monument, maybe next Thursday afternoon when I finish the morning sighting trip?"

She smiled and nodded. "I'll be here about three."

"Make it one. I'll buy you a ham sandwich and tell you about whales."

She nodded again and he straightened to his full height. She slipped the car into gear and pulled slowly away, watching him shrink in her rearview mirror.

Bree was right. The man was in love with his whales. No doubt she was also right about his having no time for romance, although today he had been friendly, definitely friendly. Bree would say that's all it was. But she had also said the professor was dull, and he wasn't. Not at all. He was fascinating. He listened and understood. He knew things and wanted to know more. Actually, she thought he knew too much sometimes, made her think too much.

He's not at all like Charlie, she told herself. *Maybe it's just that Adam is older, or at least he seems older. He must be over thirty, maybe even thirty-two or thirty-three, but not the thirty-five Bree estimated. To Bree at her young twenty-four, that would seem older than it does to me. To me, thirty-three seems quite a sensible age.*

"Especially for a friend," she said, then smiled to remember his having caught her talking to herself.

She was still smiling to herself when Bree came in that night.

"Tell me all about it," Bree demanded before she even shut the door.

Muffie looked up from the letter she was writing and gestured at the room in general. "I cleaned," she said, as if that were the subject.

Bree stared around the orderly room. All the furniture was visible and uncluttered. The ironing board stood folded in its corner and their meager supply of food was tidily stashed in plastic containers on one end of the otherwise empty table.

"Your clothes are in there," Muffie added.

They were neatly arranged in more boxes from the grocery and on another rope across the room. Bree glanced quickly at the unaccustomed order.

"Thanks," Bree said. "I was going to do it myself as soon as I got the time. Really."

Muffie nodded.

"But tell me what happened," Bree demanded.

Muffie shrugged with careful casualness. "He's very nice, not dull at all. I like him."

"Of course you like him. Everybody likes him. Tell me, did he actually come up there and ask you for a date?"

"Oh, you mean Charlie. Yes, he did."

"Who did you think I meant?" asked Bree, puzzled for a moment. "Oh, the professor. Yes, he's nice, but tell me exactly what Charlie said, word for word."

Bree sat down and leaned forward to listen. Muffie told her, as well as she could remember, in spite of Bree's frequent interruptions.

"Fantastic!" was Bree's verdict. "I never thought he'd do it. And it didn't hurt anything to have the professor right there to make him jealous. Pretty neat, if I do say so myself."

"What do you mean?" asked Muffie.

Bree grinned with mischievous pride. "Who do you think planned all this? Did you think the professor just happened to bump into you on the boat, just happened to know you would be there in a blue slicker? And how do you think Charlie knew where to find you?"

"You didn't."

"I did, with a little help from Jack, of course. And some good luck at having them run into each other. You should be grateful. You weren't doing very well on your own."

Muffie's smile disappeared, along with her confidence. "I'm not grateful at all," she said. "I'm embarrassed. They'll think I asked you to do this."

Bree shook her head. "No, they won't. Charlie knows better. He knows you're too stubborn."

"But Adam—"

"Adam? You call him Adam? Well! Maybe I've underestimated you if the reserved old professor got first-name friendly with you in one afternoon. Nobody else calls him that, except maybe his mother, and I'm not sure she does either. Don't worry about the professor. Jack told him you didn't expect to see him. Besides, I told you before, he's a waste of time unless you're a whale. Stick with Charlie."

"That's what Charlie says," mused Muffie.

"It's good advice. Take it from an expert."

Muffie didn't ask what Bree meant by that last remark. She thought she was probably happier not knowing.

Chapter 5

For Saturday night's party, Muffie dressed very carefully in the new lavender shirtwaist dress she'd been saving for a special occasion. It fit well, not too tight and not too short. The color suited her too, softening the brightness of her hair and bringing out the whiteness of her skin. She turned in front of the cloudy mirror. *Yes,* she thought, *it's just right.*

But no, Bree didn't think so. "The lavender is too pale and makes you look washed out," she said. "It's too long and baggy—a great dress for an old lady—and worst of all, it looks like something you made yourself."

"I did," Muffie admitted, looking at the dress again and wondering what was wrong with homemade.

So for Saturday night's party, Bree dressed Muffie in Bree's own skin-tight designer jeans and Bree's own backless, shoulderless, sleeveless black-and-silver knit top. Muffie's bone-colored high-heeled sandals were not quite right, but they would have to do. Bree would have preferred black or silver, but at least the high heels were better than the moccasins Muffie seemed determined to wear. Huge silver earring loops completed the gear.

"You need a little more green on your eyelids and just a touch more lipstick," said Bree, applying colors liberally to an impatient model.

When she was at last permitted to see her new image in the mirror, the dressed and redressed Muffie stared at the stranger staring back at her. She squinted and moved closer to see more clearly, but it didn't help. She blinked at the mirror up close, fascinated by the snaky effect of green and silver on her eyelids. *Creepy,* she thought.

"I can't go out in public like this," said Muffie, kicking off the shoes.

"Do you want to be seen or do you want to be ignored?" demanded Bree.

"Ignored," answered Muffie.

"You've already tried that. Now try it my way. If you don't like it, you can always go back to your old—and I do mean old—look."

"These pants don't fit. I can't sit down. I can't even bend over very far. And they're too short."

"Perfect," said Bree. "They were too big on me anyway."

Muffie looked at Bree's tight jeans and electric blue bare-midriff top, then looked back at her own reflection. They were dressed much alike, but on Bree the look seemed normal.

"Come on," Bree said. "Don't scowl like that. Charlie will love it. You'll see."

Charlie did love it. He couldn't keep his eyes off her. She tried to avoid his eyes, but there was nowhere else to look. He was everywhere.

"I can't get over it," he said. "Miss Puritan herself, and now she's a rock star. I had you figured all wrong."

"It was Bree's idea," Muffie explained, feeling awkward and miserable. She tried to straighten her right knee where the jeans were cutting into her flesh. There wasn't room. She shifted in the seat and found she had shifted closer to him. She tried to shift back but his arm over her shoulders held her where she was.

"Excuse me," she said and stretched arms and legs out in a giant fake yawn. She made certain one of her elbows stabbed sharply at his chest and that the sudden motion pushed his arm off her shoulders. She stretched again to make more room. "Claustrophobia," she said.

He grinned and moved away, slightly.

Muffie caught Jack's eye in the rearview mirror long enough to see that Jack was enjoying her maneuvers. He leaned over to whisper something to Bree, who laughed and glanced quickly over the seat at Muffie.

I hate this, thought Muffie.

Pulsing rhythms of heavy drum and augmented electric guitar shook the air as far as a full block away from the party. From the front yard, the sound was aggressive. From the back yard, where the party was in full boom, the music bordered on debilitating. None of the forty or fifty party-goers, a few of them from the staff of the National Seashore, were attempting to dance to the live music. Impossible as it seemed to Muffie, they were engaged in conversation. How could they hear?

"Charlie!" The crowd shouted a general welcome for the life of the party, and he made it include her. She smiled politely as Charlie propelled her to the middle of the largest group. In five minutes, Charlie had put a soft drink in her hand and started on his first beer. In ten minutes, she had been sized up by every girl there and by several of the nearer men. They were not subtle in their looking, and she was not subtle in the icy reception she gave their stares. In twenty minutes, she was alone.

If there were a tray, I could pass it around, she thought, *and that way I would at least be doing something useful.* There was no tray. She minced toward the house, fighting the jeans all the way, to find the hostess, whom she knew slightly, to offer help.

The kitchen, jammed with talkers and drinkers, was hotter and noisier than the yard. Getting in was difficult. Getting out became essential. As soon as she could slither between incoming guests, she escaped to the relative peace of the outdoors. Looking about for an inconspicuous place, she struggled toward a corner of the porch, where she leaned uncomfortably against the railing and wished the jeans would permit her to sit.

Now and then she could hear Charlie's laughter from the other side of the yard, usually followed by a general burst of hilarity from the crowd that always seemed to be around him. Gradually, her ears dulled to the music, and she found she could make out a few voices around her. How long she leaned there listening to snatches of conversation she did not know. It seemed a very long time before an unfamiliar voice said in her ear, "How about another drink?"

"No, thank you."

"Dance?"

She saw that a few couples had begun to dance in the area in front of the little band. She thought they were couples. Since no one was actually touching anyone else, it was hard to tell.

"No, thank you," she said, without explaining that her clothes barely let her walk, much less dance. It didn't matter. She didn't dance anyway.

The owner of the voice pushed his face close to hers and laid one heavy, possessive hand on her shoulder. She could not avoid the sour smell of beer. He said, "Well, then, if you don't want to dance, how about a kiss?"

She pushed his hand off her shoulder. "No, thank you."

Arguing and protesting, he followed her as she moved back into the kitchen, pushing her way into the midst of the throng. She lost him in there somewhere. When she squeezed out the other side, he was gone.

Her ears were beginning to hurt from the weight of the huge silver earrings. She took them off and tried to stuff them in her jeans pocket. It was no use. She put them back on. Now and then she found a girl to talk to, but the conversations didn't last long. The girls were interested in the men and drifted off with them as soon as they could. She had several conversations with men too, but these didn't last long either.

By ten, she had had more than enough. By midnight, she was miserable, but the party showed no sign of breaking up. She began to realize that the party would stop when the beer finally ran out. For a wild moment or two she considered dumping the rest of the beer. She could sneak over there to the keg and turn the tap on. The beer would run out onto the yard and that would end the party. It was tempting.

At one A.M., when the band took a break, she discovered that she could still hear drums when the music wasn't being played. On longer reflection, she decided that what she was hearing was the thump of her own nervous system as it still reverberated to the attack it had received.

She checked the level of the beer supply again and was relieved to learn that little was left. The hostess made the same discovery and brought out more. Muffie sagged wearily against the side of the porch to wait for the party to end.

She never did see the end of it. At three thirty, Charlie's singing had reached the pitch, or lack of pitch, that proved beyond doubt that he had had more

279

party than he could handle. Jack led him off, still singing, and sent Bree to fetch Muffie. That Bree had been drinking too, was evident, but Jack seemed as sober as Muffie herself.

It took all three of them to stuff Charlie into the backseat. He just barely fit. Muffie wondered if he had grown since they'd arrived. She pushed his feet over and crowded in next to him. He didn't notice or didn't care. She couldn't tell which.

Jack was quiet at the wheel, but Charlie and Bree sang loudly all the way to the main highway. Muffie vainly attempted to quiet them. They bounced along the twisty road and took one final sharp turn to meet the main highway. The suddenness of the turn threw the extremely relaxed Charlie in her direction and his weight crushed her against the side of the car.

"Hey! Here's little Duffie!"

She didn't correct her name. There wasn't any point. She was simply grateful that he had stopped singing. She thought that would be an improvement. It wasn't. Now that he had discovered her, he reached for her.

"Come here, Fluffie." His arm reached around her and pulled her in his direction in spite of the fact that there was no room for her to move. His other hand landed on her knee. She pushed it off and it came right back. She pushed it off again and planted it firmly on his own knee.

He laughed and used that hand to turn her face up to his. "Huffie," he said, and laughed again, filling her nose with beer fumes. "Come on, Beautiful, let's have a kiss for Ol' Charlie."

She pulled her chin to free it from his hand, but her chin didn't move. Her hands fighting against his were useless. Against his chest, they were nothing. Against his face, they were an annoyance, a part of the game, no more than that. His face was next to hers, then his mouth was on hers.

She struggled and kicked and came up fighting. "No!" she shouted. "No! Let me go!"

"Aw, come on, Tuffie. You know you like it. You've been prancin' around in those little tight pants all night just waitin' for Ol' Charlie to get around to kissin' you."

"Get away from me," she threatened.

"Or you'll do what?" He laughed again and tried for another kiss.

She fought him off again. She was much smaller than he and should have realized it was useless, but the fighting came from fear and disgust. He had her solidly pinned against the door, her wrist in his crushing grasp, and she hid her face against his chest in the only protection she could find until the car stopped in front of her apartment.

Jack was out of the car and at her side in a moment. He opened the door and reached in to pry one of Charlie's hands free. In a carefully ordinary tone,

Jack said, "Easy, Charlie, easy. You'll hurt her. You don't want to hurt Muffie."

"No," said Charlie, slowly changing to a new thought. "Don't want to hurt Muffie."

Jack said, "Let her go, Charlie. She's home."

To Muffie's relief, Charlie did let her go. Jack helped her from the car and asked quietly if she was okay. She nodded.

"You'd better take Bree in," Jack said. "Can you manage?"

Muffie said, "I think so. How will you manage Charlie by yourself?"

"I've done it before," Jack answered. "I'll be okay as long as he doesn't get belligerent. If he wants to fight, I'll let him sleep in the backseat."

"Why do you do this, Jack?" Muffie asked.

Jack shook his head and went back to Charlie.

Once upstairs with the sagging, giggling Bree, Muffie dragged the heavy weight of the small girl onto the bed. She pulled off Bree's high-heeled shoes and left her there. She put water for tea in the small electric hot pot and tried to sit down to wait for it. Sitting was impossible. She changed into cool, loose pajamas and padded barefoot back to the table. *This is crazy,* she thought. *I'm too tired for tea and too upset.*

She unplugged the hot pot and lay down on the sofa. What a night! She was exhausted, drained. More than anything else she could think of right then, she wanted a soothing hot shower. She looked at the clock. Four-thirty. If she took a shower now, she'd wake up everyone in the house except Bree. Nothing would wake Bree. In three more hours, she could have her shower.

Shutting Charlie solidly out of her mind, she concentrated on the party, working through it in her mind. She could still hear music in the back of her head, where it seemed to have taken up permanent residence. Maybe it was an age thing, she reflected. Maybe if she were sixteen. . .

Nobody at the party was sixteen. Maybe it wasn't age at all, but some personality difference that made her more comfortable with quiet. Noise had always grated on her. It was only reasonable that extreme noise would be repugnant.

There was something else too, some kind of noise of the spirit that had destroyed her peace, a kind of spiritual static. The guests had seemed desperate in their search for a good time. They had tried too hard. They had talked too loudly, laughed pointlessly, drunk without satisfying thirst. In retrospect, she saw them as some kind of imprisoned souls grasping for a taste of pleasure. Especially Charlie. He had grabbed at the noise and the laughter, desperately greedy for it.

I'm tired, she thought. *My imagination is running away with me. They probably had a wonderful time at the party. Jack and Bree seemed to, and Charlie. If I had tried harder, maybe I could have had a good time too.*

No, on second thought she knew she wouldn't. If having a good time meant drinking too much, she was never going to have a good time. It was that simple. Being drunk was repulsive and foolish. She could never allow herself to be like that. Even lovely Bree had lost her grace and her quick wit. What had Jack thought, Muffie wondered, when he'd seen Bree like that, especially since Jack had stayed sober.

She wished Charlie had been sober. She shuddered again at the memory of the struggle in the car. He wouldn't have been that way if he had been sober. Or would he? She didn't know. For the first time it occurred to her that Charlie might have expected her to cooperate in his backseat gropings even if he had been cold sober. He must have pawed dozens of other girls. Had they cooperated? Some of them must have.

Oh, Charlie, she mourned, *beautiful Charlie. Why do you have to be like that?*

She lay there watching leaves move against the window screen. Expecting them to make a dry, scratching sound, she listened for it. From someplace close by, her bird sang, sometimes trilling, sometimes striking single, clear notes. His voice was clear and strong in the night stillness. And very loud.

Now? she thought. *In the middle of the night? I thought birds slept all night, except for owls and such. This songbird should be asleep with his head under his wing. What bird is this?*

She concentrated on the melody, willing away the rude battle with Charlie and the lonely discomfort of the party. As the melody swelled, the party faded. The pounding in her brain eased and her tense muscles relaxed.

"What a blessing you are," she said drowsily to the bird and fell asleep.

The church bell woke her, or maybe it was habit that made her eyes open. Either way, it was too early and she turned her face to the darkness of the sofa back and tried to go back to sleep. She couldn't.

If she had followed her own natural inclination, she would have bathed, dressed in her best white dress, and gone to church. She rose and moved to do just that, but in the shower the contrast between the party last night and church this morning made her ashamed to go to church. She couldn't face herself this morning. How could she face God?

She wasn't due at work until later, but she didn't want to stay around until Bree woke up. She decided to go in to work early, reasoning that she might feel better if she was busy.

It was just as well for the crew on duty that she did go in. Richard definitely was feeling the effects of the party, and at the desk, a pale Mary Lou was glad to see her. These two, who had scarcely spoken to her the night before, welcomed her this morning with as much genuine enthusiasm as they could feel over their headaches.

Muffie was glad to be there. If she had stayed home, she would have had too much time to think. She had thought enough last night, more than enough, and now she simply wanted to empty her mind and forget. Besides, she liked to be useful.

Richard didn't look good, so she volunteered to be the guide for the film that ran at intervals in the auditorium. She didn't have to do much but welcome the audience and introduce the film. The auditorium was more than half full when she saw Charlie standing in the right-hand aisle. He gestured to her to meet him outside and she nodded. Once she had the audience settled and the film started, she could slip out the back and meet him.

Did she want to? Absolutely not, but she did want some peace of mind, so she went.

"How do you feel?" she asked in greeting.

"Rotten. How about you?"

"Okay," she said, which was true, if she considered only how she felt physically.

He rubbed the back of his thick neck and looked down at her with what she thought must be embarrassment. It was hard to tell with Charlie. He said, "Listen, about last night. Uh. . .great party, wasn't it?"

"Wild," she said, absolutely without enthusiasm, and wondered why she'd said it.

"I mean, you had a good time, didn't you?"

"Did you, Charlie?"

"Yeah. So how about next Saturday? There's a party over at the beach."

"I don't think so, Charlie. Thanks anyway. I don't think I'm the party type."

"Sure you are. You just need to loosen up and thaw out a little. Once you relax and start to talk to people, you'll be fine. What's wrong?"

The tight jeans were wrong, she thought, *and that ridiculous non-blouse, and those enormous earrings. I tried to fit in and I didn't.* She said, "It's not for me, Charlie. Ask Anita."

"I don't ask Anita; I tell her. You're different. You I ask, so I'm asking. That's what you want, isn't it?"

"Yes."

"So?" he insisted.

She thought. "No," she said finally.

"What kind of answer is that!" Charlie's exasperation was loud in the echoing hallway. She turned away, embarrassed. His huge hand caught her shoulder and spun her around to face him. "What kind of answer is that? Tell me."

She tried to turn, but he held her fast. She looked straight up at him and kept her voice as firm as possible. "Let go of me, Charlie."

He gave her shoulder a little shake and pushed her away, his eyes blurred with confusion, his mouth hard with anger.

"Charlie, I do not want to go to the party with you. I do not like your parties. I do not even like me when I go to them. Okay?" She enunciated each word very distinctly, telling him with her voice what she was not saying with her words.

He stood as though stricken. She knew intuitively that he had almost never been turned down by a girl and that what he was hearing was a shock. *It's about time*, she thought. *Charlie ought to learn that other people have feelings too.* Just because he was the handsomest man she'd ever seen, with the warmest smile and the most appealing eyes, he didn't have the right to. . .

Right now his eyes looked confused and hurt. Poor Charlie. It wasn't his fault she didn't like his parties. She said, "I'm sorry, Charlie. I like you. I really do. It's just that—"

It was the wrong thing to say. Charlie recoiled from her in anger. "Forget it," he growled and stalked off in the direction of the exit. She watched him slam open the door, ignoring the already open door next to it, and disappear.

"Good-bye," she said when he was gone, and strode in the opposite direction, back to the auditorium. *That wretched party*, she thought. *And those clothes! If I had worn the lavender dress the way I wanted to, I wouldn't feel so ashamed.*

Yes, ashamed. She was ashamed of the way she had dressed, practically advertising for those unwelcome advances she had gotten. No wonder those men had thought she wanted them. Her stomach quailed at the memory.

It wasn't Bree's fault. Bree had meant well. Even Muffie recognized that those awful clothes looked like what most of the other girls had worn. The lavender dress would have looked out of place.

It should have looked out of place. *I was out of place*, she thought. *What was I doing there?*

Trying to have fun, only it wasn't fun, not then and not later and not now. Charlie wouldn't understand that. He couldn't have known that she wouldn't like the party or the music or the beer. Or the backseat struggle.

Her arm, just above the wrist, was bluish where he had bruised it in that struggle. She lightly touched it, feeling the tenderness beneath the skin. She supposed he hadn't realized he had held it so tightly in that crushing grip of his.

He was not going to do that again. That was the last time she would allow him to hurt her like that. If he couldn't control his own behavior, she certainly could control hers. She would simply see to it that she wasn't near him when he had been drinking.

But he liked beer and drank it as she drank water. To avoid him when he drank meant she'd have to avoid him totally.

Okay, she thought. *He won't ask me out again anyway. Fine. He overreacted to the whole thing. I have a right to prefer other kinds of recreation. He's angry over nothing. I'm the one who should be angry. I'm the one who had a boring evening with a rude date who left me alone for the whole evening and then tried to paw me on the way home.*

And then, once she thought of it, she was angry. No, she had been angry since the beginning of the party. Even before that. She had been angry ever since she'd rigged herself up in those ridiculous clothes. After that point, nothing had pleased her. Surely there had been people to talk with at the party or something she could have done to help if she had really made an effort.

For that matter, now that she was taking a hard look at her own behavior, she could have gone to stand near Charlie instead of finding corners to hide in. Perhaps he would not have had so much to drink if she had been there, if she had relaxed and enjoyed what there was to enjoy.

No. For her there was little to enjoy there, and it was no use pretending otherwise. What she should have done was go home and let Charlie have his "good time" without her. But that was the problem under it all. She wanted to have a good time, and she wanted to go out with Charlie. She hated the way he had acted the night before, and she found his drinking repulsive. She knew she was just one of the dozens of girls around him and that she should walk off and wash her hands of him while she still could do so without getting hurt. She knew that, but. . .

Charlie had something that drew her, even against her will. Some spark in his zest for life that caught her, even though she sensed a desperation under that zest.

What was it, she wondered, that drove him to such frantic play? Why was he bored one minute and rushing through life the next? How could he paw her and bruise her when he was the same gentle giant who had taught her to fly the dragon? She'd been nervous about his closeness that first day, and she was certain he knew it. He had been careful to let her know that he would not harm her, and she had gradually accepted his arms around her, had felt safe enough inside their circle to learn from him about the dragon.

He was a puzzle, a helter-skelter mixture of wonderful and terrible. She didn't understand him and didn't think she ever would. He was the adventurous hero one minute and the source of fear the next.

The one thing she knew was that he and she had nothing in common. Nothing. Whatever it was between them was finished before it started. She would be better off if she had nothing to do with him at all. Safer.

I wish I'd told him off, she thought. *I should have told him to keep his hands to himself and to. . .*

Next time I see him I'll. . .

She sighed. She was better off without him.

What she needed was somebody stable and solid, somebody she felt safe with, somebody she understood. Like Ewald Phipps. That's what her parents said.

Often. Usually right after they reminded her that she wasn't getting any younger.

Mrs. Ewald Phipps. Mrs. Martha Phipps. She sighed again. Not that, please not that.

She would have to try harder to have this one summer of good times, just this one, before she gave up. But how? So far she was doing very badly indeed. About the best thing she had done was meet Charlie. And go on the whale watch. And meet the professor. Adam.

Adam was good looking. Even Bree thought so. And he was adventurous. Nobody else she knew spent days on boats and in helicopters searching the sea for whales. Certainly not Ewald. Ewald was a good man with a good job, a respected place in the community, and not one ounce of excitement. He was familiar, comfortable, dull.

Adam was comfortable too. He was quiet, like she was, and religious. She hadn't expected that. She'd grown up with serious Christians and was accustomed to them as a part of her life, so of course she was more comfortable with Adam. She hadn't expected to run into a Christian who acted like the other Christians she knew, not way out here, not in her new lifestyle. She wasn't sure she liked it. It bothered her. If Adam had been an atheist, she would have found that easier to deal with, almost. As it was, as long as Adam was there to remind her, she would have a harder time closing the doors to her old ways. She halfway resented him for reminding her of what she was at home.

The other half of her reached toward the comfort he offered. With Adam, she didn't have to explain her background. He would understand why she didn't know how to be a good-time girl. He might even understand why she wanted to try. He just wouldn't approve.

She wondered what he would have said if he had seen her in the party get-up last night. She could imagine. It would be approximately what her father would have said. It would be close to what she herself would say, if someone asked her.

Adam would never see her like that because she would never look like that again. On Thursday, when she and Adam would go to the Pilgrim Monument, she would wear one of those print skirts and soft blouses that she felt comfortable in. She would dress the way she liked to dress, no matter what Bree said.

She would enjoy another afternoon with Adam. It would be a relief after being with Charlie. With Adam there was no romantic pretense, only friendship, possibly the beginnings of a very good friendship. She didn't have to try to be mysterious or amusing. She could just relax. They would talk and see new things and she would get to know this tall, lean, quiet man.

And she would forget about Charlie.

Chapter 6

At one o'clock Thursday afternoon, two bells by ship's time, Muffie parked her car near Macmillan Pier in Provincetown and walked toward the end of the pier. She didn't get far before she saw Adam striding to meet her, extending his hand in greeting and looking glad to see her again.

She took his hand and smiled up at him.

"You came," he said.

"Of course. I said I would."

He acknowledged that with a nod and with the smallest of smiles. They stood there awkwardly for a moment, then he pulled her hand through his other arm, holding it there, and she did not pull away.

The walk to the monument was more like a hike than a stroll. Adam walked in the same manner he did everything else—purposefully. His step was long and his pace fast. He moved through the pedestrian and motor traffic in a direct line and nothing stayed in his path. Muffie wondered if others got out of his way because of his serious look or because he seemed unlikely to stop.

She was walking faster than she ever did by herself, trying not to lag behind, following the pull on her hand. She took a little running step to keep up.

He turned. "Too fast?"

"A little."

"Sorry. I'm not used to walking with anyone. There isn't any hurry." He slowed down and she began to catch her breath. Once or twice, Adam picked up speed without seeming to realize it, but the tug of her hand on his arm reminded him and he slowed down again.

He didn't talk. She didn't either, at first because she needed her breath for keeping up with him, then because he seemed preoccupied. After that, she kept her silence out of curiosity. She wondered what he would say, finally, and when.

Atop the highest hill in town, the obelisk monument rose needlelike toward the sky. Although the road approached it as gradually as possible, the walk was steep. The professor, however, climbed at the same speed he walked and she panted along behind, arriving quite out of breath. He didn't turn to look at her, not once.

At the entrance, he paid their admission, and they pushed through the turnstile. He turned left and she followed. The museum was small, but the exhibits were interesting. She wandered along slowly, trying to take in each item. He moved ahead of her, sometimes finding himself too distant and returning to where she lagged behind, inspecting some antique tool or item of clothing.

While she studied the exhibits, he studied her. In the few quick glances she gave him, she caught a look compounded of surprise, a little impatience, and something else she couldn't identify—possibly a trace of reluctant admiration.

Adam only partly understood these things himself. He was an expert on whales, not on young ladies. He knew the feeding habits and behavioral characteristics, as much as they were known by anyone, of several varieties of cetaceans. He lived as closely with them as he could.

His recent experience with young ladies was both wider and more limited. He had met many more of this species than he had of the whales. Smiling lips and fluttering eyelashes were part of his daily milieu. He was aware that several of these ladies had tried to encourage his friendship, and he recognized that they seemed unaccountably taken by him. Indeed, he had overheard enough of their comments to know that some of their behavior was directly attributable in some way to the blueness of his eyes.

However, so far, the young ladies had been remarkably similar. Quite a number of them belonged to the student-in-love-with-the-professor subspecies, a most annoying variety that tended to cluster in groups and giggle. They often hung around at the end of class to ask endless pointless questions about subjects they cared nothing about.

Another subspecies he knew well was the professional woman. These were easier for him to be with, since they had given up giggling and tended to be more sensible, more practical. One of these had almost become his wife, until she had become discouraged by his refusal to follow her aggressive plan for his career advancement.

Some of the women he had met fit a category he loosely labeled "available." These were pleasant company, agreeable, and eager to be whatever he wanted them to be. Since he wanted them to be themselves, not a mirror of his ideas, he found them empty.

To be fair to all these ladies, he would have admitted readily that he was not at all interested in romantic entanglements. If a woman was independent, she interfered with his work. If she was dependent on his moods, he found her hollow. If she adored him, he doubted her intelligence.

This one, with her quiet manner and slender grace, was different. Her looks were more than satisfactory. She might even be called beautiful. Her hair was rich, with reddish glints in the warm brown, and her skin was a delicate peach that still, after several weeks on the cape, was almost as light as it had been when he'd first met her. And her eyes, with their sudden flash of green— she was most definitely beautiful.

She was serious. He liked that. The girl had depth and a lively mind. Her questions were thoughtful and seemed to spring from a genuine desire to know. There was so much he could teach her.

She was beginning to matter to him, and he didn't know if he liked that. If she stayed in his thoughts as she had the last week, she would interrupt his work, become a nuisance. The sensible thing to do would be to see her now and then but not get too involved.

She looked up at him just then and he caught the flash of green eyes. *Too late*, he thought, impatient at his own weakness. *Too late*.

He led her out to the grassy terrace surrounding the monument. In this area of sand and sparse grass, the putting-green perfection of the carefully tended grass was a striking setting. In its way, it was more impressive than were the beds of flowers around it.

"Grass," she said in a surprised voice, and he felt a race of satisfaction in her perception.

"It's difficult to grow grass like that here," he responded. "Too much salt."

She said, "I wondered what you'd say first." When he blinked, caught off balance by her comment, she went on. "You haven't spoken since the pier. I haven't either."

He said no more but led her to the monument itself and into the base, then followed her up the tight winding stairs toward the top. She tried to climb quickly, knowing he would move quickly if alone, but she ran out of breath and stopped twice, briefly. Along the way, she noticed that some of the stones of the outside wall were engraved with names of states or of organizations or of communities. On her second stop, she asked about them.

"Gifts for the construction of the tower," he said. "They wanted to have a part in it. The blocks are granite and very expensive, particularly since there is no granite around here. It's the tallest all-granite monument in the United States."

From then on, she read each block until at last she reached the open observation platform on the top. She looked out over the nearby houses and shops to the sea, which beckoned her as it always did. She inhaled deeply, smelling that indefinable sea smell.

"That's Long Point Light, that last one on the end of land curving around the harbor. Then Wood End Light to the right. We passed those on the way out to search for whales."

She nodded at his explanation. "Stahlwagon Banks are. . .?"

"Over there," he finished, pointing the opposite direction, and they walked around to look from the opposite side of the observation platform. "From here they are only water, indistinguishable from the rest of the sea, but when you get closer in the helicopter, they are a different color. The water is shallower, not so deep a blue."

They looked from each of the four sides, and he identified the sights she knew along with others she had never heard of. It all looked different from up here—older, quainter, and more sprawling than she had thought it was. She wished she had brought her camera, but then she remembered she always took pictures and afterward forgot to look at them. *I might just as well try to keep it in my memory with the rest of this summer,* she thought, and looked long and hard before turning to descend. On the way down, she reread some of the stones, in case she had missed any. It was her nature to see it all, everything, instead of breezing past.

For lunch, he took her to a tiny restaurant with umbrella tables on a back deck overlooking the beach. She sat in the blue-and-white director's chair next to his.

"It's a lovely day," she said, looking out over the water.

"Yes," he said, seeing the way she leaned her determined little chin on her hand and following with his eyes the graceful line of her forearm. It was the same delicate peach as her cheek, except for a blue-black mark above the wrist. He reached out to touch it, to pull it toward him. She winced as his hand closed over the mark.

"What happened?" he said, inspecting the bruise.

"An accident," she said, not meeting his eyes.

He stroked it lightly with his finger, then carefully fitted his hand around her wrist and measured his grip against the bruise. "It looks like the mark of a hand, a very big hand."

She tried to withdraw her arm, but he held it gently out between them. The waiter appeared at that moment, and she pulled again at her arm. This time Adam released it.

They ordered and the waiter was gone before Adam asked again, "What happened?"

She shrugged.

He said, "How's Charlie?"

She tried to brush the question away. "There's nothing between Charlie and me. There never was, really. I'll probably never see him again."

"You said that last time we met, just before he showed up on the beach looking for you. Did Charlie do this?"

"He didn't mean to," she said.

"What else did he do to you?" demanded Adam.

"Nothing." She saw the concern in his face and deliberately laughed lightly. "Don't worry about me. I can take care of myself."

He said, "I don't know about that."

She didn't know about that either, right at that moment, but she said no more on the matter. Instead, she led him into a discussion of the preservation of whales, and by the time her lobster roll appeared, he seemed to have forgotten the bruise.

She hadn't, though. She listened to Adam, trying to concentrate, trying to put in an appropriate word here and there, but it was difficult to brush aside his concern. It was tempting to tell him the whole story, about how frightened she was and how helpless. What would he say to that? She decided against it.

Adam is a gentle man, she thought, *but this would make him angry. He would not placidly accept hurt to a friend. And he likes me. I can tell by the way he studies me when he thinks I'm not watching and by the way he anticipates my questions sometimes.* She smiled to herself and refocused on the wanton destruction of whales.

They lingered over lunch until time for supper. Then they wandered out to the end of the pier to watch for fishing boats coming in with their catches. There were no boats to watch, but it didn't matter.

"Are you hungry?" he asked, very much later.

"I should go," she answered.

At her car he said, "My church has a chowder supper every Tuesday night. Do you like chowder?"

"I don't know."

He said, "They also have corn on the cob."

She smiled. "I like corn."

So it was settled and they parted, he to walk back to his single room and she to drive back to Wellfleet.

It was a pleasant afternoon, all in all—a quiet one. When she was with Adam, things seemed to settle down to a calm that she absorbed. With Charlie, she was always on edge, off center, trying to say and do the right thing without making a fool of herself, then finding herself in difficulty. Each time was like that. Every single time she saw Charlie was a challenge that ended in a fight.

Okay, not a fight. A struggle, a shout, or a battle for her survival. Why couldn't he be gentle like Adam?

But Charlie was gentle, she thought, remembering the tentative way he had touched her cheek and his patience when they had flown the kite. He just. . .lost it sometimes. There was so much of him that he seemed almost unable to manage it all. He needs. . .

She didn't know what he needed. Control, for a start. And some maturity. Peace? Yes. Definitely, he needed peace. A solid shaking up of his thinking? "A good swift kick," she said aloud, then she regretted it. He would get one of those someday. Somebody would see to it. Not her. She was too small, too insignificant to matter to him, but somebody would really hurt him. Then what?

Not that it mattered to her, of course. She wouldn't be seeing Charlie.

She didn't see him. She worked at the Salt Pond Visitors' Center giving out information and he, apparently, stayed on the beach.

On Saturday, she gave her shipwreck talk, her best one yet, and she loved it. She didn't think of Charlie at all then, except for one tiny part when she filled waiting hands with sand to make waves.

She volunteered to work Sunday, knowing that most of the crew would be recovering from the beach party Charlie had asked her to. Charlie didn't appear, but she kept too busy to notice. Almost.

She wouldn't think about him anymore. She had Tuesday to look forward to. Charlie never crossed her mind at all, except that now and then she saw the bruise. It was lighter now and would soon disappear, then she could forget Charlie entirely.

Tuesday, after work, she showered and dressed carefully, wearing the lavender dress she had waited so long to find an occasion for. Bree watched without comment until she was giving a last brush through her hair.

"You look nice," Bree conceded.

Muffie said, "I thought you didn't like this dress."

"I was wrong," said Bree. "Evidently, I was wrong about the professor too. You don't think he's dull at all, do you?"

It wasn't a question, so Muffie didn't answer it except to smile. Her relationship with Bree had changed after that party, had lost its easy openness. Since then, they were careful what they said to each other. Neither wished to bring unspoken irritation into the open for fear of causing a rift they could not heal.

"Aren't you going to ask about Charlie?" Bree ventured.

"No."

Bree said, "He asks about you."

Muffie pretended serious interest in a wayward curl. She asked, very casually, "What do you tell him?"

Bree said, "What do you want me to tell him?"

"Nothing," said Muffie. "Tell him nothing." She flipped her curl one last time, picked up her little matching jacket and her purse, nodded a good-bye, and went out and downstairs to wait outside, away from Bree and her questions.

She didn't have long to wait. Adam was as punctual as the town clock, driving up in his battered gray pickup just as she heard the seven bells for seven-thirty. Six bells for seven o'clock, she counted, and one more for the half hour.

His car was like his clothes, she thought: good quality, serviceable, clean, and full of wrinkles and holes. It was unimportant as a status symbol, but essential to maintaining his everyday life.

He was dressed up tonight. He had exchanged his usual garb for gray trousers and a light blue shirt, both fairly wrinkle-free, and his shoes had evidently had a recent near-miss with the polish. His hair was shower damp and still looked combed in back, although the front had begun to go its own way.

Amused by his efforts and flattered, Muffie wondered why she had fussed over each curl and smoothed each wrinkle in her dress. She might as well have tumbled downstairs in something from the unpressed pile Bree was accumulating in her corner again. Adam would never notice.

But he did notice and was impressed. He said so and his expression confirmed it. She imagined that he stood a bit straighter next to her and walked more jauntily than usual. As he drove, his eyes lingered on her more than they should have if he wanted to see where he was going. She found herself keeping watch on the road for him, in case he forgot.

"It's green," she pointed out when they had sat through most of their turn at the light. "Watch that red car," she said at one point, and, "You're over the line, I think." He was over the line at least four feet.

"Sorry," she said. "You don't need me to tell you how to drive."

He smiled into her eyes and went through a stop sign.

"Yes, you do," she said. "Slow down!"

She was thoroughly nervous by the time they parked behind the church. "Do you always drive like that?" she wanted to know.

"Like what?"

She didn't answer. At least she knew now why his car was battered. It had probably gotten crunched in the first week of his ownership. If that's what happened to his car, she wondered what had made his clothes go to pieces. That man needed a keeper—someone to sew his buttons on and keep him from getting killed in traffic.

Considering his interest in food (minimal) and his manner of getting to it, she was afraid to speculate on the quality of the chowder dinner. It was probably one of those potluck dinners where it was better not to know who cooked it. She decided to try to ignore, as much as she could, any foreign objects floating in her soup and any unknown substance glued to her spoon. She braced herself and entered the fellowship hall.

A recent addition, it was built onto the back of the church and shared, at the opposite end, a corridor with the main part of the church. The original section was traditional Cape in style and the new part was a modern variation on the same theme. One whole side of glass and greenery gave an open, airy feeling to the interior, a melding of inside with outside.

Everyone knew Adam and wanted to know Muffie. They greeted her warmly, extended their obvious friendship for him to her, and made room for Adam and Muffie at the long table in the center of the hall.

Muffie tried so hard not to notice dirt that she actually hunted for it so she could overlook it. There wasn't any. The serving table and what she could see of the kitchen through the pass-through window were spotless, as clean as her mother's own kitchen.

The food smelled good. She sniffed it as unobtrusively as possible as she carried her tray to the table and sat down. After the prayer, she took a good look at her dinner. The corn looked perfect and the hot biscuit was tempting. The chowder—it was clam chowder. Those gray-brown lumps lurking about near the top of the hot milky liquid had to be clams.

She stirred and watched the lumps circle. They bore little resemblance to the raw clam she had somehow downed in P'town, but the memory was difficult to push aside. She looked at the chowder and saw raw clam on the half shell.

A furtive glance at Adam told her he was involved in active conversation with the older man across the table. She pushed the chowder to one side and ate the corn. The biscuit went in a few bites. The chowder remained.

She stirred it again and watched the lumps float. She took a spoonful and raised it to her mouth. She put the spoonful back in the bowl and the spoon on the tray and turned to the lady next to her to seek diversion in conversation.

Did she like the new fellowship hall? Was she here for a visit? Mrs. Beale was easy to talk to and reminded Muffie of people in her home church. The conversation moved from general to specific without being uncomfortably prying. Even a tentative query about her relationship to Adam was gently phrased and easily answered: "Friends, just friends."

Another lady across the table entered the conversation, then introduced the young couple next to her, and Muffie felt on friendly terms with a tableful of people. It was fun, like the carry-in suppers in the church basement at home. She hadn't realized how much she missed them.

Of course, the food at home was better. She didn't have gray-brown lumps of dead clam to contend with. One good thing about Indiana was the almost total absence of clams. She looked down at her bowl with regret, wishing she could pay her host church the compliment of eating what they offered.

Her bowl was empty. Except for her biscuit, there was no food on her tray. Biscuit?

She looked at Adam. He was still involved in conversation with the man across from him and still finishing his chowder. Her chowder? She stared at him suspiciously. He felt it and looked directly at her with no change of expression at all, none that she could see.

He said, "If you'd like more chowder, help yourself."

She was almost sure she saw a trace of a smile as he turned away.

Mrs. Beale was watching, twinkling with secret knowledge.

Muffie said, "Did Adam. . .?"

Mrs. Beale nodded and laughed, then passed the butter for Muffie's second biscuit.

Later, in the car, he said, "Would you like to get a bite to eat? You didn't have much supper."

"I wasn't very hungry," she said.

"Clams?"

"Clams," she agreed and allowed herself to shudder. "Sorry. I could have eaten them if I had tried harder. I think. Charlie says. . ."

"Charlie? Are we talking about the same Charlie who bruised your arm?"

"Yes, but—"

"I know," said Adam, "he didn't mean to do it and besides, you don't see him anymore."

"That's right," she said.

"I hope so," said Adam.

"Red light," said Muffie. "How do you drive when I'm not with you?"

He said, "It's easier. I concentrate on the road."

"Concentrate," she said. "We can talk later."

He did, and she didn't have to warn him about his driving again, not once, all the way to the ice cream stand.

"Stay in the car," he ordered.

She stayed. At last he returned, bearing two enormous ice cream cones. "Coconut almond or cranberry?"

She took the cranberry.

"Now," he said, "we talk. You are going to tell me who you really are and what you want."

"I've already told you who I am."

He said, "Yes, a girl from Indiana who is spending the summer lecturing about shipwrecks and listening to my lectures on whales."

"Right."

"That's not enough. There are too many gaps. First of all, you're a teacher, but you never mention your students. You're the only teacher I've ever met that doesn't mention her work. Why? And why do you try so hard to fit in with Bree and her crowd? And what's with you and Charlie? What are you going to do when—"

"I don't have to answer all these questions," she said.

He said, "But I wish you would."

"Why?"

"Because it's important to me. You're important to me."

"Then let me alone," she snapped. His deep blue eyes widened, but his gaze was steady. Hers faltered and shifted away. "I'm sorry," she said.

"Tell me."

"There's nothing to tell."

"All right," he said at last. "I suppose I have to accept that, for now. But I'd feel better about it if I thought you really knew what you are doing."

"That's what my father said," said Muffie. "Let's talk about something else."

"Not whales," he said.

They talked about the chowder supper and the new addition and the people she had met. He told her about the Sunday school class he taught and about his concern for the young people of the church. He would be here only a year and most of that was gone. His sabbatical ended with the beginning of the fall term and after that he would be back only for summers to continue his research. The church here was important to him in offering him a spiritual home away from his own home and in offering a place to be of service. He would miss it when he left.

She mentioned that she missed her church. Sundays didn't feel like Sundays without it. She told him how she had thought about going to church in Wellfleet and how the bells on Sunday reminded her each week. "I almost went last Sunday, but—"

"Come with me next Sunday," he said. "You already know some of the people and you know me. You can even drive, if you feel safer."

She laughed. "It's a date."

He drove her home, concentrating. She listened to the rattles of the car and tried not to think about his driving. They parked in front of her apartment. He killed the engine and the rattles, and they could hear the night sounds of the quiet neighborhood.

She heard the bird first, her bird, and called his attention to it. "What is it?" she asked.

Adam listened. "A mockingbird, close by."

"He must be very beautiful," she said.

"He looks like a thinnish robin," said Adam, "but gray with white patches on his wings and tail. To look at him you'd never suspect him of cleverly mimicking the songs of the other birds, but that's what he does. In fact, it's his name—*Mimus polyglottos*—many-tongued mimic."

"What does his own song sound like?"

"He doesn't usually sing his own song, not like most other birds, although sometimes he seems to sing something original. Mostly he copies other birds, or music on the radio, or even a passing cat. He's so good at it that people tend to forget which part of his song is his own. They recognize him by the way he tries to sound like the others, although he never quite matches exactly. He is also loud, as you notice, and he sings at any odd hour. It's like he's determined to be noticed even if he has to be somebody he isn't."

"That's rather sad, isn't it?" Muffie asked.

"I don't imagine he thinks so. No more than you think it's sad when you—"

"When I what?" asked Muffie.

"Never mind. Forget I said it." Adam reached for her hand and held it in his own, inspecting it, weighing it, memorizing it. "Muffie, I—"

He felt her hand stiffen and saw she was watching the open four-wheel drive that was just parking across the street. Adam recognized them all but the dark-haired girl in the backseat with Charlie. They all were watching, but neither he nor Muffie greeted them as he got out and opened the door for Muffie. He walked her up the stairs and, at the door, Adam said, "I'd like to kiss you, but I won't."

"Thank you," she said, and went in, leaving Adam standing there listening to the song of the mockingbird.

Chapter 7

B ree, we've got to talk," said Muffie over the morning tea and blueberry
muffin.

Bree looked pained. "Not you too," she said. "Don't tell me. You
want me to settle down and be serious, right? That's all I hear from Jack and
now you're starting in on me too. Forget it. I can put up with your stuffy attitude until September. I can tolerate your compulsion for neatness. I can even
overlook your disapproval of me and my friends. But I am not going to listen
to you tell me how to live. Forget it."

"That's not what I want to say at all," said Muffie. "All I meant was that
you and I have been distant from each other since the night we went to the
party and that I wanted to see if we could get back to the way we were. This
chilly truce is hard to live with."

"You started it," Bree charged. "You with your snobby attitude. You go to a
party and spend the whole time looking down on all of us. Then you act like you
never saw anybody with a little too much to drink, like it was all beneath you or
something. How do you think I feel? How would you feel?"

"Angry, I guess," said Muffie.

"Right."

Muffie nodded. "I don't blame you. I'm sorry. The truth is that before the
party, I really never did see anyone with too much to drink—not up close. I
didn't know how to handle it—I still don't. I wasn't looking down on you, at least
I don't think I was. I was just confused and lost. I felt like I didn't belong there,
and I probably didn't. Those things are not fun to me. I felt safer on the sidelines."

"I thought you wanted to be the original good-time girl," gibed Bree. "You
can't even survive one party. You don't know what you want."

"I guess that's about it," Muffie said. "I know you tried to help, and I appreciate it, even if it didn't work out. I just don't think I'm the party type. I don't
like the drinking, and I don't like what happens to people when they drink too
much."

"Are you trying to say I shouldn't drink?" Bree sounded angry again.

"I think you wouldn't if you could see what it does to you."

"Jack always tells me I should quit too, but he doesn't really mind."

"Are you sure? Did you ask him?" Muffie asked. "If he really loves you, he
would want you safe. I want you safe, and I'm only your friend, not the man

who loves you." Muffie knew from the look on Bree's face that she had said more than Bree wanted to hear. "Please try to understand," she said. "I don't mean to tell you what to do. It's only that I'm not comfortable with these things. I tried to explain that to Charlie, but it made him angry."

"It sure did. Charlie's still angry. What did you do to him, anyway?"

"I told him no."

"Everybody says no, but nobody means it," said Bree.

"I meant it," said Muffie.

She told Bree about the last conversation she'd had with Charlie, the one where he'd walked off angry, then she had to explain about the struggle in the backseat, which Bree knew about because she had been there. Bree seemed to think Muffie was being prissy.

Muffie showed Bree the blue mark around her wrist. "I have a couple of other bruises that don't show, places that caught the wrong side of his elbow or something. I'm not sure exactly how I got them. I was too scared to think about anything but getting out of that car."

Bree inspected the mark. She said slowly, "Charlie would never do this. He couldn't. He doesn't have a mean thought. I know him. There must be some mistake."

"My mistake," said Muffie. "I shouldn't have been there, and I really don't think Charlie knew what he was doing. Charlie scares me, especially when he drinks."

"You'd rather go out with Professor Dull."

"Adam doesn't get drunk, and he doesn't hurt me. And he's not dull. You wouldn't say he was dull if you ever saw the way he drives." Muffie laughed and explained about Adam's driving and soon the two were laughing together almost as easily as they had at the beginning of the summer.

In no time, they were laughing about the raw clam and Bree's piles of clothing and were filling each other in on the latest news about the professor and Charlie and Jack.

Jack wasn't so much fun anymore, not to Bree. He was too serious, she said. He was getting annoying about it, complaining that party life was tiresome and that he wanted to quit playing games. He was pressing her to marry him, to settle down, raise a family. She'd been putting him off since last summer, but it was getting more difficult. One of these days, she'd have to give a definite answer and she didn't want to.

"I need more time," she said. "I'm not ready for marriage. I can't take the serious stuff."

"Being serious has its advantages," suggested Muffie.

"For you, maybe," was Bree's answer. "If Jack would forget this nonsense about marriage, we could relax and have a good time. I'd like just once to go through a whole week without explaining why I can't accept that diamond ring he carries around in his pocket. I ought to just take it; then he'll be satisfied."

Muffie said, "Not for long. He would expect you to marry him and he might not be willing to wait ten years for the wedding. Do you love Jack?"

"Probably. Who knows? I'd hate to lose him; he can be a lot of fun. But. . ." Bree shrugged. "I just know I'm not going to do what my mother did—fall in love and get married to someone who leaves me and my kid when times get tough. All Mom ever did was work. Not me. I'm going to make my good times last as long as I can."

Now that she and Bree were friendly again, Muffie felt better, although she was sure the conversation had changed nothing. Maybe she should have kept her mouth shut about the drinking, but it really wasn't good for Bree and—

Martha was at it again, putting her nose in everybody's business, taking care of people, trying to make things work out right. Just when she thought she was getting the feeling of being a Muffie, she was back to being a Martha, worrying about people who were important to her. *That's what's wrong with me,* she thought. *I always worry about other people, making them and their worries the center of my life. I'm not that important to them.*

But Adam thought she was important. He had said so and he wouldn't say it lightly. He wouldn't do anything lightly. She tried to imagine him at play, hitting a baseball perhaps. She could picture that. He would concentrate on the weight of the bat and the speed of the ball, compute the physics involved, and hit at the angle and speed he calculated would send the ball in the direction he had judged to be most effective.

She smiled at her own exaggeration, recognizing the grain of truth in it. Adam was serious and solid, not like Charlie.

What difference did it make what Charlie was like? *Forget him,* she told herself. She had already begun, hadn't she? She had mentioned him only in passing in her letters home—those long, general letters she wrote once a week. How could she explain him? Instead, she wrote of Bree and Jack and of Adam. She wrote about her job and about the shipwreck presentation, which was the best part of the job. Too bad it was only forty-five minutes long and only once a week. In winter, she could spend her whole day teaching.

The part she liked best about her job here was the part she had done at home for years. She had come here to be different, or at least to begin being different, to forget who she was in the rest of her life and begin again. She had rarely been cornered the way Adam had cornered her with his persistent questions. He would ask again and what would she tell him? That she was in disguise as a Muffie? She hadn't even mentioned that part to her parents.

She never phoned home, but hid from their questions in letters. Their letters to her were warm and loving, with no criticism. They asked about her job, her friends, her health, but they never asked if she was living the exciting new life she had come there for. They always ended the same way, with a promise to keep her in their prayers.

At night, she lay awake listening to her bird with his counterfeit songs, wondering which part of the melody was his own. Poor bird. He had lost his own song, his own identity. *Like me,* she thought. *Whose song do I sing? Am I a sober, serious, intellectual match for a sober, serious professor, or am I a good-time girl who hasn't figured out how to have the good times?*

I'm all of those and none, she decided. *I'm a teacher who loves to teach but wants more in her life than just teaching. I'm a daughter who wants the love of her parents without being the person they know. I want the laughs, but I want them with serious people. I found the party depressing and empty, but how full am I?*

If I'm not careful, she realized, *I will lose myself in this muddle. I'll try so many ways of being that I won't know who or what I am. Just like the mockingbird.*

She heard Jack's car drive up and looked out to see only Jack and Bree in it. Concluding that Charlie must be out with Anita, Muffie went to sleep thinking about that.

In the morning, Bree was nervous and snappy and didn't want to talk. The ride to work was unnaturally quiet. Muffie opened the conversation several times, but Bree let it die. After awhile, Muffie quit trying, deciding that something must have happened with Jack, but Bree wasn't ready to talk about it.

Fridays were busy days at the center. Most tourists came and went on Saturday, so the lobby was full of people leaving the next day who wanted to squeeze in one last attraction or buy one more poster before they had to leave their vacations behind. A few of the people, the paler ones, were newcomers who asked the usual questions about what the center offered. By closing time, she was exhausted and ready for a can of soup and a hot shower. She was not ready for Charlie.

He was leaning against her car door when she came out. He lounged there, dwarfing the car and looking almost plastic in his perfect tan and perfect muscles. He didn't move when she approached with the key in her hand.

"Excuse me," she said, holding the key out and waiting for him to move away from the lock.

He didn't move except to grasp the extended arm firmly but very gently and lift it to inspect her wrist. It was perfectly all right. "The other one," he said, then raised that wrist for inspection. She winced but said nothing, hoping he had not seen, but he had. He fitted his hand over the mark, circling her delicate arm with his fingers and looking to see that the marks on her arm did indeed match the placing of his fingers.

"I did this," he said, stroking the bruise lightly, very lightly with the back of his hand.

"Yes."

"I didn't know till Bree told me. I'm sorry."

She said, "It's all right."

"It's not all right. I don't know what happened. I would never—I mean—Bree said you had some other bruises."

"They'll go away," she said. "It wasn't the bruises as much as the way you were that night. You—"

"I scared you. Bree told me."

She looked up at him and into his eyes. "You just wouldn't stop," she said, "and I tried to tell you no, but you wouldn't listen. I tried to stop you, but it was. . .very difficult."

"I'm sorry." He looked sorry. His eyes were softer and sadder than she had ever seen them, softer than she had imagined they could be. His laughter was gone for a change, and he looked down at her with his plea for forgiveness written across his face.

She said, "I know you didn't mean it. I'm just not used to the way you do things. Where I come from, no means no, and I've never had to fight to keep it that way. I've also never been out with anyone who was drunk. I didn't like that part either."

"You'd better get used to it if you're going to get along in the world," he said.

She thought it over and said, "I don't think so. I think I can get along without that. I don't like what it does to people. I don't like what it does to you. If that's what I have to do to get along in the world, then maybe I won't get along. Maybe the world will have to go on its way without me."

He regarded her thoughtfully. "You really mean that, don't you? You're ready to take on the whole world."

"No," she said, "I'm not ready for that, but I will stand my ground if I have to."

"Even if you get bruised?"

"Even then," she answered.

They studied each other for a moment. She saw a giant of a man quieted by his own guilt and made serious by his effort to understand. He looked so forlorn that she only narrowly resisted the impulse to reach out to him with a comforting hand on his arm. Her hand paused in midair between them.

He reached out as if he wanted to pull her into his arms, but stopped.

They spoke together. "It's all right," she said, and "I'm sorry," he said. In different circumstances it would have made them smile, but not now. She merely nodded and looked steadily into his sad brown eyes as he went on.

"I'll never hurt you again," he said, "and neither will anyone else. Not if I can help it. I swear it."

"Don't swear."

"But I promise—"

"Don't. You can't be sure what you'll do next time you drink too much. What good is a promise you can't keep?"

"It's a promise all the same, whether you accept it or not," he said.

"As long as you drink, there's only one way to keep that promise," she said. "Stay away from me. Far away, so that I don't begin to trust you too much again."

"That's unreasonable," he objected. "I can understand that you're cautious about trusting me, but we can still—"

"No," she said, watching the softness in his face give way to frustration.

"Okay," he said. "Have it the way you want it. You go hide in your own little corner and let life go by without you." His volume increased with his frustration level. "Not me. Not Charlie. I've got a lot of living to do yet and a lot of parties to go to, and a lot of girls to take to those parties. There's no use wasting my time and sympathy on a girl who's too dumb to know what she really wants." He straightened, glared once at her, then marched off.

"Have a good time," she called.

"I intend to," he shouted, not turning around.

"Good-bye," she said firmly, but he could not have heard. "Good-bye," she whispered and swallowed, holding back tears. "So much for the party girl," she said to herself in the car. Her head ached with the effort of not crying. Her body ached from the day at work. And her spirit ached from. . .she didn't know what her spirit ached from.

She stopped at the gas station to telephone Adam. No, she couldn't go out with him tonight. No, not church either. Nor lunch after church. Thanks anyway. Maybe another time, maybe when she felt better. Sorry.

By the time she stretched out on her own bed, still in her work clothes, she knew she didn't really want to feel better. Not then. Not if it took any effort. She just wanted to lie there and sink into the mattress and rest.

Bree didn't come home for supper. The radio was too much bother to turn on. Supper didn't sound good. Through closed windows, voices came and went on the street below, but none interested her. She simply lay there, absolutely still, until she dozed off.

She awoke to stifling heat and darkness. She looked at her watch. Almost eleven. Bree would be home in two or three hours. Until then, there was no one around but that bird, that loud-mouthed mockingbird with everybody's song but his own. Even with the window shut she could hear him. If she opened the window to let fresh air in, the song would be inescapable. She felt trapped.

She rose and left the apartment, driving through the cool darkness to the harbor. She parked near the end of the lot nearest the boats and sat listening to the night sounds of water slipping and slurping about the piling, boats nudging each other gently in the dark, teenagers at the ice cream stand at the far opposite end of the lot.

She listened sharply. No mockingbird. Fine. Just fine.

She slid down in the front seat so that her nose was just at windowsill level. She took a deep breath of the sea air and tried to make herself relax. *My car is like a capsule,* she thought, *and I'm closed neatly inside it like an animal invisible in his burrow, seeing but not being seen.* She liked that. It had a separate, unreachable feel to it that she found comforting. She needed to be separate for awhile so she could think, could center in on important things, the truth. Alone, she could feel closer to God.

And there she was, at the heart of it.

She sighed.

In the harbor, the small boats bobbed gently against the piling. Far out a tiny light shone from a moving boat. *He's a long way out,* she thought. *I wonder if he feels lost out there. Like me. He must know the way home. When he's done, he'll go home again and tie up, another little boat safe in the harbor. And me?*

I don't even know which direction to head in. I want too many things that don't go together. I want fun and friends and. . .too many things.

Should I pray for all these things I want? Would God listen to such a selfish prayer?

Of course He'll listen, but that doesn't mean He'll give me what I ask for. Besides, He already knows what I want, even if I don't.

What do I want? "Please, God, help me know what I want," she prayed.

The little boats bobbed gently on the water and the tiny light stayed tiny. She listened to the night noises and thought. There were no answers.

Well, I can at least make peace with Charlie. Poor Charlie. Why "poor"? Because he's so unhappy. He scares me, but I think he scares himself more. If I'd spent more time listening to him and less time worrying about myself, I'd have realized that sooner. There must be some way I can help him. If only. . .

She sat up straight and started the car. With a little luck, she might get back in time to catch Jack so he could help her find Charlie.

When she reached the apartment, Jack's car was parked out front. She parked and went up to Bree's side. "Hi," she said before she saw the huge person slouched down in the backseat.

"Hi," said all three, then there was silence.

She took a deep breath and said, "Charlie, could we talk?"

"Sure. Talk."

"In private?" she said.

"Are you sure it's safe?" he asked.

"No," she said, "but I'll risk it."

"She'll risk it," Charlie told the others. "She'll risk talking with big bad

Charlie." He didn't move.

She bristled and snapped back, "Forget it, Charlie. I thought we might be able to talk, but it was a dumb idea. Forget it."

"Feisty," said Charlie, with a touch of admiration, and hauled himself up and out of the car. "Let's walk." He led off toward the harbor in the direction she had just come.

For awhile they only walked, she hurrying to keep up with his long, easy strides. At the center of town, he stopped and faced her.

"Well?" he demanded.

She began walking again, more slowly, letting him match his steps to hers. At the bottom of the main street, she said, "I'm sorry, Charlie. I should have accepted your apology the way you meant it instead of—I'm sorry."

"You accepted my apology," he said. "It's me you don't want."

"That's not true, Charlie. I don't want to be angry with you for something you have no control over, and you know you have no control when you drink. I know you wouldn't hurt me on purpose, but. . ."

"But?" he prompted.

She didn't answer. Instead she said, "You're right about me hiding in my own little corner."

"I shouldn't have said that," he said. "I was angry."

"You were also right," she said. "And right about my not knowing what I want too. I mean, I know I want to have a good time and all that, but when it comes down to the real thing, I back off. It doesn't make sense."

"It does to me," said Charlie. "You're just out there playing in the wrong game, that's all. You don't even know the rules. No wonder you come out on the losing side."

"So teach me the rules, Charlie."

"No," he said. "Let's play a different game."

"I don't understand," she said.

As they made their way up and down the shadowy streets of the little village, he explained. He had done some thinking too, he said, and had decided he could not take the chance of hurting anyone because he lost control of himself. He was done with that. He had meant it when he'd said he would never hurt her again, and he intended to keep his promise whether she accepted his word or not. If that meant he had to give up drinking, then he would give it up. "I can and will give up drinking, if that's what it takes. In fact, I already have. I haven't touched a drop since the last time I talked to you."

"Why did you drink?"

"To shut off my thoughts," he said. "If I think, I'll remember that I'm only a small-time coach in a small-time high school instead of a power running back on a pro football team. I'll remember what my father wanted me to be and what a disappointment I am to him. I'm not a star, not a big name bringing big business to his firm, not even a little partner. Just a coach."

"Are you a good coach?"

He considered. "Yeah. Yeah, I guess I am."

"Do you like coaching?"

"Yeah. You should see those kids. They're quite a team. Last year we almost—yeah, I like it. I like it a lot."

"That's important, Charlie. You matter to all those kids, and you are happy being there. Why do you need to be something else?"

"Because," he said.

"No," she said. "In a few years those pro players will get hurt or old and have to quit. Then they'll have to find something else to do. If they're truly blessed, it will be something worth doing. You're already there, ahead of them, doing it. You're a winner the way you are, Charlie."

"You think so?" he asked. He stopped her and turned to read her eyes. "Am I a winner?"

"Absolutely," she said.

They walked on. After awhile she wondered aloud if he would be able to get along without drinking. "I can," he said. "I will, although I would do better if you were with me. Would you go to the beach party with me tomorrow? It'll be a tamer party, and I won't make you ashamed of me or afraid of me. I promise," he said. "Deal?"

"Deal," she said, and they shook on it. He kept her hand tucked inside his own as they walked on in silence, past the library and the church, past the shop on the corner, and up the silent street to her apartment.

At her stairs she said, on impulse, "Do you ever go to church, Charlie?"

He laughed. "If you've got any ideas about dragging me to church with you, now is the time to give them up. You've already made me give up my beer. If word ever gets out that I've done that for a girl, I'll never live it down. Don't make it any worse."

"I wasn't going to," she said. "I'm trying to make it better."

He took her hand, still enveloped in his own, and held it up to his eyes in the dim light. He rubbed a tentative thumb over the place where he thought the bruises were. She winced. He looked at her solemnly, and she saw the sadness in his eyes. He bent lightly to kiss the damaged wrist, then let her go, holding her only with his steady gaze.

She smiled slightly in understanding, and turned without another word and went upstairs.

Chapter 8

Muffie worked the next day, Saturday, glad to have something on her mind besides the beach party. She was going for Charlie's sake, but she wasn't looking forward to it. Until she had to think about the party, she would think about what she was doing at work. On Saturdays, she always did her shipwreck talk.

She showed her map, demonstrated the abrasive action of the waves, showed photos of recent storm damage. The crowd, larger than usual, responded enthusiastically. They were absorbed in the presentation, and so was she.

Here is where I belong, she thought. *Whatever else I am or want, I am a teacher, a good one.*

"Your talk was very effective," said a quiet baritone voice near her. It so closely echoed her thoughts that she wondered if she had spoken them aloud.

She turned to find Adam smiling at her from the doorway, and she answered with a welcoming smile of her own. "Thank you, Adam. I love to teach."

"I can see that," he said. "How's the headache?"

"Better," she said.

"Good enough for church tomorrow?"

"No," she said. "I mean, I don't know. I mean. . .it's hard to explain."

"Care to try?" he said.

She shrugged and looked away, toward the sea. He lifted her knapsack with one hand and put the other arm around her shoulder. She stiffened, then gradually relaxed enough to lean trustingly against him for a moment, long enough for him to sniff her clean smell of soap and to feel a kind of astonished pleasure at having her close, long enough for him to want to keep her there. Too soon she stood away from him again, leaving an empty place near his heart.

Easy, Adam, he thought, catching his breath.

She stepped away from him, to the opposite side of the hut, and stood gazing at the sea. He crossed to that side, not too near her, and put the knapsack down on the bench against the wall. Then casually, as if the earth had not just quaked beneath him, he swung himself up onto the low wall. He sat facing the sea, legs swinging over the sand dune. Next to him, he heard her sandy shoes scrunch on the cement floor, heard her hesitate, then heard her climb onto the bench and the shelf to sit next to him, not touching him.

After a little silence, he turned enough to lean his back against the corner, enough to see her. She flicked a glance at him, saw that he was watching, and looked away.

"I'm a good listener," he said. "A good teacher has to be a good listener. You know that."

She nodded. He waited. At last she said, "I did have a headache, but that's not the reason I don't want to go to church with you. I can't go. I. . ."

He waited.

She said, "I don't want to go. If I go to church and start my ordinary life all over again, I might as well go home. All my life I've gone to church, been well-behaved, done what I was supposed to do. I'm so used to doing what other people want that I don't even know what I want or who I really am. I'm not a real person. I'm just whatever I'm supposed to be, just dull old reliable M—" She stopped, closing her lips on the name.

He said nothing.

She sighed. "I want something else, something more."

"What do you want?"

"I don't know," she admitted in a very small voice. "I don't know. I asked God to help me know, but He didn't."

"When did you ask?"

"Yesterday," she said, then smiled ruefully. "That isn't much time to wait for His answer, is it? I guess I'd better wait a little longer. Only, what if I never find out? What if He answers and I don't understand the answer? What if I don't even hear it?"

"Are you listening?" asked Adam. "Are you opening your heart to Him and really listening?"

"I don't know," she answered. "Things keep getting in the way. I keep getting involved with people and losing my focus. First there's Bree and the way she is afraid to settle down. Then there's Charlie."

He answered carefully, "I thought that was over."

"It was," she said. "But he's so unhappy."

"I know."

"You do? Then you understand why that bothers me. He's too good to waste, too beautiful to destroy himself. How can I not try to help him?" She was almost pleading with him.

"And what about yourself?" Adam asked.

"I don't know," she said forlornly, holding back her tears.

He slid his hand across her shoulders, pulling her to lean against him, and she came into his arms. He circled them around her, protecting her, and she turned her face into his shoulder, tears finally spilling freely, silently.

"I'm sorry," she said when the tears had nearly ended.

He wiped away the last of her tears very gently with his soft sleeve and touched her face where they had been. "Don't be," he said, holding her.

They talked long after that. She told him about the horrible party and how ashamed she was and about how she wanted to be like Bree, except that she didn't really want to be like Bree, and about the way she wanted to have fun and was finding nothing really fun. Mostly he listened.

Suddenly, it was late and she realized she had to go get ready for the beach party.

Reluctantly, he released her. She hopped down.

"Thanks," she said. "Thanks for being my friend."

He winced, then said, almost ruefully, "I really am your friend, you know. Remember that. You might need a friend sometime."

She nodded and touched his arm in acceptance.

"Church tomorrow," he ordered. "I'll pick you up at nine. Be ready."

She hesitated, then shook her head. She raised one hand in farewell and ran off toward the parking lot, leaving him sitting alone on the wall.

By the time Charlie and Jack got to the apartment, she and Bree were ready in warm clothes, carrying jackets. Bree was edgy, restless, unhappy. Concerned, Muffie asked her what was wrong.

"What's wrong?" she answered. "You know what's wrong. Jack is wrong. All he talks about is getting married. I don't want to get married. He says I love him, but I don't want to. What good is love? People stop loving when they marry, so love doesn't count."

"It counts," said Muffie. "For some people it counts all their lives. You just have to work at it. At least that's what my parents say, and they ought to know. They've been married almost thirty-five years, and they still love each other."

"Imagine!" said Bree. "Thirty-five years. I wish—oh, there's Jack and Charlie." They snatched up their jackets and hurried out the door.

The crowd on the beach gathered in early dusk. The group laughed and played, running and rough-housing on the sand. A glow-in-the-dark Frisbee sailed back and forth until the darkness grew too deep. The diehards, like Charlie, gave up the games then and joined in roasting hot dogs and toasting marshmallows at the huge bonfire. Chips and watermelon, washed down with cold drinks, completed the menu. Some of those cold drinks may have been beer, but Muffie didn't have any and neither did Charlie. When the heavy fog rolled in from the water, the air was heavy and wet and Muffie was glad to have her warm jacket and cap. The crowd settled into relative quiet around the fire. Charlie sprawled on the sand and pulled Muffie down to sit next to him in the glow of the fire. Somebody started a camp song, then another and another.

Muffie shivered and Charlie wrapped a heavy arm around her and pulled her inside his jacket. She welcomed the warmth, but she was wary, ready for another defensive fight against this huge, aggressive man.

"Relax," he whispered. "I won't hurt you."

She wriggled free, but when she found that he'd made no move to prevent her going, she settled back into the warmth of his jacket and gradually relaxed. He seemed less threatening than he had before. She didn't know how carefully he wrapped her, how aware he was of her beginnings of trust in him. She only knew that this Charlie was the Charlie who'd taught her to fly the dragon, and she was grateful to have him back.

The fog lifted, leaving a clear sky with a huge moon. The night was quiet now, except for subdued conversation and the steady rush of the waves. The beach at night was magic, a memory to keep, she thought, snuggling in silence next to the great warmth that was Charlie.

She studied him in the moonlight and found him magnificent. He turned to her and smiled, ruffled her curls with his free hand, and looked back toward the flames. They were content to sit in silence, listening to the sea and the crackling of the fire.

Jack and Bree were among the first to rise, and the four went home, still speaking in hushed tones. In the car, Charlie took his usual two-thirds of the backseat, but he came no closer. Except for his arm on the back of her seat and his hand ruffling her hair, he made no attempt to be familiar. She yawned contentedly and he grinned.

At the apartment, he suggested, "Let's walk," and they did, for half an hour, saying little, thinking much. At her stairs again, she said, "Thank you. It was beautiful."

"Yes," he said and bent to kiss her lightly on the forehead. He ruffled her hair once more and was gone.

From her window in the dark apartment she could see him in the backseat, patiently waiting for Jack and Bree. *Charlie*, she thought, *beautiful Charlie*, and smiled to herself. *It was a lovely night.*

The glow from the beach bonfire lasted well into the next week. She discovered, when he came for her Sunday evening, that he had his own car. For no good reason, she had never given it a thought, but when he drove up in a red Corvette, she laughed. "Of course," she said to herself. "Of course he has a red Corvette. What else would he have?" She tried to picture him with her own old blue car or with Adam's gray pickup, but it was an impossible picture. Anyway, it was pleasant to go out, just the two of them, to eat pizza together and walk the pier. Monday, there was a band concert at the Visitors' Center. Tuesday, they flew kites above the beach. Wednesday, they swam at one of Wellfleet's kettle ponds. Thursday, they took sandwiches to Sunset Point. Friday, they went to P'town. Saturday, they borrowed bicycles to ride the bike trail at Cape Race. Always they talked.

They talked of teaching and of learning, of what they liked and didn't like.

He teased her about being out of condition and pushed her to use muscles she hadn't used in a long time. She tried to keep up, worrying that he would lose patience with her. She needn't have worried; his patience seemed endless. He called her Puffie and Snuffie and Guffie until she gave up trying to teach him her name and laughed, saying it didn't matter what he called her as long as he didn't forget who she was.

He had grown serious then, out on Sunset Point in the orange-red light of the giant setting sun. He had turned to look deep into her green eyes, tracing her chin with a careful touch of his fingers. "I know who you are," he said. "You're my angel. You keep me from being what I don't want to be. As long as you're with me, I know everything will be all right."

"No, Charlie, I'm not an angel. I'm just a person who cares about you. I can't make everything all right for you. I'm not powerful enough for that. I can't even do that for myself."

He had said, "Yes, you can. You're different from all the others. You're stronger, cleaner, braver. You know what you think is right and you live by it."

"I try, Charlie; I really try, but that doesn't make me an angel. It just makes me serious and dull."

He shook his head slightly, shushing her words with one finger against her lips. "You're not dull, Angel. You are definitely not dull." He brushed her lips lightly with the finger. She sat mesmerized, seeing his eyes focus on her lips, his head close and closer. His lips touched hers, very softly. She sat still, watching, barely breathing. He pulled away to study her, then bent close again for a second kiss, a firmer kiss, and she shut her eyes to close out the rest of the world.

He straightened and cleared his throat. "Sorry," he said. "I shouldn't have—"

Then she in turn silenced him with her slender finger on his lips and smiled, turning back to the sunset.

That was Thursday. On Saturday, they argued. The crowd was having a party and he wanted to go. She didn't.

He went.

She didn't.

Bree argued and fussed, but Muffie held firm. She did not want to go and she was not going. She didn't want Charlie to go either. It wasn't good for him, she knew. She watched him from the apartment window as he appeared with Jack to pick up Bree. He had no girl with him, but she knew he wouldn't stay alone.

"You're making a mistake," said Bree.

"I think you are too," said Muffie. "You're going out to drink until you don't have to face the fact that you're not happy."

"Right," said Bree. "I'm going to have a good time if it kills me."

"I can't do that and I can't watch you do that either," said Muffie. "It's not for me."

311

Then Bree was gone, and Jack's car roared away. Muffie sat in the quiet room. She could use the time, she reasoned. She could wash her hair, rinse out a few things, straighten the mess. She was glad, really, or so she tried to convince herself, to be staying home after such a busy week. She sighed and began to pick up Bree's clothes.

When they came home, she was in bed, but not asleep. From where she lay she could easily have seen the car from the window, could have looked to see if Anita sat in the backseat. She didn't look, didn't intend to let them know she was awake. On the stairs too many feet rumbled, and she could hear Jack fumbling with the key. She rose, grabbed a robe, and went to take a clumsy Bree from his care.

"Again?" she said.

Jack nodded.

"But you're sober," Muffie said. "Why do you let her do this?"

"I love her," he said.

"This is not loving her," she said. "If you love her, you can't allow this to happen. Let me put her to bed and we'll talk. Wait for me."

She was struggling with Bree's shoes when she heard the car leave. Evidently, Jack didn't want to talk. She sighed. There must be something she could do, but she didn't know what it was.

It was a restless night. Between her worry about Bree and that stupid loud bird, she got very little sleep. At five she quit trying, rose, dressed, and went out. She walked aimlessly, her steps taking her toward the harbor. She hadn't been there for awhile, not alone, not since she had prayed to know what she wanted.

She still didn't have an answer, but then, she hadn't been doing a lot of listening. Adam had said she had to keep her heart open for the answer. Well, her heart had been busy lately. She'd had a lot to think about. Charlie, for one thing. It had been a wonderful week, a dream week, right down to the end, and then it had collapsed. His angel, he had called her, and the kiss had been real. But Charlie wanted what Charlie wanted, and she didn't fit the party plans.

He's stubborn, she thought, *and so am I. But at least he knows what he wants. I only know what I don't want. I don't want to go to those parties. I don't want Charlie to drink. I don't want Bree to mess up her life. I want...*

I want times like last week, with Charlie kind and fun. I want to help him and help Bree. I want Bree and Jack to be happy, really happy.

She smiled. She had answers. She didn't know when she had gotten them, but she knew she had—not the whole answer, but a beginning. She still didn't know what she wanted for herself, but things were much clearer than they had been a week ago. She was absolutely certain that she would have the rest of the answer if she would wait patiently and listen. When? She didn't know, but she believed she would have her answer when she needed it. Meanwhile, she had work to do. She had to try to help Bree and Jack and Charlie.

"Thank you, Lord," she said.

How good it was to be able to talk to God! She wanted to be with others who felt this way. In the distance she could hear the church bell. She rose and started back. She had plenty of time to make it to church, even all the way over to Adam's church. She hurried.

She entered the cool, white church about twenty minutes early, in time to hear the last of choir rehearsal and watch the choir file out. Then, except for the ushers, who were just coming in, and the organist, she was alone. This was the reason she had come early, to be alone in God's house to settle her thoughts and make herself ready for worship.

It was like coming home. She'd never been here before, but it was a place she knew. From her seat near the back she followed the light from the side windows to its bright patches on the pews, breathed in the summer air from the open windows, listened to the barely audible hum of ceiling fans, admired the altar flowers—orange lilies, probably from a nearby garden, and centered on the large cross in the front of the church. In the stillness, peace descended and she eased into it, belonging here, belonging to God, praying as naturally as breathing. She had missed this.

People were filling the pews now. A few looked somewhat familiar; some nodded and smiled. Mrs. Beale recognized her and stopped to say "good morning" before going out again. Soon, Mrs. Beale was back with Adam, pointing Muffie out to him. He came directly to her and sat next to her, looking very pleased.

She smiled and rose with the congregation to begin the service. They sang together, sharing the same hymnal, prayed together, listened together. It felt right and good to worship with a friend. It would be right and good to phone home today too.

Afterward, there was coffee in the fellowship hall, and she was warmly greeted by those she had met before and by others who came to be introduced by Adam.

"I'm glad I came," she said on the way out. "Sunday isn't Sunday without church."

He said, "I've called several times, but no one was home."

"I've been busy," she said.

"Charlie?"

She nodded. "Charlie."

"At least let me take you to dinner," he said, walking her to her car.

She declined, saying she had to hurry to work. Then she was gone.

That wasn't nice, she thought in the car. *I shouldn't have rushed off like that. I rushed off from him last time. Adam is going to think I don't want to be around him.*

He'll think I'm avoiding him. Am I? Maybe. With Adam it would be too easy to slip back into Empton ways. I don't want to go backward, especially not now. I feel like my life is almost making sense. Almost. If I can just straighten a few things out. Things are so complicated with Charlie that I can't think straight.

As usual after one of their parties, the crew at work welcomed her and she carried more than her share of the work. She didn't mind. It was a good day. When she left work to find Charlie waiting for her in the parking lot, it was an even better day.

"Hi, Angel."

"How was the party?"

"Okay. It would have been better if you had been there. I'm not used to going to parties alone."

"Alone? Where was Anita?"

"There, but not with me. You were with me, all evening. Because of you I didn't touch a drop, not a drop. Did you know there is a whole little group at those parties that never take a drink?"

"Including Jack," she said.

"Yeah. I think he stays sober just to watch out for Bree. She drank too much."

"She often does," said Muffie. "You just never noticed before. Now she looks different to you."

"The whole party looked different," he said. "Everything looked different. I understand now what you meant about it not being for you. You knew it was wrong for you, and you stayed away even though I. . .I wish I had your strength."

"You can get strength the same place I get it. From God. Without Him I wouldn't be half this strong," she said.

"No thanks," said Charlie. "None of that religious stuff for me. I just need my angel."

She laughed. "Angels are very much involved with religious stuff."

"Do angels eat pizza?" he asked.

"This one does," she said.

And so the next week began, as the last one had, with Charlie and Muffie together most of the time. It was fun. *This is what I came for*, she thought. *I'll have to tell Adam about this when I see him.*

She didn't see Adam. She was never home to see him. On Thursday, her day off, she thought of surprising him in P'town with a picnic lunch, but it seemed foolish when she reconsidered. He wouldn't be expecting her. He probably had other plans. He might even have another girl watching the whales with him.

Bree had told her girls were always interested in the professor, but it had never occurred to Muffie before that he might be interested in them. What an idea! What an unpleasant, unwelcome, uncomfortable idea!

"Don't be childish," she scolded herself aloud. "He has every right to do as he pleases. I certainly don't mind. Not a bit. After all, I'm busy with Charlie, and he is the stuff dreams are made of."

She decided not to surprise Adam. Instead, she shopped for groceries and did her laundry. Even party girls have housekeeping chores, she told herself, although Bree seemed to have very few. Bree rushed from one activity to another with a desperation that left little energy for ordinary chores. In all the time that Jack and Bree spent with Charlie and Muffie, Muffie never saw Bree truly at ease. *What drives her at this frantic pace?* Muffie wondered.

She watched closely that night, with Bree's desperation in mind, and saw that she was right. Bree was in almost constant motion, chattering nonstop, turning about in the front seat to laugh and wrinkle her perfect little nose at Charlie, pointing a polished fingernail at interesting things for Charlie and Muffie to see. Through it all, Jack remained steady and calm, though watchful. Now and then, Muffie met Jack's glance and knew that he and she shared those thoughts about Bree. Once Muffie tried to engage Jack in conversation apart from Bree, hoping that Jack could give her some hint about Bree's behavior, but Jack neatly avoided Muffie.

To Charlie, Muffie said, "Bree seems anxious to have a good time."

"That's just the way she is," said Charlie, dismissing the subject. "Are you coming to the party Saturday? I know you don't care for parties, but this one is at the director's house and I practically have to go. I wish you'd go with me."

"It's a command performance for me too, I guess. Sure, I'd love to go with you, Charlie."

At the bottom of her stairs, he kissed her gently but firmly, ruffled her hair, watched as she climbed to the door, and left her to fumble with the key. As she pushed open the door, she heard a small thump and felt something move by her foot. A package. She took it into the light to see what it was. She opened it to find a beautifully illustrated book, *The Audubon Society Field Guide to North American Birds,* and a tape marked "Songs of North American Small Birds." The notecard tucked inside the front cover of the book said:

To help you find your own song.
Adam

Adam. He had not forgotten her, had thought of her on the very day she had thought of surprising him. She took the book to the table and opened it carefully, turning pages to look at one bird after another, reading about them. Page 549–550 was turned down: "Mockingbird."

She read carefully. The mockingbird did have his own song, after all, but it was mixed in a tangle of imitations of other birds. Interesting. He hadn't lost his own song. He had only confused it with the songs of all those other birds.

Maybe she hadn't lost her own song either. It must be still with her. All she had to do was find it, listen for it.

"Listen with an open heart," she said, remembering what Adam had told her.

That night, the mockingbird sang long and loudly, but his song didn't annoy Muffie. She was busy listening to find the mockingbird's own song.

Friday was busy, as usual, and Saturday was busier. The group for her shipwreck talk was the largest yet, and the time sped. When she finished, she looked up to find Adam waiting and realized she had expected him to be there.

"Thank you for the book," she said. "I was hoping you'd come by so I could tell you how much I appreciate it. I have to go out tonight—party at the director's house—but there's time for a walk on the beach if you like."

He liked the idea, so they strolled barefoot on the hard, wet sand at the edge of the surf. They talked of whales and waves and work, and the time passed quickly. Back at the starting place, where they had left her knapsack and their shoes, they brushed the sand from their feet and put their shoes back on.

"I have to go," she said. "The party starts at seven."

He said nothing at all, but picked up her knapsack to carry it to her car. They started their separate cars, waved lightly, and drove toward the main road. Looking back at his car, she saw him watching her and waved again, hoping he remembered to look where he was driving. "Stop sign," she said, as if he could hear her. He stopped. She turned right and he turned left. She watched his car disappear in the traffic.

She took care with her looks that night. She didn't know the director well, but she liked what she knew and wanted to make a good impression. At least she knew how to dress for this kind of party. Her white silky pants (not real silk, of course) and sea-green blouse, the color that brought out the green in her eyes, were just right. She knew she looked neat and clean and, according to the mirror, rather pretty.

Bree looked perfect, as usual, also in white silk (real silk) pants and royal blue silk shirt. This was a conservative look for her, but in some ways it suited her better. In these clothes, Bree seemed elegant but fragile—lovely. She was slow getting ready, though, moving as if half asleep.

"What's the matter, Bree?" Muffie asked. "Are you all right?"

"Sure. I'm fine."

Only three words? Muffie thought that was odd all by itself. She watched Bree move clumsily across the room to find her sandals. She moved almost like she did when she had been drinking.

"Have you been drinking?" Muffie asked.

"Just a couple of drinks. Getting a headstart on the party. Director doesn't serve alcohol, so I have to bring my own."

A car pulled up in front and they heard Charlie call, "Angel?"

"Angel!" Bree exclaimed. "He calls you Angel. What have you done to Charlie?"

"Nothing," said Muffie.

"He's crazy about you," said Bree. "Charlie Cooper is so crazy about you he doesn't even see all the girls trying to get his attention. I don't know how you did it, but nobody else ever did."

"That's what you wanted, isn't it?" Muffie asked.

"Yeah, but I didn't expect it to go this far. And I expected that you'd be crazy about him too."

"I am," said Muffie. "He's terrific fun."

"And handsome and intelligent and kind, and you don't sound like a girl who's crazy about him. What's the matter with you? Charlie's a one-in-a-million man and you treat him like he's an ordinary guy. He's not. He's wonderful."

"Like Jack?"

"No," said Bree. "Like nobody else. There's only one Charlie and if I had your chance, I'd jump at it."

Muffie said, "You have a chance—Jack, only you won't accept his love."

"Jack isn't Charlie," said Bree. "I like Jack, but Charlie I lo—" Bree broke off suddenly, hand over her mouth, eyes wide.

"Love," finished Muffie, softly, knowing as she said it that this was true. "You love Charlie. That's the whole trouble, isn't it? That's why you never say yes to Jack." Muffie thought a moment, then added, "But if you love Charlie, why did you try to fasten him to me?"

"It was a mistake," Bree said bitterly. "I thought he'd get tired of you and see me waiting right there under his nose. I thought if we four spent enough time together, he'd remember what fun he used to have with me. I thought you were too dull for him. I was wrong. He thinks you're his angel."

"I'm sorry," said Muffie. "I didn't know."

"Neither does Jack. And Charlie can't see anybody but you."

"And you're miserable."

"Yes," said Bree, "I'm miserable. I tried to hate you, but I can't. I try to be in love with Jack, but I'm not. I try to forget Charlie, but I can't."

"So you drink."

Bree nodded, tears in her eyes.

"It won't help, Bree."

"I know."

"You have to stop. You're too important to do this to yourself, Bree. You're important to Jack and to me. We care what happens to you."

"Charlie doesn't," she sobbed. "Charlie doesn't even notice."

Muffie held her while she cried, then Bree dried her tears, blew her nose, washed her face. They both exchanged their wet blouses for fresh dark blue blouses.

"I wish I could hate you," said Bree, sniffling.

"I'm glad you don't," said Muffie. "Just let me help you."

Bree nodded and came quietly down the stairs with Muffie to the car. Jack took one close look at Bree and turned a questioning glance at Muffie, who shook her head to indicate that it was better to pretend not to notice the reddened eyes and sniffly nose. Charlie helped Muffie into the backseat and they were off.

This party was better, in Muffie's opinion. It was quieter, more civilized. Subtle music filled the empty corners of the background; the buffet was a feast of beautifully prepared delicacies; the evening air on the huge deck overlooking the sea was balmy. It was a lovely party. Muffie lost sight of Jack and Bree and began to relax. Charlie moved with her from group to group, doing what he was so good at, mixing with people of all kinds. Somehow they got separated, but that was all right. Her mother had taught her that the way to be a good guest was to try to talk a little bit with each guest, as well as with the hosts, so she began to search for those she had not yet spoken with.

That was when she noticed Adam. He was standing in the corner of the deck with two people who were carrying on a conversation that should have involved him, but he was not really involved. He was standing absolutely still, watching her. Their eyes met and he smiled a very small, private smile. She smiled back and moved toward him.

"You didn't say you were coming," she said.

He said, "The director is an old friend of mine. You look beautiful tonight."

"So do you," she said, seeing the way his blue blazer made his deep blue eyes even bluer. "I've never seen you so dressed up before. I almost don't recognize you."

"It's just me," he said. "Me and my brand new jacket. I was hoping to impress you."

"I'm impressed. I'm seriously impressed. It still has all its buttons and not one wrinkle. You must be—"

Glass shattered somewhere across the room, and Bree's laugh rang out in the abrupt silence. Muffie started immediately toward Bree, saying a hurried "excuse me" and easing through the crowd.

Jack was there before her. "I'll take her home," he said.

"I'll come too," said Muffie. "You might need me. I'll tell Charlie."

In no time they had made a quick, not too graceful exit and deposited Bree in the front seat.

"What happened?" asked Muffie, as they drove off.

"Put her glass down on a table that wasn't there. She acts like she's had too much to drink," said Jack. "Brought it with her, I think. I don't know. I've never seen her like this."

"It's not just the drinking," said Muffie. "She was upset before we came. If we get her home, maybe I can get her quieted down."

Bree was not quiet now. She laughed and shouted and bounced, while the other three tried to calm her.

Charlie said, "Maybe I can hold her in her seat if you put her back here with us."

Bree unfastened her seat belt and turned to him. "Yes, let Charlie hold me. I want Charlie to hold me." She lurched to her feet to reach to him.

"Look out," shouted Charlie, springing up to catch her.

He missed.

Bree wavered, screamed, and was gone.

Jack slammed on the brakes and swerved, throwing Charlie out onto the pavement. Muffie screamed, the car screeched to a stop, and all was still.

Jack was out first, bending over Bree, who lay crumpled and broken in the gravel at the side of the road. Charlie was closer to the car and in the road. Muffie ran to him. He was breathing, but unconscious. He didn't move. "Help us, Lord," she prayed, not caring who heard as long as God was listening.

A car was coming. Visible in the night because of her white pants, she waved it down. The car had a CB and in a very few minutes the police and the rescue squad arrived. They took Bree and Charlie.

"Go with them, Jack," she said. "I'll bring your car."

The rescue team vanished in the flash of lights, and she followed the police car more slowly. The hospital was far, very far, or it seemed far. It seemed to take years to get there. She arrived numb and frightened. One of the policemen led her to the emergency room, where she found Jack. She hugged him and held him, but she knew he didn't feel it.

The policeman wanted a statement. She answered his questions as well as she could, trying to remember details, losing them in the confusion. Jack was being questioned on the other side of the room. He submitted to the breath test the police requested when they learned the hospital had found alcohol in Bree's blood.

One of the police officers asked if she wanted him to call someone. Muffie couldn't think. There was no one. She couldn't—Adam. He would know what to do. He was probably still at the party.

"Call Adam," she said, searching her purse for the phone number.

Chapter 9

Minutes passed, stretched long by anxiety. Jack paced and sat and paced again. Muffie sat on the edge of a chair, alert to the comings and goings of the professional staff. Surely someone would come soon to tell them Bree and Charlie were all right. What was taking so long?

Adam came at last, but Muffie remained tightly tuned to the people around her. Adam spoke quietly to the staff and returned to say there was no news yet, but that they would hear as soon as the doctors knew anything.

Almost on his heels came a doctor. Muffie tensed and moved to Jack's side.

The doctor spoke in even, quiet tones. "The young man is suffering some broken bones and some severe bruises. He's in the operating room right now. He should be all right, but he's going to need some care."

Muffie felt weak with relief. Charlie was going to be all right.

The doctor continued, "I'm afraid the young lady is gone. There was nothing we could do. She seems to have struck her head in the fall, and there was only the slimmest chance she could live. I'm sorry."

"She's dead?" came the strangled cry from Jack.

"I'm sorry," said the doctor.

Bree! Perfect Bree! thought Muffie. *She can't be dead. She can't be!* She heard sobbing and remembered Jack, turning to him in shock and grief. They sat together, huddling in misery on the green plastic sofa.

"I'll take you home," said Adam at last.

Muffie shook her head. "I'll wait for Charlie," she said and settled down to wait next to Jack, who sat where he was, too stricken to respond.

Adam nodded and went to bring coffee, then to call a friend to take Jack in for the night, rather than leave Jack alone in his house. For Muffie, there was no family nearby. Adam's instinct was to keep her with him, watching over her until he was sure she would be all right, but on careful thought he decided to call Mrs. Beale. Muffie would be safe at her house.

At the same time, Muffie began going over and over her failure to help Bree. If only she had done more. If only she had warned Jack of Bree's dangerous mood or done more to slow down Bree's drinking. If only she had stayed closer to Bree at the party, if only. . .

"You couldn't have known this would happen," said Adam.

"I have to—there must be something I can do. Let me think," said Muffie.

She searched for something, something to make it all better. "Someone should call Bree's mother," she said.

Perhaps the phone number would be in Bree's belongings. Adam asked the nurse for them and found a home address.

"I'll call," Adam said.

"I'll do it," Muffie said. "I have to do it."

The operator found the number and Muffie woke Bree's mother to say the words that would bring her such terrible pain. Struggling for words of comfort, she left her number with Bree's mother, saying she would call again tomorrow to see what she could do to help.

She should call Charlie's family, she supposed, but that could wait until morning, until he could tell them himself.

What else? Notify the Visitors' Center in the morning. Get Jack's car back to him. She groped for other details to make right. "Adam, what should I do?"

"Wait. Pray. It's all you can do. For now it's enough."

It was a long time. They kept their vigil into the small hours of the morning. Somewhere in that time Adam took her hands. Sometime he put his arm around her and pulled her close. She was unaware of these things when they happened, but his strength comforted her. From time to time she spoke, not always coherently. He listened to her go over the accident again and again. He watched her pale face for signs of tears, but there were none. She carried on an irregular conversation with God, a painful conversation that was part prayer, part search for understanding, part simple awareness of His presence.

Almost three hours after the accident, Charlie was wheeled out of the recovery room. The nurse said they could see him, so they followed her directions to his room.

He lay still, a mound of white bandages on a white bed. Muffie came to stand near him, taking the fingers of one bandaged hand in her hand.

"Angel?" he whispered.

"Here, Charlie."

"Angel, Bree—"

"She's dead, Charlie."

"I couldn't. . .she. . ."

"I know, Charlie. It's not your fault."

Charlie struggled to sit up and barely moved. "Jack?"

"Here," said Jack.

"I'm sorry, Jack. I'm—" Charlie whispered, ending in a choked sob.

Still holding Charlie's fingers, Muffie murmured. "It's not your fault, Charlie. It's not your fault. Sleep. Go to sleep." She brushed the loose hair from his temples and stroked his cheek. His breathing gradually steadied and quieted. He slept.

She released his fingers and leaned to kiss him gently on the forehead.

Adam said, "The nurse says he'll sleep until late morning. We need to get Jack home. He's exhausted. You can come back tomorrow when he's awake." He pulled her firmly to the door. With one arm on Jack's shoulders and one on Muffie's shoulders, he managed to guide them out into the night.

In the crowded pickup, Jack hunched against the door in silent grief. He was aware of the things around him, but they didn't matter. Muffie sat in silence too, staring blankly at the road. She began to shiver, lightly at first, then violently. Adam stopped the car to wrap her in his new jacket, heedless of wrinkles. He held her close, murmuring to her. He didn't know what the words were or even if they were real words, but they didn't matter. They soothed her so that she grew calmer.

He began to drive again, trying to keep one hand free to hold her next to him. She took no notice of his driving, but it was all right. He was concentrating, taking no chances with this precious cargo.

They delivered Jack to his friend's home, where the friend led him inside. Then Adam drove Muffie to Mrs. Beale's home, coming to a gentle stop in front of the small white cottage. He turned to hold her in his arms as the first of her tears came, then grew to great gulping sobs.

"I should have stopped her," she sobbed. "I didn't try hard enough. I should have been—"

"Hush," he said.

"I have to call the Center," she sobbed, "and get Jack's car, and—"

"Hush," he said.

"I have to—"

"No, you don't. You don't have to do anything at all. Hush."

"But I have to take care of—"

"You don't always have to be the one who takes care of things."

"Yes, I do," she wept. "I always do. That's who I am. I'm not a Muffie. I'm a M. . .Mar. . .Martha," and she sobbed harder.

In spite of himself, Adam chuckled. "I'm so glad you're a Martha," he whispered, "but even a Martha can't take care of everything. Hush, Martha, hush."

Eventually, the sobs subsided and he eased her out of the car and into the arms of Mrs. Beale. "I'll take care of her," Mrs. Beale promised.

"She needs—"

"I know," said Mrs. Beale. "I'll take good care of your Muffie."

"Martha," he said, tasting the new name and finding it good. "Her name is Martha."

She should have slept all day, according to Mrs. Beale, but Martha was up by nine, wakened by the smell of breakfast and the distant peal of a bell. A church bell—and she knew immediately she must go to church. She had only the clothes she'd come in and they were crushed. No, Mrs. Beale had run them through the washer and dryer and they were fresh and clean. She showered and dressed, distantly aware of the pleasure of being in a real house with plumbing that worked and rooms that were neat and uncluttered. That was a big improvement over the mess Bree always—

Bree.

After church she must phone Bree's mother again to see what she could do to help. And she must talk to Charlie's father to make sure he understood how Charlie had tried to save Bree. It was important that Charlie's father know that, and she knew Charlie wouldn't say it. She had to see Charlie today, had to be there when he was awake, had to help him. And Jack would need someone too. There was so much to do, ". . .but even a Martha can't take care of everything."

Adam had said that last night. This morning.

She needed to see him, to thank him for being there. And she still had his jacket.

Adam was already in church when she and Mrs. Beale arrived. They joined him in his pew halfway down the center aisle. *This must be his regular seat,* thought Martha; Mrs. Beale knew just where to find him.

He looked a little tired, but not bad. He looked better than she felt she looked. Her eyes still burned from crying, and she knew they were puffy. Charlie should like that; he had called her Puffie once and now it fit.

She was weary, too weary to take in all the details of the service or to follow the sermon as carefully as she should have, but the feeling of worship restored her, rested her in ways the short sleep had not. How foolish she had been to avoid church! For that matter, how foolish she had been to try to change herself into a good-time girl. She was what she was—a Martha. She sighed.

Adam turned at the sound of her sigh, lifting his brows in question. She smiled slightly to let him know it was all right and tried to concentrate on the sermon.

She had to call Bree's mother. She wanted to call her own mother and father too.

She tried to concentrate on the sermon. Then they were singing and closing with prayer.

"I'm glad I came," she whispered in the general subdued murmur of after-church exodus.

Adam smiled, "You said that last time."

"It's always true," she said.

She was anxious to get to Charlie, she explained to Mrs. Beale, so she would have to miss the coffee hour this time. She hugged Mrs. Beale and thanked her, but Mrs. Beale wouldn't accept so quick a dismissal of her aid. She insisted that Martha stay with her another night and refused to think otherwise. Martha was grateful to accept. Going back to an apartment devoid of Bree's chatter would be hard enough in daylight. Night alone there would be difficult.

Jack and his friend would pick up his car today, Adam said, so all they had to do was call the Center, which Martha did from the church office. She told them only that Bree and Charlie would not be in, and that she'd be a little late. She would explain later.

She also called Bree's mother and offered to send Bree's things home.

They picked up a sandwich and a Coke at a fast food place and ate in Adam's car. It was a good enough lunch. She didn't taste it anyway. It didn't occur to her to wonder why he was driving her down there. He just seemed to assume he would, and she accepted that.

Charlie was awake but a little hazy. He remembered little of the night, but the accident itself was clear and immediate in his mind. He wanted to talk about it, so they did, several times over. He couldn't get past the part where he reached for Bree and missed her. He seemed to feel that if he had been quicker or stronger or something, she wouldn't have fallen. They reassured him, but they knew it would take awhile for him to learn to live with the memory.

He hadn't called his father, so Martha called and held the phone for him to talk. Then she talked, explaining that Charlie had been wonderful, that he was hurt because he had tried to save Bree at great risk to himself, and that Charlie's family should be proud of him. It was quiet on the other end of the line as Mr. Cooper absorbed all this. He asked to speak to Charlie again, so she held the phone for him while Charlie nodded and said "Uh huh," and "Goodbye," and finally smiled. She hung up.

"Thanks, Angel," he said. "He's coming here. He says he's proud of me. He wouldn't have said that if you hadn't talked to him." To Adam he said, "That's why I call her Angel. She makes things come out right for me."

Martha said, "I'm not an angel, Charlie."

He said, "You are to me. Besides, I can't call you Muffie. It doesn't fit you."

"Call me by my name then, Charlie," she said. "I'm Martha."

"Martha? Really?" He sounded doubtful. "I don't know about 'Martha.' I like 'Angel' better. Either one is better than Muffie. What did you want to be called that for?"

"It sounded fun," she said, feeling foolish.

Charlie said, "You've seen one Muffie, you've seen 'em all."

She laughed. "You always say that, Charlie, and you know you don't believe it."

"I know," he laughed. "It's a habit left over from college. I guess I've outgrown it. It's time I outgrew a lot of things. I haven't grown enough; I only got bigger."

"You're going to be all right, Charlie," Martha said. "You're going to be terrific. Got to go to work, but I'll be back." She kissed him lightly on the forehead.

Charlie said, "I'll wait here for you, Angel."

Driving back in the Sunday afternoon beach traffic was slow, but Adam drove carefully, refusing to rush. She was a little late for work, as she expected, but no one objected, especially when she sought out her shift manager and explained about Bree and Charlie. The shift manager seemed to be impressed that Martha was there and said she could go home if she liked, but Martha wanted to stay, wanted to be too busy to think.

The news about Bree and Charlie traveled fast, and she spent most of the afternoon answering inquiries about the accident. Saying over and over that Bree was dead didn't make it seem real to her, but she knew she would have to face it. It simply seemed impossible. She was still a little shaky, and she knew Jack would be too.

She phoned him and he responded listlessly, but with more life than he'd had when they'd brought him home.

"I loved her," he said over and over. "I loved her."

At least Charlie will be fine, she thought. As soon as she left work, she would go see him again, pick up clean clothes at home, and go back to Mrs. Beale's.

That's exactly what she did, except that Adam was there to meet her after work and drive her to Charlie. Adam didn't have much to say during the visit, not as much as he had to say at their earlier visit. He sat in a far corner of the room and watched. She didn't notice; Adam was often quiet.

She was very tired when they left the hospital. To Adam's suggestion that they stop for supper, she said she'd rather not; she wasn't hungry. He was hungry, he said, so if she didn't mind watching him, he'd like to eat something. They stopped at a modest-looking family restaurant and she ordered iced tea. He got the whole meatloaf dinner, complete with fruit cup, salad, rolls, fries, and green beans.

"Want a bite?" he said, holding out the fruit cup and the spoon.

She ate a bite. Then she ate the whole fruit cup. He asked for an extra fork so she could have some salad, and she did. Then she ate the rolls, half the meatloaf, and most of the fries.

"It's a good thing you weren't hungry," he said.

She blinked and looked embarrassed. He laughed and ordered two strawberry shortcakes, then watched her methodically eat her way through the large dessert.

"I feel better," she said.

"You will tomorrow, when you've had some sleep. Let's get you home."

At Mrs. Beale's front door she said, "Thank you for taking care of me. I'm not used to it."

"You must have someone at home that you go out with. He must take care of you," he said.

"I don't think I ever let him take care of me," she said. "I was too busy taking care of everything else."

"In that case," he said, "he wasn't the right person for you."

"No," she said.

She wanted to think this strange conversation through that night, tried to stay awake to reason out what it meant, but she was too tired. She slipped into deep sleep almost as soon as she laid her head on the pillow.

In the morning, she returned to the apartment to pack Bree's things, using all those boxes from the grocery that she had used to make temporary shelves. She folded each lovely item carefully, feeling that this was something, a last something, she could do for Bree. As she packed, she thought of the sparkling, lively girl who had loved Charlie and wondered if Charlie knew how much Bree had loved him. Martha would never tell him. If he didn't know, perhaps it was better he didn't. It certainly would be better for Jack not to know.

She found a few pictures of Bree and kept one for herself and one for Jack. She also found a small box of keepsakes from special times—a seashell, a button, a program from a concert, and other things of little value except for memory. Perhaps Jack would want these.

She called him and he came over. He was still distant and a little vague, but he was making an effort. Yes, he wanted the picture. The box of keepsakes? He opened it and thoughtfully handled each item, putting each back in the box and closing the lid.

"These aren't mine," he said quietly. "These must be Charlie's. She loved him. I knew it, but I thought maybe, if I waited and loved her long enough, she'd get around to loving me back. She never did."

Martha said, "She must have loved you in her own way. She just didn't know it yet. Maybe, if there'd been more time—"

"Yes," he said. "Maybe." He handed her the box. "Thanks."

He helped her seal the boxes and send them. That was all there was to do. "Thanks," he said again.

"Visit Charlie," she said, "for your own sake as well as his."

He nodded.

She worked, ate, visited Charlie with Adam, phoned home, slept. Tuesday was much the same. Wednesday, she got the day off to drive with Adam and Jack to a small New Hampshire town for Bree's funeral. They stood together in the cemetery, saying good-bye to Bree, then went back to her mother's house for coffee and cake before returning late at night to Cape Cod. It was all so fast.

Charlie was restless and moody. He was discontent, eager to be on his feet. She could understand that. He must also have been lonely, although that seemed impossible considering all the company he had. Someone had brought a guest book and the signatures went on and on. His room was filled with cards and flowers. Nurses came and went constantly, glad to do whatever they could think of to spend time with this handsome, charming man. He had music in the room and newspapers. The phone rang all day.

His family spent time with him, pleasantly supportive and encouraging. She had met the formidable father and had words with him about Charlie. His father seemed taken aback by her forthright statements, but he listened and came to a different, broader appreciation of his son's success.

Charlie seemed to have everything, but he was not satisfied.

She asked him about it the next Sunday. "What's wrong, Charlie? What can I do for you?"

"What is it you have that gives you the power to make your life worth living?" he said. "I lie here and think about how empty my life is. Then I see you and see how you live and wonder what makes you like you are. You're a tough lady. You stood right up to me and right up to my father. I think you could stand up to anybody. Adam has this strength too."

"I told you, Charlie," Martha said. "That strength comes from the Lord. When you belong to Him, you become different. You think different things; you want different things. Your values change. Some things you just don't do because you know He doesn't want you to."

"Like drink," Charlie said.

"Like drink," she agreed. "The Bible says that we should not be drunk, and so we avoid it."

"The Bible actually says that?" asked Charlie.

From his corner Adam said, "It's in Ephesians, chapter 5, I think." He pulled a small Testament from his pocket and flipped pages. "Here it is. Ephesians 5: 18. 'And be not drunk with wine, wherein is excess; but be filled with the Spirit.' "

"I want this strength," Charlie said. "I want strength like yours."

"Are you sure?" Martha asked. "If you turn your life over to God, you don't know where you'll end up. You might find yourself going to church."

"I can do that," Charlie said.

"Then all you have to do is pray to God and ask Him to come into your heart. Adam and I will pray with you, but you have to do your own asking. I can't do that for you."

Charlie nodded. The three joined hands in the hospital room and prayed, and Charlie opened his heart to God. Afterward, they hugged and smiled and laughed.

Martha was still smiling in the car. "I don't know when I've felt so good about anything," she said. "Charlie is special; he's wonderful. I've been so worried about him, and now I know he's going to be all right."

"Yes," said Adam. He hesitated, then he said, "Do you know the rest of that chapter in Ephesians?"

"No," she said. "I must have heard it and read it, but I don't remember it. Why?"

He handed her the Testament. "Find it," he said. "Ephesians 5."

She found it.

"Read it," he said.

She read, " 'And be not drunk with wine, wherein is excess; but be filled with the Spirit. . .' "

"Go on."

" 'Speaking to yourselves in psalms and hymns and spiritual songs, singing and making melody in your heart to the Lord'. . .I like that," she said. "It's like having your own song to sing in your heart."

"Exactly," he said. "Your own song, not somebody else's."

"My song."

"Yes."

"My song for the Lord."

"Yes."

She lay awake that night, listening to the mockingbird, trying to find his own song in the tangle of measures borrowed from other birds. Poor bird, she thought, and was glad she had her own song. She had her own self too, such as it was. She was Martha—serious, responsible Martha—but she sang in her heart. And she had learned a few things. She knew how to have fun, thanks to Charlie. Thanks to Adam, she knew how to accept kindness and caring.

This wasn't what she had prayed for. She had prayed to know what she wanted, and she didn't exactly know yet. Not all of it, anyway. She had wanted Charlie to be happy, and she felt certain he was on the way to that happiness. She had wanted to help Bree and Jack, but she hadn't been able to do that. She would probably always wish she had done more, but it was too late for Bree. Muffie had wanted to be a party girl and she wasn't, but she did know how to have fun. She had wanted a summer to remember. She had that. She had wanted to be different; she wasn't entirely different, but there were changes. At least she knew who she was. She knew now that she could learn to be content to be herself.

Martha visited Charlie every day. Occasionally, Martha visited without Adam, but usually he drove her there and sat quietly in his corner listening to them talk, hold hands, laugh. Each time they left, Adam stood to shake hands and watched as she kissed Charlie lightly on the forehead or cheek in good-bye.

Charlie seemed to improve almost as they watched. He sat up. They pushed him in a wheelchair. He stood. He walked a little. Then, one evening, he told them he was to be released in a day or so. For the rest of the summer he would be useless as a lifeguard and really couldn't work at much else for awhile, but he should be able to start teaching on time when school started. His father wanted him to come home until he could take better care of himself.

"Wonderful," said Martha.

"But I don't want to go," Charlie said. "I can't go. I can't lose you. I've finally found my own angel and I want to keep her. I need you, Angel."

"No, you don't. You just think you do. You'll see."

He reached for her and pulled her close, kissing her firmly on the lips. "Marry me, Angel."

Marry Charlie! Beautiful Charlie wanted to marry her.

"Angel?"

"But Charlie. . ."

But Charlie, I'm Martha, dull, reliable Martha, she thought. *How can you want to marry me?*

"I need you, Angel. Marry me."

"I—yes. Yes, Charlie."

Neither of them noticed Adam leave as Charlie kissed her again.

Charlie said, "We'll be a great team, you and me. We'll raise a family, take them to Sunday school, love them to pieces. I'll coach and make you proud of me."

"I'm already proud of you, Charlie."

"Yeah, I know. You make me better than I am. You make me worth something." Charlie spun the future before her, and it floated there like a shining ribbon, like a rainbow dragon in the sky.

He needed her. She had always wanted to be useful and here it was, a future of being important to him and useful. Listening to his plans, she pictured it all, growing old with him, laughing.

"Angel?"

"Yes?"

"What do you think?"

"About what?"

"Weren't you listening? I was telling you about the house I want to build for us."

"Yes, Charlie. I guess I'm still getting used to the idea."

He talked on and on and she listened, or she thought she was listening. Evidently she wasn't, for she came to attention to find him silent, watching her. Had he asked her something she hadn't heard? She tried to remember.

"I'm sorry," she said. "I must have—" She stopped, confused.

"Look at me, Angel," he said. "Do you want to marry me?"

She thought. *Any girl in her right mind would want to marry Charlie. Of course I want to marry Charlie.* She said, "Don't be silly, Charlie. Any girl in her right mind would—"

"Not any girl," he said. "You. Do you want to marry me?"

She hesitated. "No," she said, her voice so low he couldn't hear it. She cleared her throat. "No," she said a little louder, her own voice sounding foreign in her ears. But it was true. It was crazy, but it was true. She didn't want to marry Charlie. "I'm sorry," she said.

He studied her in her confusion. She was lovely—an angel, but not his angel. He held her hand in his, stroking the long, strong fingers. He hadn't anticipated this and neither had she. She was struggling to regain her composure, but she was losing the struggle. He needed her, he wanted her, but what did she need? What did she want? He wished he knew so he could give it to her. She had given him so much.

Adam might know, he thought. *Adam seemed to know her better than anyone else. He was always with her, always in the background, watching over her.*

Adam, he thought. He said it aloud, "Adam."

She looked at him blankly. "Adam," she said. She turned to him in his corner, but he was gone. "Adam? Oh, Charlie, I—"

"I know, Angel."

She shrugged helplessly.

"Good-bye, Angel," Charlie said, but she was already gone.

Adam wasn't in the hall. She moved more rapidly to the elevator, pushing the down button, impatient for it to open its doors, impatient for it to close its doors. She willed it to hurry. On the main floor, she looked quickly around. Not there. She sped to the door, then to the dark parking lot and his car.

She saw him then, in a circle of light in the parking lot. He was slouched against the far side of his car, bent over, alone.

"Adam," she called. He didn't look up. She ran to him. "Adam," she said in barely suppressed excitement.

"Congratulations," he said, raising his head and forcing a smile. "I hope you'll be very happy."

"I will be, Adam," she said, "but not with Charlie."

"Not with Charlie? But you said 'yes'."

"Charlie doesn't need me, not anymore. And I don't want to be an angel. I'm a real person and I want—"

"What do you want, Martha?"

"You, Adam. I want you."

He folded her in his arms, burying his face in her hair. "Are you sure?"

"I love you, Adam. And you need me. I can sew on your buttons and tell you when the light is red. I can—"

"You can let me love you, honor you, and cherish you. I love you, Martha. I've loved you since the day we met in Provincetown. I loved you when you tried to be a Muffie. When you said yes to Charlie I thought my heart would stop. Marry me, Martha."

"Yes, Adam," she said, from safe in his arms. "That's exactly what I want to do."

JANET GORTSEMA
Janet lives in Pleasantville, New York, with her husband, Frank, and two cats. *Mockingbird's Song* was her second **Heartsong Presents** novel.

RETREAT TO LOVE

Nancy N. Rue

Dedication

For Glenda Allen who has helped me
listen to that still, small voice.

Chapter 1

Even in the velvety darkness of the restaurant, Alexis Riker had no trouble locating Lance. He was the one who looked like a model for *GQ*.

As she glanced down at her baggy pants and sandals, then at Lance's navy blue silk suit, she wished she'd opted for a floor-length gown.

"Can I help you find your party?" the maitre d' asked her.

Alexis grinned and shook her head. "No, I see him. At the corner table, by the window."

The maitre d' twitched an eyebrow. "Looks like you're in for quite an evening." He leaned in as he took her elbow. "He's already ordered the lobster appetizer."

Lance stood as soon as he saw her, one hand smoothing his lapel, the other brushing a stray curl off her cheek.

"Have you been waiting long?"

"Long enough to order the—"

"I know, the lobster." Alexis looked at him sideways as she slipped into her chair. The maitre d' unfurled the napkin with an expert wrist and spread it across her lap. Alexis tried to smother a smile as he glided away. "Excuse me if I use the wrong fork or something," she said. "You have to admit this is a little classier than Grinder's Deli."

"You want a club soda?" Lance said.

She nodded. Lance beckoned the waiter as Alexis tucked her hands into her lap. If she had known Omar's of Philadelphia was this ritzy, she would have—what? Had her nails done? She snorted to herself. She was lucky to have run a brush through her tangle of sandy blond hair.

"Did you really do all this to celebrate my going to Rockport tomorrow?" she said. "What a sweetheart." She squeezed his hand. "I didn't think you were all that excited that I was going up there with all those 'weirdo artist types,' as you call them."

Lance cleared his throat and seemed determined to focus on the menu. "That's not exactly why we're here. Shall we order?"

Alexis perused the entrees and snorted again. "Lance, did you win the lottery this afternoon? Look at these prices." She closed the menu. "I'll have the small dinner salad and a water."

Lance propped her menu up in front of her. "Order whatever you want. You like swordfish."

"Not at twenty-one dollars and ninety-five cents a pop!"

"Lexy."

She looked up at him. Candlelight danced in his gray eyes.

"We're not celebrating your going away. We're celebrating my arriving."

A tuxedoed waiter sidled up to their table.

"Good evening. I'm Damon and I'll be your server tonight." He set a club soda and the lobster hors d'oeuvre in front of Alexis with a flourish and folded his hands behind his back.

"She will have the swordfish," Lance said smoothly.

Alexis narrowed her brown eyes at him as he requested over fifty dollars' worth of food. Her mind raced. She was fresh out of grad school at the University of Pennsylvania. Lance had just finished at the law school. Neither of them ever had a dollar they could spend on anything but rent or books, and the most expensive meal they had ever ordered together had been a steak to share at a Sizzler over in Jersey. She watched the waiter walk away with a seven-course feast tucked into his head and frowned. What did Lance mean, he'd "arrived"?

She reached for a piece of lobster swathed in butter and dropped it on the plate.

"Lance!" she cried. Three couples at nearby tables stopped in midbite to stare at her. "You passed the bar exam!"

Lance let a smile spread slowly over his face as he pulled both of her hands into his.

"Just got the notice this afternoon. And you know what that means."

"Bailey, Logan, and Markowski want you."

"Mr. Logan called me ten minutes after I found out. He said to come to work Monday morning."

Alexis squeezed his hands. "I'm impressed, Counselor."

"I probably won't see the inside of a courtroom for about two years, but I'm on my way."

"And you deserve it," Alexis said. "I've seen how hard you've worked. I barely laid eyes on you for three weeks before the exam. You had your head buried in books the size of uptown buses."

Lance brought her hands up to his lips and kissed them.

"I think that's all going to change now," he said. "That's why we're celebrating."

Salads arrived and Lance watched with relish as Damon ground fresh pepper over his. But Alexis watched Lance, and her mind ground to a halt.

"What do you mean?" she said when Damon moved away.

Lance shimmered as he chewed. "Now we don't have to wait any longer. We can set a date. We can get you a real engagement ring instead of that." He waved his fork toward the three tiny diamond chips on a silver band on her left hand. "We can even look for a house when you come back. Matter of fact—" He set his fork down and took her hands again. "You don't even have to go to that retreat and put up with those flaky artist types because you won't have to work if you don't want to. We have a real future ahead of us now. Everything we've prayed for. God opened the doors today."

Alexis pulled her hands away and put them in her lap. Her head was reeling.

"What's wrong?" His brows pulled together. "I thought you'd be jazzed about this."

"I am excited, for you," Alexis said. "But Lance, I don't even know where to start."

She raked her fingers through her hair.

"Start what?" Lance said. "What gives?"

"I don't know. I mean, you have it all planned out. I'm surprised you haven't set the date and ordered the invitations."

"We've been talking about marriage for months, Lexy."

"Talking about it doesn't mean I'm going to go pick out a gown! We said someday."

"Someday is here. What's to stop us?"

"Maybe money isn't all there is to it," Alexis said.

He leaned back and crossed his arms across his suit coat. Alexis could see the attorney's objectivity descending in his eyes like a window shade. "This is the first I've heard of anything else holding us back," he said. "What's the problem?"

Alexis yanked back a handful of hair and let it drop against her neck. "My photography doesn't constitute part of a real future? You know why my father gave me this trip to Rockport for graduation. So I can spend six weeks with me. I have spent so much time studying photography the past three years, I haven't been able to find out how my career is going to fit into my need to do something meaningful for God, besides teaching, like I'm going to be doing in the fall. I would also like to spend some time with other artists, and no, I do not think they are all espresso-drinking weirdos."

"Lexy, most of them aren't even Christians. They believe in all this hocus-pocus stuff—"

"And you, of course, trust my faith completely." She stopped and took a breath. "I'm going specifically so I can spend some decent time alone with God and get recentered in my faith. If you don't think that has anything to do with the future, I think we have a real problem here."

The muscles were working in Lance's square jaw as he picked up his salad fork and examined it. "I wasn't belittling your career," he said tightly. "I just meant the pressure was off."

"I never felt like the pressure was on, until now."

Lance looked up at her sharply. "Hey, no pressure here. If you don't want—"

Alexis put her hand on his arm. "What I don't want is for us to plan the rest of our lives tonight."

He looked at her inky-fingered hand on his silk sleeve before he shifted his gaze to her eyes.

"That is what I want," he said. "But it sounds like you still have decisions to make."

She watched him for a minute before she answered. He was always like this. Controlled. Sure of exactly who he was and where he was going. Total grip on what he wanted and how he was going to get it. She was the one whose hands flew to her hair while her mind bounced all over the possibilities.

"Look," she said finally. "I think we should use this time while I'm at the artists' retreat to sort things through for ourselves before you budget your next twenty years' salary."

"I told you, I already know what I want," he said. "I knew it the first time I met you in the singles' group, the first time I saw you flip your hair around while you were playing charades, the first time we talked about what we believed. I'm never going to find another girl like you. And I don't want to."

Alexis leaned across the table. "I'm not asking you to. I'm just asking you to give me time to be sure." There was a long pause. *He's preparing his closing statement*, Alexis thought. Irritation clawed at the back of her neck.

"Okay," he said finally. He pushed his salad plate aside and took her left hand. "Because I know you're going to decide that we were meant to be together." He pulled the diamond chips to the top of her finger. "Just don't take the ring off while you're there, okay?"

"Why would I do that?" she said. "Lance, I'm not going to Massachusetts to look for somebody else. I'm going to look for myself."

Lance smoothed his napkin across his lap and gave her his I-have-no-further-questions-your-honor look. "I hope you find her," he said evenly. "Because I already have."

Chapter 2

L exy, I wish you'd take my car."

Alexis didn't look at Lance as she put the last of the boxes of developing equipment into the trunk. "I don't see why."

"You're driving a '57 Chevrolet through New York City, and I have a life-size picture of you breaking down in the middle of the street and having the whole thing dismantled around you."

"You're insulting Clifford!" Alexis lovingly patted the red fender, then turned to caress Lance's cheek. "This car and I have logged a lot of miles together—"

"That's exactly my point."

"And he's never let me down yet." She planted a kiss on Lance's nose and backed away. "I've really got to get going if I want to beat the morning traffic on the Betsy Ross."

"Why are you taking that bridge—"

"La—ance."

He stopped and slowly pulled her into his arms.

"I love you," he whispered.

"I know you do. Why else would you get up at the crack of dawn to come over here and see me off?" She smiled against his cheek.

He held her out at arm's length and searched her eyes. "You'll call me as soon as you get there?"

"Before I even start to become a weirdo artist."

One side of Lance's mouth went up and he shook his head. "Just call me before you go to bed, okay?"

"I'll do it. You want me to sign an affidavit?" She gave him another quick kiss and turned toward the car.

"I'll miss you," he said.

The anxious edge in his voice made her stop with one foot in. "You'll be so busy becoming Bailey, Logan, and Markowski, you won't even have time to think about me."

"Don't bet on it," he said.

"I'm not a betting woman," she said, slipping into Clifford's front seat. As she pulled out of her apartment complex, she glanced into the rearview mirror. He was still standing there, eyes riveted to the tailpipe for signs of suspicious exhaust. Her mental shutter clicked, and she slid this newest "picture" of Lance into the private photo album she kept in her head, a treasured file of moments they had shared in the last two and a half years.

Maneuvering Clifford through the still-drowsy traffic of the hazy morning, Alexis scanned a few of those moments in her mind. The first one, of course, was her favorite. She'd "taken" it a few months after she'd come to Philadelphia for grad school.

Growing up in Haddonfield, New Jersey, she had been to Philly more times than she had fingers and toes. But going there to live, even in a graduate student apartment, was different from watching the parade on Thanksgiving from her father's shoulders. Some afternoons she just wandered the streets, trying to find a way to belong.

It was on one of those walks that she had stopped in front of a gray-stone church that looked as if it had been around in Ben Franklin's time. The front door had opened, and a small herd of children bolted out and ran down the front steps, chattering about choir practice. The door hung open for a minute, and inside the vestibule, Alexis could see a bulletin board, overflowing with announcements and fliers. The crudely tacked-up papers seemed to announce, "There is a real life going on in this church."

As the door closed, a thought came into her mind, one she knew didn't come from her. Many times she had heard a still, small voice urging her to do something she might not otherwise have done. She had always somehow known it was God, and now He seemed to be telling her to go after those notices.

She must have stood in front of the bulletin board for twenty minutes. One flier seemed to beckon to her like a finger.

"Hey, Singles," it read, "Tired of the Chilly Philly Scene? Want some real people to hang with?"

The flier went on to say that singles, ages twenty-one to thirty, who were looking for Christian fellowship should join the group Friday nights in the "Singles' Room" in the church hall.

Scribbling the time on the back of her hand, she left the church with the wheels starting to turn in her head. The church had always held center stage in her life, from Sunday school to junior choir to youth group. Even in undergraduate school she had spent as much time in the Christian Union building as she had in her dorm room. But since arriving in Philadelphia, she had only gone to services at the nondenominational chapel on campus and let it go at that. God's still, small voice seemed to be saying it was time to jump in with both feet again.

That Friday night she went to the singles' group.

She wasn't in the room five minutes before somebody got her name and shouted it to the crowd of people, and somebody else plunked a soda into her hand. Within ten minutes, she was deep in the throes of charades.

Alexis drew Genesis to act out and began madly pantomiming action on a Sega Genesis video game machine. Soon people started shouting, "Computer!" "Video game!" and "Don't be an idiot, this is Bible charades!" Then a smooth voice had bored through the whole mess, right to her.

"Genesis," the voice had said.

Alexis stopped, hair flying to a halt with her, and peered through her tangle of curls. Looking at her with amused gray eyes was the best-looking guy she had ever seen outside a men's cologne ad.

Forget it, Pal, Alexis had immediately told herself. *He's Perrier water and you are lemonade. You might as well hope Tom Cruise would ask you out.*

Lance had patted the seat next to him.

"Me?" she said with about as much poise as a camel.

He nodded and she slid into the chair, and they were an "item" a week later.

Now, Alexis gave the moment one last thought as she pulled onto the New Jersey Turnpike. It had been the first of a long line of other "snapshots": she and Lance bowling together, doing budget grocery shopping with carts in tandem, and holding hands to pray.

"I must be crazy, Clifford," Alexis said to the dashboard, "to leave a guy like that for six weeks. And not just leave him, but tell him I'm going to think about whether I even want to marry him when I get back!"

As the exits flipped by, she remembered that when Lance had given her the promise ring, they had talked about someday.

"I can't afford to ask you to marry me now, Lexy," Lance had said that night as they bobbed past Independence Hall in a horse-drawn carriage. "If I do pass the bar, and I do get a decent job, I want to be sure you're still here with me, ready to talk about the future."

Ready to talk about the future, not ready to buy an expensive diamond and plan the honeymoon. Last night he made it sound as if they were all set to walk down the aisle now that he was Bailey, Logan, and Markowski-bound. That had annoyed her.

Oh, Lex, get real, she thought. *Lance is the best thing that could ever happen to you.*

"You help me stay centered," she had told him more than once. But in an even more important way—his commitment to Jesus Christ—he was her identical twin. She could never even consider a guy who wasn't a Christian.

"How could we be a more perfect match?" she asked Clifford. His engine purred on toward Massachusetts, and Alexis settled in the driver's seat. *I'm just an artist who can never settle on anything because there's always one more idea,* she decided.

But Lance wasn't a subject for a photograph. He was a guy, her guy, her almost-fiancé. She knew she ought to pull off in Providence and call him and tell him to start ordering those invitations. But Providence disappeared behind her, and so did Pawtucket and even Boston. When she finally stopped for gas, she gave the telephone booth a wide berth.

What was it about that conversation last night that had pulled her away from Lance? She dug a sandwich out of her bag and munched it thoughtfully while she drove. Was it the part about buying a house for her to stay home in all day while he worked?

Another photograph popped into her head, one she hadn't taken yet. There was Lance, sitting straight up at the head of a table with a little blond girl on one side and a little gray-eyed boy on the other. Alexis, of course, was taking the picture while the turkey steamed in front of them, the closest she was ever going to get to a camera if she followed his plan.

"That isn't what Lance wants!" she blurted out. He had been at her side all through graduate school, coming to her exhibits and studying her work as if he had a clue to the art of it. He knew how much being a photographer meant to her. He couldn't really expect her to put it all behind her, to be only his wife.

"No way, Cliff," she said. "He's just afraid I'm going to get up here with all these artists and flip out. He'll see when I come back to Philly in six weeks and—"

And what? She focused on the rotary that spun her crazily to Route 128 and Rockport. When she came back, she would decide not whether to marry Lance but when to marry him. He was the right guy, but this wasn't the right time.

What it was time for was some concentration on her art. After three years of graduate courses in photography, she was lined up to teach for the fall semester. But she had never seen teaching as a goal. Right now it was a means for paying off grad school loans. But what about after that? Despite her bravado with Lance, she was a loosely wrapped package of uncertainties.

She rounded a slow curve on Route 128 and a sleepy seaside village suddenly came into view. She could smell the salt air and hear the calling of seagulls even above the revving of cars vying for parking spots in front of the quaint-looking shops.

She swerved into a parking space, her head spinning. What was she doing here, really? Was she an artist? Would she fit in here? Or was she bound for a life of sittings at Olan Mills? Did she really have something to say for God as a photographer? She hadn't heard that still, small voice in a long time.

She sat with her eyes closed for a minute as the thoughts chased around in her head. Then she sat up and put the red Chevy into gear.

"Well, Clifford," she said, "there's only one way to find out."

As she inched down Eden Road outside Rockport proper looking for a sign directing her to Rocky Shoals Artists' Retreat, her uneasiness was shoved aside by the display of inns and houses on her right facing the ocean. Every idyllic turn-of-the-century mansion she passed she hoped was the one, then was glad it wasn't when she saw the next one. But when the Rocky Shoals sign at last appeared on the top of an imposing boulder, she gasped out loud.

The classic nineteenth-century manor was high on a hill as if standing watch over the sea. Its confident façade was reinforced by stately columns holding up the second-floor balcony and a veranda stretching from one end to the other.

Graceful cabins were scattered across a grassy emerald carpet behind the main house, each one reminiscent of the big house in some miniature way. As Alexis eased Clifford up the long sweeping driveway that ran past the front cabins, she found herself already taking up residence in her imagination.

She followed the drive behind the main house, then stopped with a jolt behind a sleek black limousine. *I doubt that's one of Lance's "weirdos,"* Alexis thought. She grinned to herself. With Lance's taste for extravagance, he would be changing his tune about her becoming "one of them."

She put Clifford in neutral and switched off the ignition. It was going to be good to stretch her muscles. But as she reached for the door handle, a male face sporting sunglasses and a big square grin poked in her window. Folding his muscled arms on the window frame, he leaned in casually, energy and charm gleaming from every tanned pore.

"Welcome to Rocky Shoals," he said. "May I take your order, please?"

Chapter 3

"Excuse me?" Alexis said.

He stuck his palm inside the car. "Name's Ty Solorzano."

She looked doubtfully at his hand for a minute before she took it. He pumped hers enthusiastically. Maybe Lance was right. If the bellboys were this off-the-wall, what were the others going to be like?

He nodded toward the limo. "I don't think Princess Di is planning to move until after the Grey Poupon arrives, so you might want to get out here and find out which cabin's yours."

His eyes were glinting mischievously behind his sunglasses, and his full lips were twitching. Alexis resisted the temptation to look in the rearview mirror to see if she had a piece of lettuce stuck in her front teeth. She had the distinct feeling he was making fun of her.

"I'm Alexis Riker," she said. "Which cabin is mine?"

"You got me."

Alexis stared at him. It must be hard to get good help up here. She opened the door and nudged him back gently with it.

"Are Mr. or Mrs. Goedert around?" she said. "That's who I was told to ask for."

"That's Sigrid over there," he said.

As she headed for the slight woman with the salt and pepper hair who was holding a clipboard and pointing directions to the limousine driver, she heard Ty say behind her, "Nice talking to you."

I don't mean to be rude, she thought. *But I didn't come up here to listen to the valet do a stand-up comic routine.*

"Ah, you must be Alexis!"

The thin woman's face crinkled as she skittered toward Alexis. The trace of an Austrian accent curled charmingly around her words.

"Are you Mrs. Goedert?"

"Please, it's Sigrid. How was your trip from Philadelphia?"

As the last syllable sprang from her mouth, Alexis had to smile. With her little sparrow face and bright, darting eyes, Sigrid reminded her of a tiny, twittering bird.

"Now you must meet Franz—Franz! Miss Riker is here!"

A tall man with an ample waistline and a thin shock of white hair that stood straight up in the sea breeze came toward them. He smiled a little formally at Alexis as he shook her hand.

"Alexis is our photographer from Philadelphia," she told her husband.

Before he could even nod, Sigrid Goedert chirped on. "Now, Alexis, I know you'll want to get settled. Your cabin is number three, right up there on the hill, you see, between the two pines there."

Alexis nodded, but she wasn't sure she heard most of it. Her eyes were fastened on the clapboard cottage with the white shutters that was about to become her home for six weeks. It had a tiny porch and bay windows that hinted of windowseats. It was everything she hadn't dared imagine.

"You can drive your car into the circle, and Franz will help you take your things inside," Sigrid said.

Alexis looked at the elderly Franz, then at Ty, who was leaning against a four-wheel-drive vehicle talking to a perfectly matched white-haired couple.

"I have a lot of heavy developing equipment," Alexis said. "I probably ought to have the bellboy help me."

Franz gave her a puzzled look and Sigrid's feathery eyebrows shot up. "Bellboy, Dear?"

"Ty," Alexis said.

Their eyes followed Alexis's pointing finger.

"Oh, no, that isn't a bellboy!" Sigrid said loud enough to make Ty turn to look. "That's one of your fellow artists. He's a sportswriter from Chicago." She took Alexis's arm as she led her toward Clifford. "His book on professional rock climbers is doing quite well, you know," she said. "He's seen his way clear to come up here and start a novel. You'll have a chance to share those kinds of things with each other when we have our meeting in the main house right before dinner. That's the only meeting we'll ask you to attend, you understand. The rest of your time here will be completely your own."

Sigrid prattled on while Alexis's mind flipped back to the tall, tanned writer she had mistaken for a bellboy. *I hope he didn't hear that,* she thought. Then she found herself smirking. *No, in a way I kind of hope he did. He's pretty full of himself. Professional rock climbers. And I wondered if I were an artist!*

But Ty Solorzano faded from her mind the minute she opened the front door of her cabin. The charm—the softness, the breeziness, the yellowness— flooded over her.

Shiny hardwood floors and pale yellow walls framed the cabin's one room. To the left was a sitting area with an overstuffed couch that seemed to be exploding with tapestried pillows and two equally contented-looking chairs that cozied up to a white fireplace. A round mahogany table pulled them together, and a potted plant next to the cushiony windowseat hovered over it all.

A look to the right took in the sleeping area, which was on a raised platform, the mahogany sleigh bed looking peacefully majestic. A cotton lace bedspread hung lazily from it, and the same irrepressible pile of pillows beckoned her to snuggle in for a nap. A tall dresser with a vase of fluffy zinnias stood on one corner, a curl-up chair in another.

Light seemed to blow in with the breeze on the wings of the sheer curtains that draped several inches onto the floor when they came to rest.

"You have the cabin with the largest bathroom," Franz said as he appeared in the doorway behind her with one of the developing boxes. "She said you'd need a darkroom, so we thought here would be good."

It was the first time she had heard him speak, and she smiled at his quiet voice and clipped accent.

"That's wonderful," she said.

She followed him in and peeked over his shoulder as he set the box down on the floor. Even with the tub on its four feet there was enough room to set up a darkroom.

"This will be perfect!" Alexis said. But Franz had already left to bring in the rest of the boxes. Her need to be alone with her thoughts had just possibly found a home in this sunny cottage.

This room might be a little too feminine for me, she thought. The Alexis Riker she knew was too horsey and down to earth for lace and geraniums. Her apartment didn't have a decor at all. If Mrs. Goedert could see it, she would call in the decorating police.

Well, this will be me for six weeks, she thought. *I think I can live with a few pillows and ruffles.*

By the time she was unpacked and had the darkroom equipment separated from the blow dryer and the bath towels, it was time for the meeting in the main house. She barely had a chance to put her hair up in a ponytail with a slightly dingy white "scrunchy" and change into jeans.

As she headed for the imposing main house, she thought warily about Ty, the "bellboy." She hoped she could find a seat far away from him and his quips. If he had heard Sigrid proclaiming that Alexis thought he was a blue-collar worker, he would be sure to have a jab or two for her. What was it about him that had turned her off from almost the first second?

But it wasn't Ty who made her want to scurry back to her cottage. It was a magnificent-looking woman standing on the back porch, obviously taking in the ocean air with her nostrils.

Her short, dark hair swirled in the breeze, then settled back down into its perfect wedge as she held onto the railing with meticulously manicured hands and smiled, eyes closed. Her jade green silk palazzo pants and tunic jacket floated up and down on the wind like elegant palm fronds. This had to be the lady in the limo, Alexis decided. She had to get out of these jeans.

And into what? she thought wildly. She hadn't brought anything but shorts, jeans, denim shirts, and T-shirts that shouted "Phillies" or "Choose Life." The woman opened her eyes and transferred her smile to Alexis.

"Hi, there," she said in a soft drawl that conjured up images of southern belles on porches like this one. "Are you one of my fellow artists?"

No, Alexis wanted to say. *I'm the cleaning lady.* But she nodded and smiled back. "I'm Alexis Riker."

"Jacquie D'Angelo. I'm a children's playwright from Dallas."

The words "you must have heard of my work" didn't follow as Alexis would have expected from someone dangling an emerald and diamond tennis bracelet on one hand and a topaz ring as big as Alexis's watch on the other.

"And what do you do? I mean, besides stand there and look like a natural beauty."

Alexis looked behind her.

"I'm talking about you, Darlin'," Jacquie said. "If I could get away without wearing a speck of makeup and look like you, Clinique would go out of business. What do you do?"

"I'm a, well, I just got my master's in photography. I'll be teaching in the fall."

"So you're a photographer."

"Well, yeah, I mean I haven't actually started to make a living as one."

Jacquie looked at Alexis a moment longer, then said, "Have you seen the inside of this gorgeous house yet?"

"No, I haven't had the chance."

"Well, let me be the one to introduce it to you. I like to see people's faces when they take in that sitting room for the first time."

"You've been here before then?" Alexis said as she joined her on the porch and followed her in through the back screen door.

"This is my second time," she said.

She swept through a wide foyer and pulled Alexis with her by the hand through a pair of French doors and into another world. Alexis heard herself gasp.

"I love it!" Jacquie clapped her hands delightedly as Alexis gazed wide-eyed around the room.

The wood-covered walls were celery, but she could barely see them for the seascapes, the bold Renaissance-style armoires, and the ivy that billowed from pots and baskets from over the stone fireplace. Chairs and couches of every period snuggled around a round table that was dotted with trays of crab and shrimp. Flowers and stripes, pillows and pottery, art books and miniature sculptures, the room was a comfortable tribute to all that is art.

"Let's join the Coxes," Jacquie said. "I met them just a little earlier. They seem darlin'."

The "darlin'" people in question were the same elderly couple Alexis had seen

Ty regaling with bad jokes earlier. They were even better matched than Alexis had thought. Same thick white hair, cut short around their ears. Both had elfin faces and eyes that crinkled when they talked. They were even wearing matching red shirts with neatly ironed white slacks.

I can't even imagine Lance and I dressing alike, Alexis thought as Jacquie led her over for introductions.

Mr. Cox hopped up excitedly and shook Alexis's hand as if he had been waiting for her to come in the door and become his best friend. Mrs. Cox was no less delighted.

"You just sit down here with us," Mr. Cox said. "Pretty thing like you—"

"Stop, Will, you'll embarrass her," Mrs. Cox said. She leaned over and put a soft, grandmotherly hand on Alexis's leg. "We can't wait to get to know you."

For some reason, Alexis believed her, just as she had believed Jacquie earlier when she wanted to take her under her wing. She looked around the room. So far, Lance would have to eat his words if he saw this little gathering. They were all interesting people, but certainly not weirdos. Could it be that artists were just normal-looking people like her after all?

As if in answer to her question, the French doors pushed open, and a slight young woman with eyes almost too big for her face slid in and looked openly at all of them.

The girl could have walked right out of photographs from the sixties of hippies in San Francisco. Her long, reddish hair was parted in the middle and lay flat against her round face as it hung straight to her shoulders like arrows. A T-shirt, multiple strings of beads, a calf-length skirt, and clunky combat boots made up her outfit. Alexis thought she looked vaguely like an unmade bed Lance would be saying, "I told you so."

From another set of French doors, Sigrid Goedert sailed in with a tray of pitchers, and she smiled unflinchingly at the girl. It was obvious to Alexis that this wasn't the first time she had seen her because she didn't drop the tray and stare.

"Marina-Natasha!" Sigrid said. "Please, find a seat, ah, and Ty!"

Ty stood in the doorway, grinning as if he had just made a joke no one had gotten. Alexis patted the chair next to her and said to the free-spirited young woman, "Please, sit here." Anything to keep him away from her elbow.

The move wasn't lost on Ty. His eyes, which she could now see were fudge brown without his sunglasses, met hers, and he held them as he said to Jacquie "Is this seat taken?"

"Doesn't look like it, Sugar," she said. "Come on."

He was still looking at Alexis as he sank into a striped armchair. Then his eyes went deliberately to Jacquie. "So, let me guess, romance novelist."

Jacquie laughed and Alexis looked away in disgust.

"Help yourselves, everyone," Sigrid sang out. "The crab and shrimp are fresh, of course."

"And the bread's homemade," Ty put in. "I've been smelling it all afternoon."

"It's hard not to when you won't get out of my kitchen," Sigrid said, her eyes twinkling.

Mrs. Cox handed Alexis a plate. "You don't want to miss any of this," she said. "The food was the one thing in the brochure that stood out for me. I saw a picture of a spread like this and I said, 'Will, we've got to go.'"

"You a big eater, Mrs. Cox?" Ty said, loading his plate with what looked to Alexis like an oceanful of seafood.

"Can't you tell?" Mrs. Cox said, patting a negligible tummy.

"Not by looking at you," Ty said.

Oh, brother, Alexis thought. *He's a charmer, too.*

"Now then," Sigrid began, "it's our tradition here at Rocky Shoals to start off with introductions, so that when you see your fellow artists, you can do more than nod."

Sigrid stood behind her husband's chair with her arms around his neck. He just smiled his quiet smile and listened.

"I'm Sigrid Goedert, and this is my husband, Franz. We're from Austria. Both of us grew up with the arts, and when we came to the United States ten years ago, we were scandalized to find out that Americans do not support their artists, except to buy their work. We saw too many talented people drawing ads for the peanut butter instead of painting what their souls told them to, so we decided to do our part by creating Rocky Shoals."

Franz cleared his throat, and Sigrid nodded to him. "Of course, the building itself and the cabins were already here. It was an inn, built in 1905 as a summer home by a wealthy Texan." She smiled at Jacquie. "You know about those."

Ty lifted Jacquie's studded wrist. "She is one of those."

Alexis tried not to roll her eyes.

"He chose a prime hilltop location here on Land's End," Sigrid went on, "which is the easternmost part of Cape Ann. Our panoramic views of the Atlantic Ocean are unmatched anywhere, eh?" She gave Franz a little nudge, and he nodded.

"Franz, of course, can tell you all about the inn itself. You will observe all the features of a grand manor, including a magnificent staircase of Canadian pine, beautiful woodwork, and seven fireplaces."

Alexis caught Jacquie's eye, and they exchanged smiles. Maybe Franz could tell them, but he wasn't going to have the chance.

"We think it is the perfect place for artists to be inspired," Sigrid continued, "and that is why we have opened it up to you. Now, perhaps we should have you all tell us just what you're going to do here."

She looked at Jacquie. "Would you like to begin, Mrs. D'Angelo?"

"Only if you call me Jacquie," she said. Although she obviously had social graces she hadn't even used yet, she seemed warm and genuine, drawing everyone in with her sincerity.

"I'm Jacquie D'Angelo from Dallas—I'm forty-seven—"

"Oh, dear!" Mrs. Cox said. "Do we have to tell our ages?"

"That shouldn't bother you," Ty said to her. "You're still wet behind the ears."

Mrs. Cox waved him off good-naturedly, and Alexis shifted the neck of her T-shirt. These people sure were easily taken in.

"I'm a children's writer," Jacquie went on. "I write plays mostly, and I'm here to get away from my husband!"

There was a round of snorts and gasps as Jacquie dazzled them with a smile. "I love that man, but in the summer, with the round of picnics and barbecues the corporate world calls us to, I'd be doing nothing but buying potato salad and doing flower arrangements. I wouldn't get a word written."

"You have a play in progress, then?" Ty said.

"I do, and it better be in much better progress before I leave, because it's scheduled for a trial run production this fall in Fort Worth!"

Alexis looked at her enviously. That sureness of where she was going with her talent. . .Alexis would have given her share of the spread in front of her to have that.

Sigrid nodded to the unmade bed.

"I'm Marina-Natasha," the girl said.

"Do you have a last name?" Ty said.

The melting look from her big eyes was surprisingly innocent. "I don't use it," she said. "I've tried to streamline my life. I have gotten rid of all the unnecessary amenities."

"You know, a last name really does get in the way," Ty said. "I've been thinking about doing away with mine."

"Really?" she said. She looked at him searchingly before she continued.

"I'm from Oregon and I'm a songwriter. I came here to compose because, it's like, I wanted the fresh feel of a different environment. I think change is good for the soul." She nodded at all of them, and for lack of any other way to respond, they all nodded back.

This girl was born twenty-five years too late, Alexis thought. *Next thing you know, she's going to be flashing us a peace sign.*

"Don't worry," Marina-Natasha said finally.

"About what?" Ty said.

"About my music."

Ty looked at everyone and they all returned his gaze blankly. "Should we be?" he said.

"I mean it, like, won't be loud when you're trying to, like, sleep or write or whatever. I'm in that cabin that's set off all by itself."

"That's nice of you to be concerned—" Jacquie started to say.

"But I think music, especially music while it's actually, like, being created, is beautiful no matter what time of night it is."

"I'm sure you'll inspire us all," Sigrid said. Her voice was like a placating hand on the head of a restless child, but Marina-Natasha seemed satisfied with that and settled back in her chair.

"What about you, Alexis?" Sigrid said. "Would you like to go next?"

Alexis wouldn't, actually. What was she going to say to these people who were all so sure of their creative direction? But there was no way to get out of it without sounding like a whining high schooler who wanted to be coaxed to take the stage, so she pulled her knees up to her chest, hugged them, and started. *Lord, please help me with this, big time!* she silently prayed.

"I'm Alexis Riker," she said. That was easy enough. So far, so good. "You can call me Lexy, which is what most of my friends do. Or you can call me Alex, if you want—"

"Can we call you a taxi?" Ty said.

Jacquie tossed her head back and laughed, and the Coxes grabbed each other's arms the way couples do when they love a good howl together.

If he'd known how hard this was for me, he wouldn't have made a crack like that, Alexis thought. *Then again, maybe he would have.*

She tightened her grip around her legs. "I just finished my master's in photography. I'm here to recover from that."

Jacquie led the delighted laughter around her.

"But what I'm really here for is to find out how I can use my, my art, I guess you could call it, for God. I'm a Christian, so it's important to me that my work have some significance to Him."

There was a silence. No one was curling her lip or studying his shoelaces or asking for a refund. They all just looked back at her for a moment, then the nodding and smiling started. Ty didn't do anything except study her face. The Coxes looked as if they were going to burst.

"We'd like to go next," Mrs. Cox said, eyes bubbling. "We're Christians, too!"

"We know just what you're saying," Mr. Cox put in. "The wife here is an illustrator, has been drawing for Sunday school magazines for years. She knows how God fits into her talent."

"But Will has just entered the art world," Mrs. Cox added. "Ever since he retired he's had a paintbrush in his hand. Wants to paint the sea in every one of its moods so he can turn the walls of our home in Colorado into a complete seascape. Bring God right into the living room."

"But Virginia, she says she thinks there's more to it spiritually for me," Will said. "She's probably right. She usually is."

Alexis watched them in awe. These people were so intertwined, they could even talk for each other. Would it really be that way for Lance and her if they got married, when they got married? She tried to imagine Lance knowing what she was going to say next, but she gave up and shook her head.

The Coxes were beaming at her, and she beamed back. Six weeks without fellowship with people who believed as she did would have been like being forever on a crosstown bus by herself. Lance had been wrong about that too.

"I think that leaves you, Ty," Sigrid said. "Are you ready to tell all?"

Alexis put her legs down and leaned forward. She couldn't wait to hear this. And he obviously couldn't wait to tell it. "I'm Ty Solorzano," he said immediately. "Age, twenty-nine. Height, six-foot three. Weight, one hundred eighty-five pounds."

"Stop!" Jacquie said, smacking his arm playfully.

"I'm a sportswriter from Chicago, because you can get the best sausage sandwiches in that town."

"I've heard that," Will Cox said.

"I have a book out and it's getting decent sales, so I decided I could afford to take a little time off to work on the great American novel."

Everyone nodded in serious approval, and he guffawed. "And if you believe that, I've also got some poetry I'd like to sell you."

"Oh, you're a stinker," Virginia Cox said. "I bet you're a wonderful writer with that sense of humor."

Is that what you call it? Alexis thought. *Twenty-nine and you can't hold a serious conversation, at an artists' retreat? I may not know what I want to do, but at least I treat the whole thing with respect.*

But it didn't seem to bother anyone else as they decided unanimously that they were a wonderful group, and great things were going to arise from their six weeks here. Sigrid directed them toward the dining room, through the second set of French doors, where dinner was steaming on tables set with crystal and candles.

"Sit with me?" Jacquie said to her.

Alexis watched as Ty folded his frame into a table with the Coxes and nodded. "Sure. I'd really like to hear about your play."

Ty let out another guffaw and Alexis added mentally, *And I wouldn't like to hear what's going on at that table. At all.*

Chapter 4

The sleigh bed looked inviting, perched on its platform in a square of moonlight. But Alexis was still restless when she went back to her cabin. As she sat uneasily in the overstuffed chair, the moon seemed to beckon to her more than the mountain of pillows.

She grabbed the light jacket Lance had told her to pack—"Because it cools off up there by the ocean"—and crept out her squeaky screen door. Maybe a walk would make her sleepy.

All of Rocky Shoals was quiet. *I guess everyone who knows what they're doing with their lives can sleep like babies,* she thought. The chill of that thought and the misty dampness in the air made her shiver and walk faster.

But when she reached the front of the main house, a soft gasp escaped her lips.

The ocean, black and shiny in the moonlight, stretched before her in secret splendor. Only those patient enough to visit her at night were so rewarded. And off to Alexis's right, two beams swirled and sought out searchers like her.

"That's Thacher Island!" Alexis said out loud. The two beams must be the twin lighthouses she had read about in the brochure. She hadn't been able to see them from her window, and she could feel the awe coming up in her throat. No description of Sigrid's could capture what she was seeing now.

Clutching her jacket tighter around her, Alexis hurried across the silent lawn and down the road toward the beach. If she could get closer, maybe she'd be able to make out the lighthouses themselves.

The edge of the road was suddenly rocky, and even with the moon, it was hard to see what was in front of her. Before she could examine her next step, the rock she was standing on shifted and began to roll. She lunged forward to catch her balance, but her feet hit rocks slick with sea mist. As both feet slithered, her arms flailed about for something to hold onto. Suddenly, from behind her, two strong, warm arms folded around her waist and pulled her back up.

"Watch it now, Taxi," someone said. "They make them slicker than goo on a glass eye up here."

Alexis whipped her head up and looked straight into the dark, teasing eyes of Ty Solorzano. With a jerk she pulled away.

"Careful," he said.

"I'm fine. I just lost my balance."

"Hey, it was no problem to save your life, really. No thanks necessary."

There was a gentle taunting in his voice that set Alexis's teeth on edge. She muttered, "Thanks," and started to head back toward the house. The spell of the lighthouses had been broken by the appearance of this watchdog. Something about him made her squirm.

But Ty seemed more than ready to make casual conversation as he took her elbow to steady her. "Let me ask you this. Have you ever walked out here before, in the daytime?"

"No," she said, trying not to rip her elbow out of his hand as she took it away.

"Then you have no idea what you were just flirting with?"

Alexis gave an exasperated sigh. "I was looking at the lighthouses, okay? I'd never seen them before and I wanted a closer look. That's the news. You want the weather?"

She could see his full lips go into their square smile as he chuckled. A stubborn cowlick at the top of his close-cut dark hair blew up in the night wind and lent him an air of boyishness.

"No," he said, looking down at her, "but I'll give you the accident report. Two more steps and you'd have been over a cliff with a fifty-foot drop to the next cliff, which then dumps you off into the ocean."

Alexis resisted the temptation to peek over the side to see if he were right. It was so hard to give this guy the satisfaction.

Instead, she said tightly, "Thanks. I'd hate to be bumped off my first night here."

"Yeah, I'd always rather wait a night or two. So let me ask you this—"

But Alexis did back away this time. "I've really got to go," she said.

"You want me to walk you back? There's that one hedge you might have a little trouble with."

His mocking ran up her spine like sand spurs and she cut him off. "I've got it handled. Good night."

As she half-ran across the road, she heard him say behind her, "Good night, Taxi."

What is it about that guy that drives me up the wall? Alexis asked herself as she sped back up the hill toward the main house. *He's so sure everyone is going to find him hilarious, and I just think he's obnoxious. Has he explored every inch of Cape Ann so he knows right where the next damsel in distress is going to lose her footing?*

Glancing behind her to be sure he'd faded off into the mist, she slowed down and watched for the hedge.

When Alexis reached the bottom step leading up to the porch of the main house, she looked up at its welcoming white railing and the clean wicker furniture that looked so restful under the soft glow of the porch light. Slipping off her shoes, she took the steps two at a time and nestled onto the love seat, piled with the inevitable pillows. She pulled one onto her lap and hugged it against her as she looked out at the lighthouses again.

Those two sweeping, searching beams scanning the ocean together, in perfect sync with each other, had captured her as nothing had in a long time. Maybe she'd start tomorrow by capturing them with her camera. She didn't know why, but maybe God was leading her somewhere.

As she gave the lighthouses one last look, Alexis heard a telephone ringing from a room just off the porch.

Oh, no, Alexis thought with a chill. *I forgot to call Lance. I hope that isn't him, waking everybody up to check on me.* She sat up straight and listened as footsteps entered the room, and the ringing halted with an abrupt hello from Sigrid.

But unless Sigrid and Lance went way back, it was obvious from the first three lines of the conversation that it wasn't Alexis's almost-fiancé on the phone. Sigrid's voice went up in sleepy delight, then dipped down into concern. Alexis scooted to the edge of her seat to leave so she wouldn't eavesdrop, but a sharp turn in Sigrid's voice fastened her to the cushion.

"No, Lisl, that is not acceptable. We have people here, you know that. It isn't a matter of having room, it's a matter of its being inappropriate. I know he is my grandson, Lisl, but you know what his being here involves. I do not have time to watch over him. Ach, fifteen and a bigger handful than twenty toddlers put together, and you know it. If you will recall what he did last time, I won't have that again. . . . Then we will be good for him in the winter months when we do not have six artists here expecting peace and inspiration. I do not know, Lisl, but I'm sure you will figure out something. Lisl, here, speak to your father."

Sigrid stopped talking, and a low muttering began that Alexis could only assume was Franz delivering his clipped and quiet tones into the receiver. Her stomach grew queasy, and she crept off the love seat and down the steps.

When Alexis slid into bed, she yawned and started her prayers. "Help me, Father, to find Your way in my life," she prayed. "Be with Lance and ease his worry. Bless my fellow artists, and the one who thinks he's an artist, and be a guide for Sigrid and Franz. Please don't let the lighthouses be gone when I wake up—" And with that last fuzzy thought, she was off to sleep.

❧

Most artists didn't do breakfast. Only the Coxes were huddled cozily at a table by the window in the dining room when she arrived at eight. Virginia's eyes crinkled, and Will waved her over.

"Come join us, our little Christian friend!" he said.

"I'm far from little, Mr. Cox," Alexis said, smiling ruefully. "And if I keep eating all of Sigrid's cooking, I'm going to be twice this size before I leave."

Virginia shook her head and pushed a sweetgrass basket toward her loaded with scones, muffins, and croissants. "You young girls, always worrying about your figures."

"I like a woman with a little meat on her bones myself," Will said.

"You're robust and healthy and beautiful," Virginia said.

Alexis laughed and pulled out a muffin studded with blueberries. "I'm going to have breakfast with you two every morning if I'm going to get this pep talk!"

"Butter?" Will said, his eyes twinkling.

"Do you need more butter?" Sigrid bustled up to the table, running the palms of her hands against her apron. Her eyes sagged with fatigue, and although she smiled, Alexis could see that her thoughts weren't happy.

"We're fine!" Virginia said. "We're just giving Alexis a hard time."

Sigrid nodded vaguely. "Have a good morning, then."

It must be tough to turn away your own grandson, Alexis thought.

❧

A glance toward the ocean after breakfast told Alexis there'd be no seeing the lighthouses until the morning fog burned off. She probably ought to start by setting up her darkroom. She knew once she did get some shots, she'd want to develop them right away.

Heading to her cabin with a determined stride, she was caught off-guard when a nearby cabin's screen door squeaked open and Jacquie's head poked out. She was in a cream-colored bathrobe and her eyes were puffy with sleep, but her hair looked as if she'd just been coiffed by Vidal Sassoon himself. Alexis wanted to ask her if she'd slept sitting up.

"Are you one of those disgusting morning people who thinks this hour is the best part of the day?" Jacquie asked drowsily.

Alexis laughed. "I hardly ever get to sleep this late. I'm usually hard at it by this time."

Jacquie wrinkled her nose. "Hard at what? What could be that important?"

Alexis opened her mouth to answer, but nothing came out. "At this point, I don't know," she said.

Jacquie's face softened, and she let the screen door close behind her as she emerged onto her porch and leaned down over the railing at Alexis. "Then that must be what you're here to find out," she said. "What is important enough to get out of bed for."

At that moment, Alexis decided she liked this woman. Jacquie was warmth and compassion and who knew what else beneath the silk blouses and perfectly glossed smile.

"So will I see you at lunch?" Jacquie said.

"If I get my darkroom set up and have a chance to get some shots of the lighthouses. Have you seen them?"

"They're half the reason I keep coming back here. Those two are like an old married couple, you know?"

Alexis snorted. "I hadn't thought of comparing them to my parents!"

"I wasn't thinking of myself and Michael D'Angelo either, Sugar. But when it really works—your lights shining out together, searching together—I think that's what it should be like." She wiggled her shoulders and grinned. "Ooh, that's good stuff. I better go in and write that down!"

Alexis promised to look for her at lunch, but it was noon by the time she had her enlarger, safelight, and processing trays set up in the bathroom. She didn't want to stop before she covered the window with aluminum foil to reflect the heat and block most of the light, then covered the window and its frame with dark cloth.

She turned off the light and set her watch. If she still couldn't see any light after two minutes in the dark, she would know the room was safe for printing with most papers. After five minutes she would see it was okay for film loading and processing. It was actually looking good for light.

Too bad it doesn't close out sound, Alexis thought.

Just outside her cabin, the ever-present guffawing and joking of Ty Solorzano filtered in as if he were standing right in her sitting room regaling her with one-liners.

"So what did you do this morning, Cosmic Traveler, get up and whip out a few tunes before breakfast?"

He had to be talking to Marina-Natasha. *Slick, Pal,* Alexis thought. *You really know how to talk to an artist. If you took your own art seriously, you'd know you don't just "whip out a few tunes."*

"That's, like, so cool that you would ask that," she heard Marina-Natasha say in her self-interrupting voice. "Because I did actually do that this morning. Everything was, you know, like, so together when I got up this morning and—this is intense—my mind was full of, like, chords and progressions. My hands—"

There was a pause, and Alexis could picture Marina-Natasha holding up her hands and gazing at them in one of her interminable pauses. She didn't get to hear Ty's response to that because they had evidently moved on toward the main house. A few minutes later, she caught one of his guffaws.

Maybe I'll just skip lunch, Alexis thought. She wasn't sure she could listen without becoming sarcastic. He sure brought out the worst in her.

But the smell of homemade soup and bread was too much for her, and she grabbed the other seat at Jacquie's table just as everyone was starting to serve themselves.

At the next table, Ty moaned ecstatically over his clam chowder, and Alexis glanced over at him involuntarily. He was in shorts damp at the sides from being pulled over a bathing suit, and his hair was still spiky and wet from a recent swim.

"You are an artist in that kitchen, Sigrid," he said. "If I catch you some fish, will you cook them?"

"Don't do it unless he promises to share with us," Will said.

"Feast for all," Ty said. "I'm going out early in the morning. How's the snorkeling here, Franz?"

Alexis turned to Jacquie. "Is this guy on a vacation or what?"

"Whatever it takes to be inspired. The view is enough for me. Have you seen your lighthouses yet?"

Alexis shook her head and Jacquie pointed to the window. "You can get a peek from here."

Alexis pushed aside the lace curtain and let her spoon drop. There they were, standing tall and stately on either end of their island like proud, protective parents. The mist was gone and they stood out vividly against the ocean sky. There was a strength there; she could feel it even from here. What must it be like to be out there—on the island with them—close enough to see their shining eyes and smooth, rounded walls?

A guffaw from the next table broke her reverie. "Virginia won't let you go sailing, Will? I'll take you."

"So much for the great American novel," Alexis mumbled.

"What was that, Sugar?" Jacquie asked.

"Nothing," Alexis said, and she reached for the bread.

"If those lighthouses do it for you, Honey, I'd follow my instincts."

Alexis looked up at her. "I was thinking about that. I would just be taking pictures, but somehow I want to."

Jacquie's dark bob nodded softly and she put her hand to her chest. "That's where it starts, Darlin'. Right in here."

≈

How does God fit into "right in here"? Alexis wondered later as she hiked with her camera bag out to the scene of last night's fiasco with Ty.

She took a minute to look down from the spot where she had slipped. Ty had been right. There was a fifty-foot drop to the next ledge and a treacherous plummet from there to the beach. Lance would have said more than "I told you so" if she had to spend the rest of the summer in traction.

A flutter of guilt arose in her stomach. She still hadn't called him. Maybe she could manage a postcard tonight.

Take pictures, Alexis, she told herself firmly. *Just do it.*

Then she was lost in the craft of photography. Adjusting the light so her first photographs of the lighthouses wouldn't lose their depth in the bright sunlight, she attached her telephoto lens to keep the proportions natural. She then tested the film speed to catch the tossing of the waves. The afternoon passed in a series of clicks and whirrs.

≈

She had intended to develop the roll that night after dinner, but as the sun started to set over Rocky Shoals, the waves pulled her out to the ocean as if she were part of the tide. The darkroom was forgotten the minute she found The Rock.

The Rock was located several yards down the beach from the cliff in a crag on the way down the path to the beach. Flat, smooth, and gray, it was a welcome change from the pillow-prone chairs at Rocky Shoals.

Cushions are okay, Alexis thought as she eased herself onto the cool, hard seat. *But this is an Alexis place. It's like me*, she decided. *I'm so plain. I take pictures because it's fun and the process gives me joy. Aren't artists supposed to have deeper motives than that, God?*

She listened, but no answer came. Even so, she knew she'd be back to this spot.

✻

And so the routine began. An early start every morning to go to The Rock to pray, then breakfast with the Coxes in the dining room. Will usually had the extra butter waiting for her and made sure there were plenty of blueberry muffins in the basket. Virginia would say grace and go on about Will's paintings while he raved over Virginia's sketches. Alexis loved the way they talked for each other.

Right after breakfast, she headed out with her camera. She still hadn't developed anything. It was always so much more delicious to be outside. She shot the lighthouses from every angle, at every time of day. And when there seemed to be no other way to capture them, she roamed around Rocky Shoals looking for what Lance would have called "Kodak moments."

The thought of Lance always made her a little uneasy. She had called him the afternoon after she had arrived and left a message on his machine to let him know she was safe. On purpose, she had not given him the number for Rocky Shoals. The idea of talking to Lance didn't click with the approach she was taking here. Wouldn't he have a field day with the explanation that she was doing what she wanted to do and hoped God would tell her why!

Lunch and dinner she usually chatted with Jacquie. Marina-Natasha joined them when Ty started eating with the Coxes. Every morning at breakfast, Alexis wanted to blurt out to them, Why are you spending time with this guy who is obviously a flake? How much writing can he be getting done on a sailboat?

Or a snorkeling exhibition. Or a fishing trip. One afternoon she'd even seen him headed back to Rocky Shoals with a bunch of rock-climbing gear over his shoulder.

The only time she saw Ty sans sporting equipment—or when he wasn't entertaining everyone in the dining room—was during one of her early morning sessions on The Rock. The morning fog had draped a cloak of secrecy all around her. The fog was a mysterious thing. You could be sitting in the middle of it, thinking you were completely alone, and suddenly, without warning, some form or figure—a seagull, a crab, a waving piece of seaweed—would appear next to you. One morning, Ty appeared that way.

She didn't hear his steps, but all at once he was there, just a few feet from her, standing on a jagged piece of rock and staring out to the ocean. Alexis held her breath, hoping he wouldn't discover her.

He stuffed his hands in his pockets and the square, athletic shoulders gave way to a sagging sigh as heavy as the fog around them.

This is a surprise, she thought as he took one last look and picked his way on down toward the beach. *Maybe there is something going on in there.*

But that night, Ty showed his usual colors as he presented his fish to Sigrid like a proud little boy. They all had to squeal over it at the dinner table until Alexis thought she'd choke.

"Is this guy for real?" she said to Jacquie.

"Who, Ty?" Jacquie sounded surprised.

"Yeah, I mean every minute is a sporting event."

"Of course. He's a sportswriter. That's his niche." Jacquie picked up her water glass and watched Alexis.

"Well, fine, but do we all have to be taken along for the ride?"

"I don't know what you mean."

"Everything's a joke or a party or a whitewater rafting expedition. We don't get to choose whether we're part of it or not because he fills up the whole room with it."

Alexis looked up from her plate to find Jacquie staring at her.

"Where is this coming from?" Jacquie asked.

"From me," Alexis said.

"I don't believe that for a minute."

Jacquie's eyes flashed as if she had some piece of wisdom. It was Alexis's turn to stare.

"You actually like him, don't you?"

"I find him absolutely delightful and refreshingly honest," Jacquie said. "And I'm completely baffled that you don't."

Alexis shifted uneasily on the chair pad. "I hope you don't think I'm being un-Christian. I would never be hateful to him or do him any harm. I actually pray for him like I do everyone else. But he bothers me."

"Hmmm," Jacquie said and asked for the tartar sauce.

❧

The next morning, Alexis awoke earlier than usual, as if some unseen hand were nudging her out of bed. After pulling a sweatshirt on over her jeans and applying the usual scrunchy in her hair, she set off across the lawn for a peek at the light-houses in the fog. If she were lucky, she'd hear the horns of the fishing boats groaning mournfully as they passed in the thickness.

She hadn't gotten halfway down the hill in front of the main house when a figure whipped past her like a spooked rabbit, knocking her elbow with a smack as it went and hurling itself toward the slope in twisted fury.

Instinctively, she grabbed her elbow as she watched the figure disappear over the hill. Then she heard what could only be described as a bleating cry of pain. Alexis ran toward the sound and skidded to a halt at the base of the boulder that announced the entrance to Rocky Shoals. Lying beside it, curled up and clutching his knees, was a teenaged boy.

Chapter 5

"Are you okay?" Alexis said.

The boy didn't look up, but she could see the pain writhing through him as he continued to clutch at his leg. Alexis squatted down beside him.

"How badly does it hurt?" she said. "Here, let me help you."

She reached out to touch his arm, but he jerked away as if she were a copperhead striking out at him.

"Just leave me alone! I'm okay."

"You took a dive against this monster rock. I did something like that myself my first night here. It's easy to do if you don't know the place—"

"Oh, I know the place," he said, his upper lip curling.

"Fine, but you've got to be in pain—"

"I'm not in pain!" he cried. And finally, he whipped his face around to look at her. His eyes were seething with anger.

Alexis rocked back on her knees. "I didn't put the rock there, Pal. Lighten up and let me help you."

"Nobody said you did, and nobody asked you to help me, okay? I'll get up when I'm ready."

Alexis forced herself to bite back her next reply—"Which will be after about six weeks in a body cast."

Here in the serenity of Rocky Shoals, the intrusion of this rebellious boy was jarring. His head of dark brown hair was partially shaved, and he wore one earring. Even in this position, Alexis could see that his pants were fashionably three sizes too big for him. She was afraid to try to read what was on his T-shirt. She was pretty sure it wasn't "Phillies" or "Choose Life."

"Come on, give me a break here," she said. "Just show me where it hurts. If it looks like it's broken, we'll call somebody, and if it doesn't, I'll leave you alone."

He viewed her with small, brown, hawklike eyes that reminded her of someone. "You a doctor?" he said.

"No, but I've had first aid training. I know what a broken bone looks like. I could get us that far."

Still eyeing her, he pointed to his left ankle, just above a bulky black shoe with yellow stitching. Such footwear, Alexis remembered, were known as Doc Martens. A kid on this beach ought to be barefoot, dashing around like a deer, not crashing into rocks.

Alexis looked at his ankle and touched it gently. Her dad had insisted she and her sister and brother take the EMT course that had been offered in Haddonfield a couple of summers ago.

There was no swelling in the boy's ankle yet, and he didn't wince when she touched it.

"Are you some kind of stoic?" Alexis said.

"What's that?"

His demeanor was brusque and defensive, like that of a boxer waiting for the next punch.

"Do you stand up to pain like a knight, never flinching, that kind of thing?"

"No," he said. "That's lame."

"Then I don't think it's broken," she said.

He started to struggle up from the ground when the front screen door slammed on the main building. Alexis shaded her eyes with her hand to see Sigrid standing there rigidly. The kid got to his feet and limped off in the other direction like a wounded soldier fleeing the enemy.

Sigrid's voice shot after him. "Karl! What happened? Where are you going?"

Sigrid marched down the steps as Karl beat a hasty retreat down the hill.

"Karl! What—" Sigrid stopped in midsentence. She noticed Alexis, and a scarlet flush began to blotch her face. "Alexis, I am so sorry. Did he—" Sigrid stopped again and clutched her tiny hands together, looking over the hill with eyes that were more angry than anxious. Now Alexis knew where she'd seen Karl's eyes before.

"He fell over the sign boulder when he was running down the hill," Alexis said. "His ankle is probably going to be bruised, but I'm pretty sure it's not broken."

Sigrid grunted. "He let you look at it?"

"Under duress."

"Karl's business is strictly off-limits to the rest of us as far as he's concerned," Sigrid said. Then she put her hand on Alexis's shoulder. "Thank you for being concerned. I am somewhat embarrassed to say that he is my grandson."

So Lisl won after all! Alexis almost blurted out. *Karl must be the one who was a bigger handful than twenty toddlers put together. The one whose presence was inappropriate and unacceptable because of something that had happened last time.* Alexis squirmed a little. She would hate to think her presence was ever unacceptable to anybody, especially her own grandmother.

"There's no need to be embarrassed," she assured Sigrid, whose face was by now drawn up into a knot. "He's a kid."

Sigrid looked directly at her. "Were you like that when you were a 'kid'?"

"No, but—"

Sigrid seemed to force a smile as she took Alexis's arm and gave her a tiny push toward the hill. "I'm sure you were a delightful child, and I would have been charmed to have you here with my artists. Karl is a different story. Franz and I will be certain he is no trouble to any of you."

"I'm sure he won't be—" Alexis started to say. But Sigrid patted her arm and marched back up toward the main house.

Looks like you have your work cut out for you, Alexis thought as she watched her go. Still, as she headed across the road for her spot on the ocean rock, she decided Karl had just as difficult a journey ahead.

Alexis spent most of the morning wandering with her camera, snapping whatever begged to be caught on film. To her own surprise, most of her subjects turned out to be the other guests. They were all engrossed in their gifts, and the camera wanted to know why.

What makes you do it? the lens seemed to ask. What drives you to spend an hour penning the right line of dialogue or listening to your own melody like an entranced bird?

She caught Jacquie on the front porch of the main building, her feet up on the railing, her rayon pants spilling away from her shiny calves, gnawing the words gently out of her pen as her tennis bracelet sparkled in the sun.

"Oh, Sugar, I must look a mess!" she exclaimed when she heard the shutter click. And then she smiled her splendid smile.

Alexis got a picture of Marina-Natasha twirling along the beach with her hands over her head, her eyes closed in blissful reverie. She would have loved to have known what was going through her mind, but she didn't have two hours to listen to the answer.

Just before lunch, she discovered Virginia Cox settled in with her sketch pad on the cliff.

"Is it okay that I took your pic?" Alexis inquired when Virginia looked up with a start.

"Of course, long as it didn't break the camera!" she said gaily. "I didn't even hear you come up, I was so involved."

Alexis sidled up shyly to her. "Can I ask what you're sketching?"

"Better yet, you can see."

She tilted the sketch pad toward Alexis, who leaned over her shoulder. It was a zany pencil drawing of a sailboat bobbing on the waves with two caricatures of men swaying out from port and starboard. One had a square smile like the opening to a mailbox, while the other sported a grin that crinkled even in pencil strokes.

Alexis looked up at the ocean. Just a few yards out, tacking and coming about for all they were worth, were Will and Ty in a sailboat. Even above the crash of the waves, Alexis could almost hear Ty guffawing.

"They're getting a lot done," Alexis said wryly.

"Aren't they, though? These little jaunts with Ty have been so good for Will. He comes back just bubbling over with details of the ocean he's never noticed before. I mean, you can't, really, when you're a Colorado landlubber."

Alexis stared as Virginia went on. "If it weren't for Ty and that little Sunfish, Will would still be stuck on seashells and sandcrabs. He can't swim, you know."

"He can't swim and he's out there with him?"

Virginia chuckled. "I did my wifely duty and made sure he was going to be in a life jacket, but Ty had already taken care of that. He seems to have taken a real liking to Will."

"What's not to like?" Alexis said automatically. Ty's voice was now clearly audible, hooting into the wind. *Probably chortling over some ridiculous joke*, Alexis thought.

"I'm certainly grateful," Virginia said. "Will just wants to get some of it on him."

"Some of what?" Alexis asked.

"Some of life. The academic world he worked in for thirty years as a college professor didn't leave much room for experiencing God, you know? I just thank the Lord for Ty."

What is it with me? Alexis thought. *How can I be the only one who doesn't see all this benevolence in Ty? He is just so superficial to me.* Alexis patted Virginia's shoulder and moved away. *I think they'll probably find out what I've already seen: He's a flake.*

At lunch, Sigrid was only in evidence long enough to be sure there was enough crab salad to go around and to give Alexis a pink message slip. She then hurried off to the kitchen.

Alexis unfolded the slip and saw Sigrid's message: Call Lance today. She didn't recognize the phone number. He must be at Bailey, Logan, and Markowski.

"Anything wrong?" Jacquie was looking at her curiously over her water glass.

"No, I don't think so. I just have to return a phone call."

Jacquie cocked an eyebrow. "Would it have anything to do with that ring on your left hand?"

Alexis followed her eyes to the three diamond chips and slid her hand into her lap.

"Sort of," she said. "We're kind of engaged—"

Jacquie pressed her palms together and rested her chin on the tips of her fingers. "Lexy honey, I don't think you can be 'kind of engaged.' That's like being a little bit pregnant. You either are or you aren't."

"Did you say Taxi was pregnant?"

Alexis jerked her eyes up. Ty was standing at the edge of their table, holding a pitcher of iced tea.

"Heavens, no!" Jacquie broke out into a rippling laugh.

"Not even a little bit?" Ty said.

Jacquie smacked him playfully on the arm, but Alexis glared.

"I'm sorry if I've embarrassed you," Ty said. But Alexis could hear the guffaw teetering at the edge of his voice. She stabbed her fork into a piece of crab.

"Yes, you have embarrassed her," Jacquie said. "Now sit down here and make it up to her."

Was there no sensitivity in these people? Couldn't they see she didn't want to be giggling buddies with this guy, the way everybody else did? She stuffed in three mouthfuls and chewed with a vengeance.

Ty turned to Jacquie. "So how are you, Duchess?"

"I'm fine, thank you. How was the sailing?"

"Great. I think Will had a good time. He was out there howling like a dog."

Are you sure that wasn't you? Alexis wanted to say.

"Let me ask you something, Duchess. Do you mind?"

"You can ask me anything, Darlin'. As long as it isn't my beauty secrets."

"What I want to know about is this bracelet here." He ran a finger along the diamonds and emeralds that ringed her wrist. "I bet there's a story behind it."

"If I tell you, will it appear in the great American novel?" Jacquie said teasingly.

Alexis stifled a snort. *Written aboard a sailboat or up El Capitan? Right.*

Before Jacquie could launch into her story, the kitchen door swung open, and a hush settled over the room. Karl had sauntered in.

As Alexis watched Virginia and Will exchange glances and Jacquie shoot her eyebrows up to her hairline, she was sure none of them had caught a glimpse of Sigrid's grandson before. He cut a disturbing figure here in the dining room, with the baggy shorts and neck chains in sharp juxtaposition to the lace tablecloths and crystal bud vases.

But what looked completely out of place to Alexis was the white towel-apron that had been tucked around his waist. Resentment had pulled his face into a knot so painful, Alexis had to look away. When she did, her eyes caught Ty's.

"Look at this." Ty's voice was surprisingly hushed, but Alexis shot him a warning look. His face had lit up with fascination, and she wanted to clap her hand over his mouth if he threw out one "Let me ask you this" at Karl.

"It's Sigrid and Franz's grandson," Alexis said.

"He's a piece of work," Ty said.

"Already got him figured out, do you?"

Ty looked at her in surprise. "No, do you?"

"Stop it, you two," Jacquie said. "We don't need to talk about Sigrid's family behind her back."

What about Karl's back? Alexis wanted to cry. But then Karl was suddenly there at their table, unceremoniously stabbing dessert dishes onto the tabletop.

"How ya doin'?" Ty said. Alexis stiffened to keep from kicking him under the table.

"Swell," Karl said. He curled his upper lip so hard his eyes turned to slits.

"I understand you're a Goedert."

"No," he said. "My mother's a Goedert. I'm a Barrett. Impressed?"

Ty looked blankly around the table. "Should I be?"

"They own television stations," Karl said, his lip still folding into his nostrils. "Most people are really impressed by that."

"You're obviously not."

Karl hissed through his lips and moved on to the Coxes' table.

"Whoo!" Jacquie said softly. "I'd hate to meet that sweet thing in a dark alley."

"Okay, Duchess," Ty said, "let's hear this bracelet story. Start with whether that's the real thing or it's a paste and you have the original locked in a safe."

"Don't be ridiculous! Darlin', if something means something to you, you don't hide it."

Alexis guiltily twisted her ring.

"Oh, so this is a special bracelet," Ty said. "Twenty-fifth wedding anniversary."

"No." Jacquie let her bell-like laugh ring out over the table. "Longer ago than that. When my Michael signed his first big deal, he came home to me with this. Now mind you, the two of us and the two schnauzers were still living in a studio apartment, and I was seven months' pregnant. We didn't even have a crib for the baby yet. Here he comes home with this."

"Did you let him have it for spending the money on that instead of diapers?"

Alexis gaped at Ty, but Jacquie nodded. "I carried on, really lit into that poor man. And when I was all through, he said, 'Darlin', today I realized that I have what it takes. We're going to have plenty of chances to move out of this hole and have a nursery right out of *House Beautiful* and all that. But I wanted to bring you something to commemorate this day—the beginning—and show you that every bit of it is because I love you.'"

Alexis felt a lump forming in her throat. *If you make one joke about that story, Ty Solorzano, I will let you have it under the table.*

But Ty was looking long and hard at Jacquie.

"He's bought me more expensive jewelry since then," she said. "I'm embarrassed to wear some of it. But this bracelet is the most special. I only take it off when I go swimming, something like that."

"Finished with these?"

Alexis looked up to see Karl at her elbow again, a tray slung against his hip like a skateboard. It was hard to say how long he'd been lurking there. In spite of his collision with the boulder, the kid seemed to slither about without making a sound.

"I think we're finished," Jacquie said, sliding her dessert dish toward him. "You can take these."

Jacquie's voice was suddenly strangely formal, and as Alexis handed her dish to Karl, she caught him looking coldly at Jacquie.

"So what are you up to this afternoon, Duchess?" Ty said.

"I wrote two scenes this morning, so I'm taking the afternoon off and going for a swim. Although you never really take time off, do you?" she added. "It's always there in your head."

"I was going to ask if I could join you," Ty said, "but if you're going to be lost in thought—"

"How about we meet later for a walk or something," Jacquie suggested. "I would love the company, Sugar, after I get my head cleared."

"I'll meet you—where—on the cliff?"

"I'll be there if you are."

Ty unfolded himself from the table and towered over the group for a minute. "Nice talking to you, Taxi," he said.

Before Alexis could decide how thick the sarcasm was, he was gone. Alexis felt herself letting go of her breath.

"Why does he call you Duchess?" Alexis could feel the words spitting out of her.

"Duchess of Dallas," Jacquie said, grinning. "Isn't that precious? He started calling me that right after we got here."

"Why do you let him do that?"

Jacquie cocked her head. "Why shouldn't I? I think he does it to tease me about being well off. He's letting me know he's not put off by my money because I don't flaunt it. I take it as a compliment. Nicknames like that are very flattering."

Alexis twisted her mouth. "I'm supposed to be flattered because he calls me Taxi? What does that mean? I'm always around but never where you need me?"

Jacquie grew still as she rested her chin on her hand. "My, Lexy, I'm hearing some anger here!"

"You seem so astute, Jacquie. I just don't get why you want to hang around with that—cad."

"Oh, Honey, I think there's a lot more to Ty than meets the eye, if you don't mind a cliché."

"I just—"

Jacquie put her hand up. "Then let's agree to disagree for now," she said. "No hard feelings—just two friends with a difference of opinion—how's that?"

Her eyes were genuine as she leaned across the table, waiting to smile again.

"Okay," Alexis said.

"All right then. So what about this weekend? Do you want to meet in Rockport and have lunch? You haven't really seen the town, have you?"

"No," Alexis said. "That would be great."

"That's that, then. You just drive that darlin' ole red car of yours into town, and we'll meet at noon, Saturday. How about in front of the Toad Hall Bookstore?"

Alexis grinned and nodded, and all the tension of the last hour melted off. She had been itching to get into town, and it would be fun to spend time with Jacquie, without other people butting in. She watched Jacquie scoot off toward her cabin. Then Alexis took a deep breath and headed for the back porch to the pay phone.

"Bailey, Logan, and Markowski," announced the polished voice on the other end of the line.

Alexis caught her breath. Was she going to ask for Lance and hear this woman say, "Who?"

"May I help you?" the voice said.

"May I speak with Lance Bodin? He's a new—"

"I can connect you with Mr. Bodin's office. One moment, please."

Mr. Bodin, Alexis thought as the line gave way to classical music. *Mr. Bodin's office?* Why did that make her think of summers buying potato salad and doing flower arrangements?

"This is Lance Bodin."

Alexis tightened her grip on the phone. The voice was smooth and quiet. It was Lance she was hearing, but it was someone different too. Already.

"Hello?"

"Lance!" she said. "I'm—hi—I'm returning your call!"

"Hi, Lexy," he said. "That was nice of you."

Alexis groaned inwardly. There were two ice cubes in his tone. If she weren't careful, this entire conversation would be on the rocks.

"I left you a message," she said lamely. "You knew I got here—" She didn't finish. Of course, she should have kept trying until she talked to him personally. Why hadn't that occurred to her until now?

"So how are you?" she said. "How is it at Bailey and those guys, or can't you talk about that while you're in your 'office'? I'm impressed, Lance. Your own office already—"

"I miss you, that's how I am."

"I miss you too."

There was a silence. Alexis knew he was analyzing her voice.

"I'm in another world up here, Lance. It's not like I don't think of you, but my whole reason for being here is to think about me and God. You're in the same position, new job and everything. I'm sure you can't sit around mooning over me."

"No, I can't," he said, control tugging at every word. "But you're on my mind constantly. I want to know what you're doing, what you're thinking about."

The last phrase hung on the line between them like a lead weight.

"You want to know what I'm deciding about us, isn't that what you mean?" she said.

"All right, yeah, there's some of that," Lance said. "What do you expect? You leave things up in the air between us; what am I supposed to do? Bury myself under a bunch of legal briefs and wait for you to come back and tell me what the rest of my life is going to be like?"

Alexis gasped. "Is that the way you see this, Lance? I have your life in my hands? That is not why I came up here!"

She pulled the receiver closer to her mouth, the anger still pumping through her veins like a locomotive.

"Lance, if I am not happy with myself, and with God, and with what I'm supposed to do with my life, I can't make anybody else happy either."

He cleared his throat. "Am I getting equal time in this search?"

"You're not listening to me!"

She knew she had exploded, and so did whoever was standing on the other side of the screen door. She was aware of someone there, someone too embarrassed to come out at this point. Alexis turned her back to the door and talked tightly between her teeth.

"I think it would be better if you and I didn't talk while I'm up here, Lance," she said.

"Oh, great. This reassures me."

"I'm sorry. But this isn't getting us anywhere. I need time away from everything. I also need to know that the voices I'm hearing are mine and God's, not yours or anyone else's."

"So after two years, I get no input."

"You gave me your input. You told me what you wanted before I left. It's here in my heart. Okay?"

It wasn't okay. She could tell by the silence that roared from Philadelphia like a shout.

"Do I have a choice?" he managed icily.

"In a way you do. You can say, 'No, Lexy, I can't do it this way.' "

"And what would you do?"

"Tell you I was sorry, but I had to do it this way."

"Some choice."

"Or you could pray, which is what I'm doing."

"All right, then," Lance said. "I guess we do it your way."

"I hate that it's 'my way,' " she said. "I wish you could see—"

"I see," he said. "I'll talk to you when you get back. I love you, so I'll give you your space. But I don't have to like it."

Somehow they both hung up. Alexis stood for a minute, her hand on the receiver as it dangled from its hook, and tried to decide whether she wanted to cry. There weren't any tears in her throat, really. There was some frustration tied up around her shoulder blades and some unsaid words scrambling around for a resting place in her mind. But what else could she have done? She had to do it this way, for both their sakes.

She took her hand off the receiver. That decision had been awfully easy. And the next one was easier. She was going to get her camera and finish off that roll of film.

※

Sigrid was typing rapidly when Alexis snapped a picture from the door of her flowered, cluttered office. The look Alexis captured was pensive, but the faint smile Sigrid gave her was vacant. Although Karl was nowhere to be seen, his abrasive teenage presence was all around his grandmother.

Franz, on the other hand, seemed unaffected by his grandson's sudden appearance. The old man was headed toward his truck, his shock of white hair sticking upright in the breeze, whistling as if he were headed for some pleasant outing.

Why doesn't he take Karl with him? Alexis thought. But as she snapped Franz polishing the side mirror of the already gleaming green Ford, she had to shrug. *That isn't what you're here for, Alexis,* she told herself. *You're here to find out what God wants you to do, not to solve the Goederts' problems.*

She spent another hour taking pictures before she picked her way down to the beach. As long as she was fooling with the f-stop and the focus, she didn't have to think about things. But as soon as she was finished, the thoughts rushed back in like a dam that had burst. The Rock was the only place to go when that happened.

As she headed down the rocky path, she began to sift through her cluttered thoughts. All her prayer sessions had been peaceful and soothing, but she didn't feel she was any closer to God's purpose for her photography than when she'd arrived. There was still no small voice.

Maybe it was time to develop all the film she'd taken and see where the pictures led her.

She sank down on the smooth top of The Rock. The thought of going into the darkroom made her anxious somehow. *I'm afraid I'm going to find out I'm destined for Olan Mills,* she thought. *Not that that's bad, but I kind of hoped for something different, God.*

She was about to get up and head for her cabin when her eye caught movement on the beach just below. Somebody else was sitting on a rock, thinking even darker thoughts than hers.

That somebody was Karl.

Chapter 6

There was something disjointed about the way he was sitting there. Alexis stared at him for a good three minutes, trying to figure out what it was.

The rebellious haircut, the earring, the clothes that shouted, "Just try to make me change these!" were still there. But the profile that cut sharply into the sky was searching. *Searching for something outside that getup,* Alexis thought, *searching for a way to say, "Please, try to find me."*

The trouble was, there wasn't a soul in this place who seemed to care anything about Karl beyond how to keep him out of everyone's way.

If I could just capture this moment, Alexis thought. She slowly brought her camera up to her face and framed Karl in the viewfinder. She snapped softly and he didn't move. *His mind is really out there someplace,* she decided. *If I could just see where he's looking; if I could just see into his eyes before he catches me.*

Alexis let the camera rest against her chest on its strap. The rocks were slippery from the incoming tide, but if she picked her way carefully, she could wedge her foot between those two pieces that jutted up and get a steady shot.

She rose slowly like a snake coming out of a bottle and placed her feet carefully on the jagged path, glancing up just long enough to make sure Karl hadn't seen her. Three more teetery steps and she'd be in the perfect position. Finally, with her tennis shoes squeezed between the rocks, she squatted down and focused on Karl's face.

But for a fleeting second, she couldn't take the picture.

The eyes that scanned the ocean sky were so filled with hurt, they drove a stake into her chest. He was gnawing at his lip, and his face worked as if tears were doing battle behind it. The picture she took when she snapped the shutter was the picture of loneliness.

This time he heard it, and his eyes flashed to hers. The transformation from heartbroken little boy to arrogant teenager was so abrupt and so practiced, Alexis almost shouted, "Karl Barrett, you're a fake!"

Instead, she jerked to a standing position, and her left foot slid crazily from its nest in the rocks across a wet, stony surface. Her leg jutted away from her, and she thrashed her arms to keep from plunging headfirst into the shallow water.

"Hey!" Karl cried out. His hands shot up to grab her arm, and she clawed at his sleeve to break her fall. They seesawed while Alexis shrieked, "Ah! No!"

"Hold on!" he yelled. He leaned forward in one last balancing act and they got their bearings. As soon as Alexis was sure she wasn't going to go backward into the rocks, she let go of his shirt. He straightened it as if it were a Brooks Brothers suit.

"What did you do that for?" he said.

"I didn't do it for anything," Alexis answered, looking down to make sure her camera hadn't taken a dive into the water.

"I meant that." He pointed to the camera. "You took my picture."

"I've been taking everybody's picture."

If it were possible, he curled his lip even more. "Why?"

Alexis hesitated a minute, trying to get her heart to slow down. "I'm not sure, exactly. I just want to capture people when they're really being themselves, and then—"

"Then what?" He couldn't have looked more disgusted if he'd smelled rotten eggs.

"I haven't figured that out yet. When I do, I'll tell you."

"Oh, yeah. You just do that thing."

Alexis waited and watched. The face, squinted up in insolence, watched back. As she looked into his eyes, she saw them waver. And she thought she saw the pain flicker in them.

"You don't really want to be here, do you? At Rocky Shoals, I mean," she said.

"What was your first clue?"

"So why'd you come?"

"Like I had a choice. My stepfather decided it was time to escape to Europe again, and he wasn't going without her—"

" 'Her' being—"

"The witch. My mother."

"And you weren't invited."

"They won't even take me to McDonald's. They might be seen with me by the wrong people."

"What do you do, throw french fries?"

"Oh, yeah, I spit Coke through my straw."

Alexis wasn't quite sure he wasn't telling the truth, but she nodded. "So you're pretty ticked off that they dropped you here."

"Dumped me off here is more like it. Let's get the right verb."

Alexis could feel her eyebrows shooting up.

"See, I'm not an idiot," Karl said. "I know from verbs. I can also do simple computations. I know the scientific method. I color in the lines."

It was Alexis's turn to curl her lip. "Could you be a little more sarcastic, Pal?"

"Excuse me, but it's either dress in the wardrobe they hang in your closet and speak the lines they hand you in the script, or hurry up and grow up and get out. Yeah, I'm sarcastic."

Alexis was tempted to ask him if he were sure he was only fifteen. This was an intelligent kid. She had the sinking sense that something valuable was being wasted right before her eyes.

"Look," she said, "if you really didn't want me to take your picture, I can just not develop yours. Or I'll give you the negatives. I should have asked."

He regarded her suspiciously. "For real?"

"I always ask people's permission at some point. Why should you be any different?"

Karl shrugged. "No big deal. You can do whatever you want with them. Only don't show them to her."

" 'Her' being—"

"Sigrid."

"I won't show anybody until you've seen them."

He shrugged again, but she could feel his eyes on her as she picked her way back up the path toward the road. She was pretty sure if she'd turned back, she wouldn't have seen a curled lip. But Alexis had seen enough sadness for one afternoon.

✤

I think a darkroom is one of my favorite places in the world, Alexis decided that night as she hung the drying film from a clip in the bathroom linen closet. There was something about the whole process of taking a roll of black plastic from a reel, putting it through its paces and coming out with real images that tell a story. And the darkroom was where it happened. It had been a place of endless magic for her ever since she'd set foot in one in high school.

But as she closed the linen closet door to let the film dry and began to wash the chemicals off her equipment, a thought popped into her head. *Then why does this one seem so lonely?* She stopped, a stainless steel funnel in hand, and looked at herself in the mirror above the sink. *Where did that come from?* she asked the brown eyes that looked back at her. Lonely? Hadn't she come here just for that, to be alone?

As if on cue, there was a rap at the front door. Alexis swiped her hands across the back of her jeans and crossed her sitting room. Jacquie had poked her head in the screen door.

"I didn't catch you taking a bubble bath, did I?" she asked.

"Not unless I wanted to do it in a tank of developer!" Alexis said. "Come on in. Have a seat." She snapped on a lamp and turned to smile at Jacquie.

But Jacquie sank wearily into the tapestried pillows and her eyes drooped.

"Is something wrong?" Alexis said.

Jacquie raked her hand through her shiny wedge. "Yes."

"What's up?"

"It's silly, really, to get so upset over something like this." Tears gathered over her lower lids.

"Jacquie, what is it? Is it something with Michael?"

"No, well, yes. Aaah!" Jacquie shook both her hands and pulled them to her mouth. "I've lost my tennis bracelet, the one I was telling ya'll about at lunch."

"Oh."

"See, it's silly. Michael will be wonderful about it, but that isn't the point."

"Of course not. It's a symbol of his love."

Jacquie looked at her in surprise.

"So where do you think it is?" Alexis said.

"Lost."

"Well, yeah, temporarily. But let's find it. Let's retrace your steps. When do you remember having it last?"

Alexis was standing up, searching under the pile of photography books for her tennis shoes. Jacquie didn't move.

"When I took it off to go swimming this afternoon, I put it in my jewelry box on top of the dresser"

Alexis stopped and looked at her. "What are you saying, that it was taken from your room?"

"Yes, I am." Jacquie pulled both hands through her hair this time and held it back tightly on the sides of her head so that her face looked pinched. "And thank you for not asking me if I'm sure I put it in there. Everybody else has, except Ty. He was no help at all."

"Of course not."

"He just kept saying, 'I'm so sorry for you. This must really hurt.' "

Alexis lowered herself slowly back onto the couch. "Jacquie, this is too weird. Who else knew you took your bracelet off to go to the beach, besides Ty and me?"

"Nobody! There were only three of us at the table. And it would break my heart to think anybody here would take it. I'm thinking maybe somebody from outside, some transient."

"Jacquie, this isn't Dallas. They don't have a large homeless population here on Cape Ann."

Jacquie chewed on her thumbnail and shook her head. "I do have one thought, but I don't want to even say it because it's so hateful."

"You've never had a hateful thought in your life," Alexis said.

"What about that boy, Sigrid's grandson?"

"Karl? No, that's impossible. He was with me."

"You?"

"We were talking down on the rocks."

Jacquie went back to her thumbnail, and Alexis got up to pace the hardwood floor. Karl had been with her, but that had been after her entire phone conversation with Lance, and her trip back here to get her camera, and her picture-taking session. He could have had time.

"That kid has as much money as you do, even though he dresses like a vagrant," Alexis said, a little too gruffly. "What would he want with your bracelet?"

Jacquie glanced at her sharply and pulled her knees up against her. "I don't know whether to say anything to Sigrid or not. She would be so embarrassed."

Sigrid would be embarrassed, Alexis thought. *And what about Karl?* He really was the most likely candidate, Alexis knew. Yet as she chewed her lip, she couldn't bring herself to say it. Somebody had to be on that kid's side.

Jacquie sighed heavily and stood. "I should go. There really isn't anything more we can do about it tonight anyway."

Alexis got up too, and stood helplessly in front of Jacquie. She wanted to hug her, to tell her she'd pray for her, but this woman was the self-sufficient corporate wife.

"Is there anything I can do for you?" she said instead.

"Just think good thoughts," Jacquie said.

When she was gone, Alexis did think a few, but most of what went through her head was about Karl. He could easily have overheard Jacquie talking in the dining room at lunch about taking the bracelet off to go swimming. No one would have thought anything of it if they'd seen him go into any of the cabins, since it was obvious Sigrid was using him like the hired help.

He couldn't have done this, she decided. As she began to set up her enlarger to make a proof sheet from the negatives, her mind was racing so fast she knew she wouldn't sleep anyway. There was just something about this that didn't set right.

But, by the time she got to the last stage, the fixer, and pulled the contact sheet out by the corner to check for contrast, she knew it had to be Karl.

"Okay, Alexis," she said. "He's a messed-up kid, and if nobody else has been able to keep him from ripping people off, you sure aren't going to be able to. You don't know anything about teenagers."

She let the proof sheet wash and started cleaning up the chemicals.

"He did it, Alexis," she said. "And now you have to help Jacquie decide how to handle it."

She pulled the proof sheet out of the washer and laid it on a clean blotter. As she scanned the sheet with a professional eye, even the potential for some incredible prints didn't run off the sadness that had collected around her. Straightening her shoulders, she tried to concentrate on her photos.

The ones of the lighthouses were decent, she decided, especially the one of sea foam splashing up against the rocks that fringed Thacher Island. Jacquie was so photogenic, in spite of her protest that she "looked a mess." There was Virginia Cox completely absorbed. That little wrinkle between her eyebrows was going to come out as if it were etched in stone. Then Sigrid at her desk. Franz cleaning the mirror of his truck, parked out behind the main house with the cabins in the background. Not much there to write home about.

Then Alexis stopped and pulled the contact sheet up to her eyes.

She had purposely focused so that Franz would be in sharp contrast against a soft, blurry background. But there was a figure back there, a person. He was on the porch of Jacquie's cabin.

Alexis gripped the contact sheet and tore into the sitting room where she could get it under the light. She grabbed the magnifying glass.

There was a person on Jacquie's porch. The one other person who had heard the story of Jacquie's bracelet. The person who had brought up the subject in the first place. The person who had made it a point to find out what the Duchess of Dallas was going to be doing all afternoon.

The person was Ty.

Alexis sank into a chair and shoved the pillows onto the floor. *No wonder I couldn't accept that it was Karl,* she thought. *I knew all the time Ty was a flake.*

But a thief?

She stopped and scanned the contact sheet for his face, but she hadn't taken any shots of him. There was nothing to study except her memory, and that was vivid enough. Strolling around the place with sports equipment thrown over his shoulder, casing the joint.

"Oh, Lord," Alexis prayed softly. "What do I do now? I've got the evidence right here in my hand. What do I do?"

"Anybody home?"

Alexis lurched up from the chair and shoved the proof sheet behind her back. Standing outside her screen door was Ty.

Chapter 7

Alexis stood in the middle of the floor and stared at the door.

"Hey, Taxi," Ty said. "Are you all right in there?"

He put his ear to the screen door. Slowly, Alexis slid the contact sheet between two books and crept to the door.

"I'm fine," she said. She pressed her hand against the doorjamb and peered out at him. She tried to glance surreptitiously down at the doorknob to make sure the lock was set. It wasn't.

When her eyes came up, she knew his gaze had followed hers. His face was mystified as he strained to see her through the dark screen.

"I'm fine," she said again. She let her hand drop to her side and feathered her fingers toward the latch. "So, I guess that's it."

"I was just coming back from a walk, and I saw your light," he said. "I didn't know anybody else stayed up until three in the morning. I didn't know if you were sick or—"

"I'm fine, okay!" She tried to say it loud enough to cover the clicking of the lock, but the snap seemed to echo through the cabin. Ty looked down at the latch. His eyes clouded.

"I didn't come here to try and put a move on you," he said.

"Good." She tried to sound flippant.

"Look, what's the deal?" His hand slid up the door frame and he shifted his weight abruptly. "I'm out here brooding over something I think you might be concerned about too. I'm thinking about how I'm going to broach the subject tomorrow when you're shooting bullets at me with your eyes across the dining room. And then I see your light on. I think you might be going through the same torment I'm feeling. I do the neighborly thing—I knock on the door—and you check the locks like you've got the Boston Strangler standing out here."

Alexis clung to the inside of the door frame with both hands and prayed *Please, God, make him go away. He's a lying thief and I'm going to scream if You don't make him go away.*

Ty ran one of his mighty hands over his short-cut hair. He tilted his head at her. "You really think I'm a jerk, don't you?"

Alexis felt her knuckles turning white. "Look," she said tightly, "it doesn't really matter what I think of you, all right? I came up here for my art and if I make friends, fine, but I'm not looking for—"

378

"Teenage boys to rescue?"

She stared hard at him.

"You have compassion for the kid," Ty said. "That was obvious today at the lunch table. You looked like you wanted to pull up a chair for him and make sure he ate all his chicken soup."

"Do you have a problem with that?" Yanking a handful of hair to the back of her neck, Alexis pressed on. "He's messed up, and it's easy to see why. He needs somebody to—" She stopped abruptly and crossed her arms over her chest. "Why am I telling you this?"

"Because it's how you feel. It's nice to know you have some honest feelings in there."

"Excuse me?"

Ty looked down at his sandals. "Look, that was out of line. Forget I said that." He put his hand to his eyebrows. "Let me just get back to the point—"

"Would you, please?" Alexis said angrily.

"I'm taken in by the kid too," Ty said.

"Oh, that shows."

"I thought you might want to know he took Jacquie's bracelet."

It took every ounce of Alexis's strength to keep from clawing through the screen door to get at him. *You would use that poor, tragic kid to cover your own tail? Flake? Cad? I wasn't even close.*

"I decided to sail out to Thacher after lunch," he continued, "and when I was on my way to my cabin to change, I saw—what's his name—Karl?"

"Yes," Alexis said sharply.

"He was going into Jacquie's place. It just seemed off. So, I just hung out on the path, but he never came out. Then I started thinking—corporate wife, stressed-out half the time—Jacquie might have some kind of tranquilizers in there and maybe that kid got hold of some."

The thoughts were slamming down in Alexis's mind like angry palms. *Oh, now you're going to come off like the rescuer. Sportswriter saves delinquent from suicide.*

"Anyway, I went up on the front porch, and then I thought, what am I going to do now, knock on the door? So I'm standing there like some kind of NYPD wannabe when I hear him coming through the room. He must have seen me, because I could hear him going the other way, and next thing I know, I'm leaning sideways over the porch railing, watching him take off up behind the cabins."

By this time, Alexis had come to a decision. She wasn't going to confront this guy with what she knew. She was just going to get him out of here as fast as she could and go to Sigrid in the morning, before he had a chance to spin out this fantasy for her. Right now, she had to measure her words cautiously.

"So are you saying he crawled out the back window?" she said.

"That's the only thing I can figure out."

"Well—" She tried to look casual as she shrugged her shoulders. "I guess Sigrid's going to have to know. Why don't you let me tell her?"

"I definitely think you should be there," Ty agreed. "But you don't have to go it alone. Let's both meet with her in the morning. I'll tell her what I saw, and you can tell her whatever your concerns are."

The fear started to lap at her insides again. This guy was a pro. She had just been manipulated into a corner, and she wasn't sure she could get out.

Maybe there was no way out but through.

"I was just developing some pictures," she said.

He shifted his eyes, and even in the darkness she could see the gleam of humor come back into them. "And this connects to what we're talking about because—"

Alexis tried to keep her eyes steady on his face. "I have a picture of you on Jacquie's porch this afternoon. You're in the background, but it's you."

"Right. You must have snapped it when I was up there waiting for Karl to come out."

Her thoughts shifted to a halt. He admitted he was on the porch. He'd given a perfectly logical explanation for being there. Why would he have volunteered this whole thing, unless he knew she'd taken the picture and was providing his alibi even before she could start the interrogation?

"Did anyone else see you on the porch?" she asked carefully. "I mean, that might have seen him go in?"

"Herr Franz was giving his truck a manicure, but he had his back to Jacquie's cabin. By the time Karl took off, Franz had left too."

Alexis wanted to ask, *Did you see me taking a shot of Franz? Is that why you're being so sure to tell me all this?*

"Look," Ty said, "we'll work it out tomorrow. Man, I hate doing this to these people. Herr Franz and the Austrian innkeeper over there aren't going to win any Grandparent of the Year awards, but this is still going to be rough on them. What time do you want to meet?"

"You pick," she said. *Then I'll get to Sigrid first—and Karl before that—and tell them what? That I have a picture of Ty doing exactly what he says he was doing, while he has this nice little story of himself watching Karl take off out the back window?*

Her word against his, and everybody loved funny, charming Ty.

"Are you sure you're okay?"

She looked up from the toe she'd been staring at. His face was close to the screen, his eyes shielded by his hand so he could see her. She could see his eyes were filled with a mixture of concern for her and sympathy for the "kid." This guy was an artist, an actor. No wonder everyone had been so taken in.

"I'm fine," she said. "What time?"

"They start serving breakfast at seven o'clock, so let's say six-forty-five after

Sigrid has everything on the table. She's usually just standing around double-checking the bun cozies at that point anyway."

Boy, you really have cased the joint, haven't you? Alexis thought. But she nodded firmly. "Six-forty-five, in the sitting room." She began to push the wooden door closed, but Ty put a hand up.

"I know it's late," he said. "But let me just say this, okay? Part of what I do as a writer is just meet people. They're where the stories are and I enjoy it. I don't usually step on people's toes, and I've obviously tromped on yours. I mean, we're dealing with a bunion here."

Alexis looked at the ceiling. He wasn't going to go away until she said something.

"Look," she said, "we're here for different reasons, okay? Not everybody has to be best friends. Thanks for the information about Karl. Now, I've really got to go to bed."

"Sigrid has two of your prints from Philadelphia that you sent with your application on her desk," he said. "I was impressed with the way you capture people. I'm assuming those were just strangers passing by, but you've got the drama of the human soul going on there." He pulled back from the screen. "Too bad you can't capture that in person."

Even if she'd known what to say, he was gone before she could have uttered the first word. She could only slam the door after him. Hard.

"The gall of that man!" she muttered as she hurled herself into a chair and gripped the arms.

"I don't know the 'drama of the human soul' when I see it in person? Oh, excuse me. I guess you have to walk up to people and charm their stories out of them by pretending to be their best friend and then steal them blind!"

She pounded the arms of the chair with both fists, then sat up abruptly. She snatched the contact sheet out from between the books and examined it under the magnifying glass again. There had to be something in that picture, something she could use to turn that convenient little story of his right back on him.

She scrutinized the shot of Ty lurking fuzzily in the background behind Franz and his truck. But there was nothing incriminating there: no burglary tools bulging from his pockets, no neck craned to see if anyone were watching. From what she could tell, he was staring right at the door, with his back to the camera.

Quite possibly, he'd never seen her at all.

"But Karl did not take the bracelet and jump out the window," she said to the sheet. "Look at this face. This is not a thief. This is an orphan."

She moved the glass to the shot of Karl, fixed to his rock, clutching his knees and searching the atmosphere for someone to care. If they could all just see this, the way she had, they'd know there was no way.

Why can't they? she thought. *If I show them this, they'll see the real Karl, and they won't be so quick to hang this whole thing on him.*

Alexis glanced at her watch. It was already three-thirty. It would be dawn by the time she got out the enlarger and set up the trays again. The print would still be dripping when it was time to meet Sigrid. But it was the only chance she had. She went into the darkroom and started filing through the negative sleeves for Karl.

❧

The foghorns on the water told her she was nearly out of time. When Alexis finally brought the print out into room light, her eyes were burning, and the cobwebs of sleeplessness clung to the corners of her brain. She tried to shake them off as she climbed onto her bed and propped the print up on the covers. Karl's distant, longing face confronted her.

It really was good work, she decided, considering the contortions she'd had to go through. After all, she hadn't had time to look at anything but his face when she set up the shot.

Karl's lean body was a study in itself, caught up in almost a fetal position, looking vulnerable amid the folds of those oversized clothes. *He hides in those,* Alexis thought. *It's like he wants to be in a pocket where no one can find him unless they really want to.*

Involuntarily, her eyes went to his actual pockets, big gaping things with a chain crawling out of one and attaching itself to his belt loop. Who knew what was on the other end, although she was pretty sure she didn't want to.

The other pocket fell open forlornly, empty, just like Karl himself. There was a shimmer there that broke up the dark, morose plaid of his pants.

Alexis squinted at it. Her fingers closed tightly around the edges of the picture.

The gleam was the end of Jacquie D'Angelo's tennis bracelet.

She dropped the picture onto the bed and clawed both hands through her hair. She'd been about to accuse an innocent person of a crime—a real crime—just because she didn't like him. And she'd almost stood up for a guilty one as a result. The horror of it gripped her like the fingers that clung to her hair.

"What do you do now, oh, All-Seeing One?" she whispered to herself.

Then a lump gathered in her throat, and she could feel the tears coming. She rarely cried, but several drops spilled over her lower lids as she leaned back and closed her eyes.

"Oh, dear God," she said. "I am so sorry. What am I doing?"

She cried soundlessly for a few minutes. And from somewhere in the silence, a still, small voice came to her.

You're a human being. You made a mistake. Find out why later. Fix it now.

Alexis's eyes sprang open. She hadn't dreamed it. It was that quiet voice of guidance she knew had to be God.

"Fix it?" she prayed softly. "How?" There was no answer. Alexis sat up and reached for the picture.

382

She could see movement through the kitchen window. Sigrid and Franz looked like shadows moving around in the 6:00 A.M. light, waking up the day with rolling pins and spatulas. Alexis stood in the path below, craning her neck for sight of Karl. When his voice grumbled behind her, she convulsed as if she'd been shot.

"What are you doing out here?" Karl said.

She put her hand over her mouth and let her heart settle.

"Man, you're jumpy," he said. His voice had the early-morning sound of gravel, but his face was as soft and shapeless as a toddler waking up from a nap.

But two year olds don't commit larceny, Alexis told herself firmly.

"Can we talk?" she said.

Karl tried to curl his lip but only one side would go up. "No," he said, "I'm expected for oatmeal duty."

"I'll cover for you," Alexis said. "Come on."

Before he could shrink away, she steered him toward the south side of the house and around to the front.

"What, am I being abducted?" Karl said. "Where are we going?"

"To the beach." It was the only place she could think of where no one else would see them or overhear this confrontation. As she led him down the path to a crag that was hidden from the house, she brushed aside the thought that this kid could shove her over the cliff without so much as a by-your-leave.

"Sit down, Pal," she said.

"Who died and made you warden?"

"I'm holding all the cards and you're going to want to stay on my good side." She locked her gaze onto his. For an instant, a tiny flame of fear flashed across his face, then disappeared just as quickly. Once again composed, he sat down.

"What cards?" he said.

"Well, only one, actually," she said. She reached inside her sweatshirt and produced the picture.

Karl glanced at it and shrugged. "I hate having my picture taken. That doesn't even look like me."

"Not the 'me' you let us all see, no," Alexis said.

The other side of the lip came up this time. "Oh, here we go with the psychoanalysis. I've heard it from the pros, Lady. How I hide my true self so I can stay in this protective shell of rebellion and anger—"

"And grand larceny?"

The slits that were his eyes opened up. "Oh, yeah, I forgot to mention that I steal."

"You also forgot to conceal the evidence," Alexis said. She brought the photograph up to his face and stabbed at it with her finger.

He was frozen for only an instant before he grabbed at the picture. Alexis pulled it out of his reach and held it over her head.

"So what are you going to do now?" he said. "Blackmail me?"

"Nah," Alexis said. "I'm not going to lower myself."

"To my level, you mean?"

"To that level. I don't think it's really your level."

"Man, get a clue!" The words exploded out of Karl like a spray of bile. "I've had all the psychological games played on me and I'm sick of it! Just tell me what you're gonna do and get it over with, because you're not going to 'cure' me!"

Alexis could feel her heart pounding, but the words came by themselves. "I'm not playing psychiatrist, here. I'm going to be straight. I know you took the bracelet."

Karl gave a hard laugh.

"This isn't funny," she said. "You took something that was not only monetarily valuable but really meant something to somebody."

"Like that rich broad has any feelings at all besides how much it hurts when you break a nail."

"You heard Jacquie talk for five minutes, and you've got her all figured out?"

"I've seen it, okay? My parents hang with people like that. They're just a bunch of—"

"Fine," Alexis cut in sharply, "but you don't deal with that by ripping them off."

"Now you're going to tell me I wanted to get back at her for making me feel like some jerk busboy."

"The issue is that you committed a crime, and you have to make it right or else you're lost. So I'm your only out."

Karl's eyes came unsquinted, and a slow smile twisted his face. "You're going to get me off?" he said.

"No, Pal, you are."

Alexis thought the close-shaven scalp around his ears went white. But he didn't let the fear touch his eyes. "What am I gonna do about it?" he said.

"Part one: You're going to find a way to get the bracelet back to Jacquie before lunch today."

"I'm going to walk right up and say, 'Hey, rich lady, I stole this from you, but now I'm repenting of my sins.'"

"I think you'll be a little more creative than that," Alexis said. She leaned in and brought her face close to his. "But number one, you do it, and number two, you don't mock something that means everything to me."

"What, are you churchy?"

"I'm a Christian. I'm asking you to respect that."

The gleam went out of his eyes, and he glanced jerkily over his shoulder. Alexis waited.

"Okay," he said finally. "No Jesus jokes."

"Part two: You're going to spend some time with me every day."

"Doing what?" Karl said.

"Talking."

"What's the catch?" Karl focused his eyes suspiciously at her like a pair of gun barrels.

She put up her hand. "No psychoanalysis," she said. "Just straight talk with no garbage floating around in it. If I think you've been totally up front by the time I leave, I'll keep your little dip into crime a secret. If I don't, you're busted."

The bony legs inside the baggy denim shorts began to twitch. He curled and uncurled his lip, and his eyes darted across the horizon as if an escape route lay within reach. He was the picture of anxiety pumping.

"I don't have to do this, you know," he said. "All's you have is that lame picture. A good lawyer could—"

"You'd need Johnnie Cochran, Son," said a voice from the fog. "Because we also have an eyewitness."

Both Alexis and Karl jumped from their places on the rock.

Ty put a firm, tanned hand on Karl's shoulder. "What do you say we talk about this a little more?"

Chapter 8

Alexis dug her fingers into the rock. She hadn't thought what she was going to do about Ty. There was a good chance he'd told Sigrid already, and that chance made her heart plunge.

"I think we've got this worked out—" she said.

But Ty's eyes were on Karl, and so was his pawlike hand. Karl stopped squirming and stared stubbornly at his Doc Martens.

"I saw you go into Jacquie's cabin," Ty said evenly. "And I saw you take off out the back. I can only assume you climbed out the window, unless you have bionic powers."

"Nobody saw me take it!"

"Give it up, Son. All the evidence points your way, and nobody's going to give you a spot on *Larry King Live* to defend yourself. I suggest you take the lady's offer."

Alexis felt her chin drop to her chest.

Karl didn't take his eyes off his clunky shoes.

"She sees some hope that you're figuring out you're a decent human being, and I keep the thing to myself."

"Man, you two are slick," Karl said. His eyes shifted from one to the other. "When did you work this out together, in the middle of the night?"

"Yeah, we meet on a regular basis behind the sign boulder after midnight," Ty said.

Karl's face contorted into a twisted smile as Ty continued to weave an image of the two of them poring over Karl's juvenile record by matchlight. But Alexis's mind was careening in another direction. Ty must have been standing there in the fog for a long time to have overheard the deal she was cutting with Karl.

She watched as Ty met every one of Karl's barbed comebacks with one of his own. His brown eyes, alive with concern, stayed as firmly on Karl's face as his hand did on his shoulder.

"So, what's your answer?" Ty said. "The lady is waiting."

Karl shrugged his shoulders inside his big T-shirt. "I guess I don't have much choice."

"No, Son," said Ty. "I guess you don't."

Karl gave them one last lip curl before he headed for the road.

"You know I'm going to get busted big time by Sigrid when I get up there," he tossed back over his shoulder.

"I said I'd cover for you," Alexis said. "That's my part of the deal."

He hissed through his teeth and was gone.

A silence as thick as the fog fell between Alexis and Ty, and Alexis wasn't sure how to break it. *If I say a word, I know the guilt will come spilling out,* she thought.

"I know you feel pretty stupid right now," Ty said.

Alexis felt her eyes widen.

"But don't. I wanted to believe he didn't do it too. I've just been around his type enough to know that no matter how much you may feel sorry for them, you can't overlook what they're capable of."

Alexis pulled her lips into a knot to keep from blurting out something vile. Just when she'd decided maybe he wasn't so bad, he said something like that.

"No," she said, trying to keep her words even. "I don't feel stupid. I just like to trust people until I have a reason not to."

"So what did you find in the picture that tipped you off?"

Reluctantly, Alexis thrust it at him. Ty peered at it closely.

"He wasn't too careful about hiding the evidence, was he? Amateur."

Alexis stood up. "And I intend to try to keep him an amateur."

She turned to go, but Ty cocked his head at her. "Let me ask you this. You're going to spend some time with the kid. What are you planning to say to him?"

Alexis crossed her arms uncomfortably over her chest. The truth was, she had absolutely no idea. But she'd sooner have hurled her whole darkroom into the ocean than admit that to Ty. What was it with this guy? A few minutes ago he'd been the image of tough love, brimming with concern. She'd almost felt—what?—drawn to him.

Right, she thought, *then what does he do? He turns around and taunts me, like he's the only one who can handle a kid.*

"Look, I'm going to bed," she said, wrapping her arms tighter around her. "I was up all night." She turned and got as far as the top of the rocky path.

"Hey," he called from below.

She didn't turn around. "What?"

"You really know how to talk to Karl."

She forced herself to face him. "Well, thank you so much. Coming from you, that's quite a compliment." She expected a retort, barb for barb. She got only a baffled look.

"It was a compliment," he said. "One human being to another."

There was more he wanted to say. She could see the words teetering precariously on his lips. His brown eyes gripped hers as if he were holding both her shoulders. Then he dropped his gaze and went back toward the beach. As she watched him disappear into the fog, the sensation that she'd been very, very wrong sank over her.

Alexis shook her head and picked her way up the path. Nothing was making sense. Maybe she just needed to get some sleep.

❧

Her cabin was a flurry of books and photo paper, and she remembered she hadn't even cleaned up the darkroom. *I'll do it later,* she decided. *My brain is too foggy to do anything but sleep.*

But as she burrowed under the cream-colored comforter, she heard it again. That still, small voice.

You've done the right thing, the voice said.

Funny, Alexis thought as she turned over and drifted off. *I've been waiting for that voice ever since I got here. But I wanted it for my art, not for this. How does this kid fit in? How does Ty fit in?*

Before she could swat that last thought aside, she was asleep.

❧

"More shrimp salad, Lexy?" Sigrid asked. "After all, this is your breakfast, the most important meal of the day."

Alexis smiled sleepily and helped herself to seconds. She'd almost slept through lunch and would have if Jacquie hadn't banged on her door. Jacquie couldn't wait to share some good news with the group.

Tapping her spoon on her glass, Jacquie beamed at the entire dining room. "I have an announcement to make!" she said. She held up her wrist and dangled the tennis bracelet. "What was lost has been found."

Virginia Cox squealed delightedly, and Will started a round of applause. Marina-Natasha looked as if she had no clue anything had ever been misplaced.

Sigrid looked the most relieved of all as she stood clutching the front of her apron. "Where did you find it?"

"In the strangest place," Jacquie said. "In a bush outside my cabin."

Alexis caught her breath, and before she could think, her eyes went to Ty. His look confirmed what was in her mind. Karl was definitely an amateur.

But Jacquie was bubbling on about her absentmindedness while gazing at the bracelet as if it were a rediscovered puppy. "I know ya'll think I'm silly," she said. "But Michael D'Angelo means more to me than anything in this world. When I'm not with him, this little memento is as close as I get."

"I'd like to have a little memento valued at a couple thousand dollars," Ty said.

Alexis tried to roll her eyes, but she couldn't. Ty had caught them with his gaze, and he was staring her down.

❧

At almost sunset that night, Alexis was strolling across the lawn toward the beach when a voice hailed her from the sign boulder.

388

"I'm over here," he said.

Alexis stopped. "That's good, Karl."

"Aren't I supposed to talk to you or something?"

Her heart lurched. He looked almost hopeful, as if he had been waiting since dinner for her to appear.

"Yeah, I was just looking for you," she said. She perched next to him on the rock and began to pray, fast. She still had no idea how she was going to approach any of this with Karl. Her eyes lit on the sketch pad he held in his lap.

"Doing some drawing?" she said. "You told me you could stay in the lines."

He sneered. "Yeah, that's about all."

"May I see?"

He passed the sketchbook to her without looking at her, and he didn't say a word as she lifted each page. She wished he would. It might cover the soft gasps that wanted to come out of her with each new drawing.

There were several cartoon characters she vaguely recognized as action heroes. But there was something off about them. Oddly, they all seemed more angry than heroic.

But the sketches that took her aback were the ones of Rocky Shoals. While her own photos portrayed the serenity and gentleness of the retreat, Karl's drawings depicted an almost prisonlike structure staring starkly out over a ring of jagged rocks. Alexis felt trapped just looking at them.

Maybe I've taken on something I can't handle here, she thought. She closed the sketchbook and handed it back to Karl.

"What will you draw next?" she said. "That's always my biggest problem. What do I shoot next?" She looked at him sideways.

"I don't know, I can't really draw," he said. "It's stupid anyway."

"I don't think there's an artist on earth who hasn't felt that way about his or her stuff. I know I do from time to time."

"Yeah?" He was trying not to look interested. "So what do you do?"

"Pray," she said automatically.

Contempt lowered over his face like a welder's mask. "Oh," he said. "I'm not supposed to cut down your religion, right?"

"Right," she said.

"Okay, but I don't believe in praying. I don't believe there's anybody to pray to."

Alexis pulled her arms around herself. She suddenly felt as if Karl were exhaling arctic air. "Listen, I'm going to bed early because I was up all night. What do you say we meet tomorrow sometime?"

"Whatever," he said. "It's your deal."

"It's our deal," she said. But beyond that, she couldn't think of another thing to say.

"I'll look you up when I get back from Rockport," she said. "Fourish?"

"Fourish," he said, a mocking tone in his voice. "Will there be hors d'oeuvres?"

"Karl-kebobs," she muttered as she walked away. Then she added, "What have I gotten myself into?"

ॐ

Standing on Bradley Wharf in Rockport Harbor, camera in hand, Alexis snickered to herself. After taking half a roll of shots of what was touted to be the most painted and photographed building in America, she wondered if she'd ever feel this good again.

It was just an old fishing shack, built in the 1880s, but everyone oohed and aahed over it as the ultimate artist's subject of the New England coast. *I'm just like any other tourist*, she thought happily. *And I'm loving it.*

After all that had happened with Karl and Ty at Rocky Shoals, it was freeing to be away from there.

She popped her camera back into its case and made her way toward Main Street. Today it seemed right to just wander and be.

Toad Hall Bookstore was where Jacquie had said to meet her. It was next to the Tom Nicholas Gallery, and since she was a few minutes early, Alexis wandered in. Rockport was a virtual haven for artists, writers, and musicians, and its shaded, sleepy streets were lined with museums and galleries that seemed to exude inspiration. As she immersed herself in a photo display, Alexis licked the salt air off her lips and sighed. She was feeling a kind of peace, one that had been unfamiliar lately.

But when she drifted out half an hour later, there was still no Jacquie. Alexis looked around for a bench on which to park herself.

The only one she found was taken, and her heart did a flip-flop when she realized the occupant was Ty.

She didn't recognize him at first. There was no catcher's mitt or tennis racquet in evidence, for starters. He was leaned over at the waist, intently studying a small book that looked even smaller in his hands. In place of the mischievous look he always wore, there was a glow of total enchantment, as if he were someplace far away from the mundane world.

Alexis grinned in spite of herself. The girls in back of him definitely knew he was there. Two willowy females in flowery sundresses were passing behind him, and neither was concealing the fact that she found this tanned tower of muscle most attractive.

Stay right there, Alexis said to them mentally. She pulled her camera out of the case and gave it a quick focus. They were still looking wistfully back at him when she shot the picture.

As they moved on, whispering and giggling, Ty turned a page without looking up, his brown eyes hanging on the words as if they were magic. Alexis clicked the shutter again.

Great shot, she thought. But as she tucked the camera back into her bag, there was less satisfaction than guilt.

She sighed as she watched Ty continue to read. He was actually looking kind of vulnerable. Yet, if she walked over there to him and maybe even apologized for being so abrupt about Karl, would he stay that way? Or would he flip out some comic retort and send her reeling back into her own sarcasm?

Does it matter? said that still, small voice. *Does it matter how he reacts as long as you're doing the right thing?*

She slung the camera bag over her shoulder and went toward him.

Chapter 9

"Hi," she said.

Ty turned another page and a sound of sheer appreciation blew from his lips.

"Ty?"

He looked up then, his eyes shining. "Hey, Taxi," he said. His voice was faint, as if he hadn't really focused on her yet.

"I just took your picture," she said. "I like to ask people's permission, just to be professional."

"Sure," he said vaguely, then he waved the book in front of him. "Hey, Taxi, have you ever read this stuff?"

"What is it?" Alexis peeked curiously at the worn volume.

"It's some poetry I just picked up at Toad Hall."

Alexis snorted. "I haven't read a poem since the last one they made me read in high school. Unless it was on a birthday card."

"You've got to hear some of this stuff," he said. "Listen to this—sit down—I'll just read you a little."

Alexis was pretty sure it didn't matter who had come up to speak to him. He would have grabbed them and demanded an audience. Those two girls who were eyeing his legs would have been prime candidates.

As he was licking his thumb and flipping back through the pages, Alexis stuffed her bag under the bench and slid in beside him. There was something engaging about him trying to find just the right passage to show her. She cleared her throat to chase that thought away.

"Okay, Taxi, I know the meter's running," Ty said. "Just hold on. Okay, here it is. Listen to this."

He turned his body to face her and his eyes started to shimmer again as he read.

> "The voice of my beloved! Behold, he cometh leaping upon the mountains, skipping upon the hills.
>
> "My beloved is like a roe, or a young hart: behold he standeth behind our wall, he looketh forth at the windows, shewing himself through the lattice.
>
> "My beloved spake, and said unto me, Rise up, my love, my fair one, and come away.

"For, lo, the winter is past, the rain is over and gone;

"The flowers appear on the earth: the time of the singing of birds is come, and the voice of the turtle is heard in our land.

"The fig tree putteth forth her green figs, and the vines with the tender grapes give a good smell. Arise, my love, my fair one, and come away."

He shook his head and looked at her, the magic glowing in his eyes. "This is exquisite."

Alexis stared at him. "It's the Song of Solomon," she said.

His dark brows went up. "You know it, then?"

"It's from the Bible. The book has always been one of my favorites, in fact."

"You're serious?"

"As a heart attack."

He studied the book's title page and grunted softly. "That goes to show what I know about the Bible. Professors in college always used to say it was great literature and we all ought to read it cover to cover."

"I have read most of it," Alexis said. "Only I didn't do it for the literature."

Ty looked at her for a long moment, his brown eyes searching her face. She'd always tried to meet him stare for stare, waiting for the next, "Let me ask you this," but this time she had the urge to shyly look away as he watched her.

"Is the rest of the Bible this rich?" he asked finally.

"From a literary standpoint I can't tell you," she said. "But in terms of its meaning, oh, yeah. But I don't think that's what you want to hear from me."

"What do I want to hear from you?" He leaned back and laid his arm along the back of the bench. His face was somber.

Alexis turned her gaze to her lap. "I know what I would want to hear from me, and that's an apology. I didn't exactly thank you for stepping in with Karl. That whole thing was getting way out of control, and I'm not sure I could've gotten a yes out of him if you hadn't been there."

He shrugged lightly. "It's okay. I didn't do it for the thanks, but that's nice to hear."

They were quiet and Alexis wasn't sure what to do. There was no reason to stay—she'd done her thing—but she wanted to, and for no reason she could think of.

"So, can I ask you this?" he said.

She glanced at him sharply, but there was no mockery in his face. "Sure," she said.

"Did you think I took the bracelet?"

Alexis felt a stab in her stomach and she knew her eyes had jolted open. It was probably scrawled across her face like an unmistakable signature. "Yeah," she said softly. "And right now I couldn't even give you one good reason why."

"I can give you a few." He crossed one leg over the other knee. "Number one, you caught me in a photograph on her front porch. Number two, I was one of the few people who knew she took the bracelet off to go swimming. Number three, I even brought the subject up at lunch, and number four, I was the first one to accuse Karl." He cocked his head to the side. "There are probably other reasons too."

There were. But Alexis didn't want to get into them. Still, she couldn't get off the bench. "Do you know what time it is?" she asked.

He turned his wrist to reveal the face of his diving watch. "Twelve-forty-five."

"I wonder where Jacquie is."

"You were supposed to meet her?" he said.

"For lunch, forty-five minutes ago."

Ty sat up and looked down Main Street. "Even figuring in the Jacquie factor, that's pretty late."

Suddenly, an idea sprang up in Alexis's head, and she gave it words before she had time to stop herself. "What do you want to bet she's wrangling with some antique dealer someplace? I hate to eat alone."

The mischievous glimmer returned to Ty's face. "Are you asking me to have lunch with you, Taxi?" he said.

"I think I am," she said.

He stood up and grinned down at her. "Where to?"

⁂

Brackett's Restaurant was right on Main Street with an ocean view that captivated Alexis more than the menu.

"Your shutter is clicking," Ty said. "I can hear it."

Her first impulse was to snap back with something cheeky. But his eyes were smiling at her, as if he were enjoying the sight of her pressing her forehead to the glass to get a closer look at the seagulls wading in the low tide. Maybe it was time to stop this clever repartee thing.

"How can you tell?" she asked.

"You're so wrapped up in the photo opportunity out there, you haven't thought about what you want for lunch." He grinned. "That's a sure sign. I've seen how you go after Sigrid's cooking."

Alexis opened her mouth, but he raised his hand in protest. "I didn't mean it like that. You have a great figure, but I just like watching you eat. Most women pick at their plates like it's unfeminine to enjoy a meal."

Alexis let out a big breath. "That's one thing you and I have in common, then. You're no slacker when it comes to appetite either."

"Life's too short and too full of jagged places not to enjoy the pleasures."

It looked as if they were going to enjoy most of the pleasures on the menu by the time Ty finished ordering the combination platter for both of them. They were digging into shrimp cocktails and moaning deliriously when Ty said, "I still can't get over the material in this Song of Solomon. Somebody published it as a separate volume in the 1800s, and they had it on the antique bookshelf. I don't think I would have picked up the Bible, then I'd have missed it."

Alexis rested her fork against the shrimp glass. How sad to think someone had never read the Bible, not even a little bit.

Ty's eyes lit up again, and he left a jumbo shrimp dangling in midair as he talked. "It isn't just the language that's beautiful. It's the passion of the writer's soul, you know? There's more to it than just these two people in love with each other. I knew that even before I knew where it came from."

Alexis looked at him in surprise. He was right, of course. Some people said the Song of Solomon was an allegory of the love story of God and his people Israel. Others just said these were poems about true love and marriage. Either way, it wasn't simply beautiful language. And he had seen that.

By the time the platters arrived, overflowing with clams and scallops and oysters, Ty had finished raving about Solomon. He munched happily for a few minutes, and Alexis watched him with amusement as his cheeks bulged with seafood.

"So let me ask you this," he said.

"How can I 'let' you? You're going to do it anyway," Alexis said, laughing.

Ty's face went blank. "What?"

"You always say that," Alexis said. " 'Let me ask you this.' But I'm not doing the 'letting.' You're doing the asking, so just ask me."

"You're a strange model, Taxi," he said.

He was grinning. Slowly, Alexis grinned back. "I'm going to take that as a compliment."

"Good, because that's how it was meant. Now—"

Alexis Riker, she scolded herself, *are you flirting with this guy? Number one, he's not your type. And number two, what about Lance? Get over it, Girl!*

"So, have you figured out what you're going to say to him?" Ty was saying.

Alexis shook herself back to the table. "Who?"

"Our little fugitive from justice."

"Oh, Karl." A shadow fell across her mind. "No. I don't know if this is a mistake or not. I mean, the only thing I really know to say to him that would save him is to convince him of the love of Jesus Christ, and he isn't open to that at all. Jesus leads you to the right things to do to help yourself, but I don't even think I can get him introduced."

"I wouldn't even try if I were you," Ty said. "Your faith's pretty strong, then?"

"It's the center of my life."

He took a long drink of his iced tea before the next "let me ask you this" came out. "So, if Christ is at the center," he said, "where does Ring Man fit in?"

Alexis felt her face squeezing into a question mark. "Ring Man?"

Ty nodded toward her left hand. "The other day when I was teasing you about being pregnant—and by the way, that was in bad taste—I'm sorry."

Alexis nodded and twisted the ring around her finger.

"But you were talking about the guy who gave you the ring. You're engaged?"

Alexis took her time wiping her mouth with her napkin. "We're not seeing anybody else," she said carefully. "And we've talked about marriage."

"A little bit engaged," Ty said, his eyes twinkling.

Not even that! she wanted to blurt out. It would be easy to tell the whole confusing tale right now. But Lance would have his necktie in a cinch if she talked about their private life with a guy she didn't even know.

Ty was chewing thoughtfully and watching her from across the table.

"I don't know," she said. "That's part of what I'm here to find out. Lance is a wonderful person—and a Christian. I couldn't be with anybody who wasn't. But there's just stuff I have to find out about me, not him. Doesn't have much to do with photography, does it?"

His brown eyes widened. "I think it has everything to do with photography. I don't think your art and your life are two separate things."

"Is that why you're never without a golf ball or a badminton birdie?" Alexis asked.

Ty slathered butter on his roll. "That's part of it, but you want to know something?"

"Sure."

"I'm not sure what I'm doing here either. I'm out there playing around on the waves in a Sunfish with Will Cox, and the whole time I'm thinking, okay, the royalties are coming in, now what?"

Alexis stopped with her fork in a scallop. It was her turn to search his face. His eyes were wistful, and the full lips were pursed in a sad little smile. "Have you found any answers yet?"

"Nah, but I'm having a good time!" He laughed and stuffed the rest of the roll in his mouth.

Alexis shook her head. "Can you ever hold a serious thought in your head for more than seven seconds?"

"Yeah, but there's no future in it," he said. "What about you, any answers yet?"

She toyed with a fried clam. "I'm getting answers, but I don't think they're to the questions I'm asking."

"What are you getting?"

"I'm getting 'Help Karl.' 'Take pictures of people.' " She shrugged. "That kind of thing."

"And you're thinking that doesn't have anything to do with your future as an artist."

"Right."

He sat back and studied her. She went for her iced tea glass.

"I think it does," he said. Then he laughed again, a husky chuckle Alexis hadn't heard before. "I don't know what, but then, I can't even get any answers to my own questions, so what do I know? Let's get the garçon over here and get a dessert menu. What do you say? Big, sloppy something with a bunch of whipped cream on it, huh?"

Alexis groaned, but she nodded and laughed. Inside, a nagging thought said, *Lance wouldn't like this.* But Alexis listened to the waiter's rundown on taste temptations and half-pushed that thought aside. *There is nothing wrong with having lunch with somebody,* she told herself, *and besides, this is the most fun I've had since I've been here.*

Suddenly, a big, tanned hand came down over hers. "Thanks for giving me a chance to show you that I'm not a complete jerk."

"Same here," she said.

"I hope you find all your answers."

"You too." She felt a little pang. *That sounds kind of final. Does that mean we won't get to talk about this again?*

"Look at this show," Ty said.

The waiter produced two pieces of fluffy cheesecake with blueberries drooling over the sides.

"I'll never be able to eat all that!" she exclaimed.

"I have confidence in you, Taxi. Now man your fork."

❧

When they emerged from Brackett's onto the sunny sidewalk, Ty looked down at her almost shyly. "I've got one more question for you, Taxi," he said.

"I'm afraid," she said, laughing. "What?"

"Can I have a ride back?"

"How did you get here?"

"Hitched a ride with a fisherman I ran into this morning. Fascinating character. He's been fishing these waters since Billy Budd was a boatswain."

"What?"

"I know these literary allusions are lost on you, Taxi. Let me see, how about Noah?"

Alexis stiffened. "You're not making fun of me, are you?"

"Would you lighten up? I admire your faith. I wish I had a little of it myself." He pinched his full lips ruefully, then broke into his familiar square smile.

❧

As Alexis pulled Clifford into the driveway behind the main building at Rocky Shoals, Ty interrupted his rendition of Marina-Natasha discussing sixties' folk singers and pointed toward the back porch. Karl was sprawled on the steps, glaring up at the sun.

"He's such a rebel, he won't even let the sun make him squint," Ty said. "Look at that."

"Yeah," Alexis agreed. Once again a shadow fell across her thoughts. What was she going to say to this kid?

But Karl himself had the first words when they climbed out of the car. "I wouldn't go in there," he said, jabbing a thumb toward the back door.

"Why not?" Alexis said.

"Because that rich lady, you know, who I—" He waved his hand around to fill in the blanks.

"Jacquie, yeah," Ty said. "What about her?"

"She's in there bawlin' her eyes out," Karl said. "Sounds like somebody died."

Chapter 10

K arl wasn't exaggerating. Jacquie was doubled over on the couch in the sitting room of the main house, sobbing from the pit of her soul. Ty covered the room in two long strides and curled his arm around her. Alexis joined them, kneeling in front of Jacquie.

"Duchess, hey, what's going on?" Ty crooned to her hair.

Jacquie couldn't answer except to shake her head.

"It's her husband," Sigrid said from the French doors. "He's had a heart attack. It's serious," Sigrid added. "Jacquie, we have you on the six o'clock flight to Dallas."

Jacquie nodded against Ty's shoulder. "Did you get the limo?" she ouid, her voice barely audible.

"Franz is still working on that. And if not, he can always take you to Boston in our car."

Jacquie pressed her hands over her face. "I can't get a handle on this," she said. "I can't believe this is happening."

"Of course you can't," Ty said soothingly. "Nobody can get a handle on something like this." He pulled her into the circle of his arms and rocked her like a child. She cried softly into his chest.

Alexis leaned forward. "Let us get the handle, Jacquie," she said. "Why don't I drive you to Boston in my car?"

"I can't ask you to do that."

"Why not? You'd do it for me. I know you would."

"I tell you what," Ty said. "I'll drive down there with you so Alexis doesn't have to come back by herself at night. Would that make you feel better?"

Jacquie nodded and cried some more. "You two are so good, thank you. I don't think I could go down there alone anyway."

"Are you packed?" Ty said.

"No, I haven't put the first thing into a suitcase. I have stuff from here to kingdom come in my cabin. I can't even think straight."

Alexis said, "I'll go throw stuff into bags, okay?"

"Would you?" Jacquie said.

I'm better at that than I am at this part, Alexis thought. Ty, on the other hand, was an amazingly good comforter. With his brawny arms around Jacquie and his usually raucous voice now soft and soothing, she was almost as calm as a baby with a warm blanket.

⁂

Alexis was just finishing packing Jacquie's myriad of cosmetics when Ty tapped at the cabin door and poked his head in.

"Jacquie said to tell you there's stuff under the mattress," he said.

"Where doesn't she have stuff? I'm not this settled in my apartment at home."

Ty lifted the corner of the mattress, and Alexis slid her hand under it. She came out with a velvet-covered jewel box.

The corner of Ty's mouth lifted as they looked at each other. "She wasn't fooled by the bracelet on the bush, was she?"

Alexis shook her head. "Nope. She was guarding against the next invasion of the jewel snatcher."

Ty grinned at her, and once again Alexis felt shy.

"Here are my keys so you can bring the car around," she said, tossing them to him. "How's Jacquie doing?"

"As well as can be expected. She's so in love with this guy. I don't know how she'll deal with it if she loses him."

⁂

When they were finally cruising down Interstate 93 toward Boston, Jacquie sat silently between them, one hand clutching her purse, the other wrapped around Ty's fingers. Tears ran down from bottomless blue eyes that seemed to see nothing.

"How are you doing, Jacquie?" Alexis asked softly.

"Horrible," she said. A fresh flood of sobs choked her throat.

"It's okay," Ty said. "It's good to get it out. Go ahead and cry, Jacquie."

But Jacquie turned abruptly to Alexis. When Lexy glanced down, she saw a surprising spark of anger in her eyes. "You have faith in God, Alexis," she said, her voice breaking. "Why does He let things like this happen? Michael never did anything to anyone. He's honest in business. He's a wonderful husband. He has so many good years left!"

Alexis gripped the steering wheel. She wasn't good at this at all. She knew the answer, but giving it to Jacquie in a way that made sense was something else all together. *God, help me say the right thing,* she prayed.

"Can you tell me?" Jacquie said.

Alexis took a deep breath. "No, I can't," she said. "I don't think anybody can give you an exact answer. We know that God allows all things to happen. Some are the result of His will, and some are because of the things people do."

Alexis glued her eyes to the road. "Where God comes in," she went on, "is in helping us through hard things when they come along. If it makes sense later, great; but at the time something like this happens, you don't need reasons, you need strength and support. God gives you that."

"I don't feel any strength and support from God," Jacquie said stubbornly.

Alexis chewed at her lower lip for a second before she answered. "Then how come Ty is holding your hand and I'm driving you to the airport? God's working through us."

"Why?" Jacquie said. "Why would He do that for me? I'm not a believer."

"Because I asked Him to," Alexis said.

She could feel two pairs of eyes on her, one streaming and blue, the other warm and brown.

❧

Jacquie was still wiping her tears when Ty and Alexis saw her down the corridor toward her plane. She turned once to wave to them and blow a kiss. Ty blew one back.

"She's a neat lady," he said. "I hate to see her hurting."

"Yeah," Alexis said. She gave him a sideways glance as they walked away from the gate. "You really handled her well. She trusts you, and I think you gave her strength."

He didn't answer her, and he remained silent as they left Logan Airport and drove toward Rockport. Alexis glanced over at him a few times, but he was staring out through the windshield. He seemed as far away as he had earlier that day when the Song of Solomon had commanded his attention.

"Let me ask you something," he said when they turned onto Route 128 and were passing Salem. "What you said to Jacquie, does that really work?"

"Yeah," Alexis said. "I wouldn't have told her that if I didn't believe it were true."

"Has it actually worked for you?"

Alexis squirmed. "It isn't like taking an asprin, if that's what you mean. It 'works' if you believe in the Lord and have a relationship with Him."

"Jacquie doesn't. I don't. So it won't work for us."

Before Alexis could answer, a still, small voice seemed to whisper in her ear. *This is your chance,* it said.

"A lot of times people come to the Lord for the first time when they're hurting, like Jacquie is," she began carefully.

Ty shook his head. "I can see God now if I came running to Him with my problems after all this time. 'Where you been, Pal? Little late, aren't you?' "

"Are you mocking me?" Alexis said.

"No, not at all. Look, could you pull over?"

Alexis whipped her gaze away from the road for a second. "What for?"

"Because I can't talk about this driving down the road. I think we need to be face to face. There's a parking lot over there."

Alexis pulled Clifford into the empty lot in front of a closed cafe, her heart beating like a jackhammer. Ty's face was somber in the soft glow of the streetlight.

"So, what you're telling me is that Jesus takes all comers as long as they believe."

"Right."

"Then what?"

"Then you keep believing and reading the Bible, and you find a church. Your faith starts growing and becomes the center of your life."

There was a silence in which he seemed to be waiting for her to say something else.

"That's it," she said. "Once you make a commitment, a lot of things will happen, but that's basically it."

Ty's eyes narrowed so suspiciously that Alexis had to bite back a laugh.

"But what do you need that big book of instructions for?"

She did laugh this time. "You mean the Bible? It isn't just an instruction manual. The Bible tells the story of God's love for all people. As believers, we get inspiration from that."

As he considered that, his brown eyes seemed on fire with his thoughts.

"Yeah, I can maybe see that," he said. "The Song of Solomon did something for me."

"You haven't seen anything yet," Alexis said. "The Gospels will really blow you away."

"Do you have a Bible?"

"I have two in my cabin."

"Can you spare one for a seeker?" His pensive face creased slowly into a grin.

"Yeah," she said.

&

Later that evening, Alexis handed a Bible to Ty in the sitting room of the main house. Over cups of herbal tea, Alexis watched as he leafed reverently through the pages. He was entranced already.

This was a mini-miracle, she decided. Yesterday, she was still sneering at his jokes. Today, she had spent a whole afternoon and evening with him, and now she was sharing the most important thing in her life with him. Hard to believe, but it looked like she and Ty Solorzano were friends.

&

But Alexis didn't talk to Ty again for three days. She only saw him trek across the lawn toward the beach, flippers in hand, or emerge from the kitchen with a sandwich and head off down the road with it while the rest of them lunched or dined together.

Sigrid brought them news that Jacquie's husband was going to have bypass surgery but so far was holding his own. Alexis met with Karl a few times, just long enough to say, "Hey, are you staying out of trouble?" She still wondered why she was in this situation in the first place. And, of course, she took pictures as the spirit moved her.

Through it all, she pushed away the nagging questions.

What was with Ty? Had she said something to put him off that night? There was always that chance when you witnessed to somebody. But Ty had asked; he had seemed open to God. And there had been that still, small voice too.

But the most irritating question was the one she couldn't shove off to the side. Why did it bother her so much that he seemed to be avoiding her? Sure, she'd seen different sides of him that she genuinely liked, but so what? She liked Will Cox and Franz, and even Karl, but she didn't go to pieces when she didn't see them for a whole day. She wasn't even that bummed out that she couldn't see Lance. That was the thought that set the anxiety sizzling.

"Where has our Ty been?" Will Cox inquired at dinner the second night Ty didn't appear.

"Ty?" Marina-Natasha said, looking around vaguely.

"I think he's doing some serious thinking, myself." Virginia cocked her pixielike head, and the crinkles around her eyes spread out into merry cobwebs. "You need to be alone to do that, you know."

Alexis concentrated on buttering a roll. "What do you think he's thinking about?" she said, trying to sound casual.

"A woman," Will said.

Alexis stared. Virginia smacked him playfully on the arm. Coffee splashed over his hand, and he wiped it off with his napkin, still grinning at her.

"You are incorrigible!" his wife said. Then her crisp eyes grew soft as she turned to Alexis. "Not that it wouldn't just tickle me to see that boy in love, but I think he has much higher concerns. I saw it the first time I met him, under all the joking around and the constant activity." She leaned in as if she had a secret, and Alexis found herself leaning in with her. "I think God may be doing some work here. Wouldn't that be excellent?"

Will winked at them both. "God works in mysterious ways. I think He's working on a good woman for Ty."

Alexis stuffed the whole roll into her mouth.

❧

After dinner, Alexis was headed across the lawn toward the beach when she caught a glimpse of Karl. A guilty pang went through her as she watched him settle himself on the front porch railing and swing his legs rebelliously against the poles. She really needed some time alone on the beach. There seemed to be so much to sort out and so little headway being made. But she'd made a deal with the kid.

I don't know what I'm doing, she thought as she changed course and went toward the house. *God, just help me make whatever it is the right thing.*

It wasn't until she got to the porch that she realized Karl held his sketch pad in his hand and had a death grip on a pencil. When he saw her coming, he slammed the pad shut and hurled himself off the railing right at her feet.

"You're determined to rack yourself up, aren't you?" she said.

He shrugged and walked toward a dark-green wicker umbrella-topped table surrounded by four cozy chairs on the lawn. Alexis followed him, groaning inwardly. *Who do I think I am?*

Karl slumped into one of the chairs. Alexis sat on one facing him and cleared her throat.

"Hairball?" he asked.

"Yeah," she said. "I get them often. Doing some drawing?"

"No, I was catching up on my calculus." The face squinted at her.

Don't let him get to you, Alexis, she thought. *Just keep going.*

"I guess you decided what to draw next," she said.

Karl spread his hand out over the cover of his sketch pad and massaged it for a minute. Alexis watched him carefully as his fingers inched toward the edge of it as if he were going to open it. But then he closed them into a fist and sat back, arms folded tightly against his chest.

"I can't draw."

There was no hiding the pain in that statement. Alexis wanted to leave her chair and hug him.

Instead, she pulled the sketch pad toward her. "Do you mind?"

He shrugged.

But, as she turned to the last page, which hadn't been filled before, Karl suddenly reached across the table and snatched the pad from her. She let it go.

"It's okay, it's your private stuff," she admitted. "But I did ask."

"I just didn't want you to see the last one, okay?"

"Okay."

His squint loosened a little. "Don't you want to know why? My shrinks always want to know why."

Alexis pushed out a sharp sigh. "I'm not your shrink. I think I'm your friend. At least I'm trying to be. I'm just trying to be here so you have somebody to talk to."

Where that had all come from, she had no clue. But her heart slowed down and she sat back in the seat.

"Okay," Karl said finally. She could see it was an effort for him to keep his lip curled. "So, I'll play shrink. Why are you doing this for me?"

She folded her hands on the table. "I know you're not into this," she said. "But I've got to be honest with you. It's God."

A laugh contorted Karl's face. "God talks to you?"

"In a way."

"You're—" He stopped, the word "crazy" left unspoken on his lips. He set the chair back on its two back legs and stared hard at the tabletop.

"What else is He saying about me?" he said.

He hadn't said much of anything until now. But once again, words flowed out of Alexis's mouth. "That right now you're a really unhappy person so you're acting like some kind of macho criminal type. There's a lot of good in you, and if you had someone who believed in you, you could probably be okay. More than okay. You could be an artist, be happy, have a life."

Karl rocked the chair. "He doesn't think I have a life?"

"Not the one you're supposed to live."

Karl let the front legs down onto the ground with a jerk. "What life am I supposed to live?"

"I don't know," Alexis said. "I don't even know what kind of life I'm supposed to live. But I'm working on it."

"What are you doing? I mean, how do you work on it?"

She looked at him closely. It wasn't a sarcastic question. His eyes were wide open now, making him look vulnerable.

"I pray a lot. And I spend time alone thinking. And I work on my art, see where He leads me through it."

Karl thought a minute, then poked his finger at his sketch pad. "So I draw pictures and I find God?"

Alexis twisted her mouth. "Not totally. I mean, you have to have a relationship with the Lord before He can really work in your life, but sometimes He can show up when you're working at your art, and you find out you need Him."

He looked at her for such a long time, she thought there was going to be a conversion right here at the table. But the open innocence he let her see for those few moments curled back up, and he gave a short laugh. "I don't know about God," he said. "I was trying to draw you."

Alexis felt a twinge in her stomach. "Me?"

"Yeah, but you can't see it. I can't draw."

He was pulling away, detaching himself from her again, and she couldn't let him go.

"A sundae at that ice cream store on Bearskin Neck says you can," Alexis said quickly.

"Sundae?" he asked sarcastically. "Goodie."

"Okay, what then?"

She prayed he wouldn't just get up and saunter across the lawn. He didn't. His eyes lit up momentarily. "A bag of saltwater taffy from Tuck's. It's on Dock Square."

"You're on," she said and stuck out her hand. He slapped it cautiously and grabbed his sketch pad. "So if I can't draw you, I buy, and if I can, you buy."

"Deal," Alexis said.

"I'm gonna lose," he said.

"If you see yourself as a loser, you probably will be one," she said.

405

"We're placing bets here?" said a voice. "I didn't think you were a gambling woman, Taxi."

Alexis whirled around to see Ty strolling toward her, hands in his pockets, head cocked as if he'd heard the whole conversation. She could feel her face wreathing into a smile.

"She isn't," Karl said. "She just placed a pretty lame bet. She hopes she loses."

"Sounds like the odds are in your favor, then," Ty said.

Karl grunted, got up, and ambled away. To Alexis, every I-don't-care step looked carefully planted.

"Did I interrupt when you were making headway?" Ty asked.

"I don't know how much headway I was making." Suddenly, she felt awkward talking to him.

"I think you're wrong," Ty said. "He actually looked like a young boy there for a minute."

Alexis's gaze flew up to him. "You saw it too? It wasn't just my imagination?"

"No." He pointed to the chair next to her. "Do you mind?"

"No!" she said, and then groaned inside. Why couldn't she just calm down?

"Before you go any further with this kid, though," Ty said, "there's something I think you ought to know."

"I already know he lies and steals. I don't think I want to know anymore."

"You want to know this. Sigrid told me today that the last time Karl was here, he made off with one of the patron's cars."

Alexis sat straight up.

"Grand theft auto," Ty said. "Only it didn't exactly turn out that way. Franz found him down near Salem with it and got it back here before the owner found out. But that's just his activities here in Rockport. In Connecticut, he has a record as long as your leg. Karl is only free, as opposed to sitting in some juvenile detention facility, because they got him a good lawyer and lucked out and drew a soft-hearted judge last time. But one more offense and he's behind bars. Possibly in an adult facility."

Alexis looked at him blankly. The wheels in her head were turning slowly. "You mean, if they found out about Jacquie's bracelet, he'd be—"

"Busted," Ty said.

Alexis sat back in the chair and grabbed a handful of hair, letting it fall as the thoughts tumbled around in her head. "Do you think I did the right thing? Did I do him any favors by getting him off again?"

"I don't know. You have to figure Sigrid and Franz suspect him on this bracelet thing and they're letting themselves believe she 'lost it.' Maybe that's your cue."

Alexis frowned. She wasn't crazy about taking "cues" from Karl's grandparents.

"Look," Ty said, "I didn't tell you so it would mess up your head. I just don't want you to think that if this doesn't work out, it's your fault. I mean, they've tried everything."

Alexis tightened her hands on the arms of the chair. "I know. I've thought of that. But there's one thing they haven't tried, and it's about the only thing that's going to work."

Ty pulled at his lower lip with his fingers. "You're talking about God, right?" Alexis nodded.

He let his lip go and stood up. "Well, look, I just thought I'd pass that along, for what it's worth."

Alexis felt her heart sinking, but she plastered on a smile as he pushed in the chair. "Thanks," she said.

"Listen," he said.

She waited, hoping for something she couldn't identify.

But he shrugged and said, "I'll see you later, huh?"

Yeah, she thought sadly. *Whenever.*

As he left the table and moved toward the main building, she tried to look as if she had planned to sit there for the duration of the evening all along. Ty had only taken a few soft steps across the grass when he stopped.

"I'm reading the book," he said.

Alexis turned sharply to face him. "What?"

"I'm reading the book. I'll get back to you on that."

Then he was gone. Alexis watched until he disappeared around the side of the house. Then she sighed from somewhere deep inside.

Chapter 11

I'm sick of this darkroom! I'm sick of this camera! If I never see another roll of film or photo opportunity, it'll be too soon!" Alexis slammed out of the bathroom and flopped onto the windowseat.

It's probably a good thing nobody heard that, she thought. *I think I'm getting a little whiffy. I'm talking to the walls!*

She peeked outside through the filmy curtain. She'd been stuck in the darkroom all morning, trying to make some sense out of the work she'd been doing. Usually, she came out of a session of trays and chemicals with a sense of having accomplished something. But it seemed as if all she was doing was developing pictures. There was no purpose. No passion.

The time she had here was slipping away. Three weeks and she'd be back in Philadelphia, tail between her legs, telling Lance she was no closer to the answers than she had been when she'd left.

And what else was she going to tell Lance? she thought desperately.

One thing was for sure. She had to get out of this cabin before she started doing worse than talking to the walls.

With tennis shoes on and her hair brushed up into a scrunchy, she opened the door for the first time that morning. She hadn't even gone to breakfast. With Jacquie gone and Will and Virginia wanting to discuss Ty's mysterious behavior with every forkful, meals had become a tedious chore. Her stomach was growling now, though. Maybe she could mooch a muffin from Sigrid in the kitchen or get Karl to abscond with one for her.

Karl. She hadn't seen much of him either. She wondered if he were working on her drawing.

I'm almost afraid to see what he comes up with, she thought.

As she swung open the screen door, a piece of paper floated to the ground. Someone had stuck it in the crack between the screen door and the door frame. For a minute, she thought it might be Karl's rough sketch, but that idea vanished.

Taxi,
I let my own world fade for awhile
And wrapped myself in yours
I peep out now like a child awakening
With more questions than before

Maybe you can answer them for me.
There's a cliff where you nearly met your demise—
will you meet me there at noon?
Wear tennie pumps and don't eat lunch.

Ty

He'd wrapped himself in her world? She hadn't even seen him for three days.

I do not get this guy, she thought as she tucked the note into her jeans pocket and headed for the main building. *I'm thinking we're starting to be friends. Then he disappears for half a week, and I get this note requesting some strange rendezvous.*

But she stopped with one foot on the bottom step of the back porch.

What was it he'd said the other night when he'd walked away from her?

I'm reading the book. I'll get back to you on that.

The book. The Bible.

Alexis backed down from the step. Was that the world that he'd wrapped himself in?

"Wow," said a voice behind her.

Alexis looked up at Marina-Natasha, who was standing in the path, observing her with awe.

"What's wrong?" Alexis said.

"You look like you just, like, had some revelation or something." She tossed her panels of red hair so that her beads jangled. "That's so awesome."

"Yeah," Alexis said, and started down the path.

"Aren't you coming in for lunch?" Marina-Natasha asked.

"No," Alexis told her, "I have other plans." Then she looked down to make sure she was wearing tennie pumps.

❧

It was the kind of Massachusetts summer day they describe in travel brochures. There had been a squall the day before, but the morning had dawned splendidly, as if it were washed and brushed. A salty sea breeze flowed deliciously across the water and rippled through Alexis's hair. A row of fluffy clouds sent feathery tendrils dancing through the sky, almost touching the sea. *A sky so blue it hurts your eyes,* Alexis thought. She had been stuck in the darkroom for too long.

She hurried across the road and was almost to the cliff when she stopped again. What was she doing here, exactly, meeting Ty like this? Was it really to see what he thought of the Bible, or was it something else?

Alexis, don't be a geek, she told herself firmly. *You had no intention of coming here, tennie pumps or no tennie pumps, until you figured out what he was talking about. Isn't this what a Christian is supposed to do?*

If that hadn't convinced her, she would have had no choice anyway. A voice hailed her from the rocky shelf below.

"Hey, Taxi, you made it."

Alexis peeked over the edge. There was Ty, perched on the next level down. He had a rope apparatus in his hand that was attached to two nylon straps up on her level. One was wrapped around a tree and the other around a rock that jutted up out of the ground.

"What's all this?" Alexis said.

"It's your lifeline. Have you ever rock climbed before?"

"I've free climbed and been around some equipment, but—"

"Okay, you just do as I tell you and you'll be fine."

"What?" Alexis stared at him. "What are we doing?"

"We're lowering you down here. This is a killer; you're gonna get a real rush out of this."

"I get a rush just thinking about it. I don't need to do it."

"Come on, Taxi, where's your sense of adventure?"

Actually, it was pumping inside her as she looked down the fifty-foot drop. Her dad had taken all of them on hikes when they were kids and shown them how to scale a simple rock slope. But she had always wanted to do something more challenging. Once she had mentioned it to Lance when they were driving in the Poconos. He had told her it was a good way to break your neck.

"This better be worth it," she called down to him. "I'm missing Sigrid's lunch for this."

"No, you're not," he called back, grinning squarely. "I've got a Sigrid lunch for two right down here." He nodded toward a picnic basket, its contents bulging under a red-checked napkin.

"Start giving those instructions," Alexis said.

"Okay," he said, "you see how my rope is connected to the ribbons?"

"Yeah."

"Okay, those are tied to the rock and the tree. That means you aren't going to come crashing down when you—"

"When I what?"

"Rappel down the wall."

Alexis went down on her knees and looked him full in the face. "Rappel? You mean, walk down the face of the wall with nothing but a rope—"

"And me."

Alexis looked doubtfully back at the setup Ty had installed.

"You see that doohickey that attaches the strap to the rope?"

She zeroed in. "Yeah, the carabiner."

"I'm impressed. Do you know what it does?"

She flipped back through her foggy memory file. "It's going to let you stop me if I get going too fast."

Ty grinned. "See, I got it handled."

410

"That's what I'm worried about," she said.

But she found herself grinning back at him. For some reason, she did trust this man. He might be obnoxious, but there was something about him that had slowly dawned on her. He wouldn't hurt another human being if his own life depended on it.

"All right," she said. "Where do I hang on?"

"You see that red thing that looks like a harness, there on the rock?"

Alexis picked it up. "Is this some kind of medieval torture device?"

"Just step into it. It's called a seat."

She held the beltlike contraption out in front of her and put first one leg, then the other into its openings as if she were putting on a pair of shorts. It was obvious that its belt fit into a loop and tightened around her stomach.

"Okay, you got that tight?"

"Yeah."

"Now pick up the rope. See, I have the other end."

She took the line into her hands and waited for the anxiety to start. She was, after all, about to walk down a fifty-foot wall. But there was only excitement and a dude with arms like pistons at the bottom.

"You still want to do this?" he called up to her.

"Try and stop me. What next?"

"Just turn backwards at the edge of the cliff and take a step down. Put your foot on the wall itself."

"Talk about a leap of faith!"

"Hold the rope in your right hand and let it go across your body so you can guide it with your left hand. If you were to hold the rope way out behind you with your left hand, you'd stop. So, that's what slows you down." She heard him give a husky chuckle. "That and me down here at the other end."

The thought that Ty liked being her safety net fluttered across her mind.

"All right," he continued, "start walking backwards. You're just taking a stroll down the wall."

Gingerly, Alexis lowered her foot over the edge and found the wall. Stretching the rope across her and hanging on with a death grip, she let the other foot go.

I'm going to go plunging into the ocean! she wanted to scream.

But both feet were planted firmly on the stone face of the wall, and she began to walk down it.

Ty howled. "Whoo, look at you, Girl! You're doing it!"

Alexis nodded and kept walking, one tenuous step at a time.

"Hey, Taxi!"

"What?" she said.

"Don't forget to breathe."

Alexis let out a guffaw. She actually hadn't drawn a breath since she'd left the top. With the jerk of her laugh, she let her left hand go slack and began to drop faster. Quickly, she pulled her hand behind her, but not before Ty gave his end a gentle yank and slowed her down.

"What a team, Taxi," he said, his voice calm and soft.

Alexis took the rest of the wall grinning. When her feet touched the bottom, she smiled delightedly up at him. "That was so cool."

"You're a natural."

He was looking down at her with shining, magic eyes that didn't let go of hers until she forced herself to look away.

"I don't know," she said quickly. "I'm not ready for Mount Everest." She sniffed in the direction of the picnic basket. "I am ready for lunch."

She could feel him looking at her for a moment longer before he pulled the napkin off the basket. "I think the Austrian innkeeper outdid herself," he said.

"You have a nickname for everybody, don't you?" As Alexis pulled off her gear, Ty set the basket between them and pulled out two chilled bottles of sparkling cider.

"Do you have a problem with that?" he said.

"No. I really didn't mean it that way. I'm just curious."

"Because I'm an odd duck, and you want to figure me out."

"I guess so," she said.

"Okay, let's see what we've got here. Three kinds of sandwiches—egg salad, crab salad—okay, she grabs that out of my hand, no need to go further—"

Alexis looked guiltily at the hard roll dripping with mayo and fresh crab and laughed. "It's my favorite. I didn't want you getting it first."

"No danger of that. You're like a steam shovel. Okay, we've got grapes. Some kind of pâté for crackers. Oh, don't tell me, it's Sigrid's fruit salad. I don't know what her secret is, but it's to die for. You want some?"

Alexis nodded happily as he loaded up her plate. Below them, the ocean merrily splashed foam, leaving an occasional droplet sparkling on Ty's dark hair. She could feel the breeze tossing her own ponytailed mass of curls. She leaned against the warm rock wall and savored her sandwich under the jealous gaze of a scavenging seagull.

"No way, Pal," she said to it. "I'm eating every bite of this."

"And then some," Ty said.

"This was a great idea. Thanks for including me."

"You're the whole reason I'm doing it," he admitted.

Alexis looked at him carefully. "What do you mean?"

"Well, you're responsible for opening up a can of worms," he said. He dug into the bottom of the picnic basket and pulled out a book. The leather of the Bible Alexis had lent him gleamed in the sun.

I was right, Alexis thought. *But what do I do now? Where do I go from here?*

But there it was, the still, small voice of calm. *The words will be there.*

"You okay?" Ty asked, his lips working against each other.

"Yeah." She nodded toward the Bible. "What did you think?"

He stretched out to his full length on the shelf and went to work on a container of pâté and some stone-ground wheat crackers.

"I read the Gospels," he said.

Alexis stopped in midbite. "All four of them?"

"I pretty much immersed myself in them. I shut out all outside distractions and went for it. That's the way I like to work."

"What did you think?"

Ty carefully spread pâté on his cracker. "That's just it. I don't think I thought so much as I felt, you know? I had some pretty strong reactions. This guy Jesus, He's tough."

Alexis put her sandwich down. "What kind of reactions?" she said.

"Okay, He's telling me that basically He wants me to let Him run my life. I'm supposed to pack everything in, leave everything I own, and follow Him. Where are we going?"

Alexis groped for an answer. *Excuse me, God,* she prayed wildly, *but I thought You said the words would be there.*

She looked helplessly at Ty. "I don't know," she said.

He grinned. "Great. Thanks."

"I'm serious. I don't know what the Lord has planned for you. Once you—a person—start following, that's when you find out."

"So if I want to be a Christian, I have to go back to Chicago and sell my apartment, give away the cat—"

"No!" Alexis said. "You just do whatever the Lord asks, and you'll know, because it won't leave you alone until you find out what it is. So, yeah, I guess He might want you to leave Chicago and do something else, but if you believe and pray and have a relationship with Christ, He'll let you know that. Then you have to be willing to follow through. He wouldn't ask you to do anything you couldn't do."

He finished off a cracker and surveyed her thoughtfully. She grabbed a plastic container and peeked in at the dessert offering.

"Is that how you do it?" Ty said.

"I try." Alexis shrugged ruefully. "I haven't had much success lately, but I keep praying and listening."

He took off his sunglasses and chewed on the earpiece. "So what you're telling me is that you pray, then you wait, then you know, then you do whatever God tells you."

Alexis twitched an eyebrow. "That's basically it. And you have faith because you've committed your life to Christ, and He's your Savior. You don't have to worry about what happens." She gave him a half-smile. "Of course, you do worry and you do go off on your own thing and you do misinterpret because you're human, then God comes in and forgives you, then you start again."

"What, no guilt?" he said. "Where do I sign?"

Alexis laughed and looked up at his tanned face. "Supposedly no guilt. It does creep in."

There was a long silence while Ty poked through the containers as well. But Alexis could tell his mind wasn't on the choice between strawberry shortcake and Sigrid's blueberry cobbler.

"I don't know," Ty said finally. "It's a lot to absorb all at once. I'm gonna have to go back and read some of that again."

"Will it take you three days of isolation?" Alexis asked impulsively, then chomped down on the inside of her mouth. *Why did I say that?* she thought. *Why would I care?*

"No, I think the saturation period is over. What I do want to do is process it with somebody, though. Are you game?"

"Game?" Alexis said. "Does that mean we discuss it over tennis?"

He stuck his fork into the cobbler and grinned at her. "You don't play tennis?"

"Not in public."

"What's your pleasure—besides running around behind a camera and hiding in a darkroom?"

"I can do other stuff," she protested. "I love to swim."

"I haven't even seen you in the ocean."

"I came here to work."

"Ah. What else?"

"I'm a bicyclist. I go everywhere on my bike in the city. Weekends I like to go out in the country. Of course, I haven't been able to do that since I've been in school."

"Did you bring your bike?"

"Up here?" Alexis frowned. "No. I didn't think I'd have time."

Ty nodded thoughtfully. "You like to sail?"

"I haven't done it in years."

"Deep-sea fish?"

"That I haven't tried, but I've always thought—"

"Taxi," he said.

She stopped and looked into his brown eyes, now wide and earnest. "What?"

"Girl, you need to get a life."

"I have a life!"

"Right. Look, I'll make you a deal. You answer all my questions about this Christianity thing, and I'll show you the smorgasbord of life. You can pick your pleasures. You've got to get some pleasures in there—"

The idea settled over her like a strong, warm handclasp. She sat back against the rock wall and studied her knees.

There was something about this "deal" that made sense. She had been fighting so hard, and nothing she'd found so far had come close to feeling this contented. It must be okay. It must be right.

"You know that I'm kind of spoken for," she said.

Ty nodded. "I'm not taking you on dates, Taxi. You'll pay your way." Then he stuck out a big tanned hand. She slipped hers into it. "We're friends," he said. "Right?"

She couldn't hold back a smile, nor did she want to. "Yeah," she said. "We're friends."

✼

And so began a week of whirlwind activity. After breakfast with the Coxes—during which Virginia and Will spent most of their time winking back and forth at each other every time Ty's name was mentioned—she'd pack her camera into a waterproof bag and be whisked off somewhere by Ty.

"You can't give yourself permission to take a day away from that thing, can you?" he said to her the second day.

"It isn't like writing," she told him. "You can't just save the details and put them down later. If the picture's there, you have to take it."

But there was really no time for shooting, not while bobbing atop the Atlantic in a sailboat, following Ty's instructions, and she had to admit, howling the entire time. And not while standing on the deck of a deep-sea fishing boat, fighting over a bent-double rod for a tuna with Ty hanging on behind her. And definitely not while tooling down Eden Road in Ty's wake on the ten-speed Franz had dug out of his garage. But her mental photo album filled up fast with memories of gathering seashells, lying on her back making angels in the hot sand, and laughing up into Ty's tanned face.

Lunches they usually spent on the cliff. Once, Ty even produced one of Sigrid's baskets at dusk when they were digging for clams, complete with cloth napkins and stemware for their sparkling cider. Those were the times when Ty asked his questions about the Bible and about Christ, and Alexis prayed for the right answers. She wasn't altogether sure they were coming out. Ty was making no move to commit himself to the Lord. But, she reassured herself, he wasn't backing away either.

Most evenings, they mixed with the other artists. Alexis found out that no one worked past dinner the way she did. The Coxes usually got a game of Monopoly going in the sitting room, and Alexis derived great satisfaction from beating Ty out of Boardwalk and Park Place. Twice, they joined Marina-Natasha on her porch and sang along with the guitar.

When the lights began to wink out for the evening, Alexis would then find Karl. He was elusive during the day, but when everyone else was going peacefully off to sleep, Karl's inner turmoil brought him outside. Alexis knew she could usually find him on the front porch, parked defiantly on the railing.

Alexis still didn't think she was getting anywhere with him, but he seemed to curl his lip and squint his eyes less, so maybe that was enough.

"How's the drawing coming?" she asked one night.

"What drawing?"

"The one you're doing of me."

He shrugged.

"So, the bet's off?"

"I didn't say that."

"Then you do want that saltwater taffy."

"Big deal."

Alexis jerked her face toward him. "You know what, Karl? It is a big deal. It's a big deal to me."

He looked at her out of the corner of his eye.

"Has it ever occurred to you that somebody else might have feelings too?" she said.

"They don't care about mine, why should I care about theirs?"

"I don't care about yours? What am I doing here, then?"

He didn't say anything.

"Y'know, Karl," she said. "I can understand your feeling like trash because nobody in your family seems to care. I hurt for you, seriously, I do. But that doesn't mean the rest of us are going to do the same thing. It hurts when I reach out to you and you just slap me in the face."

A minute passed before he said, "You're not going to cry, are you?"

Alexis blinked. His face was uncurled and concerned.

"No," she said.

"I didn't mean anything by that. But it's like, I could never trust anybody else, so why should I trust you?"

"Because I'm a Christian."

He considered that for a minute while he studied his Doc Martens. "Where do you guys go all day?"

"Who?"

"You and Ty. Are you guys, like, together?"

"No!" Alexis realized she was shaking her head faster than she needed to. "We're just friends. He's kind of showing me the other side of life. We go fishing and swimming and stuff."

"That's better than what I'm doing."

"Which is?"

Karl rolled his eyes. "Peeling potatoes. Carting stuff up and down the stairs for Sigrid."

"Do you ever get a day off?"

"What would I do with it?"

"You could come with us."

He grunted, and for an instant, Alexis wished she hadn't said it. For openers, what was Ty going to say? And what would it be like to drag this kid on a sailboat?

But Karl suddenly looked at her full in the face. There was something unfamiliar in his eyes.

"What are you doing tomorrow?" he asked.

Alexis's heart took a dive. They were going on a ferry out to Thacher Island to see the lighthouses up close. She'd been dying to do that since the first night she'd arrived, and Ty had worked out the trip for them. If they took Karl along, that would give the adventure an entirely different focus.

She hoped none of that was showing on her face as she closely surveyed the tops of her knees. She could feel him watching her.

"Well," she said, then she looked up at him. His eyes were shining. The words came out before she could stop them. "We're going out to the lighthouse island," she said. "We'd love to have you come along."

"I might," he said. Then he pulled back inside like a turtle into a shell. But before he disappeared into Karl again, she saw the look in his eyes one more time.

Ty was probably not going to like this. She wasn't sure she did. *But how could you turn your back on the first glimmer of hope?*

Chapter 12

Y ou did what?" Ty said.

"I couldn't help it. He looked so hopeful there for a minute. It's what I've been working and praying for."

Ty gave an exaggerated shrug. "All right. You have everything we need then?"

"Sigrid packed the lunch—"

"I'm talking handcuffs. Permission from the parole board—"

"Stop it!"

"Okay, okay, look—" Ty leaned against her car door and put his palms up in protest. "I really don't have a problem with Karl going with us, as long as you aren't doing it out of guilt. I mean, the whole purpose of this is to give you a chance to lighten up and let some answers come in. I don't want you to sacrifice a day for this kid if that's not really what you want to do."

Alexis stared at him. He wasn't kidding; he was adamant. Yet, even as she watched, his face softened, and he put a hand gently on her arm.

"I didn't mean to sound like a drill sergeant," he said.

Her eyes went to his hand. His grasp was surprisingly tender.

Quickly, he pulled away and peeled himself off the car. "Really, it's okay. Bring the kid. Bring the whole juvenile detention center."

"Ty—"

"Wardens can come too—"

"Ty—"

"Parole officers—"

"Just Karl will be fine!"

He grinned his square grin. "I'll go tell Grandmama we're stealing him away."

For a minute, Alexis watched him amble up the back steps. There was no end to the surprises with him.

❧

Karl spent most of the boat ride to the island leaning over the rail, staring morosely into the churning water. Alexis nervously avoided the I-told-you-so look in Ty's eyes.

But as the twin lighthouses of Thacher Island grew larger, Alexis thought less about Karl. Her hands gripped the railing and her mind filled with the wonder of the two structures.

The lighthouses were so much bigger than they appeared from Rocky Shoals. Towering hundreds of feet into the air, their walls were massive, curved feats of stone that appeared impenetrable to the constant battering of the wind and ocean. Side by side, they were like soldiers, standing guard, searching and warning. There was something secure about them.

"Those are some serious lighthouses," Ty said behind her.

"Aren't they amazing?"

"You aren't the only one who thinks so. Take a look at our little inmate."

Alexis shifted her eyes casually over her shoulder. When she did, she couldn't take them away.

Karl's usually squinted eyes were riveted like bolts to the two lighthouses looming over them. Awe spread across his face.

"Can you stand it?" Ty whispered to her. "He's mesmerized."

"He'd never admit it," Alexis whispered back.

"You got that right. I don't think we ought to tell him."

"Just let him have his day."

And Karl did. It occurred to Alexis as she watched him follow the guide up the winding staircase inside the first lighthouse, reaching out like a little boy to touch the damp walls and feel their chill, that he must have had plenty of opportunities when he was growing up to go places, with all the money his family had. It wasn't just "getting out of Rocky Shoals" that was putting that playful, curious look on his face.

❧

"No hogging all the crab sandwiches for yourself this time," Ty said to Alexis on the beach at Loblolly Cove as he handed her a hunk of French bread oozing seafood salad.

Alexis blew the sand off the wrapper. "You've just got to be quick. Karl, what are you having?"

Karl rolled to his back from a prone position on the sand. He squinted at the basket. "Did she put any pizza in there?"

"Good luck!" Alexis said.

"What's the matter, Guy, sick of your grandmother's cooking?" Ty said.

"Sick of my grandmother," he muttered. "You can give me a turkey, I guess."

Ty dug through the lunch and pulled out a sandwich bulging with sliced white meat. Karl opened it as if it contained nitroglycerin and gave it a suspicious sniff before he took the first bite.

"I don't think she poisoned it," Ty said drily.

Karl snorted. "I'm sure she'd like to."

Alexis sat up on her knees. "No way. She may be hard on you, but come on!"

"She hates my guts."

"She's your grandmother, Man," Ty said.

Karl pulled his lips into a bunch. "And your point is—"

"That is the point," Alexis said. She knew she had to tread carefully. "Family means no matter what you do, they love you."

"No," said Karl bitterly, "it means no matter what you do, they have to take you in. I don't think love has a whole lot to do with it."

Alexis looked helplessly at Ty. He warmed his brown eyes toward Karl. "What makes you say that, Guy?"

Karl set the sandwich down on the plastic wrap and glared at it. The words squeezed out like an embedded splinter. "You guys have spent more time with me today than my 'family' has my whole life, practically." He propped himself up on his elbow, the sandwich forgotten at his side. "It's like, my parents, before the divorce, would take me to Disneyland and stick me on all the rides by myself while they stood there at the exit smoking a cigarette. Some of the lines were so long, they'd go have a drink at the hotel while I waited to get on. You want to hear about my whitewater rafting experience?"

"Sure," Alexis said. A pain was beginning to twist around her heart.

"We're in Oregon, after they split up. My old man and his girlfriend want to 'commune with nature.' So they're sitting there by the pool at the Hilton one night, and I say that I want to do something. Go canoeing or whitewater rafting or something besides sit there and watch them feed each other cocktail peanuts. So you know what my father does?"

Alexis and Ty shook their heads.

"He wakes me up the next morning and says, 'You wanted to go whitewater rafting? The bus'll pick you up in twenty minutes.' It did, and there I am with all these families getting ready for a day on the river." Karl's face was so tightly squinted, he could barely get the words out.

"They stick me on a boat with these people I don't even know and who can't remember my name from one minute to the next. They basically ignore me the whole time. I could have jumped out of the raft, and I don't think they would've noticed until they came up one wetsuit short at the end of the trip." Karl attempted a wry smile. "That's how my 'family' shows their love for me."

Alexis sat silently. There was nothing to say. If even half of that were true—and from the almost imperceptible tremor that threatened in Karl's voice, she suspected the worst—it was no wonder he was angry at the world. What would it have taken to have gone on one ride with him or sat on the beach and shared the sand?

"That's the pits," Ty said.

Karl wriggled his shoulders inside his too-big T-shirt and tried to look detached. "Whatever."

"Nah, 'whatever' doesn't work for me," Ty said without hesitation. "What did you miss? What do you want to do today, on this beach, that you never got to do?"

Karl tried to grunt, but Ty scooted toward him. "Come on, you're dying to tell me. Spill it."

"You're weird."

"That's a given. Now come on."

Karl looked at Alexis, but she nodded. "Go for it. What have you got to lose?"

"My self-respect for one thing!" he said. "You don't have to try to make up for my lost childhood. I can handle it."

Ty put his hand on Karl's arm. For an instant, Alexis remembered how tender his hand had felt on hers.

"I don't do anything I really don't want to unless I have to," Ty said. "Here's your chance to have one good day and see what it feels like."

Karl got his arm away from Ty and tilted his head back. They waited while his face worked, and his crossed Doc Martens jiggled feverishly. Finally, he said, "I want somebody to ride the waves with me."

Ty closed his eyes and caught at his lower lip with his teeth. Alexis knew if he felt anything like she did, he was trying not to cry.

"Then let's do it," Ty said huskily.

And they were off. Ty got to the water first, still ripping off his shirt, with Karl on his heels whipping off nothing except the Doc Martens. The two of them hit the ocean with knees pumping, and both bodies disappeared under the surface, only to come up shaking like drenched dogs.

Alexis took out her camera and caught a few shots of them waiting for a swell big enough to hitch a ride on. *Too bad I can't capture the howling on film,* she thought. *Ty's even got Karl doing it.*

"Hey, Taxi!" she heard Ty call. "Come join us!"

She cupped one hand around her mouth. "I don't have a swimsuit!"

"And I do?" Karl hollered.

Alexis grinned at the soaked T-shirt that stuck to his skinny body like a second skin. "Okay!" she called out. "I don't know if you can stand the competition, though!"

But the need to win was the furthest thing from any of their minds as they spent the afternoon buoyed by water and laughter. Alexis reflected at one point that she had never heard Karl laugh before. She'd heard grunts and snorts and hisses, but the deep, mischievous chortles that bubbled out of his throat that day didn't come from a rebellious teenager who was full of anger and disappointment. They flowed from a kid who was having a good time and feeling loved.

By the time they headed for Clifford that afternoon, Alexis was too tired to even collect her own belongings off the beach.

"You get the car started. I'll get everything else," Ty told her.

Even at that, she let him drive back to Rocky Shoals. On the way, she sat in the middle in the front seat, and Karl fell asleep with his head against the window.

"He looks like a little kid when he's like that," Ty said.

"He is a kid," Alexis said.

Karl squirmed. "I'm not asleep," he said. "So be careful what you say." Then he added, "You two oughta be somebody's parents."

Alexis knew as soon as she opened her eyes that she'd slept through dinner. The shadows were already slanting across the yellow walls of her cabin, turning them to evening gold. She sat up and hugged one of the pillows, sleep still clinging stubbornly to her eyes.

Something woke me up, she thought, *because I could probably sleep for days.*

Then she heard it, the screen door squeaking quietly, then banging softly against the door frame.

She made her way to the front door and opened it. A piece of paper fluttered out. Her heart gave a pleasant quiver as she leaned over to pick it up. Another poem from Ty?

But the flutter faded as she perched on her porch railing and unfolded the paper. It was a drawing from Karl.

Spreading it open on her lap, Alexis gazed at it through the gathering darkness. Even with the shadows creasing it, the drawing leaped off the page.

There she was, leaning against a rock on a beach, her feet dug into the sand, her face radiantly looking up. There were clouds over her head, big fluffy ones, the kind you saw stuff in when you were a kid.

As she looked closely at them, Alexis caught her breath. There were faces and figures in those clouds, skillfully merged with the tufts and puffs.

In one there was a camera, in another Clifford with an almost zany life of his own, and in another, what? Alexis laughed out loud. It was a sandwich, comically drooling its contents onto the cloud.

He's included all the things he knows I love! Alexis thought happily.

But on the fourth cloud, her laughter stopped. Etched clearly into this frame was a portrait of Ty.

There was no mistaking it. The close-cut hair with its stubborn cowlick. The intense eyes, eyebrows lifted above them like arrowheads. The square smile, ready to let its next piece of drollery escape, straight in her direction.

Alexis quickly folded the drawing and tucked it into her pocket. She was going to have to set Karl straight on that posthaste. She and Ty were just friends, period.

With a jacket thrown around her shoulders, Alexis crossed to the main building, then hesitated on the steps. She wasn't even sure where Karl stayed. It was probably too early for him to be in for the night anyway. She decided to try the front, where he usually hung out.

But there was no Karl on the front porch, and for obvious reasons. Sigrid and Franz were sitting on the wicker furniture, and she knew she'd caught them in the middle of some silent crisis. Sigrid couldn't hide the pinched look around her mouth, and Franz had picked up a newspaper.

"Hi," Alexis said uneasily. "Have you seen Karl?"

Franz grunted from behind the paper. Sigrid painted on a smile. "We just had a chat with him," she said. "I believe he headed for the beach."

I bet that was some "chat," Alexis thought.

"I'll look for him down there, then," she said.

But as Alexis turned to go, she heard the wicker loveseat creak. Sigrid got to her feet and followed her down the steps.

"Alexis, forgive me," she said. "But I must say this to you." She rubbed her tiny hands together. "You seem to have taken a liking to my grandson, or perhaps you have some idea of rescuing him, I don't know. But I must tell you his family has tried everything. I cannot imagine that someone outside, no matter how well meaning, could have any effect on him. Sometimes we have to let matters run their course."

Alexis gripped the stair rail. *Let matters run their course?* she wanted to scream. *You mean, let the courts take care of him, because none of you ever cared enough to!* But she kept her hold on the rail and looked into Sigrid's birdlike eyes, so much like Karl's.

So very much like Karl's. Cold. Hard. Blocking out all feeling. Sigrid was obviously treating Karl the way she had been treated. You toe the line, you follow the rules, you are happy.

You can't change her, Alexis, she thought. *But there's still hope for Karl.*

It was the still, small voice. There was nothing else to do but follow it. She let go of the railing.

"I'm sorry," Alexis said. "But I am going to keep my friendship with Karl. It can't hurt, can it?"

Sigrid drew herself up like a condor, her eyes snapping. "It can hurt you, my dear. Karl has hurt all of us deeply, and we are his family. He won't hesitate to hurt you too, believe me."

Alexis took a step down the stairs. "I'll take my chances," she said. "Good night, now."

Her heart was still slamming against the inside of her chest when she got to the beach. It was almost completely dark, and there weren't any shadowy figures in the moonless night to scrutinize for Karl.

Maybe that was better, she decided. What would she say to him at this point, with her anger still pumping in her fists? Hey, Karl, you were right. I'd have somebody test my food for strychnine before I ate it if I were you.

She sat down hard on a rock and put her face in her hands. How could people be so willing to nurture and encourage strangers, then be so blind to the agonizing need of a child in their own family?

And what was worse, what could she do about it?

Slowly, Alexis sat up and looked out at the waves washing rhythmically on the shore. She could no more stand in the way of those people and whatever they wanted to do with their grandson than she could stop the ocean from rolling in and out.

But if I don't, she thought, *a human being is going to be lost.*

A pain started deep in her chest, and she leaned back on the rock to breathe through it.

"Taxi, are you all right?"

Ty was suddenly there, settling his brown eyes on her. Seeing him was like getting permission to open a floodgate.

"No, I'm not," she said bitterly. "I just had a nice little 'chat,' as she calls it, with Karl's grandmother."

Ty wiggled an eyebrow. "It's 'Karl's grandmother' now."

"And she doesn't even deserve to be that!"

"It was more than a 'chat,' then."

"As far as I'm concerned it was." Alexis folded her arms tightly against her chest. "Basically, she told me to stay away from Karl because they'd done all they could, and they were just waiting for him to be incarcerated."

"She used the word 'incarcerated'?"

"No, but she might as well have." Alexis stirred restlessly on her rock. Ty reached over and put his hand on her arm again. It was as gentle as before, and this time she didn't look at it. She didn't want him to move away.

"She pretty much told me the same thing," Ty said.

"And what did you say to her?"

"I told her I'd think about it. She knew I wasn't buying it."

"Why is she doing this?"

Ty slid his hand under her arm and brought her to her feet. "You want to walk down the beach and talk about it?"

Alexis nodded and pulled her jacket sleeves down over her hands.

"Too cold?" Ty asked.

"No, I'll be okay."

"Here." Ty linked his arm through hers and took off in long strides down the beach. Alexis scurried to keep up, carried along on his arm with her feet barely touching the ground.

"Sigrid's doing the best she can," he said.

"Oh, right. That's good enough for me—"

"She comes from a different generation, a different culture entirely. She doesn't know what else to do with Karl except treat him the way she was treated."

Alexis stopped. "Do you really think that?"

"It's the best I can come up with."

"That's kind of what I thought too, only I didn't see it as an excuse."

"It's not an excuse, it's a reason. Which doesn't mean it's necessarily good for Karl."

"It's horrible for Karl! Especially since it doesn't apply to his parents, who obviously have other problems."

Ty chuckled. "Poor little duffer. He wants us to be his parents."

Alexis looked up at him. His eyes were soft as they looked down at her, with the sad twinkle of Karl's words lingering in them. She couldn't pull her own eyes away from them. And she didn't want to.

But you have to, she thought with a jolt. *You can't do this. You can't.*

"What's wrong?" Ty said.

"You know what, Ty?" she said. She took a step backward, and as she did, the concern that sprang into his eyes went right through her. "I'm cold. I think I ought to get back."

"Okay. I'll walk you."

"No, really, I'll be okay. I've got to, you know, clear my head."

He looked hard at her before he nodded.

The thoughts pounded as she made her way back up the beach. *What is the matter with me? Why can't I just be friends with this guy without all this other stuff crowding in? He's not for me. I didn't come here for this. I'm not interested in him; he's not interested in me. . . .*

By the time she got to her cabin, she had to stop and put her fingers to her forehead to stop her racing pulse. This, she decided, was getting out of hand. She needed to get off by herself and think this through before she did something stupid.

She reached for the doorknob and pushed the door open. A pink piece of paper drifted to the floor.

What is it this time? she thought as she reached for it. *Another invitation to disaster? An incriminating drawing?*

It was a message in Sigrid's handwriting: *Call Lance.*

Chapter 13

The only light on the back porch by this time came from the pay phone. As soon as she dialed, Alexis slid down the wall out of the glare and onto the floor.

Let him be asleep, she thought as she listened to the empty ringing on the other end. *If I could have until tomorrow, I'd have this all sorted out.*

But the voice that answered was sharp and awake.

"Hi!" she said, perhaps too brightly.

But her attempt to sound cheerful was lost on Lance. His words cut her off at the knees. "Lexy, what's going on?"

"I'm returning your call," she said.

"Don't turn this around," he replied testily. "The woman who took my call earlier, the one with the accent—"

"Sigrid."

"She said you were out walking on the beach with some guy named Ty."

Alexis gave an exasperated snort. "I went down on the beach, and I happened to run into Ty—"

"Who is this Ty?"

"He's another artist here. Lance, what are you saying?"

Lance's voice was tight. "I'm saying that I thought you went up there to explore your creativity and get close to God, not get involved with some other guy."

"I am not involved with some other guy!" Alexis sat straight up and squeezed the receiver. "Where did you get an idea like that?"

"Innuendo."

"What?"

She could picture Lance running his hand down the back of his head in a familiar gesture of frustration. Her own free hand was digging through her hair like a steam shovel.

"Sigrid let it slip that you two have been spending a lot of time together," he said. "Is that true?"

Alexis bristled. "I don't like your tone, Lance."

"And I don't like what I'm hearing. You're several hundred miles away, and what you're saying you're doing doesn't match the facts."

"I have a friendship with Ty. We're both really interested in a teenage boy who's here—"

"Teenage boy? Lexy, what are you doing up there?"

Alexis gritted her teeth. "If you'd let me finish one sentence, I'd tell you."

There was silence. Lance pinched it off with a gruff, "I'm sorry. Go ahead."

Alexis sighed. "Sigrid's grandson is up here, and I've gotten attached to him and so has Ty. In fact, I was looking for Karl tonight when I happened to run into Ty on the beach. Am I acquitted?"

"Come on, Lexy, you're not on trial."

"Then why do I feel like I am?" she said. "Why did you call me? To interrogate me about my every move?"

"No."

He was trying hard to stay in control, Alexis could tell. She changed ears and waited.

"I called because we have an opportunity for a great deal on a house," Lance said.

"What?"

"One of the guys in the office just made junior partner, so he and his wife are upgrading to a larger home. He wants to sell his, and I think it'd be perfect for us, just starting out. Three bedrooms, two baths, study downstairs for me, and there's a screened-in porch we could turn into a studio for you."

Alexis scrambled to her feet and strangled the phone receiver. "I thought we weren't going to make any decisions like this right now," she said. She knew she was barking, and Lance growled back.

"If we want this deal, we have to take it now," he said. "We can't expect Keith to wait."

"I can't run my life on Keith's timetable, whoever he is!" Alexis said. "I'm not ready to commit to buying a house and all that. You know that!"

"What I know is that you're not ready to commit to me." His voice was icy and Alexis pulled back from it in pain. "Isn't that right?"

It was right. *But I don't know why you're right, Lance!* she wailed inside. *If I can't tell myself, how can I tell you?*

"Isn't that right?" he repeated.

"I don't know, Lance!" she cried. "The only thing I'm sure of is that I'm not ready to make a commitment. If you want the house, go for it. But I can't, I just can't."

"Why?"

"I said I don't know."

"And when were you planning to find out, Lexy? I'm a little sick of hanging in limbo. I'd like to get on with my life."

Alexis dragged her fingers through her hair again, this time holding onto a glossy handful at the base of her neck to keep from screaming. "I don't have an estimated time of arrival," she said tightly. "I'm doing my best. But I don't expect you to wait. Do what you have to do."

She anticipated a click in her ear. She wouldn't have blamed him if he'd hung up. But he let out air into the receiver.

"No, I'm going to wait," he said. "What else am I going to do? I love you."

Alexis closed her eyes and leaned her forehead against the porch wall. "You don't have to."

"Yes, I do," he said. "But, Lexy, please don't muddy the waters."

Long after he'd hung up, she stood on the porch, her head against the wall. She was letting Ty muddy the waters, and that wasn't fair. Not to Lance, not to her, and not even to Ty. Even if Ty were interested in her as anything other than a summer project, it could never work. He wasn't even a Christian, and it didn't look as if he was ever going to be. All their discussions had been purely intellectual; she'd seen no sign that Ty was ready to make a commitment to Christ.

But what about my feelings? she asked herself. *What about the way it felt when he touched my arm? The way our eyes connected when we talked about being Karl's parents? The way I hoped the drawing was another poem from him?*

Alexis pulled herself away from the wall and left the porch for the cabin at a march.

If you didn't spend so much time with him, you wouldn't have those feelings, she told herself firmly. *You owe it to Lance to just chill before this gets out of hand.*

She closed her cabin door resolutely behind her. Lance was right. She needed to focus on him, and on her art, and on God.

"Lord, please," she whispered to the darkness. "Help me to stay away from Ty."

She stared for a minute. That wasn't the prayer she had intended to pray.

�֍

After the longest night she had ever spent, Alexis hurried into the dining room the next morning for a last-minute breakfast. At the sight of Ty saving a place for her at his table, she knew it was going to be an even longer day.

In the gray hours near dawn, she had come to a decision. She would not see Ty anymore, except to exchange hellos and pass the salt. If she couldn't control her feelings, at least she wouldn't let the feelings control her. Before drifting off into a fitful sleep, she had thanked God that things had gone no further.

Not that Ty had any intention of taking their relationship further, she'd reminded herself. But why risk making a fool of herself for nothing?

Alexis stopped in the doorway and tried to look past Ty as he nodded ultra-casually toward the chair next to him, his tongue parked whimsically in his cheek. But there was no looking past Ty, anymore than there was any ignoring him when he said, "Let me ask you this." Alexis felt a pang she couldn't brush aside.

She straightened her shoulders and strode across the room toward Will and Virginia's table. "Morning, Ty," she said with forced cheer as she passed him. She pulled out a chair between the Coxes and sat down. She wasn't sure whose eyes were boring into her more deeply, Ty's or the elderly couples'.

"Did you save me a muffin, Will?" she said.

Harrumphing, he passed her the basket.

Breakfast was definitely longer than the night she'd spent. The only saving grace was the appearance of Karl. While he shuffled through and grunted at everyone else, he sneaked her a significant look. She slipped up to the beverage table where he was piling unused juice glasses onto a tray.

"I got the drawing," she said.

He shrugged.

"You did it. It's me, all right."

"I can't really draw."

"Enough with that. I love it, Pal. Period. End of discussion."

He tried to smother a smile, but it coaxed irresistibly at the corners of his mouth. "What about the bet?"

Alexis poured herself some cranberry juice and swept him a sideways glance. "You won."

"Yes!" he hissed, pumping his fist.

"Where is this candy place?" she said.

"Downtown. Next to that restaurant, Brackett's or something."

Alexis put her hand on her stomach to stop another pang. "Okay. Finish up what you have to do for your grandmother and meet me at my cabin. Just knock on the door."

"We never talked about how much candy I was getting."

"Don't push it, Pal," she said.

When she returned to the table, Sigrid was refilling the coffee cups.

"None for me, thanks," Alexis said.

Sigrid gave her a chilly nod that sent shivers up Alexis's spine. *What had Lance said about Sigrid the night before?* "*Innuendo. Sigrid sort of let it slip that you two have been spending a lot of time together.*"

That was true. But why had Sigrid "let that slip"? She didn't even know Lance.

Alexis looked up at her now. Sigrid's tiny eyes flitted over her, filled with resentment. There had been no "letting it slip" at all. She'd done it on purpose. Alexis scraped her chair back.

"Would you all excuse me?" she said.

Sigrid's chin came up and she walked away.

֍

An hour later, there was a knock on Alexis's cabin door.

"You ready?" she called before she got the door open.

"For what?" Ty said to her.

She couldn't say anything. He was standing there, one arm leaning on the door frame above her head.

"I thought you were Karl." Her voice sounded limp. Inside she was caving in.

"He was still scrubbing the omelet pans when I left the kitchen," Ty said. "Look, I'm sorry to barge in on you, but have I done something to upset you?"

Alexis looked down at her bare toes in agony.

"I have," he said. "Look, I've really been trying not to be so caustic around you, but sometimes it just happens. But I thought we were—"

"I did too," Alexis said hastily. "But I just feel like—"

Feel like what, Alexis? she asked herself. *What I feel like is spending the whole day with you again. Getting to know you better, feeling your hand on my arm and your eyes linking up with mine. . .*

"Hey, cool! You coming too, Ty?"

They both snapped like whips as Karl took the porch steps in one stretch of his bony legs. He stood in front of them reveling in the delicious anticipation. Alexis closed her eyes.

"No, I can't make it this morning," Ty said. "But what do you say we do some rock climbing this afternoon, you and I? Unless you've got him booked for the day."

Alexis knew Ty was talking to her, but she couldn't look at him. She leaned over to put her shoes on. "No, we'll be back by lunch."

"Yeah, I gotta be," Karl said, his voice dipping into his old sarcasm. "She can't make the peanut butter sandwiches without me."

"I assume you're talking about Sigrid," Ty chided him gently as they went down the steps together.

The conversation continued as they drifted off toward Clifford. Alexis tied and retied her shoes three times. Ty didn't get it. He was just going to be angry now because she was snubbing him, and it was all going to go back to the way things were before, when they sniped at each other.

Well, that's the way it is, she thought as she closed up the cabin. *I'm doing what I think is right.*

Then why, she wondered as she pulled the Chevy onto Eden Road, did she get another stabbing pain right in the pit of her stomach when she looked in the rearview mirror and saw Ty standing by the sign boulder? There was nothing in his eyes but hurt.

She swallowed hard and said, "Look for a radio station."

Karl fumbled with the knob through several sets of static, then flipped it off. He slung his arm across the back of the seat and crossed one boot over his other knee.

"So, what's up with you today?" he asked in a way beyond his years.

"We're going to go get candy. I'm into it."

"Right. Did you know that's how my family turned me into a delinquent?"

"What?"

"That's what one of my shrinks said."

Alexis snorted. "Your parents paid good money to have some guy tell you you're a delinquent because they took you to get candy when you met a commitment?"

"No. She said when my parents would be all messed up about something and I'd say, like, what's wrong or something, and they'd say, 'Oh nothing—everything's fine—you just run along and play,' that's crazy-making. Sure looked like they were messed up to me, but if they said they weren't, then I must be the one who's messed up."

Alexis tightened her grip on the steering wheel. It made sense.

"So," he went on, "they'd hit the bottle and I'd hit the streets. You gotta do something with how messed up you feel inside."

"You think I'm messed up inside?" Alexis said.

"Why else would you be white knuckling the steering wheel?"

Alexis looked down at her hands. Her fingernails were meeting her palms as if she were in danger of falling from a trapeze.

"It's Ty, huh? You guys have a fight?"

"No," she said firmly. "Contrary to what you put in my drawing, we don't have enough of a relationship to have anything to fight about."

"Oh. I thought you guys were, like, an item."

Alexis looked at him quickly. Karl was playing with his fingers as if he were disappointed.

"We were just getting to be friends," she said more softly. "But I don't think it's going to work out."

"Why not?"

Alexis actually opened her mouth to answer, then clamped her lips shut.

"None of my business." His voice was suddenly chilly.

"I'm just really confused," she said. "Ty is confusing me more. I've got to do what I think is right, and that isn't always the thing that makes everybody happy."

"And that's why I should get a thing going with God?" Karl said. "So I can be even more miserable doing the right thing than I am now?"

Alexis pulled Clifford into a parking place in front of Tuck's and turned to face him. "You have to look at the long run. When you do what God wants you to do, it might hurt for awhile, but eventually you get a peace and it's all right."

Karl shrugged. "I don't think I can wait," he said.

I don't know if I can either, she thought.

❧

As it turned out, there was nothing like a candy store to take the edge off the ache in Alexis's chest. It took Karl thirty minutes to select just the right combination of saltwater taffy. Alexis took almost as long to decide between the peanut turtles and the divinity fudge, and at Karl's suggestion she opted for both.

They sat on a shaded bench out front and dug into their bags. It was the same bench, Alexis realized, where she'd found Ty engrossed in the Song of Solomon. Suddenly, the ache returned, and she focused on Karl.

"So, you're surviving your visit with your grandparents," she said.

Karl stuffed a third piece of soft taffy into his mouth. "This isn't like when you visited your granny when you were a kid, okay? This is more like a continuation of my parole."

Alexis nodded ruefully. "I know. I was just trying to, you know, make you feel better."

Karl concentrated on folding a taffy paper into the tiniest square he could. "You already have." His voice was unnatural, but Alexis knew the words were sincere. "Ty, too. I wouldn't mind being like him because he isn't a dork. He does cool stuff, and he thinks for himself. Nobody tells him who to be or what to do—"

He suddenly stopped and shrugged. Alexis watched as he withdrew into his oversized T-shirt. She reached across the bench for his arm.

"What, Karl?" she said. "What were you going to say?"

"Nothing."

"No fair! We've come this far. Come on."

But he got up and took off down the street, the candy bag clutched under his arm. Alexis snatched up her own sack and went after him. He took a sharp turn down a side street and led her to the Lumber Wharf. Halfway down the pier, he stopped and leaned heavily on the railing. Alexis reached him, out of breath, in time to hear him say with a voice full of tears, "I want to be like Ty is, but it's never gonna happen."

It was all Alexis could do not to put her arms around him. As it was, she put a hand on his shoulder and squeezed. He didn't pull away. His head was down on the railing, and the tears were running down his face without a sound.

"I know it looks like it can't happen, Karl," she said. "I don't blame you for believing that. But that isn't all there is, really."

"That's all there is for me, and I've got the record to prove it," he answered bitterly.

"The record of the past, but what about today?"

"Today—"

Alexis put her head on the railing so that her face was right beside his. "Today you're walking around Rockport eating as much candy as you want with somebody who cares. And today you're going to go rock climbing with somebody else who cares about you. That's more than most people have—today."

"What about tomorrow?" he asked. He lifted his head and searched her eyes in desperation.

"I don't know about tomorrow," Alexis said. "I try to let God take care of that."

"I knew we'd get to that," he said. But this time no protective shade came over his face.

Alexis gave his arm another squeeze before letting go. "We don't have to talk about that now. But if you're ever ready, you know where to find me."

He stared at the splintering boards of the pier for a minute and then abruptly stuck out his candy bag. "You want to try any of this?"

"Yeah. I saw you got root beer flavor."

"They're pretty lame. You can have all of those."

They strolled back down the pier toward Front Beach, dipping into each other's bags. Karl sprawled out on the sand and stuffed two pieces into each cheek. Saliva ran out of the corners of his mouth and his eyes closed as he savored the moment. He was the picture of pleasure.

"I wish I had my camera," Alexis said.

Karl sat up and shifted the candy to one side of his mouth. "I have your camera," he said, his squirrellike cheeks bulging.

"How did you end up with it?"

"When we left the beach yesterday, Ty and I picked up everything because you were too wiped out. He picked up the bag, but I got the camera. I guess you didn't put it back in."

"That's right. You guys made me come in the water right after I took that last shot."

"I wrapped it in my towel, and it ended up getting in with my stuff."

"Don't worry about it. I'll get it later. But I hate missing this shot. Look at you!"

Karl propped himself up on one elbow and wiggled his eyebrows. "We can always come back and do it again."

Alexis cuffed him across the top of his brown head and sprawled out in the sand herself. A family passed them with a stroller, the wife in matching top and shorts casting a puzzled look behind her at the young woman with the wild hair entertaining the scary-looking adolescent in the skater pants.

Alexis smiled at her. *Hey, Lady,* she wanted to say to her, *with God the possibilities are endless.*

But then she thought of Ty and her thoughts clouded. He wasn't even a possibility, and she needed to stop thinking of him that way.

"We'd better get back if you're going to do your lunch thing," she said to Karl.

"Yay," Karl said without emotion. "I have a real future as a short-order cook."

"But today," Alexis said, "you're a candy-eating rock climber."

"Yeah," Karl said. She couldn't tell whether he meant it.

When they got back to Rocky Shoals, Franz was sitting in his truck at the bottom of the driveway.

"What's up with this?" Alexis asked Karl.

He grunted, the way Franz himself always did.

Franz leaned out the driver's side window and waved.

"I think he wants me to stop," Alexis said, chuckling. "Do you think he's actually going to say something to me?"

"Sigrid's not with him," Karl said.

"That would be the difference."

But Alexis's laugh died away when Franz got out of the truck and hurried stiffly over to Clifford. There was a sense of urgency in the way he held his shoulders, and his face was as stiff as his walk. There was no hello, no smile. Only, "Karl needs to come with me."

Karl lifted himself out the passenger window. "What for?"

"You just come," Franz ordered. He turned and headed for the passenger side of his truck.

"Is there a problem, Mr. Goedert?" Alexis called after him.

The old man jerked his white head around, and even the shock of hair on top seemed to stand on end as he glared. Alexis felt a shock go through her.

"This is a family matter, thank you," he said coldly. "Karl!"

Karl didn't look at Alexis as he slithered out of the car and stomped, head down, to his grandfather's truck. The boyishness was gone from his shoulders, the hope vanished from his face. The candy bag was left crumpled on the seat beside her.

Franz climbed into the driver's seat and waited. There was nothing else for Alexis to do but pull up the driveway. She watched in her rearview mirror and saw Franz wait until she was behind the main building before he pulled out.

I'm not going to follow you, Pal, she thought angrily. *I'm going to go inside and get some answers!*

But Sigrid met her halfway across the wide hall, and her sparrow's eyes were snapping. "I warned you, Alexis," she said. "You cannot say I did not warn you!"

Chapter 14

Alexis stared at her.

"I'm involved whether you like it or not—"

"Just as I warned you not to be." Sigrid's voice shook like a brittle leaf.

"You warned me that I would get hurt," Alexis said, seething. "But so far I haven't found anything but joy in my friendship with Karl."

"Really?" Sigrid arched her neck and drew her shoulders up as if she stood at five-foot-ten. "Come with me," she said.

It was more a command than a request. Sigrid marched through the French doors and into the sitting room with Alexis filing behind her.

The only thing missing is the handcuffs, Alexis thought angrily.

But when Sigrid reached for the object on the table and held it straight out in front of her, Alexis's anger faded to bafflement.

"That's my camera," she said.

"Indeed. I found it in Karl's room."

Alexis put her hands up to stop her. "I know, Sigrid," she said. "He picked it up on the beach yesterday, and it accidentally got mixed up with his stuff."

Sigrid didn't blink. "There are no accidents with Karl. He knows exactly what he is doing."

"He told me outright what had happened. It was completely innocent—"

"It is innocent because he told you it is?" Sigrid gave a hard laugh. "You are fifteen years behind the rest of us, Alexis. We have been learning Karl's tricks almost from the day he was born. There is no innocence. The boy has—what do you call it?—hoodwinked you."

She was still holding out the camera and Alexis snatched it from her.

"I understand your anger," Sigrid said. "But don't direct it at me. I tried to tell you—"

"You're wrong!" Alexis cried. "He didn't steal this, and I won't press charges!"

"What you are doing is covering up for your failed attempt to rehabilitate a boy not even his own family has been able to change."

"No!" Alexis could barely keep from stamping her foot.

"No?" Suddenly Sigrid's snapping eyes narrowed hawkishly. "Then tell me something, my dear. Did you not cover up for Karl when Jacquie D'Angelo's bracelet was stolen?"

Alexis froze as Sigrid studied her face, her chin pulled up in an attitude of triumph.

"He took her bracelet," Sigrid said. "You knew it, and you allowed him to get away with it."

It's as if she's winning something here, not losing her grandson, Alexis thought. *I have to stop this.*

But nothing would come out of her mouth.

"Your silence is admission enough," Sigrid said.

"Admission of what?" said a voice from the doorway.

Alexis closed her eyes. She had never been so glad to hear Ty enter a room.

Sigrid turned toward him, her voice commanding. "Come in, Ty," she said. "You are part of this as well. I warned you too."

"So you did," Ty said.

Alexis could feel him behind her. Her chest ached.

"So what's the deal?" he said. "You're accusing Alexis of helping Karl cover up for Jacquie losing her little bauble? That makes no sense.

"In the first place, your grandson is extremely intelligent. Why would he take Jacquie's bracelet, then drape it on a bush for her to find? And if he did, what would Alexis have had to do with it? I think she's smarter than that too. Hey, Alexis."

He touched her elbow lightly. Alexis didn't dare look at him.

"Yeah?" she said.

"If you were going to cover Karl's crime, wouldn't you have found a better spot than a bush to hang the evidence on?"

Alexis almost hugged him.

"I'd definitely have gone with sending it through the mail—" she said.

"Slipping it under the mat—"

"Dropping it into her soup at dinner—"

"Stop it, both of you!" Sigrid's tiny hands were bunched into balls. "When Jacquie's bracelet was taken, I knew it was Karl, but I didn't want to believe it. I wanted to think Franz and I were doing some good for him here. When she found it, I rejoiced with the rest of you, but inside," she paused to tap her chest, "I knew that it was only a matter of time before something else was missing. I cannot close my eyes to it anymore." She nodded toward the camera in Alexis's hand. "I don't care what he has told you. Karl took that with the intention of keeping it. He was only covering for himself this time."

"Sigrid, that's absurd!" Alexis cried.

"It is a crime, and the boy must be punished. I have told his mother before the only way he's going to learn is to be held accountable for what he does. No more psychiatrists and therapists and counselors and social workers and tests to determine whether there is some hormonal imbalance. We turn him over to the proper authorities, and they do with him what they will."

"Come on, Sigrid," Ty said. "That would be appropriate if Karl had actually committed a crime, but he didn't steal Alexis's camera. Besides, we've seen some real progress in the kid."

"We have," Alexis said. "Just today he was talking about—"

"He has fooled the best in the business," Sigrid said imperiously. "I have made up my mind, and neither of you has the power to stop me. Now," she held up a finger as if she were scolding two mischievous children, "if there is anymore interference in this, I will have to ask you both to leave as well."

She turned on her heel, but Alexis couldn't let her go.

"Sigrid, what's going to happen to Karl now?"

Sigrid didn't turn around as she answered. "Franz has taken him to the police station to find out the proper procedure. I have a call in to his mother in Paris. We shall just have to see."

And with that she did go. Alexis felt as if a hole had been drilled into her heart. She raked her hands through her hair, but what she really wanted to do was throw her arms around Ty and let him hold her.

"I don't care what she says, we can do something about this," Ty said.

Alexis swallowed hard. "What?"

"I don't know yet. Look, what do you say we take a walk on the beach and try to process this? Between the two of us, we should be able to figure out something."

Alexis held onto the arm of the chair. She wanted nothing more than to hike down the sand with her arm crooked through Ty's, venting her anger, basking while he vented his, then stopping at a pile of rocks to sort it through.

But I can't, she railed at herself. *I can't because there's so much more to it than that. I wouldn't be doing it just for Karl, I'd be doing it for me, and against Lance.*

"Or not," Ty said softly.

There was a tangle of emotions in his brown eyes, a little confusion, a touch of understanding. But all she could remember as he shook his head and left the room was the sadness.

❧

Alexis spent the afternoon listlessly photographing the lighthouses again. There was a storm brewing, and the tall towers looked braver than ever, standing up to the threatening wind and the ever-rising waters.

Braver than I am, she decided. She knew now how Karl must feel all the time: Nothing you do will make any difference in the way things turn out.

Just before dinner, Franz's truck pulled into the driveway, and Alexis openly craned her neck toward the front seat. Karl was there beside his grandfather, his face nearly suctioned to the side window, lip curled.

Alexis followed them around to the back of the main building in time to see Franz jam the Ford into park and point toward the garage that stood apart from the rest of the structures. She'd never noticed the room above the garage, but now as she watched Karl amble toward it, willing himself not to care, she realized that was where he stayed. As the rain started to slice at a slant across the compound and across Karl, Alexis folded her arms around herself. Just what the boy needed—isolation from the very people who were supposed to love him.

To her left, Marina-Natasha skittered across the lawn toward the main building for dinner, her boots sucking at the mud that was already forming.

There's no way I'm going in there and eat the food those people serve, Alexis decided bitterly. *Maybe Sigrid's right. Maybe I ought to just leave.*

As she watched Karl disappear into the garage where there was obviously an inside staircase, she turned back toward the beach. She'd stay at Rocky Shoals until he left. For where? A boys' home? Juvenile detention? Jail?

Alexis shuddered and broke into a run.

❧

By six o'clock the wind that kicked up whitecaps and brought in the haze at four each afternoon had usually died down. But tonight the wind had shifted to the east instead, and a shelf of high clouds was hurling in. The inshore waters had whipped into a nasty chop as Alexis started down the beach. Still, it rained every two or three days along the seaboard, and Alexis just tucked her head down and plodded through it. The rain would stop soon, but she wasn't sure the ache in her chest would.

I've prayed so hard, she thought miserably. *All I wanted was some peace about my art, and what have I gotten?*

More confused about Lance. Less sure that she wanted to spend her life being the lawyer's wife.

More befuddled about what her photography could possibly mean to God. During those days with Ty, she had felt closer to an answer. But nothing was really resolved, and she suspected now she'd only been using her confusion as an excuse to be near him.

And she had become more depressed about Ty. She couldn't deny her feelings for him. She was drawn to him, and what future was there for them? He obviously liked her and wanted to do things for her, but he'd done almost the same for Marina-Natasha and the Coxes, and certainly Karl. Besides, the bottom line was, he wasn't a Christian. And it didn't look as if he was ever going to be.

Which meant she was more disappointed in herself as well. She'd had three opportunities to bring other people to God since she'd been here, and she'd blown all of them.

If things work out according to God's plan, maybe that's my answer, she thought *I never should have come here. I'm not an artist, and I'm not even strong enough to b a witness.* She stopped in the rain with a jolt and threw her head back. *I need t go back to Philadelphia and be a teacher and a wife and be content with that.*

As she looked out over the blackened water, she saw an angry swell rolling in from the open sea. The ocean was churning in a violent attempt to take over the shore. Alexis wrapped her arms tightly around her body and headed for the bath.

❧

By the time she reached Rocky Shoals, her clothes and hair were plastered against her, and she was gasping for air in the wind as she angled to keep herself upright. When she reached the front porch of her cabin, she had to grab onto the railing to keep from careening sideways on the slick floorboards.

Take a bath. Get on dry clothes. Pack suitcases. That was all she could think of. And if the lines weren't down, she'd call Lance and tell him she was on her way as soon as Karl was taken away.

"Alexis!"

Alexis groaned out loud. Marina-Natasha was splashing toward her, panels of red hair stuck comically against the sides of her round face.

"Come into the main building!" she called out.

"No, that's okay!" Alexis shouted back. The wind seemed to suck the words right out of her mouth.

"Sigrid says we should all come!" Marina-Natasha shouted. "These cabins aren't safe in this kind of storm!"

Alexis nodded and backed into her cabin as Marina-Natasha slid her way back down into the mud. Alexis had no intention of joining any of them. She'd rather tough it out here.

But as she soaked in the footed bathtub, the window above her rattled as if it were being shaken by an unseen hand. Then while she was standing with her head poked into the closet looking for something to wear, the lights went out. She fumbled in the darkness for a flashlight and finally gave up. Throwing on a big sweater with her jeans and tossing a rain slicker over her head, she ran for the main building.

I'll just get a flashlight and come back, she promised herself.

But as she hurried toward the main house, she thought of Karl. He was sitting up there in that dark garage apartment, waiting for the axe to fall. Nobody should have to do that alone. What she would say to him now, she didn't have a clue, but at least she could be with him.

Darkness was fast consuming Rocky Shoals as she leaned into the wind and crossed the compound to the garage. She had to feel her way to the inside staircase, which, to her dismay, shifted under her weight as she gingerly took the steps.

Alexis tapped on the door at the top of the stairs. "Karl? It's me, Alexis."

There was no answer. Alexis stood with her hand on the doorknob, gnawing at her lip. It could be that he didn't want to talk to her. After all, none of the stuff she'd tried to tell him about hope was panning out. She'd let him down just as hard as anyone else because she'd promised more.

But something made her turn the knob and push her way inside. And something told her even as she called out his name that Karl wasn't there.

But she crept around the room, trying not to trip and calling out to Karl in the corners.

She'd been right. He wasn't there, and Alexis felt herself starting to shake.

She hurried to the large picture window that ran along the ocean side of the room. Though rain and darkness obscured it now, Karl had almost the entire shoreline framed in this window.

He had probably been standing here watching the storm and thought—what?

What thoughts ran through the head of a fifteen-year-old boy whose last hope for being anything other than a loser had just been snatched away unjustly? Did he decide there was no point in even trying anymore? Did he see more of a future out there in the storm than in this dingy room?

Somebody does care. You care. Go to him.

"Go to him, Alexis," she said aloud to herself. "You've got to find him."

She took the rickety staircase two steps at a time, but three steps across the compound she knew she wasn't going to pull this off alone. The wind was blowing so hard she could barely keep her footing.

Ty, she thought wildly. *Ty's the only one who can help me. Just one more time—we'll find Karl—then I'll go home and I'll never see Ty again.*

Breathing like a freight train, Alexis swung around and drove for the back door of the main building.

Sigrid met her in the foyer. Alexis stiffened and tried to get past her, but the elderly woman groped at her sleeve.

"Alexis," she said, "have you seen Will Cox?"

"No, I'm looking for Ty and—" She stopped. "What's going on, why are you looking for Will?"

Sigrid didn't answer but nodded grimly toward the sitting room and led the way there.

Virginia Cox was hunched into a striped chair by the fire. Ty was kneeling in front of her.

"What did he say when he left?" Ty was saying to her. "Come on, Mrs. Cox, try to think."

Alexis flew to the arm of the chair. Virginia's pixie face was swollen and blotchy and her lower lip was trembling like a child's. She latched onto Alexis's hand, though Alexis was sure she didn't know whose fingers she was clutching.

"He wanted to see the ocean in a storm," Virginia got out. "I told you, he wanted the sea in all its moods. I told him it was too dangerous."

"Do you know exactly where he was going?" Ty said.

Virginia shook her head, and her body quivered with sobs. Alexis put her arm around her and felt the rain from Virginia's jacket ooze through her own sweater. The cap of white hair stood up in wet spikes.

"You've already been out looking for him?" Alexis said.

Virginia nodded.

"Where did you go?"

Virginia clutched the sides of her face. "All the usual places he goes. Up on the hill, down Eden Road where the fishermen come out of the water, on the rocks, just above your cliff."

She looked at Ty, and so did Alexis, just in time to see fear flicker through his eyes. He stood up quickly as Sigrid hurried into the room carrying two blankets and a pile of sweats.

"Come on, my dear," she said to Virginia. "Let's get you into dry clothes and pour you some hot tea. We'll find Will, but he'll do you no good if you're in bed with pneumonia."

Her voice was warm and soothing, but the sound rattled through Alexis like a chain of icicles. She followed Ty to the window where he was staring out at the storm.

"Ty, could we go out on the porch?"

He looked down at her as if she hadn't spoken. The fear in his eyes was full blown.

"Yeah," he said. "We have to talk."

They slid out where the wind and the slicing rain drove them against the wall. Ty put his mouth close to her ear.

"This doesn't look good. Virginia said Will always went to the cliff. With this wind, he could have been washed over."

Alexis pulled her face back to search his eyes. "Ty, no. He can't even swim!"

"I'm going to go look for him, and I want you to help me if you will. You've climbed with me. I know how strong you are."

"What about the Coast Guard or somebody?" Alexis's pulse was hammering so hard she could hardly get the words out.

"They've been called, but I can't just sit around and wait. I'm the one who got him all excited about 'getting some of it on him.' I feel responsible."

He was shouting over the wind, but his words caught at Alexis's heart.

"I'll go with you," she shouted back. "But we have to look for Karl too. He wasn't up in his room where they sent him. I'm afraid he's taken off."

Ty steered her toward the door. The fear was gone from his eyes. Something iron hard and determined had taken its place. "Let's get you a hooded jacket you can move around in. Franz probably has one."

"Ty." Alexis folded her fingers around his arm. "Don't tell him or Sigrid that Karl's missing yet, please."

"Never entered my mind."

"Gusts are up to forty miles an hour," Franz told them gruffly as they started down the front steps, laden with climbing gear. "You'll be smashed against the rocks."

"And Will may already be." Ty hooked his hand around Alexis's arm and said, "Let's go."

They bent their heads against the wind and ran down the hill toward the road, which was by now a succession of rapids under the angry storm.

"Get up on my shoulders," Ty shouted. "I'll carry you across."

"I can make it!" she called back.

Ty leaned over and hauled her onto his back by one leg and one arm. "If you're going to help me, you have to do exactly as I say," he shouted.

She tucked her head down and nodded.

He slid her off at the edge of the path and pulled her arm through his. "Hold on," he said. "These gusts will lift you right off your feet. Don't let go."

Alexis locked her hand into the crook of his arm. "Holding," she shouted.

Inching his way along the slippery rock, Ty moved closer to the edge, with Alexis hanging from his arm like a ball and chain.

Alexis screamed Will's and Karl's names into the wind. But her voice was swallowed almost instantly by the jealous storm.

"Okay, we're close enough," Ty called to her. "I'm going to get down on my knees and see if I can see anything down below. Hold onto this rock, and don't let go!"

"Okay!"

Ty watched as she wrapped her arms around a piece of jutting rock, then he went down on all fours and crawled cautiously toward the edge.

"Will!" Alexis cried out again. "Karl, where are you?" She had no hope that they would hear her, but she had to do something. She couldn't just sit here and watch Ty go over the side.

But as she opened her mouth to scream again, the ocean seemed to erupt. A violent swell crashed against the rock wall and spewed its angry venom on top of them. Alexis buried her face against the rock and hung on. Just as brutally as it had collided with them, the wave then receded back into the ocean, tugging at Alexis to let go.

Tearing her face away from the rock, she strained her eyes toward the cliff. "Ty!" she screamed. "Ty, are you all right?"

There was a returning shout, and Ty's long legs disentangled themselves from a rock a few feet away.

"I heard somebody yell!" he shouted to her. "There's somebody down there!"

He crawled toward the edge again. Alexis watched in horror as another black and monstrous wave gathered speed and charged toward him.

"Hold on, Ty!" She flung her arms around the rock as the water smashed into the cliff once more. It was sucked with a vengeance back to the sea, and once again Alexis shouted to Ty and squinted through the rain and the tears to see him.

He was on his belly at the cliff's edge, shouting.

Then she heard it. A voice was answering from somewhere in the storm. Alexis sat up straight.

"Will?" she screamed.

"Lex—"

This wasn't an old man's voice. It was strong and clear, and scared.

"Karl?" she shouted.

Ty pulled his head up from the edge and whirled to face her. "It's them," he said. His voice was like lead. "They're down on the ledge, Taxi. They're fifty feet down."

Chapter 15

Ty held out his hand, and Alexis grabbed onto it while he pulled her to the edge. Fear laced her insides like strands of barbed wire, but she willed herself to look over the side.

Karl was kneeling on the second level. With his wedge of dark hair pasted to his head by the rain and his face chapped crimson by the punishing wind, Karl looked like a little boy banished to the corner.

As Ty shone his flashlight down on them, Alexis gasped when she realized Karl was holding a limp body across his lap.

"It's Will!" Alexis cried.

"Karl!" Ty shouted down. "Is he breathing?"

It looked as if Karl were frozen with his eyes round as wafers.

"Put your face close to his!" Alexis cried out.

With a jerk, Karl bent over, and Alexis held her breath. Finally, he nodded up at them.

"Are you hurt?" Ty called down.

Karl shook his head, then shouted something Alexis couldn't hear.

"What did he say?"

"I can't hear him. I think he's trying to tell us something about Will."

Alexis slid down on her stomach and stuck her head out over the edge. "Show us!"

Karl nodded and put his hand in the air, then ran it slowly down his back. When he brought both hands together in front of him as if he were breaking a stick, Alexis looked at Ty. His eyes were closed, and his jaw muscles wrenched.

"He thinks Will has a broken back," Alexis said.

"We've got to get down there and bring him up before they both get washed away," Ty said.

Alexis looked down at the ocean churning violently below them. How Karl had kept himself and Will from being dashed from the shelf she had no idea, but she was sure he couldn't do it for much longer.

"Can you get back to the main house and tell them where to send the rescue squad?" Ty shouted to her.

Alexis looked doubtfully up the rocky path she'd barely been able to navigate with Ty holding her up.

"Whoa!" Ty cried. "Get down!"

He brought his arm down on her back and flattened Alexis to the rocks. Seconds later, another vicious breaker surged over them. Alexis clung to Ty with both hands, and as the water ran back into the ocean, she was afraid to look over the side again.

"Karl!" Ty shouted. His voice was raucous and hoarse as he craned his neck over the edge. He stuck his forefinger to his thumb and held it out.

Alexis scrambled to the edge and started to cry. Karl was giving the okay sign back; Will was still strung across his lap.

"I'll go!" Alexis shouted to Ty.

"Just hold onto rocks!" Ty said. "And please be careful."

She nodded with more bravery than she felt and started for the path. The stony surface of the ground was like a sheet of ice, and her left boot shot off to the side. Alexis curled up and rolled, then scooted herself along on her stomach. She was in several inches of water. It wouldn't be long before the cliff would be completely submerged.

Alexis looked back over her shoulder. A flash of light swooped over her through the blinding rain, and for a moment she froze in its beam.

Of course, she told herself, *the twin lighthouses.* The lighthouses were still standing tall in the tempest, still searching. Alexis got up on her hands and knees.

"Dear God, please let me get there," she cried. "And please let them be there when I get back."

Behind her, Alexis heard another swell crash against the cliff, but she didn't look back.

Praying and crying and clawing her way along the rocks, Alexis finally reached the rain-swollen road. Water was racing down it like an avalanche.

Wildly, Alexis looked around and saw a thick branch floating toward her. She grabbed it and stuck it end-down into the water. The water was only about knee-deep, and she knew if she used the stick as a crutch, she could probably get across without being swept away.

"Please, God," she kept praying. "Please, just let me get there in time."

Clutching the top of the branch with both hands, Alexis pulled herself into the water. The stick held fast in the muck below her.

"Okay, okay, I can do this, I can do it."

She yanked the branch up and stuck it in farther ahead. Just a few more yards and she'd be there. Her hands ached from hanging on, but she clutched harder. As she did, her fingers slipped and the branch careened out of her hand. When she lurched to reach for it, her body tumbled face-first into the water.

Alexis tried to scramble up, but the flood was moving too fast. She could feel the water pulling her under, relentlessly, like a lead ball. Frantically, she flailed her arms, but the surface surged above her as the weight of her boots and the rush of the water held her down.

I'm drowning! was all her mind could tell her. *Please, God, no! I'm drowning.*

Then her arm caught on something hard, and she grabbed at it. Alexis heaved herself to the surface on the point of a rock. A pair of arms reached down and pulled her up the rest of the way.

"You're all right now, Girl," someone shouted. "I've got you, you're all right."

Alexis clung to his sleeves and let herself be dragged halfway up the hill before she could get enough air to shout.

"Franz!" she cried. "We've found Will and Karl!"

The old man held her by the shoulders as he peered into her face. "What? Karl?"

The wind whipped the words away as soon as they left her lips, but Alexis kept shouting. "He's down on the second ledge with Will. Will's unconscious; they need help!"

Franz bolted toward the road, but Alexis grabbed at his jacket. "Get the rescue squad, Franz!" she cried. "Ty is going down for them, but he needs a stretcher! Karl thinks Will has a broken back! I have to go back and help."

Before her eyes, Franz's face went blue. Alexis grabbed at his collar. "Are you all right? Franz?"

He nodded vaguely, then his eyes took fire again. "They're on their way," he shouted to her. "I'll get you across the road again, then I'll wait for them."

Alexis nodded and took the old man's arm. Unsteadily, they made their way to the surging road, and Franz led her across. His gnarled hands shook in hers, but his feet were steady. She watched from the other side long enough to be sure he got back across, then she went down on her hands and knees and began to crawl toward the cliff.

The rain was blowing across her in sheets by now, and it was so dark she couldn't see farther than her hands could reach. Only the beams from the lighthouses illuminated the way ahead in periodic sweeps.

"Taxi, over here! Just a few more feet!" a chopped-up voice cried to her.

Alexis stuck out her hand, and a strong wet one curled around it. Ty pulled her into the circle of his arm.

"I told Franz!" she shouted to him above the din. "The rescue squad is on the way."

"We can't wait for them!" Ty shouted back. "It's getting higher. I have to go down now!"

Alexis looked over the edge of the cliff. Karl, waist-high in water, was holding Will up against his chest to keep his face above the surface. The sight slammed into Alexis like an axe.

"What do we do?" she asked Ty as calmly as she could.

"We're already set." He pointed to the two nylon straps that held a line to two rocks. The carabiners were already in place and Ty had the rope in his hand.

"Where's your seat?" Alexis shouted to him.

Ty handed the red webbed apparatus to her. "You'll need it."

"Does Karl have the rope on the other end?"

"It'll be all right. Put that on, and when I get down, I'll be your safety person."

"Ty—"

"We don't have any choice."

Helplessly, she watched Ty lower himself over the side, wind whipping at his face and nearly blowing his cheeks sideways.

"Put that on!" he barked at her before his head disappeared from view.

It was hard to tell the tears from the rain that smacked at her face as she stepped into the harness and went to the edge to wait. Through the relentless rain and the plunging sea, she saw Ty reach the bottom, just as another wave crashed against the wall and obliterated all three of them.

"Ty!" Alexis screamed. Then she pulled herself into a fetal position on the ground and let the water flood over her. *If he's gone when I pull my head up*, she thought frantically, *what will I do? Oh, God, please help us.*

"Alexis!"

She clung to the edge of the cliff and looked down. Ty was on the shelf, his streaming face turned toward her.

"I need you to rappel down!" he shouted. "Just like you did before."

It isn't just like before, she wanted to cry. *I'll be smashed against the rocks if another wave comes.*

Her heart slamming against her chest, she searched the ocean with her eyes. The storm was still roiling the water into angry points, but in the lights from Thacher Island, she could see that there were no monstrous breakers threatening on the horizon. If she were going to go, she had to go now.

"I'm coming down!" she cried over the edge.

"Okay. Don't worry! I've got you!"

Muttering one long rambling prayer, Alexis took the rope in her hands and backed slowly over the wall. She held her left hand out to her side to keep from sliding down too fast, but she also knew from the tug on the rope that Ty was holding her back as well.

"One foot at a time," she said out loud.

Slowly, she made her way down. She didn't dare look down, but she could tell from the nearness of Ty's voice that she was almost to the bottom.

"Please, just let me get there," she prayed. She pulled her left arm in and quickened her steps. Her right foot slid crazily, and she thrust out her left hand to stop herself.

"Keep going!" Ty shouted. "Don't stop, come on!"

Alexis jerked the rope toward her and tore down the side of the cliff, both feet flying away from her with every slippery step. Out of control, she slithered to a halt into Ty's arms. Before she could pull away, he flattened her to the ground and fell on top of her. Seconds later, they were covered with water.

An eternity passed before the water receded and Alexis came up choking. Ty had already pulled himself up and was leaning over Karl's lap. He tilted Will's head back with his mouth open and listened. His hand fumbled for Will's wrist.

"Is he okay?" Alexis shouted.

Ty gave her a panic-stricken look. "He's not breathing. I can't get a pulse!"

Alexis crawled to him and watched in horror as Will's face turned blue in the circle of light from Ty's flashlight.

"Can't you do something?" Karl cried. His ruddy, storm-torn face was gathered into a knot of fear. He clung to Will's limp body as if he held a cherished teddy bear in his arms. "We can't just let him die!" he screamed.

"We won't," Alexis shouted back. "Ty, do you know CPR?"

He looked at her and she read the answer in his eyes, the same answer she would have had to give him: *I've had the training, but I've never done it on an actual person.*

"Let's go," she said. "Karl, keep his head back in your lap and hold his wrist. Let us know the minute you get a pulse."

Karl nodded numbly.

"I'll do mouth to mouth. You start on his chest," Alexis said.

Ty nodded grimly and they went to work.

She felt rather than saw Ty put one hand over the other over Will's heart and heard him count one, two. When she heard three, she put her mouth over Will's and breathed. As she pulled her head up to look, his chest began to fall. Ty gave three more quick pushes with his hands, and Alexis leaned over to breathe again.

"One, two, three!" Ty shouted. Again, Alexis breathed. Over and over they took their turns, Alexis listening to Ty, Ty watching her.

Please, Alexis's soul shouted. *Please let him live. Let this be Your breath I breathe into him, Lord.*

"I got it!" Karl cried.

Alexis glued her eyes to Will's chest. With a jerk it rose on its own, and Will gasped and coughed. Ty snatched up the old man's wrist and hung on. He closed his eyes in relief.

"He's back. Okay, Taxi, let's get his knees propped up, right?"

"We need something to cover him with! Here, Karl, help me get this jacket off."

"Hello! How are we doing down there?"

All three heads bent back. From above a brilliant light shone down on them, the bright red slicker of a rescue worker reflected in the glare.

"We've got him breathing again, but hurry!" Ty shouted.

"We've got a stokes!" the man called down. "We'll just lower it down to you. There's a backboard on it. Can you handle that?"

Alexis whispered, "Thank You, God."

It took less than three minutes for the paramedics to lower a basket stretcher down over the cliff and for Alexis, Karl, and Ty to slide the backboard under Will and lift him onto it. It didn't occur to Alexis until Will's cradle had reached the top that there hadn't been a major wave since she'd first reached the bottom. Fearfully, she looked over her shoulder. The ocean was still choppy, but the rain had slowed to a miserable drizzle, and even the wind was no longer whipping brutally against them.

"Okay, let's get you folks up now," someone called down to them.

Alexis unbuckled her harness. "Karl first," she said.

"What?" he said.

"We have to get you to the top, Guy," Ty said. "Just slip into this little gadget here, and they'll pull you right up."

Karl stared in terror at the harness Ty was pulling over his legs.

"You got down here," Ty said. "Getting back up's the easy part."

"How did you get down here?" Alexis asked as she cinched in the belt.

Karl looked at her blankly, his eyes still round with fright. "I have no idea," he said.

Karl was hoisted to the top like a fish being reeled in. The rescue workers tossed the harness back down and Ty held it out for Alexis. When she was firmly tucked into it and the rope was checked, she felt Ty wrap himself around her from behind.

"You don't mind if I hitch a ride, do you?" he said. "I've been down here about long enough."

Alexis leaned back against his wet chest and closed her eyes. With a gentle jerk, they left the ground.

At the top of the cliff, three paramedics were huddled around Will. Virginia was at his head, her hands around his oxygen mask, her voice praying tremulously into the rain. Karl stood apart from the scene, and even through the darkness and the mist, Alexis could see his shoulders shaking.

With fumbling fingers, she unhooked the rope from her harness and ran to him. His arms went around her and hung on like the frightened child he was, and he sobbed into her neck. Sobs broke out of Alexis's chest too. It was several minutes before she realized a third set of tears had joined theirs. She and Karl and Ty held on and cried until Will was loaded into the ambulance.

"We've got him stabilized," a paramedic said to them. "You guys did a great job."

"What a team," Ty said into Alexis's hair.

Alexis closed her eyes to savor the moment.

❧

Sigrid was standing in the foyer when Alexis, Ty, and Karl straggled in through the back door of the main building with Franz and one of the rescue workers behind them.

"We've got some heroes for you!" the rescue worker called out to her. "These people do nice work."

Alexis turned to grin at him. When she pivoted around, Sigrid had Karl by the arm.

"What were you thinking of?" she shouted at him. "Yourself, just as always! People had to risk their lives to come after you!"

In a horrible frozen moment, Sigrid raised her hand behind her head, and Karl flinched like a cowering dog. In that same moment, Alexis tore her arm away from Ty and flew at her.

"Don't touch him!" she screamed. "Don't you touch him! He risked his life! He was the one who found Will and went after him, only you would never think that. You have never looked to see who he is! Never!"

"Easy, Taxi."

Ty's voice eased into her ear as he took her by the shoulders and pulled her back. Alexis tried to wriggle away, but he held on. Another pair of hands wrapped themselves around her arm, and she realized it was Karl.

"This is a good boy, Sigrid," Alexis said, her breath coming on like a smoking engine. "It's about time you stopped judging him and punishing him and started loving him."

Sigrid jutted out her chin and stared at Alexis with glittering eyes. Before she could open her mouth, heavy boots thumped the wood floor and Franz crossed the foyer in two steps.

"Sigrid," he commanded. All heads turned toward him. "Enough."

She didn't move, except to clamp her lips together.

"I'd suggest some hot soup and dry clothes for these folks," the rescue worker interjected. He clapped his hand on Ty's back, then turned and left.

I don't blame you, Pal, Alexis thought wearily. *I'd want out of this crazy place too, if I were you.*

Alexis wasn't sure how she ended up with a cup of soup in her hands or how she came to be wrapped in a blanket next to the fire in the main sitting room. By the time she was aware of where she was, the only other people around were Ty, sitting on the floor beside her in his own blanket, and Karl, curled up, asleep, on the Victorian sofa.

"Poor guy," Alexis muttered. "He's been through a lot tonight."

"And you haven't?"

"You did all the work. I just took orders."

Ty grinned down at her. "I wasn't talking about going over the cliff. I was talking about Sigrid."

Alexis shuddered and groped for a new subject. She looked up at the spikes of hair that stuck out of the top of Ty's head and chuckled. "Nice 'do. Although, I'm sure I'm looking particularly attractive myself."

"I love a woman with mud in her curls."

Ty reached up and touched a tendril that had escaped from her ponytail, then pulled his hand away. Alexis felt a pang that was becoming painfully familiar.

"You were amazing out there," she said. "Will would have died if it hadn't been for you. Maybe Karl too."

"You've got some guts yourself."

Before she could stop herself, she said, "Do you love a woman with guts too?"

His eyes widened and she jerked her face away.

Alexis, why did you say that? she thought. And then she felt a warm hand cup under her chin. Ty pulled her face toward him.

"I do, Taxi," he said huskily.

Her voice came out in a whisper. "You do what?"

"I do love a woman with guts."

Ty's hand slid to her hair and pulled her face to his. His kiss was soft and warm, and endless.

She didn't open her eyes until her face was safely buried in his blanket. When she did, she saw Lance's face, hurt and angry and confused.

She put her palms against Ty's chest and pushed away. He let her go easily.

"I'm sorry, Taxi," he said. His face was smeared with guilt. "I shouldn't have done that."

Alexis got to her knees and let her blanket drop behind her. "It's okay. I shouldn't have let you."

A "let me ask you this" trembled on his lips, but before the words came, she scrambled to her feet. "I think I better go."

"Yeah," he said softly. "I think you better."

The tears came before she got to the back porch, but she held back the sobs until she was face down on the sleigh bed. Before she tumbled off into an anguished sleep, one last thought burned all the way to the bottom of her soul.

She had never felt like that when Lance kissed her.

Chapter 16

As the sun filtered through the curtains the next morning, Alexis fumbled her way to the window seat. Only hours before, the sky and the ocean had thrown a tantrum that seemed never-ending. Yet, the morning had dawned clean and bright.

But despite the unblemished azure overhead and the crisp shine of the sun reflecting off of windows and doorknobs, the evidence of the storm was strewn everywhere. Tree branches were scattered around the compound like blown-away garbage, and chunks of glass from broken windows glinted on the lawn.

Alexis slumped against the curtains and wrapped her arms solemnly around one of the ubiquitous pillows. The storm might be over outside, but it still raged inside her. Her heart felt as if it, too, had been broken into countless jagged pieces.

What happened last night? she asked herself. And yet she already knew the answer. She'd known it since—when?

The day she and Ty shared the picnic on the cliff?

The afternoon they rode the waves with Karl?

The night they took Jacquie to the airport and she gave him the Bible to read?

Alexis tossed the pillow aside and paced across the hardwood floor. "I know exactly when it was," she said out loud to the golden walls. "It was the day he stuck his head inside Clifford and said, 'Welcome to Rocky Shoals. May I take your order?' " She raked her hands through the hopeless tangle of her hair. "It was the first time I saw him. That's why I forced myself to dislike him."

She flopped down on the bed. What did she really know for sure? There had to be something that was clear in her muddled mind.

I know Ty's an incredible man. I was wrong about him. He's sensitive and unselfish and warm. But he isn't a Christian.

Still, I'm drawn to him. I love being with him. I trust him.

But she was betraying Lance. She had told him there was nothing between her and Ty, and now there was, and it was wrong.

I've learned so much from Ty. I'm not the same person I was when I came here. I want him to know that. I don't want him to think I'm angry with him for what happened last night.

There was no answering voice for that one. There couldn't be anything wrong with letting Ty know that she thought he was a wonderful human being.

You don't have to tell him you're in love with him.

Alexis sat straight up on the bed and held her head in her hands. She knew it was true. She did love him.

"But there's no future with him!" she cried hopelessly. Her voice broke. She could love Ty all she wanted, but she couldn't do anything about it. He moved in a different world. Sure, he had shown an interest in the Lord, but it had proven to be nothing more than intellectual curiosity. The Bible was good literature to him.

And there was Lance.

Pain shot through her, and she got up again and moved restlessly to the sitting room. Even if there were some purpose in telling Ty she loved him, she couldn't do it before she saw Lance again. No matter what happened, she owed him that. They had a history together. They were brother and sister in Christ.

There was a soft knock on the door.

"Just a minute!" she called.

She made a dive for a pair of shorts to slide on under her T-shirt and swiped at her face with the back of her hand before she opened the door a crack. Karl peered back at her. With a guilty pang, she pulled it open the rest of the way. She hadn't even given him a thought since she woke up.

"Good morning!" she said. "Last time I saw you, you were in a coma on the couch."

"Yeah. She dumped me off of there about eight o'clock this morning."

"Sigrid?" Alexis bristled. "She woke you up to work breakfast? After what you went through last night?"

"No," Karl looked at the floor. "She woke me up to tell me they called off the dogs."

"You mean the police?"

"Yeah. Big of them, wasn't it?"

Alexis looked at him closely. He couldn't hide the moisture that had collected in his eyes. "That's cool. You showed them who you really are."

Karl shrugged. "I didn't do it to prove anything to anybody."

"I know," Alexis said softly. "And I'm sure they do too."

"Don't bet on it."

She caught his arm. "Come on, sit down. Tell me exactly what they said. I want all the details."

Karl followed her to the sitting room and dropped into one of the overstuffed chairs, but he was shaking his head and digging into his pocket. "I didn't come over for that. I got a message for you."

Alexis sank down on one leg on the corner of a chair. "Is it Will? Have they heard anything?"

"He's gonna be okay."

Alexis glared at him. "Don't strain yourself, Karl. Come on, what's going on?"

"He didn't have a broken back like I thought. What am I, a doctor?"

"How is he?"

"He has some internal stuff. And he already had a bad heart, so that's why he almost bought it."

"He would have 'bought it' if you hadn't gone down there. How did you know he was there?"

"I was looking out the window up in solitary confinement, planning how I was going to run away, when I saw the old dude down on the cliff. I was thinking, 'That's pretty stupid, you know,' then he biffed and went right over the side. So, I ran down there."

Alexis stared at him. "Just like that. You didn't come get anybody or anything?"

"I didn't figure there was time. Besides—" Karl folded and refolded the piece of paper he had dug out of his pocket. "I was kind of hoping I'd just go down with him. It seemed like it would have been better than jail."

Alexis took hold of his hands. "Ty and I wouldn't have let you go to jail. We'd have done something, and your grandparents really had nothing to go on. I think they were just at the end of their rope with you, and they were trying to shake you up."

"Does that mean I'm not supposed to hate them anymore?" His eyes were in slits.

"It's okay to be mad at them. I'm not into hate, myself."

He shrugged, then with an abrupt thrust, poked the piece of paper at her. "I'm supposed to give you this."

"What is it?" she asked as she accepted the now-mangled wad.

"I didn't read it!" he said defensively. "He just said give it to you, so I am."

"He?" Alexis felt the pang go through her again.

"Ty, Sherlock. You think my grandfather's writing you love letters?"

"I don't think Ty's writing me love letters either," she said quickly.

A slow smile spread over Karl's face. "Why not? You guys kissed, didn't you?"

She opened her mouth to protest, but Karl was watching her, grinning an elfin grin.

"Okay, so I wasn't asleep," he said. "As long as you were talking, I was kind of drifting around, but when it got quiet, it was weird, so I woke up and opened my eyes." He puckered his mouth. "And there you were, lips locked—"

Alexis stood up. "Thanks, Pal. And forget you saw that, okay? It was a one-time thing."

She pushed him toward the door, but he dug his boots in. The face that looked over his shoulder at her was suddenly pensive.

"What do you mean a 'one-time thing'? You guys are, like—I don't know—like a matched set or something."

The pain in her chest was pushing so hard, Alexis could barely breathe. She steered Karl firmly to the door. "Look, I'll talk to you later, okay? I better see what he has to say and I'll get back to you."

"Your people can call my people and we'll do lunch," he said coldly.

She halted in the doorway and pulled his face toward her with both hands. "It isn't like that, Karl. I just have things to figure out. I'm not putting you off, honest. We've been through too much together."

"Yeah, well, so have you and him. You dump him now, it'll be the stupidest thing you ever did."

She gave his face one last squeeze and pushed him gently out onto the porch. She was sure he was still standing there when she closed the door.

She started to peel apart the folds of the paper, damp from Karl's sweaty hands, but she went to the window seat with it still unopened between her fingers.

Did she really want to read what was on Ty's mind? Was it going to confuse her more? Or was it going to hurt?

I have to face it, she thought. *No matter what it says, I have to face it now. No more hiding. No more denying.*

Her fingers shook as she unfolded the paper and spread it out on her lap. The words swam as she read.

Taxi,
I've sought refuge behind every rock and shoal and every quip and grin
Last night I found it in the warmth of your soul
But that's a place not mine to win—
I'm leaving Rocky Shoals today
Forgive me for not saying good-bye
I can't.
Call me a coward
Call me a wimp
Call me anything you want
But please, please, please—
Don't call me a Taxi.
She's not mine to call.
> *God bless you,*
> *Ty*

Alexis blinked at the words until she couldn't see them anymore. Then she pulled the poem up to her face and cried into it. She barely heard the door creak open, then Karl was there, his arm around her shoulders.

"He said good-bye to you, didn't he?" she said bitterly. "He gave you a chance—"

"Yeah," Karl said. "But he's not in love with me."

✻

Sigrid set a table for two on the dark green wicker set on the front lawn at lunchtime. Marina-Natasha was already there, gazing dreamily out at the lazy ocean over a glass of lemonade. Alexis sat stiffly in her chair, watching the pulp dip and dive in her own glass and trying not to think of Ty. She could almost hear his banter: "Ah, the Cosmic Traveler. Did you whip out a few tunes this morning?"

"It's like it's totally resting after the storm," Marina-Natasha said.

Alexis looked up absently. "What is?"

"The ocean. But, it's like, we all do that—you know—there are storms in our lives and we fight and toss and pitch—" She paused, the last word still formed on her lips.

I've got the tossing and pitching part down, Alexis thought. *Tell me something I don't already know.*

Marina-Natasha gasped, as if the next thought had sprung unbidden into her brain. "Then, wow, there's this incredible, like, peace thing that settles in. You never thought you'd have it, but it's intense."

Alexis rested her chin in her hand. "Do you ever actually feel that?"

Marina-Natasha looked at her blankly. "What?"

"That 'incredible, like, peace thing.' "

"Totally. I feel it right now, don't you?"

Alexis picked up her fork. "No, as a matter of fact, I don't."

"Oh," Marina-Natasha said. "Drag."

They ate in silence for several minutes.

"It's awfully quiet without your friends, isn't it?"

Alexis jumped. Sigrid was at her elbow with a frosty lemonade pitcher.

The red panels of Marina-Natasha's hair bobbed in agreement. "But silence is like music in itself, you know?"

Sigrid nodded vaguely and filled their glasses. "I have news. Will Cox is out of the woods. Virginia called just a little while ago. As soon as he's able to travel, they'll be returning to Colorado. Franz and I are going to take some of their things to them at the hospital as soon as we can get away, but there's so much to be done here after the storm."

Her face was pinched and white, and her once ramrod posture was sagging under the weight of an invisible burden. She was deliberately avoiding Alexis's eyes.

"Would you like for me to take the stuff to them?" Alexis said. "I'd love to see the Coxes before they leave anyway."

Sigrid stood very still. "It's all the way in Boston."

"I don't have a problem with that." Alexis cocked her head sideways. "I'll do it if you'll let me take Karl."

Sigrid's eyes flew to hers. They were wet with tears.

"You need to do it today, then," she said. "Karl leaves tomorrow."

Alexis let her fork clatter to her plate. "Where is he going?"

"To his mother in Paris, where he belongs."

"Lisl has agreed to that?"

Sigrid looked at her sharply, and Alexis met her gaze with her pulse pounding. "I overheard, by accident," Alexis said. "But I think we're even. I think some things were told to Lance that would have been better left unsaid, if you get my drift."

Sigrid picked up their soup bowls and nodded grimly. "After we talked last night, I passed on to Lisl some things I have learned. What one night can teach you, eh? Let us hope she can apply them."

Before she could stop herself, Alexis put her hand on Sigrid's arm. "If she can't," she said, "I'm sure Karl can."

"Thank you," Sigrid said to Alexis without looking at her.

As she crossed the lawn toward the main building, Alexis heard a sigh that seemed to come from the pit of her stomach.

❧

While Sigrid packed a bag for the Coxes, Alexis wandered down the path to The Rock and sat listlessly watching the ocean lap at her feet.

It's like last night never happened, she thought. *Maybe I ought to do the same thing. Just pretend it never happened. Act like I never knew Ty Solorzano. Forget I ever came here.*

But I sent you here, and you'll know why. The still, small voice had spoken.

Alexis sat up straight on The Rock. *Dear God, You haven't answered any of my questions. How can You say You sent me here?*

There was no answer. The only thing she knew was that if God said it, sometime she would know for sure.

❧

Karl and Alexis were quiet in the Chevy until they got onto Interstate 93 and the traffic thinned out. Alexis gave him a sideways glance and noticed that he had pulled a red nylon strap out of one of his enormous pockets.

"Where'd you get that?" she said.

"Ty," he said.

"Oh." The pain in her chest hadn't gone away all day. Now it just stabbed harder.

"He said it was a souvenir of our 'little adventure.' I'm going to give it to the old man," Karl said. "You're pretty ticked at Ty, aren't you?"

She pulled her eyes away from the road long enough to give him a surprised look. "Why do you say that?"

"Because you don't want to talk about him."

Alexis held on hard to the steering wheel. She couldn't start hedging with the kid now. "I don't want to talk about him because it hurts too much."

"Because he's gone."

"Yeah."

"So, that means you love him."

"It isn't that simple."

"You either do or you don't."

"I do!" Alexis put her hand to her mouth and blinked hard to keep the road in view.

"So what's the problem?" Karl asked. "If you got it that bad for the guy, why aren't you with him?"

"I told you, it isn't that simple."

"What's complicated about it? He's hot for you too." She gave him a dark look, and he grinned wickedly. "Okay, he 'loves' you. So go for it."

"I can't."

"What's the bottom line?"

"He isn't a Christian."

There was a stunned silence. "That's it?" Karl said finally.

"That's enough for me."

"That's enough for you to settle for being miserable."

Alexis pulled to a stop behind a line of traffic waiting to exit into Boston and put her hands up to the sides of her face. Hair tumbled down between her fingers. "God won't let me be miserable for long. I'll get over it."

"You know, it's weird."

"What is?"

Karl shifted in his seat. "I was starting to believe some of the stuff you said about God. Now I don't know."

Alexis looked at him sharply. "What do you mean?"

"I've been miserable enough in my life. I don't want to believe in a God who only shovels in more."

Alexis jammed Clifford into gear and inched behind the traffic. "I'm telling you it's only temporary, Karl. It will all work out for the best in the end. God knows what He's doing."

Karl sniffed and reached for the Boston street map that lay on the seat between them. "You gotta turn in two blocks, then that turns into a one-way street, which means you have to then make a right—"

God does know what He's doing, Alexis thought as she half-listened. *I just hope I do.*

❧

Will Cox looked rested and chipper propped up in his bed, despite two IVs that ran from his arms and a plastic yoked tube that still rested under his nostrils. Virginia sat in the chair beside him, beaming even through the dark smudges of worry and fatigue that circled her eyes.

"God bless the two of you!" she cried when she saw them.

Alexis stifled a grin as the elderly woman put her arms around Karl's neck. He stood like a mortified stick.

"You precious child!" she said into his half-shaved head. "Thank the Lord you were there and that you had the courage to go down—"

"Let the man go, Virginia!" Will said. "He and I have things to discuss."

Karl wriggled away and practically ran to Will's bedside.

"Alexis." Virginia put her arms around Alexis's neck. "Thank God for you too, my love. You and Ty were amazing." She pulled away suddenly and looked around. "Where is Ty?"

Alexis took the bag to the closet. "He left this morning."

"He's not finishing the retreat?"

Alexis didn't trust herself to answer. She shook her head.

"You'll see him again, though. You two were inseparable."

When Alexis said nothing, Virginia crept up beside her and slipped an arm around her waist. "What is it?" she said. "You didn't part on good terms, after all that happened?"

Alexis looked down at her, and the tears came again.

"No one seems to understand," Alexis whispered. "I can't get involved; he's not a Christian. It would only end up hurting worse."

Virginia shook her head. "I'm so sorry. What will you do now?"

Alexis shrugged and took the tissue Virginia pulled out of the cuff of her blouse. "Go home. Maybe see if I can patch things up with my—with Lance."

Virginia glanced over her shoulder at the bed. Karl was standing with one leg propped up on the bed frame, snickering while Will recounted the tale from his viewpoint. When she turned back, she leaned in close to Alexis's ear.

"I'm not one to give advice about most things," she said. "But marriage is one thing I do know something about. You may not be able to be with Ty because he isn't a Christian, but don't go be with Lance just because he is. God wants you to be in love too."

"We're going to have to frame this strap, Honey," Will called across the room. "We'll hang it right next to Karl's work. He's already twice the artist I'll ever be."

Viriginia moved over to the bed, and Will proudly held up a sheet torn from a sketch book. Curiously, Alexis crept over and looked over Will's shoulder.

It was a pen and ink drawing of a large, cradlelike basket being hoisted up over a cliff, waves grabbing at the bottom like flames.

"Where are you in the picture, Karl?" Virginia asked.

Will put his hand on his chest. "He's right here," he said. "And that's where he's going to stay."

They didn't go straight back to Rocky Shoals. Alexis pulled into a cafe in Marble-head and phoned Sigrid to tell her their estimated time of arrival was unknown.

They spent most of dinner laughing over anything they could think of. Virginia's won't-take-no-for-an-answer hugs. Will's plans to hold an exhibit in Boulder when Karl became a famous artist. Alexis knew their silliness was only to keep down the sadness that was pushing up inside both of them, but she went along willingly. She'd had more sadness than she could handle already today.

When they reached the retreat center, they decided to go down to The Rock one last time. Karl grew serious.

"I have to tell you this one thing, then I'll shut up," he said.

"You won't either."

"Bet me."

Alexis punched his arm lightly. "No way. You broke me on Tuck's candy with the last wager."

He tried to look casual as he leaned back against his own rock, but Alexis could see the gears churning in his head.

"I heard you talking to that guy on the phone that day," he blurted out.

Alexis sat up. "What guy, you mean Lance?"

"Yeah, that's what you called him. The dude back home, right?"

"Right. So, what's to confess? I was probably being pretty loud out there. You couldn't help but hear."

"No, I stayed and listened on purpose, and I figured something out," he said. "I figured out if you marry him, you're going to end up like my real parents did."

Alexis put her hand to her chest to keep the pain from tearing it open. "Why do you say that?"

"Because that's the way they did it. My mother always wanted one thing, and my father wanted something else. They never should have gotten married in the first place."

"Did they have awful fights?" Alexis asked.

Karl shook his head and concentrated on the toes of his Doc Martens. "Nope," he said. "All I heard was silence. It'll kill ya."

Alexis cleared her throat. "Well, thanks."

"No problem."

The only sound for awhile was the constant washing back and forth of the waves. Alexis struggled to find something to say, but every new ebb and flow brought them closer to the moment when they'd have to say good-bye.

So much needed to be said before then. There was no way to say it all, and she couldn't seem to say any of it.

If you had to choose one thing. . ., her thoughts said to her.

"Karl," she said.

"Yeah?"

"It's my turn now. I'm going to tell you this one thing, then I'll shut up."

"You gonna preach?"

"Nope. I'm going to tell you that I'm going to pray for you. I just want you to know that."

Karl looked up at her. "That's it?"

"That's all I can do," she said.

"What are you going to pray for? That I won't go back to being a little shoplifting, graffiti-painting jerk?"

Alexis shook her head. "I don't think you will, and if you did, you'd have to take the consequences because now you know you don't have to do stuff like that. Nope, I'm just going to pray that, someday, you'll be able to pray for yourself."

"You were praying that whole night when me and the old man were down on the shelf, huh?"

"You better believe it."

"I kind of thought about it, but it sounded lame when I did it."

Alexis peered at him through the darkness. "It doesn't matter," she said. "God doesn't care. It's the believing that God cares about."

Karl seemed to be mulling that over in his mind. "You probably ought to go ahead and do it anyway," he said. "It works when you do it."

Silently, she started in right then.

⁂

It was dawn when they crossed the lawn at Rocky Shoals. Franz began loading Karl's bags into the back of the truck while Sigrid stood on the porch, watching.

Karl jammed his hands into his oversized pockets and stared at nothing in the sky. His face was working hard.

"You don't have to say anything," Alexis whispered to him. "Just remember, God loves you, and so do I."

Like a spasm, Karl lunged for her. His arms went around her neck and his face nuzzled her hair.

"I'll never see you again," he said in a broken, little boy's voice.

"I'm betting that you will," she said. "And this time I'm going to win."

Slowly, he peeled himself away from her, and without looking at her again, went to his grandfather's truck and climbed in. As Alexis turned to go, there was a grunt behind her. She looked over her shoulder at Franz.

"I want to say—" He stopped and looked at her miserably, his white shock of hair blowing helplessly in the wind.

"You don't have to say anything," Alexis said. "You never do! The other night, I saw how much you care about Karl. Just show him that you love him. That's enough thanks for me."

Franz looked at her for a moment. Then he nodded and walked stiffly to the

461

truck. As he went, he put up a hand in a grateful wave. Although he wasn't looking at her, Alexis waved back.

Karl, on the other hand, kept his eyes glued to the window on the other side of the truck while Franz rearranged his belongings in the back. Karl wasn't going to risk another look at her at this point, she knew.

As Alexis turned to go toward her cabin, out of the corner of her eye she saw Sigrid still on the porch. She was dusting the already immaculate railing with her apron. Alexis went up the steps and put her hand on the old woman's arm.

"Aren't you going to say good-bye to your grandson?" she said.

Sigrid pulled her arm away and shook her head stiffly. "I'm sure he has nothing to say to me."

"What about you?" Alexis would not give up now.

"He doesn't want to listen to me the way he does to you."

"Sigrid," Alexis said, "if I'd waited for Karl to want to hear me, we never would have talked at all. He's just a little boy. He still doesn't know how to ask for what he needs."

Sigrid didn't answer. For the thousandth time in twenty-four hours, tears welled up in Alexis's throat and she turned to go through the main building to her cabin. It was hard enough to watch Karl leave. But it was harder to watch his own grandmother let him go without saying a word.

From the back porch, she heard the truck start up and its wheels crunch along the gravel driveway. Alexis went down the back steps two at a time and headed across the compound. Just as she got to her cabin, the gravel stopped crunching and the engine of the green Ford idled.

"Franz, wait! Wait just a minute!" cried a frail voice.

A car door opened and closed. Alexis slipped silently into her cabin.

"Thank You, God," she whispered.

❦

During her last five days at Rocky Shoals, Alexis was more alone than she had ever been. And yet, unlike her first days there, when she'd been surrounded by the laughing voices of Jacquie and Ty and the others, she wasn't lonely.

She spent most of the time either on The Rock, listening for God's still, small voice, or in her darkroom preparing gifts. One afternoon, she spent in Rockport purchasing the finishing touches. She went out of her way to avoid Brackett's and Tuck's and the bench in front of the Toad Hall Bookstore.

The day before she left, she went to Sigrid's office with four brown packages piled in her arms.

One contained a photo of Virginia out on the rocks, laughing into the wind as she pencilled a caricature of Ty and Will howling from the Sunfish. Alexis had framed that one in ocean blue with a green mat. Her note said, "Thank you for being my model for a Christian marriage. I hope someday I have the chance to perfect the art the way you have."

Alexis had tucked that one quickly into the package and sealed it up before she started crying again. She wasn't at all sure she was ever going to have that chance.

The second box held the delightful picture of Jacquie, pen in hand, feet propped up on the porch railing, her amazing smile dazzling the world. Nothing but a pewter frame would do for that one. She hadn't been able to hold back the tears when she'd written Jacquie's note. "I was wrong about Ty," it said. "And you were right."

The third was her favorite: Karl on his rock, searching for understanding in the ocean. "Remember who loves you," she'd written to him. "God and I."

The last one she couldn't think about. She just wanted to mail it.

When she reached the office, Sigrid was at her desk, poring over a flood of papers that seemed to flow right out of the flowered wallpaper and the chintz chair. She looked up sharply when Alexis tapped on the door. The same expression crossed her face that Alexis had seen every time their eyes had met for the last five days.

"Has the mailman come yet?" Alexis asked.

Sigrid held out her arms. "No, you're just in time. Are these what I think they are?" She nodded toward the pair of framed photos Alexis had taken of her and Franz, now placed proudly on her desk.

Alexis poked a hand into her pocket. "I have some money for postage—"

But Sigrid held up a palm. "Please, no, Alexis, you've done so much already."

"Can we talk about that?" Alexis said. "I'm leaving early tomorrow morning. I'd like to clear the air first."

Sigrid, Alexis thought later, looked as if she would rather have given up her last antique than "clear the air," but she nodded and sank back into her chair.

Alexis took a deep breath. "I know we disagreed about Karl, and I know I went against your wishes."

"And I know you were right."

Their eyes locked together. Sigrid's face wrestled for control.

"I don't think that's what matters," Alexis said gently. "What matters is that we all saw who he really is. I just want you to know I didn't do any of it to spite you."

Sigrid pushed back a few wisps of gray that had escaped onto her weary forehead. "Alexis, my dear," she said, "you never did anything to spite anyone in your life. You have touched us all this summer."

Alexis picked up the package she held on her lap. "I have one more thing. Did, um, did Ty leave a forwarding address?"

Sigrid shook her head. "He left a thank-you note and a generous gratuity. I tried to call him at the number on his application, but the phone had already been disconnected. It is as if he has dissolved."

Alexis stood up and blinked fast. *And maybe that's the best thing*, she thought. "Is that his picture?" Sigrid said.

Alexis nodded. It was the one she'd taken that day in Rockport, when he'd first discovered the Song of Solomon. The two girls behind him were gazing at him enraptured.

"Would you like me to keep it and mail it if he ever gets in touch with me?" Sigrid said. "He was such a good friend, I'm sure he will."

Alexis hugged the box to her. "No, thanks. I think I'll keep it."

As she left the office, she added to herself, *Because this is all I have left of him.*

꙾

The lighthouses stood clear and proud that night when Alexis came to say goodbye. She had been avoiding this moment since Ty had left and now the sight of them brought back Jacquie's words: *They're like a married couple.*

"Like a team," Alexis said out loud. "Like Ty and I were."

But "were," she knew, was the operative word. Now as she gazed out at the two strong towers lighting up the darkness in long, slow swoops, a thought came to her.

Our time together is the time we've already had.

Whether that was the still, small voice or not, she couldn't tell. But at least God had answered some of her questions.

She was going to be a teacher, for now. Somehow she connected with young people. Karl had shown her that. And she was going to keep taking pictures as the Spirit led her, because somewhere out there, at the right time, she was going to find a purpose for her art.

And Lance. No, she couldn't marry him. She'd always love him, but not in the way Jacquie adored Michael or Virginia had pledged herself to Will. And not the way she loved Ty, wrong as that had turned out to be.

But the most important thing was what God had told her about Himself. He was there, no matter what. The still, small voice would always guide her, whether it came in her thoughts or out of the mouth of someone else, or showed up in something as unlikely as a lighthouse. And it would take her where she needed to go, because it was obvious she didn't always know the way. If it hadn't been for Him, there would have been no Karl, and no rescue, and no. . .

Pain seared through her chest. There was nothing to do now but go home and get on with her life.

"And I have one now," she whispered tearfully to a Ty who wasn't there.

꙾

Rocky Shoals looked dark and empty as she crossed the lawn. But when she reached the bottom of the steps, she heard the wicker loveseat creak. To her surprise, Marina-Natasha was settled in among the cushions.

"Alexis?" she called out.

"Yeah, hi." This was not a person Alexis wanted to spend her last evening with, but she politely went up a few steps.

"I want to thank you for the photo," Marina-Natasha said. "It's intense."

Alexis had never been sure exactly what "intense" meant when Marina-Natasha used it, but it seemed to fit this time. The picture of the Cosmic Traveler on the beach, hands lifted in the ecstasy of creation, was a portrait of someone giving herself up completely to her art.

"You're leaving tomorrow too?" she said.

"Yeah, first thing."

"Going to meet Ty?"

Alexis felt her heart jump. "Ty? No!"

"Oh." Marina-Natasha cocked her head and frowned. "I just thought you two would be together. You're soul mates."

Alexis closed her eyes. "No. It would never work out."

Marina-Natasha considered that for a minute. "Your religion?"

"Basically."

"So what do you do?" she continued. "Do you pray that somehow it will happen?"

Alexis sighed and began to back down the steps. "No," she said, trying not to sound condescending. "You don't pray for impossible things."

"Oh." Marina-Natasha looked at her oddly, her brows knotted together, then she sniffed. "It doesn't sound like much of a faith to me, then, if you can't ask for a miracle."

✣

As Alexis pulled Clifford out onto Eden Road in a shroud of fog the next morning, those were the words from Rocky Shoals that echoed in her ears. With the lighthouses fading behind her, she started to pray for the impossible.

Chapter 17

Somebody's got a fire going in their fireplace, Alexis thought as she crossed the street to her townhouse. She grabbed the mail from the box by the door, put her key in the lock, then stopped to take a longer sniff.

She loved that smell. Leaves burning. Smoke curling out of chimneys. She could almost swear the scent of gingerbread was wafting from someone's window.

Alexis leaned against the door. *What a magnificent autumn this has been in Philadelphia,* she thought. The oaks and maples that lined the street and framed the long row of narrow houses were ablaze in reds, rusts, purples, and golds. No wonder she'd decorated all four of her rooms with the same bonfire of colors.

She was about to go in when footsteps on the sidewalk stopped her. It wasn't fear of a stranger but fear of the familiar that made her pause. Her fingers tightened around the doorknob as she looked up at Lance.

"Hi, Lexy," he said.

The usually smooth, clear voice was shaky. Alexis tried to keep hers steady as she answered. "Lance, I really don't want to go over everything again. We've both said what we have to say. I want to let it go."

She turned the key in the lock, but Lance curled his fingers around her wrist. His touch was gentle, but she stared at his hand until he let go.

"I didn't come to stir things up," he said. "I want to put them to rest too. Please hear me out."

She looked at him for a long moment. The gray eyes were calm and not filled with the hurt of a month ago, the last time they'd talked. His square jaw was tense, but he didn't seem ready to spew out the accusations he'd showered on her then. Not to mention the time before that, and the horrible first time before that. His hands were jammed into the pockets of his tweed suit pants, like a little boy afraid of being misunderstood.

"Okay," Alexis said. "I'm listening."

Lance nodded toward the door. "Can't I come in?"

Tongues of uneasiness lapped at her insides. "I don't want you yelling at me in my own home, accusing me of things I didn't do."

"I'm not going to yell at you, Lexy." His voice wavered. "I just want to talk."

"Last time we 'talked,' you as much as called me a tramp."

Lance closed his eyes. "Please, Lexy, you know I didn't mean that."

Alexis watched as he swallowed and dug his hands deeper into his pockets.

Slowly she nodded. "Come on in, but I've got a lot of stuff in here that means something to me. Don't throw anything, okay?"

His hands came out of his pockets. "I never threw anything at you!"

"Only because I never let you in." She nudged open the door.

He continued to protest until Alexis led him through the narrow foyer and into her tiny living room. There his mouth fell open into a stunned O.

Alexis dropped the mail onto a square padded footstool she used for a coffee table and stripped off her jacket. Lance stood in the middle of the striped rug, a relic from her mother's attic, and stared.

"What's wrong, you don't like Au Yard Sale?" she said.

He didn't answer but swept his eyes over the room. He'd never seen the inside of the townhouse she'd gotten a lease-option on in September. He'd only stood in the street and shouted at her as she'd carried in boxes, telling her she could spend her life alone in some pitiful little apartment for all he cared. He was going to have a real life, in a real home.

Little did Lance know that Alexis had spent the last two months raiding her parents' attic and basement for rejected chairs and a couch. Little did he realize the pleasure she derived from covering them with bright brick-colored throws and smothering each one with pillows in green, orange, purple, and gold. He had no idea how many garage sales she'd scoured, picking up stools and end tables and funky lamps, or how many hours she'd spent sanding and varnishing her treasures.

The treasure hunts had been the most fun. Digging through trunks and boxes for mementos of her childhood. Selecting just the right shells from her Rockport collection. Painting frames for her favorite photos.

And she was sure he wouldn't understand the delight she was taking in continuing to create a collection of every piece of her life, a life that was becoming clearer to her every day.

"This is incredible, Lexy," he said finally.

She cocked an eyebrow. "Really? I thought you'd hate it."

"Why would I hate it? It's you." His eyes met hers sadly.

"Why don't you sit down?" she said. "Just toss that on the floor."

Lance picked up a photo album from the chair and set it on the footstool, but his eyes lingered on it.

"Those are my pictures from Rockport," she said. "You can look at them if you want. I don't have anything to hide."

Lance's hands were clasping and unclasping between his knees. "I know you don't," he said. "And that's one of the things I want to say. I was too hard on you."

She didn't disagree with him. In their three major arguments since she'd come home, in the scathing letters he'd written, and in the phone calls she slammed the receiver down on, he'd taken every piece of her heart and chewed it up and spit it out. He accused her of going to Rockport specifically to find another guy. He told her she had a cheating, conniving nature. He made it abundantly clear that he found her irresponsible and selfish. He had ripped open her soul.

"I've spent the last three weeks beating myself up over the things I said to you, Lexy. There's no excuse for it, really, but I know God has forgiven me. I just hope now you can."

Alexis leaned back against the mountain of pillows on the couch. "I want to," she said. "But it's hard when I don't understand. I was up front with you. I asked you to forgive me for hurting you. I tried to make you see that I didn't do anything wrong except be led momentarily by my feelings."

"I know. Believe me, I know. I don't have any excuses, but I do have a reason."

She looked up at him. "Why don't you tell me, because I don't want to feel this ugly stuff about you for the rest of my life."

Lance scooted to the edge of the chair and leaned toward her. "All I can say is that I was hurt. But I know now that you and I just weren't meant to be. If we had been, you'd never have fallen in love with somebody else, especially somebody you can't even have. You're not like that, Lexy. You're too close to God."

Slowly, Alexis slid forward and took one of Lance's well-manicured hands. "I don't think you'll ever know what that means to me."

"I will," he said, "if you'll tell me you forgive me."

She closed both hands over his and smiled into his pensive face. "Without a doubt," she assured him. "It's done. It's over. Let's get on with our lives."

Lance looked around. "It looks like you already have. I never knew you to care about interior decorating before."

"It's not interior decorating I care about," she explained. "It's me. It's all starting to come together."

"You like teaching?"

"I do for now. I love interacting with the students, and I'm finding time to do some of my own stuff. There's still something else out there for me. I don't know what it is yet, but it'll come."

His eyes fastened on the wall by the window behind them, and he stood and wandered toward it. "This is a beautiful piece."

Alexis snorted softly. The minute she'd seen the picture of the two light-houses on her contact sheet at Rocky Shoals, she had known that Lance would want an enlargement hanging in their living room. Now it was in her home, for reasons she couldn't even begin to explain to him.

"Every photographer in New England has caught that same shot," she said.

"Not like this, I bet." He ducked his head. "I hope you can forget that I said that retreat was a waste of time for you."

Alexis didn't say anything. It would be a long time before she'd be able to put that out of her mind. He'd stabbed a hole in the middle of her memory of a time that had completely changed her life.

"You're living the life you're supposed to live," he said. There were tears shimmering in his gray eyes. "Now I need to go out and find mine. I'm just so sorry you aren't going to be sharing it with me."

"But I still can, just not in the way we planned."

Lance put up his hand. "If you're talking about 'let's be friends,' I'm not ready for that. I don't know if I ever will be. It hurts too much. You'll always be here, though." He put his hand on his chest.

Alexis nodded. When the front door closed, she sank back against the pillows and waited for the tears. But instead, there was a still, small voice.

It's done, and it's good. No need to cry.

She let the words roll around in her head and savored the sound. Smiling to herself, she picked up the pile of mail from the footstool. The top letter was from Jacquie, and she opened it hungrily. Amazing things were happening in Jacquie's life, and Alexis had been waiting for two weeks for the next "chapter."

> *Michael has been given a clean bill of health. We're going to the islands for thirty days and I'm leaving the work behind. I have to if I'm going to expect him to! I just hope we can find a church down there that we like as much as the one here. Now, when we get back, I want you to think about coming to Dallas for Thanksgiving. We have so much to be thankful to you for.*

Alexis folded the letter back into the envelope and popped it into the red and gold stationery box on the footstool. All her letters from her Rockport family were in there, including the first one from Jacquie, telling her that she and Michael had become Christians in the hospital in Dallas with the chaplain beaming over them.

But it was you who got the whole thing started, Alexis, she had written. *Just seeing the way you live opened the door for us.*

Alexis was about to close the lid when she saw the corner of Karl's letter peeking out. She could never resist rereading it or gazing at his pencil drawing of her praying, which she had hanging over her bed upstairs.

> *I think about you praying for me, and I guess it's working. I haven't ripped anything off since we got home from France. I've thought about praying, but I still sound lame to myself. You oughta come up here and teach me.*

Christmas break. Alexis closed the box and pawed through the stack of mail on her lap. Her plane ticket ought to be arriving any day. Here was the electric bill. An ad for a credit card.

There was one last piece of mail, and the familiar scrawl of the handwriting caused a strange sensation to sweep through her.

It was a letter from Ty.

Fingers trembling, she slowly ran a letter opener under the seal. A poem unfolded in front of her, just as if it had been tucked in the screen door of her little yellow-walled cabin. Eyes already swimming, Alexis sat back onto the pillows.

Taxi,
I've walked through the shadows and stared in every window
Looking for myself in the glass.
Because, you see, I came back home
And only found that I was lost.
I was not uncovered beneath the words, "Best Sausage in Chicago"
I was not discovered in the tinted plates of Copeland's Sporting Goods
My soul came into view in the scattered bits and pieces of stained-glass art
And the spectacles of a balding shepherd
Who said, you have a home here.
Say a prayer for me, Taxi,
As I start my partnership with Christ.
You and He were like twin lighthouses, searching for me.
Now I am come into my garden, my sister.

                                                            Ty

The last line, she knew, was from the Song of Solomon. She'd read all eight chapters at least a dozen times since she'd been back. But the rest was from the deepest part of Ty's soul, and tears streamed down her face as she reread his words.

Ty had committed himself to Christ. He'd captured the picture in his words the way she wanted to with her camera. Wandering the streets of Chicago, empty and searching for something to fill up a hole. Finding a church with stained-glass windows with probably half of the pieces missing. She chuckled through her tears. He would have been fascinated with that, of course.

And she could picture him shaking hands with a balding pastor and saying, "Now, let me ask you this—"

A sob collided with a laugh and she clutched the poem to her and let both flow freely. "I have to write to him," she said out loud. "I have to tell him how happy I am for him."

She fumbled with the envelope for a return address, and her heart sank. Nothing, not even a postmark.

Alexis turned the letter over in her hands. Not only was there no postmark, there was no stamp. Now that she looked at the envelope closely, there wasn't even a full address for her. He'd simply written Alexis Riker, Philadelphia, PA.

Her heart seemed to stop completely. The letter hadn't been mailed at all. It had been hand delivered.

Pillows, photo albums, and the electric bill all scattered to the floor as she scrambled up and went for the door.

What am I doing? What am I expecting to find? she thought crazily as she flung it open.

A square smile greeted her. "Did you call for a taxi, Lady?"

Alexis stared at the tall, lanky form that lounged in the doorway, then she felt a smile tremble its way from one ear to the other. "Let me ask you this," she managed to say. "How did you find me?"

"One artist can always find another. Besides, I haven't been a journalist all these years for nothing. I have connections."

She looked at him and grinned. The cowlick was still standing up on the top of his dark head. The lips were still full and twitching. The legs were still the longest in masculine history.

"Now let me ask you this," he said.

Alexis closed her eyes. Those were the six most beautiful words in the English language. "Ask me."

He picked up her left hand, and she opened her eyes to see him inspecting her fingers. Then he grinned and said, "Can I come in?"

He didn't let go of her hand as she led him into her living room until he stopped to look around.

"Great room," he said. "It's you."

"So they tell me," she said.

He turned to look down at her. "Taxi, nobody ever had to tell you who you were. Now, I, on the other hand—"

Alexis smiled up at him. "You and Christ. You've met."

Ty motioned to the chair, his face suddenly serious. "May I?"

"Please, do."

He sank slowly into a chair and she settled on the couch. Her heart pounded. Ty stared at the ceiling for a good minute before he said anything. When he did, it was in a voice far different from any he had used before.

"Look," he said, "I've had an incredible experience, and I knew I had to come and share it with you. I get the feeling you still want to hear it."

Alexis almost choked. "Yes, I want to hear it!"

He put his fingers to his forehead for a second, as if he were trying to center his thoughts there. "I went home from Rockport," he said finally, "and I thought life as I knew it was basically over. I couldn't write. I couldn't pick up a tennis racquet. I couldn't even go back to my old apartment. I checked into a hotel, and I started literally walking the streets. It got to the point where it was either start all over or not."

Their eyes clinked together.

"I get it," she said.

"So I'm wandering down the sidewalk one day and I see this church. It's always been there—I mean, literally, built in 1882—and anyway, it just drew me in. There were some bricks missing in the steps. Trees needed pruning, that kind of stuff. But the door comes flying open, and all these teenagers come pouring out." He shook his head.

"I thought I was losing it, because every one of them looked like Karl. I mean, we're talking the half-shaved heads, the pants ten sizes too big. Screaming past me with their earrings dangling, and that's the boys. And up on the steps waving good-bye like they were a herd of angels going off for milk and cookies was this guy. I'm telling you, Taxi, he must be a hundred years old. Thick glasses, bald except for this little fringe, I mean, he's a dead ringer for some country friar. There he is in the middle of downtown Chicago, smiling like a saint. And every one of those juvenile delinquents, to a kid, turned around and said good-bye. Some of them even said 'I love you.'

"I had to go in there. I told myself at first that I was doing it for Karl some how, but after about thirty seconds with George White—that's the old guy's name—I knew I was doing it to save my own life."

"What happened?" Alexis was enthralled.

"Six weeks of spiritual direction. Baptized September thirtieth. Wheels turning so fast in here—" He tapped his forehead. "I can't even sleep most nights."

Alexis put her hands to both sides of her face and let the tears come.

Ty nodded. "That's what I do a lot too. I don't know how to tell you, it's like a miracle."

"The impossible," she whispered.

"You could say that." He shrugged. "I just wanted to come and tell you in person. You started it, Taxi."

For the first time since he'd appeared in the doorway, Alexis couldn't look at him. She was glowing for him, and yet little points of fear began to poke at her insides. *What now?* she wanted to say to him. *What does this mean now?*

It probably means what has always been the case, she thought. Ty was going to get on with his life with a spirit no one could keep up with. But at least now they could be friends.

Strangely, Lance's voice cut in. *"If you're talking about 'let's be friends,' I'm not ready for that."*

"It's basically changed everything," Ty was saying.

Alexis picked up a pillow to hug.

"Did I tell you I have a new book contract?"

She shook her head.

"A Christian publisher. I'm doing an exposé of what Christianity could be oing for kids—should be doing—you know, kids like Karl. There's some travel nvolved. I'm doing research on the existing programs, interviewing kids on the treet."

Travel. The points of fear stabbed at her. A visit now and then. A few laughs ver a crab sandwich downtown, then he'd be off to the next stop.

"I can't think of anything in my life that hasn't changed," Ty said. "And let ne just ask you this. What does it mean that you aren't wearing that ring on your ft hand?"

Alexis felt her pulse stop. She stared stupidly at her finger.

"I checked it out when I came in," Ty said. "Can I ask what that means?"

She curled her right hand around her left fingers. "It means Lance and I are nished. I figured out when I was in Rockport that it wasn't going to work. We ant different kinds of lives, and I don't love him."

Ty searched her face for a minute, then he got up. Alexis put the pillow aside nd watched as he paced around her living room, looking at books, picking up nickknacks, straightening pictures.

He stopped in front of the lighthouse picture and gazed at it. Alexis couldn't and it any longer.

"Ty, what are you doing?"

He didn't look at her. "I'm trying to get up the guts to tell you—"

He cut himself off and stepped over an end table to join her on the couch. e smothered her hands with his oversized ones.

"Just listen to me, okay, and if I'm way off base, just throw me out."

Alexis forced herself to meet his gaze. Every nerve in her body stood on end.

"You set me up for God. You opened doors, gave me the example. I was ready r Him when I finally gave myself over, you know what I'm saying?"

Alexis nodded.

"But I didn't become a Christian just so I could come back here and—I hon- tly thought you might already be married to what's-his-face. I mean, I hoped ou wouldn't be, I prayed— But it just seemed like your faith was so strong, you uld handle anything, maybe even me."

Alexis searched his face. His lips were quivering, just like hers were, she new.

"What are you saying?" she said.

"I want you to come with me—take pictures for my book—team up with me th the kids—be my partner—"

"Oh."

Alexis studied her hands. A business proposition. That was almost as un- arable as "let's be friends." She started to shake her head when a warm hand me up under her chin and tilted it toward him.

"Be my wife," he said in his husky voice. "I love you, and I need a Taxi."

Alexis opened her mouth, but Ty took both of her hands again and squeeze[d] them. "You don't have to give me an answer right away. I know how you like [to] think things through. Or you might want to say no now and spare me the agon[y,] which is fine. I'm out the door—"

"Ty—"

"Yeah—"

"Shut up." Alexis put her fingers to his lips. "I will be your Taxi, and I'll g[o] anywhere with you, as long as we take God along."

The squarest smile yet took slow shape on Ty's face. "Do we have a choice[?]"

"Absolutely not." Then she said the second most beautiful set of words in t[he] English language, words she'd been holding back almost since the day his fa[ce] had first appeared in Clifford's window.

"I love you, Ty."

Ty's hand slid to her hair and pulled her face to his. His kiss was soft a[nd] warm, and endless.

This is the beginning, said a still, small voice.

Alexis thanked Him as she buried her face against Ty's strong chest. A[nd] this time, she didn't pull away.

ANCY N. RUE

ancy is the prolific author of many books for teenagers. A former high school
acher, she resides in Nashville with her husband and daughter. *Retreat to Love*
her first inspirational romance.

A Letter to Our Readers

Dear Readers:

In order that we might better contribute to your reading enjoyment, we would appreciate you taking a few minutes to respond to the following questions. When completed, please return to the following: Fiction Editor, Barbour Publishing, Inc., P.O. Box 719, Uhrichsville, OH 44683.

1. Did you enjoy reading *New England?*
   □ Very much. I would like to see more books like this.
   □ Moderately —I would have enjoyed it more if _____
   _____
   _____

2. What influenced your decision to purchase this book?
   (Check those that apply.)
   □ Cover   □ Back cover copy   □ Title   □ Price
   □ Friends   □ Publicity   □ Other

3. Which story was your favorite?
   □ *Mountaintop*   □ *Mockingbird's Song*
   □ *Sea Escape*   □ *Retreat to Love*

4. Please check your age range:
   □ Under 18   □ 18–24   □ 25–34
   □ 35–45   □ 46–55   □ Over 55

5. How many hours per week do you read? _____

Name _____

Occupation _____

Address _____

City _____ State _____ ZIP _____

E-mail _____

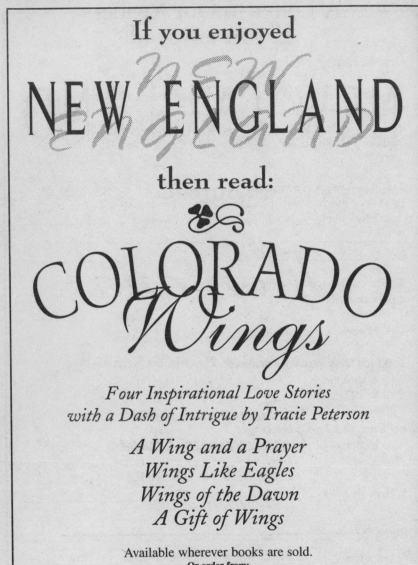

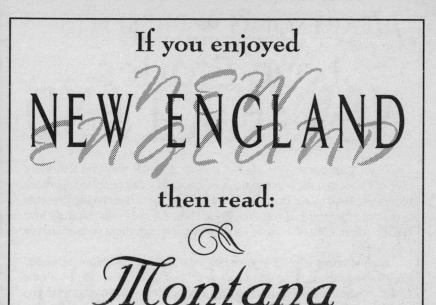